AF512023

Microbiology for Dental Students

With 555 MCQs

Third Edition

Microbiology for Dental Students

With 555 MCQs

Third Edition

BS Nagoba, MSc (Med), PhD (Med)
Assistant Dean (Research & Development)
and
Professor of Microbiology
MIMSR Medical College
Latur, Maharashtra

Wolters Kluwer

Publishing Manager: P Sangeetha
Development Editor: Dr Vallika Devi Katragadda
Production Editor: K Annie Devi
Manager-Manufacturing: Sumit Johry

Copyright © 2018 Wolters Kluwer Health (India)

10th Floor, Tower C, Building No. 10
Phase – II, DLF Cyber City, Gurgaon, Haryana – 122002

All rights reserved. This book is protected by copyright. No part of this book may be reproduced in any form or by any means, including photocopying, or utilized by any information storage and retrieval system without written permission from the copyright owner.

The publisher is not responsible (as a matter of product liability, negligence, or otherwise) for any injury resulting from any material contained herein. This publication contains information relating to microbiology for dental students that should not be construed as specific instructions for individual patients. Manufacturers' product information and package inserts should be reviewed for current information, including contraindications, dosages, and precautions. All products/brands/names/ processes cited in this book are the properties of their respective owners. Reference herein to any specific commercial products, processes, or services by trade name, trademark, manufacturer, or otherwise is purely for academic purposes and does not constitute or imply endorsement, recommendation, or favouring by the publisher. The views and opinions of authors expressed herein do not necessarily state or reflect those of the publisher, and shall not be used for advertising or product endorsement purposes.

Care has been taken to confirm the accuracy of the information presented and to describe generally accepted practices. However, the authors, editors, and publishers are not responsible for errors or omissions or for any consequences from application of the information in this book and make no warranty, expressed or implied, with respect to the currency, completeness, or accuracy of the contents of the publication. Application of this information in a particular situation remains the professional responsibility of the practitioner. Readers are urged to confirm that the information, especially with regard to drug dose/usage, complies with current legislation and standards of practice. Please consult full prescribing information before issuing prescription for any product mentioned in the publication.

The publishers have made every effort to trace copyright holders for borrowed material. If they have inadvertently overlooked any, they will be pleased to make the necessary arrangements at the first opportunity.

Third Edition, 2017

ISBN-13: 978-93-86691-42-2

Published by Wolters Kluwer (India) Pvt. Ltd., Gurgaon
Compositor: maniworks.com
Printed and bound at Sanat Printers

For product enquiry, please contact – Marketing Department (marketing@wolterskluwerindia.co.in) or log on to our website www.wolterskluwerindia.co.in.

Dedicated to the sweet memories
of my beloved grandfather
Shri Hanmant Nagoba

Preface to the Third Edition

I am extremely delighted to place before the readers the third edition of Microbiology for Dental Students. The second edition, published in the year 2011, was devised as per the recommendations of the Dental Council of India; however, while recently going through the syllabus of the health universities across the country, it was observed that a few topics have been added to their syllabus. The constructive suggestions from senior microbiology teachers from various dental colleges and the feedback received from the students also spurred me to revise the book. The third edition has not only been thoroughly revised but made complete with respect to the syllabus of all health universities in the country through the addition of two new chapters and also extra content wherever necessary.

I hope this book will fulfil the requirements of dental students in pursuance of their course in microbiology and also prove to be useful to the dentists all over the country and nearby countries.

I am extremely thankful to the students and teachers of microbiology for overwhelming response to the previous two editions and for the suggestions for the third edition. I sincerely hope that they will continue to support with valuable suggestions and comments in future also.

BS Nagoba

Preface to the First Edition

This book has been tailored to the needs of the dental students, highlighting the importance of Microbiology for dentists.

An attempt has been made to cover the entire course of Microbiology as per the recommendations of Dental Council of India, to offer a text that is concise, easy to understand and user friendly. Instead of traditional lengthy text, bulleted points are used to make understanding of the subject easy. A few chapters not prescribed in the course have been deliberately included for better comprehension of the subject. A special care has been taken to give detailed information wherever necessary.

Though this book has been designed for dental students, it will also be of help to paramedical students such as DMLT, Pharmacy and Physiotherapy in comprehending the basic concepts of Microbiology.

I hope this book will prove very useful for dental students in pursuance of their course in Microbiology, and will receive attention and appreciation from teachers.

BS Nagoba

Acknowledgements

I am very happy to express my gratitude to Hon. Prof. Dr VD Karad, Executive President and Director General, MAEER's MIT, Pune, a dynamic personality and a renowned educationalist. He has always been a source of inspiration, guidance and help to me.

I am thankful to Hon. Mr RK Karad, Executive Director and Dr SB Mantri, Principal, MIMSR Medical College, Latur for their constant support and valuable guidance.

My special thanks are due to Dr Milind Davane, Assistant Professor, Department of Microbiology for his wholehearted support in proofreading the manuscript.

I am also thankful to Mr VN Kale, Senior Librarian; and Mr Kashinath Karad, Mr Vinod Jogdand, Assistant Librarians for their timely help.

I would like to thank Miss Namita Surwase, Senior Clerk in Microbiology; Mr Dayanand Ghante and Mr Pandurang Jadhav, Photographers; Mr SS Gutte and Mr Datta Shinde, Technicians in Microbiology; and Mr Kaule MJ and Mr Kadam SS, Laboratory Assistants in Microbiology for their sustained efforts in the preparation of manuscript.

I am also thankful to my better half Mrs Karuna; my dear daughters Miss Pallavi and Ramani; and other members in my family, namely, Mr Ravindra Mule, Miss Anita Mule, Mr Preetam Mule, Mr Jitendra Mule and Mr Gaurav Mule for their kind support.

Finally, I would like to thank Wolters Kluwer, in particular P Sangeetha, Publishing Manager; Dr Vallika Devi, Development Editor; and Miss Annie Devi, Production Editor for their cooperation and sustained efforts in the publication of this book.

BS Nagoba

Acknowledgements to Reviewers

The publisher and author gratefully acknowledge the reviews by the following experts:

1. Dr Aparna Dave, Professor & Head, Department of Oral Pathology, Microbiology & Forensic Odontology, SGT Dental College, Hospital & Research Institute, Gurugram
2. Dr Manpreet Arora, Professor, Department of Oral Pathology, Microbiology & Forensic Odontology, SGT Dental College, Hospital & Research Institute, Gurugram
3. Dr Pulin Saluja, Associate Professor, Department of Oral Pathology, Microbiology & Forensic Odontology, SGT Dental College, Hospital & Research Institute, Gurugram

Contents

Abbreviations

G	–	Glucose
L	–	Lactose
S	–	Sucrose
M	–	Mannitol
I	–	Indole test
MR	–	Methyl red test
VP or Vi	–	Voges–Proskauer test
C	–	Citrate test
H_2S	–	Hydrogen sulphide test
+	–	Positive
–	–	Negative

1 Introduction and History

The organisms which are invisible to naked eye are called **microorganisms** and the science that deals with the study of microorganisms is called **microbiology** (*micro* means small, *bious* means life). It involves the study of the following aspects of microorganisms:

- Form and structure
- Physiology and metabolism
- Reproduction
- Identification
- Distribution in the nature
- Relationship with each other and with other living organisms
- Physical and chemical changes induced by them in their environment

Medical microbiology

Medical microbiology is the branch of microbiology that deals with the study of disease-producing microorganisms in human beings. It is also concerned with the prevention and control of infectious diseases.

Branches of medical microbiology

The important branches of medical microbiology are as follows:

- General microbiology
- Bacteriology
- Immunology
- Virology
- Mycology
- Parasitology

Different groups of microorganisms

- All microorganisms are not alike.
- Some of them are very small while others are relatively larger in size.
- Some of them possess plant-like characters, while others have animal-like characters and few of them have neither plant-like nor animal-like characters.
- Based on the morphological and functional properties, they are grouped as follows:

Bacteria They are small, unicellular, microscopic organisms with primitive nucleus.

Fungi They are unicellular or multicellular microscopic organisms with well-developed nucleus. Fungi possess plant-like characters but are devoid of chlorophyll and are not differentiated into root, stem, leaves, flowers, etc.

Algae They are unicellular or multicellular microscopic organisms possessing plant-like characters. Algae possess chlorophyll but are not differentiated into root, stem, leaves, flowers, etc. Most of them possess well-developed nucleus, except blue-green algae.

Protozoa They are unicellular microscopic organisms possessing animal-like characters, that is, they do not possess rigid cell wall. Protozoa possess well-developed nucleus.

Viruses They are very small, ultramicroscopic, (seen under electron microscope), non-cellular microorganisms, which are capable of multiplying only inside the living cell.

Position of microorganisms

In the early history, living organisms were classified into two kingdoms:
1. Plant kingdom
2. Animal kingdom

After the discovery of microorganisms, they were initially placed either into plant or animal kingdom based on their characters. With the increase in the understanding of microorganisms, it was found that many microorganisms possess both plant-like and animal-like characters and neither plant-like nor animal-like characters. Because of this problem, a new kingdom, ***Protista*** was proposed for microorganisms. All bacteria, fungi, algae and protozoa are grouped under the kingdom *Protista*. Viruses are not included because they do not have cellular organization.

The kingdom *Protista* is further divided into two groups, based on structural (cellular organization) differences among the microorganisms, as:
1. Prokaryotes
2. Eukaryotes

The differences between *prokaryotes* and *eukaryotes* are given in Table 1.1.

Are microorganisms useful to us?

Microorganisms are useful to us in different ways.

Table 1.1 Differences between prokaryotes and eukaryotes

Prokaryotes	Eukaryotes
Size Less than 5 μm	Greater than 5 μm
Nucleus Primitive type	Well developed
• Nuclear membrane—absent	Present
• Nucleolus—absent	Present
• Chromosome—single (circular)	One or more (linear)
• Mitotic division—absent	Present
Cytoplasm	
• Mitochondria—absent	Present
• Golgi bodies—absent	Present
• Endoplasmic reticulum—absent	Present
• Ribosome—70S	80S
Chemical composition	
• Sterols in plasma membrane—absent	Present
• Cell wall—complex; peptidoglycan—present	Simple; peptidoglycan—absent
• Muramic acid—present	Absent
Respiration	
• Respiration is part of plasma membrane (mesosomes)	Mitochondria are responsible for respiration
Examples	
• Bacteria, blue-green algae	Algae, fungi, protozoa

- Some microorganisms produce
  - Organic acids such as citric acid, lactic acid and acetic acid
  - Wines and alcohols
  - Vitamins, amino acids, enzymes, etc., which are essential for us
  - Antibiotics, which can be used in the treatment of infectious diseases caused by pathogenic microbes
- Some microorganisms which are normally present in/on our body help in the nutrition of the host by producing various vitamins and by degrading mucins, carbohydrate fibres, etc. They also prevent or interfere with colonization/invasion of the body by more pathogenic organisms.
- Some microorganisms are able to fix atmospheric nitrogen into organic matter and thus help to increase the soil fertility.
- Methanogenic bacteria produce methane gas—biofuel.

Are microorganisms harmful to us?

Many microorganisms are harmful to us in different ways which are as follows:

- Many microorganisms cause diseases in man, animals and plants.
- Many of them spoil our food.
- Some of them spoil water—produce odour and make water unsafe for drinking.
- Some microorganisms spoil books, leather, furniture, rubber, iron pipes, wall paints, etc.

Oral or dental microbiology

Oral or dental microbiology is the study of microbes present in the oral cavity and their role in health and disease. It is also concerned with study of orodental infections and general infections caused by microbes.

History of microbiology

- The concept that contagious disease was caused by invisible living things was known from ancient time but the definitive knowledge about microbes had to wait till microscopes were developed.
- The microbes were first observed and described by **Antony van Leeuwenhoek** (1632–1723).
- Leeuwenhoek (Dutch draper) was able to produce an instrument having a magnification of 40–300X.
- He observed minute organisms in rainwater and other materials using this instrument and designated them as **animalcules**.
- In 1678, Robert Hook developed a compound microscope and confirmed Leeuwenhoek's observations.
- The present day science of microbiology is greatly influenced by the contributions of Louis Pasteur and Robert Koch.

Ignaz Semmelweis (1818–1865)

- Ignaz Semmelweis, a Hungarian physician, discovered in 1847 that washing hands with chlorinated lime solution drastically reduces the number of women dying after childbirth.
- He introduced rigorous hand washing rules in the maternity ward.
- Because of his discovery of the value of hand washing, he is considered as a pioneer of antiseptic procedures.
- Semmelweis's germ theory was introduced when he saw a connection between puerperal fever and disinfected hands of the hospital staff.

Louis Pasteur (1822–1895)

- Known as the **father of modern microbiology**
- Was a chemist from France but his studies on fermentation led him to take interest in microbiology
- Important contributions include the following:
  - Established that fermentation was the result of microbial activity (1857)

- Introduced the techniques of sterilization, for example
  - Steam sterilizer
  - Autoclave
  - Hot air oven
  - Flaming
  - Pasteurization
- Established the importance of cotton plugs for protection of media from aerial contamination
- Accidentally, he observed that culture of chicken cholera bacillus left on the bench for several weeks lost its pathogenic property but retained its ability to protect the birds against subsequent infection by chicken cholera bacilli led to the concept of attenuation and development of live vaccines (1880)
- Developed the anthrax vaccine by attenuating anthrax bacilli at a high temperature (42–43°C) in 1881 and coined the term **vaccine** for such prophylactic preparations
- Developed the vaccine for rabies in 1888

Joseph Lister (1827–1912)

- Known as the **father of antiseptic surgery**
- Realized that microorganisms prevalent in the atmosphere might be responsible for postoperative wound infections
- Was interested in the prevention of postoperative sepsis and introduced antiseptic techniques in surgery (1867) using carbolic acid as a spray during operation or on the wound in postoperative stage. It was a revolution and an important milestone in surgical practice.

Robert Koch (1843–1910)

- Known as the **father of bacteriology**
- Was the first to isolate anthrax bacilli in pure culture and to show spores in anthrax bacilli (1876)
- Introduced staining techniques and methods of obtaining bacteria in pure culture by using solid media
- Discovered tubercle bacilli (1882) and cholera *Vibrio* (1883)

Koch's postulates

- Robert Koch postulated the criteria for proving that a microorganism isolated from the lesions of a disease was indeed causally related to it.
- According to Koch's postulates, a microbe can be accepted as the causative agent of the disease only if the following conditions are satisfied:
  - The microbe should be constantly associated with the lesions of the disease.
  - It should be possible to isolate the microbe in pure culture from the lesions of the disease.
  - Inoculation of such pure culture in suitable laboratory animals should produce a similar disease.
  - It should be possible to re-isolate the microbe in pure culture from lesions produced in the experimental animals.
  - An additional criteria introduced subsequently requires that specific antibodies to causative microbe should be demonstrable in the serum of patients.

Exceptions to Koch's postulates It is not always possible to satisfy all the postulates in every case. Some exceptions are as follows:

- *Treponema pallidum* and *Mycobacterium leprae* are unable to grow on artificial media
- Many viruses and *Rickettsiae* are unable to grow on artificial media

Germ theory of disease

- The **germ theory of disease** was proposed by *Girolamo Fracastoro* in 1546, but scientific evidence in support of the theory accumulated slowly.
- *Fracastoro* proposed that epidemic diseases are caused by transferable seed-like entities or germs that transmit infection by direct or indirect contact, or through air to long distances.

- This view was largely forgotten by the time microorganisms were first directly observed in the 1670s by Antony van Leeuwenhoek.
- Agostino Bassi, an Italian, was the first to prove that a disease is caused by a microorganism during his work on disease in silkworms; this disease was devastating the French silk industry at the time.
- The more formal experiments on the relationship between germ and disease were conducted by Louis Pasteur between 1860 and 1864. He conclusively proved the aetiology of many diseases.

Chemotherapeutic agents

- With the identification and confirmation of bacteria as cause of human diseases, efforts were made to develop effective chemotherapeutic agents, which could kill bacteria in the body without damaging the host tissue. Pioneer work in this area was done by **Paul Ehrlich**.
- **Ehrlich** is known as the **father of chemotherapy**.
- He was the first to launch a search for the **magic bullet**—a chemotherapeutic agent that destroys a pathogen without causing any harm to the infected host.
- In 1906, he discovered **Salvarsan**—an arsenic compound for the successful treatment of syphilis in early phase.
- In 1928, **Sir Alexander Fleming** accidentally discovered the antibacterial effect of penicillin produced by the mould *Penicillium.* Subsequently, stable and safe preparations of penicillin were developed by Chain *et al.* in 1940.
- Many other antibiotics were discovered thereafter using fungi as source including streptomycin by Walksman *et al.* in 1944.

Important discoveries in virology

By the end of the 19th century, many infectious diseases were proved to have bacterial aetiology. But there were large number of diseases for which no bacterial cause could be established. These included smallpox, chickenpox, measles, common cold, etc.

- Ivanovsky was the first to prove the existence of ultramicroscopic microorganisms in 1892 when he reproduced a mosaic disease in tobacco plant by applying the juice from the diseased plants to healthy leaves from which all bacteria had been removed.
- Beijerinck (1898) confirmed these findings.
- In 1898, Loeffler and Frosch demonstrated that a filterable agent is responsible for foot and mouth disease.
- The first human disease proved to have a viral aetiology was yellow fever. Its nature and transmissibility through the bite of infected mosquitoes was established by Walter Reed (1902) in Cuba.
- Landsteiner and Propper (1909) demonstrated the causative agent of poliomyelitis.
- In 1934, Ruska developed electron microscope which made morphological examination of viruses possible.
- Cultivation techniques for viruses such as chick embryo technique by Goodpasture were developed in 1930s and by 1940, tissue culture methods were developed.
- The possibility that infection with virus could lead to malignancy was first put forth by Ellerman and Bang (1908).

Important discoveries in immunology

Edward Jenner (1796) introduced the first successful immunization in smallpox by using cowpox virus. Apart from contributions of Pasteur and Jenner in the development of vaccines for immunization, the important historical landmarks in immunology are as follows:

- Von Behring and Kitasato (1890) demonstrated a specific humoral factor, an antibody produced in guinea pig's serum, by injecting a series of sublethal doses of tetanus toxin.

- Metchnikoff (1883) proposed that the phagocytic response as the prime defence mechanism against microorganisms invading blood and tissues and thus the concept of cellular immunity was established.
- The discipline of allergy and its importance in the pathogenesis of human disease came into existence after the experiment of Portier and Richet (1902) on a dog that led to the discovery of anaphylactic reaction.

Self-assessment

Short-answer questions

Write notes on

1. Difference between eukaryotes and prokaryotes
2. Important contributions of Ignaz Semmelweis
3. Important contributions of Antony van Leeuwenhoek
4. Important contributions of Joseph Lister
5. Important contributions of Louis Pasteur
6. Important contributions of Robert Koch
7. Koch's postulates
8. Germ theory of disease
9. Important contributions of Paul Ehrlich

Multiple-choice questions

1. Which of the following groups of microbes is NOT included in the kingdom *Protista?*
   A. Algae
   B. Viruses
   C. Fungi
   D. Protozoa
2. Which of the following is a prokaryote?
   A. Protozoa
   B. Yeast
   C. Mould
   D. Blue-green algae
3. The ribosome in prokaryote is
   A. 50S
   B. 80S
   C. 70S
   D. 50S
4. The function of respiration in prokaryotes is performed by
   A. Mitochondria
   B. Ribosome
   C. Cell membrane
   D. Mesosome
5. Microbes were first seen by
   A. Robert Hook
   B. Robert Koch
   C. Antony van Leeuwenhoek
   D. Louis Pasteur
6. Louis Pasteur was associated with
   A. Fermentation in brewing
   B. Vaccination against anthrax
   C. Vaccination against rabies
   D. All of the above
7. The following statements are TRUE regarding prokaryotes, EXCEPT
   A. Respiratory function is carried out by mesosomes
   B. Nucleus is primitive type
   C. Sedimentation constant of ribosome is 80S
   D. Sterols in plasma membrane are absent
8. A live attenuated vaccine was first developed by
   A. Paul Ehrlich
   B. Louis Pasteur
   C. Loeffler and Frosch
   D. Landsteiner and Propper
9. Joseph Lister was associated with
   A. Antiseptic techniques in surgery
   B. Discovery of carbolic acid
   C. Postoperative wound infections
   D. All of the above
10. The following are the properties of bacterial nucleus, EXCEPT
   A. Shows mitotic division
   B. Is a single circular molecule of DNA
   C. Nucleolus and nuclear membrane are absent
   D. Deoxyribonucleoproteins are absent

11. Which of the following statements is FALSE about Robert Koch?
    A. Is known as the father of microbiology
    B. Introduced the techniques of sterilization
    C. Was the first to isolate anthrax bacilli in pure culture
    D. Discovered cholera *Vibrio*

12. Which of the following organisms is an exception to Koch's postulates?
    A. *Staphylococcus aureus*
    B. *Escherichia coli*
    C. *Mycobacterium tuberculosis*
    D. *Mycobacterium leprae*

13. The father of chemotherapy is
    A. Alexander Fleming
    B. Paul Ehrlich
    C. Salvarsan
    D. Walksman

14. Select the most appropriate name associated with the development of stable and safe preparations of penicillins
    A. Alexander Fleming
    B. Chain *et al.*
    C. Walksman *et al.*
    D. Paul Ehrlich

15. Electron microscope was developed by
    A. Ruska
    B. Rous
    C. Ellerman
    D. Bang

16. The first successful immunization against smallpox was carried out by
    A. Von Behring
    B. Kitasato
    C. Paul Ehrlich
    D. Edward Jenner

17. The process of phagocytosis was discovered by
    A. Metchnikoff
    B. Pfeiffer
    C. Buchner
    D. Nuttall

18. A connection between puerperal fever and disinfected hands of the hospital staff is established by
    A. Robert Hook
    B. Robert Koch
    C. Joseph Lister
    D. Ignaz Semmelweis

19. The germ theory of disease was proposed by
    A. Robert Koch
    B. Girolamo Fracastoro
    C. Antony van Leeuwenhoek
    D. Ignaz Semmelweis

2 Microscopy and Staining Techniques

Microorganisms are very small and cannot be seen by the unaided eye. The size of microorganisms is measured in microns (micrometres) or millimicrons (nanometres).

- 1 micron (μ) or micrometre (μm) = 1/1000 millimetre
- 1 millimicron (mμ) or nanometre (nm) = 1/1000 micron or 1 millionth of a millimetre
- 1 Angstrom unit (Å) = 1/10 of a nanometre

Medically important bacteria generally measure 0.2–1.5 μm in diameter and 3–5 μm in length. Viruses are smaller than bacteria and are measured in nm. Fungi and protozoa are larger than bacteria and are measured in μm. Hence, microscopes of different types are required for the study of microorganisms.

Microscopy

As microorganisms are too small to be seen by the unaided eye, they must be magnified to be clearly seen and studied. This is done by using microscopes. A microscope may be defined as an optical instrument, consisting of a lens or combination of lenses for making images of minute objects enlarged or magnified.

Types of microscopes

Microscopes are of two types, based on the principle of magnification, which are as follows:

1. **Light or optical microscope**
   - Microscope in which magnification is obtained by a system of optical lenses
   - These include
     - Bright field microscope
     - Dark field microscope
     - Fluorescent microscope
     - Phase contrast microscope
2. **Electron microscope**
   - Microscope in which magnification is obtained by a beam of electrons
   - Includes electron microscope

Bright field microscope (compound microscope) (Fig. 2.1)

This microscope contains a light source and a compound lens system. The lens system consists of objective lens and eyepiece (ocular lens).

Objective lens

They are of four types which are as follows:

1. **Scanning objective (4X)** Used for examination of insect vectors such as mosquitoes, flies and bugs and for scanning of smears

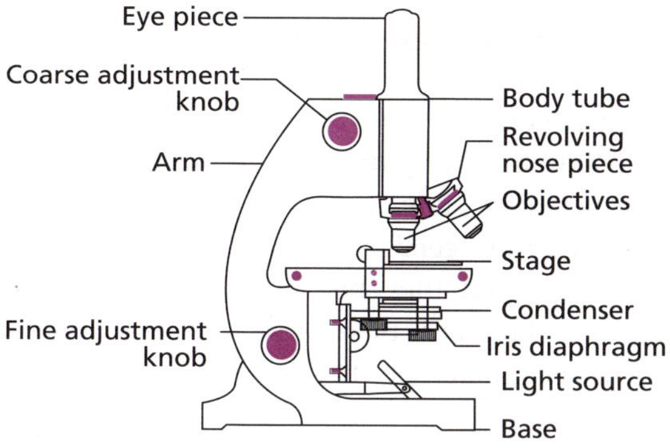

Figure 2.1 Compound microscope.

2. **Low power (10X)** Used for examination of protozoa and other larger microorganisms. It gives total magnification of 100X (10X of objective lens × 10X of eyepiece)
3. **High power (40X)** Used for examination of bacterial motility, protozoa, fungi, etc. It gives total magnification of 400X (40X × 10X)
4. **Oil immersion (100X)** Used for examination of stained smears of bacteria. It gives total magnification of 1000X (100X × 10X). The oil (immersion oil) having same refractive index (1.5) is used to fill the space between the object and objective. The use of oil avoids refraction of rays of light and passes them directly into the objective. This gives a resolution of 0.2 µm approximately

Eyepiece (ocular lens)

It is a fixed lens usually 10X (sometimes 5X or 15X). Eyepiece magnifies the real image of the object formed by the objective.

In addition to these important lenses, microscope also has the following:

- *Condenser*—whose lenses focus light from the illuminating source on the plane of the object
- *Iris diaphragm*—below the condenser to control the amount of light reaching the object and to regulate the path of light
- *Mirror*—to collect and reflect the light on object

Dark field microscope

In this type of microscope, a special type of dark field condenser with a central circular stop is used, which illuminates the object with a cone of light without allowing light rays to enter directly the objective lens; only light rays reflected or scattered from the object enter the objective lens with the result that the object appears self-luminous against a dark background.

Uses

- Extremely slender organisms such as spirochaetes, which are not visible under ordinary microscope, can be seen under the dark field microscope.

Fluorescent microscope

Fluorescence is a property of absorbing light rays of one wavelength and emitting (convert them into) the light rays of another wavelength. This property is used in fluorescent microscope.

In fluorescent microscope, the specimen is exposed to ultraviolet light of shorter wavelength that results in emission of longer wavelength of visible light. Organisms stained with fluorescent dyes become self-luminous and are seen as bright objects against dark background.

Uses

- To visualize *Mycobacterium tuberculosis* and other microorganisms
- Detection of antigen in tissue or specimen
- Detection of antibodies in serum

Phase contrast microscope

- This microscope improves the contrast and makes the structures evident within the cells that differ in thickness or in refractive index.
- When rays of light are passed through an object, they emerge in different phases depending on the difference in the refractive indices between the object and the surrounding medium and these phase differences are converted into differences in intensity of light producing light and dark contrast in the image. Phase contrast microscope uses a special condenser and a special phase objective to produce these differences.

Uses

- To observe unstained living organisms, for example, *Vibrio cholerae* in stool specimens and cultures, *Entamoeba histolytica* in stools, *Trichomonas vaginalis* in vaginal swab and other specimens and cultures
- To study the structures and structural changes in larger microorganisms and tissue cells

Electron microscope

- In this microscope, instead of ordinary light, a beam of electrons is used.
- The wavelength of electron is approximately 0.005 nm, as compared to 500 nm of visible light.
- As the resolving power of microscope is directly related to the wavelength, thus, the resolving power of electron microscope is theoretically 100,000 times that of light microscope, but in practice it is about 0.1 nm.

Uses

- The electron microscope has the advantage of tremendous magnification and is used to study the various fine structures of bacteria and viruses.

Stain and staining procedures

Microorganisms are transparent or semi-transparent. It is difficult to observe them in unstained state due to very little contrast between their cells and surrounding medium. When stained they become opaque and the contrast between them and the surrounding medium is increased. The result is that microbes become visible.

Types of staining

There are two types of staining which are as follows:

1. **Vital staining** The staining techniques in which organisms are not killed.
2. **Supravital staining** The staining techniques in which organisms are killed. These are of four types:
   - **Simple staining (monochrome staining)** Watery solution of a simple basic dye is used, for example, methylene blue or basic fuchsin. It provides the colour contrast but imparts the same colour to all organisms.
   - **Negative staining (background staining)** A drop of India ink or nigrosine is mixed with culture of organism or other material containing organisms (e.g., sputum or cerebrospinal fluid [CSF]) and a thin film is prepared and observed under microscope. In this, the background is stained and organisms appear as colourless objects against a dark background. This method is used for demonstration of capsule and spirochaetes.
   - **Impregnation staining** Organisms which are very thin to be seen under light microscope are rendered visible by increasing their thickness by impregnating silver on their surface. This method is used for demonstration of organisms such as spirochaetes and bacterial flagella.

- **Differential staining** The staining methods which differentiate two types of organisms are known as differential staining. They impart different colour to different bacteria or bacterial structures, for example, Gram stain and acid-fast stain.

Self-assessment

Short-answer questions

Write notes on

1. Dark field microscope
2. Bright field microscope/compound microscope
3. Fluorescence microscope
4. Phase contrast microscope
5. Electron microscope
6. Supravital staining
7. Negative staining
8. Impregnation staining

Multiple-choice questions

1. Spirochaetes can be best demonstrated by
   A. Phase contrast microscope
   B. Light microscope
   C. Dark-field microscope
   D. All of the above
2. Fluorescence microscope is most commonly used to visualize
   A. Meningococci
   B. Gonococci
   C. *Trichomonas vaginalis*
   D. *Mycobacterium tuberculosis*
3. The following statements are TRUE about negative staining, EXCEPT
   A. Uses India ink or nigrosine
   B. Stains the background
   C. Does not stain organisms and leave them as colourless objects
   D. Is mainly used for demonstration of bacterial flagella and pili
4. A maximum magnification achieved by using a compound microscope is
   A. 100X
   B. 400X
   C. 1000X
   D. 2000X
5. Capsule can be best demonstrated by
   A. Gram stain
   B. Negative stain
   C. Z–N stain
   D. Silver impregnation stain
6. Impregnation staining is used for the demonstration of
   A. Spirochaetes
   B. Actinomycetes
   C. Mycobacteria
   D. None of the above

3 Morphology and Physiology of Bacteria

Bacteria are unicellular microorganisms with primitive type of nucleus. A typical bacterial cell shows the structures given in Figure 3.1.

The cell wall

- Is a strong and rigid structure, immediately external to cell membrane, surrounding the bacterium like a shell
- Is 10–25 nm in thickness
- Absent in mycoplasma group of organisms

Chemical nature

- In both Gram-positive and Gram-negative bacteria, the component primarily responsible for mechanical strength is peptidoglycan (a mucopeptide, also known as murein).
- It is composed of alternating units of N-acetyl glucosamine and N-acetyl muramic acid linked together by beta 1–4 linkage and a tetrapeptide side chain attached to N-acetyl muramic acid.
- These units are linked together by peptide cross-bridges, which cross-link the monomeric units of peptidoglycan to each other.
- In **Gram-positive bacteria,** cell wall is 16–18 nm thick and is a monolayered structure. Peptidoglycan is a major component (50–80%), which is associated with polysaccharides and large amounts of a special

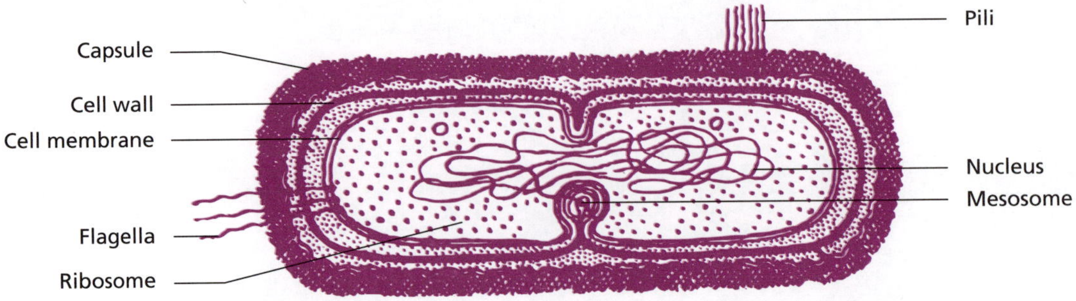

Figure 3.1 Bacterial cell.

class of polymers called teichoic acids (ribitol or glycerol teichoic acid).

- In **Gram-negative bacteria,** cell wall is comparatively thinner and multilayered. It contains an inner layer of peptidoglycan (1–10% of peptidoglycan), about 2–3 nm in thickness, and an outer layer (8–10 nm) of proteins—phospholipids and lipopolysaccharides (LPS). The wall of some Gram-negative bacteria possesses a third layer of protein.

Functions of cell wall

- Gives rigidity and shape to the cell
- Plays role in virulence and immunity
- Helps to maintain osmotic pressure and protects the cell against osmotic damage
- LPS of Gram-negative bacteria have endotoxic activity and 'O' antigen specificity
- Takes part in cell division

Cytoplasmic (plasma) membrane

- Is a thin, elastic, 5–10 nm thick, semipermeable layer lining the inner surface of the cell wall
- Is made up of lipoprotein
- Is a typical unit membrane structure composed of phospholipids and proteins in which protein molecules are embedded in phospholipid bilayer
- Also contains carbohydrates and carrier molecules (e.g., the enzyme *permease*)

Functions

- Is a principal osmotic barrier
- Acts as a semipermeable membrane and controls the inflow and outflow of metabolites, that is, inflow of nutrients and outflow of waste products
- With the help of the enzyme *permease* and others, it participates in active transport of selective nutrients
- Takes part in respiration

Mesosomes

- Are complex infoldings of the cell membrane
- Consist an invaginated cell membrane with many vesicles or tubules filling the invagination
- Chemically similar to cytoplasmic membrane
- **Functions** Possess respiratory enzymes. As mitochondria are absent in bacteria, respiratory activity is carried out by mesosomes

Cytoplasm

- The bacterial cytoplasm is a colloidal system containing a variety of organic and inorganic solutes in a viscous watery solution.
- It contains ribosomes, mesosomes, inclusion granules and vacuoles.
- Endoplasmic reticulum and mitochondria are absent in bacteria.

Ribosomes

- The tiny granules scattered in the cytoplasm are called ribosomes
- Are composed of RNA and proteins
- Are made up of two subunits:
  - Larger subunit (50S)
  - Smaller subunit (30S)
- Are 10–15 nm in size with a sedimentation coefficient of 70S
- **Functions** They are sites for protein synthesis

Inclusion granules

- Are non-living bodies deposited in the cytoplasm
- Are not permanent or essential structures and are usually deposited when large amount of nutrients are present and disappear under the conditions of starvation, for example, lipid granules, volutin granules and sulphur granules

- Are source of stored energy and present in some species of bacteria

Nucleus

- The nucleus in bacteria is not well developed and is without nuclear membrane and nucleolus.
- It contains a single, circular molecule of double-stranded deoxyribonucleic acid (DNA) and is about 1 mm in length.
- **Functions** Controls the following:
  - Growth and metabolism of the cell
  - Multiplication of the cell
  - Hereditary transmission of characters
- In addition to nuclear DNA, bacteria may possess extracellular genetic material consisting of DNA known as **plasmids** or **episomes,** which are not essential for the life of the cell. They may be responsible for properties such as drug resistance and toxigenicity.

Capsule and slime layer

- Some bacteria, for example, pneumococci and *Haemophilus influenzae,* synthesize organic polymers which are deposited outside the cell wall as a loose, gelatinous, amorphous viscid layer called capsule or slime layer.
- If the layer is loose and irregularly arranged, it is known as slime layer and if it is organized into a sharply defined structure, it is known as capsule.
- When its width is less than 0.2 µm, it is known as microcapsule and when its width is more than 0.2 µm, it is known as macrocapsule.
- Some bacteria may have both capsule and slime layer, for example, *Streptococcus salivarius.*

Chemical nature

- Water is the main component (98–99%).
- Solids form 1–2% and are generally carbohydrates in nature—these are complex polysaccharides. In some bacteria, they may be non-carbohydrate in nature, for example, in anthrax bacilli, it is polypeptide in nature.

Functions

- Enhances bacterial virulence by inhibiting phagocytosis
- Acts as protective covering against antibacterial action of substances such as lysozymes, colicins, bacteriophages and antibodies
- Acts as an antigen. Helps in identification and typing of bacteria

Flagella

- Are the hair-like structures arising from cytoplasm and extending out through cell wall
- Are 5–20 µm in length
- **Chemical nature** Chemically, flagella are proteins and are made up of flagellin (molecular weight 30000–50000 Dalton)

Structure of flagella

It consists of three distinct regions which are as follows:

1. **Basal structure (basal body)** It is a circular structure embedded in the cell envelope. It consists a central rod, which bears four rings: L, P, S and M.
   - All four rings are present in Gram-negative bacteria and only S and M rings are present in Gram-positive bacteria.
   - In Gram-negative bacteria
     - L is situated in LPS
     - P is situated in inner peptidoglycan
     - S is situated just above the cell membrane
     - M is embedded in the cell membrane

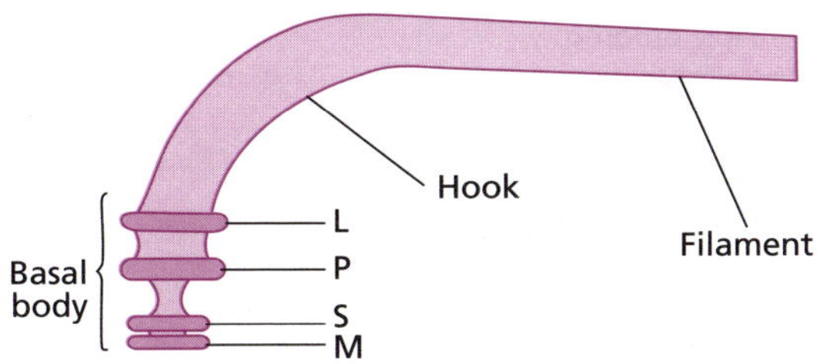

Figure 3.2 Structure of bacterial flagellum.

2. **Hook** It is a short curved structure, connecting the filament and basal body. It is broader than filament, protein in nature (but different from flagellin) and embedded in the cell envelope.
3. **Filament** It is external to the cell and connected to the hook at the cell surface. It is made up of flagellin (Fig. 3.2).

Arrangement/types

- **Atrichate** Flagella are absent and non-motile—*Klebsiella* spp.

- **Atrichate (motile)** Flagella are absent but motile—spirochaetes

- **Monotrichate** Single flagellum at one end—*Vibrio cholerae*

- **Amphitrichate** Single flagellum at both the ends—*Alcaligenes faecalis*

- **Lophotrichate** Tuft of flagella at one or both ends—*Spirilla*

- **Peritrichate** Flagella all around the cell—*E. coli, Salmonella typhi*

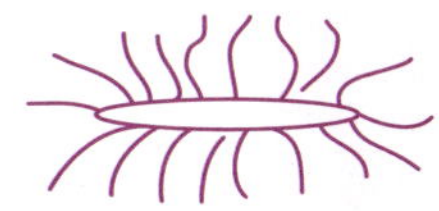

- **Function** They are locomotory organs responsible for motility (movement).

Pili or fimbriae

- Are hair-like structures arising from cytoplasm and are different from flagella
- Are shorter in length (0.1–1 μm) and breadth (10 nm) as compared to flagella
- Chemically protein (pilin)
- **Special type of pili** Sex pili are present in male bacteria which are longer than the regular type but are less in number (1–5 per cell in special type while several hundreds per cell in regular type)
- **Functions**
  - Act as organs of adhesion—virulence factor
  - Sex pili—transfer of genetic material from male to female by forming conjugation tube

Bacterial spores (endospores)

- Spores are highly resistant, resting phase of bacteria.
- They are resistant to temperature, chemicals and other abnormal environmental conditions.
- Known as endospores as the spore is formed inside the bacterial cell.
- Each bacterium forms one spore, which on germination forms a single vegetative cell; hence it is not a method of reproduction.
- Examples of sporulating bacteria
  - Aerobic—*Bacillus* species
  - Anaerobic—*Clostridium* species

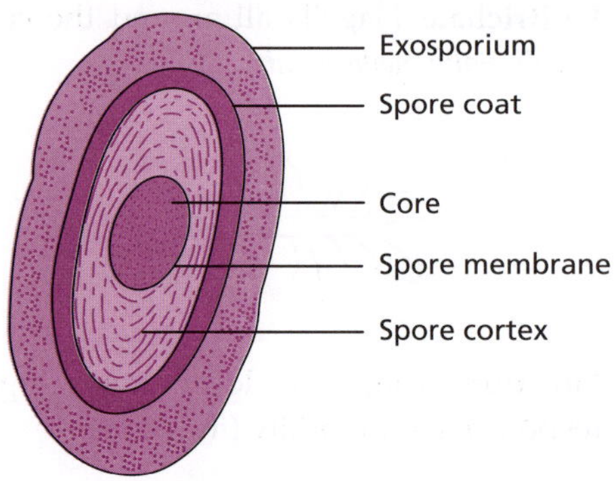

Figure 3.3 Properties of endospore.

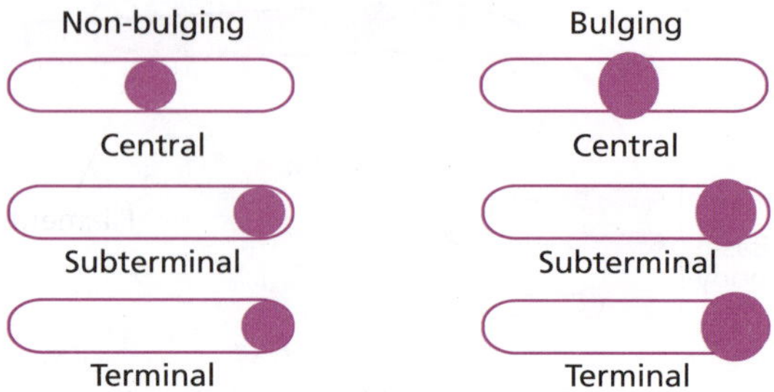

Figure 3.4 Shape and position of spores.

Properties of endospores

- **Core** It is the spore protoplast and contains nucleus and enzymes such as dipicolonic acid synthetase synthesizing dipicolonic acid (5–15%), which makes the spore resistant to heat and other components.
- **Spore wall** It is the innermost layer surrounding the inner spore membrane. It contains peptidoglycan and becomes future cell wall.
- **Cortex** It is the thick layer surrounding the spore wall. Contains unusual type of peptidoglycan which is extremely sensitive to lysozyme.
- **Coat** Composed of keratin-like protein with many disulfide bonds. It is impermeable and makes the spore resistant to antibacterial chemical agents.
- **Exosporium** Lipoprotein membrane containing some carbohydrates (Fig. 3.3).

Shape and position of spores (Fig. 3.4)

- Spore may be central, subterminal or terminal.
- It may be bulging (diameter being more than the bacterial cell) or non-bulging (diameter being the same as bacterial cell).

Shape of bacteria

Depending on the shape, bacteria are classified into different types (Fig. 3.5):

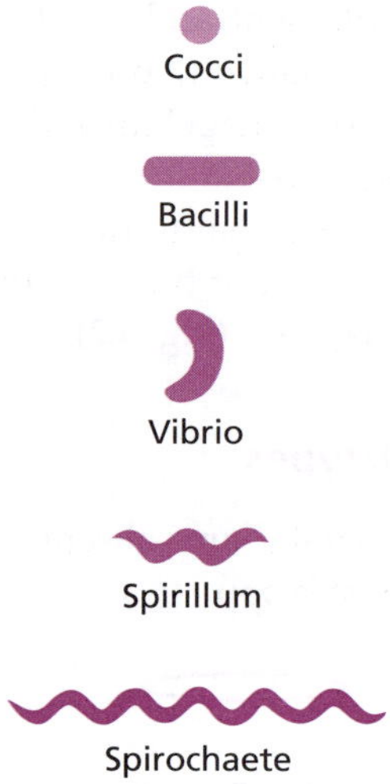

Figure 3.5 Shape of bacteria.

- **Cocci** Spherical or oval cells
- **Bacilli** Rod-shaped cells
- **Vibrios** Comma-shaped curved rods
- **Spirilla** Rigid spiral forms
- **Spirochaetes** Flexuous spiral forms
- **Actinomycetes** Branching, filamentous bacteria
- **Mycoplasma** Cell wall deficient bacteria

Reproduction of bacteria

- Bacteria multiply by simple binary fission into two equal daughter cells.
- The division starts when a bacterial cell reaches a critical mass in its cellular constituents.

- This occurs in the following ways:
  - The circular double-stranded DNA molecule (nucleus) during replication gets separated into two strands of DNA and forms new complimentary strands resulting in two identical double-stranded DNA molecules, which are distributed to two daughter cells.
  - A transverse septum grows across the cell from the cell membrane.
  - Cell wall material is deposited and the two daughter cells are separated (Fig. 3.6).
- The time required for a bacterium to form two daughter cells under optimum conditions is known as generation time.
- The generation time in **most bacteria** is **20 minutes**; however, in **tubercle bacilli**, it is **20 hours** and in **lepra bacilli**, it is **20 days**.
- Some bacteria also reproduce by budding in which a small bud develops from mother cell that separates and grows further to form a new bacterium.

Bacterial growth

Bacterial cells, like other living cells, are metabolically active. Bacterial growth means balanced increase in the mass of all cellular constituents. When the growth reaches a critical mass, cell division (binary fission) occurs.

Conditions of growth

- Bacterial growth requires
  - Water
  - Source of carbon and nitrogen
  - Inorganic salts
  - Growth factors in some cases
  - Source of energy
- Bacteria vary in their requirement of
  - Gases
  - Hydrogen ion concentration (pH)
  - Temperature

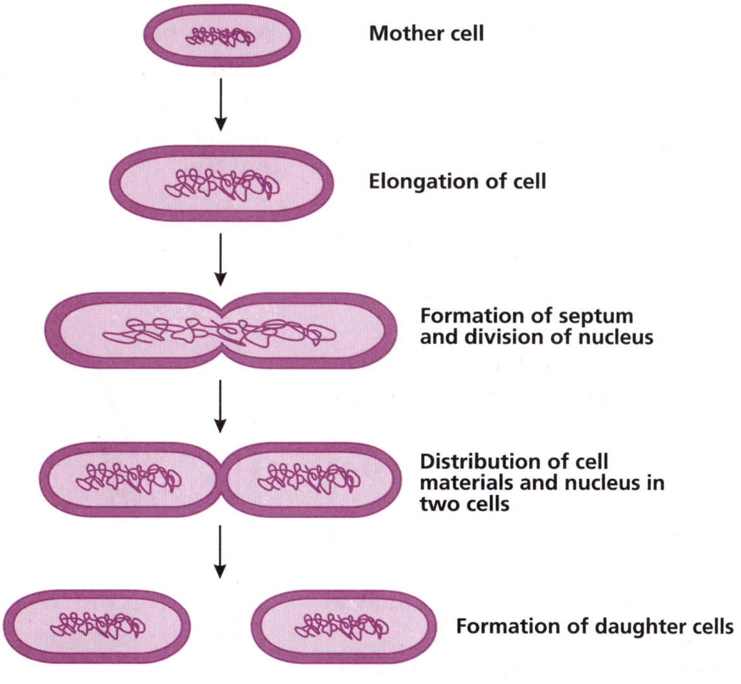

Figure 3.6 Binary fission in bacteria.

Water

- Is the most important factor for bacterial growth
- Is a vehicle for the entry of all nutrients into the cells and for the elimination of all waste products
- Participates in metabolic reaction
- Forms an integral part of the protoplasm

Carbon, nitrogen and energy source Bacteria are classified into two main groups based on the carbon and nitrogen source they utilize.

- **Autotrophs** Bacteria which are able to utilize atmospheric carbon dioxide and nitrogen (medically less important).
- **Heterotrophs** Bacteria which require organic compounds as their source of carbon and energy (medically important).

Inorganic salts Required for

- Osmotic regulation and to provide trace elements essential for certain enzyme systems
- Particularly the anions—phosphate and sulphate
- The cations—sodium, potassium, magnesium, iron, manganese and calcium

Growth factors

- Many pathogenic species require certain key substances for their growth known as growth factors.
- These include vitamins, purines, pyrimidines, amino acids, etc.

Gaseous requirements

- Bacteria require oxygen for their growth. Based on oxygen requirements bacteria are of four types:
  - *Obligate or strict aerobe*—grows only in the presence of oxygen
  - *Microaerophilic*—requires low oxygen concentrations
  - *Obligate or strict anaerobe*—grows only in the absence of oxygen
  - *Facultative anaerobe*—grows in the presence or absence of oxygen
- Bacteria also require carbon dioxide for their growth. It is produced by bacteria itself during metabolism.
- A few bacteria require additional carbon dioxide (5–10%) for their growth, for example, *Neisseria* spp. These are termed **capnophilic bacteria**.

pH

- Most pathogenic bacteria grow best at a neutral or slightly alkaline pH (7.2–7.6).
- Growth is poor below pH 6.0 or above pH 7.8 and stops at pH below 5.0 and pH above 9.0.

Temperature

- Pathogenic bacteria grow best at body temperature of 37°C.
- The optimum temperature for bacterial growth is occasionally higher (*Campylobacter jejuni* grows at 42°C) or lower (*Yersinia pestis* grows at 30°C).

Growth phases

When a bacterium is inoculated into suitable liquid medium and incubated at suitable temperature and pH, the culture passes through four different phases of growth (Fig. 3.7).

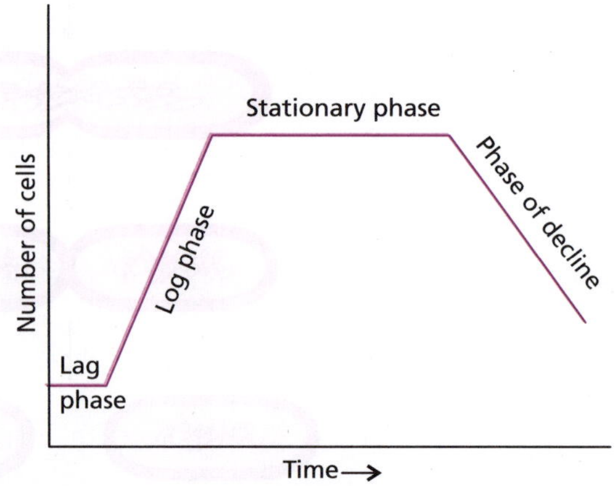

Figure 3.7 Bacterial growth curve.

Lag phase

- This phase occurs immediately after inoculation.
- During this phase no multiplication occurs.
- However, the cell size of the bacterium increases.
- Necessary enzymes and metabolic intermediates are synthesized during this phase.
- Lasts for 1–4 hours.

Log phase (exponential phase)

- Cell division occurs at a maximum rate.
- The number of bacteria increase exponentially.

Stationary phase

- The rate of growth slows down as nutrients are depleted and toxic products are accumulated.
- The rate of cell division equals the rate of cell death.

Decline phase

- The rate of bacterial division is slower than the rate of death.
- As a result of this, there is a decline in the total viable count (Fig. 3.7).

Self-assessment

Long-answer question

1. Draw a labelled diagram of bacterial cell. Describe in detail the cell wall and bacterial flagella.

Short-answer questions

Write notes on
1. Capsule and slime layer
2. Bacterial growth curve
3. Cell wall
4. Mesosomes
5. Ribosomes
6. Inclusion granules
7. Pili
8. Flagella
9. Endospore
10. Binary fission

Multiple-choice questions

1. Which of the following is a distinctive component of the cell wall of Gram-negative bacteria?
   A. Peptidoglycan
   B. Teichoic acid
   C. Lipopolysaccharide
   D. Polysaccharides
2. Bacterial cell wall has all the following properties, EXCEPT
   A. Consists peptidoglycan
   B. Is the structure responsible for Gram reaction
   C. Is sensitive to the action of lysozyme
   D. Acts as a principal osmotic barrier
3. Which of the following is a distinctive component of the cell wall of Gram-positive bacteria?
   A. Peptidoglycan
   B. Teichoic acid
   C. Lipopolysaccharide
   D. Lipoproteins
4. Which of the following components of Gram-negative bacteria has the endotoxic activity?
   A. Lipopolysaccharide
   B. Lipoprotein
   C. Phospholipids
   D. Proteins of outer membrane
5. The following statements are TRUE regarding cytoplasmic membrane, EXCEPT
   A. Acts as semipermeable membrane
   B. Participates in active transport of nutrients
   C. Acts as protective covering and gives rigidity
   D. Takes part in respiration
6. Mesosomes have all the following properties, EXCEPT
   A. Consist invaginated cell membrane
   B. Chemically similar to cell membrane

C. Responsible for respiratory activities of bacteria
D. Act as an osmotic barrier

7. A loose, gelatinous, amorphous viscid layer arranged irregularly outside the cell wall of bacteria is known as
A. Capsule
B. Microcapsule
C. Macrocapsule
D. Slime layer

8. Which of the following structures, found external to cell wall of bacteria, are involved in attachment of bacteria to cell surfaces?
A. Capsule
B. Pili
C. Flagella
D. All of the above

9. Select the most appropriate of the following statements regarding lophotrichate
A. Single flagellum at one end
B. Tuft of flagella at one or both ends
C. Single flagellum at both ends
D. No flagellum anywhere on the cell surface

10. The flagella and pili originate from
A. Cell wall
B. Cytoplasmic membrane
C. Cytoplasm
D. None of the above

11. Which of the following species of bacteria form spores?
A. *Bacillus* species
B. *Corynebacterium* species
C. *Actinomyces* species
D. All of the above

12. The following statements are TRUE about endospores, EXCEPT
A. Formed inside the bacterial cell
B. Appear as refractive bodies in unstained preparations
C. Each bacterium forms one spore, which on germination forms one vegetative cell
D. Formed during log phase of growth

13. The generation time in most of the bacteria is
A. 20 months
B. 20 minutes
C. 20 days
D. 20 hours

14. The cell division in bacteria starts at maximum rate in
A. Lag phase
B. Log phase
C. Stationary phase
D. Phase of decline

15. Microbes which require organic compounds as their source of carbon and energy are
A. Autotrophs
B. Heterotrophs
C. Chemotrophs
D. Phototrophs

16. Select the most appropriate term for bacteria that require additional carbon dioxide
A. Microaerophilic
B. Aerophilic
C. Anaerobic
D. Capnophilic

17. Facultative anaerobes grow better
A. In the presence of oxygen
B. In the absence of oxygen
C. In the presence of carbon dioxide
D. In the absence of carbon dioxide

18. The microcapsule in bacteria has width less than
A. 0.2 μm
B. 0.1 μm
C. 0.3 μm
D. 0.4 μm

4 Sterilization and Disinfection

Sterilization

Sterilization is the process by which an article, surface or medium is made free of all microorganisms. It is the process of destruction or complete removal of all kinds of microorganisms, including spores.

Methods of sterilization

Important physical methods of sterilization include the following:

- Heat
  - Dry heat
  - Moist heat
- Radiation
  - Non-ionizing radiation
  - Ionizing radiation
- Filtration

Heat

It is the most reliable method of sterilization and also the method of choice for materials that are not damaged by heat.

Dry heat

- Is preferred for sterilization of glasswares such as glass syringes, test tubes, Petri plates and materials such as oils, jellies and powders
- Is less efficient process than moist heat, as it requires longer time and higher temperature
- Kills organisms by oxidizing their chemical constituents
- Can be used in the following ways given below

Incineration

- Is the direct burning of contaminated materials
- Is the efficient method of sterilization and used for disposal of
  - Soiled dressings
  - Beddings of patient
  - Animal carcasses
  - Pathological materials

Red heat

- Is the direct heating of an instrument or object in a flame till it becomes red hot
- Is an easy way of sterilization but has limited applications
- Is a useful method of sterilization for non-inflammable materials such as
  - Inoculating loops or wires
  - Points of forceps
  - Scissors
  - Spatulas

Hot air sterilizers (ovens)

- Hot air oven is the most widely used method of sterilization by dry heat.
- It has a two-walled chamber:
  - Inner wall of copper
  - Outer wall of asbestos to reduce radiation of heat
- The cavity of the instrument is divided into small compartments with the help of removable racks.
- Thermometer is inserted at one of the corners.
- The oven is heated by electricity.
- A fan is also fitted to ensure even distribution of air and elimination of air pockets (Fig. 4.1).

Directions for use

- It is operated at 160°C for 1 hour or at 180°C for 30 minutes.
- All glasswares to be sterilized are covered with craft paper and kept in a chamber in a manner which allows free circulation of air in between the objects.
- The temperature is increased.
- The temperature is recorded with the help of thermometer and maintained for 1 hour at 160°C or 30 minutes at 180°C.
- After this specific time, electricity is cut down and material is allowed to cool.
- On cooling, the material is taken from the oven and used.

Uses

- For sterilization of glasswares such as flasks, pipettes, test tubes, Petri plates, glass bottles, slides and syringes
- For sterilization of forceps, scissors, scalpels and other surgical instruments
- Saliva ejector
- For sterilization of swabs
- For sterilization of pharmaceutical products such as liquid paraffin, sulphonamides, dusting powders, fats, grease, oils and glycerin

Precautions

- It should not be overloaded.
- Glasswares must be free from water traces and properly covered with papers.

Sterilization control

- To confirm whether the objects/articles are properly sterilized or not, the paper strips impregnated with non-toxigenic strain of *Clostridium tetani* or *Bacillus subtilis* are placed along with the material to be sterilized. After sterilization, the strips are transferred to suitable media and incubated for an appropriate time at 37°C. The medium is observed for growth. If it shows growth

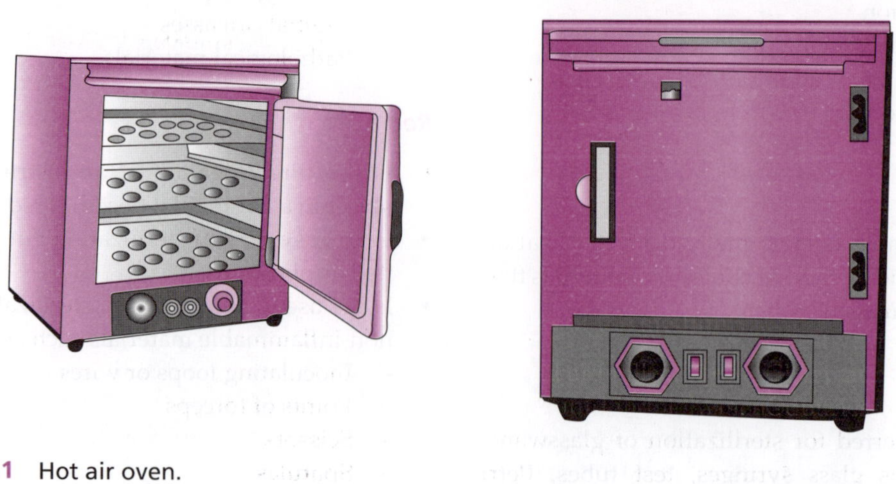

Figure 4.1 Hot air oven.

then process of sterilization is considered as faulty and if no growth is seen then the sterilization is considered as perfect.

- Browne's tube is convenient for routine use. A tube placed with the material shows change in colour from red to green depending on the temperature. Green spot indicates that the process of sterilization is perfect.
- Thermocouples may also be inserted with material and temperature can be recorded.

Moist heat

- Is more efficient than dry heat in penetrating the material
- Is commonly used for the sterilization of culture media prior to washing, laboratory coats, apron, glass syringes and surgical instruments, etc.
- Moist heat may be employed in the following ways:
  - *Temperature below 100°C*
    - ***Pasteurization***
      - For sterilization of milk
      - Includes two methods:

        Holder method—63°C for 30 minutes

        Flash method—72°C for 15–20 seconds followed by quick cooling to 13°C or lower
      - All non-sporing pathogens are killed except *Coxiella burnetii,* which is relatively resistant and may survive the Holder method
    - ***Inspissation***
      - For sterilization of media such as Lowenstein–Jensen and Loeffler's serum slope
      - *Method* Heating at 80–85°C for 30 minutes on 3 successive days in inspissator
      - *Principle* First exposure on day 1 kills all vegetative forms. Spores, which are not destroyed, would germinate to form vegetative forms and are killed by the second exposure on day 2. Spores, if at all present, germinate and would be killed on third exposure on day 3, thus ensuring complete sterilization
    - ***Water bath***
      - For sterilization of serum or body fluids containing coagulable proteins
      - *Method* Heating for 1 hour at 56°C on several successive days in water bath
  - *Temperature around 100°C*
    - ***Boiling***
      - Boiling at 100°C for 10–30 minutes kills almost all vegetative bacteria but does not ensure complete sterilization, as some spore-forming bacteria may not be eliminated completely. For example, *Clostridium tetani* may survive boiling for 1–3 hours. Addition of 2% sodium carbonate promotes sterilization
      - Recommended for sterilization of pipettes, cylinders, rubber stoppers, scalpels, forceps, scissors, syringes, etc., when absolute sterility is not required
    - ***Steaming***
      - Steaming at atmospheric pressure at 100°C is used to sterilize culture media, for example, media containing sugars and gelatin which may be damaged at higher temperature
      - A Koch or Arnold sterilizer is used
      - One exposure for 90 minutes ensures complete sterilization
    - ***Tyndallization***
      - It is an intermittent or fractional sterilization method.
      - In this method, steaming of object is done at 100°C for 30 minutes on 3 successive days.

  - This ensures complete removal of spores, which might not be killed by a single steaming.
  - *Principle* First exposure kills vegetative forms. The spores present will germinate on successive days and will be killed by second and third exposure.

– ***Temperature above 100°C***
  - It is the most widely used method of sterilization.
  - Sterilization by steam under pressure is carried out at temperature between 108°C and 147°C.
  - Several types of steam sterilizers are available. The commonest one is autoclave.

Autoclave

- Water boils at 100°C when its vapour pressure is the same as that of atmospheric pressure.
- When the vapour pressure is increased, the temperature at which water boils also increases.
- The steam under pressure has greater penetrating power.
- The relation between pressure and temperature at which water boils is given in Table 4.1.

Table 4.1 Relationship between pressure and temperature

Pressure (lb/inch2)	Temperature (°C)
Atmospheric pressure	100
5	109
10	115
15	121
20	126
25	130
30	135

Structure of autoclave

- It consists of a vertical or horizontal cylinder of gunmetal or stainless steel, supported by a case made of iron sheet.
- The lid or door is heavy, secured by butterfly nuts and rendered airtight by an asbestos washer.
- The lid has three screws:
  - Steam outlet
  - Safety valve
  - Pressure indicator
- Heating is done by a gas burner or electricity (Fig. 4.2).

Directions for use

- Sufficient water is put in the cylinder.

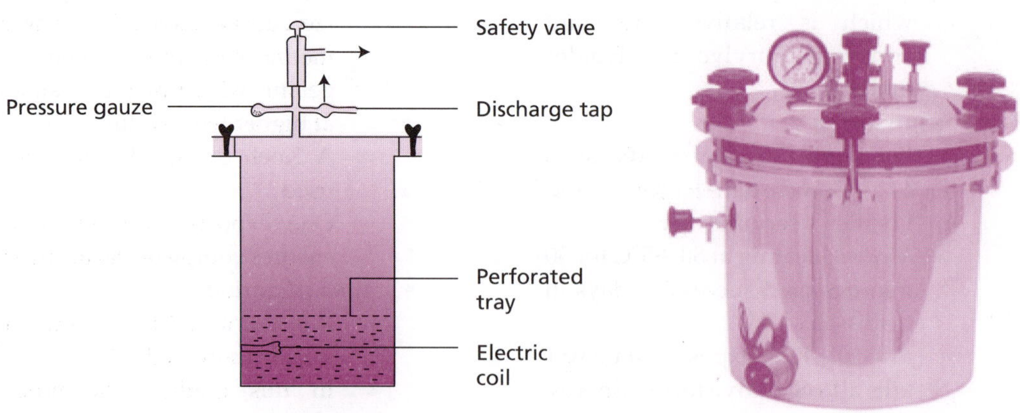

Figure 4.2 Autoclave.

- Articles to be sterilized are placed on the platform (tray).
- The lid is closed properly and screws are tightened.
- The safety valve is adjusted to the required pressure.
- Heating is started with steam tap kept open to displace air inside.
- When all the air inside is expelled out (indicated by continuous flow of steam coming out of tap after sometime), the tap is closed.
- The pressure is recorded; the pressure usually employed is 15 lbs/inch^2 (7.5 kg) above the atmospheric pressure. At this pressure, water boils at 121°C.
- This pressure is maintained for 15 minutes, which ensures killing of all microorganisms including the spores.
- After the desired holding period, the heater is turned off and the autoclave is allowed to cool till the pressure equals to atmospheric pressure (till indicator bar comes to a null point).
- The steam tap is opened slowly to allow the air to enter inside.
- The lid is opened and material is taken out for use.

Precautions

- All air must be expelled out the autoclave as the presence of air lowers down the temperature of the steam and affects the process of sterilization. Also, the presence of air forms air pockets around the materials and thereby prevents the penetration of the steam in the material to be sterilized.
- To avoid drenching by the condensed steam, the cotton wool plugs should be covered with craft paper or cellophane sheets.
- The lid should be opened only when the outside and the inside pressure is equal. This precaution is necessary because opening of lid when the pressure inside is high will cause violent boiling of medium/liquid at a temperature above 100°C and may sometimes be expelled out from the container with an explosive force.
- Opening of lid when the pressure inside is low, will cause evaporation of water and loss of water from medium/liquid reducing the quantities of medium/liquid.

Uses

- The autoclaving can be used for sterilization of anything, which is not damaged by steam. These include the following:
  - All solid and liquid media
  - Distilled water
  - Saline solution
  - Laboratory coats
  - Swabs, syringes and needles
  - Surgical instruments
  - Dressings
  - Laboratory wares
  - Pharmaceutical products
- In **dentistry**, autoclave is useful for sterilization of articles such as
  - Rubber gloves, stopper, tubing
  - Syringe and wax needles
  - Instruments
  - Enamel metal trays
  - Tongue depressor/applicator
  - Saliva ejector
  - Orthodontic pliers
  - Orthodontic kits
  - Hand pieces
  - Hand instruments
  - Steel burs, steel tumbler
  - Calverton heads

Sterilization control

- For determining the efficacy of autoclaving, the following control methods are used:
  - The paper strips impregnated with *B. subtilis* or paper strips or ampoules containing spores of *B. stearothermophilus* are introduced with the material to be sterilized. After sterilization, the strips or ampoules are transferred to a suitable media and incubated for an appropriate time at 37°C. The medium is observed for growth. If it shows growth, the sterilization is considered as imperfect and

if it shows no growth then it is considered as perfect.
  - Other methods such as
    - Chemical dyes showing change in colour at specific temperature
    - Use of thermocouples
    - Autoclave tapes

Radiation

Two types of radiations are used for sterilization:

1. Non-ionizing radiation
2. Ionizing radiation

Non-ionizing radiation

Ultraviolet radiations (UV rays)

- These are short rays (wavelength 210–310 nm) having low penetrating power. The wavelength between 240 and 280 nm, especially 254 nm is most efficient in sterilization.
- Most effective in the absence of oxygen.
- All living microorganisms (bacteria, fungi, viruses) including spores are sensitive to UV treatment. However, spores require double exposure.
- The most commonly employed one is the low-pressure mercury vapour type, which emits more than 95% radiation of wavelength 254 nm.

Applications

- In the control of air-borne infections by air disinfection, for example, disinfection of enclosed areas such as
  - Entry ways
  - Hospital wards
  - Operating rooms
  - Laboratories
- Disinfection of drinking water
- Obtaining pyrogen free water

Ionizing radiation

- Ionizing radiations include gamma rays, beta rays, X-rays, etc.
- Are highly lethal to DNA and other vital cell constituents
- Have high penetrating power
- Gamma and beta rays are extensively used in industry mainly for sterilization of instruments and dressing packs such as
  - Plastic syringes
  - Swabs
  - Culture plates
  - Catheters
  - Various types of rubbers
  - Cardboards
  - Fabrics
  - Metal foils
- Gamma and beta rays are also used for sterilization of oils and greases, food products, pharmaceutical products, etc.
- X-rays and other type of ionizing radiations (alpha particles, neutrons, protons) are not recommended for sterilization either because of poor penetration power or because they induce radioactivity in exposed materials

Filtration

- Filters are used for removal of microorganisms from the fluids or liquids that are thermolabile (sensitive to heat; hence cannot be sterilized by heat).
- Filtration is usually carried out under negative pressure.
- The fluid is sucked through the filter in a receiving flask, which is connected to an exhaust pump.
- The exhaust pump causes exhaustion of flask and fluid is sucked through the filter.

Applications

- Filtration has a number of applications which are as follows:
  - For the sterilization of medicines or other materials, which are heat labile and are damaged by heating, for example
    - Antibiotic solutions
    - Ophthalmic solutions
    - Sera

- Carbohydrate solutions
- Enzyme solutions
- Toxins or toxoids

– To obtain cell-free bacterial products such as toxins, enzymes from cultures
– To make virus (bacteriophages) containing fluids free from bacteria, that is, to obtain bacteria free-filtrates of viruses
– To separate and study microorganisms, which are scanty in fluids

Types of filters

Different types of filters, each having its own applications are available.

Candle filters

- Used for purification of water at large scale
- Are of two types:
  - *Unglazed ceramic filters* Are also called porcelain filters and are composed of hydrous aluminium silicate or kaolin, for example, Chamberland and Doulton filters
  - *Diatomaceous earth filters* Are composed of diatomaceous earth, asbestos and plaster of Paris in different proportions, for example, Berkefeld filter

Asbestos filters

- Composed of asbestos fibers
- Contain disposable, single-use discs

Examples include Seitz filter, Carlson and Sterimat filter.

Sintered glass filters

- Composed of finely powdered glass particles of different sizes according to the required pore size

Membrane filters

- Composed of cellulose esters and are called millipore or polypore filter
- Available in a range of pore sizes (0.05–12 μm)
- Most suitable for preparing sterile solutions

Uses

- Water purification and analysis
- Sterilization and sterility testing
- Preparation of solution for parenteral use

Disinfection

Disinfection is the process of destroying infectious agents. It differs from sterilization, as it does not kill the bacterial spores.

- **Disinfectant** An agent, which is usually a chemical that kills the growing organisms. It may not affect bacterial spores.
- **Antiseptic** An agent that kills or inhibits the growth of microorganisms in contact with the body without causing extensive damage to the body tissue.
- **Germicide** An agent capable of killing microbes
- **Bacteriostatic** An agent capable of inhibiting the growth of bacteria.
- **Bactericide** An agent capable of killing bacteria.
- **Fungistatic** An agent capable of inhibiting growth of fungi.
- **Fungicide** An agent capable of killing fungi.

Ideal characteristics of disinfectant

An ideal disinfectant must have the following:

- Wide spectrum of antimicrobial activity
- Stable and should not undergo any chemical changes
- Should act in the presence of organic matter
- Soluble in water or other suitable solvent
- Not be toxic to the tissues
- Effective in low concentration
- Cheap and easily available
- Odourless or have pleasant odour
- Not corrode or stain material to be disinfected

- Effective in acid as well as alkaline medium
- Speedy action
- High penetrating power
- Safe and easy to use—free from adverse effects
- Not be toxic, if absorbed into circulation
- Not cause local irritation

Action of disinfectants—how do they act?

- Produce damage to the cell wall
- Alter the permeability of the cell membrane
- Alter proteins from protein salts or cause coagulation of proteins
- Inhibit enzyme action
- Inhibit nucleic acid synthesis or alter nucleic acid molecules
- Cause oxidation or hydrolysis
- Disruption of the cell

Guidelines for use of disinfectants

- If more reliable methods are available, do not use disinfectants.
- Cleaning is the most important step in disinfection—clean the instrument/material to be disinfected.
- Total surface contact is essential.
- Use of the recommended strength of the disinfectant is essential.
- As the action of a disinfectant is not instantaneous, the recommended exposure time has to be strictly followed.
- Disinfectants may themselves be contaminated by incorrect use. Therefore, proper care must be taken to avoid contamination.
- Disinfectant may be inactivated by many materials such as pus and blood, rubbers and cellulose products, plastic (polyvinyl chloride) and nylon. Therefore, proper care must be taken.
- After disinfection, rinse the equipment in sterile water, taking all sterile precautions to avoid recontamination.

Commonly used disinfectants

Phenols

- Phenolic compounds are the most widely used disinfectants
- Bactericidal or bacteriostatic in nature depending on the concentration used; some of them are also fungicidal
- Act by damaging the cell membrane and thereby causing lysis of cells
- Different phenolic compounds are as follows:
  - ***Phenol or carbolic acid***
    - Generally not used as it is
      - Expensive
      - Low degree of activity as compared to other derivatives
      - Corrosive—not suitable for application to skin or mucous membrane as it is readily absorbed and produces severe toxic symptoms
    - It is effective against
      - Vegetative forms of bacteria
      - *Mycobacterium tuberculosis*
      - Certain fungi
    - Excellent disinfectant for faeces, blood, pus, sputum, etc.
    - Can also be used for disinfection of
      - Contaminated instruments and utensils
      - Contaminated linen and cloths (5%)
      - Carbonization of theatre (5%)
  - ***Cresol***
    - These are methylphenols
    - Because of low solubility in water, phenols are formulated with soaps, for example, cresol; because of this the bactericidal activity of phenol increases

- Cresols are more germicidal and less poisonous than phenol but corrosive to living tissue; hence prolonged contact should be avoided

Uses

- For cleaning of floors (1% solution)
- For disinfection of surgical instruments
- For disinfection of furniture, tables and other contaminated objects
  - ***Halogenated diphenyl compounds***
    - Highly effective against Gram-positive and Gram-negative bacteria
    - Examples include
      - *Hexochlorophene* As it is toxic, it should be used with caution.
      - *Chlorhexidine* It is highly effective against Gram-positive bacteria and also against Gram-negative bacteria and less toxic/non-toxic.

Uses

- Used as a skin antiseptic, incorporated in cosmetics and soaps, and used for the treatment of wounds

Alcohols

- Ethyl alcohol (ethanol) and isopropyl alcohol are used as disinfectants and skin antiseptics.
- They act by denaturing bacterial proteins. Also by disorganizing the lipid structure of the cell membrane.
- Bactericidal and fungicidal in nature. No action against spores and viruses.
- Effective at a concentration of 60–70% in water.
- Isopropyl alcohol is a better fat solvent, more bactericidal and less volatile. Commonly used as disinfectant for clinical thermometers.
- Methyl alcohol is effective against fungal spores.

Uses

- Isopropyl alcohol is used for disinfection of clinical thermometer and ethanol is used to disinfect skin prior to cutaneous injections.
- Methyl alcohol is effective against fungal spores and used for disinfection of cabinets and incubators infected by fungi. It is less effective against bacteria and injurious to eyes when exposed to its vapours.

Oxidizing agents

- This group includes halogens, hydrogen peroxide, potassium permanganate, sodium perborate, etc.
- They are good disinfectants/antiseptics but are less effective in the presence of organic matter.

Halogens

Include chlorine and iodine

Chlorine

- Hypochlorite (the most commonly used chlorine compound) and inorganic and organic chloramines are the chlorine compounds used for disinfection.
- Organic chloramines—used as antiseptic for wound dressing.
- Chlorine is bactericidal in nature and is effective against spore-forming bacteria and viruses.
- Chlorine and its compounds are used for
  - Disinfection of water
  - Disinfection of diary equipment
  - Disinfection of sanitary utensils
  - Air disinfection (sodium hypochlorite in the form of aerosol)
- Also used in food industry.

Iodine

- Commonly used as a skin disinfectant
- Bactericidal in nature with moderate action against spores; also active against tubercle bacilli and many viruses

- Usually employed as a tincture—an alcoholic solution containing iodine (2.5%) and potassium iodide (2.5%) in alcohol (90%)
- Iodine combined with surface active agents known as iodophors, for example, betadine are generally used and are claimed to be more active than tincture iodine

Hydrogen peroxide (H_2O_2)

- Is a weak disinfectant
- Useful for cleaning of the wounds and for mouthwash or gargle
- H_2O_2 in 3% solution is used

Potassium permanganate

- Is a powerful oxidizing agent
- Used in the treatment of urethritis
- Bactericidal in nature, also active against viruses
- Has antifungal activity also and is used in the treatment of fungal infections of hand and feet
- Can also be used as a water purifier and as a cholera disinfectant

Acids and alkalis

- Acids such as sulphuric acid, nitric acid, hydrochloric acid and benzoic acid and alkalis such as potassium and sodium hydroxide and ammonium hydroxide are germicidal in nature. They are rarely used as disinfectants.
- Benzoic acid and acetic acid are used as preservatives.

Dyes

- Various dyes used for staining of bacteria are bacteriostatic in nature.
- Crystal violet, malachite green, brilliant green, etc., are active against Gram-positive organisms but have less effect on Gram-negative organisms.
- They are used as skin and wound antiseptics.

Heavy metals

- Soluble salts of mercury, silver, copper, arsenic and other heavy metals have antibacterial activity, that is, bactericidal and bacteriostatic activity.
- Mercury chloride is used as disinfectant.
- Organic compounds such as thimerosal, an organomercury compound, (antiseptic and antifungal agent) and merbromin (topical antiseptic) are less toxic.
- Silver compounds such as silver sulphadiazine and silver nitrate are widely used as antiseptics, especially for burn wounds.
- Organic silver salts are efficient bactericidal agents.
- Silver nitrate is bactericidal for gonococci and is also used as a prophylactic agent in ophthalmia neonatorum (neonatal conjunctivitis caused by bacteria, viruses and exposure to certain chemicals) in newborn infants.
- Arsenic compounds were used in the treatment of syphilis in old days before the discovery of penicillin.

Alkylating agents

- Formaldehyde, ethylene oxide and glutaraldehyde are the alkylating agents.
- They exert lethal effect upon proteins.

Formaldehyde

- In aqueous solution, it is bactericidal, sporicidal and also effective against viruses.
- Formalin, an aqueous solution of 37% formaldehyde, is used for coagulating and preserving fresh tissues (specimens) and for destroying anthrax spores in hair and wool.
- The gas is used for
  - Fumigation of operation theatre, wards, sick rooms and laboratories
  - heat-sensitive of instruments and heat-sensitive catheters
  - Clothing, bedding, furniture, books, etc.
- For fumigation of 1000 cu. ft. or 28.3 cu. metre room, 150 g of potassium permanganate

is added to 250 mL of formalin after sealing the windows and other outlets to generate gas.

- After the generation of formaldehyde vapours is started, the door should be sealed and left unopened for 48 hours.
- After disinfection, all traces of vapours should be nullified by exposure to ammonia vapour to avoid irritation and toxic effects.

Disadvantages

- Is highly toxic. Ingestion of 30 mL of a solution containing 37% of formaldehyde can cause death in an adult human
- Is highly corrosive and its ingestion can cause severe injury to the upper gastrointestinal tract
- Is allergenic and carcinogenic

Ethylene oxide

- Is an alkylating agent used for gaseous sterilization
- Is a colourless liquid with a boiling point of 107°C
- Is active against all kinds of bacteria, spores and viruses.
- Acts by inhibiting proteins and nucleic acid
- Is highly inflammable, mutagenic and carcinogenic
- Can be used for sterilization of any object but it is especially useful to sterilize those objects which are damaged by heat, for example, heart–lung machine, respirators, sutures, dental equipment, fabrics, bedding and clothing, disposable instruments, blades, scalpel, scissors, talcum powder, tubing, catheters and gloves
- Is not suitable for fumigation because of its explosive property

Glutaraldehyde

- Has an action similar to formaldehyde
- Is especially effective against tubercle bacilli, fungi and viruses
- Is less toxic and irritant to eyes and skin than formaldehyde
- Can be used for cleaning cystoscopes, bronchoscopes, corrugated rubber anaesthetic tubes, facemasks, plastic endotracheal tubes, metal instruments, orthodontic pliers, orthodontic kits, three-in-one syringe and polythene tubing

Beta-propiolactone (BPL)

- Is a condensation product of ketane and formaldehyde with a boiling point of 163°C
- Has a low penetrating power but more efficient than formaldehyde for fumigation purpose
- Is active against all microorganisms and more active against viruses
- 0.2 % BPL is used for sterilization of biological products
- Is carcinogenic

Surface active agents

- These agents alter energy relationship at interfaces, producing a reduction of surface or interfacial tension.
- They are widely used as detergents, wetting agents and emulsifiers.
- They are of four types:
  - ***Cationic surface active agents***
    - Include quaternary ammonium compounds, which are more active at alkaline pH, for example, acetyl trimethyl ammonium bromide (cetavlon or cetrimide) and benzalkonium chloride
    - Act by denaturing proteins
    - Are bactericidal in nature, more active against Gram-positive bacteria and to a lesser extent against Gram-negative bacteria
    - Is no activity against spores, tubercle bacilli and most viruses
  - ***Anionic surface active agents***
    - Include soaps, which act better at acidic pH

- Are prepared by using saturated and unsaturated fatty acids
- The soaps prepared from saturated fatty acids, for example, coconut oil, are more effective against Gram-negative organisms
- The soaps prepared from unsaturated fatty acids, for example, oleic acid are more active against Gram-positive bacilli and *Neisseria*

– ***Non-ionic surface acting agents***
  - Relatively non-toxic and some of them may promote the growth of bacteria, for example, tween 80 promotes growth of tubercle bacilli

– ***Amphoteric or ampholytic compounds***
  - Are active against a wide range of Gram-positive and Gram-negative bacteria and some viruses
  - Are known as 'Tego' compounds and are not in general use

Self-assessment

Long-answer questions

1. Define sterilization. Discuss in detail the sterilization by moist heat and dry heat.
2. Define disinfection. Discuss in brief the commonly used disinfectants.

Short-answer questions

Write notes on

1. Hot air sterilizer
2. Pasteurization
3. Inspissation
4. Tyndallization
5. Autoclave
6. Non-ionizing radiation
7. Ionizing radiation
8. Sterilization by filtration
9. Phenols
10. Oxidizing agents
11. Alkylating agents

Multiple-choice questions

1. Which of the following statements is FALSE about sterilization by dry heat?
   A. Is the preferred method of sterilization for oils, jellies and powders
   B. Is more efficient method of sterilization than moist heat
   C. Requires longer time and higher temperature
   D. Kills organisms by oxidizing their chemical constituents
2. The incineration is an efficient method of sterilization of all of the following articles, EXCEPT
   A. Soiled dressings
   B. Pathological materials
   C. Animal carcasses
   D. Petri dishes
3. Which of the following statements is FALSE regarding the hot air sterilizer?
   A. Is used for sterilization of orthodontic kits
   B. Is used for sterilization of saliva ejector
   C. Is used for sterilization of pharmaceutical products
   D. Is used for sterilization of swabs
4. The hot air oven is operated at
   A. 121°C for 15 minutes
   B. 160°C for 60 minutes
   C. 100°C for 30 minutes
   D. 80° C for 30 minutes
5. Which of the following is used as sterilization control in hot air oven?
   A. *Bacillus stearothermophilus*
   B. *B. anthracis*
   C. *B. subtilis*
   D. *B. cereus*
6. Which of the following statements is TRUE regarding sterilization by moist heat?
   A. Requires longer time
   B. Requires higher temperature than sterilization by dry heat
   C. Is less efficient method than dry heat
   D. Is more efficient method than dry heat

7. Which of the following bacteria may not be killed by pasteurization?
   A. *Salmonella typhi*
   B. *Coxiella burnetii*
   C. *Brucella abortus*
   D. *Staphylococcus aureus*
8. Select the most appropriate temperature used for sterilization by inspissation
   A. 100°C for 30 minutes
   B. 90°C for 30 minutes
   C. 80°C for 30 minutes
   D. 60° C for 30 minutes
9. Select the most appropriate temperature used for sterilization by tyndallization
   A. 100°C for 15 minutes
   B. 80°C for 60 minutes
   C. 60°C for 30 minutes
   D. 56°C for 30 minutes
10. Which of the following statements is FALSE about autoclave?
    A. Is operated at 121°C for 15 minutes
    B. Is less efficient method than hot air oven
    C. Is used for sterilization of anything which is not damaged by heat
    D. Is used for sterilization of orthodontic pliers
11. Orthodontic pliers are sterilized by
    A. Hot air oven
    B. Boiling
    C. Koch steam sterilizer
    D. Autoclave
12. Which of the following statements is FALSE regarding non-ionizing radiations?
    A. Include gamma rays and X-rays
    B. Are short rays with wavelength 210–310 nm
    C. Are most effective in absence of oxygen
    D. Are used for disinfection of enclosed areas such as entry ways, wards and OT
13. The following are the features of ionizing radiations, EXCEPT
    A. Are highly lethal to DNA
    B. Have high penetrating power
    C. Are used extensively for sterilization of instruments and dressing packs
    D. Are used for disinfection of enclosed areas such as entry ways, wards and OT
14. Which of the following statements is FALSE regarding filtration?
    A. Used for sterilization of medicinal preparations such as antibiotic solutions
    B. Used for obtaining cell free bacterial products
    C. Used for sterilization of egg containing media
    D. Used for sterilization of carbohydrate solutions
15. Following are the uses of membrane filters, EXCEPT
    A. Water purification and analysis
    B. Sterilization of oils
    C. Sterilization and sterility testing
    D. Preparation of solution for parenteral use
16. Following are the oxidizing agents, EXCEPT
    A. Chlorine
    B. Iodine
    C. Potassium permanganate
    D. Chlorhexidine
17. Following agents are used for gaseous sterilization, EXCEPT
    A. Ethylene oxide
    B. Formaldehyde
    C. Glutaraldehyde
    D. Beta-propiolactone
18. Following are the alkylating agents, EXCEPT
    A. Beta-propiolactone
    B. Glutaraldehyde
    C. Formaldehyde
    D. Ethylene oxide
19. Pasteurization of milk is carried out at
    A. 80°C for 20 minutes
    B. 100°C for 20 minutes
    C. 56°C for 30 minutes
    D. 63°C for 30 minutes

20. Which of the following is used for cleaning of orthodontic pliers and orthodontic kits?
    A. Beta-propiolactone
    B. Glutaraldehyde
    C. Formaldehyde
    D. Ethylene oxide
21. Which of the following chemical agents is used for fumigation?
    A. Alcohol
    B. Iodine
    C. Formaldehyde
    D. Carbolic acid
22. Which of the following is NOT used as sterilization control in autoclave?
    A. *Clostridium tetani*
    B. *Bacillus subtilis*
    C. *B. stearothermophilus*
    D. All of the above

5 Culture Media and Culture Methods

Culture media

It is not always possible to identify microorganisms by microscopic methods alone because of their similarity in morphology and staining characters. Hence, further study of microorganisms is essential for their identification. For this purpose, organisms are to be grown artificially on artificial food materials prepared in the laboratory.

The food material on which the organisms are grown is known as a **culture medium** and the growth of organism is known as **culture**. The culture media must fulfil the requirement of organisms to be grown. The important requirements are as follows:

- **Nutrients** The medium must contain the nutrients necessary for growth—sources of energy, nitrogen, carbon, inorganic salts, growth factors and vitamins, electrolytes, water, buffer, fermentable substances, etc. The nutritional requirement may be different for different organisms.
  - For some organisms, the requirement is simple, while it is complex for others. Hence, the culture medium should be devised accordingly.
  - The composition of culture medium varies according to the requirement of a particular organism.
- **pH** Suitable degree of acidity or alkalinity is essential. For example, the fungi require acidic pH (5.3–5.6) for their optimum growth; however, bacteria grow better at 7.2–7.4.
- **Oxygen** Some organisms require presence of oxygen and are known as aerobic organisms. While other organisms grow in the absence of oxygen and are known as anaerobic organisms. A few others require microaerophilic condition (5–10% CO_2) for growth.
- **Temperature** Temperature at which maximum growth occurs is known as optimum temperature. Optimum temperature required for the growth of microbes is 37°C; however, fungi can also grow at room temperature.

Common ingredients of media

Water

- It is essential for the existence of living cells; acts as a source of hydrogen and oxygen.

Peptones

- Peptones are golden granular hygroscopic powder obtained from meat, casein fibrin or soya flour.

- They are complex mixture of partially digested proteins and contains proteoses, amino acids, polypeptides, phosphates, minerals (K, Mg, Ca, Fe, Zn) and accessory growth factors (riboflavin, nicotinic acid).

Meat extract

- It is an extract of meat, contains protein degradation products, carbohydrates, inorganic salts, enzyme exciters and growth factors—rich in vitamin B complex.

Yeast extract

- It is an extract of yeast cells, contains proteins, amino acids, growth factors (vitamin B), carbohydrates and inorganic salts. It is a substitute for meat extract.

Electrolyte

- Sodium chloride or other electrolytes are essential to maintain osmotic pressure.

Agar

- Dried mucilaginous substance obtained from sea weeds
- Does not provide any nutrition to growing organisms
- Melts at 98°C and generally solidifies at 42°C, hence used as a solidifying agent

Artificial media commonly used for growth of bacteria

Different types of culture media are used for bacterial growth. These can be classified in different ways as shown in Table 5.1.

Classification based on physical state

Based on their physical state, they may be liquid, solid and semisolid media.

Liquid media

- These media are liquid in nature and do not exhibit specific characteristics which help in identification. They also do not permit isolation of different types of bacteria from mixed populations.
- **Uses** They can be used for
  - Further testing of pure culture of bacteria
  - Preparing bulk cultures for preparation of antigens or vaccines
  - Obtaining growth of organisms from blood or water when large volumes have to be tested
- **Examples** Nutrient broth and peptone water

Solid media

- These media are solid in nature and they produce discrete visible growth
- **Uses** They can be used for
  - Obtaining a pure growth
  - Studying distinctive colony morphology and other characteristic features, for example, pigmentation and haemolysis

Table 5.1 Classification of culture media

Based on physical state	Based on nutritional factors (chemical composition)
• Liquid—liquid in nature	• Simple—simple chemical composition
• Solid—solid in nature	• Synthetic—chemically defined
• Semisolid—neither liquid nor solid	• Non-synthetic—complex; not chemically defined
	• Special—media used for special purpose, for example – Enriched media – Enrichment media – Selective media – Differential media – Indicator media – Transport media – Sugar media

- **Examples** Nutrient agar and blood agar

Semisolid media

- These media are neither liquid nor solid in nature; they have the phase between liquid and solid.
- **Uses** Used for
  - The study of bacterial motility
  - Cultivation of anaerobic and microaerophilic organisms

Classification based on nutritional factors

Based on nutritional factors, artificial media are of the following types:

- **Simple media (basal media)**
  - These are the media with relatively simple chemical composition, for example, nutrient broth and peptone water.
  - These are the basal media, which form the basis of all other laboratory media.
  - Addition of 2–3% agar to nutrient broth makes it nutrient agar, which is the simplest solid basal medium routinely used for diagnostic purpose.
  - Addition of 0.2–0.4% agar makes it semisolid medium which is used for the study of bacterial motility.
  - Addition of 6% agar makes it firm agar that prevents spreading or swarming of growth of bacteria such as *Proteus* species.
- **Complex media**
  - These are the media other than simple media which have complex composition.
  - Contain additional ingredients for bringing out certain properties or providing special nutrients required for the growth.
- **Synthetic or defined media**
  - These are the media prepared by using pure chemicals of known chemical composition; hence, the exact chemical composition of the medium is known.
  - Used for special studies.
- **Special media**
  - These are the media used for special purpose. They include the following:

Enriched media

- The basal media added with substances such as blood, serum or egg are known as enriched media.
- **Uses** For the growth of organisms which are more exacting in their nutritional needs.
- **Examples** Blood agar enriched with blood, Loeffler's serum slope enriched with serum and Lowenstein–Jensen medium enriched with egg.

Enrichment media

- These are the liquid media incorporated with substances which either have a stimulating effect on the organisms to be grown or inhibiting effect on the growth of unwanted organisms in specimens containing more than one organism.
- They selectively favour the growth of organism of interest and inhibit the growth of unwanted organisms.
- **Uses** Useful in culture of faeces in enteric fever where non-pathogenic or commensal bacteria tend to overgrow the pathogenic ones.
- **Examples** Tetrathionate broth and selenite F broth inhibit the growth of coliforms in faeces and allow the growth of *Salmonella* species.

Selective media

- These are the media incorporated with substances which inhibit the growth of a large number of organisms and selectively permit the growth of required organism in a greater number
- **Uses** To isolate a particular organism from specimens where mixed microbial flora is expected.

- **Examples** Deoxycholate citrate agar (DCA) for *Shigella* and *Salmonella,* and Wilson–Blair medium for *Salmonella*.

Differential media

- These are the media which differentiate the two different types of organisms.
- These media are incorporated with substances which help to distinguish the differing characteristics of organisms.
- **Uses** To differentiate the two types of organisms.
- **Examples** MacConkey's medium containing peptone, lactose, sodium taurocholate, neutral red and agar differentiates lactose fermenters (form pink colonies) from non-lactose fermenters (form colourless or pale colonies).

Indicator media

- These are the media incorporated with an indicator which changes the colour of the organism that grows on it. Thus, these media indicate the presence of a particular organism by imparting a particular colour to it.
- **Examples** Wilson–Blair medium containing sulphite, which is reduced to sulphide by *Salmonella typhi* producing black colonies. MacConkey's medium forms pink colonies in the presence of neutral red indicator and indicates the presence of lactose-fermenting organisms.

Transport media

- These are the media used for transportation of specimens containing delicate organisms such as gonococci and *Vibrio cholerae,* which do not survive outside the body for longer duration.
- These organisms may be killed during the transportation of the specimen or may be overgrown by non-pathogenic, organisms. Hence, to avoid these problems, special media, known as transport media, are used for transportation of specimens.

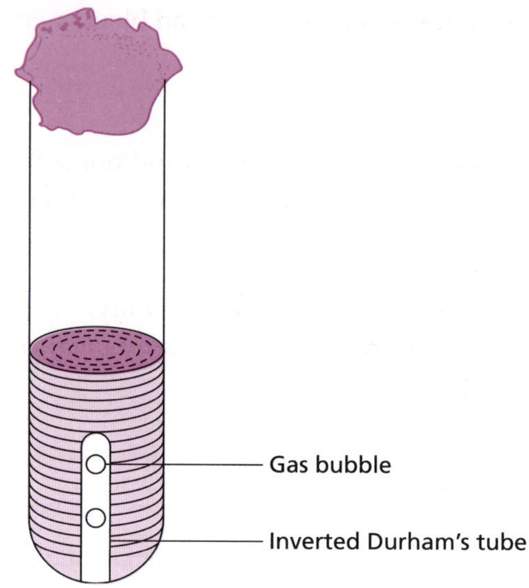

Figure 5.1 Sugar media.

- **Examples** Stuart's transport medium, buffered glycerol saline transport medium and Cary–Blair transport medium.

Sugar media

- The media containing fermentable substances (sugars) are known as sugar media.
- These media contain 1% sugar (glucose, lactose, sucrose, mannitol, etc.) in peptone water with Andrade's indicator and an inverted small tube known as Durham's tube for gas collection (Fig. 5.1).
- **Uses** Used for the study of sugar fermentation reactions. Fermentation of sugar results in the formation of acid that changes the colour of medium from colourless to pink and gas as indicated by gas bubbles accumulated in Durham's tube. These fermentation reactions help in the identification of organisms.

Culture methods

- The methods used for growing microorganisms are known as culture methods.
- Different culture methods are used for the culture of bacteria.

- Culture methods are used for the following purposes:
  - To isolate bacteria in pure culture and to identify them
  - To study different properties of bacteria
  - To obtain sufficient growth of bacteria for preparation of antigens and vaccines
  - To determine susceptibility of bacteria to antibacterial agents, bacteriophages, bacteriocins, etc.
  - To estimate viable counts
  - To maintain stock cultures

Inoculation of media

- Inoculation of media is the process of insemination of bacteria in a culture media.
- It may be done from
  - Pathological material (primary culture) for isolation of pathogenic bacteria
  - Another culture (subculture) for the further study of the isolated bacteria
- Inoculation loop, straight wire or Pasteur pipette is used for inoculating the media.

Inoculation loop

It is a platinum wire loop of 23 SWG (standard wire gauge) thickness or a nichrome wire loop of 24 SWG thickness, which is about 3″ long and is held on a metal holder or fused into a glass rod. The free end of wire is bent in the form of a loop of about 2–4 mm in diameter. A nichrome wire is cheap but takes more time to cool after flaming (Fig. 5.2).

- **Uses** Used for
  - Inoculation of culture media
  - Preparation of smear
  - Collection of specimens

Figure 5.2 Inoculation loop.

Straight wire

It is a straight wire held on a metal holder or fused into a glass rod (Fig. 5.3).

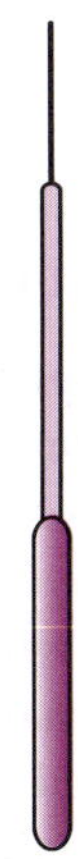

Figure 5.3 Straight wire.

- **Uses** It is used
  - To stab or shake culture
  - To pick up exactly a single colony from the mixture

Methods of culture

The different methods of culture are given in the following text.

Streak culture (surface plating)

- This is the most commonly used method for isolation of bacteria in pure form from any specimen. A loopful of specimen is taken with the help of a flame sterilized and cooled loop and placed on the surface of dried culture plate near the peripheral area. This is known as **primary inoculum**.

- This primary inoculum is then spread thinly over the plate by streaking it in a series of parallel lines in different segments of the plate.
- The loop used for spreading is flamed and cooled in between the different sets of streaks.
- After overnight incubation at 37°C, growth may be confluent at the site of primary inoculum and becomes progressively thinner and well-separated colonies are formed over the final series of streaks (Fig. 5.4).
- **Uses** For the isolation of bacteria in pure culture from clinical specimens.

Lawn or carpet culture

- In this method, a liquid culture or a suspension of the bacterium is flooded on the surface of the plate. Excess inoculum is pipetted off or alternatively the surface of the plate is inoculated with the help of a swab soaked in the bacterial culture.
- Plates are incubated at 37°C. After overnight incubation, uniform surface growth is obtained.
- **Uses** Used for
  - Antibiotic susceptibility testing by disc diffusion method
  - Bacteriophage typing
  - Obtaining a large amount of bacterial growth for preparation of bacterial antigens and vaccines

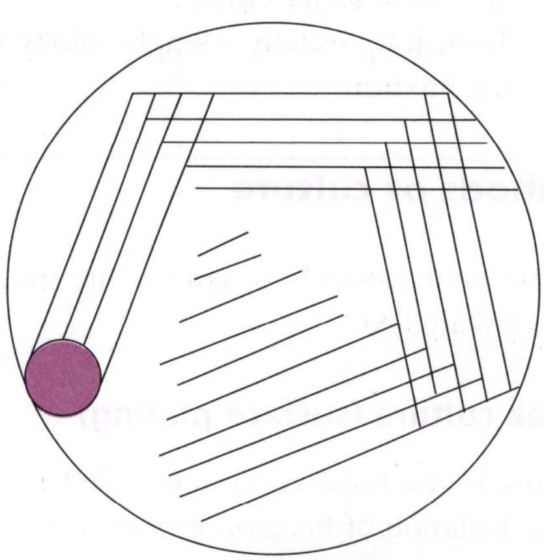

Figure 5.4 Streak culture method.

Stroke culture

- It is made in tubes containing agar slope (slant). Nutrient agar is most commonly used.
- **Uses** Used for
  - Obtaining a pure growth of bacterium for slide agglutination and biochemical reactions, etc.
  - Maintaining stock cultures

Stab culture

- In this method, culture is made by stabbing or puncturing of a medium deep inside the agar with the help of a straight wire charged with culture material.
- **Uses** Used for
  - Demonstration of gelatin liquefaction
  - Demonstration of oxygen requirement of bacteria
  - Maintaining stock cultures of bacteria

Pour plate culture

- In this method, the inoculum to be tested is serially diluted and a known amount (1 mL) of each dilution is mixed with 15 mL of melted agar at 45–50°C and mixed well.
- The mixture is poured into a sterile Petri plate and allowed to set.
- After incubation at 37°C for overnight, the colonies distributed throughout the depth of media are counted.
- The number gives the viable bacterial count in a given suspension.
- **Uses** Used for
  - Estimation of **viable count,** for example, to quantitate bacteria in urine cultures
  - Analysis of water

Liquid culture

- Liquid cultures in tubes, screw-capped bottles or flasks may be inoculated with loop, pipettes or syringes.
- Liquid cultures are preferred when large and quick yield is required.
- **Uses** Used for
  - Blood culture and sterility tests, where the number of bacteria in the inoculum is expected to be small
  - For specimens containing antibiotics and other antibacterial substances which are rendered ineffective by dilution in the medium

Incubation of culture media

Most of the bacteria are mesophilic that grow better at 37°C. Hence, the inoculated culture media are incubated at 37°C in an incubator. The incubator is structurally similar to hot air oven (Fig. 5.5).

Anaerobic culture methods

Anaerobic bacteria do not require oxygen for their growth. They grow in the absence of oxygen. The anaerobic conditions or anaerobiosis can be achieved by different methods.

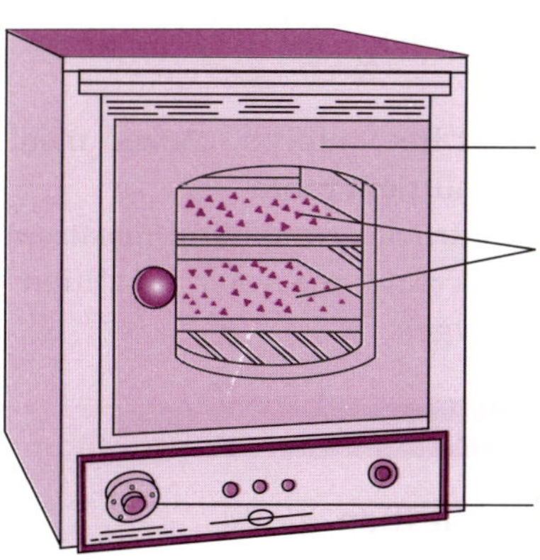

Figure 5.5 Bacteriological incubator.

Methods of anaerobiosis

Production of vacuum

- Vaccum is produced by incubating cultures in vacuum desiccators. Results are not satisfactory, hence not used.

Displacement of oxygen

- Oxygen displacement by inert gases such as hydrogen, nitrogen and helium or carbon dioxide was also tried, for example, candle jar method.
- In a **candle jar method**, inoculated plates are placed in a large airtight container and a lighted candle is kept before the lid is sealed. It is expected that the burning candle will utilize all the oxygen before it gets extinguished, but some oxygen is always left behind. Hence, it is an ineffective method of anaerobiosis. However, it provides 5–10% CO_2 concentration condition which is suitable for the growth of microaerophilic bacteria, which require 5–10% CO_2 for growth.

By displacement and combustion of oxygen

- For this, McIntosh–Filde's jar is used, which consists of a glass or metal jar with a metal lid.
- The lid has two tubes with taps—one acts as inlet for introduction of gas and the other acts as outlet.
- The lid also has two terminals, which can be connected to electric supply and a catalyst (alumina pellets coated with palladium) under the lid.
- It also has pressure gauze (Fig. 5.6).

Operation

- Inoculated culture plates are placed inside the jar and the lid is clamped.
- The outlet is connected to a vacuum pump and the air inside is evacuated.
- The outlet is closed and hydrogen is passed through the inlet till it is filled (monitored by pressure gauze).

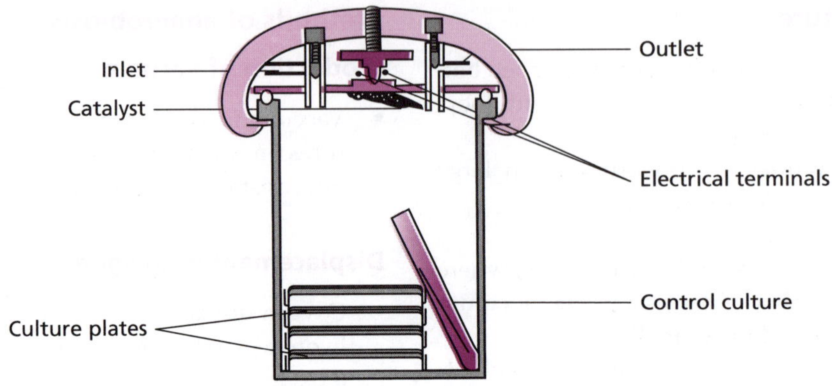

Figure 5.6 McIntosh–Filde's jar.

- Electric terminals are switched on to heat the catalyst, which catalyzes the reaction between hydrogen and residual oxygen to form water.

Absorption of oxygen by chemical or biological methods

Chemical methods

- **Pyrogallol** In this method, a tube containing pyrogallic acid and sodium hydroxide is placed inside an airtight jar that absorbs oxygen and produces anaerobic conditions.
- **Chromium and sulphuric acid** These two chemicals react in the presence of oxygen forming chromous sulphate and produce anaerobic conditions.
- **Gas-pak** It is the method of choice.
  - It is a commercially available gas-pak packet containing pellets of citric acid, sodium bicarbonate, sodium borohydride and cobalt chloride, which generates hydrogen and carbon dioxide on addition of water.
  - Hydrogen combines with oxygen to produce water and creates anaerobic conditions.
  - *Process* Inoculated plates are placed in the airtight jar and the packet of gas-pak with water is added and the lid is tightly closed.
  - *Advantages* Simple, reliable and no risk of explosion unlike McIntosh–Filde's jar.

Biological methods

- By incubating the culture of aerobic organisms in an airtight jar with the assumption that utilization of oxygen by aerobic bacteria for their growth creates anaerobic conditions.
- This method is slow and ineffective.

By using reducing agents

Oxygen in a medium can be reduced by using various reducing agents such as glucose, thioglycollate, ascorbic acid, cysteine and cooked meat pieces.

Robertson's cooked meat medium

- Is the most widely used medium for anaerobes
- Contains fat free, minced, cooked meat of ox heart in nutrient broth
- The meat particles containing unsaturated fatty acids create anaerobic condition by utilizing oxygen

Self-assessment

Long-answer question

1. Define anaerobiosis. Describe in detail the various methods of anaerobiosis.

Short-answer questions

Write short notes on

1. Simple media
2. Enriched media
3. Selective media
4. Differential media
5. Indicator media
6. Transport media
7. Sugar media
8. Streak culture
9. Lawn or carpet culture
10. Pour plate culture
11. Gas-pak jar
12. McIntosh–Filde's jar
13. Candle jar

Multiple-choice questions

1. The following are the sources of peptone, EXCEPT
   A. Meat
   B. Soya flour
   C. Casein
   D. Yeast
2. The following statements are TRUE regarding agar, EXCEPT
   A. Is obtained from sea weed
   B. Solidifies at 42°C
   C. Acts as a source of carbon
   D. Melts at 98°C
3. The following are the enriched media, EXCEPT
   A. Loeffler's serum slope
   B. Lowenstein–Jensen medium
   C. Nutrient agar
   D. Chocolate agar
4. The following are the selective media, EXCEPT
   A. Wilson–Blair medium
   B. Deoxycholate citrate agar
   C. MacConkey's medium
   D. None of the above
5. The quantity of blood added to prepare blood agar is
   A. 1–2%
   B. 3–4%
   C. 5–10%
   D. 11–15%
6. Which of the following blood is most suitable for preparation of blood agar?
   A. Human blood
   B. Rabbit blood
   C. Horse blood
   D. Sheep blood
7. Peptone water is an example of
   A. Defined media
   B. Simple media
   C. Transport media
   D. Enrichment media
8. Which of the following is a transport medium?
   A. Stuart's medium
   B. Buffered glycerol saline medium
   C. Cary–Blair medium
   D. All of the above
9. The indicator incorporated in MacConkey's agar is
   A. Bromocresol purple
   B. Methyl red
   C. Neutral red
   D. Phenol red
10. Which of the following sugars is present in MacConkey's medium?
    A. Galactose
    B. Lactose
    C. Sucrose
    D. Glucose
11. The thickness of platinum wire loop is
    A. 23 standard wire gauge (SWG)
    B. 24 SWG
    C. 25 SWG
    D. None of the above
12. All of the following methods are used for culture of anaerobes, EXCEPT
    A. Candle jar
    B. Craigie's tube
    C. Gas-pak jar
    D. McIntosh–Filde's jar
13. Which of the following is a method of choice for anaerobiosis?
    A. McIntosh–Filde's jar
    B. Candle jar
    C. Gas-pak jar
    D. None of the above

6 Identification of Bacteria

Once the bacterium is isolated from a specimen in pure culture, it has to be identified by using appropriate methods of identification. For identification, various characteristics of bacteria are to be studied. These include growth and staining characters, biochemical reactions, antigenic structure and antibiotic sensitivity.

Study of growth characters

Growth on solid medium (colony morphology) (Fig. 6.1)

The following characters of colony are to be noted:

- **Size** In millimetres
- **Shape** Circular/irregular
- **Surface** Smooth/rough/granular
- **Elevation** Flat, convex, raised or umbonate
- **Edge** Entire/undulate/crenated/ lobate
- **Opacity** Opaque/translucent/transparent
- Colour of the colony
- **Consistency** Mucoid/friable/firm/butyrous
- Other properties
  - Haemolysis
  - Pigmentation
  - Swarming

Growth in liquid media (broth culture)

In a liquid medium (nutrient broth, peptone water or other liquid media), the following characters are to be noted:

- The degree of growth—scanty/moderate or abundant
- Presence of turbidity and its nature (e.g., uniform turbidity)
- Pellicle formation on surface and its quality

Study of staining characters

Study of staining characters helps in preliminary identification of bacteria. Differential staining such as

- **Gram staining** Helps to differentiate bacteria into Gram-positive and Gram-negative
- **Ziehl–Neelsen staining** Differentiates bacteria into acid-fast and non-acid-fast bacteria and helps in preliminary identification of mycobacteria
- Various special staining methods help to bring out special characters, for example, Albert's stain and Neisser's stain for *Corynebacterium diphtheriae* and spore staining for spores.

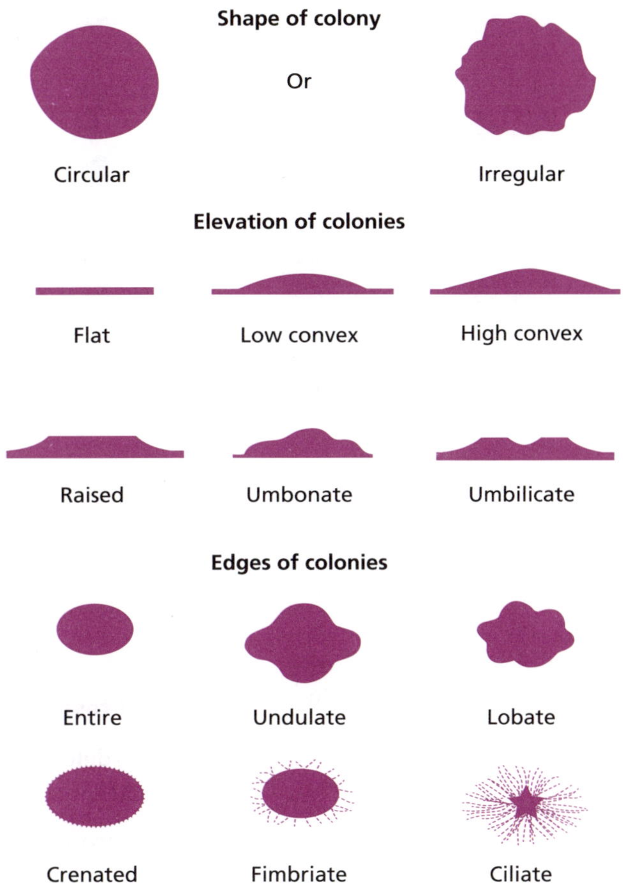

Figure 6.1 Colony morphology.

Study of biochemical reactions (Fig. 6.2)

Biochemical reactions are used for accurate identification of bacteria. The most important and most widely used biochemical reactions are given in the following text.

Sugar fermentation tests

Principle To determine the ability of a bacterium to ferment a specific sugar (carbohydrate) producing acid or acid with gas.

Fermentation medium Important constituents are as follows:

- Suitable basal medium—peptone water
- Sugar (1%)—glucose, lactose, sucrose and mannitol (routinely used)
- Suitable indicator—Andrade's indicator (sodium hydroxide + acid fuchsin)
- Durham's tube—a small inverted tube filled with liquid for collection of gases
- The constituents are dispensed in test tubes and sterilized under low-pressure steam

Test procedure A drop or a loopful of liquid culture is inoculated in the test medium and incubated for 18–24 hours at 37°C

Result

- Positive test—development of pink colour and gas production

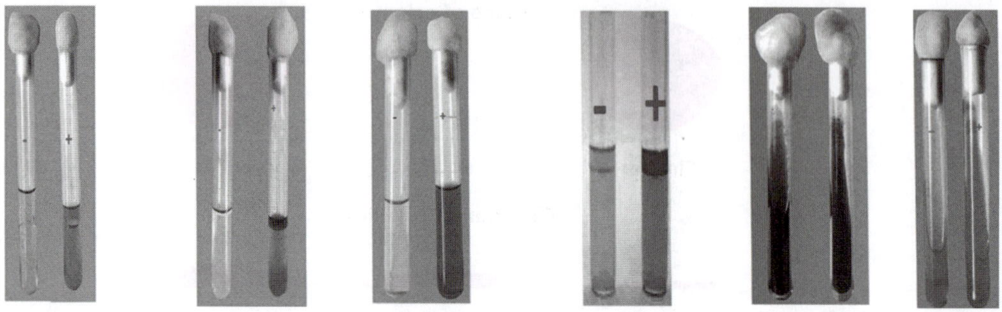

Sugar fermentation test | Indole test | Methyl red test | Voges-Proskauer test | Citrate test | Urease test

Figure 6.2 Biochemical reactions. *See the color image at the end of the book (Color Plates).*

- Negative test—no colour change

Mechanism Fermentation of sugar results into formation of acid and gas. The resultant acidity changes the pH of the medium that results in change of colour of indicator from yellow to pink and the gas formed is collected in Durham's tube

IMViC tests

Indole test

Principle To demonstrate the ability of bacteria to decompose amino acid tryptophan into indole

Medium Peptone water

Test procedure The test bacterium is inoculated into peptone water and incubated at 37°C for 24–48 hours. The production of indole is tested by adding indole reagent (Kovac's or Ehrlich reagent)

Result
- Positive test—development of pink ring at the surface of the medium
- Negative test—yellow coloured ring at the surface of the medium

Mechanism The amino acid tryptophan is converted into indole which reacts with para-dimethylaminobenzaldehyde and gives pink colour

Examples
- Indole positive—*Escherichia coli, Proteus vulgaris*
- Indole negative—*Klebsiella* spp. *Proteus mirabilis*

Methyl red test

Principle To determine the ability of bacteria to produce acid from glucose

Medium Glucose phosphate broth (GPB)

Test procedure The test bacterium is inoculated into GPB and incubated at 37°C for 24–28 hours. The acid production is tested by adding a few drops of methyl red reagent

Result
- Positive test—development of bright red colour
- Negative test—yellow colour

Mechanism Some bacteria produce acid by fermenting glucose which gives red colour when an indicator is added

Examples
- MR positive—*E. coli, Salmonella* species
- MR negative—*Klebsiella, Enterobacter* species

Voges–Proskauer (VP) test

Principle To determine the ability of bacteria to produce acetyl methyl carbinol (acetoin) from pyruvic acid

Medium GPB

Test procedure The test bacterium is inoculated into GPB and incubated at 37°C for 48 hours. After incubation, 1 mL of 40% KOH and 3 mL of 5% alpha-naphthol in absolute alcohol are added

Result

- Positive test—development of pink colour in 2–5 minutes
- Negative test—no pink colour

Mechanism Some bacteria ferment carbohydrates and produce acetyl methyl carbinol (acetoin) from pyruvic acid that gives pink colour in the presence of alkali (KOH) and atmospheric oxygen

Examples

- VP positive—*Klebsiella* species, *Enterobacter*, El Tor *Vibrio*
- VP negative—*E. coli*, *Proteus* species, *Salmonella* species

Citrate utilization test

Principle To determine the ability of bacteria to utilize citrate as the sole source of carbon for its growth

Medium Koser's citrate medium (liquid) or Simmon's citrate medium (solid)

Test procedure The test bacterium is inoculated into Koser's or Simmon's citrate medium and incubated at 37°C for 24–96 hours

Result

- Koser's citrate medium
  - Positive test—turbidity because of growth
  - Negative test—no turbidity
- Simmon's citrate medium
  - Positive test—change of colour from green to blue
  - Negative test—no colour change and no growth

Mechanism Some bacteria utilize citrate as the sole source of carbon for their growth. These bacteria utilize citrate with resultant alkalinity and make the medium alkaline that changes the colour of bromothymol blue from green to intense blue or makes medium turbid in case of Koser's citrate medium

Examples

- Citrate positive—*Klebsiella, Pseudomonas aeruginosa*
- Citrate negative—*E. coli, Shigella*

Hydrogen sulphide production (H_2S) test

Principle To determine the ability of bacteria to produce H_2S from sulphur-containing amino acids

Medium Peptone water or media containing lead acetate, ferric ammonium citrate or ferrous acetate can be used

Test procedure The test bacterium is inoculated into the medium and a strip of lead acetate paper is held over a culture in a test tube between the cotton plug and the tube

Result

- Positive test—blackening or browning of lead acetate paper
- Negative test—no change in colour

Mechanism Some bacteria produce H_2S by enzymatic action on sulphur-containing amino acids. This liberated H_2S causes blackening when it interacts with metallic salts

Examples

- H_2S positive—*Proteus* and *Salmonella* species with some exceptions
- H_2S negative—*E. coli, Klebsiella, Salmonella paratyphi A*

Urease test

Principle To determine the ability of bacteria to decompose urea into ammonia

Medium Christensen's urease agar

Test procedure The test bacterium is heavily inoculated over the entire slope surface and incubated at 37°C. The medium is observed after 4 hours and again after overnight incubation

Result

- Positive test—development of pink colour
- Negative test—no change in colour

Mechanism Some bacteria produce an enzyme urease that splits urea into ammonia. Ammonia makes the medium alkaline and changes the pH that results into colour change of phenol red from pale yellow to pink

Examples

- Urease positive—*Klebsiella, Proteus, Helicobacter pylori*
- Urease negative—*E. coli, Salmonella* species

Catalase test

Method I 1 mL of hydrogen peroxide (H_2O_2) solution is poured over a 24-hour nutrient agar slope culture of the test bacterium and observed for gas bubbles immediately.

Method II A drop of H_2O_2 is taken on a clean glass slide to which a small amount of culture of the test bacterium is added with the help of a glass rod and observed for gas bubbles.

Result

- Positive test—immediate bubbling
- Negative test—no gas bubbles

Mechanism Some bacteria produce the enzyme *catalase* that catalyzes the release of oxygen from H_2O_2. Hence, contact of bacteria with H_2O_2 causes the formation of gas bubbles indicating the formation of oxygen.

Examples

- Catalase positive—staphylococci, all members of Enterobacteriaceae except *Shigella dysenteriae type 1*
- Catalase negative—*Bacillus* species, streptococci, *Clostridium* spp.

Oxidase test

Principle To determine the ability of bacteria to produce an enzyme *cytochrome oxidase*

Test procedure

- **Plate method** A freshly prepared 1% solution of tetramethyl-p-phenylenediamine dihydrochloride (oxidase reagent) is poured on the surface of colonies of the test bacterium and observed for the development of a purple colour
- **Dry filter paper method** A strip of filter paper soaked in a freshly prepared 1% solution of *oxidase* reagent is smeared with the test bacterium and immediately observed for the deep purple colour

Result

- Positive test—deep purple hue within 5–10 seconds
- Negative test—no colour change

Mechanism Some bacteria produce an enzyme cytochrome oxidase that catalyzes the transport of electrons between electron donors in the bacteria and redox dye (oxidase reagent), which is reduced to a deep purple colour

Examples

- Oxidase positive—*Pseudomonas* species, *Vibrio* species, *Neisseria*
- Oxidase negative—all members of Enterobacteriaceae, staphylococci and streptococci

Triple sugar iron (TSI)

Principle To determine the ability of bacteria to ferment carbohydrates incorporated in a growth medium and production of H_2S

Medium TSI agar medium contains glucose, lactose, sucrose and ferric salts. Phenol red indicator is incorporated. The medium is used in the form of a butt and slant

Test procedure The test bacterium is inoculated deep in the butt with the help of a straight wire (stab culture) and incubated at 37°C for overnight

Results All three sugars positive, if the slant remains red and the butt becomes yellow.

- Gas production—if bubbles are produced in the butt
- H_2S production—if there is blackening of the medium
- No fermentation—red colour

Study of antigenic structure

Antigenic analysis of the test bacterium using specific antisera can be used for identification of bacterium or to further confirm the biochemically identified bacterium by agglutination or precipitation reaction.

Antibiotic sensitivity testing

It is important in the selection of antibiotic of choice for treatment and also helps in identification of some bacteria, for example, bacitracin sensitivity in identification of *Streptococcus pyogenes* and optochin sensitivity to identify pneumococci.

Self-assessment

Short-answer questions

Write notes on

1. Sugar fermentation reactions
2. IMViC test
3. Hydrogen sulphide test
4. Oxidase test
5. Catalase test
6. Urease test
7. Triple sugar iron

Multiple-choice questions

1. Which of the following indicators is used in sugar fermentation reaction?
   A. Kovac's reagent
   B. Ehrlich's reagent
   C. Christensen's indicator
   D. Andrade's indicator
2. Which of the following tubes is used for collection of gas in sugar fermentation reaction?
   A. Craigie's tube
   B. U tube
   C. Durham's tube
   D. None of the above
3. Which of the following statements is FALSE about indole test?
   A. Tryptophan containing medium is required
   B. Development of pink ring indicates positive test
   C. The test uses xylene as an indicator
   D. Tryptophan is converted into indole by bacterial decomposition
4. Which of the following bacteria is indole negative?
   A. *Escherichia coli*
   B. *Proteus mirabilis*
   C. *Proteus vulgaris*
   D. None of the above
5. Which of the following statements is TRUE regarding methyl red test?
   A. Detects acetyl methyl carbinol
   B. Positive test is indicated by yellow colour
   C. Uses glucose phosphate broth
   D. Is always positive with indole positive test
6. Which of the following statements is FALSE regarding Voges–Proskauer test?
   A. Detects acetyl methyl carbinol
   B. Uses glucose phosphate broth
   C. Uses 40% KOH and 5% alpha-naphthol as indicator
   D. Is always positive along with positive methyl red test
7. Which of the following statements is FALSE regarding the citrate test?
   A. Is used to determine the ability of bacteria to utilize citrate as a sole source of carbon
   B. Uses Koser's or Simmon's citrate medium

C. *E. coli* gives positive citrate reaction
D. Citrate is utilized with resultant alkalinity

8. The oxidase reagent is
A. Tetramethyl amino benzaldehyde
B. Tetramethyl-p-phenylenediamine dihydrochloride
C. Paramethyl amino benzaldehyde
D. Dimethyl-p-phenylenediamine dihydrochloride

9. Which of the following bacteria is oxidase negative?
A. *Pseudomonas* spp.
B. *Vibrio* spp.
C. *Proteus* spp.
D. *Neisseria* spp.

10. Which of the following indicator is used in urease test?
A. Methyl red
B. Neutral red
C. Congo red
D. Phenol red

11. Which of the following bacteria is catalase positive?
A. Pneumococci
B. Streptococci
C. Staphylococci
D. None of the above

7 Bacterial Genetics

Genetics is the study of heredity and variation. The hereditary characters are encoded in genes—segments of DNA that carry information for a specific biochemical or physiological property in its nucleotide sequence. Individual organisms transmit these characteristics to their offspring through genes. The chromosomal DNA plays an important role in the maintenance of characters constant from generation to generation by its accurate replication.

The genetic material

Structure of deoxyribonucleic acid (DNA)

- Nucleus in bacteria contains a single, circular molecule of a double-stranded DNA about 1000 μm (1 mm) long.
- It contains complementary nucleotides.
- The two strands are wrapped around each other to form a double helix (Watson and Crick) (Fig. 7.1).
- Each strand has a backbone of deoxyribose sugar and a phosphate group arranged alternatively.
- Each deoxyribose is attached to one of the four nitrogenous bases. These bases are
  - Adenine (A) and guanine (G)—**purine bases**
  - Thymine (T) and cytosine (C)—**pyrimidine bases**
- The purine 'A' is paired with pyrimidine 'T' and the purine 'G' is paired with pyrimidine 'C'.
- The bases are paired by hydrogen bonding at the centre of the molecule. The hydrogen bonds help to hold two strands together. A-T is held by two hydrogen bonds and C-G by three hydrogen bonds.
- The order of nitrogen-base pairs is highly specific and contains the genetic information for the organism.
- Each of the four bases is bonded to phospho-2′-deoxyribose to form a nucleotide. As the strands are complementary, if the sequence of bases in one strand is ATGC, the sequence of other strand is TACG.

Structure of ribonucleic acid (RNA)

RNA differs from DNA in the following ways:

- It is single stranded.
- It contains ribose sugar instead of deoxyribose.
- Instead of thymine (T), uracil is the base present in RNA.
- There are three different types of RNA in a cell: messenger RNA (m-RNA), ribosomal RNA (r-RNA) and transfer RNA (t-RNA).

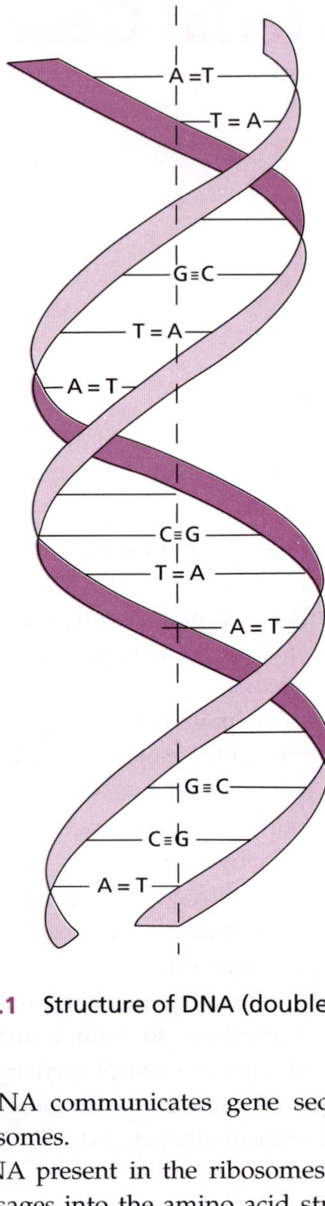

Figure 7.1 Structure of DNA (double helix).

- m-RNA communicates gene sequence to ribosomes.
- r-RNA present in the ribosomes translate messages into the amino acid structure of protein with the help of t-RNA.

Some important terms

- **Gene** It is a segment of DNA that codes or specifies for a particular polypeptide (functional product).
- **Codon** Genetic information is stored in the DNA as a code, the unit of which is a sequence of three bases (triplet). Each such triplet is known as codon. Each codon specifies for a single amino acid, but more than one codon may exist for the same amino acid.
- **Nonsense codons** The three codons—UAA, UGA and UAG—do not code for any amino acid (do not form any amino acid) and act as **'stop codons'** for terminating message for the synthesis of a polypeptide. These are known as nonsense codons.
- **Genotype** It is the genetic make-up—the information that codes for all characters of the organism.
- **Phenotype** It is the manifestation of genotype—the actual, expressed structural and physiological properties of the organism.

Functions of chromosome

- To synthesize a polypeptide, the chromosome is functionally subdivided into segments, each segment determines an amino acid sequence and hence the structure of a discrete protein.
- The different proteins thus synthesized determine the structural and physiological properties of the organism by functioning as enzymes, and as components of membrane and other cell structures.
- The way in which the genetic information in DNA is transcribed on to RNA and translated into a particular sequence of amino acids on a protein occurs as given in the following text.

Transcription The enzyme RNA polymerase attaches to a gene on DNA and synthesizes m-RNA, using one of the strands in DNA as a template. Hence, the m-RNA synthesized is complementary to one of the strands in DNA. This process is known as transcription.

Translation The m-RNA then passes into cytoplasm where it attaches to the ribosome containing r-RNA. The m-RNA possesses triplet of nucleotide bases known as codons.

These codons are recognized by the anticodon sequences of t-RNA. The t-RNA molecule contains a triplet of nucleotides complementary (anticodons) to the triplet of nucleotides on m-RNA at one end and a specific site for amino acid at the other end. The t-RNA brings the amino acid, attaches to the complementary nucleotide triplet on m-RNA and puts the amino acid into a peptide linkage with the amino acid of the neighbouring t-RNA molecule. The ribosome moves along the m-RNA until the entire m-RNA molecule has been translated into corresponding sequence of amino acids. This process is known as translation.

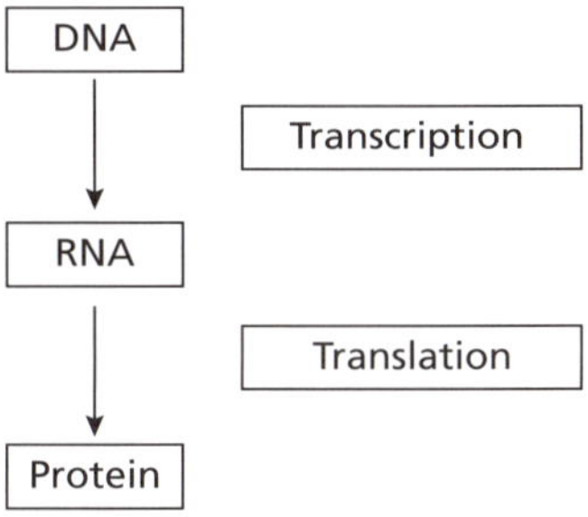

In this manner, the nucleotide sequence of a gene determines the structure of specific protein using m-RNA as mediator. Thus, chromosomes regulate the proteins of cells, which help to determine the traits of organism, contain genetic information to control various activities of cell, contain instructions to produce new progeny, etc.

Extrachromosomal genetic elements

The extrachromosomal genetic elements include plasmids and episome.

Plasmids

These are self-replicating, cyclic, double-stranded circular DNA molecules, different from those on chromosome (extrachromosomal) and present in the cytoplasm in a free state. These are of two types:

1. **Conjugative**—large and self-transferable, for example, R and F plasmids
2. **Non-conjugative**—small, non-transferable, but can be transduced; these plasmids are transferable with the help of conjugative plasmids, for example, resistance determinants (r-determinants)

Properties of plasmids

- Contain genes for self-replication.
- May express phenotypically.
- Some plasmids have the apparatus for transfer, that is, they are self-transferable. Such plasmids can mediate the transfer of chromosomal genes and other plasmids by integration.
- Some plasmids have the ability to jump from chromosomal DNA to plasmid DNA or vice versa by a process called transposition and are known as **transposons** or **jumping genes**.
- Plasmids carry genes, which are not essential for the life and function of the host but they confer properties such as
  - *Fertility (F) factor*—the cell containing F-factor (plasmid) is F^+ (male) and synthesizes sex pilus
  - *Resistance (R) factor*—attributed to resistance. These are conjugative plasmids. Contain two functionally different parts:
    - Resistance transfer factor (RTF)—contains genes for autonomous replication and conjugation
    - r-determinant—smaller component, determines drug resistance. A single factor may carry gene-controlling resistance to multiple antibiotics
  - *Bacteriocinogen*—responsible for production of bacteriocins
  - *Other plasmids*—responsible for production of exotoxins, haemolysins, surface antigens, etc.

Episome

- Is also an extrachromosomal genetic material
- Is integrated with chromosomal DNA or exists autonomously in the cytoplasm
- Is similar to plasmid—not possible to differentiate from plasmid; hence the two terms are used synonymously

Bacterial variation

Bacterial variation is of two types: phenotype and genotype.

Phenotype (phaeno—display)

Refers to the expression of various inherited traits by bacterial cells in a given environment.

Phenotypic variation

- A bacterial cell may exhibit different phenotypic appearances in different environmental conditions.
- Phenotypic changes are temporary and occur in response to the changed environmental conditions; these are reversible when the original environmental condition is restored.
- The important phenotypic variation occurring in bacteria is
  - Synthesis of enzyme, *beta-galactosidase,* necessary for lactose fermentation by *Escherichia coli,* occurs only when it is grown in lactose-containing medium. Though *E. coli* possesses the genetic information for the synthesis of *beta-galactosidase,* actual synthesis is induced by the presence of lactose (inducible enzyme). This has led to operon concept by Jacob and Monad. The operon concept explains the regulatory mechanism involving structural and regulatory genes.
- Lactose fermentation in *E. coli* requires three enzymes:
  - *Beta-galactosidase*—coded by the structural gene *lac* Z
  - *Galactosidase permease*—coded by the structural gene *lac* Y
  - *Transacetylase*—coded by the structural gene *lac* A
- The genes are arranged linearly in a sequence forming a functional unit know as *lac* operon (Fig. 7.2).
  - The regulatory gene *lac* I—codes for a repressor.

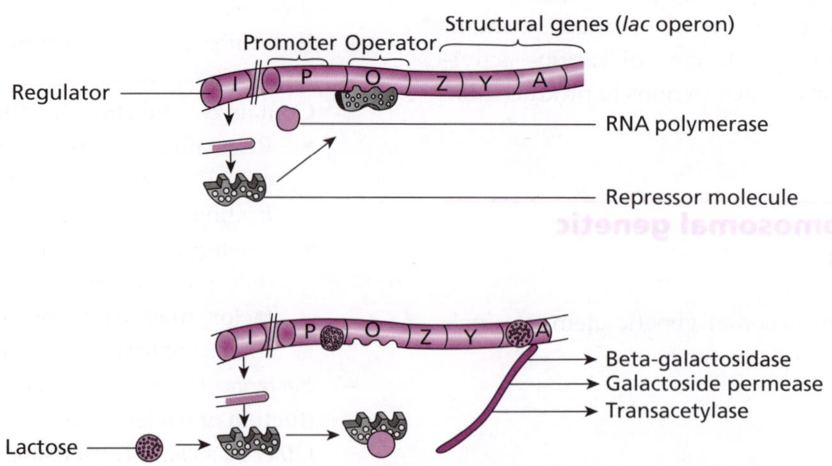

Figure 7.2 *Lac* operon.

- In addition, there are promoter and operator regions which lie between *lac* I and the structural genes
- The repressor can combine with the inducer molecule (lactose) when it is present, otherwise it combines with operator region and prevents the travel of RNA polymerase from the promoter region to the operon.
- When lactose is present, the repressor molecule, which has affinity for lactose, leaves the operator free allowing RNA polymerase to travel along the structural genes in a sequence for transcription of RNA to synthesize enzymes necessary for lactose fermentation.
- When the lactose is completely metabolized, the repressor again attaches to the operator and prevents the travelling of RNA polymerase from the promoter region thereby inhibiting transcription and enzyme synthesis.

Genotype

It is the sum total of the genes. It is the genetic constitution of an organism.

Genotypic variation

- These variations are due to changes in the genetic material and hence the genotypic variations are stable, heritable and not influenced by the environment.
- Genotypic variations occur by mutation or transfer of genetic material from one bacterium to another (gene transfer).

Mutation

Mutation is defined as a permanent alteration/change in the sequence of bases of DNA. This change may or may not lead to detectable change in the cell phenotype. When the mutations are not expressed phenotypically, they are known as **silent mutations**. The different forms of a gene produced by mutation are called **alleles**.

Mutation may be spontaneous or induced by mutagenic agents. **Spontaneous mutations** occur spontaneously in the absence of any known mutagen and appear to be due to errors in base pairing during DNA replication.

Mutational changes include the following:

- Nucleotide replacements
- Nucleotide deletions and insertions

Nucleotide replacements Mutations that occur due to replacement of bases. This occurs in two ways:

1. Transition—replacement of a purine by another purine, or replacement of a pyrimidine by another pyrimidine, for example, replacement of AT by GC
2. Transversion—replacement of a pyrimidine by purine or vice versa, for example, replacement of GC to CG

Deletions and insertions During DNA replication, there may be insertion of one or a few base pairs or deletion of one or a few base pairs. This insertion or deletion shifts the normal reading frame of the coded message forming a new set of triplet codons that specify the incorrect amino acids. These mutations are called **frame shift mutations**.

Induced mutations

Mutations induced by a variety of physical and chemical agents are called induced mutations. The agents that induce mutation are called **mutagens or mutagenic agents**.

- **Physical agents**—such as irradiations (UV rays, X-rays, visible light) and heat
- **Chemical agents**—such as base analogs (5-bromouracil, 2-aminopurine), nitrous acid, alkylating agents and acridine dyes (acridine orange and proflavine)

Nonsense mutations

Mutation that results into formation of a nonsense codon (UAG, UAA or UGA) that prematurely terminates the growing peptide chain leading to the formation of a partial polypeptide. Thus, the protein molecule synthesized is not a complete one and hence it is non-functional.

Missense mutation

Mutation in which substitution and frame shift mutation give rise to an altered codon, which specifies a different amino acid that replaces the correct amino acid normally located at a particular position in the protein. This is called missense mutation.

Gene transfer

Transfer of genetic material in bacteria occurs in three ways: ***transformation, transduction*** and ***conjugation***.

Transformation

It is the process in which the genetic information is transferred through free or naked DNA.

Discovery

Griffith (1928) observed that when non-capsulated, rough strain is injected in a mouse with heat-killed, smooth strain (capsulated) of pneumococci, the mouse dies and living, smooth pneumococci are isolated from the blood of the dead mouse. He guessed that heat-killed, smooth strain of pneumococci might have liberated something which conferred on the rough strain the ability to make a new type of capsular polysaccharide and thus might have converted the rough strain to smooth one making it virulent. In 1943, Avery, Macleod and McCarty identified the transforming principle as DNA.

Mechanism

During transformation, the bacterium becomes competent and during this period of competence, the double-stranded DNA from donor binds to sites (present during the stage of competence only). This DNA is enzymatically cleaved to form fragments and fragmented DNA is efficiently taken up and incorporated into the recipient DNA.

Transduction

It is a process of gene transfer in which a portion of DNA from one bacterium is transferred to another by bacteriophages. Transduction not only transfers chromosomal DNA but may also transfer plasmid or episomal DNA.

Discovery

By Zinder and Lederberg in 1952 in *Salmonella.*

Types

It is of two types: generalized and restricted transductions.

Generalized transduction It is the transduction in which any segment of DNA is transduced by a bacteriophage (Fig. 7.3).

Specialized (restricted) transduction It is the transduction in which only a particular segment of DNA is transduced by a bacteriophage.

Mechanism

- Bacteriophage attacks the bacterium and releases its nucleic acid in the bacterial cell and starts its replication process.
- During the maturation process of the bacteriophages, a few phage heads may envelope any fragments of bacterial DNA in generalized transduction or it may envelope only a particular segment of bacterial DNA in specialized transduction along with phage DNA.
- When such a phage infects another bacterium, it introduces bacterial DNA which

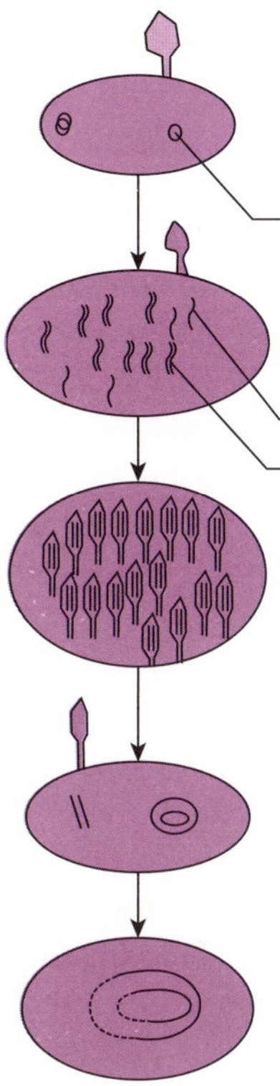

Figure 7.3 Generalized transduction.

gets incorporated into the host bacterial chromosome.

- Thus, the transfer of bacterial genes to the other bacterium occurs.

Lysogenic conversion

In the process of transduction, adsorption of a bacteriophage is followed by injection of phage DNA into the host cell. If this phage is of virulent type, the result is

- **Lytic cycle** in which new phage particles are synthesized that are released by a process of lysis of the host cell.
- **Lysogenic cycle** When the infecting phage is a temperate phage (phage which persists without causing lysis of bacterial cell), the result is lysogenic conversion/lysogeny. In this, phage DNA is incorporated into the host cell DNA (known as **prophage**), which multiplies, synchronously with the host cell DNA. It acts as an additional chromosomal element and the host acquires significant new characters, which are transferred to the progeny, for example, the diphtheria bacilli are toxigenic because of lysogenic bacteriophage, that is, beta phage. Elimination of beta phage renders them non-toxigenic.

Conjugation

It is the process of transfer of genetic material in which a 'male' or 'donor' bacterium mates or makes physical contact with 'female' or 'recipient' bacterium and transfers genetic material to it.

Discovery

By Lederberg and Tautum (1946) in *E. coli.*

Mechanism

During the process of conjugation, one partner acts as 'donor' male (F^+ cells) and the other acts as 'recipient' female (F^- cell). Bacteria, possessing a plasmid called F factor (F for fertility), is transferred by conjugation when male and female make cell-to-cell contact.

After the F-factor is transferred, every female (F^-) is converted into male (F^+). Plasmids not only determine maleness but also determine other characters. Many plasmids carry genes, which confer new properties on the host cell, for example

- Resistance to drugs—R-factors
- Production of colicins—Col factor

Conjugation process

- The cells come in direct contact through pilus retraction.
- One strand of plasmid DNA is broken down.
- The broken strand enters the recipient.
- The complementary strands are synthesized in both donor and recipient.

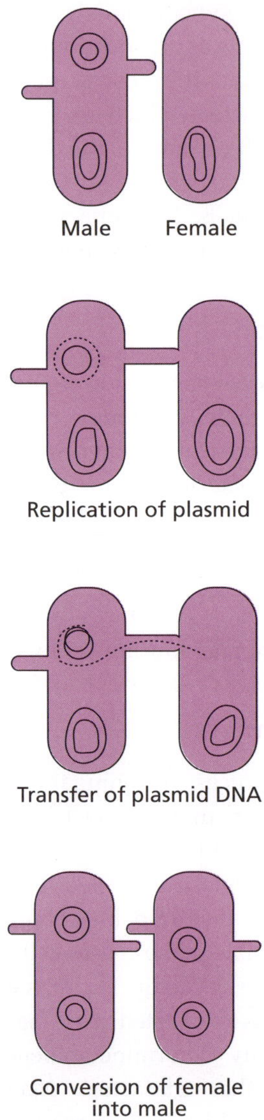

Figure 7.4 Conjugation.

- This results in conversion of female (F^-) into male (F^+), which in turn conjugate with other female (F^-) (Fig. 7.4).
- Conjugation mediates the transfer of plasmid DNA. It may also mediate the transfer of chromosomal DNA in some bacteria.

Significance

Confers new properties in recipient cell, for example, drug resistance property.

F-mediated chromosome transfer in Hfr cell

- The F-factor from the donor cell gets integrated with the bacterial chromosome and forms one large circular molecule. The bacterial cells in which this occurs and the clones that arise from them are called Hfr cells (high frequency of recombination).
- Hfr cells transfer the chromosomal DNA to the recipient cell with high frequency.
- As this process of integration is reversible, the conversion of F^+ cell into Hfr cell is also reversible.
- When the F-factor reverts from the integrated state to a free state by detaching from chromosome, sometimes, it may carry part of chromosomal DNA with it.

This F-factor carrying part of chromosomal DNA is known as F1. When F1 cell conjugates with F- cell, it transfers the chromosomal DNA incorporated with it. This process is known as **sexduction**.

Significance of conjugation in medical sciences

The two medically important plasmids, colicinogenic (Col) factor and resistance transfer factor (RTF), which confer properties of colicin production and resistance to drug are transferred by conjugation.

Col factor It is the plasmid responsible for colicin production in *E. coli*.

RTF It is the plasmid responsible for spread of multiple drug resistance among bacteria.

- RTF and r-determinant are the two components of the plasmid known as R-factor.
- The RTF mediates conjugational transfer of the r-determinant, which carries genes responsible for resistance to drugs.
- R-factor may have many r-determinants and resistance to many drugs can be transferred simultaneously.
- This is a very common mode of drug resistance particularly in enteric bacteria.

- RTF is also shown to mediate conjugal transfer of genes responsible for enterotoxin and haemolysin production in some enteropathogenic *E. coli.*

Genetic mechanism of drug resistance

- The drug resistance is acquired after a change in DNA.
- This change may occur by alteration in the structure of chromosome. The alteration in chromosomal DNA is caused by mutation or by acquisition of extrachromosomal DNA which is the result of genetic exchange, in which the sensitive organism receives extrachromosomal genetic material from resistant organism resulting into development of resistance to one or multiple drugs (Flow chart 7.1).

Mutational drug resistance

It develops as a result of spontaneous mutation in a locus of chromosomal gene that controls susceptibility to a drug. The presence of a drug serves as a selective mechanism to suppress susceptibility and promotes the growth of drug-resistant mutants.

In clinical practice, mutational resistance is very important in tuberculosis. If only one drug is given to the patient, tubercle bacilli die initially in large numbers but soon resistant mutants emerge and multiply unchecked. A serious consequence of unchecked drug resistance is emergence of multiple drug-resistant strains. Hence, to avoid emergence of resistance by mutation, a combination of four drugs is used. By using the four drugs, a mutant resistant to one drug will be killed by the other drugs as mutational drug resistance involves one drug only at a time.

Transferable (infectious) drug resistance

- It arises as a result of transfer of plasmid or episome through the process of conjugation or transduction.
- Transfer of resistance against single or multiple drugs (most common) through the plasmid known as R-factor is a very important method of drug resistance.

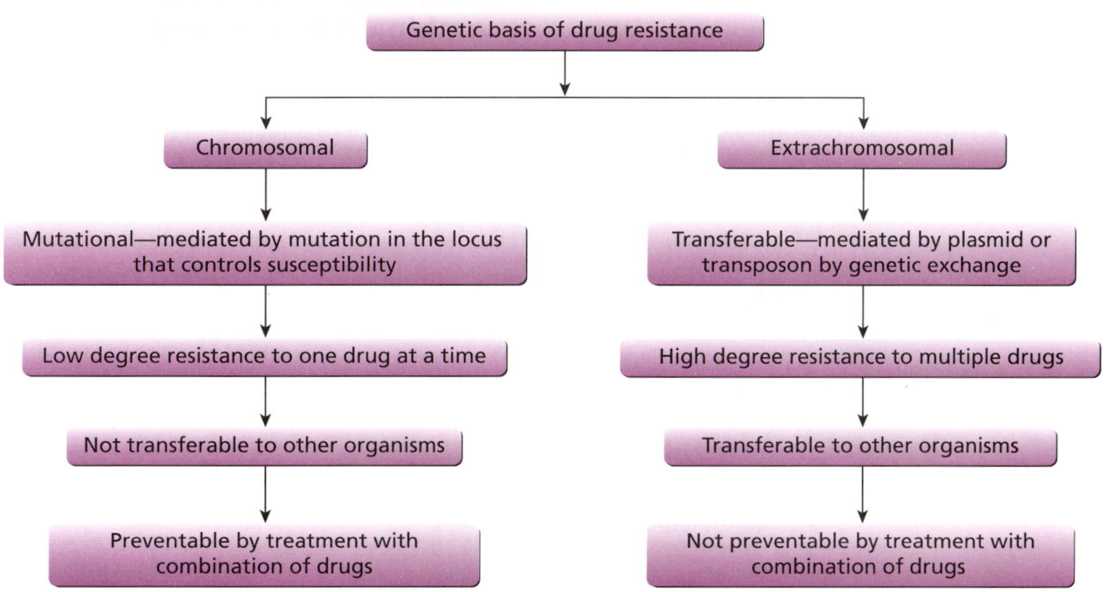

Flow chart 7.1 Genetic basis of drug resistance in bacteria.

- The R-factor contains two components:
  - r-determinant—determines resistance to drug
  - RTF—mediates transfer of r-determinant
- The transferable drug resistance is very common in Enterobacteriaceae.
- Resistance in *Staphylococcus aureus* to penicillin is due to a plasmid that produces penicillinase. This plasmid is devoid of RTF and its transfer from resistant to susceptible strain occurs by transduction rather than conjugation.

Transposable genetic material

- Transposons (Tn) are DNA sequences, which have the ability to move from one plasmid to another or from plasmid to chromosome and vice versa. Due to this property, they are also known as jumping genes.
- Because they are unable to exist independently, they are transferred from one DNA molecule to another. This process is known as **transposition,** which is different from recombination, as it does not require any DNA homology between transposable element and the site of insertion in a DNA molecule.
- Transposons are larger segments of DNA with one or more genes in the centre and the two ends carrying inverted repeat sequences complementary to each other but in the reverse order. Because of this, each strand of transposon can form a single-stranded loop carrying the gene or genes and a double-stranded stem formed by hydrogen bonding between the terminal inverted repeat sequences (Fig. 7.5).
- The gene/s contained in encode for at least one function—most often for antibiotic resistance and may also encode for toxin production.
- Another group of DNA sequences, smaller in size and has the ability to move from one DNA molecule to another genetic material is known as insertion sequences (Is).
- These elements (Tn and Is) can transpose DNA blocks to chromosome, plasmid or phage DNA and can subsequently transfer the DNA blocks to other cells and new characters thereby.
- They play an important role in bringing about various types of mutations in the chromosomes.

Genetic engineering/DNA recombinant technology

It is the technique to isolate the desired genes from one kind of organism and introduce them

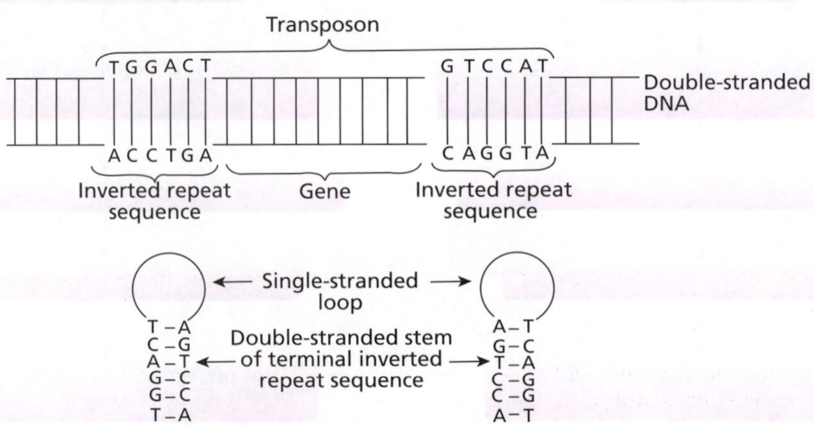

Figure 7.5 Structure of a transposon.

into another organism changing the latter's genetic make-up. The organism that received the new genes acquires new properties in addition to the original ones.

The central process in DNA recombinant technology is gene cloning which consists of

- Production of defined fragment of DNA
- Propagation and duplication of the DNA fragment in a suitable host

Steps

Generation of DNA fragments The first step is construction/generation of recombinant DNA with the help of enzymes called *restriction endonucleases*. These enzymes recognize specific sequences of nucleotides in DNA and cleave them into fragments containing the desired genes. The fragments thus formed are isolated for further processing.

Cloning vectors These are needed to insert foreign DNA. A vector is a DNA molecule on which a DNA fragment is cloned. For the purpose of propagation, a DNA fragments must be joined to a vector DNA to insert a foreign DNA into a cell. Vectors most commonly used are

- Plasmid such as R-factor
- Temperate bacteriophages
- Cosmid—a hybrid vector containing both a plasmid and a phage

Joining of DNA molecules The final step in the construction of a recombinant DNA is the joining together of a particular DNA fragment of interest to the vector molecule. This process is known as ligation and is catalyzed by an enzyme *DNA ligase*.

Introduction of recombinant DNA into the host cell The recombinant DNA prepared in vitro is then introduced into a suitable host (cloning organism) by transformation. *E. coli* is the most commonly used bacteria for this purpose. In addition to it, vaccinia virus can also be used.

Detection and characterization of recombinants Recombinant DNA (cloned genes) in the host cell is detected and characterized by hybridization and immunological methods. It can also be detected by the detection of products of recombinant DNA.

Obtaining the desired product The host cell containing a recombinant molecule is grown in a suitable medium. The host cell growth carrying specified genes are produced and desired protein is obtained in large quantities by growing the host cell (Fig. 7.6).

Applications of genetic engineering

The technique can be used for the following:

- **Production of hormones**, for example, growth hormones, insulin and thymosin.
- **Production of vaccines**, for example, hepatitis B vaccine and rabies vaccine.
- **Production of enzymes** such as urokinase used to dissolve blood clots.
- **Production of interferon** for the treatment of viral diseases and certain types of cancer.
- **Production of antimicrobial agents**.
- **Production of proteins** of therapeutic interest, for example, interleukin-2, tumour necrosis factor and factor VIII.
- It may be possible in future to alter the genetic material in human egg and treat inherited diseases such as haemophilia, thalassemia and sickle cell anaemia (gene therapy).

DNA probes

- DNA probes are radiolabelled or chromatographically labelled pieces of single-stranded DNA, which can be used for the detection of homologous DNA.
- The technique is based upon hybridization of test DNA (DNA to be detected in a test sample/culture) with a DNA probe.

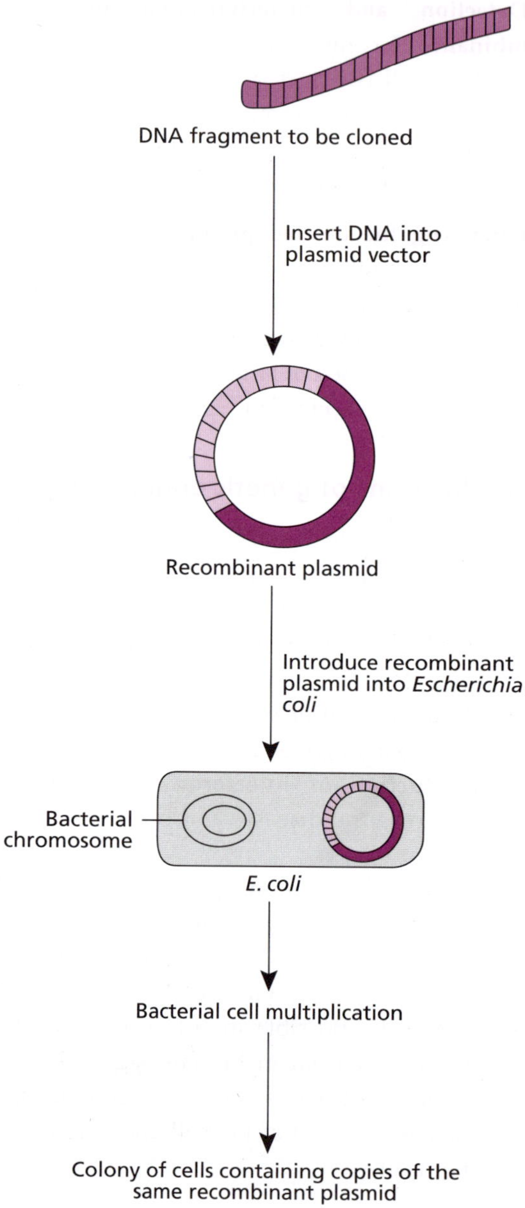

Figure 7.6 Gene cloning and recombinant DNA technique.

- Hybridization is the technique in which two single strands of a nucleic acid come together to form a stable double-stranded molecule.
- If the test DNA is present in a given sample, it will conjugate with the DNA probe forming a stable double-stranded DNA.
- All microorganisms contain some unique sequences of nucleic acid within their genome that make them different from all other organisms.
- The unique sequences of nucleic acid can be recognized by hybridization with a probe, which is unique for that particular organism.
- Various diagnostic DNA probes have been developed for identification of different microorganisms.

Procedure

- Nucleic acid of the test pathogen is extracted and denatured before hybridization with DNA probes.
- DNA probes containing unique sequences are added to the test sample.
- The double-stranded DNA formed by hybridization is then separated from the rest of the labelled probe DNA and sample.
- The amount of probe bound to sample is recorded and the degree of binding is compared with positive and negative controls and results are interpreted.

Applications

- Detection of microbes that are difficult or impossible to culture
- Detection of microbes which do not have diagnostic antigens
- To differentiate virulent and avirulent strains
- To detect a latent viral infection
- For rapid confirmation of cultured organisms
- To identify antibiotic resistance genes
- To develop epidemiological markers

Commercially available DNA probes

Some of the commercially available DNA probes are as follows:

- *Mycobacterium tuberculosis*

- *E. coli* (heat-labile toxin [LT] and heat-stable toxin [ST])
- Herpes simplex virus
- Hepatitis B virus
- Rotavirus
- HIV
- *Plasmodium falciparum*

Polymerase chain reaction (PCR)

History Developed in 1983 by Kary Mullis (awarded Nobel Prize in 1993).

Principle It is an in vitro method for producing large amounts of specific DNA fragments of defined length and sequence from small amounts of complex template. It amplifies a specific DNA sequence (or gene) of interest.

Procedure Three steps include the following:

- Melting of DNA at 94°C to convert double-stranded DNA to single-stranded DNA.
- Annealing of primers to target DNA at 50–70°C.
- Synthesis of DNA by addition of nucleotides from primers by action of *DNA polymerase*.

Newly formed DNA is melted and the process repeated again and again until an exponential increase in the amount of DNA occurs (Fig. 7.7).

RNA polymerase chain reaction

It is a modification of PCR technique in which RNA template is used for amplification. From the RNA template, a complimentary copy of DNA is obtained by using the enzyme *reverse transcriptase* and then the routine method of PCR is used, which amplifies cDNA (complementary DNA).

Applications of PCR

- It is a rapid method (1 day) that has number of applications.
- It is a versatile tool useful in
  - Diagnosis of infectious diseases
  - Diagnosis of genetic and neoplastic diseases
  - Forensic investigations
  - Evolutionary studies (in the examination of phylogenetic relationships)
- In clinical laboratory, it can be used in the diagnosis of large number of bacterial, viral, parasitic and fungal diseases.

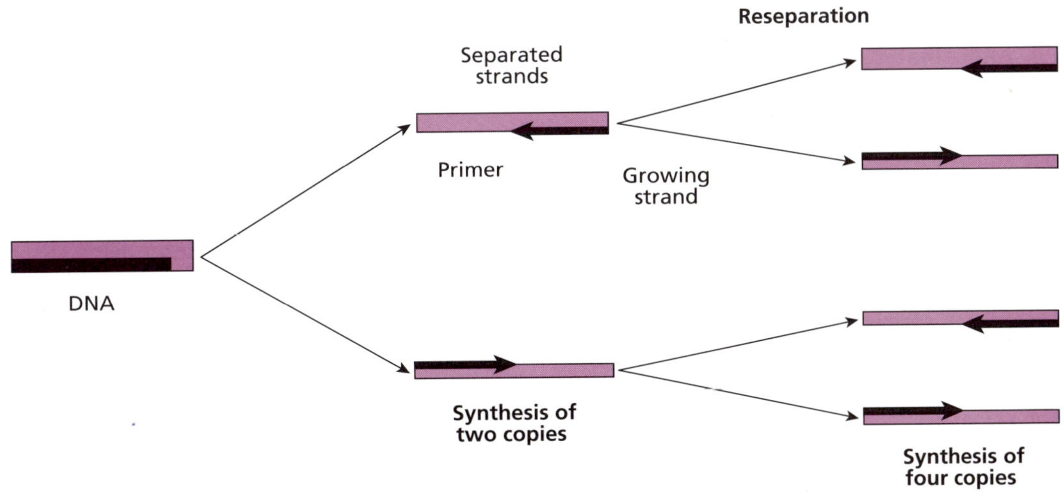

Figure 7.7 Polymerase chain reaction.

Self-assessment

Long-answer questions

1. Describe in detail the process of gene transfer in bacteria.
2. Describe in detail the genetic mechanism of drug resistance.

Short-answer questions

Write notes on

1. Structure of DNA
2. Plasmids
3. Episomes
4. Transposons
5. Spontaneous mutations
6. Induced mutations
7. Lysogenic conversion
8. DNA recombinant technology
9. Cloning vectors
10. DNA probes
11. Polymerase chain reaction
12. Transformation
13. Transduction
14. Conjugation

Multiple-choice questions

1. Length of bacterial chromosome is about
   A. 1000 μm
   B. 1000 mm
   C. 1000 nm
   D. 100 μm
2. Plasmids that have the ability to jump from chromosomal DNA to plasmid DNA or vice versa are called
   A. Plasmids
   B. Cosmids
   C. Episomes
   D. Transposons
3. Polymerase chain reaction is useful for the detection of
   A. Nucleic acid
   B. Antibody
   C. Proteins
   D. None of the above
4. Phage mediated transfer of gene from bacterial chromosome is known as
   A. Conjugation
   B. Transformation
   C. Transduction
   D. Transposition
5. Which of the following methods is NOT a method of gene transfer in bacteria?
   A. Transformation
   B. Transcription
   C. Conjugation
   D. Lysogenic conversion
6. Mutations which are not expressed phenotypically are known as
   A. Spontaneous mutations
   B. Frame shift mutations
   C. Nonsense mutations
   D. Silent mutations
7. Following are the mutagenic agents, EXCEPT
   A. 5-bromouracil
   B. Aniline dyes
   C. 2-amino purine
   D. Alkylating agents
8. The following statements are TRUE regarding conjugation, EXCEPT
   A. Mediates the transfer of plasmid DNA
   B. Mediates the transfer of chromosomal DNA
   C. Mediates the transfer of free or naked DNA
   D. Mediates the transfer of F-factor
9. The following statements are TRUE regarding R-factor, EXCEPT
   A. Mediates transferable drug resistance
   B. Mediates infectious drug resistance
   C. Mediates mutational drug resistance
   D. Is an extrachromosomal drug resistance

10. DNA with the ability to jump from chromosomal DNA to plasmid DNA or vice versa is known as
    A. Episomes
    B. Transposons
    C. F-plasmid
    D. R-plasmid

11. Which of the following is NOT a non-conjugative plasmid?
    A. Colicinogenic factor
    B. F-plasmid
    C. Resistance transfer factor
    D. Resistance determinants

8 Infection

Infection is a biological process that takes place in the body of macroorganism (*macro meaning large*) upon the penetration of pathogenic microorganisms. This penetration may result in an obvious (visible) or latent (hidden) disease or in a carrier state. Thus, infection is a successful invasion (lodgement and multiplication) of the host tissue by a microorganism that may or may not lead to disease.

Types of infection

- **Primary infection** Initial infection or fresh infection caused by a microorganism is known as primary infection.
- **Reinfection** Subsequent infections by the same pathogen in the same host are termed reinfection.
- **Secondary infection** Infection by a new parasite after the host loses its resistance due to pre-existing infectious disease.
- **Mixed infection** Infection caused by more than one microorganisms simultaneously.
- **Focal infections** Localized infections or sepsis such as sinusitis, appendicitis and tonsillitis producing generalized effects such as vague physical or mental disturbances and allergic reactions are termed focal infections.
- **Cross-infections** In a person already suffering from a disease, a new microorganism sets up a new infection from another external source is termed cross-infection.
- **Nosocomial infections** Cross-infections occurring in hospitalized patients are termed nosocomial or hospital-acquired infections.
- **Iatrogenic infections** Infections acquired during diagnostic or therapeutic procedures are termed iatrogenic infections.

Classification based on clinical effects

- **Inapparent or subclinical infections** Infections in which clinical effects are not apparent (not seen).
- **Atypical infections** Infections in which typical or characteristic manifestations of the particular disease are not present.
- **Latent infection** Infections in which microbe remains in the tissue in a latent or hidden form that proliferates and produces clinical disease when the host resistance is lowered.

Classification based on source

- **Endogenous or auto-infections** Infections in which the source is host's own body. The causative agent comes from another part of the host's own body.

- **Exogenous infections** Infections in which the source is external and not the host's own body.

Sources of infection in humans

Humans

- Man is the commonest source
- Microorganisms originate from
  - Patient
  - Carrier—a person who harbours pathogen without suffering from disease caused by it
  - Persons suffering from latent or subclinical infections

Types of carrier

- **Healthy carrier**—harbours the pathogen but has never suffered from the disease caused by it
- **Convalescent carrier**—recovered from the disease but continues to harbour the pathogen in the body
- **Temporary carrier**—carries organisms for a short duration, that is, less than 6 months
- **Chronic carrier**—carries organisms for a long duration, that is, for many years
- **Contact carrier**—carrier who acquires organism from a patient
- **Paradoxical carrier**—carrier who acquires organisms from another carrier

Animals

- Some pathogens are able to cause infections in man as well as animals; hence, animals may act as a source of infection of such pathogens.
- Infections transmitted from animal to man are called **zoonotic diseases**.
- Infections from animal to man are transmitted by
  - Contact with animals
  - Animal bite
  - Ingestion of milk, meat or other animal products
- Examples include plague, rabies, brucellosis and hydatid disease.

Insects

- Insects such as mosquitoes, ticks, mites, flies, fleas, lice and bugs may transmit the pathogen to man.
- Insects that transmit infections are known as vectors and diseases that are transmitted are known as **arthropod-borne diseases**.

Two types of vectors

Following are the two types of vectors:

1. **Mechanical vectors** They carry pathogens on their legs, wings and body and transmit these pathogens to food materials, which then act as a source of infection, for example, transmission of *Salmonella* and *Shigella* by domestic flies. No development of infecting organism occurs in the body of insect.
2. **Biological vectors** They carry pathogens in their body. The pathogens undergo development in the body of the vector with or without multiplication. For example, malarial parasite undergoes development in mosquitoes which then transmit infection to other human beings. Leishmaniasis and filariasis are the other examples of diseases transmitted by biological vectors.

Soil

- Some pathogenic organisms are able to survive in soil, hence soil can act as a source of infections.
- Soil serves as a source of infection for causative agents of
  - Tetanus
  - Anthrax
  - Hookworm disease
  - Mycetoma

Water

Water may act as a source of infections due to contamination with pathogenic organisms, for example, cholera, hepatitis A or due to presence of aquatic vectors, for example, *Cyclops* that causes guinea worm infection.

Food

- Food contaminated with pathogenic organisms may act as a source of infection.
- Food materials may be contaminated externally or microorganisms may be present due to a pre-existing infection in meat or other animal products.

Portals of entry and exit

Portals of entry

The route by which organisms enter into the body of a host is known as portal of entry. The common routes of entry are as follows:

- Cuts or abrasions of the skin
- Mucosa of respiratory tract (nose, throat and lungs)
- Eyes or mouth
- Gastrointestinal tract
- Genitourinary tract
- Parenteral route and through intraperitoneal cavity

Portals of exit

- The routes by which organisms leave the body of a patient to another person to initiate the infection are known as portals of exit.
- From the site of its entry, the organism may spread
  - Directly through tissues
  - Via lymphatic channels to the bloodstream and via blood, it reaches the site suitable for its multiplication
- After the growth and multiplication, it leaves the body of the patient by a suitable portal of exit for continuation of species.
- The different routes of exit are as follows:
  - Respiratory tract—through respiratory discharges, that is, sputum, saliva
  - Gastrointestinal tract—through faeces
  - Insects—organisms from one person to another are transmitted by blood-sucking insects and also mechanically by flies
  - Others, for example, pus, urine and other body fluids

Transmission of infections

Transmission of infection to human beings occurs in various ways.

Inhalation (transmission through air)

Respiratory infections such as tuberculosis, diphtheria and influenza are transmitted by inhalation. The organisms in the mouth and respiratory tract are disseminated into the environment during talking, coughing and sneezing in the form of droplets, which evaporate to form droplet nuclei (minute particles). The droplet nuclei remain in air for 1–2 hours, which may be inhaled by susceptible individuals.

Contact

Contact is of two types: direct and indirect.

Direct contact Contagious diseases (disease transmitted by direct contact) such as syphilis and gonorrhoea, are transmitted by sexual intercourse and close bodily contact.

Indirect contact Through the agency of fomites. Fomites are inanimate objects such as clothing, bedding, pencils or toys, which may be contaminated with pathogens from one person and act as a vehicle for its transmission to other person, for example, transmission of diphtheria in school children by sharing of pencils.

Ingestion

Intestinal infections are transmitted by the ingestion of contaminated food or drinks. Infections transmitted by ingestion may be

- Water-borne, for example, cholera transmitted by ingestion of contaminated water.
- Food-borne, for example, food poisoning transmitted by ingestion of contaminated food.
- Hand-borne, for example, dysentery in which the pathogenic organisms are transmitted during feeding through the contaminated hand, if proper care is not taken.

Transmission by insects

Insects may act as vectors and transmit infections from one person to another. The transmission may be mechanical or biological.

Transmission by inoculation

Transmission of organism in some infections may occur by direct inoculation of organisms in the tissue. Examples include

- Transmission of rabies by dog bite
- Transmission of arboviruses by insect vectors

Infection by inoculation may be iatrogenic when unsterile syringes and surgical equipment are used, for example, human immunodeficiency virus (HIV) and hepatitis B virus may be transmitted by transfusion of infected blood or by using contaminated syringes and needles.

Congenital transfer

Transmission of infection from mother to foetus in utero by crossing the placental barrier is known as congenital or vertical transfer. Pathogens such as *Treponema pallidum*, HIV, rubella virus and malarial parasites are able to cross the placental barrier and infect the foetus in utero.

Iatrogenic transfer

Transmission of infection may sometimes occur during diagnostic or therapeutic procedures such as catheterization, injection, lumbar puncture and dialysis. This type of transfer is known as iatrogenic transfer.

Spread of infections

Spread of infection occurs in various ways as given in the following text.

By water

- Water is the most important vehicle for spread of infections such as typhoid, cholera and dysentery, which are known as water-borne infections.
- As mentioned earlier, the spread of infection through water may be due to its contamination with the pathogen or the presence of aquatic vectors.
- When contaminated water is used for drinking purpose without purification, the infections spread rapidly.

By sewage

- Sewage may contain a variety of bacteria causing alimentary tract infections.
- Sewage may contaminate the water sources used for drinking purpose and acts as a vehicle for spread of various alimentary tract infections, for example, cholera, typhoid and dysentery.

By milk

- Milk from infected animals may contain microorganisms, for example, *Brucella* species and *Coxiella burnetii*.
- If milk is not pasteurized properly it acts as a vehicle for spread of various zoonotic diseases.

By food

- Food may act as a source of infection and causes the spread of infection when it is contaminated with pathogens.
- Contamination of food may occur because of
  - Improper handling of food by an infected person or a carrier
  - Preparation of food in utensils contaminated by washing in contaminated water
  - Transmission of pathogen by flies from infected faeces
  - Pre-existing infection in meat or other foods of animal origin
- When such food items are consumed, spread of infection to human beings occurs.
- These infections are known as food-borne infections.

By air

- Pathogenic microbes in infected secretions from the respiratory tract are disseminated into the environment/air.
- Air is the most important vehicle for spread of these pathogens.
- Respiratory secretions expelled out in the form of larger droplets (more than 100 μm) fall down to soil, dry there and may remain there as dust particles, which may spread by small air currents.
- The smaller droplets (less than 100 μm) evaporate to become droplet nuclei, which remain air-borne for 1–2 hours and may be inhaled into the nose, throat, and lungs.
- These infections are known as air-borne infections.

Microbial pathogenicity

- The capacity of a microorganism to produce disease or tissue injury is known as pathogenicity/virulence.
- Pathogenicity is the ability of the pathogen to inflict damage on the host; however, the virulence is the degree of pathogenicity produced by the pathogen.

Predisposing factors to pathogenicity (virulence factors)

Adhesion

Ability to adhere to the host cell surface is an important virulence factor for an extracellular pathogen. Adhesion is a complex process mediated by specific components of microbial cells known as adhesions or ligands. These include the following:

- Pili or fimbriae in piliated or fimbriated microorganisms
- Glycocalyx—a loose network of polymer fibres (polysaccharides synthesized and secreted by bacteria) extending outward from a cell
- Lectin or other cell components

Toxigenicity

- It is the ability of an organism to cause the disease by producing toxin that inhibits the host cell function or kills the host cell.
- Bacteria produce two types of toxins: endotoxins and exotoxins.
- The important properties of endotoxins and exotoxins are given in Table 8.1.

Capsule

Capsule serves as a physicochemical barrier and prevents phagocytosis and helps the microorganism to spread in the body. It also acts as a barrier against the action of antibodies and increases the invasive property of the pathogen.

Other virulence factors

A number of extracellular proteins help in the establishment and maintenance of disease. Most of them are enzymes. These include the following:

- **Coagulase**—produced by *Staphylococcus aureus* forms fibrin barrier around the bac-

Table 8.1 The important properties of endotoxins and exotoxins

Endotoxins	Exotoxins
Integral part of the outer layer of cell wall	Released into surrounding medium
Lipopolysaccharides	Protein in nature
Heat stable	Heat labile
Toxic but less potent	Highly potent
Less specific in their effect	More specific in their effect
Cannot be toxoided	Converted into inactive form known as toxoid, which is non-toxic but antigenic
Weakly antigenic	Highly antigenic
Produced by Gram-negative bacteria	Produced by Gram-positive as well as Gram-negative bacteria

terium and protects it from the attack by host cells

- **Fibrinolysin**—promotes the spread of infection by breaking down the fibrin barrier in tissues
- **Hyaluronidase**—breaks down hyaluronic acid, a polysaccharide present in connective tissues and promotes spreading of organisms in these tissues
- **Leucocidins**—cause damage to polymorphonuclear cells
- **IgA protease**—acts on IgA antibody, which plays an important role in local immunity
- **Bacterial surface antigens** such as Vi antigen of *Salmonella typhi* and K antigen of *Escherichia coli* help to resist phagocytosis and lytic action of complement
- **Other enzymes** such as proteases, nucleases and lipases that serve to depolymerize host proteins, nucleic acids and lipids and enzymes such as *catalase, peroxidase, superoxide dismutase, heparinase* produced by various organisms contribute to the pathogenicity

Host factors predisposing to infections

The important host factors predisposing to infections are given below.

General health

- General health is one of the important factors.
- Some common health problems that predispose the man to various infections are as follows:
  - General debility
  - Malnutrition
  - Deficiency of vitamins, such as vitamin A and vitamin C, increases susceptibility to bacterial infections
  - Deficiency of zinc and folic acid predisposes to some infections
  - Low protein diet makes a person susceptible to infection

Age

- The age of an individual is an important predisposing factor.
- The two extremes of life carry higher susceptibility to infection as compared to adults because of weak immunity in infants and children and in old people.

Hormonal influences

- Hormonal disorders such as diabetes mellitus, hypothyroidism and adrenal dysfunction are associated with increased susceptibility to infections.

Impaired host defences

- Deficiency of natural immunity, cell-mediated immunity and humoral immunity are the most important predisposing factors.

Other host factors

- Malignancy
- Prematurity
- Low birth weight
- Intravenous drug abuse
- Immunosuppressive therapy
- Pregnancy
- Instrumentation, for example, radiological invasive techniques, catheterization, cystoscopy
- Surgery

Focal and systemic infections

Focal infection

It is the localized infection or sepsis producing generalized effects such as vague physical or mental disturbances and allergic reactions. It occurs as a result of metastasis of microorganism or its toxin capable of injuring tissue from the focus of infection. Focus of infection is a circumscribed area of tissue, which is infected with exogenous pathogenic microorganisms and is usually located near a mucous or cutaneous surface.

Mechanism of focal infection

Two different mechanisms are involved in focal infection: metastasis of microbes and dissemination of toxin.

Metastasis of microbes The spread of microbes from an infected focus through vascular (haematogenous route) or lymphatic channels (lymphogenous route) to those particular tissues for which microbes have a special predilection.

Dissemination of toxin Toxin or toxic products formed by microbes may be carried through bloodstream or lymphatic channels and transported from the focus of infection to a distant site where they may exert a toxic effect by initiating a hypersensitivity reaction, for example, the cutaneous lesions by the erythrogenic toxin liberated by streptococci in scarlet fever; and the damage to heart tissue in rheumatic fever because of altered reaction or hypersensitization of tissues to haemolytic streptococci.

Oral foci of infection

Various infections of the oral cavity may act as sources of infection and may be responsible for spread of microbes to a distant site causing metastasis. The potential foci in the oral cavity include the following:

- Infected periapical lesions, particularly the chronic lesions such as the periapical abscess, granuloma and cyst
- Teeth with infected root canals are the potential sources of dissemination of microbes as well as their toxins
- Periodontal disease following tooth extraction or dental manipulation is also a significant focus of infection; the tooth extraction in particular is an important cause of bacteraemia

Importance of oral foci of infection

Clinical evidences suggest that oral foci of infection either cause or aggravate many systemic diseases. Most frequently encountered systemic diseases are as given below:

Arthritis Arthritis of the rheumatoid type and rheumatic fever type are manifested due to the occurrence of streptococcal infection in the mouth. The causal microbe (group A streptococci) may not be cultured from the joints and blood but the patients have a high titre of antibodies against these microbes. The presence of these antibodies suggests that tissue hypersensitivity reaction as the cause of inflammatory reactions that occur.

Subacute bacterial endocarditis (infective endocarditis) The majority of these cases are related to oral infection and occur following tooth extraction. The close similarity between the causative agent of subacute bacterial endocarditis and the *Streptococcus* of viridans group in the oral cavity, in the dental pulp and in periapical lesions, and frequent occurrence of transient streptococcal bacteraemia following tooth extraction are the indications that oral foci are the cause of this disease.

Gastrointestinal diseases It has been reported that constant swallowing of streptococci from mouth may lead to a variety of gastrointestinal diseases and gastric and duodenal ulcers are related to oral foci of infection.

Ocular diseases In many ocular diseases such as iritis, cyclitis, choroiditis and uveitis microbes associated with the teeth, oral cavity, tonsils, sinuses, etc., have been considered as primary foci of infection.

Skin diseases Some form of eczema and possibly urticaria can be related to oral foci of infection.

Renal diseases Streptococci, particularly *Streptococcus haemolyticus,* present in dental root canals or periapical or gingival areas appears to have some relation with certain type of renal diseases and may play a role causing the renal disease.

Cross-infections in dentistry

Cross-infection is the transmission of infectious microbes among the patients and staff within a hospital environment.

Microorganisms causing cross-infections

Bacteria

- *Staphylococcus aureus*
- *Treponema pallidum*
- *Streptococcus pyogenes*
- *Mycobacterium tuberculosis*
- *Bordetella pertussis*

Viruses

- Hepatitis B, C and D viruses
- HIV
- Herpes simplex virus
- Influenza virus
- Mumps virus
- Measles virus
- Rubella virus
- Epstein–Barr virus

Fungi

- *Candida albicans*
- Dermatophytes

Sources

In a dental set up, following are the sources of cross-infections:

- Patient suffering from the infectious disease—a less important source as a patient with acute illness rarely comes to the dentistry and if at all it comes, because of the apparent illness, necessary precautions are taken to prevent the spread
- Patient in prodromal phase of infectious disease—an important source
- Carriers such as convalescent carriers and asymptomatic carriers are the important sources

Transmission

The transmission of cross-infection during dental treatment can occur in the following ways:

- By direct contact with blood or saliva
- By inhalation of droplets containing infectious agent
- Through the use of contaminated instruments during procedures

Routes

Two important routes are transdermal route and respiratory route.

Transdermal route In this, microbes such as *Staphylococcus aureus, Treponema pallidum,* hepatitis B, C and D viruses, HIV and herpes simplex virus enter the tissues of the recipient by injection through the intact skin or mucosa usually due to an accident involving a sharp instrument or through the cuts or abrasions of the skin.

Respiratory route In this, microbes such as *Streptococcus pyogenes, Mycobacterium tuberculosis, Bordetella pertussis,* influenza virus, mumps virus, measles virus, rubella virus and Epstein–Barr virus enter through the mucosa of respiratory tract (nose, throat and lungs) by inhalation of aerosols.

Prevention and control of cross-infections

The following measures help in the prevention and control of cross-infections:

- Educating the staff about the basic concepts of infection control.
- Following universal safety and precaution procedures to control transmission of the infections.
- Proper sterilization and disinfection of inanimate objects.
- Applying aseptic and antiseptic techniques during dental procedures, and using protective clothing and immunization to prevent cross-infections among the staff members.
- Proper sterilization of equipment, use of disposable items, good environmental hygiene, proper disposal of hospital waste, etc., to prevent cross-infection from patient to patient.

Classification of infectious diseases

Infectious diseases may be categorized into two types: localized or generalized.

- **Localized** Infection may be superficial or deep.
- **Generalized** Localized infection may become generalized when immune system fails to check it.
  - ***Bacteraemia*** is the circulation of bacteria in blood. Transient bacteraemia may occur during chewing, brushing of teeth and straining at stools. In healthy individuals, bacteria that enter the bloodstream are quickly eliminated by immune system and hence are unable to initiate infection. Bacteraemia of longer duration occurs during generalized infections, for example, typhoid fever.
  - ***Septicaemia*** is the condition whereby bacteria circulate, multiply and form toxic products in blood.
  - ***Pyaemia*** is septicaemia caused by pyogenic bacteria with multiple abscesses in internal organs such as spleen, liver and kidneys.
  - ***Toxaemia*** is the formation of toxic products in blood. When the bacterial endotoxin circulates in the blood, the condition is called **endotoxaemia**.

Classification of infectious diseases based on the spread in a community

Based on the spread of infectious diseases in a community, they are classified as follows:

- **Endemic**—diseases which are constantly present in a particular area. The disease has special predilection for that particular area
- **Epidemic**—when the disease spreads rapidly and attacks a large number of members of community
- **Sporadic**—a few scattered cases that occur in later part of an epidemic when the virulence of organism is low and the resistance of the population is high
- **Pandemic**—when a large number of persons are affected in many countries, within a short period then it is called pandemic

Self-assessment

Long-answer question

1. What is microbial pathogenicity? Describe in detail the factors predisposing to pathogenicity.

Short-answer questions

Write notes on

1. Carriers
2. Mechanical and biological vectors
3. Portals of entry and exit
4. Transmission of infections
5. Oral foci of infection
6. Focal infection
7. Toxigenicity

Multiple-choice questions

1. Which of the following statements is TRUE about iatrogenic infections?
   A. Are cross-infections occurring in hospitals
   B. Are infections acquired during diagnostic or therapeutic procedures
   C. Are mixed infections occurring in hospitals
   D. Are latent infections occurring in hospitals
2. Following are the zoonotic diseases, EXCEPT
   A. Plague
   B. Salmonellosis
   C. Brucellosis
   D. Shigellosis
3. Following are the examples of diseases transmitted by mechanical vectors, EXCEPT
   A. Salmonellosis
   B. Shigellosis
   C. Malaria
   D. Amoebiasis
4. Following are the water-borne diseases, EXCEPT
   A. Hepatitis A
   B. Hepatitis B
   C. Cholera
   D. Typhoid
5. Which of the following diseases is transmitted by ingestion?
   A. Typhoid
   B. Syphilis
   C. Malaria
   D. Plague
6. Which of the following infections is not transmitted by inoculation?
   A. HIV
   B. Hepatitis B virus
   C. Rabies
   D. Polio
7. Which of the following microbes is NOT transmitted from mother to foetus in utero?
   A. HIV
   B. *Treponema pallidum*
   C. Malarial parasites
   D. *Mycobacterium tuberculosis*
8. Droplet nuclei are transmitted by
   A. Water
   B. Air
   C. Food
   D. Milk
9. Endotoxic activity in Gram-negative bacteria is due to
   A. Protein
   B. Lipopolysaccharides
   C. Lipids
   D. None of the above
10. The following statements are TRUE regarding exotoxins, EXCEPT
    A. Protein in nature
    B. Highly potent
    C. More specific in their effect
    D. They cannot be toxoided
11. Infections occurring in hospitalized patients are known as
    A. Iatrogenic infections
    B. Nosocomial infections
    C. Cross-infections
    D. All of the above

12. Which of the following diseases is NOT transmitted by biological vector?
    A. Salmonellosis
    B. Leishmaniasis
    C. Malaria
    D. Filaria
13. Circulation and multiplication of bacteria in blood along with formation of toxic products is called
    A. Bacteraemia
    B. Toxaemia
    C. Septicaemia
    D. Pyaemia
14. Diseases which are constantly present in particular area are known as
    A. Epidemic
    B. Endemic
    C. Pandemic
    D. Sporadic
15. Diseases which infect a large number of persons in many countries are known as
    A. Epidemic
    B. Endemic
    C. Pandemic
    D. Sporadic

9 Microbe–Host Interaction in the Oral Cavity

Interaction of a microbe with the host in the oral cavity is influenced by various factors. These factors are

- Microbial factors
- Host factors

Microbial factors

Adhesion

- Ability to adhere to the host cell surface in the oral cavity is a very important factor.
- A microbe can become a part of the oral flora only when it is able to adhere and multiply at the site where it has adhered. If it is unable to do so, it would be eliminated from the oral cavity by the washing action of saliva and by various antimicrobial activities in the oral cavity.
- Adherence to the tooth surface involves non-specific and weak attractive forces initially (reversible phase), later it becomes firm (permanent phase) by specific bridging interactions derived from both the microbe and host.
- Adhesion is a complex process involving specific components of microbial cells and receptor site on the host. These structures on microbial cells that mediate adhesion are known as **adhesins** or **ligands**—these are specific surface molecules that interact with the host cell surface. These include the following:
  - Pili or fimbriae in piliated or fimbriated organisms
  - Glycocalyx—a loose network of polymer fibres (polysaccharides synthesized and secreted by bacteria) extending outward from a cell
  - Lectin or other cell components
- Once the microbe adheres, various microbial factors such as lipoteichoic acid (component of cell wall in Gram-positive bacteria), extracellular polymers (structures that promote adhesion of microbes to acquired pellicle on enamel and to similar or different type of microbes in the oral cavity) and host factors such as salivary factors (factors inducing aggregation of microbes), food, IgA and minerals such as calcium promote aggregation of similar or different type of species.

Antimicrobial agents

Microorganisms normally present in the mouth produce a variety of chemicals and biologically active substances, for example, streptococci normally present in the mouth produce hydrogen peroxide as a metabolic end product and some bacteria produce bacteriocins. These antimicrobial agents are active against other microbes, which are susceptible to the action of these agents (their activity depends upon susceptibility of other microbes).

Metabolic capability

Only those microbes are able to survive and grow in the oral cavity which have metabolic machinery to utilize the nutrients available in the oral cavity and those that are able to neutralize the harmful effects of antimicrobial agents present in the oral cavity and saliva.

Nutritional requirements

Many nutritional sources are available in the oral cavity which support the growth of existing microbes. These include the following:

- **Microbial products** Extracellular end products of one microbe can be used as food by another microbe and intracellular food storage granules, **inclusion granules** such as lipid granules, volutin granules and sulphur granules, are sources of stored energy present in some species of bacteria.
- **Host products** Such as dietary sucrose and starch, glycoproteins, minerals and vitamins in salivary secretions and proteins present in the crevicular exudates are the important nutritional sources.

Host factors

The various host factors are mentioned in the following text.

Acquired pellicle formation on enamel

Acquired pellicle formation on a cleaned tooth surfaces occurs within a few hours of cleaning. This pellicle is composed of acidic glycoprotein obtained from saliva. The pellicle provides site for attachment of microbes. The microbes first attach to this pellicle and not directly to the enamel.

Salivary factors

Saliva is a complex mixture of the secretions of salivary and other glands of mucous membrane in the oral cavity. It is composed of 99.5% of water and 0.5% solids containing 50% of organic substances such as proteins, lipids, enzymes, hormones, ammonia, urea and antibacterial substances and 50% of inorganic substances such as chlorides, bicarbonates, sodium, calcium, potassium and dissolved gases, which play an important role in the oral ecology. The various salivary factors that influence the oral ecology are as follows:

- **Mechanical washing**—helps in prevention of overgrowth of microbes
- **Swallowing**—helps in ingestion of aggregates or attached microbes and kill them with the help of gastric juices
- **Glycoproteins in saliva**—help in adherence of microbes to enamel, may also inhibit attachment of certain microbes to the enamel and can also serve as nutrient
- **Lysozyme, lactoferrin and lactoperoxidases**—help to kill exogenous microbes
- **Buffering action of saliva**—helps to maintain pH at 6.7, which helps to prevent overgrowth of microbes
- **IgA**—present in salivary secretions which inhibits the adherence of microbes. Occasionally, it may promote the adherence of certain microbes.

Anatomical factors Different anatomical sites are created in the oral cavity because of untreated malocclusion, irregular teeth and poor restoration, which act as a special stagnation sites to reside microbes and help microbes by avoiding their contact with the natural defence mechanisms in the oral cavity.

Crevicular fluid It is similar to serum and contains albumin, IgG, IgM, IgA, complement and transferrin, which play an important role in the defence mechanisms of the oral cavity. It also contains sodium, potassium, calcium, iron and various enzymes of host or microbial origin, which include proteinases, collagenases, elastase and lysozyme.

Miscellaneous factors There are many other factors which significantly influence the microbe-host interaction in the oral cavity and the ecology of oral cavity in relation to microbial flora, these are as follows:

- A low oxidation-reduction potential (Eh), which favours the growth of anaerobic organisms in the oral cavity in the depth of dental plaque
- Administration of systemic antimicrobial agents and local application of antiseptic agents suppress the growth of sensitive microbes and allow the colonization by other microbes which are resistant to antimicrobials and antiseptics
- Heavy smoking and tobacco chewing
- High carbohydrate diet
- Oral hygiene and systemic diseases

These factors play an important role in the oral ecology and greatly influence the oral microflora.

Teeth and dental plaque

- A tooth consists of a mineral matrix of calcium phosphate crystals (enamel) within which the living tissue of the tooth (dentin and pulp) is present.
- A dense non-mineralized bacterial mass formed on the tooth surface is known as dental plaque. It is a tenacious microbial deposit formed on the hard surfaces in the mouth and consists of microbial cells and their products along with the host components derived from saliva.
- They are not removed by the flow of saliva or a gentle stream of water.

Formation of dental plaque

- The bacterial colonization of tooth surfaces occurs when a single bacterial cell attaches itself to the tooth surfaces where it grows and increases in number by forming microcolonies.
- When a tooth surface is freshly cleaned, a thin organic film (pellicle) measuring several μm in size forms owing to the attachment of acidic glycoprotein from saliva, which provides an attachment site for colonization and growth of bacterial microcolonies.
- The colonization of this glycoprotein is highly specific. It is primarily colonized by *Streptococcus sanguinis, Str. sobrinus, Str. mutans* and *Str. mitis,* which convert dietary sucrose into glucan that helps to attach bacteria to solid surface by acting as the carrier for other bacteria and thus favours accumulation and binding of microbes to pellicle. Because of extensive growth of these bacteria, a thick bacterial layer called dental plaque is formed. Thus, dental plaque is accumulation and tenacious attachment of bacteria along with their products on the smooth surfaces of the tooth.
- If plaque formation continues further, fusobacteria start growing and are embedded in the matrix formed by the streptococci making the layer thicker. In addition to fusobacteria, *Borrelia* species, *Veillonella* spp., Gram-positive bacilli, Gram-negative cocci and in heavily formed plaque, *Actinomyces* species *(A. viscosus, A. naeslundi, A. israelii and Rothia dentocariosa)* may predominate.
- Despite the availability of oxygen, anaerobic flora is predominant in mouth because of the following:
  - Development of anoxia due to the action of aerobically growing facultative anaerobic organisms, which utilize oxygen for their growth, and less diffusion of oxygen on tooth surface caused by a dense matrix of plaque.
- Microorganisms associated with plaque produce acid products and produce damage to the tooth surface causing dental caries (tooth decay).

Structure of dental plaque

- The plaque is formed by 25–30% of matrix made up of organic material derived from the host as well as microorganisms and the remaining 70–75% of it consists of a variety of microorganisms.
- The matrix acts as a cementing material and reserves food material.
- The microbes are cocci—*Str. sanguinis* is most predominant constituting 80–90% of the total flora. Bacilli, filamentous bacteria and fusiform bacilli are the other microbes found in dental plaques.
- It shows three different recognizable layers. The first layer consists of dead or metabolically inactive cells and inactive bacteria and is present near the pellicle. The second layer mainly consists of streptococci having glycogen-like storage granules. The third layer shows filamentous bacteria at right angles to the enamel surface; they have cocci attached to them which have a corn web arrangement.
- The plaques are heterogeneous. It is a unique feature of plaque. The composition of microbes not only varies from individual to individual but also varies from tooth to tooth in the same mouth and even from site to site on the same tooth. Thus, different microbial flora can be observed at different sites on an individual tooth surface.

Self-assessment

Long-answer questions

1. Describe in detail the various factors influencing the interaction of microbe with the host in the oral cavity.
2. Describe in brief the dental plaque.

Short-answer questions

Write notes on

1. Salivary factors
2. Adhesion in the oral cavity
3. Dental plaque

Multiple-choice questions

1. Of the following, all are adhesins or ligands, EXCEPT
   A. Capsule
   B. Pili
   C. Lectin
   D. Glycocalyx
2. Which of the following microbes is most commonly associated with dental plaque?
   A. *Streptococcus sobrinus*
   B. *Str. mutans*
   C. *Str. mitis*
   D. *Str. sanguinis*
3. Following are the important nutritional sources in the oral cavity, EXCEPT
   A. Glycoproteins
   B. Starch
   C. Dietary glucose
   D. Dietary sucrose
4. Which of the following salivary factors helps in adherence of microbes to enamel?
   A. Lysozyme
   B. Glycoproteins
   C. Lactoferrin
   D. Lactoperoxidases
5. Following are the microbes most commonly associated with dental plaque, EXCEPT
   A. *Staphylococcus aureus*
   B. *Streptococcus mutans*
   C. *Veillonella* spp.
   D. *Actinomyces* spp.

10 Introduction to Immunology

- Immunology is a branch of medical science that deals with the study of physiological responses by which the body destroys or neutralizes the foreign matter (living or non-living) as well as cells of its own system that have become altered or in other words, it deals with the special study of immune system and its responses to the invading pathogens.
- The physiological function of the immune system is to give protection against infections, that is
  - To prevent infection
  - To eradicate established infection by developing immunity
- Immunity refers to all the physiological mechanisms used by the immune system of the body to resist any foreign particles including microbes.
- These physiological mechanisms help to recognize the foreign materials and help to neutralize, eliminate or metabolize them by giving immune response.
- There are two types of immune responses, which protect individuals from infections. These are
  - Innate immunity
  - Adaptive immunity

Innate immunity It is the early line of defence that mediates the initial protection against infections either by blocking the entry of microbes or by eliminating the microbes that succeed in entering the host. This early response is mediated by cells and molecules, which are always present in and on our body.

Adaptive immunity It is acquired immunity. Adaptive immunity is stimulated by microbes that invade tissues. It develops slowly and mediates the later show. It is a more effective defence against infection, as it specifically acts against the foreign substances. The lymphocytes are the important components of adaptive immunity.

Types of adaptive immunity are humoral immunity and cell-mediated immunity.

Humoral immunity It is mediated by antibodies produced by B lymphocytes. Antibodies are secreted into the body fluids (humor means liquid, i.e., any body fluid) such as blood and mucosal fluids, where they neutralize and eliminate microbes and microbial products present in them and prevent the onset of infection.

Cell-mediated immunity It is mediated by specially sensitized T lymphocytes. Antibodies are unable to defend intracellular pathogens (pathogens which live and multiply inside the host cells). Immunity against such intracellular pathogens is mediated by sensitized T lymphocytes. This immune response involves the interaction of cells of immune system (i.e., T lymphocytes) with the intracellular pathogen and is known as cell-mediated immune response.

Immunity

Immunity is defined as the state of resistance or insusceptibility exhibited by the host towards the injury caused by microorganisms or their products. It is the ability of an individual to recognize and defend against infectious diseases. Types of immunity are shown in Figure 10.1.

Natural or innate immunity

This is an inherited resistance to infections, which an individual possesses by the virtue of his genetic and constitutional make-up. It develops naturally without contact with any microorganism and is non-specifically directed against any microorganism; hence, it is a non-specific defence mechanism of the body. It is also known as constitutive immunity.

Types of natural or innate immunity

Species immunity

It is the immunity existing in the members of a particular species, for example, many human pathogens do not infect animals and animals are naturally immune to many human pathogens. This is because of species immunity.

- Human beings suffer from mumps but dogs and cats do not.
- Anthrax bacillus may infect mammals but not birds.
- Amphibians are naturally immune to diphtheria and tetanus.

These differences may be due to physiological and biochemical differences between tissues of different species.

Racial immunity

Various races within the same species show marked difference in the degree of resistance to infections, for example

- Algerian race of sheep is resistant to anthrax while ordinary domestic sheep is susceptible to it.
- Blacks appear to be more susceptible to tuberculosis than whites.

These racial differences may be due to differences in diet, habits, environmental conditions, living style, economic status and genetic basis.

Individual immunity

Resistance to infection varies from individual to individual. Different individuals of the same species may show a marked difference in their immunity. This is evident during an outbreak of an infectious disease in which

- Some individuals would entirely escape from it
- Some individuals will develop subclinical infections
- Some individuals might develop a disease

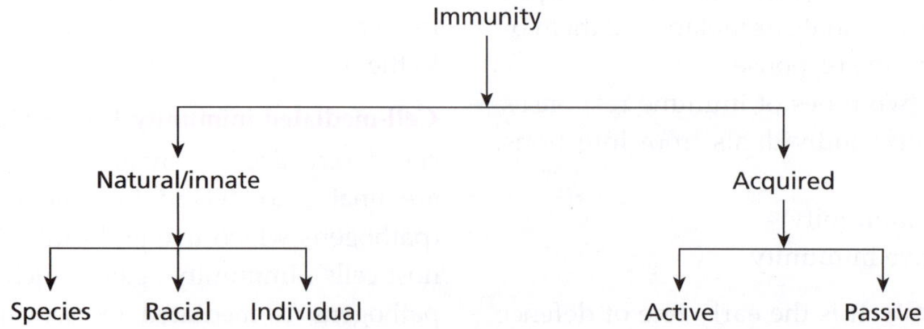

Figure 10.1 Types of immunity.

Also, the severity of a disease may be different in different individuals. This is due to an individual immunity.

The host factors

The host factors influencing the level of innate immunity are given below.

General health

- General health of an individual is one of the important factors.
- General debility increases susceptibility to infections.
- Malnutrition increases susceptibility to infections.
- Deficiency of vitamins, such as vitamin A and vitamin C, increases susceptibility to bacterial infections.
- Deficiency of zinc and folic acid predisposes to some infections.
- Low protein diet makes a person susceptible to infection.
- Presence of silica and calcium in tissue favours gas gangrene.
- Deposits of silica in lung tissue may predispose an individual to tuberculosis.

Age

- Age of an individual is an important consideration for susceptibility to infection.
- The two extremes of life carry higher susceptibility to infection as compared to adults, that is, immunity is weak in infants and children because of the immature immune apparatus, and in old people because of gradual waning of immune response.
- Adults may show increased susceptibility, in some instances, due to hormonal influences.

Hormonal influences

- Hormonal disorders such as diabetes mellitus, hypothyroidism and adrenal dysfunction are associated with enhanced susceptibility to infections. Hormones cause depression in the host's resistance by
  - Anti-inflammatory effect
  - Antiphagocytic effect
  - Suppression of antibody formation
  - Hypersensitivity

Nutrition Malnutrition predisposes to various infections. The level of immunity is reduced in malnutrition.

Mechanism of innate immunity

Innate immunity operates non-specifically in two ways:

1. **By preventing entry of microorganisms** It is the first line of defence (the external defence system).
2. **By interacting with infectious agent through activation of tissue factors (cellular and humoral factors) when the infective agent penetrates the body** It is the second line of defence (the internal defence system).

The external defence system

Epithelial surfaces

For a microorganism to cause a disease, it must enter the body. The simplest way to avoid infection is to prevent the entry of microorganisms. The intact skin and mucous membrane play an important role in external defence.

Role of skin

- The skin consists of keratin, which is indigestible by most of the microbes. Thus, it is impermeable to most of the microbes till the time it is intact.
- Most bacteria fail to survive on skin for a long time because of the inhibitory effect of saturated and unsaturated fatty acids in sweat and sebum (oily secretion of skin).
- Sweat also contains high concentration of salts, which are inhibitory to bacteria and fungi.
- Acidic pH (5.2–5.9) of the skin prevents growth of bacteria.

Role of mucous membrane

- Mucous membrane secretes mucus, which is a protective barrier.

- Microbes trapped within the adhesive mucus are removed by ciliary movements, coughing and sneezing.
- Mucous secretions of the respiratory, alimentary and genitourinary tracts contain a bactericidal substance known as **lysozyme,** which kills bacteria by acting on cell wall mucopeptides.

Role of body secretions

The body secretes various fluids, which play an important role in the defence mechanism.

- Skin secretions—sweat and sebum contain bactericidal substances.
- Tears contain lysozyme, which is bactericidal. Also, the flushing action of tears makes conjunctiva free from microbes and dust particles.
- Mucopolysaccharides in saliva inactivate bacteria and viruses.
- Gastric juice contains hydrochloric acid, which destroys bacteria and keeps the stomach free from microbes.
- Flushing action of urine eliminates bacteria from urethra.

The internal defence system

When an infective agent penetrates the body by bypassing the barriers of external defence, the internal defence comes into operation. These include tissue factors which are of two types: humoral factors and cellular factors.

Humoral factors

A variety of non-specific substances possessing antimicrobial activity are present in blood and tissue fluids. These include the following:

- **Lysozyme**—heat-labile protein present in most of the tissue fluids (except sweat, urine and cerebrospinal fluid) and in polymorphonuclear leucocytes. It is a mucolytic enzyme acting on mucopeptide of the bacterial cell wall
- **Complement**—heat-labile protein normally present in serum that has bactericidal activity. It plays an important role against the pathogens invading blood and tissues
- **Properdin**—complement-like substance normally present in serum. With the help of complement components and Mg^{++} ions, it exerts antibacterial and antiviral activity, particularly active against Gram-negative bacteria
- **Interferon**—non-specific antiviral agent that interferes with intracellular viral replication
- **Phagocytin**—heat-stable protein derived from polymorphs. It is bactericidal in nature
- **Other antimicrobial substances** such as beta-lysin in serum, plakins derived from platelets and leukins derived from leukocytes are also active against infectious agents

Cellular factors

Natural defence against microbes invading blood and tissues is mediated by phagocytic cells that engulf and digest them. Phagocytosis is the most important means of defence against microbes. There are two types of phagocytic cells:

- **Microphages** These are polymorphonuclear leukocytes or granulocytes in the blood. These include neutrophils mainly and eosinophils to a lesser extent.
- **Macrophages** These are mononuclear cells—monocytes in blood and tissue.

Process of phagocytosis

It takes place in the following steps:

- Phagocytic cell reaches the site by chemotactic mechanism where microbes are present.
- Attaches to the surface of microbe (adsorption).
- Process of engulfment starts with a deep invagination of cell membrane, which forms a thin layer around the microbes and finally it fuses to form a pouch called phagosome.
- Phagosome penetrates deep into the cytoplasm and fuses with lysosomal granules to form phagolysosome.
- The lysosomal granules rupture, releasing a variety of hydrolytic enzymes, which kill and digest ingested microbes within 15 minutes (Fig. 10.2).

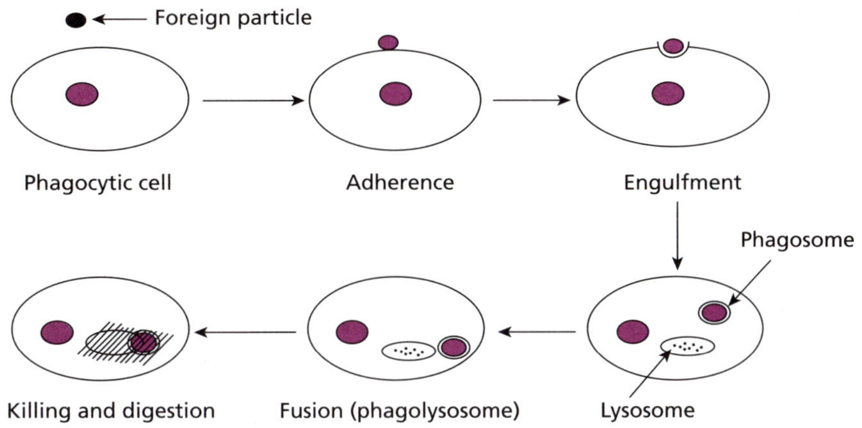

Figure 10.2 Process of phagocytosis.

Inflammation

Populations of mast cells, which are extremely sensitive to injury, are distributed throughout the connective tissue, particularly in the skin, lungs and intestine. Tissue injury or irritation initiated by the entry of microorganisms, toxins or other factors (heat, trauma, etc.) cause degranulation of mast cells releasing various mediators that are responsible for an acute inflammatory response, which is an important non-specific defence mechanism.

An inflammation occurs due to

- Increased blood flow
- Aggregation of macrophages and microphages by chemotactic mechanism

Role in defence

- The attracted phagocytic cells engulf and destroy the pathogens.
- The outpouring of plasma helps to dilute the toxic products.
- Acute-phase protein reactants including fibrinogen, transferrin, C-reactive protein, complement components and others formed during the inflammatory process serve as non-specific resistance factors and may also participate in the tissue repair process. Thus, inflammatory response helps
  - To limit tissue damage
  - To restrict infection
  - To initiate tissue repair

Fever

Fever is a protective defence mechanism of the body. Increase in body temperature increases:

- Circulation of blood and flushing of tissue that helps to eliminate toxin through urine and sweat.
- Increased body temperature may be harmful to invading microbes and in some instances, it may destroy the pathogens.
- It stimulates the production of interferon that helps in recovery of viral infections.

Acquired immunity

It is immunity specific to a disease which an individual acquires during the course of his/her life. As it is specific for a disease, it is also known as specific immunity. It is of two types (Fig. 10.3):

1. Active immunity
2. Passive immunity

Active immunity

It is the resistance developed by an individual in response to the microbes or their products (antigenic stimulus). The entry of antigen results in activation of immunocompetent cells producing antibodies (humoral/antibody-mediated immunity) or activated T cells (cell-mediated immunity).

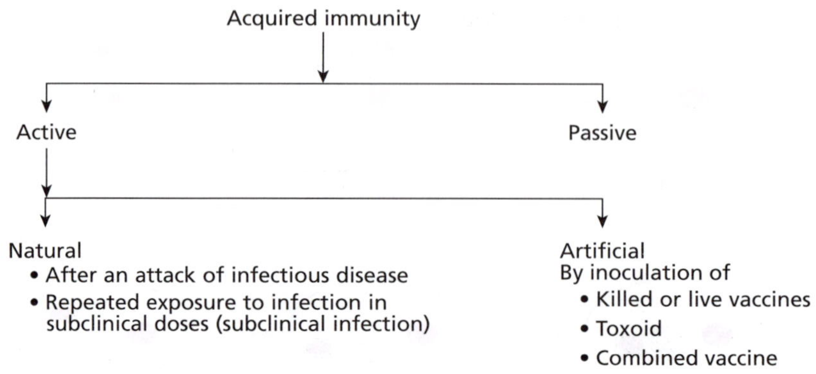

Figure 10.3 Types of acquired immunity.

Active immunity requires a considerable time for its development (weeks or months) but once developed, it persists for a long duration and may last for years.

Active immunity is of two types:

1. Naturally acquired active immunity
2. Artificially acquired active immunity

Naturally acquired active immunity

Immunity, which an individual acquires as a result of natural contact with a microbe or its product is known as naturally acquired active immunity. This contact may result in a major invasion with a clinical disease or a minor invasion without a clinical disease (inapparent or subclinical infection).

Following infection, the patient, in most cases, will be immune to further infection by the same pathogen for a period which is different for different diseases. In diseases such as influenza, common cold, gonorrhoea and staphylococcal infections, the immunity lasts for a short duration. While in other infections such as diphtheria, smallpox, measles and yellow fever, it lasts for long duration and may persist for life. In general, the immunity following viral infections lasts longer than immunity following bacterial infections.

Artificially acquired active immunity

Immunity, which an individual acquires as a result of artificial inoculation of microbes or their products, that is, immunization with microbes or their products is known as artificially acquired active immunity. For immunization, various immunizing agents such as vaccines or microbial products obtained from microorganisms, for example, toxins or extracted cellular fractions are used. Two types of vaccines are used to develop artificial active immunity: live vaccines and killed vaccines.

Live vaccines They are preparations containing live microorganisms with reduced virulence.

- Live vaccines initiate infection without causing disease.
- The level of immunity induced is same as the natural infection and immunity lasts for several years.
- Booster doses are generally not required but may be required sometimes.
- Can be administered by the route of natural infection and parenterally.

Killed vaccines They are preparations containing killed or inactivated microorganisms.

- Killed vaccines do not initiate infection and there is no multiplication of microorganism.
- The level of immunity induced is less as compared to natural infection and live vaccine and lasts for a shorter duration, hence booster doses are necessary.

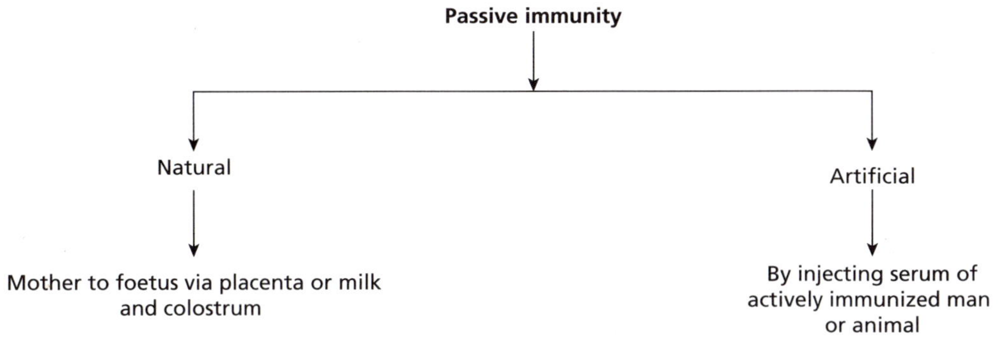

Figure 10.4 Types of passive immunity.

- Cannot be administered orally. They are effective by parenteral route.

Toxoid Certain microorganisms produce exotoxins, for example, diphtheria and tetanus bacilli. These toxins can be detoxified and used for immunization. The detoxified toxin is known as toxoid, which is non-toxic but antigenic. Toxoid when injected produces antitoxin, which specifically reacts with toxin and neutralizes it, for example, TT—tetanus toxoid for tetanus and DT—diphtheria toxoid for diphtheria. Their activity can be enhanced by mixing them with the vaccine, for example, DPT (diphtheria, pertussis and tetanus) in which pertussis is a vaccine that potentiates the activity of diphtheria and tetanus toxoids. The activity of toxoids can also be potentiated by adjuvant.

Passive immunity

The immunity, which is acquired by transfer of readymade antibodies against microbes or their products in another host, is known as passive immunity. Here, the immune system does not take any active part in the development of immunity. As compared to active immunity, it is rapidly established and immediate protection is offered which is necessary in certain clinical situations such as diphtheria, tetanus and snake bite. Passive immunity is of two types as shown in Figure 10.4.

Naturally acquired passive immunity

In newborn babies, normally there is no acquired active immunity because of immature immune system but they are resistant to a number of infectious diseases such as measles, chickenpox and diphtheria. This resistance is due to transfer of readymade antibodies from mother to foetus. It lasts for 3–4 months.

Transfer of antibody from mother to foetus occurs in two ways as shown in Figure 10.5.

Artificially acquired passive immunity

Passive immunity can be acquired artificially by injecting antibodies produced in some other human beings or animals. This immunity lasts for a short duration. This procedure is used for

- Treatment and prophylaxis and is particularly useful in clinical emergencies where immediate and temporary protection is needed, for example, snake bite, tetanus and diphtheria.
- The suppression of active immunity when it is injurious as in Rh-negative women with Rh-positive babies.
- For passive immunization, the hyperimmune serum prepared in horse (most common), sheep, goat, rabbit, guinea pigs or human being is used.

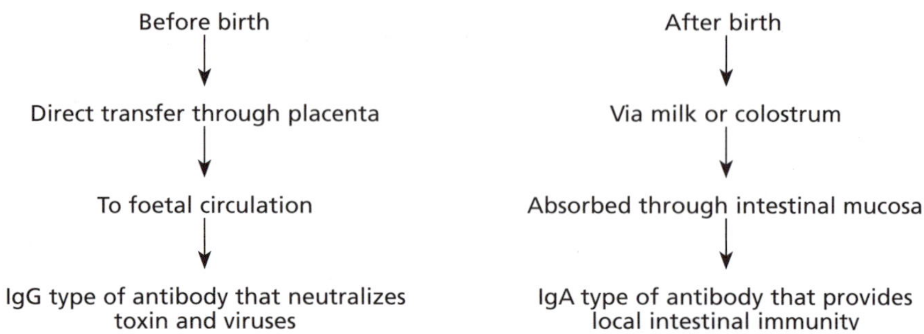

Figure 10.5 Transfer of antibody from mother to foetus.

Table 10.1 Difference between active immunity and passive immunity

Active immunity	Passive immunity
Produced actively with the involvement of immune system	Received passively (readymade antibodies) without the involvement of host's immune system
Induced by infection or by contact with antigen (e.g., vaccines, toxoids)	Induced by injecting serum containing readymade antibodies prepared in animals or man
Takes time to develop antibodies or T cells	Immediately established
Immunity lasts for long duration and effective	Lasts for short duration (10–14 days) and less effective
Negative phase may occur after injection of antigen	No negative phase
Immunological memory present; booster doses more effective	No immunological memory; subsequent administration of antibody less effective
Used for prophylaxis or treatment of subacute or chronic infections to increase resistance of the body	Used in the treatment of acute infections for providing immediate and temporary protection. Also for prophylaxis

- The serum prepared may be antitoxic, antibacterial, or antiviral in nature and termed antiserum or antitoxin.

Differences between active immunity and passive immunity are given in Table 10.1.

Self-assessment

Long-answer questions

1. Define and classify immunity. Discuss in detail the innate immunity.
2. Define and classify immunity. Discuss in detail the acquired immunity.

Short-answer questions

Write notes on

1. Differences between active and passive immunity
2. Active immunity
3. Passive immunity
4. Inflammation
5. Role of skin and mucous membrane in defence
6. Types of immunity
7. Humoral factors in innate immunity
8. Cellular factors in innate immunity

Multiple-choice questions

1. The primary natural barrier against infection is the
   - A. Acidic pH of the body fluids
   - B. Mechanical action of ciliated cells
   - C. Lytic enzymes in body fluids
   - D. Intact skin

2. The following are phagocytic cells, EXCEPT
   A. Neutrophils
   B. Monocytes
   C. Eosinophils
   D. Lymphocytes
3. The following are non-specific humoral factors, EXCEPT
   A. Beta-lysin
   B. Complement
   C. Antibodies
   D. Interferon
4. The cell types, which are extremely sensitive to injury, responsible for an acute inflammatory response are
   A. Microphages
   B. Macrophages
   C. Mast cells
   D. None of the above
5. Inflammatory response is initiated by
   A. Microbes
   B. Heat
   C. Trauma
   D. All of the above
6. Which of the following statements is FALSE about active immunity?
   A. Is established rapidly
   B. Persists for long duration
   C. Is associated with immunological memory
   D. Leads to formation of antibodies
7. Which of the following statements is FALSE about passive immunity?
   A. Is established rapidly
   B. Persists for short duration
   C. Is not associated with immunological memory
   D. Leads to formation of antibodies
8. Lysozyme is present in most of the body fluids, EXCEPT
   A. Cerebrospinal fluid
   B. Tears
   C. Mucus
   D. Intestinal secretions
9. Naturally acquired passive immunity is developed by
   A. Inoculation of microbes or their products
   B. Injection of readymade antibodies
   C. Natural contact with microbes
   D. Transfer of antibodies from mother
10. Artificially acquired active immunity is developed by
    A. Inoculation of live vaccine
    B. Inoculation of killed vaccine
    C. Inoculation of toxoid vaccine
    D. All of the above
11. Artificially acquired passive immunity is developed by
    A. Injection of readymade antibodies
    B. Inoculation of live vaccine
    C. Inoculation of killed vaccine
    D. None of the above
12. An immunoglobulin that is transferred passively from mother to foetus before birth is
    A. IgA
    B. IgM
    C. IgG
    D. IgD
13. An immunoglobulin that is transferred passively from mother to foetus after birth is
    A. IgG
    B. IgA
    C. IgM
    D. IgD
14. Which of the following is an example of naturally acquired passive immunity?
    A. Administration of antitetanus serum
    B. Administration of live vaccine
    C. Administration of killed vaccine
    D. Transfer of maternal antibody through placenta to foetus
15. Which of the following is NOT an antitoxic serum?
    A. Antitetanus serum (ATS)
    B. Antirabies serum (ARS)
    C. Antidiphtheria serum (ADS)
    D. Antisnake venom (ASV) serum

11 Antigens and Antibodies

Antigen

An antigen is defined as any foreign substance which when introduced parenterally (*para* means 'beyond' or 'outside of' and *enteron* means 'intestine', that is, by routes other than gastrointestinal tract) into the living animal body, evokes a specific immune response either by producing a specific antibody with which the antigen reacts specifically and in an observable manner or by producing specifically sensitized T cells or both. The antibodies or T cells produced are reactive against the antigen.

Any foreign substance (examples given below) may act as an antigen.

- Dead or living microorganisms
- Bacterial toxins
- Vegetable proteins
- Red blood cells
- Egg albumin
- Snake venom
- Serum
- Milk
- Plant or animal tissue

The two attributes of antigenicity are as follows:

1. **Immunogenicity** It is the capacity of an antigen to provoke a specific immune response.
2. **Immunological reactivity** It is the capacity of an antigen to induce specific reaction with the corresponding antibody or specifically sensitized T lymphocytes.

Types of antigen

Based on the ability of antigens to carry out the two functions (attributes) mentioned above, antigens are classified into two types: complete antigen (immunogen) and incomplete antigen (hapten).

Complete antigen (immunogen)

- An antigen which has the ability to induce antibody formation and reacts with it specifically and in an observable manner is known as complete antigen.
- The complete antigen can generate an immune response by itself and does not need a carrier molecule as in the case of incomplete antigen. Thus, a complete antigen can function as antigen as well as immunogen.

Incomplete antigen (hapten)

- It is a substance which is unable to induce antibody synthesis (non-immunogenic) by itself but possesses the ability to react

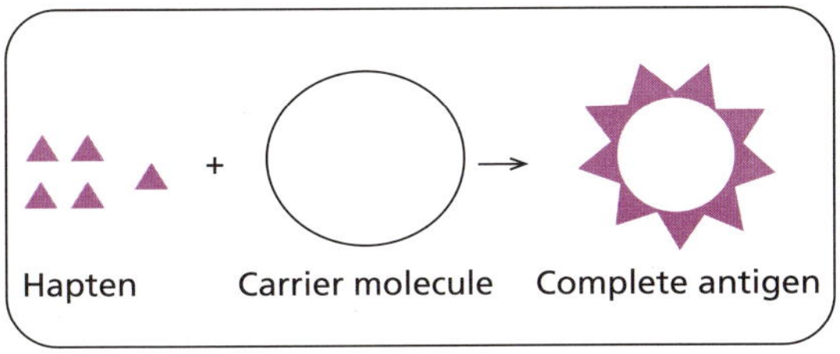

Figure 11.1 Hapten-carrier molecule reaction.

specifically with an antibody. Thus, hapten can function as an antigen but not as an immunogen.

- Haptens are incomplete antigens, which become complete antigens when they covalently combine with a **carrier molecule** or **schlepper**. After the combination with a carrier molecule, it becomes a complete antigen and can induce immune response (Fig. 11.1).
- Haptens are generally low molecular weight lipids or carbohydrates while the carrier molecules are proteins.

Chemical nature

- Chemically, antigens are proteins, polysaccharides, lipids or nucleic acids.
- Protein antigens are more effective than polysaccharide antigens.
- Lipids and nucleic acids are less antigenic. Their antigenicity can be enhanced by coupling them with proteins.
- Not all proteins are antigenic, for example, gelatin, histones and protamines are non-antigenic because they lack the presence of an aromatic radical such as tyrosine essential for the antigenicity.
- Non-antigenic substances can become antigenic after the combination with aromatic radicals such as tyrosine.
- As a general rule
  - Antigenicity increases with structural complexity
  - The substances with diverse chemical and structural properties are the most powerful antigens
  - Presence of an aromatic amino acid group increases antigenicity

Antigenic determinants (epitopes) (Fig. 11.2)

Antigens are large molecules but only a restricted portion on them is involved in the actual binding with a specific antibody-combining sites. Such areas, which determine the specific immune response and react specifically with antibody, are known as antigenic determinants or epitopes—**the basic recognition unit**.

An epitope is the smallest unit of antigenicity represented by a small area on the antigen molecule possessing a specific chemical structure and steric configuration.

Properties of antigen (requirements of immunogenicity/factors affecting immunogenicity)

The various properties of antigen are as follows:

- **Foreignness** Recognition of self and nonself is an important function of the immune system. The body does not give immune response to self-antigens, so the antigen should be genetically foreign to the host.

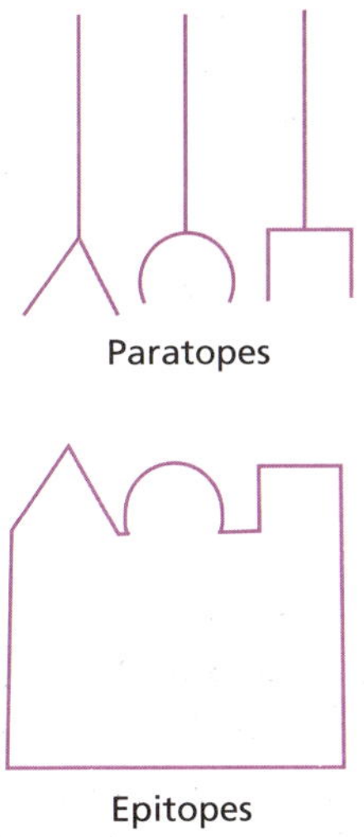

Figure 11.2 Paratopes and epitopes.

Substances that are foreign to the circulation are antigenic and are able to mount an immune response. The antigenicity of a substance is related to the degree of foreignness. Substances which are more foreign are more antigenic.

- **Size** For a substance to be antigenic, it must have a certain minimum size. Extremely small molecules are non-antigenic; however, larger molecules are highly antigenic. In general, substances having molecular weight less than 10,000 are weakly antigenic or non-antigenic. The effective immunogens have molecular weight greater than 10,000.
- **Chemical nature** Chemically, complex molecules are more antigenic. The presence of an aromatic radical, for example, tyrosine is essential for antigenicity. As mentioned earlier, non-antigenic substances can become antigenic after the combination with aromatic radicals such as tyrosine.
- **Susceptibility to tissue enzymes** Substances which are metabolized and susceptible to the action of tissue enzymes are good antigens. Antigens administered into the body are processed by phagocytic cells and intracellular enzymes into fragments containing epitopes, which are responsible for immune response. Hence, molecules which are readily phagocytosed and processed are immunogenic and molecules which are resistant to this processing are non-antigenic.

Antibodies

Immunoglobulins/antibodies are a group of glycoproteins present in the serum and tissue fluids of all mammals. They are formed in response to foreign substances (antigens) that have entered into the body with which they react specifically and in an observable manner.

Nature

- Antibodies are globulins in nature and are known as **immunoglobulins**.
- They contain sugar residues and hence are **glycoproteins**.
- Immunoglobulins constitute 20–25% of the total serum proteins.
- When electrophoretically separated, most of the serum antibodies migrate to gamma region, hence they are termed **gamma globulins**.
- Most antibodies belong to the 7S (Svedberg unit) class having molecular weight 150,000–180,000; and some belong to the 19S class having molecular weight 9,00,000 and are designated as **M** or **macroglobulins**.
- Antibodies are heat labile and denatured by heating at 70°C for 1 hour.
- Their activity is affected by the pH of the medium and other factors affecting proteins.
- They are not denatured by ethyl alcohol at low temperature (0–4°C), but alcohol at higher temperature denatures them.
- Natural salts such as magnesium sulphate, ammonium sulphate and sodium sulphate can precipitate antibodies but do not denature them.

Structure of immunoglobulin

- The detailed structure of immunoglobulin was studied by **Porter** *et al.* (1962).
- Basic four-chain model of an immunoglobulin contains two distinct types of polypeptide chains: two light chains and two heavy chains linked together by disulfide bonds (–s–s–) and non-covalent linkages (Fig. 11.3).

Light chains (L-chains)

- Smaller chains with a molecular weight 20,000–25,000. Attached to heavy chains by disulfide bonds.
- L-chains are similar in all classes of immunoglobulins and occur in two groups called *Kappa* and *Lambda*.

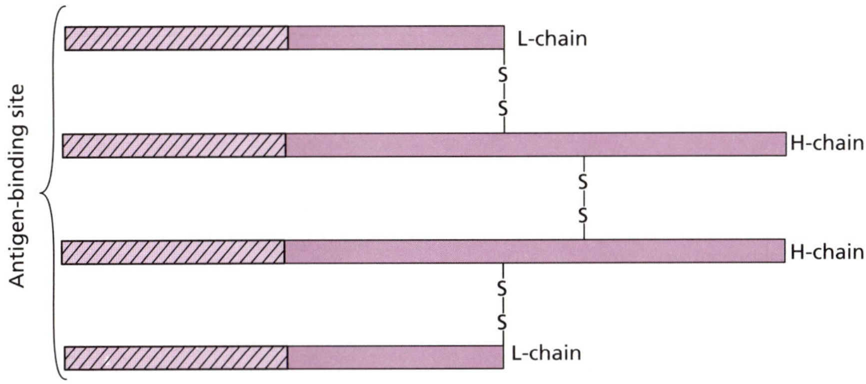

Figure 11.3 A basic four-chain model of an immunoglobulin.

- An immunoglobulin molecule may have either *Kappa* or *Lambda*—about 60% of immunoglobulin molecules possess *Kappa* type while about 30% possess *Lambda* type.

Heavy chains (H-chains)

- Larger chains with a molecular weight 50,000.
- Two H-chains are joined together by disulphide bonds.
- H-chains are structurally and antigenically different for each class of immunoglobulin and are designated by Greek letters as follows:

Immunoglobulin class	Type of H-chain
IgG	γ (Gamma)
IgM	μ (Mu)
IgA	α (Alpha)
IgD	δ (Delta)
IgE	ε (Epsilon)

- Each antibody molecule possesses an antigen-binding site known as **fragment antigen binding (Fab) portion**. It is composed of both L-and H-chains and is responsible for antigen binding. This combining site of antibody molecule possesses a specific amino acid composition that is complementary fit for specific reactive area of the antigen molecule and is known as **paratope/ hot spot**.
- Each antibody molecule also possesses **Fc portion (fragment crystallizable)**. Fc portion has no antigen-binding site but it determines the biological properties of the immunoglobulin molecule such as
  - Complement fixation
  - Placental transfer
  - Skin fixation
  - Catabolic rate
  - Secretion into the body fluid
  - Binding to phagocytes
  - Binding to mast cells

Immunoglobulin classes

Human sera contains five different classes of immunoglobulins—IgG, IgA, IgM, IgD and IgE in the decreasing order of concentration. The properties of different classes of immunoglobulins are summarized in Table 11.1.

Immunoglobulin G (IgG)

- Is the major immunoglobulin in normal serum accounting for 70–80% of the total immunoglobulins
- Is a monomer containing 2H and 2L chains (Fig. 11.4)
- Is the major immunoglobulin synthesized during secondary immune response

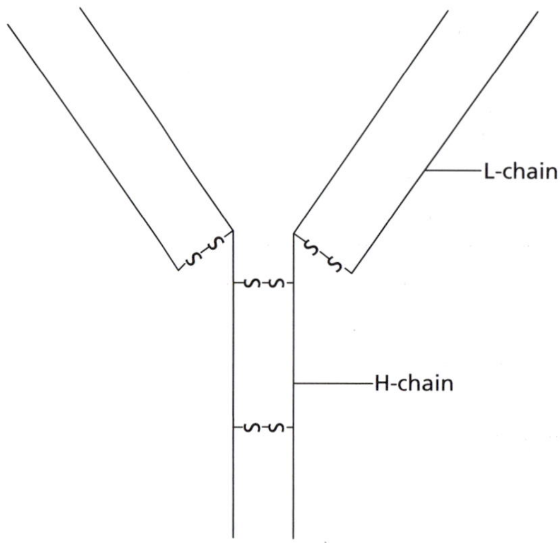

Figure 11.4 Immunoglobulin G.

- Can cross the placental barrier and provide a major line of defence (naturally acquired passive immunity) against infection in the newborn for the first few weeks
- Binds to microorganisms and enhances their ability to get phagocytosed
- Can activate complement and thus helps to attract polymorphonuclear leukocytes (phagocytic cells) by chemotactic mechanism and stimulates ingestion and killing of microorganisms
- Mediates extracellular killing of a target cell by K cells bearing the specific receptor for Fc portion of IgG
- Participates in most of the immunological reactions such as complement fixation and precipitation and neutralization of toxins and viruses
- Participates in allergic reactions, for example, Arthus reaction and also plays a role in autoimmune diseases
- When administered passively, IgG suppresses the homologous antibody synthesis by a feedback mechanism. This property is utilized in the isoimmunization of women during delivery by the administration of anti-Rh (D) IgG

> IgG protects the body fluids

Immunoglobulin A (IgA)

- Is the second most abundant immunoglobulin constituting 10–13% of the total immunoglobulins
- In human sera, more than 80% of IgA occurs as monomer containing 2H and 2L chains but in seromucous secretions, it occurs as a dimer containing 4H and 4L chains and is known as **secretory IgA**

Secretory IgA

- Is the predominant immunoglobulin present in the seromucous secretions such as saliva, tears, nasal fluids, sweat and colostrum, and in the secretions of the lungs and genitourinary and gastrointestinal tracts
- Two monomeric units are joined together by a cysteine-rich polypeptide chain called **J-chain (joining chain)**
- Possesses an additional structural unit—a glycine-rich polypeptide called the **T (transport)** or S (secretory) piece or component, which appears to protect IgA from digestion by proteolytic enzymes (Fig. 11.5)
- IgA present in secretions is synthesized locally by the plasma cells situated near the mucosal or glandular epithelium and selectively concentrated in secretions and on mucous surfaces forming an antibody paste. This IgA plays an important role in local immunity against respiratory, intestinal and urogenital pathogens by inhibiting the adherence of microorganisms to the surface of mucosal cells by coating them and thereby preventing their entry into the body tissue
- Can activate complement by alternate pathway and helps in killing certain coliforms with the help of lysozyme
- Promotes phagocytosis and intracellular killing of microorganisms

> IgA protects the body surface

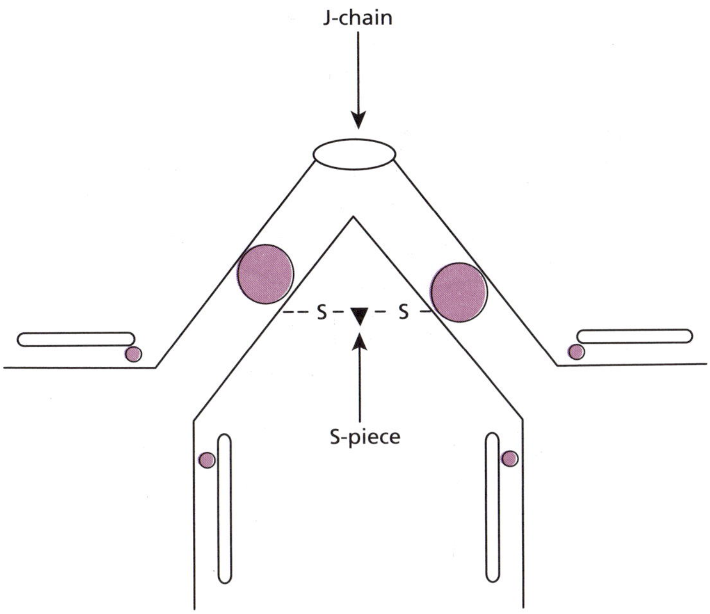

Figure 11.5 Immunoglobulin A.

Immunoglobulin M (IgM)

- Is the first antibody formed in every antibody response
- Constitutes 5–8% of serum immunoglobulins
- Is a pentamer containing 10H and 10L chains—five subunits of monomer (Fig. 11.6)
- Possesses J-chain (molecular weight 15,000) responsible for joining of subunits
- As IgM is largely confined to bloodstream, it offers protection against bacteraemia and septicaemia
- As it is not transported across the placenta, its detection in foetus or newborn indicates intrauterine infection, which is useful in the diagnosis of congenital syphilis, rubella, toxoplasmosis and HIV infection
- Activates complement by classical pathway and also neutralizes viruses and toxins
- Is the most efficient antibody in agglutination, complement fixation and cytolytic activity and is also effective in immune haemolysis, opsonization and bactericidal action
- As it is a short lived immunoglobulin that disappears rapidly, its demonstration in serum indicates recent infection

IgM protects the bloodstream

Immunoglobulin D (IgD)

- Accounts for less than 1% of the total immunoglobulins.
- Structurally, it resembles IgG (a monomer containing 2H and 2L chains).
- IgD together with IgM may function as antigen receptor on the surface of B lymphocytes for recognition of antigens to produce antibodies.

Immunoglobulin E (IgE)

- Occurs in a very low concentration, extravascular in distribution.
- Structurally, it resembles IgG (a monomer containing 2H and 2L chains).
- Normal serum concentration occurs in a very low concentration (0.00003 mg/mL)

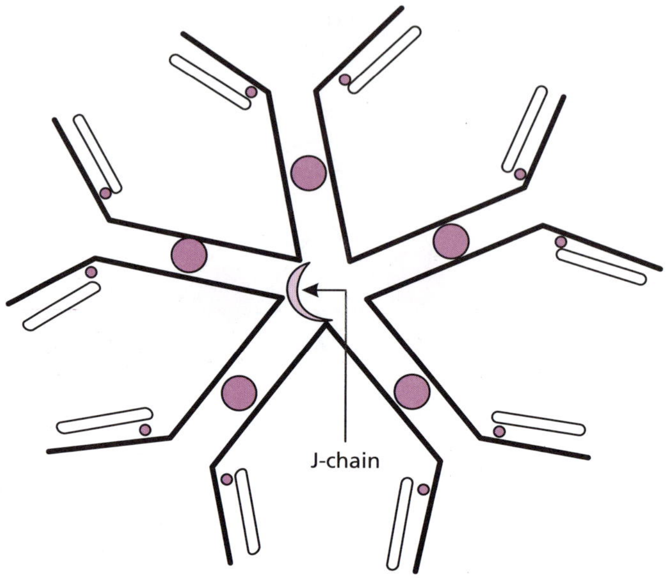

Figure 11.6 Immunoglobulin M.

but the level is greatly elevated in atopic conditions such as asthma, hay fever and eczema.

- It has an affinity towards the surface tissue cells, particularly mast cells and basophils and is responsible for degranulation of these cells, thereby releasing vasoactive amines and other mediators. Thus, it is responsible for type 1 hypersensitivity reactions (hay fever, infantile eczema, asthma and atopic dermatitis).
- It also plays an important role in immunity against helminthic parasites.

IgE mediates reaginic hypersensitivity

General properties of immunoglobulin molecules are summarized in Table 11.1.

Table 11.1 Summary of general properties of immunoglobulin molecules

Property	IgG	IgA (SIgA)	IgM	IgD	IgE
Type of H-chain	Gamma	Alpha	Mu	Delta	Epsilon
Molecular weight	150,000	160,000 (385,000)	970,000	184,000	188,000
Sedimentation coefficient	7S	7S (11S)	19S	7S	8S
Half-life	23 days	6–8 days	5 days	2.8 days	2.3 days
Carbohydrate content	3%	11%	10%	13%	12%
Valency	2	2 (4)	10	2	2
Normal serum concentration	8–16 mg/mL	0.6–4.2 mg/mL	0.5–2 mg/mL	0–0.04 mg/mL	0.00003 mg/mL
Subclasses	Four–IgG1, IgG2, IgG3, IgG4	Two—IgA1, IgA2	Two—IgM1, IgM2	Two—IgD1, IgD2	–

Self-assessment

Long-answer question

1. Discuss in detail the structure of immunoglobulins and immunoglobulin classes.

Short-answer questions

Write notes on

1. Differences between complete antigen and hapten
2. Antigenic determinants/epitopes
3. Chemical nature of antigens
4. Properties of antigens
5. Structure of immunoglobulin
6. IgG
7. IgM
8. Secretory IgA
9. IgE
10. Light chains
11. Heavy chains

Multiple-choice questions

1. Which of the following statements is TRUE regarding complete antigen (immunogen), EXCEPT
   A. Is able to induce antibody formation
   B. Is able to react specifically with antibody
   C. Is unable to generate an immune response by itself
   D. Is able to function as an antigen as well as immunogen
2. An antigenic determinant is known as
   A. Paratope
   B. Epitope
   C. Hypervariable region
   D. None of the above
3. To be antigenic or immunogenic, a substance should have molecular weight greater than
   A. 10, 000 Dalton
   B. 1000 Dalton
   C. 100, 000 Dalton
   D. None of the above
4. Which of the following is must for antigenicity?
   A. Gelatin
   B. Tyrosine
   C. Tryptophan
   D. Histones
5. Which of the following statements best describe the properties of hapten?
   A. Is able to induce antibody synthesis but unable to react with antibody
   B. Is able to induce antibody synthesis and able to react with antibody
   C. Is unable to induce antibody synthesis and unable to react with antibody
   D. Is unable to induce antibody synthesis but able to react with antibody
6. Which of the following statements is FALSE about immunoglobulins?
   A. Most of them have molecular weight of 150000–180000
   B. Most of them have sedimentation coefficient of 7S
   C. They are glycoproteins constituting 20–25% of the serum proteins
   D. They are thermostable and are not denatured on heating at 70°C
7. Which of the following statements is FALSE regarding fragment antigen binding?
   A. Contains light chain only
   B. Contains both light chain and a part of heavy chain
   C. Possesses specific amino acid composition
   D. Is known as paratope
8. The Fc portion is responsible for all of the following properties of immunoglobulin, EXCEPT
   A. Skin fixation
   B. Placental transfer
   C. Secretion into the body fluid
   D. Binding with antigen molecule
9. The binding of complement to immunoglobulin molecule is mediated by
   A. Fc portion
   B. $F(ab)_2$ portion

C. Fab portion
D. None of the above

10. An immunoglobulin that is synthesized locally and concentrated in various body secretions is
A. IgA
B. IgG
C. IgM
D. IgD

11. Following are the requirements of immunogenicity, EXCEPT
A. Foreignness
B. Size
C. Shape
D. Chemical nature

12. Which of the following immunoglobulin molecules can cross the placental barrier?
A. IgE
B. IgA
C. IgG
D. IgD

13. Which of the following immunoglobulin molecules mediates reaginic hypersensitivity?
A. IgE
B. IgA
C. IgG
D. IgM

14. Which of the following plays an important role in local immunity?
A. IgE
B. IgA
C. IgG
D. IgM

15. Which of the following indicates recent infection?
A. IgE
B. IgA
C. IgG
D. IgM

16. Which of the following protects the body fluid?
A. IgE
B. IgA
C. IgG
D. IgM

17. Which of the following protects the body surface?
A. IgE
B. IgA
C. IgG
D. IgM

18. Which of the following protects the bloodstream?
A. IgE
B. IgA
C. IgG
D. IgM

12 Antigen–Antibody Reactions

When an antigen solution is mixed with a potent antiserum (antibody), an antigen–antibody complex is formed because of the interaction of antigen with its antibody. This complex formation in an observable manner due to the combination of a specific antigen with a specific antibody and is called antigen–antibody reaction.

Antigen + antibody → Antigen–antibody complex

These reactions play an important role in

- Antibody-mediated immunity against infectious disease and tissue injury in hypers ensitivity and autoimmune diseases in vivo (in the body)
- In the laboratory, antigen–antibody reactions are useful in
  - Diagnosis of infectious and non-infectious diseases
  - Epidemiological surveys
- The antigen–antibody reactions in vitro are known as *serological reactions*

The different types of antigen–antibody reactions used in a laboratory are as follows:

1. Precipitation and flocculation
2. Agglutination
3. Complement fixation test
4. Neutralization test
5. Enzyme immunoassays
6. Immunofluorescence test
7. Radioimmunoassay
8. Immunoblotting

1. Precipitation and flocculation

Precipitation is a reaction between a soluble antigen (precipitinogen—antigen that has no particulate size) and its antibody (precipitin). This reaction takes place in the presence of electrolytes at a suitable temperature (37°C) and pH (7.4), resulting in the formation of an antigen–antibody complex which is an insoluble precipitate.

Precipitinogen	**+Precipitin** →	**Insoluble precipitate**
(soluble antigen)	(antibody)	(antigen–antibody complex)

Flocculation is a precipitation reaction in which the precipitate of antigen–antibody complex remains suspended as floccules instead of sedimentation taking place.

Precipitation reaction can take place in a liquid medium or in a semisolid medium (gels) such as agar gels, agarose or polyacrylamide gels.

Applications

Precipitation and flocculation reactions are used for the following:

- Detection of antigen (more sensitive)
- Identification of microbial components in infective tissues
- Detection of antibody (less sensitive)

Techniques of precipitation and flocculation reactions

Following are the types of precipitation and flocculation tests:

Ring test

When an antigen solution (an extract of the organism) is layered over antiserum in a test tube, a white ring of precipitate forms at the junction of two fluids (Fig. 12.1).

Uses Used for the detection of antigen, for example

- Ascoli's thermoprecipitation test for anthrax
- C-reactive protein test
- The grouping of streptococci by Lancefield technique

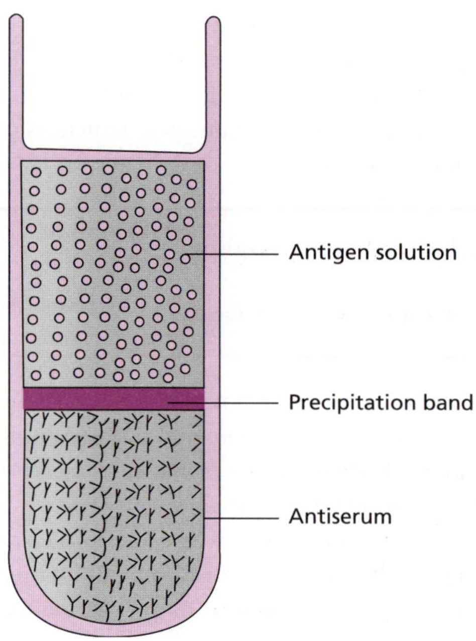

Figure 12.1 Ring test.

Slide flocculation text

When a drop of antigen solution and the patient's serum are placed on a slide and mixed well by shaking, the reaction appears in the form of floccules, for example, VDRL test for diagnosis of syphilis.

Tube flocculation test

An antigen solution and the patient's serum are placed in a tube and mixed by shaking. The result is formation of floccules, for example, Kahn test for diagnosis of syphilis.

Immunodiffusion test

It is a precipitation in gel, which is more sensitive and specific than precipitation in a liquid medium.

Important types of immunodiffusion

1. Radial immunodiffusion (single diffusion in two dimensions)

- In this test, the antibody is incorporated in agar gel and poured on a glass slide or Petri dish and is allowed to cool and set.
- Wells are cut in layers of agar and the antigen is added to these wells.
- The antigen diffuses radially and reacts with antibody in the gel forming ring-shaped bands of precipitation.
- The diameter of the ring (halos) is used to estimate the concentration of the antigen (Fig. 12.2).

Uses

- For the quantitation of soluble antigens in body fluids

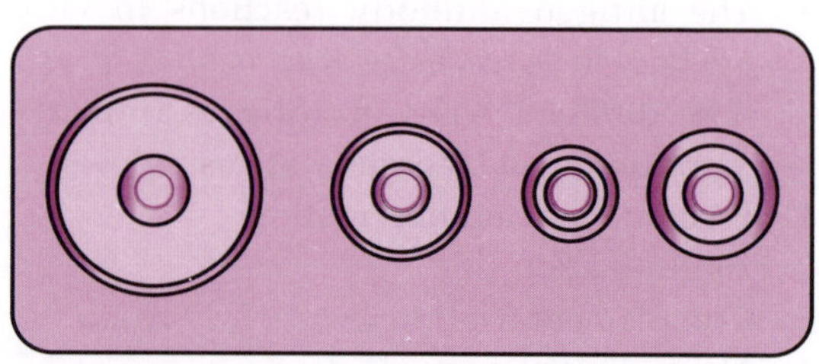

Figure 12.2 Radial immunodiffusion.

- For the quantitation of immunoglobulins, proteins and complement components in serum and other body fluids

2. Agar gel diffusion (double diffusion in two dimensions—Ouchterlony procedure)

- In this test, agar gel is poured on slide or Petri dish and wells are punched in the agar gel.
- The antiserum is placed in the central well and different antigens are placed in the surrounding wells.
- The slide/Petri dish is placed in a moist chamber to prevent drying and to allow diffusion for 24 hours or more.
- The result is the formation precipitation bands where antigen and antibody meet in optimum proportion.
- If two adjacent antigens are identical, the lines of precipitate formed will fuse. If they are not identical, the lines will cross each other. Cross-reaction or partial identity is indicated by spur formation (Fig. 12.3).

Uses

- To detect an antigen
- To compare two antigen–antibody systems

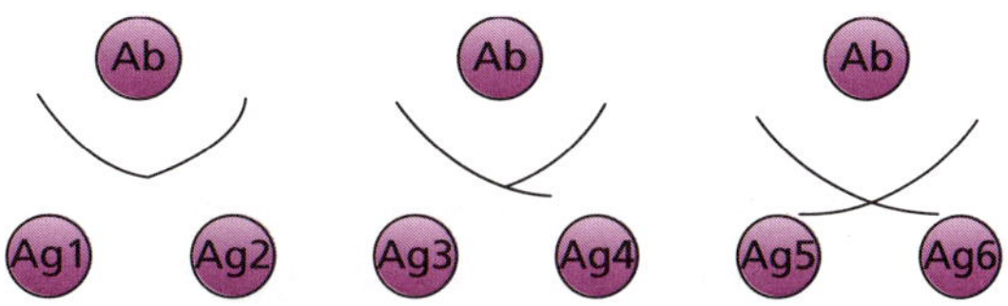

Figure 12.3 Agar gel diffusion. *Ab*, antibody; *Ag*, antigen.

- In the diagnosis of bacterial, viral, fungal and parasitic diseases, for example, Elek's test for testing toxigenicity in diphtheria

3. Immunoelectrophoresis (IEP)

- Is a combination of electrophoresis and agar gel diffusion
- Is a two-step reaction
- In the first step, the antigen is subjected to electrophoretic separation in agar gel (Fig. 12.4a)
- In the second step, a trough is cut parallel to and slightly away from the path of electrophoretic separation and is filled with antiserum and allowed to diffuse (Fig. 12.4b)
- The antigen and antibody diffuse towards each other and form precipitation bands

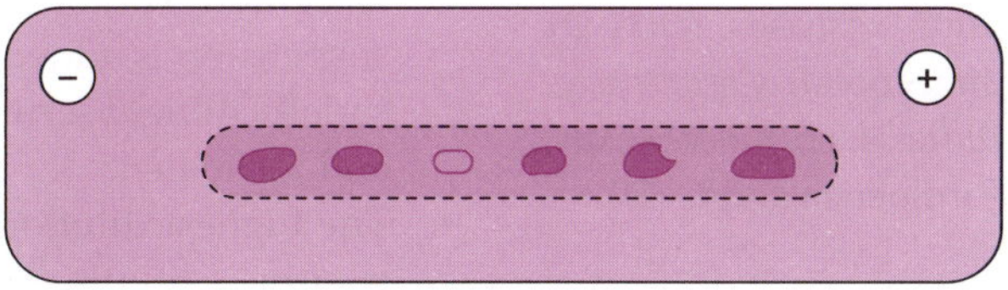

(a)

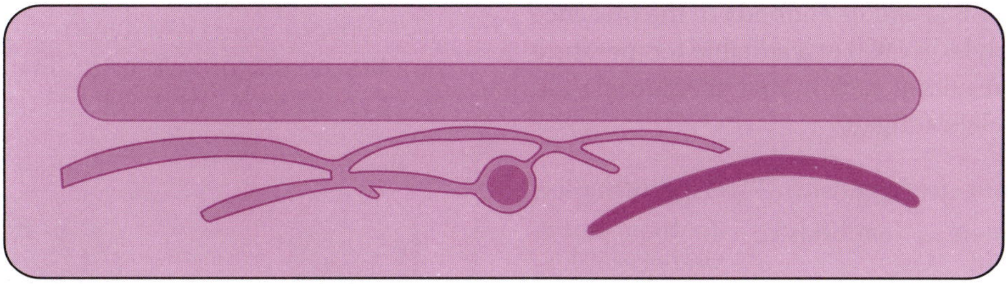

(b)

Figure 12.4 Immunoelectrophoresis. (a) First step. (b) Second step.

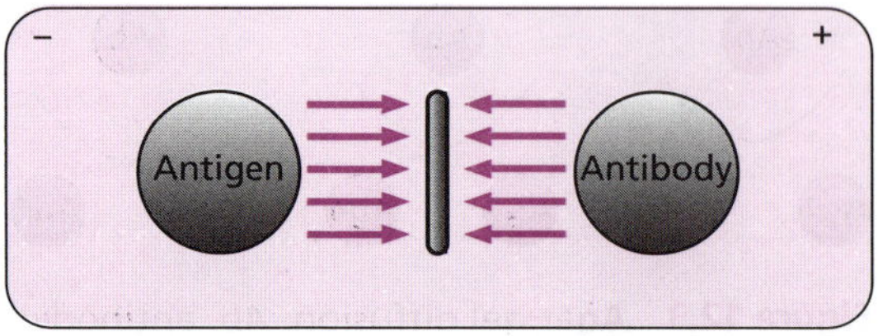

Figure 12.5 Countercurrent immunoelectrophoresis.

Uses

- Analysis of normal human serum
- Detection of abnormalities in human sera and in various body fluids in various diseases

4. Countercurrent immunoelectrophoresis (CIEP)

- In this test, antibody is placed in one well and the antigen that is to be tested in another well. These are moved through the gel with the help of electric current. The result is the formation of a line of precipitate when antigen and antibody meet in optimum proportion (Fig. 12.5).

Uses

- Detection of antigens in various body fluids
- Diagnosis of infectious diseases such as pneumococcal, meningococcal, *Corynebacterium diphtheriae*, candidiasis, cryptococcosus, histoplasmosis, HBV, influenza and CMV

2. Agglutination reaction

It is the reaction between particulate antigen (bacteria, RBC) and its antibody in the presence of electrolytes (NaCl) at a suitable temperature and pH, resulting in clumping or agglutination of particulate antigen.

Agglutinogen+Agglutinin $\xrightarrow{\text{NaCl}}$ **Agglutination**
(particulate antigen) (antibody) (antigen–antibody complex)

The test can be performed as slide agglutination and tube agglutination.

Slide agglutination test

The procedure is as follows:

- A smooth and uniform suspension of particulate antigen is prepared in a drop of saline on a glass slide or a tile and a drop of appropriate antiserum is added and mixed with a wire loop.
- A positive result, in a few seconds, is indicated by the clumping together of the particles and clearing of the drop. Clumping is visible to the naked eye but sometimes requires confirmation under the microscope (Fig. 12.6).

Antigen + saline + antibody→Clumping—positive test
No clumping—negative test

Uses

- Identification of bacterial isolates from clinical specimens
- Blood grouping and crossmatching

Tube agglutination test

This is a quantitative test for detection of antibody titre. The procedure includes the following:

- A certain volume of particulate antigen suspension is added to an equal volume of serially diluted serum in different test tubes and incubated.
- The highest dilution of serum that gives a positive agglutination reaction is recorded as antibody titre.

Uses

- Used in the diagnosis of
  - Typhoid fever (Widal test)
  - Brucellosis (*Brucella* agglutination test)
  - Typhus fever (Weil–Felix test)

Figure 12.6 Slide agglutination test.

Haemagglutination tests

The test can also be performed using RBCs as antigen or carrier molecule. These tests in which RBCs are used are known as haemagglutination tests, for example, Paul–Bunnell test for infectious mononucleosis, *Treponema pallidum haemagglutination* test for serodiagnosis of syphilis and Coombs test for detection of incomplete antibody in haemolytic diseases of the newborn due to Rh incompatibility.

Coombs antiglobulin test

- Devised by Coombs *et al.* (1945) to detect antibodies which fail to agglutinate corresponding antigen and inhibit agglutination known as **incomplete** or **blocking antibodies**.

Direct Coombs test

- It is used to detect monovalent maternal antibody present on the surface of RBCs.
- In this test, sensitization of RBCs with incomplete antibodies occurs in vivo.
- When such RBCs are treated with Coombs serum (rabbit antiserum) against human gamma-globulin, agglutination occurs (Fig. 12.7).

Uses In the haemolytic diseases of a newborn due to Rh incompatibility.

Indirect Coombs test

- Indirect Coombs test is used for detection of antibodies in the patient's serum.
- In this test, sensitization of RBCs with antibodies is performed in vitro by incubating the patient's serum with Rh-positive RBCs and then Coombs serum is added. This results in agglutination (Fig. 12.8).

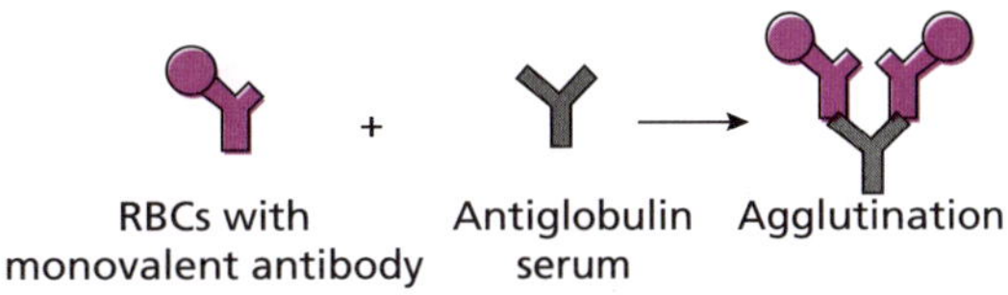

Figure 12.7 Direct Coombs test.

Uses Detection of anti-Rh antibody (free) in the patient's serum and also to demonstration of any type of incomplete or non-agglutinating antibodies.

Passive agglutination tests

Instead of RBCs, inert particles such as latex particles can be used as carriers of antigen. Addition of specific antibody transforms the latex (milk) from a milky white liquid to a coarse suspension of visible granules. These tests are known as passive agglutination tests, for example, rheumatoid (RA) factor test, pregnancy test, C-reactive protein (CRP) test and antistreptolysin O test (ASO). By attaching soluble antigen to the surface of carrier molecule, a precipitation reaction can be converted into agglutination reaction. When instead of antigen, the antibody is attached to the surface of carrier molecule and used for detection of antigen, the test is known as **reverse passive agglutination test**.

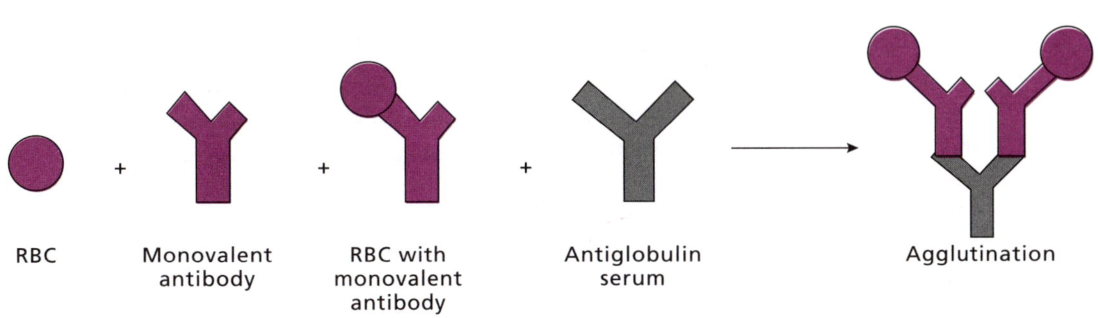

Figure 12.8 Indirect Coombs test. *RBC*, red blood cell.

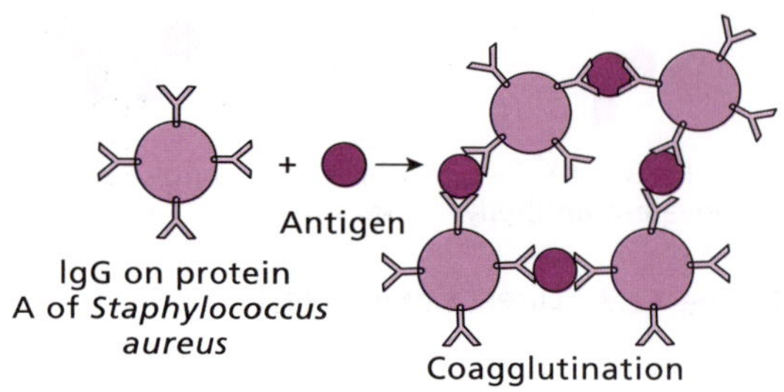

Figure 12.9 Coagglutination test.

Coagglutination test

In this test, the **protein A** of *Staphylococcus aureus* (Cowan-1 strain) is bound non-specifically with Fc portion of IgG leaving Fab portion free to react with its homologous antigen.

- The IgG on protein A of *Staphylococcus* reacts with specific antigen that causes clumping of the staphylococci.
- This clumping or agglutination of staphylococci is called coagglutination (Fig. 12.9).

Uses For detection of bacterial antigens in blood, urine and cerebrospinal fluid (CSF) in pneumococcal, gonococcal, meningococcal, streptococcal, *Salmonella*, etc.

3. Complement fixation test (CFT)

- The ability of antigen–antibody complexes to fix complement is used in CFT. It is a versatile and sensitive test for detection of antigen and antibody.
- It is a two step reaction:
  - *Step 1*
    - Inactivated patient's serum + antigen + fixed amount of complement and incubated at 37°C for 60 minutes
  - *Step 2*
    - Sheep RBCs sensitized with anti-sheep RBC antibodies (amboceptor) are added and incubated at 37°C for 30 minutes
- **Results**
  - The test is considered positive if there is no haemolysis of sheep RBCs.
  - The test is considered negative, if there is haemolysis of sheep RBCs.
- **Example** Wasserman test for diagnosis of syphilis:

> Patient's serum + cardiolipin antigen + complement + SRBCs–antibody (amboceptor)

No haemolysis indicates presence of antibodies against *T. pallidum*—positive test.

- In a positive test, the patient's serum contains antibodies, which react with antigens and fix the complement. Thus, the complement is utilized in the first step and there is no free complement present for the lysis of sheep RBCs.
- In a negative test, the serum does not contain antibodies; hence, there will be no antigen–antibody reaction and complement will not be utilized in the first step. It will be left intact to react with sheep RBCs and cause haemolysis.

4. Neutralization test

Homologous antibodies neutralize the biological effects of viruses, toxins and enzymes. Such antibodies are known as neutralizing antibodies and the test is known as neutralization test. This test is used in identification of viruses (virus neutralization test) and toxin (toxin neutralization test), for example, ASO test in streptococci, Nagler's reaction in *Clostridium welchii*.

Virus neutralization test

- Virus neutralization can be demonstrated in various systems such as animals, tissue culture and chick embryos.
- The inoculation of virus in these systems results into multiplication and growth.
- Inhibition of multiplication and growth by injecting or incorporating specific neutralizing antibodies indicates a positive neutralization test.

Toxin neutralization

When antitoxin combines with toxin, it neutralizes biological effects of toxin making it harmless. Toxin neutralization can be studied in vivo as well as in vitro.

- **Neutralization in vivo** Schick test to determine immunity or susceptibility to diphtheria is an example of an in vivo test. In this test, when diphtheria toxin is injected intradermally in a human, no reaction will occur at the site of injection if the individual possesses a circulating antitoxin in his blood. When no reaction occurs, the individual is considered immune. Other examples of in vivo neutralization tests are as follows:
  - Toxigenicity testing of *C. diphtheriae* in experimental animals
  - *Cl. welchii* toxin neutralization test in guinea pig or mice
- **Neutralization test in vitro** Examples of in vitro test are as follows:
  - ***Nagler's reaction*** When *Cl. welchii* is grown on agar medium containing 20% human serum or 5% egg yolk, it produces a zone of opacity surrounding the colonies due to lecithinase activity (phospholipase) of alpha-toxin. This zone of opacity can be inhibited by spreading antitoxin on the surface of the plate and no zone of opacity is seen due to neutralization of alpha-toxin by antitoxin.
  - ***Antistreptolysin O test*** In this test, antitoxin present in patient's serum neutralizes streptolysin O and inhibits its haemolytic activity.

5. Enzyme-linked immunosorbent assay (ELISA)

It is a type of binding assay in which antigen–antibody reaction is a base and enzyme reaction is a marker. This is a simple, versatile and highly sensitive test and needs only microliter quantities of test reagents. It can be performed as

- Sandwich ELISA
- Indirect ELISA

Sandwich ELISA

- It is used for assay of an antigen.
- In this test, the wells of microtitre plate are coated with specific antibody against antigen to be tested.
- The sample to be tested is added to the well and incubated. If antigen is present in the test sample, it reacts with antibody. To detect this antigen–antibody reaction, antibody labelled with an enzyme is added and incubated. This antibody labelled with the enzyme binds to the antigen.
- After washing, when suitable substrate is added, the enzyme acts on the substrate forming a product. The enzyme activity is measured by spectrophotometric or fluorometric or electrode method (Fig. 12.10).

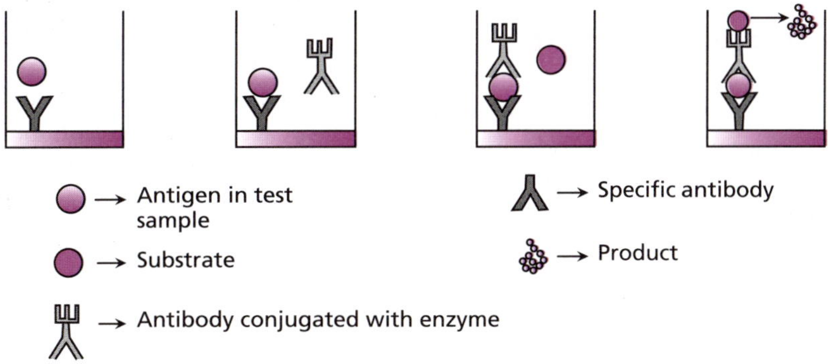

Figure 12.10 Sandwich ELISA.

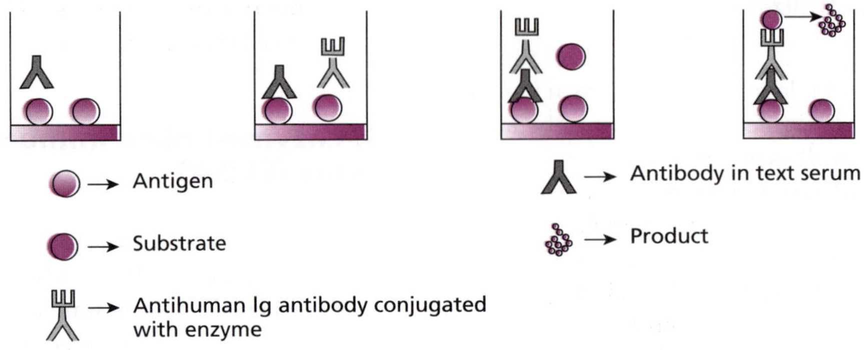

Figure 12.11 Indirect ELISA.

Uses

- Detection of antigens such as rotavirus antigen and hepatitis B virus antigen
- Detection of toxins

Indirect ELISA

It is used for detection of antibodies. In this test, antigen is coated in the well instead of antibody and treated with the patient's serum and then a goat antihuman immunoglobulin antibody conjugated with an enzyme is added. Rest of the procedure is similar to sandwich ELISA (Fig. 12.11).

Uses

Detection of antibodies in various infections such as *Salmonella, Haemophilus, Vibrio cholerae, Brucella, Treponema,* rubella, HIV, hepatitis B virus, herpes simplex virus and cytomegalovirus.

6. Immunofluorescence test

Fluorescence is the property of absorbing light rays of one particular wavelength and emitting rays with a different wavelength. Fluorescent dyes such as fluorescein isothiocyanate and lissamine rhodamine can absorb ultraviolet light and convert it into visible light. These dyes can be conjugated with antibodies and used to locate and identify antigens in tissues **(direct immunofluorescence test)**. The method can also be used for detection of antibodies directed against antigens already known to be present in a given specimen **(indirect immunofluorescence test)**. This test is more sensitive than precipitation or CFT.

Direct immunofluorescence test

- In this test, the tissue section or smear of a clinical specimen is fixed on a glass slide and specific antibody tagged with fluorescent dye is applied directly to the slide.
- Allowed to react for 30–60 minutes at 37°C and observed for fluorescence under ultraviolet microscope (Fig. 12.12).

Uses Commonly used for detection of bacteria, viruses, fungi and parasites in tissues, blood or other specimens.

Indirect immunofluorescence test

- It is used for detection of antibodies in sera or other body fluids. It is a double-layer technique.
- In this test, antigen is known. It is treated with test serum. If antibodies are present in the serum, a complex is formed. This complex is visualized by a fluorescent dye tagged with anti-immunoglobulin serum (Fig. 12.13).

Uses

- Used to detect antibodies in *T. pallidum, Brucella,* pneumococci, *Cryptococcus,* cytomega-

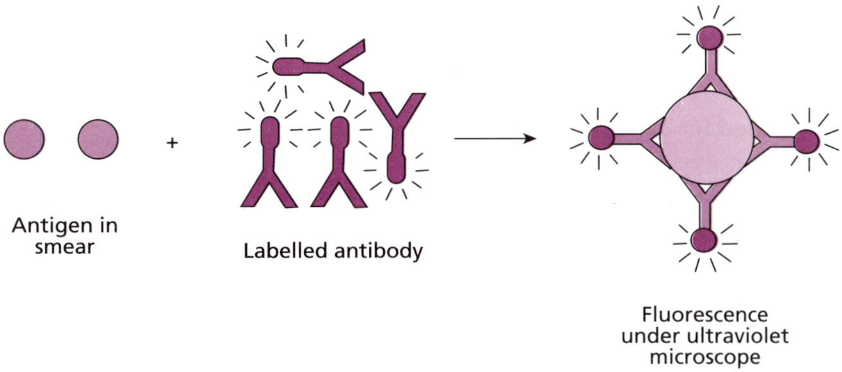

Figure 12.12 Direct immunofluorescence test.

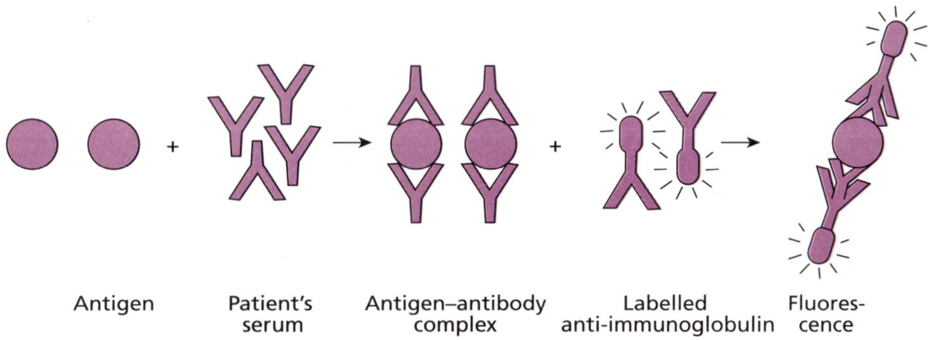

Figure 12.13 Indirect immunofluorescence test.

lovirus, rubella virus, malaria, *Echinococcus* and other infections
- In the diagnosis of cancer, autoimmune diseases, etc.

7. Radioimmunoassay (RIA)

The test uses radioactive isotopes to detect antigens or antibodies. It is highly sensitive and specific test used for quantitation of hormones, drugs, viral antigens, etc. It permits the measurement up to picogram (10^{-12} gram) quantities.

It is basically a competitive binding assay in which fixed amounts of antibody and radiolabelled antigen react in the presence of known (standard) or unknown (test) amounts of the antigen. The amounts by which the binding of labelled antigen to its antibody is competitively inhibited by the increasing amounts of standard antigen preparations are recorded and a dose response curve or standard curve is plotted. The amount of antigen present in unknown sample can be calculated from the standard curve by comparing the binding of the labelled antigen.

Procedure

- The antigen is radiolabelled and reacted with enough antibody to bind about 70% of it.
- Various known amounts of unlabelled antigen are added to allow competition for antibody.
- The labelled antigen bound to antibody is separated from unbound labelled antigen.
- From the amounts of labelled antigen bound at various concentrations of unlabelled

antigen, a standard curve is constructed which allows quantitation of unknown antigen in the test sample.

Uses RIA can be used for quantitation of hormones, drugs, tumour markers, IgE, viral antigens, autoimmune markers, etc.

8. Immunoblotting

Immunoblotting is a highly sensitive and highly specific test to detect individual proteins (antigens) in a complex mixtures. It is a combination of three different procedures which are as follows:

- **Separation**—separation of antigens by polyacrylamide gel electrophoresis
- **Blotting**—blotting or transfer of separated antigens electrophoretically from polyacrylamide gel to a sheet of nitrocellulose paper
- **Enzyme immunoassay (or radio immunoassay)** to
  - Detect antibody in test sera against various antigen fractions
  - Probe with known antisera against specific antigen bands

Different immunoblotting techniques include the following:

- **Southern blot** Nitrocellulose sheets with transferred DNA are called southern blots. It is named after Edward Southern who devised the technique.
- **Northern blot** When the above procedure is applied to analyze transferred RNA.
- **Western blot** Nitrocellulose sheet with transferred proteins is termed Western blots. It is the confirmatory test used for serodiagnosis of HIV infections.
  - In this test, the antigens are separated by polyacrylamide gel electrophoresis. The separated antigens are blotted on to nitrocellulose paper. These strips are then treated with test sera and finally with enzyme-conjugated antihuman globulin. A suitable substrate is then added, which produces a prominent colour band where the specific antibody has reacted with the separated antigen. The position of the band on the strip indicates the antigen with which the antibody has reacted.

Self-assessment

Long-answer questions

1. Enumerate antigen–antibody reactions. Discuss in detail the agglutination.
2. Enumerate antigen–antibody reactions. Discuss in detail the precipitation.

Short-answer questions

Write notes on

1. Neutralization test
2. Immunofluorescence test
3. Radioimmunoassay
4. ELISA
5. Complement fixation test
6. Agar gel diffusion
7. Immunodiffusion techniques

Multiple-choice questions

1. Which of the following is a slide flocculation test?
   A. Kahn test
   B. Ascoli's thermoprecipitation test
   C. C-reactive protein test
   D. VDRL test
2. Which of the following statements is TRUE about precipitation reaction?
   A. Is a reaction between particulate antigen with its antibody
   B. Is a reaction between soluble antigen with its antibody
   C. The nature of antigen is neither particulate nor soluble
   D. The precipitate of antigen–antibody complex remains suspended
3. Which of the following tests is an example of agar gel diffusion?
   A. Elek's test
   B. Ascoli's thermoprecipitation test

C. Wassermann test
D. None of the above

4. Slide agglutination test is used for
A. Identification of bacterial isolates from clinical specimens
B. Blood grouping
C. Cross-matching
D. All of the above

5. Following are the examples of tube agglutination test, EXCEPT
A. Widal test
B. Coombs test
C. Brucella agglutination test
D. Weil–Felix test

6. Following are the examples of latex agglutination test, EXCEPT
A. RA factor test
B. Pregnancy test
C. Paul–Bunnell test
D. Antistreptolysin O test

7. Wasserman test used for diagnosis of syphilis is an example of
A. Agglutination
B. Precipitation
C. Immunofluorescence
D. Complement fixation

8. All of the following statements are TRUE regarding Nagler's reaction, EXCEPT
A. Is an example of in vitro test
B. Is used to find out the lecithinase activity
C. Is a virus neutralization test
D. Is used for the diagnosis of *Clostridium welchii* infection

9. Sandwich ELISA is used for the detection of all of the following, EXCEPT
A. Rotavirus antigen
B. Hepatitis B virus antigen
C. Detection of toxins
D. HIV antibody

10. Which of the following statements is TRUE about indirect immunofluorescence test?
A. Is used for detection of antibodies in sera or other body fluids
B. Is used for detection of bacteria
C. Is used for detection of antigen in blood or other specimens
D. Uses specific antibody tagged with fluorescent dye

11. Which of the following tests is used for detection of maternal antibody present on the surface of RBCs?
A. Direct Coombs test
B. Indirect Coombs test
C. Coagglutination test
D. Paul–Bunnell test

12. Which of the following is used in coagglutination test?
A. Peptidoglycan
B. Lipopolysaccharide
C. Lipid A
D. Protein A

13. A nitrocellulose sheet with transferred proteins is termed
A. Southern blot
B. Western blot
C. Northern blot
D. Eastern blot

14. A nitrocellulose sheet with transferred DNA is termed
A. Southern blot
B. Western blot
C. Northern blot
D. Eastern blot

13 Complement System

The term complement is applied to a group or a complex of substances present in the normal human and animal serum. A complement has the ability to

- Lyse red blood cells (haemolytic activity)
- Destroy Gram-negative bacteria (bacteriolytic activity)
- Kill Gram-positive bacteria without lysis (bactericidal activity)
- Inactivate viruses (virus neutralization)
- Damage tumour cells

Paul Ehrlich termed this lytic agent as complement as it complemented the action of an antibody. Previously, it was known as **Alexine**.

Properties of complement

- Complement constitutes approximately 5–10% of human serum proteins.
- It is glycoprotein by nature.
- Though some of the individual components are heat stable, complement is heat labile. It undergoes spontaneous denaturation slowly at room temperature and in 30 minutes at 56° C (inactivation).
- It does not combine with an antigen or an antibody alone. It is adsorbed non-specifically by antigen–antibody complexes and mediates a number of immunological and biological activities.

Components of complement

Complement is not a single substance but a complex of different protein fractions, namely, C1–C9.

- **C1** It is a heat-labile component. C1 forms the main bulk of complement and is made up of three protein subunits—Clq, C1r and C1s.
- **C2** It is a heat-labile component.
- **C3** It is a heat-stable component, relatively a larger protein, which has the ability to combine with yeast cell wall **(zymosan)**.
- **C4** It is a heat-stable component.
- **C5–C9** These are the components of membrane attack pathway, which cause impairment of membrane function by punching holes and finally cause lysis of cell. These are the terminal components of both classical and alternate pathways required for the **final show** of immune cytolysis.

Activation of complement

Complement is normally present in the body, in an inactive form. It is activated by classical and alternate pathways.

Classical pathway (Flow chart 13.1)

- The classical activity of complement depends upon the operation of nine protein components (C1–C9) acting in a sequence.
- The classical pathway begins with the first component of C, that is, activation of C1q.
- Activation of C1q is initiated by binding with Fc portion of IgG or IgM antibody forming complex with antigen.
- When the C1q is activated, it acquires the ability to activate several molecules of the next component in the sequence.
- C1q binds to Fc portion of Ig molecule and activates C1r that subsequently cleaves C1s and forms an enzymatically active component C1s esterase.
- The activated C1s esterase acts on the next component C4 splitting it into C4a and C4b.
- The C4a has anaphylatoxin activity while C4b, which has an active site, binds to the cell membrane along with C1.

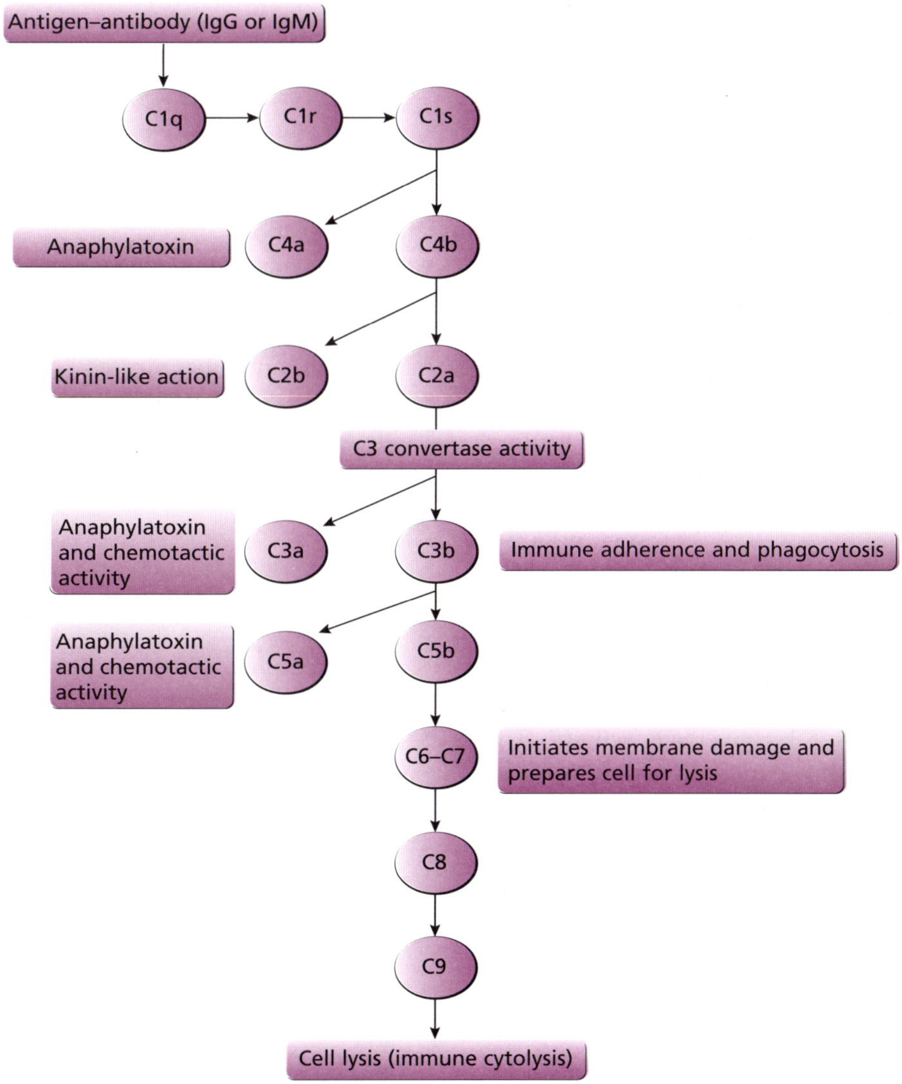

Flow chart 13.1 Classical complement pathway.

- The next component C2 is cleaved into C2a and C2b.
- C2b is released into fluid phase while C2a binds to the C4b forming C4b2a protease enzyme, which has **C3 convertase** activity.
- C3 convertase cleaves C3 into C3a and C3b.
- C3a released into the fluid phase possesses anaphylatoxin activity and is chemotactic for polymorphonuclear leucocytes.
- C3b joins the cascade and binds to the surface of the target cell along with C4b2a forming a trimolecular complex C4b2a3b, which has C5 convertase activity.
- C5 convertase acts on C5 and splits it into C5a, which has both anaphylatoxin and chemotactic activities. C5b joins the cascade and binds to C6 and C7 forming a heat-stable **trimolecular complex** (C5b67), which binds to the cell membrane of target cell and prepares it for lysis by C8 and C9.
- The addition of C8 and C9 accelerates membrane damage and lysis of the cell.
- The mechanism of lysis is by **punching holes** of approximately **100Å** in diameter on the cell membrane, causing disruption of osmotic integrity of the membrane leading to the release of the cell contents.

Alternate pathway

Activation of C3, which is the major component of C, is the central process in the complement activation. In the classical pathway, C3b is formed by the action of C42 which has got C3 convertase activity. The alternate pathway bypasses participation of C1, C4 and C2 components and activates C3 directly. This activation of C3 without prior participation of C1, C4 and C2 is known as the alternate pathway. The activation of C3 and C5–C9 causing the lysis of cells is brought out without the involvement of antigen–antibody complexes and early components (C1, C4, C2) of the complement.

The alternate pathway was described by **Pillemer** in 1954. He demonstrated alternate pathway of the properdin (a normal serum protein), which combines with **zymosan** (a yeast cell wall polysaccharide) in the presence of Mg^{++} ions and forms the P-Z complex, which activates C3 directly without the help of C1, C4 and C2.

Triggering agents In the alternate pathway, C3 can be triggered by a wide range of substances such as

- Polysaccharides, especially of microbial origin, for example, zymosan, inulin, lipopolysaccharide of Gram-negative bacteria (endotoxins) and teichoic acid of Gram-positive bacteria
- Some mammalian RBCs, for example, rabbit and certain mouse strains
- Various Gram-positive and Gram-negative bacteria
- Some parasites, for example, *Schistosoma mansoni* larvae
- Aggregated immunoglobulins such as human IgG4 and IgA, which are unable to bind with C1q and activate classical pathway
- Influenza and other viruses
- Cryptococci and other fungi
- Snake venom factor

Activation of C3

- The first step is binding of factor-B to the trace amount of C3b that exists in normal serum and forms a magnesium dependent C3bB complex, which is cleaved by a proteolytic enzyme factor-D into C3bBb and Ba.
- C3bBb complex has C3 convertase activity, which is extremely labile and loses its activity; but, by binding with properdin it forms PC3bBb, which is relatively stable.
- PC3bBb acts on C3 cleaving it into C3a and C3b. The steps of alternate pathway (Flow chart 13.2) are the same as in classical pathway.
- C3b acts on C5, which activates C6, C7, C8 and C9.

Summary of complement activation is shown in Flow chart 13.3.

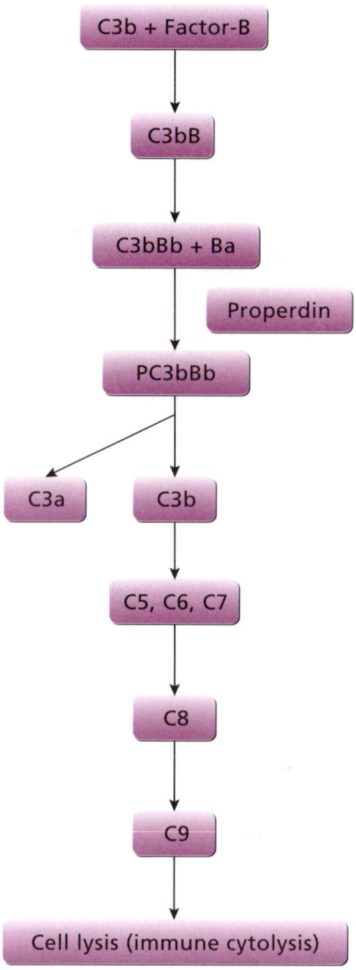

Flow chart 13.2 Alternate pathway.

Immunological and biological effects

The complement system plays an important role in various immunological and biological activities. These include the following:

- **Virus neutralization** Complement appears to play a significant role in the neutralization of viruses, particularly in the early stages of infection by either pathway.
- **Chemotaxis** C5a, C3a and trimolecular complex C5, 6, 7 are chemotactic for polymorphonuclear leucocytes (PML). They attract PML at the site of antigen–antibody interaction and enhance phagocytosis.
- **Bactericidal activity** The complement renders Gram-negative bacteria susceptible to lysozyme by digesting holes in lipopolysaccharide layer, which protects the inner lysozyme sensitive layer of mucopeptide and thus makes Gram-negative bacteria sensitive to lysis **(bacteriolysis)**. Gram-positive bacteria and mycobacteria are not susceptible to the lytic action because of their cell wall composition. However, they are killed by the complement without lysis.
- **Immune adherence** The binding of C3b to antigen–antibody complexes and viruses makes them to adhere to cells possessing immune adherence receptors (PML, macrophages, some B lymphocytes, primate RBCs, etc.) and enhance susceptibility to phagocytosis.
- **Opsonization** C1, C4, C2, C3 and C5 enhance the phagocytosis of immune complexes. This is a complement dependent opsonization and is important in limiting bacterial infections, particularly infections caused by capsulated bacteria, which are poorly opsonized in the absence of complement.
- **Anaphylatoxin activity** C3a, C5a, C4a and C2 kinins stimulate
  - The release of histamine from mast cells
  - Contraction of smooth muscle
  - Increased vascular permeability
  - Vasodilatation
  - Oedema
- **Tissue destruction** Activation of complement also causes severe tissue destruction in the pathogenesis of certain diseases in two ways:
  - ***Activation by autoantibodies*** The binding of autoantibody with self-antigen activates the complement against host's target tissue resulting in tissue injury, for example, autoimmune haemolytic anaemia, thrombocytopenia, myasthenia gravis and Goodpasture syndrome.
  - ***Activation by immune complexes*** Immune complexes which activate C leading to tissue injury and inflammation in Arthus reaction and serum sickness.

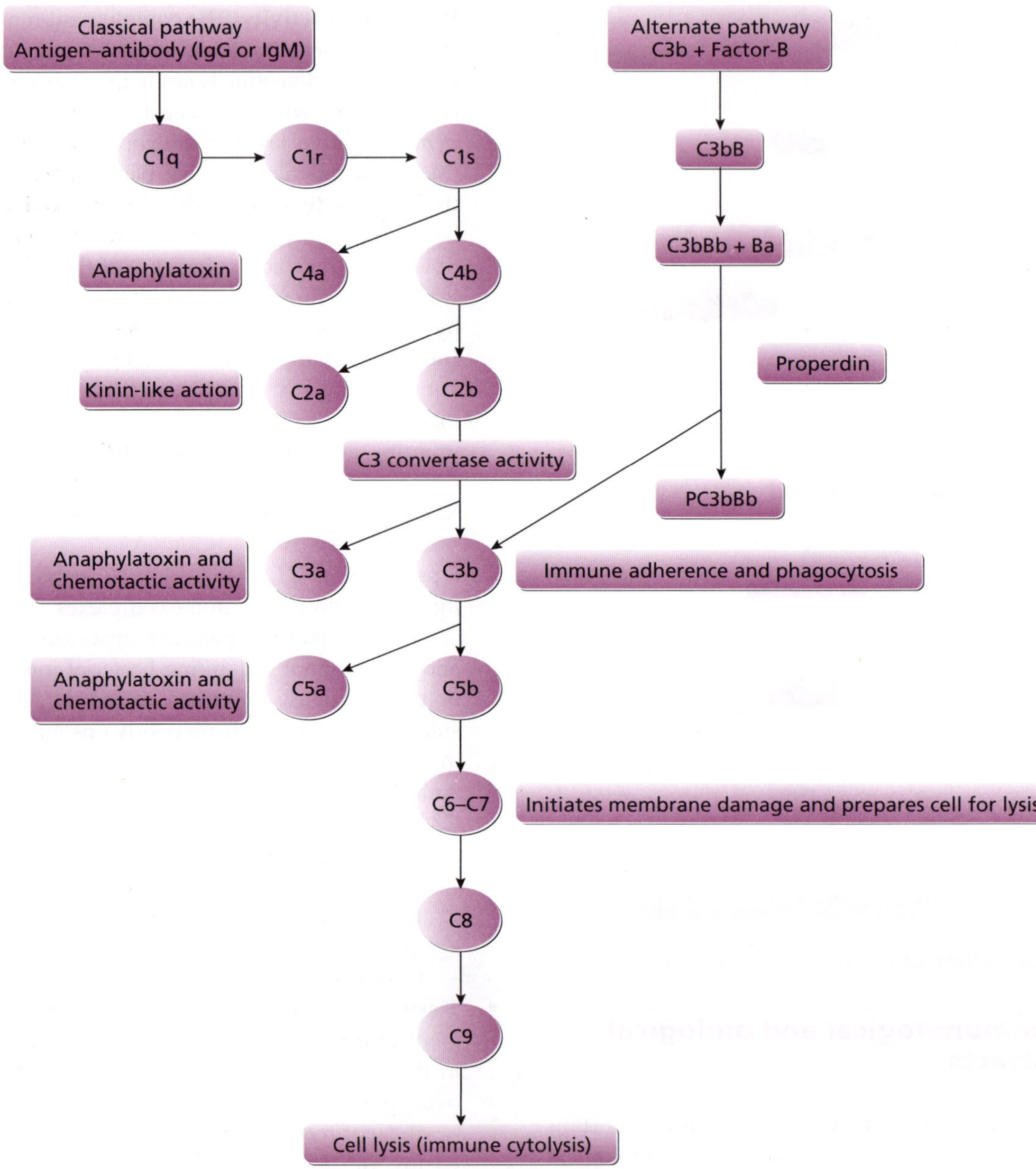

Flow chart 13.3 Summary of complement activation.

Self-assessment

Long-answer question

1. What is complement? Discuss in brief the pathways by which a complement is the activated.

Short-answer questions

Write notes on

1. Properties of complement
2. Classical complement pathway
3. Alternate pathway
4. Immunological and biological effects

Multiple-choice questions

1. Which of the following components of complement has the ability to combine with zymosan?
   A. C1
   B. C2
   C. C3
   D. C4
2. Select the most appropriate immunoglobulin molecule associated with the activation of complement by classical pathway
   A. IgM
   B. IgA
   C. IgD
   D. IgE
3. Select the most appropriate immunoglobulin molecule associated with the activation of complement by alternate pathway
   A. IgM
   B. IgA
   C. IgG
   D. IgE
4. Following are the triggering agents for the activation of complement by alternate pathway, EXCEPT
   A. Zymosan
   B. Inulin
   C. Endotoxin
   D. Exotoxin
5. The following are TRUE statements regarding complement, EXCEPT
   A. Is glycoprotein in nature
   B. Is heat labile
   C. Combines with antigen or antibody
   D. Mediates a number of immunological and biological activities
6. Which of the following statements is FALSE regarding complement?
   A. Complements the activity of antibody
   B. Causes immune cytolysis
   C. Can be activated by any antibody
   D. Is non-specifically absorbed by antigen–antibody complexes
7. Which of the following components is a major component of complement?
   A. C1
   B. C2
   C. C3
   D. C4
8. Which of the following statements is FALSE regarding biological activities of complement?
   A. Plays a significant role in the neutralization of viruses
   B. Plays a significant role in the neutralization of toxins
   C. Plays a significant role in the immune adherence
   D. Plays a significant role in the opsonization
9. Which of the following components of complement is NOT chemotactic for polymorphonuclear leucocytes?
   A. C5a
   B. C3a
   C. C567
   D. C4a
10. Which of the following components of complement has anaphylatoxin activity?
    A. C1q
    B. C3b
    C. C5b
    D. C4a
11. Which of the following components of complement has chemotactic activity?
    A. C1
    B. C2
    C. C8
    D. C3

14 Structure and Function of the Immune System

The immune system comprises a variety of organs which are responsible for the growth and development of immunocompetent cells. These are lymphoid organs and reticuloendothelial system (lymphoreticular system) (Flow chart 14.1).

- The different categories of lymphocytes, plasma cells and macrophages (phagocytic cells) are important cells, which participate in different arms of immune response to antigenic stimuli.
- Lymphocytes are the major immunological effector cells. They arise from precursors or stem cells, which originate in foetal life in the yolk sac and are found subsequently in the liver and bone marrow. The stem cells are further differentiated into two different directions. Some of them migrate to the thymus where they are processed to form thymus derived or T lymphocytes. These T lymphocytes play an important role in **cell-mediated immunity (CMI)**. Other stem cells are processed in the bone marrow or the bursa of Fabricius (in chicken) to form B lymphocytes, which play an important role in **humoral or antibody-mediated immunity (HI or AMI)**.
- Both T and B cells after maturation migrate to the spleen, lymph nodes and other organs where they initiate and participate in immune response to antigens.
- The development of principal cells of immune system occurs as given in (Fig. 14.1).

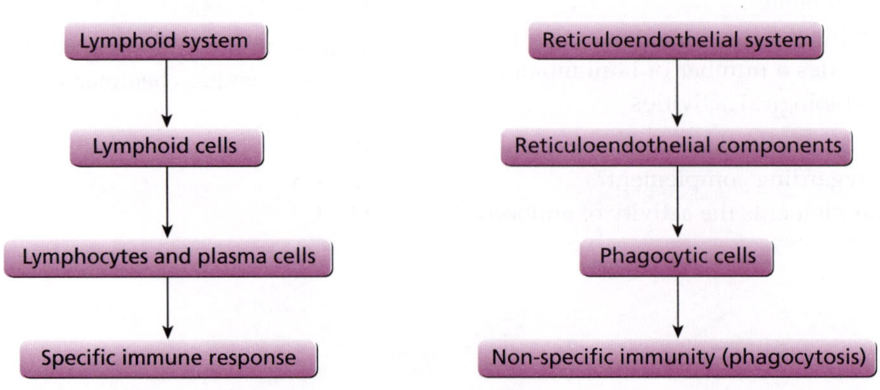

Flow chart 14.1 Lymphoreticular system.

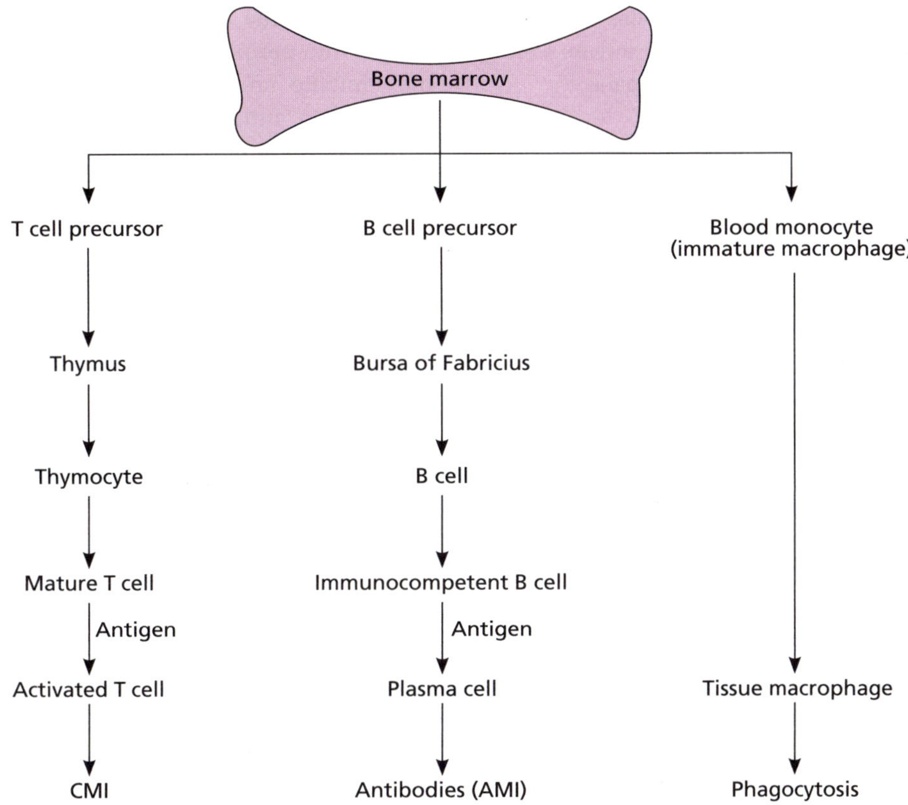

Figure 14.1 Development of principal cells of immune system. *AMI*, antibody-mediated immunity; *CMI*, cell-mediated immunity.

Lymphoid system

The lymphoid system consists of

- Lymphoid organs
- Lymphoid cells (lymphocytes and plasma cells)

The lymphoid organs are classified into central (primary) and peripheral (secondary) lymphoid organs based on the different functions they perform.

Central (primary) lymphoid organs

These are the lymphoid organs in which proliferation and differentiation of lymphocytes take place without antigenic stimulation **(antigen-independent maturation of lymphocytes)**. The primary lymphoid organs include thymus, bursa of Fabricius and bone marrow.

Thymus

- Thymus is a lymphoepithelial bilobed structure located behind the upper part of the sternum (in the anterior mediastinum).
- It is derived from the third and fourth pharyngeal pouches and gets differentiated from these pouches at about the sixth week of foetal life.
- It is capsulated. The septa arising from the capsule divide the gland into lobules, which are differentiated into an outer cortex and inner medulla.
- The precursors of lymphocytes (stem cells—immature cells) from the yolk sac, foetal liver and bone marrow reach the thymus and mature in the cortex. They acquire surface characteristics of T lymphocytes and then migrate into the medulla to complete their maturation process and exit into the blood as matured T

cells. These matured T cells are capable of responding to antigenic stimuli and are seeded into the secondary lymphoid organs.

Functions

- It is the lymphocyte educational centre—for the development and function of the immune system.
- It is the major site for lymphocyte proliferation and production of T lymphocytes.
- The thymus confers **immunological competence** on the lymphocyte. Prethymic lymphocytes are not immunologically competent. In the thymus, they are educated by hormone-like humoral factors—thymosin, thymopoietin, etc., produced by thymic epithelial cells so that they become capable of mounting CMI.

Bursa of Fabricius

- Bursa of Fabricius is a lymphoepithelial organ located near the cloaca in chickens.
- It is similar to thymus and contains lymphoid follicles, which are divided into cortex and medulla composed of immunoglobulin producing B cells.
- Precursors of B cells (stem cells) from the yolk sac, foetal liver and bone marrow reach the bursa and mature into immunocompetent bursal lymphocytes or B cells, which exit through the peripheral blood and become seeded into the secondary lymphoid organs.
- In mammals, an equivalent of bursa has not yet been identified. The maturation of precursors of B cell into functionally mature B lymphocyte occurs in the bone marrow and gut associated lymphoid tissues.

Function It is responsible for the development of immunocompetent B cells making humoral antibodies.

Peripheral (secondary) lymphoid organs

These are the organs which receive and maintain functional lymphocytes. The lymphocytes educated by the central lymphoid organs are seeded into peripheral lymphoid organs where they initiate and participate in the immune response to antigenic stimuli. The peripheral lymphoid organs include lymph nodes, spleen and mucosa-associated lymphoid tissue.

Lymph nodes

- These are small, round or ovoid-shaped organs found in various parts of the body—nodular aggregates of lymphoid tissues.
- They are located at major junctions of the network of lymphatic channels that connect to the thoracic duct, which passes lymphocytes and lymph to the large vein connected to the heart.
- They are differentiated into outer cortex and inner medulla.
- The cortex is further subdivided into an external cortex located just below the capsule and a deep cortex also known as the paracortical area.
- In the external cortex, there is accumulation of lymphocytes in regions called follicles **(primary lymphoid follicles)** within which there is a development of **germinal centres (secondary follicles)** following antigenic stimulation.
- In the medulla, lymphocytes are arranged as elongated branching bands **(medullary cords)**. In an activated lymph nodes, most of them are plasma cells secreting antibodies.
- The cortical follicles and medullary cords contain B lymphocytes (bursa dependent area) while the T cells are occupied in the paracortical area (thymus-dependent area) (Fig. 14.2).

Functions

- Act as filters for lymph draining the body tissues including foreign antigens. Hence, the antigens of microbes present in lymph are captured by antigen-presenting cells and are concentrated in lymph nodes for processing
- Provide a site for phagocytosis and antibody production
- Support the development of lymphocytes

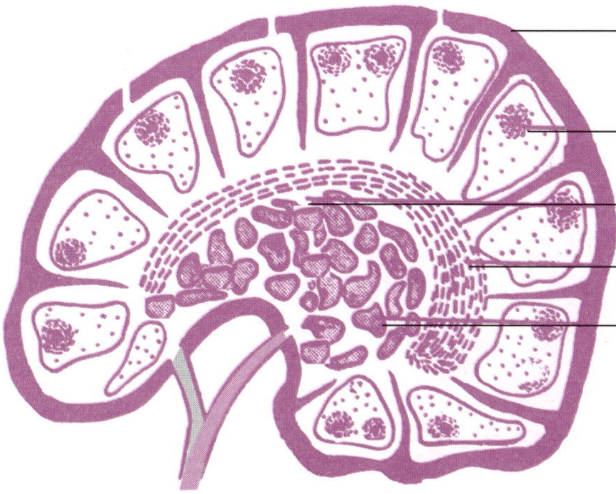

Figure 14.2 Transverse section of a lymph node.

Antigen enters the lymph node ↓ Gets trapped and processed by macrophage ↓ Presented to lymphocytes to initiate an immune response ↓ Antibodies are synthesized and released into bloodstream

Spleen

- It is the largest lymphovascular organ and weighs about 250 g in an adult man.
- The architecture is similar, but not identical to that of a lymph node.
- It has two segregated areas, the **red pulp** and **white pulp,** separated by a marginal zone.
- The white pulp is rich in lymphoid tissue, while the red pulp is abundant in RBCs.
- The white pulp is located mainly around small arteries and the periarterial lymphatic sheath is composed primarily of T lymphocytes and is called the **thymus dependent area**.
- The external lymphoid area surrounding the periarterial lymphatic sheath is a B-dependent area (perifollicular region, germinal centre and mantle layer).
- The periarterial lymphoid collections in the white pulp are called **Malpighian corpuscles** or **follicles**. Following antigenic stimulation, germinal centres are produced in the white pulp. They are composed of large numbers of rapidly dividing cells, which differentiate into plasma cells and replace the T cells in the periarterial region (Fig. 14.3).

Functions

- It is the sole lymphatic organ specialized to filter blood. Thus, it is a systematic filter to trap or concentrate circulating blood-borne particles. Any blood-borne particle is trapped and concentrated in the spleen by dendritic cells and macrophages.
- It is a major site for antibody synthesis against blood-borne particles including microorganisms.
- Its immunological role is primarily directed against blood-borne pathogens.

Mucosa-associated lymphoid tissue (MALT)

- Potentially important collections of lymphocytes, mainly producing IgA, present throughout the mucosal lining (potential portals of entry of microbes) of alimentary, respiratory, genitourinary and other

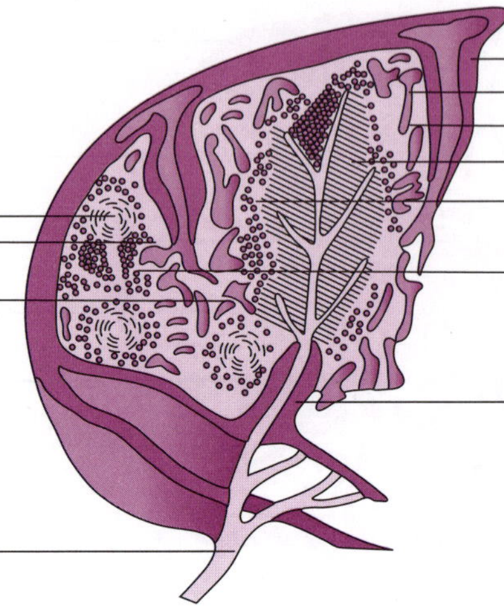

Figure 14.3 Schematic diagram of the splenic architecture.

surfaces as an isolated cells or small cell clusters, are called the MALT.

- Such lymphoid tissues of the gut are known as **gut-associated lymphoid tissue (GALT)** and those of the respiratory tract are called **bronchus-associated lymphoid tissue (BALT)**.
- The MALT structure contains a mixture of B cells, T cells, phagocytic cells and antigen-presenting cells.
- Secretory IgA is the main immunoglobulin produced by MALT.

Functions Local immunity against pathogens invading the local tissue

Important cells of the immune system

Lymphocytes

- Lymphocytes are the most important cells specialized for immunological functions. They are important mediators of adaptive immunity.
- These are small, round cells found in peripheral blood, lymph, lymphoid organs and many other tissues.
- In peripheral blood, they constitute 20–45 % of the total leukocyte population and in lymph and lymphoid organs they are the predominant cell type.

Structure of lymphocytes

- Two types of lymphocytes: small and large.
- The small lymphocytes are necessary for immune response.
- The properties of small lymphocytes are as follows:
  - *Size* 5–12 µm in diameter
  - *Shape* Round
  - *Nucleus* Spherical with prominent nuclear chromatin
  - *Cytoplasm* A thin rim of cytoplasm with scattered ribosomes but devoid of endoplasmic reticulum, Golgi bodies and other organelles (Fig. 14.4)
  - *Motility* Slowly motile. During movement, they assume a hand mirror-like form with a nucleus in the front and cytoplasm as a tail behind

Classification of lymphocytes

Lymphocytes are classified in various ways:

- **Based on morphology**
  - Small lymphocytes—5–8 µm
  - Medium lymphocytes—8–12 µm
  - Large lymphocytes—12–15 µm

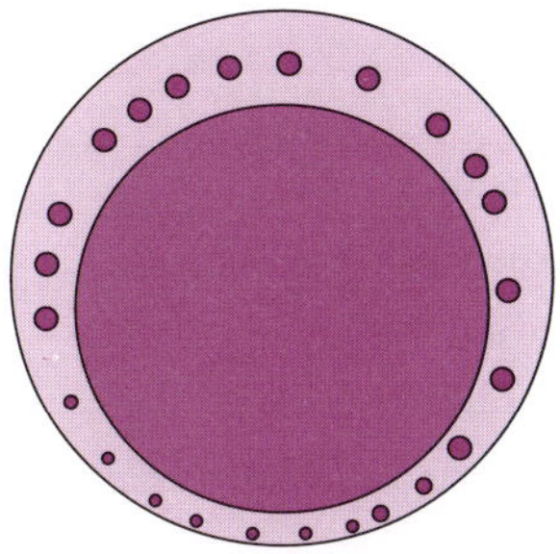

Figure 14.4 Structure of lymphocyte.

- **Based on lifespan**
  - Short lived/effector cells—2 weeks
  - Long lived/memory cells—3 years or more
- **Based on function**
  - Antibody producing B cells
  - CMI producing T cells

The T and B lymphocytes are two groups of non-phagocytic, morphologically indistinguishable lymphocytes. They are functionally different but have certain common features as follows:

- They recirculate throughout the body from blood to tissue and then again into circulation. There is constant traffic of lymphocytes through the blood, lymph, lymphatic organs and tissues. When an antigen enters into any part of the body, lymphocytes of appropriate specificity reach the site and mount an immune response. The recirculating lymphocytes can be recruited by the lymphoid tissues whenever necessary. The majority of the recirculating cells are T cells.
- Each lymphocyte possesses a specific receptor on its surface for recognition of a particular antigen. This confers specificity.
- When stimulated by a specific antigen, the lymphocytes undergo clonal proliferation. B cells are transformed into plasma cells, which synthesize antibodies while T cells produce lymphokines and induce CMI.
- They show a property of memory giving rise to a faster and powerful immune response on being re-challenged by the same antigen.

General functions of lymphocytes

The lymphocytes educated by the central lymphoid organs become **immunologically competent cells (ICC)** and serve the following general functions:

- Recognition of antigen
- Storage of immunological memory
- Immune response to a specific antigen
- Resistance to certain infections
- Transplantation immunity
- Tumour immunity
- Hypersensitivity

Functions of T cells

- Mediate CMI through the production of cytokines
- Can directly act on and destroy virally infected host cells, tumour cells and foreign cells (cytotoxic effect)
- Act as regulatory cells that modulate the activity of other T cells, B cells or macrophages. Regulation can be in the form of help or suppression
- Different T cell subsets perform different functions (Table 14.1)

Plasma cells (Fig. 14.5)

Antigenically stimulated B cells undergo blast transformation to form plasma cells. The properties of mature plasma cells are as follows:

- **Shape** Oval
- **Size** Twice the size of small lymphocyte
- **Nucleus** Small, eccentric, oval with radially arranged chromatin around the periphery that gives the appearance of a clock face or cart wheel
- **Cytoplasm** Large, contains a well-developed Golgi apparatus and abundant endoplasmic reticulum
- **Lifespan** These are end cells and have a short lifespan of 2 or 3 days

Function Plasma cell is an antibody-producing machinery, produce antibodies. It can produce

Table 14.1 T cell subsets and their functions

T cell subsets (subpopulation)	Function
Th (helper T cells)	Help B cell to produce antibody
Ts (suppressor T cells)	Suppress antibody production and Th cell activity
Tr (regulator T cells)	Regulate the activity of Th and Ts cells
Amplifier T cells	Help in the development of specific cytotoxic T cells
Cytotoxic T cells (effector T cells)	Specifically destroy virally infected cells and modified target cells
Lymphokines producing T cells	Produce lymphokines which play an important role in cell-mediated immunity and delayed hypersensitivity
Memory T cells	Retain memory of previous contact

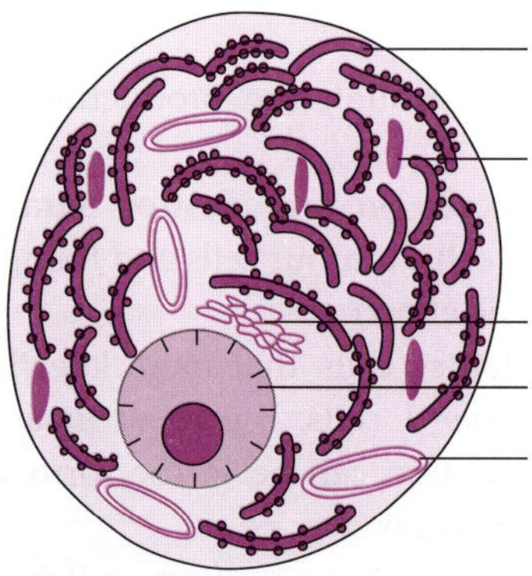

Figure 14.5 Plasma cell.

an antibody of a single specificity either IgM or IgG or IgA.

Null cells

Out of the total lymphocytes in peripheral circulation, about 5–10% of lymphocytes which cannot be classified as either T or B cells are known as null cells. The null cells are of three types:

1. Natural killer cells (NK cells)
2. Killer cells (K cells)
3. Lymphokines-activated killer cells (LAK cells)

Natural killer cells (NK cells)

- They are present naturally and are not formed in response to antigen.
- They can kill a variety of transformed and virally infected host cells.
- NK cells are present in the spleen and peripheral blood.
- They do not require antibody and their action is non-specific.
- Their activity is increased by interferon.

Functions The exact functional significance of NK cells is not known, they are believed to play an important role in

- Immune surveillance and natural defence against virus-infected cells (antiviral activity) and malignant mutant cells (antitumour activity)
- They are also involved in the early response to infection by certain viruses and intracellular bacteria

Killer cells (K cells)

- These cells possess receptors for the Fc portion of IgG.
- They lyse or kill target cells sensitized with IgG antibodies.
- K cells do not require complement for their activity.
- They are responsible for **antibody-dependent cell cytotoxicity** (ADCC) in which an antibody molecule forms a bridge between the target cell and K cell. The Fab portion of IgG binds with the antigenic determinants on the target cell and Fc portion of the IgG binds with the Fc receptor on the K cell and damage to target cell is produced without the help of complement.

Lymphokines-activated killer cells (LAK cells)

- These are null cells treated with interleukin-2 (IL-2), which are cytotoxic to a wide range of tumour cells without affecting the normal cells.
- They can be used in the treatment of some tumours such as renal cell carcinoma.

Phagocytic cells

Engulfment and digestion of foreign particles (particulate material including microbes) by a single cell is known as **phagocytosis**. The process of phagocytosis is the most important means of defence mechanism against microorganisms. The phagocytic cells were first described by **Metchnikoff (1883)**.

Types of phagocytic cells

These are of two types:

1. Macrophages
2. Microphages

Macrophages

- These are large, round or oval cells with a kidney- or oval-shaped nucleus and abundant cytoplasm.
- The blood macrophages (monocytes) are 12–15 μm in size while tissue macrophages (histiocytes) are 15–20 μm in size.
- Macrophages are widely distributed throughout the body.
- They effectively eliminate foreign substances and debris from the blood, lymph and tissues.
- They are produced from the stem cells in the bone marrow where they undergo proliferation and are delivered as monocytes in the bloodstream after a period of maturation (about 6 days).
- The blood monocytes, after few days, migrate to various tissues where they differentiate further into macrophages. During this differentiation, they undergo morphological, biochemical and functional changes, that is, the cell increases in size, show an increase in the content of lysosomal enzymes and changes in intracellular organelles.
- Monocytes in blood have half-life period of 3 days while macrophages in tissue survive for months by proliferating locally.

Microphages

- These are small, non-dividing polymorphonuclear leukocytes or granulocytes present in the blood.
- Morphologically, there are three types of cells which participate in immunological reactions. These include neutrophils (45–60%), eosinophils (1–3%) and basophils (0.3%).
- The neutrophils and, to a lesser extent, eosinophils are phagocytic.
- They contain granules and a wide range of bactericidal substances.
- They originate in the bone marrow from stem cells, undergo maturation and are finally released into the circulation.
- They are short-lived cells with a half-life of 2 days in circulation and few hours in the tissue after penetration.

Role of phagocytic cells

- The primary role is phagocytosis—engulfment and digestion of foreign particles.
- They also participate in the development of a specific immune response, for example, trapping of antigen by macrophages and its presentation to lymphocytes.
- Macrophages also participate in antitumour activity and graft rejection.
- Microphages participate in inflammation, opsonization, hypersensitivity reactions and immunity against parasitic infections.

Dendritic cells

- These are the antigen-presenting cells like macrophages.

- They are derived from bone marrow and are different from macrophages and T and B lymphocytes.
- They have little or no phagocytic activity.
- They are present in peripheral blood and in peripheral lymphoid organs, especially in the germinal centres of the spleen and lymph nodes.
- They are believed to play an important role in the presentation of antigens to T cells during the primary immune response.
- They capture protein antigens of microbes that enter through the epithelia and transport to regional lymph nodes for presentation to T cells.

Self-assessment

Long-answer questions

1. Describe the important organs of the immune system and enumerate their functions.
2. Enumerate the immunocompetent cells and discuss in detail the lymphocytes.

Short-answer questions

Write notes on

1. Mucosa-associated lymphoid tissue
2. Thymus
3. Bursa of Fabricius
4. Lymph nodes
5. Spleen
6. Lymphocytes
7. Plasma cells
8. Natural killer cells
9. Killer cells
10. Phagocytic cells
11. Dendritic cells

Multiple-choice questions

1. Which of the following lymphoid organs is NOT a part of central (primary) lymphoid organs?
   A. Thymus
   B. Bursa of Fabricius
   C. Spleen
   D. None of the above
2. In mammals, the maturation of precursors of B cell into functionally mature B lymphocyte occurs in
   A. Bone marrow
   B. Bursa of Fabricius
   C. Spleen
   D. Thymus
3. Which of the following statements is FALSE about lymph nodes?
   A. Provide a site for phagocytosis
   B. Its immunological role is primarily directed against blood-borne pathogens
   C. Provide a site for antibody production
   D. Support the development of lymphocytes
4. Which of the following statements is FALSE about spleen?
   A. It is the sole lymphatic organ specialized to filter blood
   B. Its immunological role is primarily directed against blood-borne pathogens
   C. It provides a site for antibody production against blood-borne pathogens
   D. IgA is the main immunoglobulin produced by spleen
5. Which of the following statements is FALSE about mucosa-associated lymphoid tissue (MALT)?
   A. Mediates local immunity against pathogens invading local tissue
   B. Is present throughout the mucosal lining
   C. Provides a site for antibody production against blood-borne pathogens
   D. IgA is the main immunoglobulin produced by MALT
6. Which of the following cells is converted into plasma cell?
   A. T lymphocytes
   B. B lymphocytes
   C. Macrophages
   D. Natural killer cells

7. Null cells are the type of
   A. Lymphocytes
   B. Microphages
   C. Macrophages
   D. Monocytes
8. The important function of cytotoxic T cells is
   A. To produce lymphokines
   B. To destroy virally infected host cells
   C. To suppress antibody synthesis
   D. None of the above
9. The following statements are TRUE regarding natural killer cells, EXCEPT
   A. Their activity is increased by interferon
   B. They destroy virally infected host cells
   C. They destroy malignant mutant cells
   D. They require antibody for their activity
10. Select the most appropriate statement regarding the killer cells (K cells)
    A. Their activity is increased by interferon
    B. They destroy virally infected host cells
    C. They destroy malignant mutant cells
    D. They are responsible for antibody-dependent cell cytotoxicity
11. Which of the following cells is NOT phagocytic in nature?
    A. Eosinophils
    B. Neutrophils
    C. Lymphocytes
    D. Monocytes
12. Natural killer cells are the important cells of immune system responsible for
    A. Phagocytic activity
    B. Antigen-capturing activity
    C. Antitumour activity
    D. Antibacterial activity

15 Immune Response

- Immune response involves recognition of the antigen and mounting of an immunological response for rapid and efficient elimination of an antigen. It is of two types as given in Figure 15.1.
- The adaptive immune response is highly specific and the response increases upon subsequent exposure with the same antigen. It involves T and B cells.
- The activation of T and B cells results in two types of immune responses:
  - Humoral or antibody-mediated immune response (HI or AMI)
  - Cellular or cell-mediated immune response (CMI)

Fate of immunogen (antigen)

When an antigen enters the body naturally (because of infection) or is introduced artificially (in the form of vaccine), it is readily taken up by phagocytic cells (macrophages) or dendritic cells. These are antigen-presenting cells, which process and present antigen to immunocompetent lymphocytes (T cells, B cells or both) to recognize it and initiate an appropriate immune response (HI, CMI or both).

Humoral immune response

It is mediated by antibodies and is also known as antibody-mediated immune response. Antibodies are produced by B lymphocytes with the help of T lymphocytes. When an antigen enters the body, after processing by macrophages (antigen-presenting cells), it is presented to lymphocytes of appropriate specificity, which produce antibodies of appropriate specificity with the help of T cells.

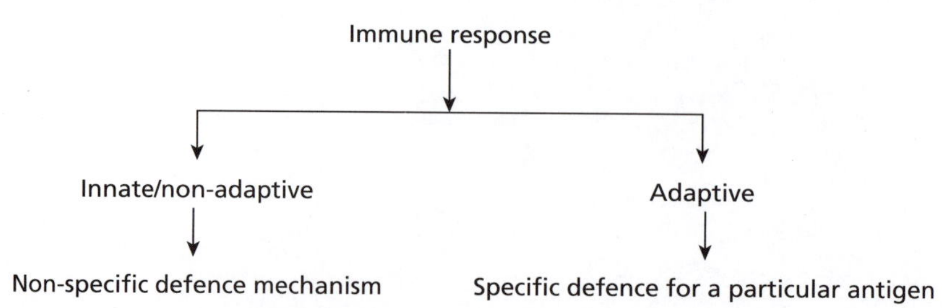

Figure 15.1 Types of immune response.

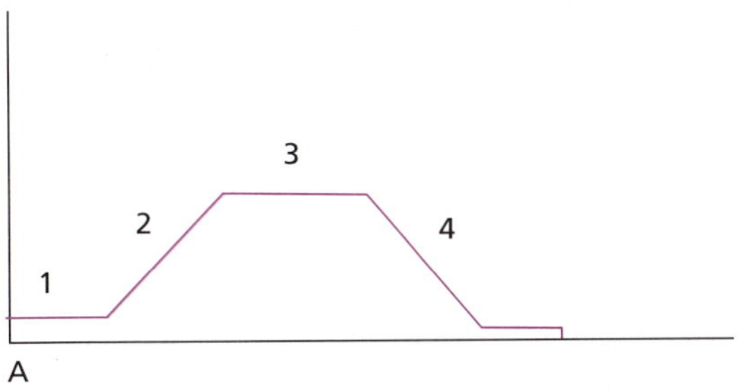

Figure 15.2 Primary response. *A*, antigenic stimulus; *1*, lag phase; *2*, log phase; *3*, plateau; *4*, decline phase.

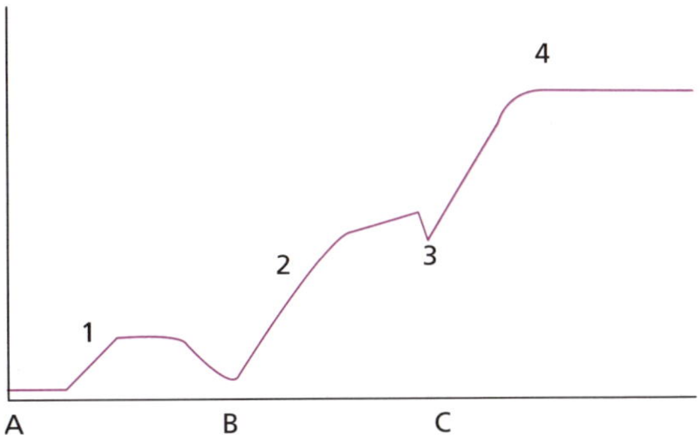

Figure 15.3 Secondary response. *ABC*, antigenic stimuli; *1*, primary response; *2*, secondary response; *3*, negative phase; *4*, high level of antibody.

- When antigen enters the body for the first time, the body gives primary response, which is
  - Slow
  - Sluggish
  - Short-lived
  - Low levels of IgM type of antibodies are produced that persist for short duration (Fig. 15.2)
- When the same antigen enters the body for the second time (booster dose) after weeks, months or even after years, the body gives a secondary response. The secondary response is
  - Prompt
  - Powerful
  - Prolonged
  - High levels of IgG antibodies are produced (Fig. 15.3).
- These differences in primary and secondary responses are due to the number of responding B cells.

B cells + antigen { Antibody-producing plasma cells / Memory cells

- In primary response, a large numbers of B cells are converted into memory cells. In secondary response, all B cells are converted into antibody-producing plasma cells so the response is more than primary. The memory cells, which are formed during primary response, are longer lasting cells which retain the memory of the first contact and respond vigorously when the same antigen enters for the second time to produce antibodies in high level.
- When an antigen enters the body, the carrier molecule reacts with Th cell (T helper cell) and the haptenic group reacts with B cell. The Th cell is activated to release helper factor, which helps B cell by giving necessary information (that is necessary for proliferation of B cell). Once the signal is received, B cells undergo clonal proliferation and blast transformation and are finally converted into plasma cells that synthesize and secrete antibodies.
- Antibodies are proteins and are synthesized like proteins on ribosomes attached to the endoplasmic reticulum. After the assembly of chains and disulphide bond formation, they are transported towards the cell surface via Golgi bodies in a secretory vesicle.
- The vesicle fuses with the surface membrane and releases the antibody molecules in circulation for its functioning.

Role of humoral immunity

- Primary defence against most extracellular pathogens

- Defence against viruses infecting through respiratory and intestinal tract
- To prevent recurrence of virus infection
- Participation in the immediate type of hypersensitivity reaction and in the pathogenesis of certain autoimmune diseases

Factors affecting antibody production

- **Age**
  - The embryo is not immunologically mature.
  - The capacity to produce antibody starts with the development and differentiation of lymphoid organs.
  - The age at which immunological competence is acquired by embryos is different in different species.
  - When the antigen comes in contact with an immunocompetent cell during embryonic life, it results into permanent inactivation or death of a cell (induction of tolerance). This is believed to be the basis for the non-antigenicity of self-antigens.
  - Immunocompetence is not complete at birth but it develops slowly as the infant grows and the full competence is acquired by the age of 4 years.
- **Genetic factors**
  - The immune response is genetically controlled and Ir genes (immune response genes) are responsible for this.
  - Response to the same antigen in different individuals is different due to genetic factors.
- **Nutritional status**
  - Malnutrition affects the immune response adversely.
  - Protein calorie malnutrition suppresses both HI and CMI.
  - Deficiencies of amino acids such as tryptophan, phenyl alanine, methionine, glycine, isoleucine and vitamins such as vitamin A and vitamin B have been shown to cause decrease in antibody synthesis.
- **Effect of antibody**
  - Animals whose blood contains preformed antibodies, which are present either owing to passive transfer or passive immunization, respond poorly to homologous antigen. These antibodies combine with antigen and prevent their contact with immunocompetent cells.
- **Route of administration**
  - The parenteral route is better for the development of HI than oral or nasal route.
  - For large particulate antigens such as bacteria or RBCs, intravenous route is more effective.
  - Soluble antigens are more effective when injected in tissues.
  - The route of administration may also influence the type of antibody production, for example
    - For IgA synthesis—oral or nasal route is more suitable
    - Inhalation of pollen antigen—induces IgE synthesis
    - Parenteral administration of pollen antigen—produce IgG
- **Dose of antigen**
  - The degree of antibody response depends on the amount of antigen.
  - Very small amount of antigen leads to no demonstrable antibody response.
  - Very large dose of antigen (beyond a level) does not increase the antibody production. In fact, very large dose of antigen may inhibit the antibody production **(immunological paralysis)**.
  - An antigen is effective only above a minimal critical dose, further increase in dose increases the antibody production up to a certain level beyond which no increase is observed.
- **Multiple antigens**
  - The simultaneous administration of two or more antigens may result into enhanced antibody response to one or other antigens or diminished antibody response to one or the other of them.

- When two bacterial vaccines (e.g., typhoid and cholera) are given together, the antibody response to each is not influenced by the other.
- When toxoids are given along with bacterial vaccines (e.g., DPT—diphtheria toxoid, pertussis vaccine, tetanus toxoid), the antibody response to toxoid is potentiated but when one of them is given in excess, the response to other is diminished, for example, when DPT is given to a person who had earlier received a primary dose of diphtheria toxoid, the response to P and T will be diminished.
- Such antigenic competitions are important in immunization with polyvalent antigens.

- **Immunosuppressive agents**
  - The synthesis of antibodies can be inhibited by the administration of various immunosuppressive agents.
  - They may be divided into two groups:
    - Agents which are effective only if given before the administration of antigen, for example, X-irradiation and cortisone. Both have a depressing effect on the lymphoid tissues
    - Agents which are maximally effective only if given after the injection of antigen, for example, purine and pyrimidine analogues, nitrogen mustards, folic acid antagonists such as methopterin, methotrexate, which inhibit the action of the enzyme, folic acid reductase; and actinomycin D, which inhibits the synthesis of RNA and cyclophosphamide
  - Analogues of purine are 6-mercaptopurine and azathioprine and analogues of uracil is 5-fluorouracil and of cytosine is cytosine arabinoside.
  - Antilymphocyte serum (ALS) raised against lymphocytes and thymocytes in horses is also used as immunosuppressive agent.
  - Cyclosporine is the most widely used agent, which is not cytotoxic for lymphocytes and has no antimitotic activity. It selectively inhibits T-helper activity.
- **Adjuvant**
  - Adjuvant is a substance, which when injected together with antigen, potentiates immune response.
  - It enhances antibody synthesis and CMI.
  - When antigen is injected alone, 98–99% of it leaves the injected area within 24 hours. The immune response can be greatly enhanced by slowing down the escape of antigen from injection site and by increasing the contact period of antigen with macrophage or other antigen receptive cells. This is done by using adjuvant, which release antigen slowly from injection site. This is known as **'Depot'** effect of adjuvant.
  - The most commonly used examples of adjuvant preparations are as follows:
    - Aluminium adjuvants—potassium aluminium sulphate (alum), aluminium hydroxide, aluminium oxide
    - Freund's incomplete adjuvant (1940)—water in oil emulsion
    - Anaerobic coryneform—*Propionibacterium acnes*
    - Bacille Calmette–Guerin (BCG)
    - *Bordetella pertussis* (DPT)
    - Freund's complete adjuvant—water in oil emulsion with mycobacterial or nocardial antigens—used in experimental animals

Cell-mediated immune response

CMI is the specific type of immune response mediated by sensitized T cells, independent of B cells and antibodies. Certain microorganisms such as the following are the intracellular pathogens which multiply inside the host cells:

- Bacteria—tubercle and leprosy bacilli
- Viruses—smallpox and measles

- Parasites—*Toxoplasma* and *Leishmania*
- Fungi—*Histoplasma* and *Blastomyces*

Antibodies are not effective against the above pathogens. Immunity against these pathogens is mediated by the T lymphocytes. This type of immune response is known as CMI.

Induction of CMI

- CMI is initiated by binding of antigen with an antigen receptor on T cell.
- The specific reaction of antigen with T cell stimulates T cells, which undergoes proliferation and a sequence of morphological and biochemical events occurs and the cell transforms into a large blast cell.
- This interaction finally results into
  - Blast transformation
  - Clonal proliferation
  - Differentiation
- The results of these events are
  - Generation of lymphokine-producing T cells
  - Generation of cytotoxic T cells
- These are the two major effector mechanisms of CMI.

Generation of lymphokine (interleukins) producing T cells

They release biologically active substances known as lymphokines. Lymphokines are **regulatory proteins** (molecular weight 20,000–80,000) whose main function is the regulation of immune response and growth and function of cells of reticuloendothelial system. They exert regulatory effect on cells such as macrophages, T and B cells and other cell types and regulate activities such as

- Localization of macrophages at the site of antigen-mediated lymphokine release
- Activation of macrophage and enhancing phagocytic ability and killing of microorganism (foreign particle)
- Helping B cell to produce antibody
- Controlling viral infection by inhibiting their replication
- Inhibiting tumours and inducing delayed hypersensitivity
- The biologically active substances released by lymphocytes, monocytes and other leukocytes during CMI are collectively known as **cytokines**

Cytokines

These include the following:

- **Lymphokines** They are biologically active substances released by activated T lymphocytes.
- **Monokines** They are soluble proteins produced by monocytes or macrophages. They are responsible for various biological effects.
- **Interleukins** The term interleukins is introduced for those products of leukocytes, which exert regulatory influence on other cells.

Most lymphokines exhibit multiple biological effects and the same effect may be caused by different lymphokines. Hence, the term interleukin is used collectively for the products secreted by leukocytes.

The cytokines have several biological activities as given in the following text.

Cytokines affecting lymphocytes

Interleukin-1 (IL-1)

- Is a polypeptide—a monokine released by macrophages and other antigen presenting cells
- Stimulates activation of T helper (Th) cells for the production of IL-2 and other lymphokines
- Stimulates B cell proliferation and antibody synthesis
- Stimulates granulocytes (neutrophils chemotaxis) and phagocytosis

Interleukin-2 (IL-2)

- Is a cytokine produced by activated T cells
- Is a powerful modulator of the immune response

- Promotes growth and differentiation of T and B cells
- Stimulates cytotoxic T cells and natural killer cells (NK cells)
- Converts large granular lymphocytes into lymphokine-activated killer (LAK) cells, which can destroy NK-resistant tumour cells

Interleukin-3 (IL-3) It is produced by T cells and acts as a growth factor for bone marrow stem cells.

Interleukin-4 (IL-4) It is produced by T helper (Th) cells; acts as B cell differentiating factor and enhances the activity of cytotoxic T cells.

Interleukin-5 (IL-5) It is produced by T helper (Th) cells; causes proliferation of activated B cells and eosinophils.

Interleukin-6 (IL-6)

- Produced by stimulated T and B cells, macrophages and fibroblasts
- Promotes terminal differentiation of B cells into antibody-producing plasma cells and encourages IgG production

Interleukins 7–13

- These are produced by various immunocompetent cells during CMI.
- They act on various immunocompetent cells and play an important role in CMI.

Cytokines affecting macrophages

Antigenically stimulated T lymphocytes produce certain biologically active soluble proteins (lymphokines), which recruit, activate and regulate effector cells with the potential to fight with the infecting agent.

The lymphokines and their biological activities are as follows:

- **Macrophage chemotactic factor (MCF)** It is chemotactic for mononuclear phagocytes.
- **Migration inhibiting factor (MIF)** It inhibits migration of phagocytic cells and localizes circulating and tissue monocytes at the site of infection.
- **Interferon-γ (IFN-γ; also known as macrophage-activating factor [MAF])** It produces significant morphological changes. It increases the content of lysosomal enzymes and their activities so that the macrophage kills ingested intracellular foreign particles.
- **Interferon-ά (IFN-ά)** It is produced by leukocytes and has antiviral properties.
- **Interferon-β (INF-β)** It is produced by fibroblasts and inhibits replication of virus in the host cell.

Cytotoxic lymphokines

Lymphotoxin (LT; also known as tumour necrosis factor-β [TNF-β]) It is a cytotoxic protein released by activated Th cells. Lymphotoxin is cytotoxic for foreign cells such as tumour cells, transplanted cells and microorganisms.

Tumour necrosis factor-ά (TNF-ά) It is produced by macrophages and monocytes—causes lysis of tumour cells and also plays role in the elimination of certain bacteria and parasites.

Other cytokines

Skin reactive factor (SRF)

- It is produced by specifically sensitized lymphocytes with antigens and mitogens.
- When injected into the skin of normal guinea pig, it produces an indurated and erythematous lesion within 3 hours.
- It facilitates the movement of monocytes from blood vessels into extravascular spaces and induces skin hypersensitivity.

Lymphocyte inhibitory factor It has T suppressor activity, suppresses antibody production.

Transfer factor (TF)

- An extract from specific antigen-sensitized lymphocytes that mediates passive transfer of CMI is known as transfer factor.
- It is highly potent; an extract from 0.1 mL of packed leukocytes is sufficient to transfer CMI.
- **Applications** It is useful for immunocompromised individuals in restoring a specific CMI, for example, in T cell deficiency (Wiskott–Aldrich syndrome, Nezelof syndrome,

DiGeorge syndrome), in disseminated infections associated with deficient CMI (tuberculosis, leprosy, mucocutaneous candidiasis, etc.) and in cancer (melanoma, sarcoma, etc.).

Generation of cytotoxic T cells (CD8 T cells)

- These are killer (K) T cells capable of killing or lysing target cells to which they bind.
- They are formed in response to viral infection and a graft from a genetically dissimilar member.
- They are cytotoxic for the host cells infected with virus, graft tissue and tumour cells.
- It is one of the major effecter mechanisms of CMI.

Mechanism of action

- The first stage is binding of effector cell to the target cell through a specific receptors. It is a calcium independent stage.
- A change occurs in the target cell, which leads to cytolysis. This phase is calcium dependent.
- These cells are cytotoxic for host cells infected with virus, graft tissue and tumour cells and play an important role in
  - Immunity against viral infection
  - Tumour immunity
  - Transplantation immunity

Role of CMI

CMI plays an important role in

- Immunity against infectious diseases caused by obligate and facultative intracellular pathogens
- Delayed hypersensitivity
- Transplantation immunity
- Immunological surveillance and immunity against cancer (tumour rejection)
- Pathogenesis of certain autoimmune diseases, for example, thyroiditis

Self-assessment

Long-answer question

1. Discuss in brief the humoral and cellular immune responses.

Short-answer questions

Write notes on

1. Humoral immune response
2. Cellular immune response
3. Lymphokines
4. Interleukins
5. Transfer factor
6. Cytotoxic T cells

Multiple-choice questions

1. Which of the following immunoglobulins is produced during the primary response?
   A. IgM
   B. IgA
   C. IgG
   D. IgD
2. Which of the following immunoglobulins is produced during the secondary response?
   A. IgM
   B. IgA
   C. IgG
   D. IgD
3. Select the most appropriate statement regarding the humoral immunity
   A. Defence against most intracellular pathogens
   B. Immunological surveillance and immunity against cancer
   C. Major role in transplantation immunity
   D. Defence against most extracellular pathogens
4. Select the most appropriate statement regarding the cell-mediated immunity (CMI)
   A. Defence against the most intracellular pathogens
   B. Participation in Type II hypersensitivity reaction

C. To prevent recurrence of virus infection
D. Defence against the most extracellular pathogens

5. Which of the following statements is FALSE regarding lymphokines?
A. These are regulatory proteins regulating immune response
B. They exert regulatory effect on macrophages, T and B cells and other cell types
C. Their molecular weight is 20,000–80,000
D. These are soluble proteins produced by B lymphocytes

6. Which of the following statements is FALSE regarding cytotoxic T cells?
A. They play an important role in immunity against viral infection
B. They participate in transplantation immunity
C. They play role in defence against extracellular pathogens
D. They participate in tumour immunity

7. Which of the following statements is FALSE about transfer factor?
A. Is an extract from specific antigen-sensitized lymphocytes
B. Facilitates the movement of monocytes from blood vessels into extravascular spaces and induces skin hypersensitivity
C. Mediates passive transfer of CMI
D. Is useful in immunocompromised individuals to restore specific CMI

8. Which of the following interleukins stimulates B cell proliferation and antibody synthesis?
A. Interleukin-4
B. Interleukin-1
C. Interleukin-3
D. Interleukin-2

9. Which of the following routes is most suitable for particulate antigens?
A. Intramuscular
B. Intradermal
C. Intravenous
D. Subcutaneous

10. Which of the following adjuvant preparations is used in experimental animals?
A. Freund's complete adjuvant
B. Freund's incomplete adjuvant
C. Aluminium hydroxide
D. *Propionibacterium acnes*

11. Which of the following is the most widely used immunosuppressive agent?
A. 6-mercaptopurine
B. Cytosine arabinoside
C. Cyclophosphamide
D. Cyclosporine

16 Immunodeficiency Diseases

Immunodeficiency disorders are conditions in which one or more components of the immune system are impaired. This leads to an increased susceptibility for microbial infections and sometimes enhanced susceptibility to malignancies and autoimmune diseases.

Deficiencies of immune system may involve

Non-specific immune functions	Specific immune functions
↓	↓
Phagocytosis and complement	Humoral or cellular or both types of immune response

Classification

Immunodeficiency diseases may be classified into two types:

1. **Primary (congenital) immunodeficiencies** These are due to abnormalities in development of the immune mechanisms because of intrinsic or congenital defects. These are genetically determined and may be congenital. Primary immunodeficiencies become clinically apparent at about the age of 6 months, when maternal antibodies transferred from mother to foetal circulation in utero start to disappear and infant becomes dependent upon its own immune system.
2. **Secondary (acquired) immunodeficiencies** These disorders are due to diseases, drugs, nutritional inadequacies, cancer and other processes that interfere with the proper functioning of the mature immune system. These immunodeficiencies can occur at any time of life, depending on the exposure to the causative factors.

Primary immunodeficiencies

Primary immunodeficiencies are further classified into four types:

1. Deficiency of innate immunity
2. Humoral immunodeficiencies
3. Cellular immunodeficiencies
4. Combined immunodeficiencies

Deficiency of innate immunity

Phagocytes and complement are the major components of the innate immunity. They may be impaired leading to various disorders.

Disorders of phagocytosis

Defects in the phagocytic cells are very important as phagocytosis is the most important means of defence against infection and participate both in innate and adaptive immune response.

The defects in the phagocytic function may be due to

Extrinsic factors	Intrinsic factors
↓	↓
External factors	Internal factors
↓	↓
Opsonic antibody, complement or other factors promoting phagocytosis	Enzyme deficiencies

Examples

Chronic granulomatous disease

- In this disease, the phagocytic cells fail to produce superoxide and hydrogen peroxide due to a defect in the **NADPH oxidase** system.
- These cells readily engulf organisms in the presence of an antibody and complement but fail to kill them intracellularly. This causes an increase in the susceptibility to recurrent infections by catalase positive pathogens such as staphylococci and coliforms.

Chediak–Higashi disease In this disease, the lysosomes present in the phagocytic cells are structurally and functionally abnormal; hence, they are unable to interact with microbes and fail to destroy ingested microbes. As a result, patients suffer from recurrent pyogenic infections, which can be fatal.

Myeloperoxidase deficiency In this disease, leucocytes are deficient of myeloperoxidase, an enzyme necessary for intracellular killing of certain microbes. Defect in the myeloperoxidase activity is associated with increased susceptibility to candidiasis and staphylococcal infections.

Lazy leucocyte syndrome

- In this disease, neutrophils are unable to respond to chemotactic stimuli (become lazy).
- Associated with increased susceptibility to bacterial infection with recurrent stomatitis, gingivitis and otitis.

Leucocyte glucose-6-phosphate dehydrogenase (G6PD) deficiency

- In this disease, leucocytes are deficient in G6PD. Hence, bactericidal activity after phagocytosis is diminished.
- Leucocytes are unable to destroy engulfed bacteria, as a result of which susceptibility to microbial infections increases.

Job syndrome

- In this disease, there is marked elevation of serum IgE, however, the levels of other immunoglobulins are normal.
- Probably, it occurs because of defect in the phagocytic function.
- It is characterized by multiple cold abscesses on the skin, subcutaneous tissue, lymph nodes, etc.
- Lung abscess, pneumonia, atopic eczema, otitis media, chronic nasal discharge, etc., are also common.
- *Staphylococcus aureus* is the commonest organism, *Candida albicans*, *Haemophilus influenzae* and *Streptococcus pyogenes* are the other organisms.

Other examples of disorders of phagocytosis

- Tuftsin deficiency
- Shwachman disease
- Hyper-IgE syndrome
- Actin-binding protein deficiency

Disorders of complement components

Complement components are necessary for proper functioning of both innate and adaptive immune response, for example, neutrophil chemotaxis, opsonization and bacterial killing. Genetic deficiencies of complement components result in the inability to eliminate microbes and circulating complexes efficiently. Hence, they are associated with increased susceptibility to microbial infections and autoimmune diseases.

Examples

- Deficiency of C1, C4 or C2—systemic lupus erythematosus (SLE)-like syndrome
- Deficiency of C3—recurrent pyogenic infections

- Deficiency of C5, C6, C7 and C8—neisserial infections
- Deficiency of factors H and I—increases susceptibility to infection
- Deficiency of factor D and properdin—neisserial infections

Deficiency of complement inhibitors

- The genetic deficiency of C1 inhibitor is associated with hereditary angioneurotic oedema. It is inherited as an autosomal dominant defect.
- The deficiency of C3b inactivator is associated with chronic recurrent pyogenic infections.

Humoral immunodeficiencies

- These are defects in antibody producing B cells that lead to deficiencies of B cells.
- The deficiency of B cell is due to non-production of B cells or due to interference with the maturation process of B cells.
- This deficiency leads to gross depletion of all immunoglobulins in the serum and a marked decrease in the number of B cells in circulation.
- An individual becomes susceptible to recurrent bacterial infections such as staphylococcal, streptococcal, pneumococcal, meningococcal, pseudomonal and *H. influenzae* infections.
- Parasitic infection by *Pneumocystis carinii* and autoimmune diseases are also seen.
- Cell-mediated immunity (CMI) remains normal and viral infections, for example, measles are readily brought under control.
- The majority of immunodeficiency diseases (more than 80%) are due to defect in the B cells.

Disorders of humoral immunodeficiency

X-linked agammaglobulinaemia (Bruton diseases)

- In this disease, the precursors of B cells fail to develop into mature B cells. The result is absence of B cells and antibody from the circulation.
- All classes of immunoglobulins are grossly depleted in the serum.
- An individual becomes susceptible to severe recurrent infections by pyogenic bacteria, for example, staphylococcal, streptococcal, pneumococcal, meningococcal, pseudomonal and *H. influenzae* infections and by protozoan parasite *Pneumocystis carinii.*
- It is seen in male infants after 6 months of age.

Transient hypogammaglobulinaemia of infancy

- In this disorder, there is an abnormal delay in the synthesis of IgG, which is expected to be initiated by the second month.
- An individual becomes susceptible to recurrent otitis media and respiratory tract infections.
- It is seen in infants of both sexes and is usually self-limited (recovers spontaneously between 18 and 30 months).

Selective immunoglobulin deficiency (dysgammaglobulinaemia)

- In this disorder, there is selective deficiency of one or other immunoglobulin classes.
- The isolated IgA deficiency has been found to be the most common and is associated with increased susceptibility to respiratory infection and chronic diarrhoea.
- Atopic disorders in children and autoimmune diseases in adults are also common.
- The selective IgM deficiency is associated with septicaemia.
- IgG deficiency is found to be associated with respiratory diseases.

Immunodeficiencies with hyper-IgM

- There is elevated IgM level while IgA and IgG levels are low.
- Patients are susceptible to infections and autoimmune disorders such as thrombocytopenia, neutropenia and haemolytic anaemia.

Transcobalamin-II deficiency

- Transcobalamin-II is a serum protein involved in the transport of vitamin B_{12}.

- Affected individuals show metabolic effects of vitamin B_{12} deficiency.
- It is characterized by diarrhoea, anaemia, agammaglobulinaemia, etc.

Cellular immunodeficiencies

- Deficiency of CMI—there is a defective T cell function.
- The thymus-dependent areas of lymph nodes and spleen are depleted of T lymphocytes and circulating T cells are also reduced in number. It also results in abnormal functioning of T cells.
- It may also result in decrease of immunoglobulin production as the T cell help is not properly received which is due to the reduction in number of T cells
- Delayed hypersensitivity and graft rejection are depressed while humoral immunity (HI) may or may not be affected.
- The individuals become susceptible to more severe and persistent infections by viruses, intracellular bacteria, fungi and protozoan parasites.

Disorders of cellular immunodeficiency

The disorders are as follows:

DiGeorge syndrome

- This occurs due to thymic aplasia or hypoplasia due to the developmental defect in third and fourth pharyngeal pouches that leads to aplasia or hypoplasia.
- It is characterized by
  - Neonatal hypocalcaemia with tetany
  - Severe cardiac disease in early weeks of life
  - Fallot's tetralogy
  - Facial and midline structures defects
- Affected individuals are susceptible to
  - Oral candidiasis
  - Chronic diarrhoea
  - Pneumonia
  - Cutaneous infections

Chronic mucocutaneous candidiasis It occurs due to selective cellular immunodeficiency to *Candida albicans* and is characterized by severe chronic candidiasis of the mucous membranes, skin and nails.

Purine nucleoside phosphorylase (PNP) deficiency

- The enzyme PNP is involved in the metabolism of purines.
- Its deficiency is associated with decreased CMI.
- The individuals suffer from recurrent or chronic infections such as pneumonia, diarrhoea and candidiasis.

Combined immunodeficiencies (stem cell deficiency)

- These are characterized by abnormal functioning of B and T lymphocytes.
- There is marked deficiency of T cells and varying degrees of deficiency of B cells.
- The affected individuals show increased susceptibility to a variety of infectious agents during early infancy.
- As CMI is depressed and no antibody synthesis occurs, patients are susceptible to recurrent fungal, bacterial, viral, protozoal infections and autoimmune diseases.

Disorders of combined immunodeficiency

The disorders are as follows:

Nezelof syndrome (cellular immunodeficiency with abnormal immunoglobulins)

- In this disorder, CMI is depressed and immunoglobulin levels may be selectively elevated, decreased or normal.
- In most cases, antigenic stimuli do not induce antibody formation.
- It increases susceptibility to
  - Pulmonary infections
  - Oral or cutaneous candidiasis
  - Chronic diarrhoea
  - Recurrent microbial infections
  - Autoimmune haemolytic anaemia

Ataxia telangiectasia

- This syndrome is characterized by
  - Cerebellar ataxia

  - Ocular and cutaneous telangiectasia
  - Sinopulmonary infection in early life
  - Endocrine abnormalities
  - Predisposition to malignancy in the second or third decade
- In most patients, IgA is deficient. IgE deficiency is also frequent and CMI is also defective.

Wiskott–Aldrich syndrome

- This syndrome is characterized by
  - Thrombocytopenic purpura
  - Eczema
  - Recurrent infections by various microorganisms
- Infected individual is also susceptible to herpes simplex, cytomegalovirus, *Pneumocystis carinii* and varicella zoster virus infections.
- Affected boys rarely survive the first decade of their life.
- Death occurs due to infection, haemorrhage or lymphoreticular malignancy.
- There is a progressive deterioration of CMI. Serum IgM level is low but IgG and IgA levels are normal or elevated and IgE is markedly elevated.

Good syndrome (immunodeficiency with thymoma)

- This occurs in adults after 40 years of age.
- It is associated with a benign or malignant thymic tumour, impaired CMI and agammaglobulinaemia.
- Complications include
  - Sinopulmonary infections
  - Septicaemia
  - Urinary tract infections
  - Chronic diarrhoea
  - Dermatitis
  - Aplastic anaemia

Severe combined immunodeficiencies

- These include many syndromes with severe deficiency of both HI and CMI.
- Many distinct patterns have been described, these are
  - The Swiss type agammaglobulinaemia in which there is defect in the lymphoid stem cells and patient lacks both HI and CMI.
  - Reticular dysgenesis in which there is defect in the bone marrow stem cells and there is a total failure of myelopoiesis because of which there is lymphopenia, neutropenia, thrombocytopenia and bone marrow aplasia.
  - Adenosine deaminase deficiency in which the low levels of this enzyme causes immunological impairment leading to greater loss of T cells and also the deficiency of B cells that makes an infant susceptible to various microbial infections.

Immunodeficiency with short-limbed dwarfism

- In this disease, CMI is defective due to thymic defects resulting from ectodermal dysplasia.
- Patients show increased susceptibility to infection.

Episodic lymphopenia with lymphocytotoxin

- There is depression of T cell function (episodic) by the action of a circulating complement dependent lymphocytotoxin (antilymphocyte antibody).
- The patients lack immunological memory, so that the secondary antibody response is abolished.

Diagnosis of primary immunodeficiency diseases

Diagnosis of disorders of phagocytosis

- Examination of blood smear—differential count
- Examination of bone marrow for abnormalities like number of phagocytic cells (count) and abnormal morphological changes
- Analysis of phagocytic cell activity by nitroblue tetrazolium dye reduction test

Diagnosis of B cell deficiency Quantitation of serum immunoglobulin levels

Diagnosis of T cell deficiency

- Skin test—patients with T cell immunodeficiency will be hypo-or non-reactive in skin test to microbial antigens
- Enumeration of T cells by sheep red blood cells (SRBC) rosette test

Diagnosis of combined immunodeficiency Quantitation of immunoglobulin levels and enumeration of T cells

Treatment of primary immunodeficiency diseases

- In a deficiency of innate immunity, the treatment is administration of antibiotics to treat pyogenic infections.
- For the treatment of B cell deficiency, parenteral administration of immune serum globulin is recommended.
- In the treatment of T cell deficiency, thymus transplantation, transfer factor therapy or injections of thymosin with limited success can be used.
- In combined immunodeficiencies, bone marrow transplantation, transfer factor therapy and thymus transplantation may be beneficial.

Summary of primary immunodeficiency diseases is given in Table 16.1.

Secondary immunodeficiencies

Immune responsiveness can be decreased non-specifically by many factors such as

- Malnutrition
- Malignancies
- Microbial infections
- Metabolic disorders
- Chronic diseases
- Immunosuppressive drug therapy
- X-ray irradiation and other factors

Secondary immunodeficiencies, therefore, are very much common than primary immunodeficiencies.

Impairment of CMI

CMI may be impaired in

- A state of malnutrition (particularly iron deficiency)
- Malignancy (Hodgkin disease)
- Metabolic disorders such as diabetes mellitus
- Cytotoxic drugs
- Obstruction to lymph circulation
- Lymphorrhoeas
- Microbial infections such as lepromatous leprosy, HIV infection, infectious mononucleosis and measles
- Immunosuppressive therapy

Impairment of HI

HI may be impaired in

- Lymphoid malignancy (chronic lymphatic leukaemia)
- Nephrotic syndrome (immunoglobulin catabolism)
- Exfoliative skin disease (loss of serum protein)
- Multiple myeloma

Table 16.1 Summary of primary immunodeficiency diseases

Deficiency	Immune response		Infection	Treatment
	Humoral	***Cellular***		
Complement	Normal	Normal	Pyogenic bacteria	Antibiotics
Phagocytic cells	Normal	Normal	Catalase-positive bacteria	Antibiotics
B cells	↓↓	Normal	Pyogenic bacteria and *Pneumocystis carinii*	γ-globulin
T cells	↓	↓↓	Viruses and *Candida*	Thymus graft
Stem cells	↓↓	↓↓	All of the above	Bone marrow

- Immunosuppressive therapy (corticosteroids and others)
- Malnutrition
- Exposure to X-rays, etc.

The patients with impaired CMI and HI show increased susceptibility to pyogenic bacteria, tubercle bacillus, Brucella, Cryptococcus, herpes zoster virus, cytomegalovirus, *Pneumocystis carinii* and other opportunistic pathogens.

Acquired immunodeficiency syndrome (AIDS)

- AIDS is an acquired immunodeficiency leading to syndrome, which increases susceptibility to various microbial infections and leads to Kaposi's sarcoma—a dermal malignancy.
- Caused by human immunodeficiency virus (HIV).
- It attacks the T helper cells (CD4 lymphocytes) leading to reduction of these cells, thus, causing loss of immunological protection.
- Infected individuals show increased susceptibility to overwhelming opportunistic infections and develop Kaposi's sarcoma and other malignancies, autoimmune diseases, intestinal infections, neurological problems, lymphadenopathy and many other symptoms.

Self-assessment

Long-answer question

1. Define and classify immunodeficiency diseases. Discuss in brief the primary immunodeficiencies.

Short-answer questions

Write notes on

1. Disorders of phagocytosis
2. Disorders of complement
3. Humoral immunodeficiencies
4. Cellular immunodeficiencies
5. Combined immunodeficiencies
6. Secondary immunodeficiencies

Multiple-choice questions

1. Chronic granulomatous disease is an immunodeficiency disorder of
   A. T cell
   B. B cell
   C. Phagocytosis
   D. Complement
2. Myeloperoxidase deficiency is associated with an increased susceptibility to
   A. Autoimmune diseases
   B. Candidiasis
   C. Cancer
   D. Viral infection
3. Which of the following is NOT a disorder of phagocytosis?
   A. Chediak–Higashi disease
   B. Lazy leucocyte syndrome
   C. Job syndrome
   D. DiGeorge syndrome
4. Which of the following is NOT a humoral immunodeficiency?
   A. Nezelof syndrome
   B. Transcobalamin-II deficiency
   C. Transient hypogammaglobulinaemia of infancy
   D. Bruton diseases
5. Which of the following is NOT a cellular immunodeficiency?
   A. Chronic mucocutaneous candidiasis
   B. DiGeorge syndrome
   C. Wiskott–Aldrich syndrome
   D. Purine nucleoside phosphorylase deficiency
6. Which of the following is NOT a combined immunodeficiency?
   A. DiGeorge syndrome
   B. Nezelof syndrome
   C. Wiskott–Aldrich syndrome
   D. Good syndrome

7. Which of the following statements is FALSE about humoral immunodeficiency?
   A. There is defect in antibody producing B cells
   B. This deficiency leads to gross depletion of all immunoglobulins
   C. T cells are also grossly depleted
   D. Susceptibility to recurrent bacterial infections is increased
8. Which of the following statements is FALSE about cellular immunodeficiency?
   A. There is defect in T cell function
   B. It does not affect the synthesis of immunoglobulins
   C. T cells are grossly depleted
   D. Susceptibility to viruses, intracellular bacteria, fungi and protozoan parasites is increased
9. Kaposi's sarcoma is a characteristic feature of
   A. Primary immunodeficiency
   B. Secondary immunodeficiency
   C. Acquired immunodeficiency
   D. Combined immunodeficiency

17 Hypersensitivity

Immune response is generally beneficial for the host, however, at times it may prove harmful. Individuals sensitized to a specific antigen may respond to subsequent antigenic stimuli in a heightened or exaggerated manner leading to

- Tissue damage
- Disease
- Even death of the individual

This type of immune response is known as hypersensitivity or allergy (meaning altered response to an antigen). This is an altered state induced by an antigen. Thus, the immune response which increases our resistance to infection is known as immunity. However, the immune response which increases our susceptibility to tissue damage or disease is known as hypersensitivity.

In allergic (hypersensitivity) reactions

- An antigen is referred as allergen or sensitizer
- Immunization is referred as sensitization
- The individual is referred as allergic or hypersensitive

Classification

Based on the time taken for sensitivity reactions

Based on the time taken by a sensitized individual to develop clinical reactions upon re-exposure to the antigen, hypersensitivity reactions are classified into two types:

1. **Immediate hypersensitivity** In this type, allergic reaction appears immediately within a short period after the contact with an antigen, sometimes within a few seconds also. It is B cell or antibody-mediated reaction, examples are
   - Anaphylaxis
   - Antibody-mediated cytotoxic hypersensitivity
   - Antigen–antibody complex-mediated hypersensitivity
2. **Delayed hypersensitivity** In this, allergic reaction appears slowly after the contact with an antigen and may take 24–48 hours to develop. It is T cell-mediated reaction, examples are
   - Infection (tuberculin) type
   - Contact dermatitis type (Table 17.1)

Classification based on pathogenesis: Coombs and Gell classification

Based on different mechanisms of pathogenesis, Coombs and Gell in 1963 classified hypersensitivity reactions into four types and recently an additional fifth type has been added to this classification.

- Type I—anaphylactic reaction

Table 17.1 Difference between immediate and delayed types of hypersensitivity

Immediate	Delayed
Appears and recedes rapidly	Appears slowly and lasts longer
Antibody-mediated reaction	Cell-mediated reaction
Induced by antigen or hapten by any route	Induced by antigen or hapten intradermally or with Freund's adjuvant or by skin contact
Passive transfer with serum	Passive transfer with lymphocyte or transfer factor
Desensitization easy but short lived	Desensitization difficult but long lasting

- Type II—antibody-mediated cytotoxic reaction
- Type III—immune complex-mediated reaction
- Type IV—delayed or cell-mediated reaction
- Type V—stimulatory hypersensitivity, an additional type that has been proposed recently

Type I—anaphylaxis (IgE or reagin-dependent)

It is an IgE-mediated immediate type of hypersensitivity reaction. An example of Type I hypersensitivity reaction is given below.

- When a guinea pig is injected with an antigen such as egg albumin (about 1 mg), no adverse effects are noted. When a second dose of the same antigen (egg albumin) is injected intravenously after an interval of 2–3 weeks, the sensitized guinea pig reacts dramatically and develops a condition known as anaphylactic shock. The animal becomes restless, cyanosed, may develop convulsions and die.
- The initial injection is termed **sensitizing dose**.
- The second injection is termed **shocking dose**.
- After the first dose, the animal forms IgE (reaginic) antibodies, which bind to the mast cells present in the submucosal layers of respiratory and gastrointestinal tract, skin and vascular endothelium and also to basophils in the blood.
- The shocking dose of the antigen interacts with these antibodies on the surface of the tissue cells (mast cells and basophils) and causes degranulation of these cells and release of pharmacologically active substances such as histamine, serotonin, heparin, eosinophil chemotactic factors, slow-reacting substance of anaphylaxis, prostaglandins and platelet-activating factor (pharmacological mediators). These mediators cause
  - Smooth muscle contraction in organs and tissues
  - Increase capillary permeability
  - Vasodilatation
- The above-described is an example of **systemic anaphylaxis**—a condition of an acute shock usually terminating in death due to suffocation from the contraction of muscles in the walls of bronchioles (Flow chart 17.1).
- This reaction can be passively transferred to another animal by injecting serum from the sensitized animal and by then injecting the shocking dose of antigen.
- Systemic anaphylaxis in man occurs following:
  - Antibiotics such as penicillin
  - Antitoxic serum such as antitetanus serum (ATS), antidiphtheric serum (ADS) or antigas gangrene serum (AGS)
  - Insect bite such as bee or wasp stings
- In man, the reaction is characterized by
  - Severe respiratory distress due to bronchiolar constriction with vascular collapse
  - Fall in blood pressure (acute hypotension)
  - Loss of consciousness
  - Death (occasionally)
- **Cutaneous or local anaphylaxis** A local wheal and flare reaction may be induced

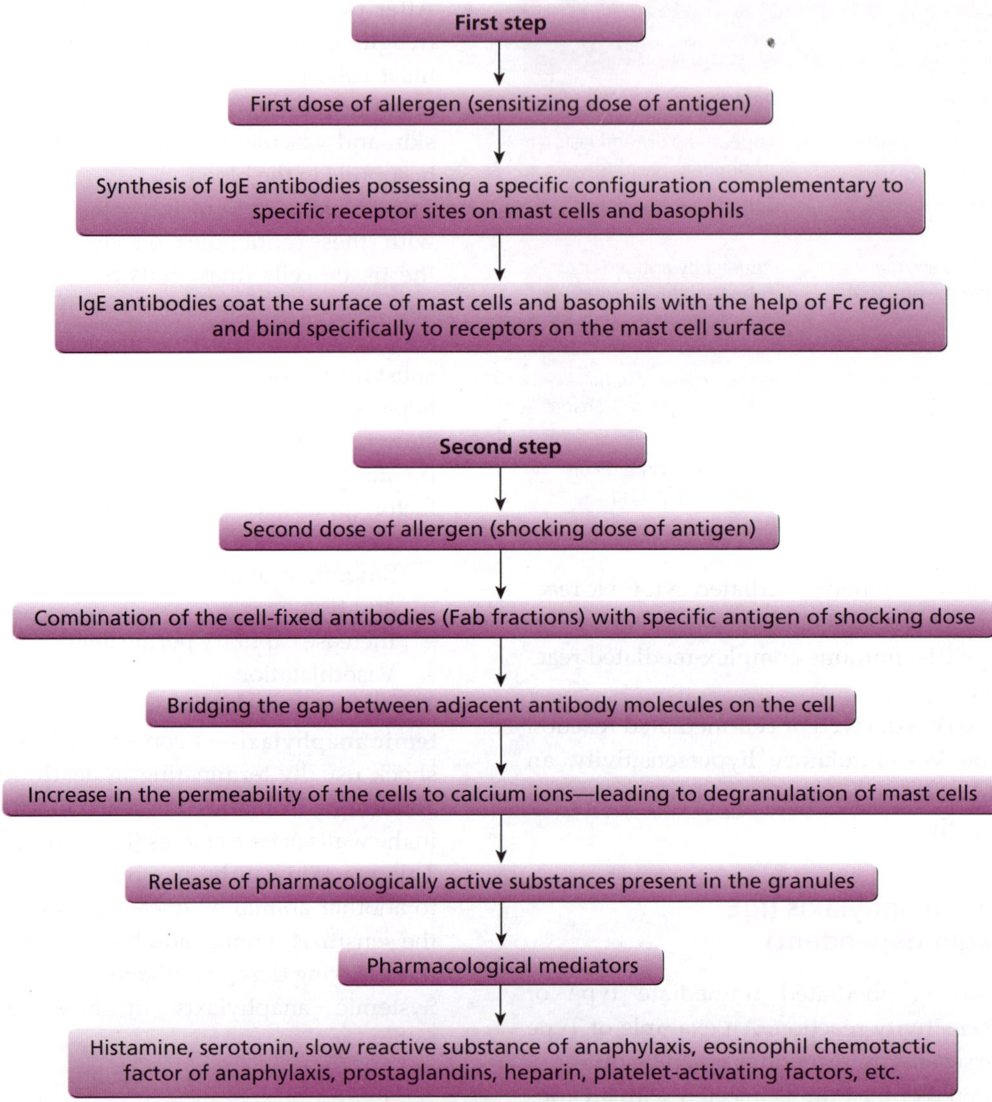

Flow chart 17.1 Mechanism of anaphylaxis (Type I hypersensitivity reaction).

by intradermal injection of antigen into an actively sensitized host. This is known as cutaneous or local anaphylaxis.

- The wheal is a pale, central area of puffiness due to oedema, which is surrounded by a flare caused by hyperaemia and subsequent erythema.
- This reaction can be used as skin test for testing Type I hypersensitivity and to identify the allergen responsible for atopic diseases.
- In highly sensitized individuals, the skin test may lead to systemic anaphylaxis, terminating in death. Hence, a syringe loaded with adrenalin should be kept ready before the test is performed.
- **Passive cutaneous anaphylaxis** Cutaneous anaphylaxis may also be induced passively by intradermal injection of antibodies. Following this, a local wheal and flare-type reaction may be demonstrated

by intravenous injection of antigen with a dye such as Evan's blue after 4–24 hours. The combination of antigen and antibody increases capillary permeability and vasodilatation permitting the escape of Evan's blue at the site of intradermal injection, resulting in an immediate bluing. This is termed passive cutaneous anaphylaxis, which can be used as an extremely sensitive in vivo method for detection of antibodies.

- **Local anaphylaxis in man (atopy)** It is a hypersensitive state in which a person reacts to the substances encountered during course of everyday life.
  - About 10% of the population suffers from atopy to allergens such as
    - Grass pollen
    - Animal danders
    - Mites in house
    - Dust
    - Food
  - Contact of allergen with the cell-bound IgE in the bronchial tree, nasal mucosa, conjunctival tissue, intestine or skin releases pharmacologically active mediators and produces symptoms of
    - Asthma
    - Hay fever (allergic rhinitis)
    - Conjunctivitis
    - Gastrointestinal symptoms
    - Dermatitis
    - Urticaria in persons allergic to food
  - The atopic sensitivity is due to excessive production of IgE antibodies known as reagins.
  - Desensitization in atopy can be achieved by injecting serum (acute or temporary desensitization) or by giving repeated injections of antigens (prolonged desensitization). Alternatively, allergen with oil adjuvant (depot therapy) can be used for prolonged desensitization.

Type II—cytotoxic reaction (Fig. 17.1)

- In this type of reaction, the antigenic component is either part of tissue cell, or microbial product or drug attached to the cell wall.
- Combination of this antigenic component with IgG or IgM antibody produces damage to cell by promoting contact with phagocytic cell or by activating the complement components.
- Contact with phagocytic cell with the help of antibody results into opsonic adherence and phagocytosis or there may be cytotoxic

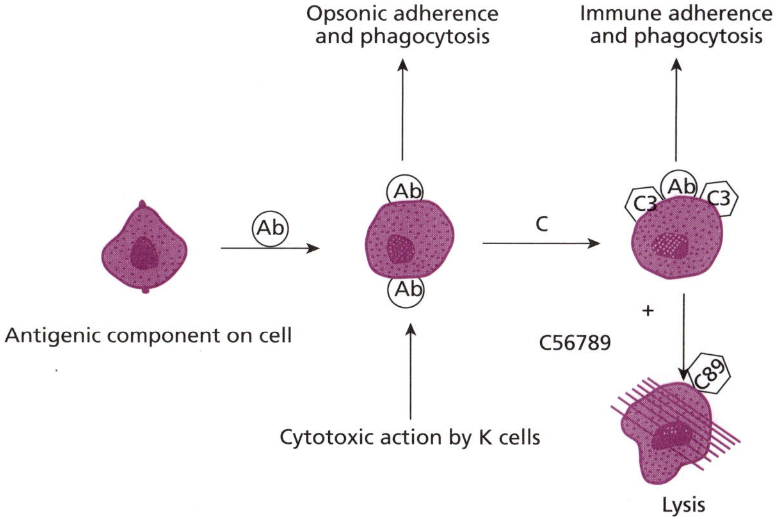

Figure 17.1 Cytotoxic hypersensitivity (Type II reaction). *Ab*, antibody; *C*, complement.

attack by killer (K) cells. If cell survives here, there is addition of complement (C3) that causes immune adherence and phagocytosis or alternatively lysis of cell occurs because of complete activation of complement.

- Examples
  - Lysis of RBCs by antierythrocyte antibodies
  - Lysis of platelets by autoantibodies leading to autoimmune thrombocytopenia
  - Drugs such as penicillin, sulphonamides and Sedormid attach to the surface of cells such as RBCs, neutrophils or platelets and cause change in antigenicity inducing antibody synthesis that causes cytotoxic reaction

Type III—immune complex-mediated hypersensitivity

- It is characterized by deposition of antigen–antibody complexes in the tissues particularly on endothelial surfaces.
- The complex formation in and around the small blood vessels may result in acute inflammatory reactions and sometimes mechanical blockage of the vessels because of platelet aggregation, causing interference with blood supply to the surrounding tissues.
- These antigen–antibody complexes may activate complement, causing release of anaphylatoxin that causes release of histamine, which is responsible for vascular permeability changes.
- Activation of complement also causes aggregation of polymorphonuclear leucocytes, which engulf antigen–antibody complexes and release proteolytic enzymes and polycationic proteins, which increase capillary permeability.
- Complement activation, massive infiltration of polymorphonuclear leucocytes and platelet aggregation lead to inflammation and tissue injury (Fig. 17.2).
- It is of two types:
  - Arthus reaction
  - Serum sickness

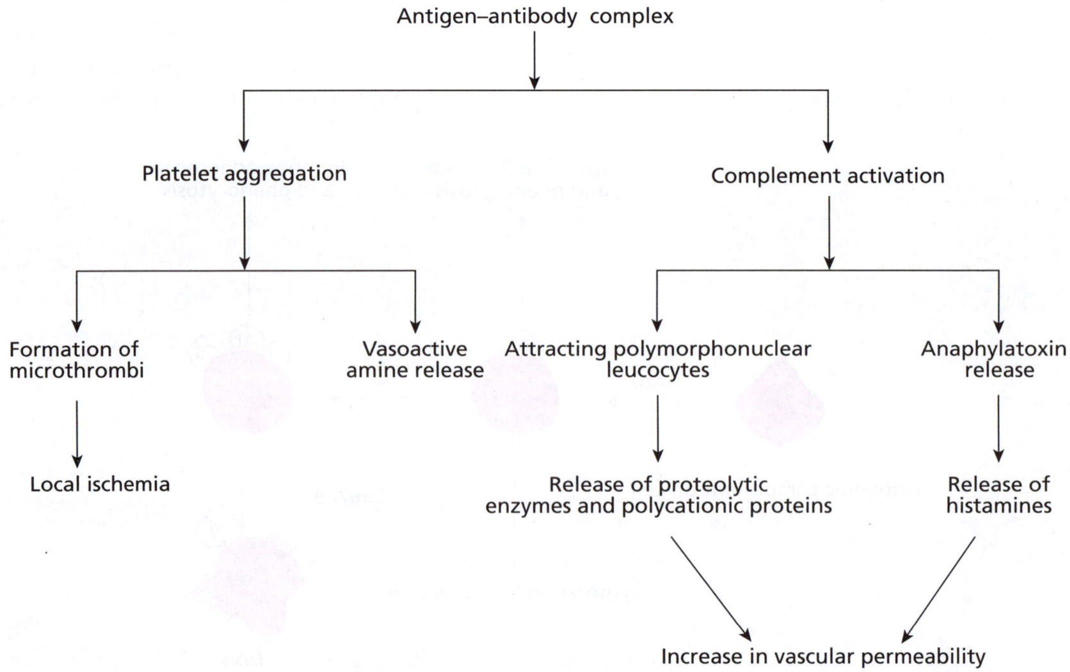

Figure 17.2 Immune complex-mediated (Type III) hypersensitivity.

Arthus reaction

It is a local inflammatory reaction with particular involvement of blood vessels. It occurs following an injection of antigen (horse serum) intradermally or subcutaneously in a hyper immunized animal (animal which has received several injections of horse serum and developed high levels of IgG antibodies). The reaction presents as an erythema, oedema, induration and haemorrhagic necrosis.

In man, Arthus-like reaction is produced in individuals who have received several injections of antitoxic sera or insulin.

Serum sickness

It is a systemic reaction that may occur in man following the injection of horse serum and sometimes following the injection of drugs such as sulphonamide, penicillin, streptomycin or organic arsenicals. A single dose is sufficient to produce symptoms. The symptoms appear after 7–14 days. The symptoms are

- Fever
- Splenomegaly
- Glomerulonephritis
- Vasculitis
- Abdominal pain
- Lymphadenopathy
- Arthritis
- Endocarditis
- Urticaria
- Nausea and vomiting

The pathogenic mechanism is the formation of antigen–antibody complexes, which get deposited on the endothelial lining of blood vessels in various parts of the body, causing inflammatory infiltration.

This is a self-limited disease. With an increase in the antibody level, antigen–antibody complexes become larger in size and susceptible to phagocytosis and immune elimination.

Type IV—delayed hypersensitivity

- In this reaction, there is an appreciable delay between the exposure to antigen and the development of symptoms.
- The reaction is mediated by sensitized T cells and not by antibodies. The reaction is demonstrated by cutaneous reactivity, which becomes visible after 24–48 hours after the introduction of antigen.
- The cutaneous reaction is inflammatory and indurate type involving lymphocytes and macrophages and not wheal and flare type as seen in anaphylaxis.
- The reaction is mediated by sensitized T cells, which on coming in contact with the specific antigen release lymphokines. The lymphokines are responsible for biological effects on leucocytes, macrophages and tissue cells. The end result is an inflammatory and indurated type of cutaneous reaction.
- Passive transfer to a normal recipient is possible with the help of sensitized T lymphocytes from a sensitized donor or with the help of transfer factor and not by serum.
- It occurs in two forms:
  - Tuberculin (infection) type
  - Contact dermatitis type

Tuberculin (infection) type

It develops due to an infection with tubercle bacillus and is demonstrated by tuberculin reaction.

When a small dose of antigen (tuberculin) is injected intradermally in an individual sensitized to tubercular protein by a previous infection or immunization (BCG), an erythema and indurated swelling develops gradually, which reaches its maximum after 24–72 hours (not wheal and flare type of reaction as seen in Type I). This type of reaction is also seen in leprosy, brucellosis, lymphogranuloma venereum, leishmaniasis and many other infectious diseases, especially in chronic infections caused by intracellular pathogens.

Contact dermatitis

- It is a delayed hypersensitivity reaction that develops from a skin contact to a variety of substances such as

  - Drugs such as penicillin, sulphonamide and organic arsenicals
  - Metals such as nickel and cobalt
  - Chemicals such as picryl chloride, dinitrochlorobenzene, formaldehyde, iodine, dyes, soaps and cosmetics
- When a sensitized individual comes in contact with these substances, it leads to contact dermatitis. It is characterized by macules and papules to vesicles that break-down leaving behind raw weeping areas, typical of acute eczematous dermatitis.
- It may be possible to identify the substance responsible for sensitivity by patch test. The procedure includes application of the suspected substance to the skin under an adherent dressing and it is then observed for itching (after 4–5 hours) and local reaction—erythema to vesicle or blister formation (in 24–28 hours).

Type V—stimulatory hypersensitivity

Certain IgG antibodies have the ability to stimulate their target cells rather than to kill or inhibit them. These antibodies react with the key surface component and stimulate the functional activity of the cell, for example, thyrotoxicosis (Graves disease) in which antibodies react with thyroid cell and stimulate the activity of these cells causing excessive secretion of thyroid hormone that leads to thyrotoxicosis.

Self-assessment

Long-answer question

1. Define and classify hypersensitivity reactions. Discuss in brief the Type I hypersensitivity reaction.

Short-answer questions

Write notes on

1. Difference between immediate and delayed hypersensitivity
2. Type II hypersensitivity
3. Arthus reaction
4. Serum sickness
5. Delayed hypersensitivity
6. Atopy
7. Contact dermatitis

Multiple-choice questions

1. Which of the following statements is FALSE about immediate hypersensitivity?
   A. Appears within a short period
   B. Is mediated by T cells
   C. Is an antibody-mediated reaction
   D. Cytotoxic hypersensitivity is one of the examples
2. Which of the following statements is FALSE about delayed hypersensitivity?
   A. Appears slowly
   B. Is mediated by T cells
   C. Is an antibody-mediated reaction
   D. Contact dermatitis is one of the examples
3. Which of the following immunoglobulin molecules is a mediator of anaphylaxis?
   A. IgM
   B. IgA
   C. IgG
   D. IgE
4. Which of the following statements is TRUE regarding the systemic anaphylaxis in man?
   A. Occurs following the contact with grass pollen
   B. Occurs following the injection of antitoxic serum
   C. Occurs following the ingestion of food
   D. Occurs following the bite of mites in the house
5. Which of the following statements is TRUE regarding the local anaphylaxis in man (atopy)?
   A. Occurs following the contact with grass pollen
   B. Occurs following the injection of antitoxic serum
   C. Occurs following the injection of penicillin
   D. Occurs following an insect bite
6. The most appropriate symptom associated with the systemic anaphylaxis in man is
   A. Asthma

B. Hay fever
C. Dermatitis
D. Severe respiratory distress

7. The most common type of reaction associated with the local anaphylaxis in man (atopy) is
A. Wheal and flare reaction
B. Erythema and induration
C. Urticaria
D. None of the above

8. Which of the following is an antigen–antibody complex-mediated hypersensitivity reaction?
A. Type IV
B. Type III
C. Type II
D. Type I

9. Contact dermatitis is a
A. Type IV reaction
B. Type III reaction
C. Type II reaction
D. Type I reaction

10. Arthus reaction is a
A. Type IV reaction
B. Type III reaction
C. Type II reaction
D. Type I reaction

18 Autoimmunity

The recognition of self and non-self is an important function of the immune system. It is a fundamental characteristic of the immune system to prevent responding to self as an antigen by appropriate mechanisms. Under some circumstances, these mechanisms might breakdown leading to an immunological response to self-antigens. This abnormal immune response, in which antibodies or sensitized lymphocytes capable of reacting with self-components are produced, is known as autoimmunity. The autoimmune response may lead to autoimmune disease. Thus, autoimmune disease is a condition in which the **'natural unresponsiveness'** or **'tolerance to self'** terminates, as a result of which antibody or sensitized lymphocyte reacts with self-antigen causing a disease.

Possible mechanism of autoimmune diseases

Different theories have been proposed to explain how the normal controlling mechanism fails to maintain self-recognition. These are

- Hidden or sequestered antigen theory
- Altered forms of self-antigens or neoantigens
- Shared or cross-reacting antigens
- Loss of immunoregulation
- Genetic abnormalities

Hidden or sequestered antigen theory

According to this theory, the tissue antigens that are exposed to the lymphoreticular system during embryonic development are recognized as self-antigens and hence no immune response is induced. However, many autoantigens are hidden within a cell or a tissue, for example, eye lens protein, brain tissue protein, thyroglobulin and sperms, which have no opportunity to develop tolerance because they are anatomically confined to sites that prevent their access to lymphoreticular system. These antigens are known as sequestered antigens and though they are self-antigens, they are treated as non-self antigens. Contact of these antigens with immunocompetent cells results in an immune response leading to the formation of antibodies or sensitized T cells that produce trauma or injury by reacting with them. Spermatozoa have no opportunity to develop tolerance because they acquire antigenicity during maturation. Therefore, they are treated as non-self and their exposure to immunocompetent cells leads to orchitis.

Altered forms of self-antigens or neoantigens

In certain circumstances, a native tissue antigen may be altered by a physical (irradiation), chemical (drugs and other chemicals) or biological (viral infections, microbial enzymes) means and thus assume a new antigenic specificity. This altered antigen stimulates an immune reaction, which damages the native tissue antigen producing tissue injury.

Shared or cross-reacting antigens

Some microorganisms carry antigenic determinants that resemble the components of host cells. These are known as cross-reacting antigens. Infection with such microorganisms may initiate an immune response that damages a particular organ or tissue in the host. For example, in rheumatic heart disease, antibodies produced against group A streptococci cross-react with human heart tissue and produce injury.

Loss of immunoregulation

The loss of normal tolerance control because of loss of immunoregulation leads to autoimmune disease. The defect or lack of efficiency in the lymphoid cell population may result in loss of normal tolerance control and autoimmune disease.

Genetic abnormalities

Genetic abnormalities such as mutation of immunocompetent cell, defect in immune response (IR) genes or immunoglobulin gene may lead to antigenic responsiveness to self-antigens causing autoimmune diseases.

Classification of autoimmune diseases

Based on the site of involvement and nature of lesions, the autoimmune diseases are classified into four types:

1. Haemolytic autoimmune diseases
2. Organ-specific or localized autoimmune diseases
3. Non-organ-specific or systemic autoimmune diseases
4. Transitory diseases

Haemolytic autoimmune diseases

Autoimmune haemolytic anaemias

- Two types of autoantibodies against RBCs are produced.
  - Cold antibodies—IgM type of antibodies that agglutinate RBCs at 4°C
  - Warm antibodies—IgG type of antibodies
- Antibodies coat the surface of RBCs and cause premature lysis in spleen and liver leading to anaemia.
- Complement-dependent intravascular haemolysis may also occur.

Autoimmune thrombocytopenia Autoantibodies against platelets are produced, which cause decrease in the number of platelets, for example, idiopathic thrombocytopenic purpura.

Autoimmune leucopenia Antibodies against leucocytes are produced which cause lysis of leucocytes, for example non-agglutinating antileucocyte antibodies causing lymphocytopenia in **systemic lupus erythematosus** and rheumatoid arthritis.

Organ-specific or localized autoimmune diseases

Autoimmune diseases affecting a specific organ are known as organ-specific or localized diseases. These include the following:

Hashimoto disease (lymphadenoid goitre) Cytotoxic autoantibodies react with thyroglobulin—a thyroid cell component—causing enlargement of thyroid gland and symptoms of hypothyroidism or frank myxoedema. The disease is frequently seen in females.

Graves disease (thyrotoxicosis) An IgG type of antibody known as longer-acting thyroid stimulator (LATS) against thyroid membrane antigen is produced, which stimulates excessive hormone secretion that stimulates cell division leading to enlargement of the thyroid.

Autoimmune orchitis Sperm agglutinating antibodies causing aggregation of spermatozoa are produced which interfere with penetration of sperms into cervical mucosa.

It occurs as a rare complication of mumps in which the virus damages the testes allowing the entry of the cells of immune system to initiate an immune response.

Myasthenia gravis In this disease, there is an abnormal fatigability of muscles due to malfunction of the myoneural junction. Autoantibodies to muscle acetylcholine receptors are produced, which prevent combination of acetylcholine with its receptors and impairs muscular contractions.

Autoimmune diseases of the eye Two types of autoimmune diseases:

1. *Phacoanaphylaxis*—intraocular inflammation due to autoimmune response to the lens protein following cataract surgery
2. *Perforating injuries*—involving the iris or ciliary bodies are followed by sympathetic ophthalmia in the opposite eye

Pernicious anaemia Two types of antibodies are produced; one is directed against parietal cells of gastric mucosa, which is believed to cause achlorhydria and atrophic gastritis. The second antibody is directed against the intrinsic factor and prevents absorption of vitamin B_{12}. The result is megaloblastic anaemia.

Autoimmune diseases of the nervous system Neuroparalytic accidents following rabies vaccination due to cross-reaction between human and sheep brain antigens.

Idiopathic polyneuritis (Guillain–Barre syndrome) is considered to be an autoimmune response against the peripheral nervous system.

Non-organ-specific or systemic autoimmune diseases

Diseases involving several organs or tissue systems are known as non-organ-specific or systemic autoimmune diseases.

Systemic lupus erythematosus (SLE)

- It is a chronic generalized disorder involving many organs/systems with remissions and exacerbations.
- SLE is mainly seen in females and is characterized by a red rash across the nose and upper cheeks, hence the name, lupus erythematosus.
- Haemolytic anaemia, leucopenia, thrombocytopenia; lesions in kidneys, vascular tissues, joints, spleen and heart are the other signs and symptoms.
- A variety of autoantibodies directed against cell nuclei, intracytoplasmic cell constituents, thyroid, RBCs, WBCs and other unknown antigens are produced.
- The important immunological feature is lupus erythematosus (LE) cell phenomenon. The LE cell is a polymorphonuclear leucocyte with ingested nuclear material complexed with antinuclear antibody.

Rheumatoid arthritis (RA)

- It is an inflammatory disease of joints and connective tissue commonly associated with serositis, myocarditis, vasculitis and other disseminated lesions.
- The synovial membranes of affected joints are swollen and oedematous with dense infiltration of lymphocytes and plasma cells. It is common in adult female.
- The striking feature is the presence of a circulating autoantibody known as rheumatoid factor (RF); it is an IgM that reacts with IgG in vitro and is found in the sera and synovial fluid of most adult patients.

Sjogren syndrome (SS)

- It is a triad of keratoconjunctivitis sicca (dry eyes), xerostomia (dryness of mouth) with or without salivary gland enlargement and rheumatoid arthritis.
- Xerostomia due to reduced quantity of saliva leads to retention of food particles in the mouth for long duration that predisposes to dental caries.

- Patient shows a variety of antibodies—antinuclear antibodies, RF, antibodies against salivary duct, lacrimal glands, smooth muscle, mitochondria, thyroid gland, etc.

Polyarteritis nodosa

- It is a necrotizing angiitis involving medium and small arteries.
- The disease proves to be fatal due to coronary thrombosis, cerebral haemorrhage or gastrointestinal bleeding. It is common in males.

Transitory diseases

- These are the conditions such as anaemia, thrombocytopenia or nephritis that occur following certain infections with microbes or drug therapy.
- The infecting agent or drug induces antigenic alteration in some self-antigens that initiates an immune response leading to tissue damage.
- The disease is transient and undergoes spontaneous cure when the infection is brought under control or the drug is withdrawn.

Pathogenesis of autoimmune diseases

The mechanism of pathogenesis of autoimmune disease is not exactly known. Antibodies or sensitized lymphocytes may cause damage through hypersensitivity reactions leading to severe and sometimes fatal reactions affecting the individual's own tissues and cells.

Type II reactions Antibodies against self-antigens may cause damage by the cytolytic or cytotoxic effects as in Type II hypersensitivity reactions, for example, autoimmune haemolytic anaemia.

Type III reactions Antibodies against self-antigens may initiate antigen–antibody complex-mediated damage to self-antigens, for example, SLE and glomerulonephritis.

Type IV reactions Tissue damage is mediated by sensitized T cells directed against self-components. The Type IV may act synergistically in association with antibody-mediated hypersensitivity reactions in a number of autoimmune diseases.

Self-assessment

Long-answer question

1. Define and classify autoimmune diseases. Discuss in detail the organ-specific and systemic autoimmune diseases.

Short-answer questions

Write notes on

1. Haemolytic autoimmune diseases
2. Systemic lupus erythematosus
3. Rheumatoid arthritis
4. Transitory autoimmune diseases
5. Mechanism of autoimmune diseases
6. Sjogren syndrome

Multiple-choice questions

1. The failure to eliminate self-reactive cells leads to
   A. Autoimmunity
   B. Immunosuppression
   C. Tolerance
   D. None of the above
2. The antibodies formed against group A streptococci producing cardiac damage is an example of
   A. Loss of immunoregulation
   B. Altered forms of self-antigens
   C. Shared antigens
   D. Genetic abnormalities
3. Which of the following is NOT a sequestered antigen?
   A. Eye lens protein
   B. Heart tissue protein
   C. Brain tissue protein
   D. Thyroglobulin

4. Which of the following immunoglobulin molecules causes lysis of red blood cells in autoimmune haemolytic anaemias?
   A. IgM
   B. IgA
   C. IgD
   D. IgE
5. Which of the following immunoglobulin molecules stimulates excessive hormone secretion in Graves disease (thyrotoxicosis)?
   A IgM
   B. IgA
   C. IgD
   D. IgG
6. Which of the following is NOT an organ-specific (localized) autoimmune disease?
   A. Polyarteritis nodosa
   B. Pernicious anaemia
   C. Myasthenia gravis
   D. Graves disease
7. Which of the following is a non-organ-specific (systemic) autoimmune disease?
   A. Pernicious anaemia
   B. Myasthenia gravis
   C. Sjogren syndrome
   D. Graves disease
8. Which of the following statements is FALSE about systemic lupus erythematosus?
   A. Characterized by a red rash across the nose and upper cheeks
   B. Lupus erythematosus cell phenomenon is an important immunological feature
   C. Swollen and oedematous synovial membranes
   D. Antinuclear antibody is the characteristic feature
9. Which of the following statements is FALSE about rheumatoid arthritis?
   A. Haemolytic anaemia, leucopenia, thrombocytopenia, lesions in kidneys are the striking features
   B. Serositis, myocarditis, and vasculitis and other disseminated lesions
   C. Swollen and oedematous synovial membranes
   D. Presence of a circulating autoantibody known as rheumatoid factor
10. Xerostomia, due to reduced quantity of saliva leading to retention of food particles in mouth for long duration, and predisposing to dental caries is a striking feature of
    A. Polyarteritis nodosa
    B. Myasthenia gravis
    C. Sjogren syndrome
    D. Graves disease
11. Guillain–Barre syndrome is
    A. Haemolytic autoimmune disease
    B. Autoimmune disease of eye
    C. Autoimmune disease of central nervous system
    D. Transitory autoimmune disease

19 Transplantation Immunity and Tumour Immunity

Transplantation immunity

- Transplantation or grafting is a replacement of an organ, which is congenitally defective or absent or an organ or tissue that is damaged because of disease or injury, by healthy ones for restoration of function.
- Transplantation of certain organs is very common procedure but high percentages of grafts are unsuccessful because of immunological response of an individual to foreign histocompatibility antigens of the donor.

Types of transplants

- **Autograft (autogenic graft)** It is a graft taken from one site and transplanted back on to the same individual to another site. Autografts are generally not rejected.
- **Isograft (syngeneic graft)** It is a graft taken from one individual and placed on another individual of the same genetic constitution, for example, grafts between identical twins or highly inbred strains of syngeneic animals. Isografts are also generally not rejected.
- **Allograft (homograft)** It is a graft taken from one individual and placed on genetically non-identical member of the same species.
- **Xenograft (heterograft)** It is grafting between members of different species, for example, animal to human. These grafts induce powerful immunological reactions and are rejected.

Rejection of graft

- Rejection may be defined as the process by which the immune system of the host recognizes, becomes sensitized against antigens of the graft and attempts to eliminate the antigenic differences of the donor organ. Except for the autografts and isografts, some degree of rejection occurs with every transplant.
- When the graft is placed, the host encounters the histocompatibility antigens on cell surface of the transplant, which are processed by macrophages locally or within the regional lymph nodes for sensitization. The sensitized lymphoid cells—both T and B cells—initiate immune injury, either the cell-mediated or humoral immune response.
- Lymphocytes, particularly T lymphocytes, play a primary role in shortening the graft survival.
- Sensitized T lymphocytes initiate immunological injury in various ways:
  - Direct cytotoxic attack by T cells

- Direct attack by natural killer (NK) cells
- Indirectly by releasing soluble T cell mediators of immune injury (lymphokines)
- By antibody-dependent cell-mediated cytotoxicity (ADCC) attack by killer (K) cells

- The B lymphocytes and antibodies activate the complement system and the coagulation system, which result into
  - Deposition of fibrin
  - Infiltration of site with polymorphonuclear leucocytes (PML)
  - Platelet thrombosis
  - Prompt coagulative necrosis
  - Antibodies also help K cells to attack target organ (ADCC)
- Immunological response against transplant is due to the presence of antigens in grafted tissue, which are absent in recipient. These antigens responsible for rejection are known as **transplantation antigens** or **histocompatibility antigens**. The synthesis of transplantation antigens and graft rejection is genetically controlled by the histocompatibility-linked immune response (Ir) genes. The major antigens determining histocompatibility in human beings are alloantigens found on the surface of leucocytes, hence are known as human leucocyte antigen (HLA). These constitute the major histocompatibility complex (MHC) and are known as the **HLA system**.

HLA complex (Fig. 19.1) The HLA complex of genes is located on the short arm of **autosomal chromosome-6**. It is divided into three separate clusters of genes, each of which codes for one of the major classes of antigens:

- Class I—A, B and C loci
- Class II or the D region—DR, DQ and DP loci
- Class III or the complement region—C2 and C4 of the classical pathway, properdin factor of the alternative pathway and tumour necrosis factor α and β

The products of these genes occur as transmembrane glycoprotein antigens, namely, **class I antigens** (strong transplant antigens responsible for graft rejection and elimination of virus infected cells), **class II antigens** (responsible for graft versus host response, immune response, cellular recognition, cellular interactions, mixed lymphocyte reaction, etc.) and **class III antigens** (include complement components responsible for the formation of C3 convertase).

Prevention of graft rejection

- **Tissue matching** Graft rejection can be minimized by matching the donor and recipient at HLA loci. This matching is known as histocompatibility testing. This can be performed by
  - Microcytotoxicity test
  - Mixed lymphocyte reaction
- **By using immunosuppressive agents** The graft rejection can be minimized, delayed or avoided by using immunosuppressive agents such as anti-inflammatory agents,

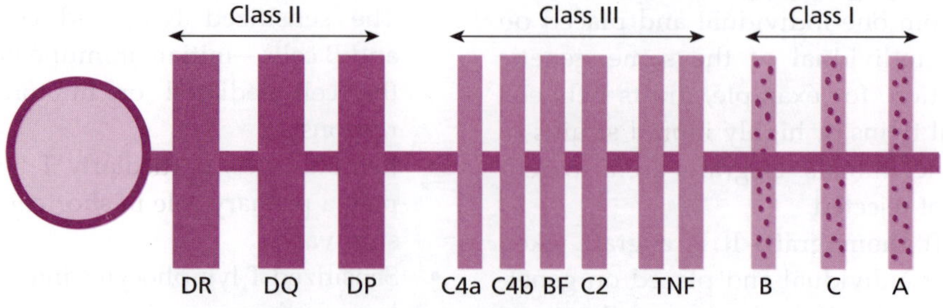

Figure 19.1 Human leucocyte antigen complex.

antimetabolites, cytotoxic agents such as steroids, azathioprine, 6-mercaptopurine, methotrexate, methopterin, cyclophosphamide, **antilymphocyte serum** against thymocytes/lymphocytes and **cyclosporine**, the most commonly used immunosuppressive agent.

- **Lymphoid cell ablation**
  - Removal of lymphoid cells by extracorporeal irradiation of blood and thoracic duct cannulation are helpful in depressing immunological reactivity non-specifically and increasing the graft survival.
  - Injections of antilymphocyte serum or monoclonal anti-T3 antibodies successfully reverse acute kidney graft.
- **Immunological enhancement**
  - Under certain circumstances, antibodies produced against graft antigens act in opposition to cell-mediated immunity (CMI) and protect the graft from CMI by inhibiting graft rejection.
  - This phenomenon is known as 'immunological enhancement'.
  - This happens when the recipient is immunized with one or more injections of killed donor tissue and then a transplant is applied subsequently, the graft survival is increased.

Tumour immunity

Tumour is a swelling or enlargement, especially due to a pathological over growth of tissue. Malignant transformation of cell leads to expression of new surface antigens, which makes the tumour antigenically different from normal tissue of the host. These new antigens are recognized as **'non-self'** and hence immune system tries to eliminate these antigens.

Tumour antigens

Tumour antigens are antigens present on the cancer cells. These antigens include the following:

- Antigens induced by viruses
- Antigens induced by chemicals
- Carcinofoetal antigens
- Carcinofoetal enzymes

Antigens induced by viruses

- The oncogenic viruses such as herpes simplex viruses, adenoviruses, papovavirus, hepatitis B virus, human T cell leukaemia virus and Rous sarcoma virus cause malignant transformations and induce new protein and antigens on the cell surface.
- These are tumour-associated transplantation antigens (TATAs).
- These evoke powerful immune responses in experimental animals.

Antigens induced by chemicals

- Chemically induced tumours express different antigens.
- These evoke weak immune responses in experimental animals.

Carcinofoetal antigens

- Certain tumours in adults show presence of antigens of foetal or embryonic cells, which are absent in normal adult cells. These include the following:
  - **Carcinoembryonic antigen**—found in human embryonic gut and is an important marker of cancer of gut (colonic cancer) in adults
  - **Alpha-fetoprotein**—normally present in foetal serum in high concentration. It is an important marker of hepatoma in adults

Carcinofoetal enzymes

- Carcinoplacental or carcinoembryonic enzymes originating from trophoblastic tissues are associated with cancerous states.
- These include Regan isozyme of alkaline phosphatase, glycogen phosphorylase, glucosamine 6-phosphate synthetase, amino acid transaminase, etc.

Immune response in malignancy

Specific immune response

- Immune response to tumour is primarily cell-mediated—T lymphocytes play an important role in destruction of tumour cells.
- Antigens shed by cancer cells are presented to T lymphocytes, which initiate antitumour activity by releasing lymphokines such as migration inhibiting factor, lymphocyte inhibiting factor, macrophage activating factor and interferon γ (IFN-γ).
- Activated T lymphocytes also cooperate B cells and activate B cells to produce antibodies, which play an important role in destruction of tumour cells.

Non-specific immune response

- Activated macrophages and NK cells non-specifically destroy tumour cells.
- Macrophages can destroy tumour cells by phagocytosis as well as by cytolysis. However, NK cells have cytolytic activity against tumour cells.
- Macrophages also secrete cytokines, which have antitumour activity, for example
  - Tumour necrosis factor-α (TNF-α) and TNF-β stimulate necrosis of the tumour cells
  - Interferons such as IFN-α, IFN-β and IFN-γ have been shown to have antitumour activity

Immunological surveillance

- Immunological surveillance is based on the concept that tumour cells display antigens, which are treated as non-self by the host's immune system.
- Transformed cells display different antigenic determinants, which induce an immune response that destroy transformed cell and thus immune system acts as an active guardian against transformed cells carrying foreign or non-self antigens.
- Burnet (1970) proposed that the immune system keeps a constant vigilance on transformed cells that arise by mutation of somatic cells and destroy them.
- Development of tumour indicates an escape from the surveillance mechanism according to this hypothesis.
- Insufficiency of the surveillance mechanism, due to ageing or congenital or iatrogenic immunodeficiencies, leads to an increased incidence of cancer.
- If immunological surveillance is effective, cancer should not occur.
- The development of tumours represents a lapse in surveillance. This may be due to the fast rate of proliferation of malignant cells because of which they may escape before the development of an effective immune response.
  - Circulating tumour antigens may coat the surface of lymphoid cells and prevent their contact with tumour cells.
  - Contact of tumour antigens with immunocompetent cells may be prevented because of the cover of antigenically neutral substances—no immune response.
  - Humoral antibodies may cause immunological enhancement.
- The tumour immunity does not appear to be strong and effective mechanism, as evidenced by the high prevalence of cancer.

Immunotherapy of cancer

Immunotherapy of cancer includes the following:

- Non-specific active immunotherapy
- Specific immunotherapy

Non-specific active immunotherapy

Treatment with certain microbial and synthetic products can cause regression of some tumours.

- **Microbial products** such as BCG vaccine, non-living *Corynebacterium parvum* and glycan—a glucose polymer derived from microorganisms—have been shown to induce immunity by activating macrophages, NK cells, T and B lymphocytes.

- **Synthetic products** such as levamisole—an antihelminthic drug and dinitrochlorobenzene—have been found effective in stimulating CMI and macrophage function. These agents have been used in different types of cancers with some degree of success.

In addition to these, thymic hormones (thymosin, thymopoietin, thymic humoral factor, etc.), interferon-γ (IFN-γ), tumour necrosis factors, interleukin-2, etc., are also found effective against tumours of different types.

Specific immunotherapy

This includes passive, active and adoptive immunotherapy.

- **Passive immunotherapy**—passive administration of serum containing a high titre of antibodies to tumour-associated antigens have been tried with limited success
- **Active immunotherapy**—by injecting tumour cell vaccines was tried in the past. At present, vaccine prepared by using purified tumour cell antigen is being tried
- **Adoptive immunotherapy**
  - Specific adoptive immunotherapy with the help of lymphocytes, transfer factor and immune RNA from persons who have been cured of their neoplasms or specifically immunized against the patient's tumour have been found to boost immunity.
  - Lymphokines-activated killer (LAK) cells obtained by treatment of NK cells with interleukin have been found useful in the treatment and preventing metastases of tumours.
  - Thymosin, a hormone extracted from bovine or human thymus, has been reported to have antitumour effects recently.
  - The immunotherapy is effective and works better only after surgery, radiotherapy and chemotherapy.

Self-assessment

Short-answer questions

Write notes on

1. Graft rejection
2. Prevention of graft rejection
3. Types of transplants
4. Immunosuppressive agents
5. Tumour antigens
6. Immunological surveillance
7. Immunotherapy of cancer
8. Immune response in malignancy

Multiple-choice questions

1. Select the most appropriate option for allograft
   A. A graft taken from one site and transplanted back on to the same individual
   B. A graft taken from one individual and placed on genetically non-identical member of the same species
   C. A graft taken from one individual and placed on another individual of the same genetic constitution
   D. A grafting between members of different species
2. Which of the following statements is TRUE regarding immunological injury initiated by B lymphocytes?
   A. Initiate attack by natural killer cells
   B. Initiate cytotoxic attack by killer cells
   C. Initiate cytotoxic attack by T cells
   D. None of the above
3. Which of the following statements is FALSE regarding immunological injury initiated by sensitized T lymphocytes in rejection of graft?
   A. Initiate attack by natural killer cells
   B. Initiate cytotoxic attack by killer cells
   C. Initiate cytotoxic attack by T cells
   D. All of the above
4. Which of the following is the most commonly used immunosuppressive agent?
   A. Cyclosporine
   B. Azathioprines

C. 6-Mercaptopurine
D. Methotrexate

5. The following are the microbial products used for non-specific active immunotherapy of cancer, EXCEPT
A. BCG vaccine
B. *Corynebacterium parvum*
C. Glycan
D. Levamisole

6. Which of the following is a synthetic product used for non-specific active immunotherapy of cancer?
A. BCG vaccine
B. *Corynebacterium parvum*
C. Glycan
D. Levamisole

7. The following are the agents used for adoptive immunotherapy of cancer, EXCEPT
A. Tumour cell vaccines
B. Lymphocytes
C. Transfer factor
D. Immune RNA

8. Following are the components of non-specific immune response to tumours, EXCEPT
A. Tumour necrosis factors
B. Interferons
C. Activated macrophages and natural killer cells
D. Lymphokines

20 Immunizing Agents (Vaccines and Sera)

Immunization is the method by which artificial immunity, that is, resistance to a particular infection, in an individual is developed artificially by giving immunizing agents.

Purpose of immunization

- To provide protection against infectious diseases in children by routine immunization of children, this forms the part of basic healthcare system of communities
- To raise the overall level of immunity in a community (herd immunity) to control infections in the community in addition to providing individual protection
- To provide protection in selected groups or individuals having a risk of particular infection (risk groups) by immunizing them against particular infection

Immunizing agents

These agents may be classified as follows:
- Vaccines
- Immunoglobulins
- Antisera

Vaccines

- Any biological product prepared from microorganisms or other biological substances, for example, allergens or tumour products, useful in the prevention or treatment of a disease.
- These are immunological substances designed to confer specific protection against diseases.
- Vaccines may be prepared from live or killed organisms, toxins, extracted cellular fractions or combination of these to develop active immunity.
- Vaccines are used for
  - Routine immunization of children which forms the part of basic healthcare system of communities
  - Immunization of selected groups or individuals having risk of a particular infection (risk groups)

Types of vaccines

Live attenuated vaccines

- Live vaccines are preparations containing live microorganisms with reduced virulence.
- **Preparation** They are prepared by using naturally attenuated strains or strains are attenuated by cultivating the organisms serially into various hosts (unfavourable host) or cultures (repeated subcultures).

- Live vaccines initiate an infection without causing disease; hence, the immunity developed is same as that following natural infection and lasts for several years.

Examples

- **Live bacterial vaccines**
  - BCG (Bacille Calmette–Guerin) vaccine for tuberculosis
  - Typhoral (typhoid oral vaccine) for enteric fever
- **Live viral vaccines**
  - OPV (oral polio vaccine) for polio
  - MMR (mumps, measles, rubella vaccine)
  - Measles vaccine

Advantages

- A single dose is usually sufficient and booster doses are generally not required, but may be required sometimes
- Can be administered by the route of natural infection to induce local immunity
- Also induce humoral and cell-mediated immunity (CMI)
- Induce longer and effective immunity

Disadvantages

- Risk of reversion of virulence
- Microbe in vaccine may spread from vaccinee to contacts
- May cause local and remote complications

Contraindications

Live vaccines should not be administered in

- Pregnancy due to risk of foetal infection
- Immunocompromised individuals such as leukaemia, lymphoma, AIDS, other types of malignancies, immunodeficiency and in whom there may be an increased risk of severe complications

Killed vaccines or inactivated vaccines

- These vaccines are preparations containing killed or inactivated microorganisms.
- **Preparation** They are prepared by inactivation of microorganisms by heat, phenol, formalin or β-propiolactone.
- Killed vaccines do not initiate infection and there is no multiplication of microorganism.
- They induce active immunity but immunity developed is less as compared to live vaccine, also the protection lasts for a short duration. Hence, booster doses are necessary.

Examples

- **Killed bacterial vaccines**
  - TAB (typhi, paratyphi-A, paratyphi-B) vaccine for enteric fever
  - Cholera vaccine
- **Killed viral vaccines**
  - Salk polio vaccine
  - Rabies vaccine

Advantages

- Safe and stable
- Can be given in combination as polyvalent vaccines
- No danger of spread of organism from vaccinee to contacts

Disadvantages

- Multiple injections are needed (booster doses)
- Cannot be administered orally. Oral route is not suitable (effective by parenteral route)
- Unable to induce local and CMI
- May sometimes cause complications (hypersensitive reactions)

Toxoids

- Certain organisms produce exotoxins, for example, diphtheria and tetanus bacilli, which play an important role in pathogenesis.
- In such infections, the toxins can be detoxified by heat, formalin or phenol and used for immunization.
- The detoxified toxin is known as **toxoid,** which is non-toxic but antigenic.

- Toxoid produces antitoxin (antitoxic antibody), which specifically reacts with toxin and neutralizes it. Examples include
  - TT (tetanus toxoid)
  - DT (diphtheria toxoid)
- The toxoids are prepared by treating toxin with formalin or heat.
- The antigenicity of toxoids can be potentiated by **adjuvant**. Alternatively, their activity can be enhanced by mixing them with a bacterial vaccine, for example, DPT (diphtheria, pertussis and tetanus) in which pertussis is a vaccine that potentiates the activity of diphtheria and tetanus toxoids.

Cellular fractions

- Some vaccines are prepared using extracted cellular fractions. These include the following:
  - Meningococcal vaccine prepared by using the cell wall antigen.
  - Pneumococcal vaccine is prepared by using the capsular polysaccharide.
  - Vaccine for *Haemophilus influenzae* type B is prepared by using a purified capsular polysaccharide.

Subunit vaccines

- In this, detergents or chemicals are used to split the microorganism and only the relevant antigens, which are immunogenic components, are used for vaccine preparation, for example, rabies and influenza vaccines.

Recombinant vaccines

- In this, the genes responsible for specific antigens from organisms difficult to grow in vitro are cloned in organisms such as *Escherichia,* vaccinia virus or other suitable vectors and then the antigen is obtained in large amount. The technique is known as DNA recombinant technology, for example, vaccine against hepatitis B virus and influenza virus.

Combined vaccines

- These are the vaccine preparations containing more than one immunizing agents. They are also known as mixed vaccines. These include the following:
  - DPT (diphtheria, pertussis, tetanus)
  - DT (diphtheria, tetanus)
  - DP (diphtheria, pertussis)
  - MMR (mumps, measles, rubella)
  - DPTP (DPT + polio)

Advantages

- To simplify administration
- To reduce costs
- To minimize the number of injections and contact with health system

Immunization programme

A routine immunization programme for immunizing children against common infectious diseases have been developed for different countries and modified from time to time based on

- The prevalence of infectious diseases
- The public health importance of infectious diseases
- Availability of suitable vaccines
- Cost-benefit factors

The diseases against which routine immunization is advised in India include the following:

- Tuberculosis
- Diphtheria
- Pertussis
- Tetanus
- Poliomyelitis
- Measles
- Hepatitis

National immunization programme

The national immunization programme in India is depicted in Table 20.1.

- Two doses of Japanese encephalitis (JE) lyophilized vaccine are recommended at

Table 20.1 National immunization programme in India

Visit	Age	Vaccine
01	At birth	BCG OPV Hepatitis B
02	6 weeks	DPT-1 OPV-1 Hepatitis B BCG if not given earlier
03	10 weeks	DPT-2 OPV-2 Hepatitis B
04	14 weeks	DPT-3 OPV-3 Hepatitis B
05	9 months	Measles
06	16–24 months	DPT OPV
07	School entry (5–6 years)	DT
08	10 years	TT
09	16 years	TT
10	Pregnancy	TT two doses

BCG, Bacille Calmette–Guerin; *DT*, diphtheria, tetanus; *DPT*, diphtheria, pertussis and tetanus; *OPV*, oral polio vaccine; *TT*, tetanus toxoid.

9–12 months of age and 6–24 months of age in selected high disease burden districts.

- Three doses of *Haemophilus influenzae B* (Hib) given as pentavalent vaccine containing Hib + DPT + Hep B are recommended at 6, 10 and 14 weeks of age in selected states.
  - This is a routine immunization programme. In addition to these vaccines, other vaccines may also be given along with these routine vaccines. These include the following:
    - Rotavirus vaccine
    - Injectable polio vaccine
    - MMR vaccine
    - Varicella vaccine
    - Hepatitis A vaccine
    - Typhoid vaccine
    - Pneumococcal conjugate vaccine
    - Influenza vaccine

BCG

- **Preparation** It is a live attenuated vaccine prepared by *Calmette* and *Guerin* in 1921 by using attenuated strain of *Mycobacterium bovis.*
- **Dose** It is given soon after the birth in a dose of 0.1 mL. Booster doses are not necessary as tuberculosis is common in India. Natural infections maintain immunity but in developed countries where tuberculosis is not common, the booster dose may be indicated at school entry.
- **Route of administration** Intradermally over the deltoid.
- **Protection offered** It gives protection against tuberculosis for about 10 years.
- **Advantages** It stimulates T lymphocytes, it may offer protection against leprosy and leukaemia.
- **Type of immunity** CMI.
- **Contraindications** Contraindicated in patients of
  - AIDS
  - Measles
  - Pertussis
  - Eczema
  - Patients on steroids
- **Complications** Occasional complications include the following:
  - Local complications—abscess, keloid formation and indolent ulcer
  - Regional complications—lymphadenitis
  - Systemic complications—fever, mediastinal adenitis and erythema nodosum

DPT

- **Preparation** Prepared by mixing the toxoids of D and T and a killed suspension of pertussis bacilli.
- **Doses** DPT is given at the age of 6 weeks as the children are protected by maternal antibodies. Three doses are given at an interval of 4–6 weeks. Booster dose is given at 18 months. Diphtheria and pertussis are uncommon after

5 years, hence only booster dose of tetanus is given at school entry and thereafter also.

- **Route of administration** Intramuscularly.
- **Protection offered** Diphtheria, pertussis and tetanus are the important diseases of childhood. DPT gives protection against these infectious diseases.
- **Advantages** It not only minimizes the number of injections but also improves immune response as pertussis acts as an adjuvant for D and T toxoids.
- **Type of immunity** Antibody mediated.
- **Complications** Rarely neurological complications such as encephalopathy and convulsions may occur.

OPV

- **Preparation** Prepared by Sabin in 1962. It is a live attenuated vaccine prepared by attenuating strains of poliovirus types 1, 2 and 3.
- **Doses** In developed countries, three doses are sufficient to induce satisfactory immune response. However, in developing countries like India, more doses are required (up to 5) as seroconversion is poor because of
  - Poor potency of vaccine
  - Improper storage
  - Interference by other enteroviruses in gut
  - Neutralization by antibodies in breast milk
- **Route of administration** Oral.
- **Protection offered** Lifelong protection against poliomyelitis.
- **Type of immunity** Local intestinal immunity—antibody-mediated.
- **Contraindications** Include the following:
  - Immunodeficiencies
  - Immunosuppression

Measles vaccine

- **Preparation** It is a live attenuated vaccine prepared by attenuating strains of measles virus.
- **Dose** A single injection is given at the age of 9 months. Booster dose is not necessary.
- **Route of administration** Subcutaneously.
- **Protection offered** It is very effective in prophylaxis and gives lifelong protection against measles.
- **Type of immunity** Antibody-mediated immunity.
- **Contraindications** Include the following:
  - Any febrile illness
  - Immunodeficiencies and AIDS
  - Untreated active tuberculosis
  - Malignancies
  - Immunosuppression
  - Pregnancy

Other vaccines

Other vaccines such as typhoid, cholera, influenza virus and rabies are given during or before expected outbreak of the particular disease or when an individual is at risk of getting infection, for example, rabies vaccine after dog bite.

Immunotherapy (passive immunization)

For this purpose, immunoglobulins and antisera are used.

Immunoglobulins

Immunoglobulins are of two types:

1. Normal human immunoglobulins
2. Specific human immunoglobulins

Normal human immunoglobulins

- It is an antibody rich fraction derived from blood, plasma or serum of human donors.
- It is obtained from a pool of at least thousand donors.
- The preparation contains high levels of appropriate antibody mainly IgG.

Uses

- It is used to prevent measles in highly susceptible individuals and to provide temporary protection.
- It is also used against hepatitis A infection for travellers to endemic area and to contacts of cases of hepatitis A in an outbreak.
- Its use has also been suggested in immunodeficiency diseases.

Specific human immunoglobulins

These are prepared from serum or plasma of convalescent individuals (patients who have recently recovered from infection) or those who have been hyperimmunized with a specific antigen. These preparations contain high level of specific antibodies.

Examples

- – Rabies immunoglobulin
- – Hepatitis B immunoglobulin
- – Tetanus immunoglobulin
- – Pertussis immunoglobulin
- – Rh (D) immunoglobulin
- – Varicella zoster immunoglobulin

- These are usually injected by intramuscular route.
- Peak blood levels are attained in 2 days after intramuscular injection.
- The average half-life is 20–35 days and protection may last up to 3 months or more.
- They should not be given before or after active immunization.

Antisera and antitoxins

- The term antiserum is applied to materials prepared in animals, usually horses.
- The antiserum is prepared by injecting specific antigen that leads to formation of specific immunoglobulin.
- Antitoxin is prepared by injecting toxin or toxoid.
- Examples of antitoxins—tetanus, diphtheria, gas gangrene, botulinum and snake venom antitoxin.
- Examples of antisera—rabies antiserum and antilymphocyte serum.
- Route of administration—parenteral route.
- The half-life of antisera is half of the human immunoglobulin and elimination occurs rapidly than human immunoglobulin.
- Antisera and antitoxins are used only in clinical situations in which there is no alternative because they present the problem of possible hypersensitivity reactions such as development of anaphylaxis or serum sickness.

Self-assessment

Short answer questions

Write notes on

1. Live vaccines
2. Toxoid
3. Killed vaccines
4. Recombinant vaccines
5. National immunization programme
6. Normal human immunoglobulin
7. Specific human immunoglobulin
8. Antisera and antitoxins
9. BCG
10. DPT
11. Oral polio vaccine
12. Measles vaccine

Multiple choice questions

1. Which of the following is NOT an example of live vaccine?
   A. Typhoral vaccine for enteric fever
   B. Salk vaccine for polio
   C. Measles vaccine for measles
   D. Bacille Calmette–Guerin vaccine for tuberculosis
2. Which of the following is NOT an example of killed vaccine?
   A. Sabin vaccine for polio
   B. Cholera vaccine

C. TAB vaccine for enteric fever
D. Rabies vaccine

3. Which of the following statements is FALSE regarding the live vaccines?
   A. Preparations containing live microbes with reduced virulence
   B. Risk of reversion of virulence
   C. Immunity developed is less as compared to killed vaccine
   D. Initiate an infection without causing disease

4. Which of the following statements is FALSE regarding the killed vaccines?
   A. There is no multiplication of microbes
   B. There is no risk of reversion of virulence
   C. Immunity developed is less as compared to live vaccine
   D. Initiate an infection without causing disease

5. Which of the following is an example of recombinant vaccine?
   A. Rabies vaccine
   B. Salk vaccine
   C. Measles vaccine
   D. Hepatitis B vaccine

6. Which of the following vaccines is given at the age of 9 months?
   A. Bacille Calmette–Guerin vaccine
   B. Oral polio vaccine
   C. Measles vaccine
   D. DPT

7. Which of the following statements is FALSE regarding the DPT vaccine?
   A. Is prepared by mixing the toxoids of D and T and a killed suspension of pertussis bacilli
   B. Is given intramuscularly
   C. Minimizes the number of injections and also improves immune response
   D. Is given at the age of 6 months

8. Which of the following statements is FALSE regarding the BCG vaccine?
   A. Is a killed vaccine
   B. Is given intradermally over the deltoid
   C. Gives protection against tuberculosis for about 10 years
   D. Is given soon after the birth

21 Normal Flora of the Mouth and Respiratory Tract

A variety of microorganisms are normally present on or in our body. The population of microorganisms regularly present is known as 'natural', 'indigenous', or 'normal flora' or normal microbiota'. The normal flora is the part and parcel of the host and includes the following:

- Saprophytes
- Commensals
- Facultative pathogens
- True pathogens (occasionally)

Most microorganisms normally present are commensals that exist in a symbiotic association with the host and obtain their nutrients from the secretions and waste products of the body.

Normal flora of the oral cavity

Despite the activity of antibacterial substances such as lysozyme and peroxidase in saliva, the mouth has more complex and mixed flora. The normal oral microflora is a complex mixture of bacteria, fungi and protozoa. Occasionally, viruses are also present as a part of normal flora.

The abundant moisture and the presence of small food particles provide an ideal environment for microbial growth. The normal oral flora is not static, and it is divided into two types:

1. **Constant flora** Organisms which are almost always present in a normal oral cavity.
2. **Transient flora** Organisms which stay for a short duration in the oral cavity of a few individuals. It is a variable flora and may include both pathogens and non-pathogens.

Bacterial flora

- Bacterial flora is the most predominant flora in the oral cavity; 500–600 different kinds of bacteria are present in the mouth.
- Both aerobes and anaerobes are present normally. These include the following organisms:

Aerobic bacterial flora

- Micrococci—most common
- Staphylococci—*Staphylococcus albus* is the commonest; *Staph. aureus* is also present
- Streptococci
  - Non-haemolytic streptococci such as *Streptococcus faecalis*
  - Alpha-haemolytic streptococci—*Str. salivarius* is the most common, followed by *Str. mitis, Str. sanguis, Str. milleri, Str. gordonii, Str. mutans* and *Str. oralis*
  - *Enterococcus* spp
- Gram-negative bacilli—include members of the *Coliform* and *Proteus* group, *Haemophilus* species such as *H. aphrophilus,*

H. parainfluenzae, H. paraphrophilus, H. segnis and *Campylobacter* species
- Gram-negative cocci—*Neisseria* species, *Moraxella* species
- Gram-positive bacilli—*Bacillus* species and *Corynebacterium* species
- *Mycoplasma* species—*Mycoplasma salivarium* is common
- *Nocardia* species

Anaerobic bacterial flora

- Gram-negative cocci—*Veillonella* species such as *V. parvula, V. dispar* and *V. atypical* are also present. These are the first to appear and the most numerous
- Gram-positive cocci—peptococci, peptostreptococci
- Gram-negative bacilli
  - *Bacteroides* species such as *B. oralis, B. gingivalis, B. denticola, B. intermedius, B. oris, B. buccae, B. endodontalis* and many other species
  - *Prevotella melaninogenicus*
  - *Fusobacterium* species—*F. nucleatum* is the most common
  - *Leptotrichia* species
  - *Porphyromonas* spp.
  - *Capnocytophaga* spp.
  - *Wolinella* species
  - *Selemonas* species, etc.
- Gram-positive bacilli
  - Lactobacilli such as *L. acidophilus, L. salivarius, L. fermentum, L. casei* and many other species
  - *Actinomyces* species—*A. odontolyticus, A. viscosus*
  - *Arachania* species
  - *Propionibacterium* species
  - *Bifidobacterium* species
  - *Eubacterium* species, etc.
- Non-pathogenic spirochaetes—which are almost invariably present between the gums and the teeth. These include *Treponema buccalis, T. dentium, T. intermedium, T. microdentium* and *T. macrodentium*
- Microaerophilic spirochaetes—*Borrelia vincentii* is normal commensal in mouth but it is a potential pathogen
- Other bacteria normally present in the mouth are
  - *Stomatococcus*—Gram-positive cocci
  - *Campylobacter* spp.—Gram-negative bacilli
  - *Rothia*—Gram-positive bacilli
  - *Actinobacillus spp.*—Gram-negative bacilli
  - *Eikenella spp.*—Gram-negative bacilli
  - *Selenomonas spp.*—Gram-negative bacilli

Fungal flora

- *Candida* species—*C. albicans* is the commonest fungus found in the mouth. *C. tropicalis, C. stellatoidea* and *C. pseudotropicalis* are the other species normally found in the oral cavity. Cryptococci are also present normally.

Protozoal flora

Among the protozoa, *Entamoeba gingivalis* and *Trichomonas tenax* are normally present in the oral cavity.

Viral flora

Viruses are not normally present in the oral cavity. Some viruses such as herpes viruses, myxoviruses, hepatitis B virus and human immunodeficiency virus (HIV) are found in the mouth or saliva during active infections or during asymptomatic carrier stage, which are not considered as resident normal flora.

Acquisition of normal oral flora

- An infant's mouth is microbiologically sterile at birth but becomes colonized shortly within few hours after birth with streptococci, staphylococci, lactobacilli and coliform bacteria.
- With the increase in age, kind and amount of microflora increases dramatically.

- The maternal vagina, the upper respiratory tract of mother and birth attendants and the environment are the sources of colonizing organisms.
- During the first year of life when no teeth are present, the oral flora mainly consists of aerotolerent anaerobic organisms such as streptococci and lactobacilli, which are predominantly seen with other bacteria including some aerobes in small numbers.
- *Str. salivarius* and *Str. mitis* are the first to colonize, which alter the environment of mouth making it favourable for colonization by other organisms such as *Veillonella* species, other streptococci, staphylococci, *Neisseria* species, lactobacilli, Actinomyces and fusobacteria.
- When teeth appear and the solid surface becomes available, the flora becomes more anaerobic, that is, especially adapted for growth on teeth surface and gingival crevices. *Str. mutans, Str. sanguis,* Actinomyces along with anaerobic organisms such as anaerobic streptococci and anaerobic Gram-negative bacilli become established on hard dental tissues.
- With adolescence, spirochetes and *Bacteroides* species appear as normal flora.
- With the loss of teeth, the flora again changes and reverts to pre-eruption days.
- The use of artificial dentures favours colonization by organisms, which are able to colonize hard surfaces.

Normal flora of respiratory tract

- The lower respiratory tract is normally sterile and generally no microbes are present.
- The upper respiratory tract is normally heavily colonized.
- Non-pathogenic corynebacteria are the organisms most frequently and most constantly present in the nose.
- The nose is also the natural home of *Staph. aureus.*
- Other organisms, normally present, are
  - *Staph. epidermidis*
  - *Str. viridans*
  - *Neisseria catarrhalis*
  - *Moraxella lacunata*
  - *Haemophilus* species

In throat

- *Str. viridans* and *Neisseria catarrhalis* are commonly present.
- Pneumococci and Friedlander's bacilli are also frequently seen.
- Nasopharynx is a natural habitat of the common pathogens causing infections of the nose, throat, bronchi and lungs.
- *Pseudomonas aeruginosa, E. coli* and *Proteus* species may also be seen occasionally in normal individuals.

Advantages of normal oral flora

The normal microbial flora of oral cavity is beneficial to the host in the following ways:

- They prevent or interfere with colonization/invasion by exogenous pathogenic organisms. This exclusion may be by simple competition with the pathogen, for example, prevention of colonization *of Str. pneumoniae* by *Str. mutans,* prevention of colonization *of Str. pyogenes, Corynebacterium diphtheriae, Staph. aureus* and *E. coli* by *Str. mitior* or by producing inhibitory substances by the organisms normally present in the mouth, for example, hydrogen peroxide by streptococci, enocin by *Str. salivarius* or by producing cross-reacting antibodies.
- The organisms normally present in the mouth produce the vitamins, for example, vitamin K and riboflavin and cofactors. They also produce certain nutrients and thus contribute in the nutrition of the host.
- They help in digestion of food by producing digestive enzymes such as amylase, lipase and protease.

- The organisms of normal flora increase the overall immune status of the host against pathogens having related or shared antigens.

Disadvantages of normal flora

- The organisms of normal flora can become pathogenic and cause disease when resistance of the host is lowered.
- They cause confusion in the diagnosis.
- They can aggravate infection, for example, penicillinase-producing bacteria can aggravate infection by interfering with the therapy.

Self-assessment

Short-answer questions

Write notes on

1. Normal flora of the oral cavity
2. Aerobic bacterial flora of the oral cavity
3. Anaerobic bacterial flora of the oral cavity
4. Normal flora of the respiratory tract
5. Advantages of normal oral flora

Multiple-choice questions

1. Which of the following alpha-haemolytic streptococci is most commonly found in the mouth as a normal flora?
   A. *Streptococcus milleri*
   B. *Str. mutans*
   C. *Str. sanguis*
   D. *Str. Salivarius*
2. Which of the following anaerobes is the first to appear in the mouth as a normal flora?
   A. *Veillonella* species
   B. *Bacteroides* species
   C. *Fusobacterium* species
   D. *Leptotrichia* species
3. Which of the following protozoan parasites is found as normal flora of the mouth?
   A. *Trichomonas hominis*
   B. *Endolimax nana*
   C. *Entamoeba gingivalis*
   D. *Leptotrichia* species
4. Which of the following microbes is most frequently and most constantly present in the nose?
   A. *Staphylococcus aureus*
   B. Non-pathogenic corynebacteria
   C. *Haemophilus* species
   D. *Neisseria catarrhalis*
5. Which of the following is occasionally present as a part of normal flora?
   A. Saprophytes
   B. Commensals
   C. True pathogens
   D. Facultative pathogens

22 Laboratory Diagnosis of Bacterial Diseases

Collection of specimens

The first and most important step in a diagnosis is collection of specimen. Different specimens are collected in different diseases based on the site of infection.

General considerations for specimen collection

- Appropriate specimen should be selected based on the site of infection, for example, urine in urinary tract infection, sputum in respiratory tract infection, stool in intestinal tract infection and pus in pyogenic infection.
- Specimens should be obtained before starting or altering antibiotic therapy.
- Specimens should be collected from the site where the suspected organism is most likely to be found.
- Specimens should be obtained while avoiding external contamination as much as possible.
- Sufficient quantity of specimen should be collected to allow complete examination.
- It should be collected in a sterile container.
- It should be correctly labelled and accompanied by a statement of the patient's symptoms, clinical diagnosis, current antimicrobial therapy, date and time of collection of the specimen and clinical details of the patient (and other relevant information if necessary, to select proper investigative procedures).
- Information regarding the risk of infection (hepatitis B, HIV, etc.) associated with handling of the specimen, if necessary.
- Appropriate specimen based on site of infection should be collected with the help of sterile cotton swab, syringe, catheter, etc.

Collection procedure for different specimens

Collection of urine

As urethra and perineum are normally colonized, specimens of urine are frequently contaminated with normal flora from urethra and perineum. Contamination can be prevented by using the following:

Clean-catch midstream urine collection

- It is the most convenient and most commonly used method for urine collection.
- In this method, the periurethral area (i.e., tip of penis, labial folds and vulva) is carefully cleaned with two separate washes of soap and water or mild detergent.
- It is then well rinsed with sterile warm water to remove detergent.

- The first portion of voiding is discarded and the subsequent midstream urine is voided directly into a sterile wide-mouth container and is used for culture and other investigations.
- For diagnosis of tuberculosis of the urinary tract, early morning specimens are collected on 3 consecutive days in sterile containers and preserved in refrigerator till they are examined. An alternative is collection for 24-hour sample of the urine.
- Specimen of urine can also be obtained by catheterization or suprapubic aspiration.

Collection of genital tract specimens

- A sterile bivalve speculum moistened with warm water is inserted.
- Specimen is collected with the help of cotton swab from cervix (cervical swab).
- Swabs are also taken from urethra in urethritis and vagina in vaginitis.

Collection of cerebrospinal fluid (CSF)

CSF is collected in a sterile container by lumbar puncture under aseptic conditions before the administration of antibiotics. Preferably, CSF should be collected in three different tubes: one for cells count, one for biochemical examination and one for culture. If a delay is expected then CSF for culture is collected into glucose broth and incubated to avoid death of some organisms at freezing temperature.

Collection of stool

- Collect in a plastic or waxed container and transport immediately.
- If a delay of more than 2–4 hours is expected, then it should be collected in a suitable transport medium such as
  - Cary–Blair transport medium
  - Stuart's transport medium
- If a stool sample is not available, a rectal swab can be taken.

Collection of sputum

- Specimen of sputum should be obtained from a deep cough (tracheobronchial sputum).
- A morning sample of sputum should be collected in a wide-mouth container.
- If tuberculosis is suspected, a morning specimen should be collected on 3 successive days.

Collection of throat swab

- The tongue is depressed, exposed and illuminated.
- A swab is then rubbed firmly over the back of the throat (posterior pharynx), tonsils, tonsillar fossae and other areas of inflammation, exudation or ulceration.
- Touching of the swab with tongue, cheeks, lips, etc., should be avoided.
- The swab is placed in a sterile test tube and sterile saline is added to prevent drying.
- If a delay is expected, the swab is collected in a suitable transport medium such as Stuart's medium.

Collection of serous fluids

- Serous fluids—pleural, synovial, ascitic fluids—should be collected in a sterile container with citrate to prevent clotting.

Collection of pus

- A specimen of pus is collected with the help of sterile cotton swab in a sterile test tube.
- It is transported immediately for processing.
- If a delay is unavoidable, it should be collected in a suitable transport medium (Stuart's transport medium).

Collection of blood

- Two per cent tincture iodine is applied to the skin over the area of vein.
- Allow it to dry.

- Remove the iodine with the help of sponges saturated with 80% isopropyl alcohol.
- The entire procedure is repeated.
- Apply tourniquet.
- Collect 10 mL of blood with the help of sterile syringe and needle.
- The blood should be diluted to inactivate antimicrobial component present in the blood. Minimum dilution of blood required is 1:10. Hence, 5 mL of blood is collected in 50 mL of glucose broth and another 5 mL of blood is collected in 50 mL of bile broth (total 10 mL of blood is collected as the number of organisms in the blood may be very less, may be one per mL).
- When the broth media are not available, the blood should be collected with an anticoagulant such as sodium polyanethol sulphonate (SPS) also known as Liquoid in the concentrations of 0.025–0.035%.
- Transported immediately for incubation at 37°C.

Collection of specimens from oral cavity

Specimens from sites such as dorsum of the tongue, lateral sides of the tongue, buccal fold, soft and hard palate, labial gingival, and tonsils of soft tissue surfaces are collected with the help of sterile swab brushes. Supragingival and subgingival plaque samples are collected with a sterile Gracey curette. Specimen from root canal is collected aseptically by using sterile paper points. If the canal is dry, it is moistened first with sterile fluid and then the specimen is collected. The specimen collected with the help of paper points is placed in a suitable anaerobic transport media, for example, Robertson's cooked meat medium or thioglycollate broth and then transported.

Transport of specimens

- Delays in transportation to laboratory may cause
  - Death of delicate organisms
  - Overgrowth of other organisms
- Specimen should be transported immediately.
- If a delay is inevitable, specimens should be collected in a suitable transport media such as Stuart's transport medium or Cary–Blair transport medium. Alternatively, it can be collected in a special container to avoid death during transport.
- Specimens should be transported in leak-proof containers as per the safety guidelines.

Direct microscopy

Wet mount

- Specimens can be observed directly, for example, urine or in an emulsified suspension, for example, stool
- Used to assess and enumerate inflammatory cells, for examination of urine deposits, bacterial motility, etc.

Hanging drop preparation

- To study motility of *Vibrio cholerae* in stool samples
- To study motility of fluid cultures

Gram stain

Gram stain is performed routinely

- To reveal the shape and size of bacteria
- To classify organisms into four categories:
  - Gram-positive cocci
  - Gram-positive bacilli
  - Gram-negative cocci
  - Gram-negative bacilli

Gram stain gives a clue to plan further diagnostic techniques and therapy.

Ziehl–Neelsen stain

Z–N stain is performed on specimens, including sputum, urine, pus, etc., when infections by mycobacteria are suspected.

Other special staining techniques

- Number of other techniques can be used for identification of different bacteria.
- These include the following:
  - Fluorescent microscopy for tubercle bacilli
  - Dark ground microscopy for *Treponema pallidum*
  - India ink (negative staining) for capsulated bacteria
  - Albert's and Neisser's stain for *Corynebacterium diphtheriae*
  - Spore staining for sporulating bacteria
  - Direct immunofluorescence stain, etc.

Culture

Culture is the most reliable method for confirming the diagnosis and regulating the treatment by performing antibiotic susceptibility tests. Most of the medically important bacteria grow in vitro on artificial media.

Media for culture

- Majority of pathogenic bacteria grow on blood agar—the most widely used culture media.
- Routinely, a specimen is inoculated on blood agar and MacConkey's agar.
- If indicated, various selective media are used. These are detailed in Table 22.1.
- Inoculated media are incubated aerobically for 12–24 hours (up to 48 hours).
- For anaerobic organisms, methods of anaerobiosis (inoculated plates are placed in McIntosh-Filde's jar or gas-pak jar and incubated for 48–72 hours) are used.

Identification

The organisms grown in culture are identified based on the following:

- Growth characteristics, for example, aerobic or anaerobic

Table 22.1 Selective media used for culture

Name of selective media	Uses
Chocolate agar	For *Haemophilus influenzae, Neisseria* species
Deoxycholate citrate agar	For *Salmonella* and *Shigella* species
TCBS agar	For *Vibrio cholerae*
Wilson and Blair's medium	For *Salmonella* species
Lowenstein–Jensen medium	For mycobacteria
Robertson's cooked meat medium	For anaerobes
Other selective media	As required

TCBS, thiosulfate-citrate-bile salts-sucrose.

- Colony morphology—helps in presumptive identification of most of the pathogenic bacteria
- Microscopic examination of colony smear
- Standard biochemical tests include the following:
  - Sugar fermentation reactions, for example, fermentation of glucose, lactose, sucrose, mannitol and other sugars. These reactions are observed for acid and gas production
  - Indole production
  - Methyl red test
  - Voges–Proskauer test
  - Citrate utilization test
  - H_2S production
  - Oxidase test
  - Catalase test
  - Urease test

Serological tests

- Serological tests are useful in the diagnosis of infections in which causative agent is difficult to culture, for example, *Treponema pallidum*, *Mycoplasma pneumoniae* and *Chlamydiae*.
- Diagnosis is done on the basis of detection of specific antibody to the infectious agent.

- Active infection is diagnosed by demonstrating specific IgM or a fourfold increase in IgG antibodies in paired sera taken 10–14 days apart.
- The commonly used serological tests in different bacterial infections are as follows:
  - Agglutination test, for example, Widal test in enteric fever, *Brucella* agglutination test in brucellosis
  - Complement fixation test for diagnosis of 'Q' fever, syphilis, etc.
  - Flocculation test, for example, venereal disease research laboratory (VDRL) test for syphilis
  - Indirect immunofluorescence test—for antibody detection in syphilis, *Legionella*, *Mycoplasma*, *Borrelia* and other infections
  - Enzyme-linked immunosorbent assay (ELISA) and radioimmunoassay (RIA) test are also used for detection of antibodies in a number of bacterial infections

Detection of pathogen-specific molecules

Detection of bacterial antigens

- Different tests are used for detection of bacterial antigens. These are given in detail in Table 22.2.

Molecular detection of microorganisms

- Nucleic acid probe tests and polymerase chain reaction (PCR) are used for molecular detection of microorganisms.
- These tests are highly sensitive and are particularly important in the identification of organisms that are difficult or slow to grow.

Antimicrobial susceptibility testing

Susceptibility testing to different antimicrobial agents is important to institute rational antimicrobial therapy. This is a very important test to guide the therapy, particularly in cases not responding to routine antibiotic therapy or in infections caused by drug-resistant pathogens. Susceptibility testing methods used commonly are

- Disc diffusion method—the most commonly used
- Dilution methods

Disc diffusion method

Principle The placing of a filter paper disc (measuring 6 mm in diameter) containing a known amount of an antimicrobial agent on the agar surface, previously inoculated with

Table 22.2 Different tests used for detection of bacterial antigens

Name of test	Bacterial antigen detected
Precipitation reactions such as Elek's test	Diphtheria toxin
Latex agglutination test	Detection of soluble antigen in specimens such as urine, CSF and serum in infections due to *Haemophilus influenzae*, streptococci (group A and B) and *Neisseria* species
Coagglutination test	Detection of antigen in streptococcal, pneumococcal, neisserial, *Salmonella*, *H. influenzae* and other infections
ELISA test	Detection of antigen in various bacterial infections
Slide agglutination test	For identification and confirmation of bacteria grown in culture

CSF, cerebrospinal fluid; *ELISA*, enzyme-linked immunosorbent assay.

bacterium to be tested, will result in a zone of inhibition of growth around the disc. Following two methods are used:

1. Kirby–Bauer disc diffusion method
2. Stoke's disc diffusion method

Kirby–Bauer disc diffusion method

- It is a simple and reliable method applicable in routine clinical bacteriology.
- **Requirements**
  - ***Discs of antimicrobial agents***—discs of a standard filter paper charged with appropriate concentration of the antimicrobial agents
  - ***Culture medium***—which supports the growth of most of the organisms. The following media are used:
    - Mueller–Hinton agar
    - Nutrient agar
    - Blood agar/chocolate agar—for fastidious bacteria, which do not grow on nutrient agar
  - **Inoculum** of test bacterium in a suitable broth medium (e.g., peptone water). For preparation of inoculum, pure culture of the organism is inoculated into a broth medium and incubated at 37°C for 2–4 hours.
- **Procedure**
  - A standardized inoculum is inoculated with the help of a sterile cotton swab on the surface of the agar plate.
  - Discs of antimicrobial agents are placed on the surface of agar plate.
  - The plates are incubated at 37°C for 16–18 hours and susceptibility is determined based on the zone of inhibition (Fig. 22.1).
  - A standard control strain is also tested for comparison.
- **Interpretation** The diameters of the zones of growth inhibition around each disc are measured and compared with zones of inhibition of the standard control strain and results are interpreted as follows:
  - ***Sensitive*** When zone diameter of the test organism is greater than, equal to or not more than 4 mm less than that of the control strain
  - ***Moderately sensitive*** If its zone diameter is at least 12 mm but reduced by more than 4 mm as compared to the control strain
  - ***Resistant*** If it shows no zone of inhibition of growth or if the zone diameter is not more than 10 mm

Stoke's disc diffusion method

This method is similar to Kirby–Bauer disc diffusion method. The only change employed

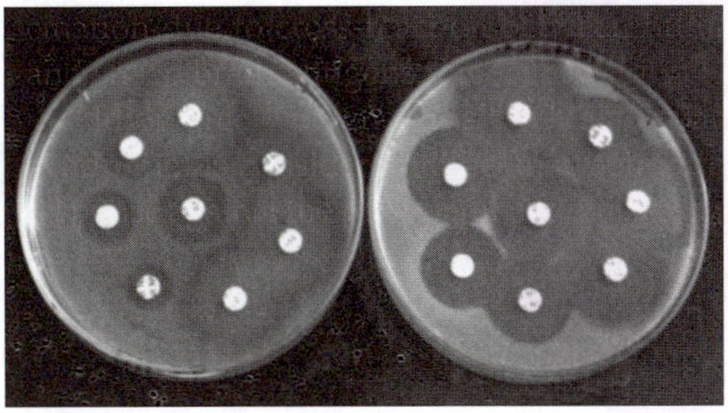

Figure 22.1 Kirby–Bauer disc diffusion method.

in this method is that the control culture and the test culture are grown on the same plate to compare the zones of inhibition produced in two cultures by the same disc.

- **Procedure**
  - The test bacterium is inoculated on middle third of the culture plate and control culture on upper and lower thirds of the plate. An uninoculated strip of about 5 mm between the test and control areas is left for placing of discs. After inoculation, discs are placed (maximum 6), three on each side between the control and test inocula.
  - The plates are incubated at 37°C for 16–18 hours and observed for zones of inhibition (Fig. 22.2).
  - The results are interpreted by measuring and comparing the zones of inhibition of control and test bacterium.
- **Dilution methods**
  - These are of two types:
    - Broth dilution test
    - Agar dilution test

Broth dilution test

- In this test, increasing concentration of antimicrobial agents is incorporated into Mueller–Hinton broth in test tubes.

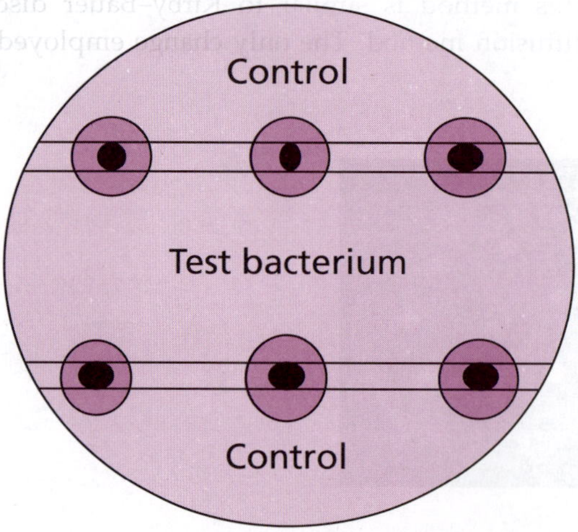

Figure 22.2 Stoke's disc diffusion method.

- The test bacterium is then added to these test tubes and incubated at 37°C for 16–18 hours.
- **Results**
  - The end point is taken as MIC (minimum inhibitory concentration)—is the amount of antimicrobial agents required to inhibit growth—and MBC (minimum bactericidal concentration)—is the amount of antimicrobial agent required to kill the bacteria.
  - The MIC is detected by noting the lowest concentration of the antimicrobial agent showing no visible growth and the MBC is detected by subculture from each tube showing no growth on a suitable medium without any antimicrobial agent.
  - For MBC, a loopful from each tube is inoculated over suitable medium and incubated at 37°C for 16–18 hours. The tube containing the lowest concentration of the antimicrobial agent that fails to show growth on the subculture is taken as MBC.
- **Uses**
  - To find out the amount of antimicrobial agent required to inhibit or kill the bacterium. It is a quantitative test.

Agar dilution test

- Serial dilutions of antimicrobial agents are prepared and 1.5 mL of each dilution is added to 13.5 mL of melted agar suspension and poured into the plates.
- In this way, plates with different concentrations are prepared.
- Bacterial pathogens to be tested can be inoculated on each plate and incubated at 37°C for 16–20 hours.
- After incubation, the results are recorded. The lowest concentration of antimicrobial agent that allows no more than one or two colonies is taken as MIC.
- **Uses**
  - To find out antimicrobial sensitivities and to determine the MIC values (Flow chart 22.1).

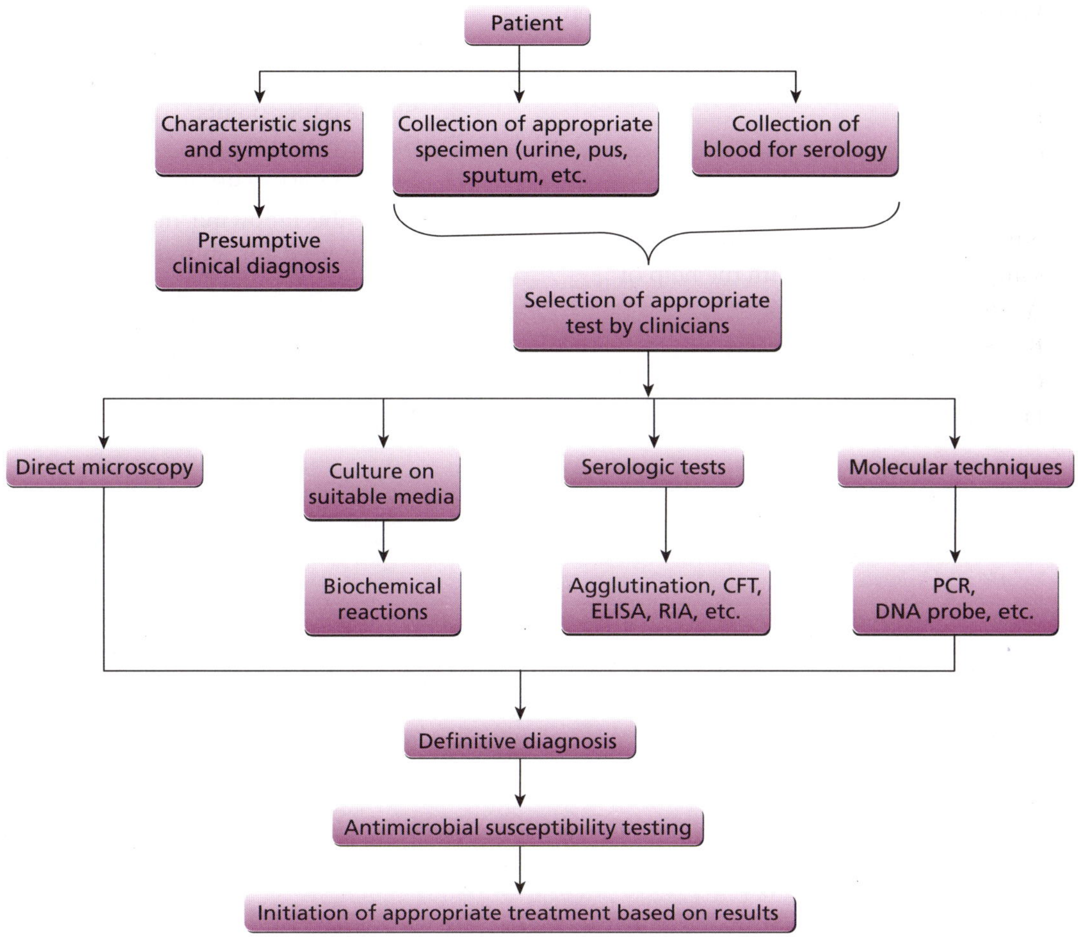

Flow chart 22.1 Summary of diagnosis of bacterial infection. *CFT*, complement fixation test; *ELISA*, enzyme-linked immunosorbent assay; *RIA*, radioimmunoassay; *PCR*, polymerase chain reaction.

Self-assessment

Long-answer question

1. Discuss in brief the methods used for collection and processing of specimens in the diagnosis of bacterial diseases.

Short-answer questions

Write notes on

1. Clean-catch midstream urine collection
2. Collection of specimens from oral cavity
3. Kirby–Bauer disc diffusion method
4. Stoke's disc diffusion method
5. Broth dilution test
6. Agar dilution test

Multiple-choice questions

1. Which of the following is the most convenient and most commonly used method for collection of urine?
   A. Catheterization
   B. Suprapubic aspiration
   C. Clean-catch method
   D. None of the above

2. Which of the following is an ideal dilution of blood required for blood culture?
   A. 1:4
   B. 1:10
   C. 1:8
   D. 1:5

3. Supragingival and subgingival plaque samples are collected with the help of
   A. Sterile swab brushes
   B. Sterile paper points
   C. Sterile cotton swab
   D. Sterile Gracey curette

4. Specimen from root canal is collected with the help of
   A. Sterile swab brushes
   B. Sterile paper points
   C. Sterile cotton swab
   D. Sterile Gracey curette

5. Which of the following methods is most commonly used for antimicrobial susceptibility testing?
   A. Disc diffusion method
   B. Agar dilution method
   C. Broth dilution method
   D. None of the above

23 Gram-Positive Cocci

Medically important Gram-positive cocci include the following:
- Staphylococci
- Streptococci
- Diplococci
- Peptococci—anaerobic Gram-positive cocci in clusters
- Peptostreptococci—anaerobic Gram-positive cocci in chains
- Micrococci—opportunistic pathogens

Staphylococci

Medically important species

The medically important species are *Staphylococcus aureus*, *Staph. epidermidis (Staph. albus)* and *Staph. saprophyticus*.
- Staphylococci are Gram-positive cocci occurring in grape-like clusters (Fig. 23.1)
- Size is 0.8–1 µm in diameter
- Non-motile, non-sporing and usually non-capsulated—some strains possess capsule
- Aerobes and facultative anaerobes
- Optimum temperature is 37°C, optimum pH is 7.5
- Cultivated on ordinary media such as nutrient agar and blood agar and selective media such as milk salt agar

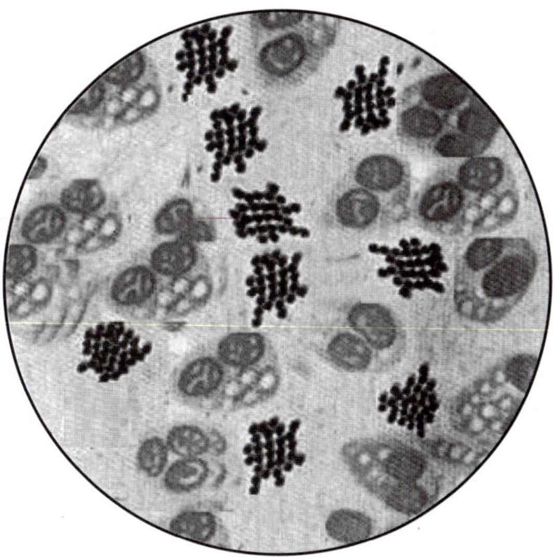

Figure 23.1 Staphylococci.

- On nutrient agar, they produce 2–3 mm, smooth, circular, opaque and pigmented colonies. Pigment formation forms the basis of their classification
- Based on pigment production and coagulase test (coagulase—an enzyme that plays role in pathogenicity), staphylococci are classified into three types (Fig. 23.2) as follows:
  - ***Staph. aureus***
    - Produces a golden-yellow pigment
    - Coagulase positive

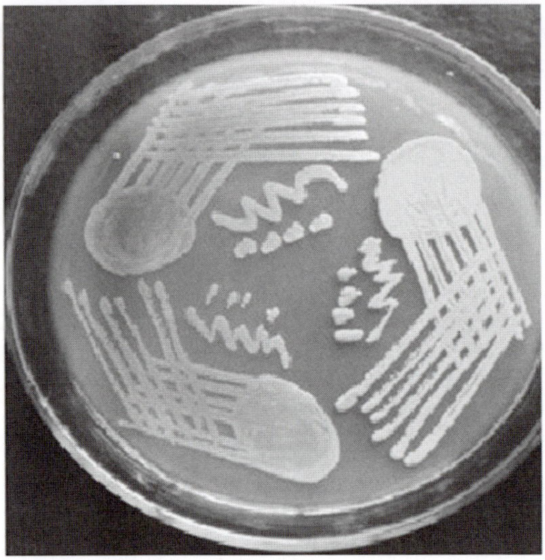

Figure 23.2 Types of pigments produced by staphylococci. *See the color image at the end of the book (Color Plates).*

  - Mannitol fermentation positive
  - Most pathogenic
- *Staph. albus*
  - Produces a white pigment
  - Coagulase negative
  - Mannitol fermentation negative
  - Less pathogenic
- *Staph. citrus*
  - Produces a lemon-yellow pigment
  - Coagulase negative
  - Mannitol fermentation negative
  - Least pathogenic

- They are relatively more resistant to physical and chemical agents. They are resistant to drying, desiccation and sunlight.
- They survive at 70°C for more than 1 hour and get destroyed at 80°C within 10–15 minutes.
- They are killed by 5% phenol in 10–15 minutes.

Staphylococcus aureus

Pathogenesis

Staph. aureus is ubiquitous in nature. It is normally present in the nose (10–30%) of healthy individuals and may also be found on the skin and hairs. It causes infections at sites with lowered host resistance, for example, damaged skin and mucous membrane.

Pathogenicity

Virulence factors

Staph. aureus produces various virulence factors. These include

- **Capsular polysaccharide**—inhibits opsonization and phagocytosis
- **Teichoic acid and protein A**—on cell wall also contribute to pathogenicity

Toxins

- **Haemolytic toxins**—alpha, beta, gamma and delta. Alpha is most important
- **Leucocidin**—produces damage to polymorphs and macrophages
- **Epidermolytic toxin**—responsible for staphylococcal scalded skin syndrome (SSSS), an exfoliative skin disease
- **Enterotoxin**—responsible for staphylococcal food poisoning
- **Toxic shock syndrome toxin (TSST)**—responsible for toxic shock syndrome

Enzymes

- **Coagulase**—causes clotting of human plasma. It acts with coagulase reacting factor present in plasma, binds to prothrombin and converts fibrinogen to fibrin
- **Lipases**—degrade lipid and help in infecting skin and subcutaneous tissue
- **Hyaluronidase**—acts on hyaluronic acid—a cementing substance of ground tissue—and facilitates spread
- **Nucleases**—degrade nucleic acid
- **Fibrinolysin or staphylokinase**—has fibrinolytic activity that helps in spreading of *Staph. aureus*

Sources of infection

- Patients, carriers and infected animals are the most important sources.
- Patients with superficial infections such as large infected wounds, burns and skin lesions and respiratory tract infections disseminate large number of staphylococci into the environment.
- Healthy carriers harbouring *Staph. aureus* on the moist skin and in nose are also the potential sources.
- Infected animals may also disseminate *Staph. aureus* and cause infection in human beings.

Modes of infection

- Body surfaces of human beings and animals are main reservoirs.
- *Staph. aureus* infection may be exogenous (from external source) or endogenous (from patient's own body, i.e., either from carriage site or from staphylococcal lesion in the body). Important modes of transmission of infection are as follows:
  - Direct contact—direct spread by doctors and nurses having discharging lesions on the hands
  - Inhalation of aerosols containing staphylococci
  - Ingestion of contaminated milk from infected animals or food articles contaminated by food handlers
  - Indirect contact—through the fomites contaminated by patients and carriers

Clinical infections

- Staphylococci enter the body through skin or mucous membrane and may further penetrate the bloodstream.
- By producing various virulence factors, they produce various clinical symptoms.
- Staphylococcal infections may be classified as follows:
  - **Cutaneous infections,** for example, carbuncles, furuncles, styes, boils, abscess, impetigo and pemphigus neonatorum, sepsis in wounds and burns
  - **Deep infections,** for example, osteomyelitis, breast abscess and abscess in other organs
  - **Respiratory tract infections,** for example, tonsillitis, pharyngitis, sinusitis and pneumonia
  - **Septicaemia**—rare but serious—may lead to meningitis, endocarditis and renal abscess
  - **Staphylococcal enterocolitis**—following the administration of broad spectrum antibiotics
  - **Staphylococcal food poisoning**—food items such as meat, milk, fish, milk products contaminated with enterotoxin producing staphylococci when ingested lead to food poisoning, characterized by nausea, vomiting, gastroenteritis, etc.
  - **Exfoliative skin diseases**—bullous impetigo, pemphigus neonatorum, toxic epidermal necrolysis and Ritter disease
  - **Toxic shock syndrome (TSS)**—characterized by fever, hypotension, vomiting, diarrhoea and scarlatiniform rash
  - **Nosocomial infections**—infections in hospitalized patients—staphylococci are the important and most common causative agents
  - **Oral manifestations**—staphylococci are involved in the pyogenic granuloma of the oral cavity—the lesions appear on the gingiva, lips, tongue and buccal mucosa

Laboratory diagnosis

- **Collection of specimens**—based on type of lesions
  - Pus—in pyogenic infections (wounds, burns, abscesses, etc.)
  - Sputum—in respiratory tract infections
  - Blood—in septicaemia, osteomyelitis, endocarditis, etc.

  - Stool—in food poisoning
  - Urine—in urinary tract infections
- **Direct microscopy**—useful with pus
  - Gram stain shows Gram-positive cocci in clusters
- **Culture**—on blood agar
  - In case of faeces—selective media—salt milk agar is used
  - Growth on culture—observed for Gram-positive cocci in clusters
  - Coagulase test is performed to differentiate them from coagulase negative staphylococci; two methods are used:
    - *Slide coagulase test* Detects clumping factor (bound coagulase). This test is performed by mixing emulsified suspension of staphylococcal colonies with a drop of undiluted rabbit or human plasma and observed for prompt clumping, which indicates positive test. No clumpin g indicates negative test.
    - *Tube coagulase test* Detects real coagulase (free coagulase) hence commonly used. The test is performed by mixing 0.1 mL of an overnight broth culture or an agar suspension of staphylococcal colonies with 1:5 dilution of rabbit or human plasma and observed for plasma clot after 3–6 hours of incubation at 37°C in a water bath. Formation of plasma clot that does not allow flowing of plasma when tube is inverted is considered as positive test. No plasma clot indicates negative test.

Antibiotic sensitivity testing by disc diffusion method is performed to guide the treatment as multiple antibiotic resistance is common.

Treatment

- Benzyl penicillin—most effective if the strain is sensitive and patient is not hypersensitive
- Other antibiotics
  - Methicillin, Cloxacillin, Flucloxacillin } For strains resistant to penicillin
  - Vancomycin—for strains resistant to methicillin
  - Cephalosporins
  - Aminoglycosides
  - Clindamycin
  - Fluoroquinolones
  - Macrolides
  - Tetracycline
  - Chloramphenicol

Staphylococcus epidermidis

- It is coagulase-negative staphylococci, normally present on the skin.
- Usually, non-pathogenic and contaminant present on the skin.
- May act as an opportunistic pathogen when the host immunity is lowered or there is an indwelling medical device/implant (intravascular catheters, prosthetic heart valve on which they may colonize and grow.
- They are associated with minor infections such as stitch abscesses, urinary tract infections, endodontitis, peritonitis, bacteraemia and septicaemia in individuals with defective resistance or structural abnormality. It also causes subacute endocarditis.
- It is also an important cause of hospital-acquired infections.

Staphylococcus saprophyticus

- It is coagulase-negative staphylococci.
- Normally present on the skin and in the periurethral region.
- Causes urinary tract infections in young, sexually active women.

Micrococci

- These are Gram-positive cocci in clusters, may occur in groups of four or eight cocci and are larger than staphylococci.

- They are catalase positive and coagulase negative.
- They are saprophytes and commensals and may cause opportunistic infections.

Streptococci

- These are Gram-positive cocci arranged in chains (Fig. 23.3)
- Size is 0.5–1 µm in diameter
- Non-motile and non-sporing
- Some strains have capsule
- They require blood agar and chocolate agar for their growth and are not cultivable on nutrient agar
- They require 5–10% CO_2 for their growth
- On blood agar they produce three types of haemolysis: alpha, beta and gamma
  - ***Alpha haemolysis*** It is a partial haemolysis, greenish zone, 1–2 mm in width, for example, *Streptococcus viridans*
  - ***Beta haemolysis*** It is a zone of complete haemolysis, clear zone, 2–4 mm in width, for example, *Str. pyogenes*
  - ***Gamma haemolysis*** It means no haemolysis and it does not produce any change in media, for example, faecal streptococci

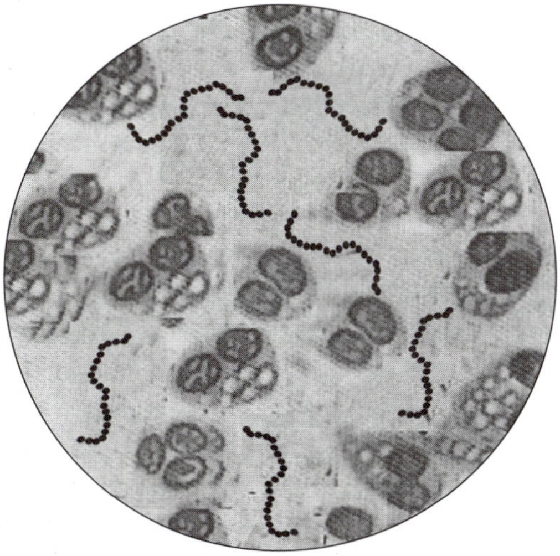

Figure 23.3 Streptococci.

- **Classification** Based on oxygen requirement and haemolysis, they are classified into different groups as given in Flow chart 23.1. *Str. pyogenes,* medically most important species, belongs to Lancefield group A
- Streptococci in general are sensitive to heat (54°C for 30 minutes) and antiseptics but relatively more resistant to crystal violet

Streptococcus pyogenes

Virulence factors

- **Antigens**
  - ***Capsular antigen***—present in some strains, it inhibits phagocytosis
  - ***Protein antigen***—inhibits phagocytosis
  - ***Carbohydrate C antigen***—plays role in non-suppurative sequelae of streptococcal infection because of antigenic cross-reactions with antigen of heart and kidneys
- **Toxins**—haemolysins and erythrogenic toxin
  - ***Haemolysins***—two types: haemolysin O and haemolysin S
    - *Haemolysin O*—is oxygen labile, strongly antigenic and induces ASO (antistreptolysin O) antibodies, which help in diagnosis of streptococcal infections
    - *Haemolysin S*—is soluble in serum, produces haemolysis around the surface of colonies. It is non-antigenic, inhibits chemotaxis and phagocytosis
  - ***Erythrogenic toxin***—is responsible for rash in scarlet fever. It is pyrogenic and can cause immunosuppression
- **Enzymes**
  - ***Streptokinase***—has fibrinolytic activity, prevents formation of fibrin at the infected site and is hence responsible for spread of infection
  - ***Streptodornase or deoxyribonuclease***—degrades DNA, which is accumulated in pus as a result of disintegration of neutrophils and contributes for spread of infection

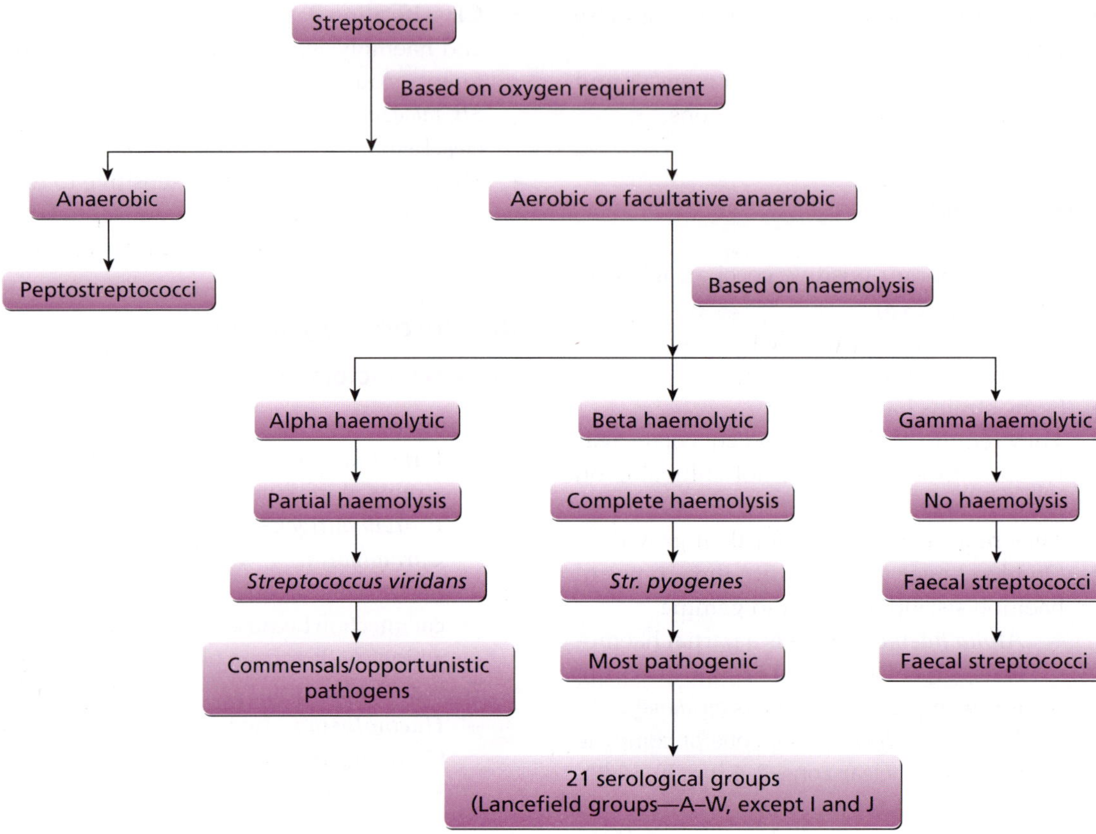

Flow chart 23.1 Classification of streptococci.

- ***Hyaluronidase***—splits hyaluronic acid, which binds the tissue cells together, and facilitates the spread of *Str. pyogenes*
- ***Proteinase***—destroys protein

Pathogenicity

Str. pyogenes causes

- Suppurative infections
- Non-suppurative complications

Sources of infection

- The major source of *Str. pyogenes* is the upper respiratory tract—throat, nose or nasopharynx—of patient or carrier.
- **Transmission**—by inhalation, direct contact or through contaminated dust or fomites.
- *Str. pyogenes* produces various exotoxins and enzymes, which contribute to pathogenicity of streptococcal diseases.
- *Str. pyogenes* produces the following:
  - ***Respiratory tract infections*** Sore throat, tonsillitis, pharyngitis, scarlet fever
  - ***Skin infections*** Erysipelas, impetigo, suppurative infections of skin, wound infections, burns infection, cellulitis, lymphangitis, etc.
  - ***Genital infections*** Puerperal sepsis
  - Abscesses in internal organs such as brain, lungs, liver and kidneys
  - Septicaemia and pyaemia
  - ***Non-suppurative complications*** Occur after 1–4 weeks of acute streptococcal infection. The exact pathogenic mechanism is not known and they are believed

to be the result of hypersensitivity reaction to some streptococcal components. These complications include:

  - *Acute rheumatic fever* Occurs most often following streptococcal sore throat. It is believed to be caused by cross-reacting antigen present in some streptococci and heart tissue because of which antibodies produced against streptococci cross-react with heart tissue (myocardium and heart valve) and cause cellular destruction and damage to heart.
  - *Acute glomerulonephritis* Occurs most often following streptococcal skin infections. It is believed to be caused by cross-reacting antigen present in cell membrane of nephritogenic streptococci and components of glomerular basement membrane because of which antibodies produced against streptococci cross-react with glomerular basement membrane and produce damage to the kidneys. Another possibility is deposition of streptococcal antigen–antibody complexes in glomeruli. In both the cases, there is activation of complement that causes tissue destruction.

- ***Oral manifestations***
  - Stomatitis scarlatina in scarlet fever characterized by congested palate mucosa and fiery red throat with swollen tonsils and faucial pillars.
  - Streptococci are also involved in the pyogenic granuloma of the oral cavity—the lesions appear on the gingiva, lips, tongue and buccal mucosa.

Laboratory diagnosis

- In acute infections—diagnosis by culture
- In non-suppurative complications—diagnosis by demonstrating antibodies

Collection of specimens

- Pus in pyogenic infections
- Cerebrospinal fluid (CSF) in meningitis
- Throat swab and sputum in respiratory infections
- Vaginal swab in genital infections
- Blood in septicaemia and in non-suppurative complications
- **Direct microscopy** For presumptive diagnosis, demonstration of Gram-positive cocci in chains in specimens such as pus and CSF
- **Culture** On blood agar, incubation at 37°C under 5–10% CO_2; observed for haemolysis. Confirmation by Gram stain, bacitracin sensitivity test (*Str. pyogenes* is susceptible to bacitracin) and other tests such as hippurate hydrolysis, esculin fermentation and CAMP (Christie, Atkins, Munch-Peteren) test
- **Serological tests** ASO titre and antideoxyribonuclease B antibody for retrospective diagnosis of non-suppurative complications

Treatment

Penicillin is the drug of choice. In a patient allergic to penicillin, erythromycin or cephalexin/ other cephalosporins can be used.

Prophylaxis

- For primary prevention of rheumatic fever, adequate antibiotic therapy is recommended
- For prevention of recurrence of rheumatic fever and prevention of development of rheumatic heart disease, long-term administration of penicillin in children who have developed early signs of rheumatic fever. The antibiotic prophylaxis prevents reinfection by streptococci and damage to the heart

Viridans group (*Streptococcus viridans*)

- These are alpha-haemolytic streptococci.

- Five species—*Str. salivarius, Str. mutans, Str. sanguis, Str. mitor* and *Str. milleri.*
- Normally present in the mouth and throat.
- Normally non-pathogenic. In persons with predisposing factors such as valvular disease of the heart, they cause subacute endocarditis.
- Diagnosis of subacute bacterial endocarditis is established by repeated blood cultures.
- Generally, sensitive to penicillin but may develop resistance to penicillin, hence treatment should be guided by antibiotic sensitivity testing.
- These are commonly associated with the following infections:
  - ***Dental caries***
    - *Str. mutans* is associated with dental caries.
    - It breaks down the dietary sucrose and produces acid and dextran, acid damages dentine and dextran binds with food debris, mucus, epithelial cells and bacteria to form plaques leading to dental caries (*see* Chapter 50, *Oral and Dental Infections*).
  - ***Endocarditis***
    - *Str. sanguis* and *Str. mitor* are commonly associated with subacute endocarditis.
    - They enter the bloodstream during tooth extraction or other dental procedures and cause transient bacteraemia that may further lead to subacute endocarditis.

Group D streptococci

- These are the faecal streptococci (enterococci), appear in pair (cocci in pairs).
- They are relatively more resistant to heat (60°C for 30 minutes).
- They are present in intestine, genital tract and saliva and are frequently isolated from urinary tract infections and wound infections.
- They may cause subacute bacterial endocarditis, infection of biliary tract, septicaemia, peritonitis and intra-abdominal abscess.

Pneumococcus (*Diplococcus pneumoniae*)

- Pneumococci are Gram-positive, flame-shaped cocci in pairs—diplococci (Fig. 23.4)
- Size is 1 µm in diameter
- Capsulated—capsule can be demonstrated by
  - ***Negative stain (India ink)*** Capsule is seen as a clear halo around bacteria
  - ***Quellung reaction*** It is a capsule swelling reaction in which capsule can be seen as refractile halo after mixing with homologous type-specific antibody, which combines with capsular polysaccharide
- Non-motile and non-sporing
- Complex growth requirements grow on enriched media only—blood agar and chocolate agar
- Require 5–10 % CO_2 for their growth
- **On blood agar**—small, moist, mucoid, transparent colony with zone of alpha haemolysis. Further incubation leads to central umbonation with raised edges. Concentric rings are seen when viewed from above giving a draughtsman or carom-coin appearance to the colony

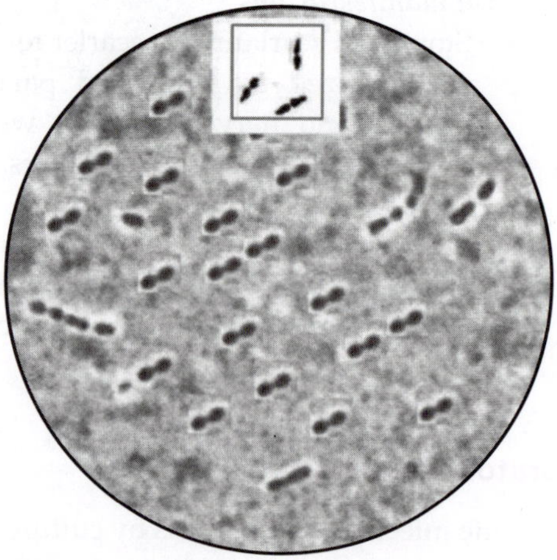

Figure 23.4 Pneumococci.

- They are delicate organisms readily destroyed by heat (52°C for 15 minutes) and antiseptics

Virulence factors—determinants of pathogenicity

- Polysaccharide capsule is the most important virulence factor—inhibits phagocytosis. Uncapsulated strains are readily destroyed by phagocytosis
- IgA protease—enzyme acting on IgA antibodies synthesized locally
- Pneumolysin—an intracellular membrane damaging toxin released by autolysis inhibits neutrophil chemotaxis, phagocytosis, lymphocyte proliferation and antibody synthesis
- Cell constituents such as teichoic acid and peptidoglycan also play role in pathogenesis

Pathogenicity

- Cause pneumonia and suppurative infections in other parts of the body
- **Source**—respiratory tract of carriers and less often of patients
- **Transmission**—by inhalation of contaminated dust, droplets or droplet nuclei
- Pneumococci produce various virulence factors, which contribute to pathogenesis, for example, capsular polysaccharide, IgA protease, protein adhesin, pneumolysin and leucocidin
- Pneumococci cause
  - Pneumonia
    - Lobar pneumonia—over 80%
    - Bronchopneumonia—60%
  - Meningitis
  - Chronic bronchitis
  - Suppurative lesions in other parts of the body such as empyema, pericarditis, otitis media, sinusitis, conjunctivitis, suppurative arthritis and peritonitis

Laboratory diagnosis

- **Collection of specimens**—sputum, CSF, pus, laryngeal swab and blood
- Transported immediately
- **Microscopy**
  - Gram stain—shows Gram-positive diplococci
  - Negative stain for demonstration of capsule
  - Quellung test—capsule swelling reaction for demonstration of capsule
- **Culture**—on blood agar and chocolate agar at 37°C under 5–10% CO_2
  - Growth after incubation confirmed and differentiated from *Str. viridans* by using the following tests:
    - Bile solubility
    - Inulin fermentation
    - Optochin sensitivity
  - These tests are positive in pneumococci and negative in *Str. viridans*
- **Rapid diagnostic methods**—demonstration of
  - Capsular polysaccharide in infected body fluid by countercurrent immunoelectrophoresis
  - Antibodies by agglutination, precipitation, indirect haemagglutination, latex agglutination test and ELISA

Treatment

Penicillin, cephalosporins, erythromycin, chloramphenicol or vancomycin

Prophylaxis

- **Vaccination** Vaccine containing a highly purified capsular polysaccharides extract from pneumococci is used.

Features of clinically important Gram-positive cocci are summarized in Table 23.1.

Table 23.1 Summary of features of clinically important Gram-positive cocci

Cocci	Important properties	Important virulence factors	Modes of infection	Important clinical infections
Staphylococcus aureus	• Gram (+) cocci occurring in grape-like clusters • Golden-yellow pigment • Catalase (+) • Coagulase (+) • Mannitol (+)	• **Protein A** evades phagocytosis • **Coagulase** forms fibrin clot around organism, protecting it from phagocytosis • **Toxic shock syndrome toxin**—responsible for toxic shock syndrome • **Epidermolytic toxin**—responsible for scalded skin syndrome • **Enterotoxin**— responsible for food poisoning	• Transmission can either be endogenous or exogenous • Direct contact • Inhalation • Ingestion • Indirect contact	• Wound infections • Respiratory infections • Septicaemia • Nosocomial infections • Food poisoning • Exfoliative skin diseases • Toxic shock syndrome
Streptococcus pyogenes	• Gram (+) cocci occurring in chains • Lancefield Group A • Beta haemolytic • Bacitracin sensitive	• **Protein antigen**—inhibits phagocytosis • **Streptolysin S**—inhibits chemotaxis and phagocytosis • **Erythrogenic toxin**—responsible for rash in scarlet fever, pyrogenic, immunosuppressive • **Streptokinase**—fibrinolytic activity • **Hyaluronidase and streptodornase**—facilitate spread in tissue	• Transmitted by inhalation, direct contact, through fomites	• Sore throat/ pharyngitis /tonsillitis • Scarlet fever • Skin infections • Puerperal sepsis • Acute rheumatic fever • Acute glomeruolnephritis
Diplococcus pneumoniae	• Gram (+) cocci occurring in pairs • Flame shaped, capsulated • Alpha haemolytic • Bile soluble • Sensitive to optochin	• **Capsule**—inhibits phagocytosis • **Pneumolysin**—inhibits phagocytosis • **IgA protease**—acts on IgA antibodies	• Transmitted by inhalation	• Pneumonia • Meningitis • Chronic bronchitis • Suppurative infections

Self-assessment

Long-answer questions

1. Discuss in brief the pathogenesis, modes of infection, clinical infections and laboratory diagnosis of staphylococcal infections.
2. Discuss in brief the pathogenesis, modes of infection, clinical infections and laboratory diagnosis of streptococcal infections.

Short-answer questions

Write notes on
1. Classification of staphylococci
2. Classification of streptococci
3. Coagulase test
4. Infections caused by staphylococci
5. Virulence factors of *Streptococcus pyogenes*
6. Infections caused by *Str. pyogenes*
7. Viridans group of streptococci
8. Pneumococci

9. Non-suppurative complications of acute streptococcal infections

Multiple-choice questions

1. Which of the following statements is FALSE about *Staphylococcus aureus?*
   A. Is coagulase positive
   B. Ferments mannitol
   C. Is most pathogenic
   D. Produces a lemon-yellow pigment
2. Which of the following statements is FALSE about *Staphylococcus albus?*
   A. Is coagulase negative
   B. Does not ferment mannitol
   C. Is an opportunistic pathogen
   D. Produces a golden-yellow pigment
3. Which of the following is the most important virulence factor of *Staphylococcus aureus?*
   A. Coagulase
   B. Hyaluronidase
   C. Lipase
   D. Staphylokinase
4. Which of the following toxins of *Staphylococcus aureus* is responsible for staphylococcal food poisoning?
   A. Epidermolytic toxin
   B. Enterotoxin
   C. Haemolytic toxin
   D. All of the above
5. Which of the following is an oral manifestation seen in staphylococcal infections?
   A. Pyogenic granuloma
   B. Stomatitis
   C. Pemphigus neonatorum
   D. Gingivitis
6. Which of the following is an oral manifestation seen in *Streptococcus pyogenes* infections?
   A. Dental caries
   B. Stomatitis scarlatina
   C. Periodontitis
   D. Gingivitis
7. Which of the following statements is FALSE about acute rheumatic fever?
   A. Occurs following streptococcal sore throat
   B. Is a suppurative complication of streptococcal infection
   C. Caused by cross-reacting antigen
   D. Damage to heart is a feature
8. The following are the enzymes produced by streptococci, EXCEPT
   A. Streptokinase
   B. Hyaluronidase
   C. Coagulase
   D. Deoxyribonuclease
9. Which of the following streptococci does not belong to viridans group?
   A. *Streptococcus salivarius*
   B. *Str. mutans*
   C. *Str. sanguis*
   D. *Str. agalactiae*
10. Which of the following statements is FALSE about *Diplococcus pneumoniae?*
    A. Polysaccharide capsule is the most important virulence factor
    B. Require 5–10 % CO_2 for their growth
    C. Simple growth requirement
    D. All of the above
11. Quellung reaction is used for demonstration of
    A. Flagella
    B. Pili
    C. Spores
    D. Capsule

24 Gram-Negative Cocci

Gram-negative cocci having medical and dental significance include two species of genus *Neisseria*—*N. gonorrhoeae* and *N. meningitidis.*

Neisseria gonorrhoeae (gonococcus)

- Gonococci are Gram-negative, oval cocci arranged in pairs (Fig. 24.1).
- They are non-motile and non-sporing but capsulated.
- They are aerobes but may grow anaerobically as well.

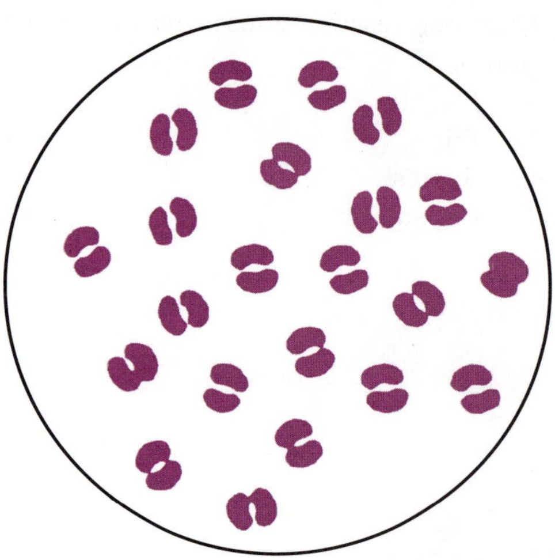

Figure 24.1 Gonococci.

- They are difficult to grow and require enriched media like chocolate agar for growth and also require 5–10% CO_2 for growth.
- Optimum temperature is 35–36°C.
- Growth is slow, grey, glistening colonies of 0.5–1 mm diameter appear after 24 hours of incubation.
- Thayer–Martin medium is selective medium—inhibits the growth of other bacteria including the non-pathogenic *Neisseria.*
- They are catalase and oxidase positive.
- They utilize glucose only with production of acid.
- They are very delicate organisms and do not survive outside the body for a long time (1–2 hours) and are readily killed by heat, drying and antiseptics.

Pathogenicity

Virulence factors—determinants of pathogenicity

- **Capsule**—found in fresh isolates. It allows intracellular survival of organisms
- **Pili**—help in attachment to specific receptors on host cells and also inhibit phagocytosis
- **Outer membrane proteins**
  - **Protein I** (*por* protein) and **protein III** (*Rmp* protein) act as ligands to attach to host cells

- **Protein II** (*Opa* protein) is associated with adherence of gonococci to host cells and for clumping of cocci in urethral exudates and has antiphagocytic role
- **Lipopolysaccharide**—endotoxic activity
- **IgA protease**—cleaves IgA and inactivates it

Clinical disease—gonorrhoea

Gonorrhoea is a venereal disease primarily affecting the male and female genitourinary tract.

- **Sources** *N. gonorrhoeae* is an exclusive human pathogen, hence patients or carriers are the important sources of infection.
- **Modes of infection** It is transmitted by sexual contact.
- **Clinical presentation** Most commonly, it occurs as an acute urethritis characterized by purulent urethral discharge.
  - In males, it may spread to the prostate, testes, seminal vesicles and epididymis.
  - In females, asymptomatic infection is common. Primary infection of urethra and cervix may spread to Bartholin's glands, uterus, fallopian tubes and ovaries and may cause pelvic inflammatory disease resulting in sterility.
  - Vulvovaginitis in prepubertal girls.
  - It also causes ophthalmic neonatorum—a non-venereal conjunctivitis in a newborn through infected birth canal.
  - Rarely, the disease may involve rectum (proctitis) or oropharynx (pharyngitis) in persons indulging in abnormal sex (anal or oral sex).
  - Disseminated gonococcal infection is common in women and may present with painful joints, fever and septic skin lesions on extremities. Rarely, it may present as endocarditis or meningitis.
- **Oral manifestations** Gonococcal stomatitis, gonococcal pharyngitis and tonsillitis; other lesions include ulceration of lip, tongue and lesions on the buccal mucosa and palate

Laboratory diagnosis

- **Collection of specimens**
  - Urethral discharge in both sexes
  - Cervical discharge, vaginal swab in females
  - Urine, blood, anal swab, conjunctival swab, material from oral lesions, etc.
- **Transport**
  - As gonococci are delicate organisms, sample should be transported immediately after collection.
  - All swabs are transported to the laboratory in Amies transport media.
  - Blood is collected in trypticase soy broth.
- **Direct microscopy**
  - Gram stain shows Gram-negative cocci in pairs—not reliable in females, as organisms with similar morphology are normally present in vagina.
  - Fluorescent antibody tests are more sensitive and specific for microscopic diagnosis.
- **Culture** Specimen is inoculated on chocolate agar and selective medium and incubated at 35–36°C under 5–10% CO_2 for 24 hours. Growth on culture is confirmed by
  - Gram staining
  - Biochemical reactions
- **Antibody detection** Antibody detection is useful in patients with metastatic lesions, especially when culture result is negative. The antibodies can be detected by using
  - Radioimmunoassay
  - Enzyme-linked immunosorbent assay (ELISA)
  - Haemagglutination test

Treatment

- Penicillin—is preferred if strain is sensitive and an individual is not allergic
- Ceftriaxone—extremely active
- Cefotaxime
- Ciprofloxacin
- Tetracycline
- Spectinomycin

- Co-amoxiclav—for β-lactamase producing gonococci

Neisseria meningitidis (meningococcus)

- Meningococci are Gram-negative diplococci arranged in pairs with adjacent sides flattened (Fig. 24.2)
- Size is 0.6–0.8 µm in diameter
- Shape is spherical or oval
- Non-sporing and non-motile but capsulated
- They are strict aerobes; growth is enhanced by supplement of 5–10% CO_2
- Optimum temperature is 35–36°C
- Optimum pH is 7.0–7.4
- Do not grow on ordinary media
- Growth occurs in media enriched with blood or serum—blood agar, chocolate agar, Muller–Hinton starch casein hydrolysate agar, etc.
- Modified Thayer–Martin medium (chocolate agar + vancomycin, colistin, nystatin) is used as selective medium for contaminated specimens
- It forms small colonies, 1 mm in diameter, round, convex, grey, translucent, smooth, glistening with entire margins on solid media
- On chocolate agar, colonies are slightly larger than that of blood agar

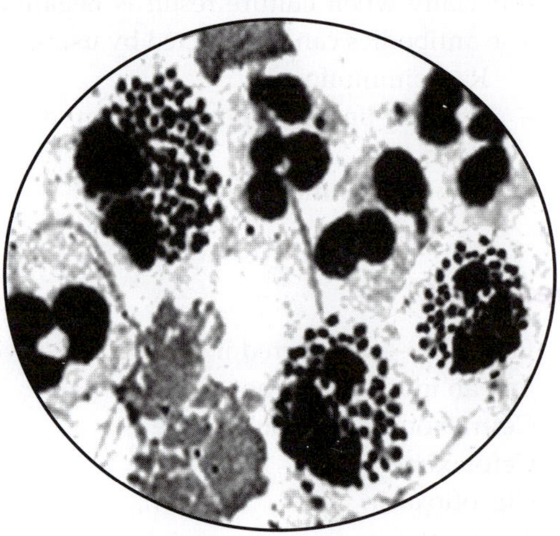

Figure 24.2 Meningococci.

- They are catalase and oxidase positive and utilize glucose and maltose by oxidative attack
- They are delicate organisms, highly susceptible to heat, drying and disinfectants

Pathogenicity

Virulence factors

- **Capsular polysaccharide**—acts by inhibiting phagocytosis
- **Pili**—help in adhesion to mucosa
- **Endotoxin**—induces inflammatory response and causes vascular necrosis. It is involved in causing petechial haemorrhages in **Waterhouse–Friderichsen syndrome**
- **IgA protease**—cleaves and inactivates IgA—an immunoglobulin involved in mucosal defence
- **Outer membrane proteins**—some outer membrane proteins are involved with attachment to the host cell

Meningococcal infections (Flow chart 24.1)

- Meningococci cause meningococcal septicaemia (meningococcemia) and acute pyogenic meningitis.
- **Pyogenic meningitis** It is more common in children and young adults.
- **Sources** Infected cases and carriers are the important sources. Human nasopharynx is the reservoir of meningococci.
- **Mode of transmission** Infection occurs by inhalation of droplet.
- Spread of organism from nasopharynx to the meninges occurs along the perineural sheath of the olfactory nerve or through the bloodstream (meningococcemia).
- **Meningococcemia** It is characterized by acute fever with chills, malaise, prostration and petechial rash and may cause lesions in lungs, joints, adrenals and other internal organs due to endotoxin.
- A fulminant meningococcemia called **Waterhouse–Friderichsen syndrome** char-

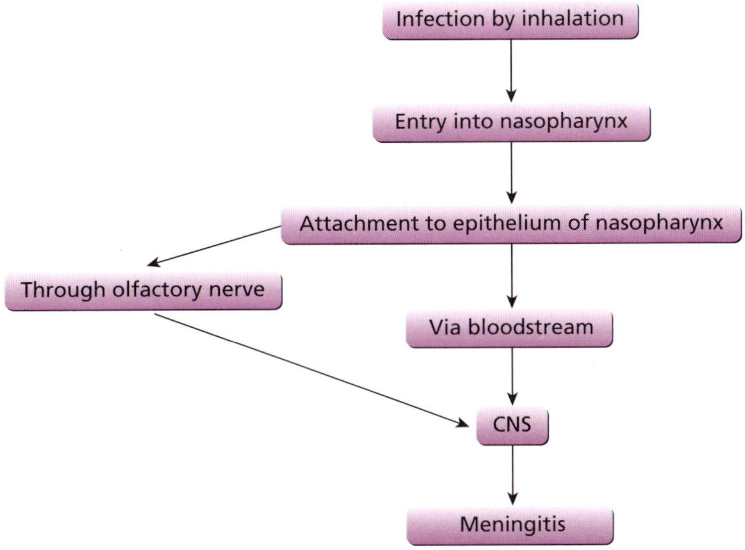

Flow chart 24.1 Pathogenesis of *Neisseria meningitidis. CNS*, central nervous system.

acterized by shock, disseminated intravascular coagulation and multisystem failure may develop.
- It also causes pneumonia, pericarditis and endocarditis, purulent conjunctivitis and purulent arthritis.

Laboratory diagnosis

- **Collection of specimens** Cerebrospinal fluid (CSF) blood and nasopharyngeal swab
- **Transport** As it is a delicate organism, a sample of CSF should reach the laboratory immediately. Nasopharyngeal swab should be transported in Stuart's transport medium. Blood should be added to glucose broth and transported
- **Direct microscopy**
  - **Gram stain**—shows Gram-negative cocci in pairs
  - **Direct immunofluorescence test**—smears treated with antibody conjugated to fluorescent tag shows presence of meningococci
- **Culture** Specimen is inculcated on blood agar and chocolate agar. Incubated under 5–10% CO_2 at 35–36°C for 24 hours. Growth on culture is confirmed by
  - Gram staining
  - Biochemical reactions
  - Slide agglutination test
- **Antigen detection** In supernatant of cerebrospinal fluid by using
  - ELISA
  - Counterimmunoelectrophoresis
  - Latex agglutination test
- **Antibody detection** Haemagglutination test is used to detect antibodies in chronic cases
- **Nucleic acid detection in samples** By polymerase chain reaction

Treatment

- Intravenous penicillin, cefotaxime or ceftriaxone
- Chloramphenicol is also effective

Prophylaxis

- Antibiotic treatment with rifampicin or ciprofloxacin after treatment to prevent development of carrier state

- Chemoprophylaxis with rifampicin or ciprofloxacin for persons who are in close contact of patients
- Vaccination—using capsular polysaccharide vaccine in older children and adults is protective

Self-assessment

Long-answer question

1. Discuss in brief the pathogenesis, modes of infection, clinical features and laboratory diagnosis of acute pyogenic meningitis.

Short-answer questions

Write notes on

1. Gonorrhoea
2. Laboratory diagnosis of gonorrhoea
3. Meningococcal infections

Multiple-choice questions

1. Which of the following oral manifestations is NOT seen in *Neisseria gonorrhoeae* infection?
   A. Stomatitis
   B. Gingivitis
   C. Pharyngitis
   D. Tonsillitis
2. Which of the following media is used as selective medium for *Neisseria gonorrhoeae?*
   A. Chocolate agar
   B. Blood agar
   C. Modified Thayer–Martin medium
   D. Thayer–Martin medium
3. Which of the following media is used as selective medium for *Neisseria meningitidis?*
   A. Chocolate agar
   B. Blood agar
   C. Modified Thayer–Martin medium
   D. Thayer–Martin medium
4. Which of the following statements is FALSE regarding *Neisseria gonorrhoeae*?
   A. Causes an acute urethritis characterized by purulent urethral discharge
   B. Is transmitted by sexual contact
   C. Requires 5–10% CO_2 for growth
   D. Is the cause of Waterhouse–Friderichsen syndrome
5. Which of the following statements is FALSE regarding *Neisseria meningitidis*?
   A. Rarely, it produces lesions in rectum or oropharynx
   B. Causes acute pyogenic meningitis
   C. Requires 5–10 % CO_2 for growth
   D. Is the cause of Waterhouse–Friderichsen syndrome

25 Gram-Positive Bacilli—*Corynebacterium diphtheriae*

- *Corynebacterium diphtheriae* are thin, slender, Gram-positive bacilli (Fig. 25.1).
- Size is 3–6 µm by 0.6–0.8 µm.
- Non-sporing, non-motile and non-capsulated.
- Club shaped due to metachromatic granules at one or both ends.
- Show a Chinese letter arrangement (V or L shapes).
- Club shaped due to granules consisting of polymetaphosphate are seen in cytoplasm situated at the pole of bacilli (hence also called as polar bodies). They are called metachromatic granules as they become bluish-purple in colour when stained with methylene blue. They are also known as volutin granules or Babes–Ernst granules.
- They can be stained using special stains such as Albert's stain, Neisser's stain and Ponder's stain.
- Three biotypes—*gravis, intermedius* and *mitis*—based on the colony characters on blood potassium tellurite agar and other properties such as morphology, haemolysis, biochemical tests and virulence.
- Bacilli of biotype *gravis* are short, whereas biotype *mitis* are long and pleomorphic and biotype *intermedius* are very long to short.
- *C. diphtheriae* are aerobes and facultative anaerobes; require an optimum temperature of 37°C and an optimum pH of 7.2.

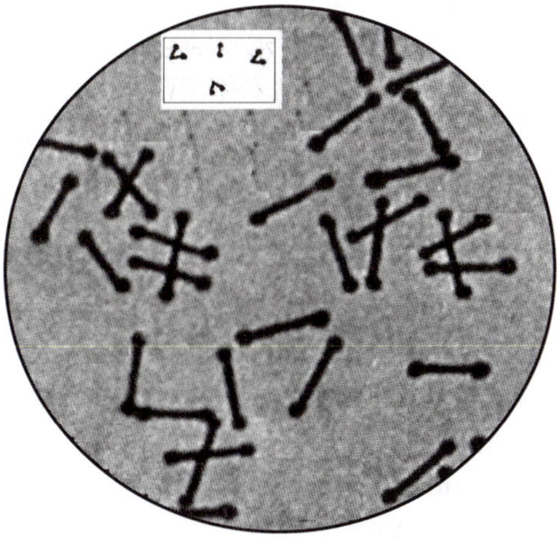

Figure 25.1 *Corynebacterium diphtheriae.*

- Grow best in media enriched with blood or serum—blood agar and Loeffler's serum slope.
- On Loeffler's serum slope, *C. diphtheriae* grows rapidly in 6–8 hours producing small, white, circular, glistening colonies with irregular edges.
- Blood potassium tellurite agar is used as selective medium. *C. diphtheriae* grows slowly on this media producing grey to black colony due to reduction of potassium tellurite to potassium tellurium.
- Diphtheria bacilli ferment glucose with acid. *Gravis* ferments glycogen and starch.

Intermedius and *mitis* are unable to ferment glycogen and starch.
- They are sensitive to heat but resistant to drying and easily destroyed by antiseptics.
- Remain virulent in blankets and dust for 5 weeks.

Pathogenicity

C. diphtheriae invades, colonizes and proliferates locally. It does not penetrate deeply into the mucosal tissue and usually does not cause bacteraemia. It produces exotoxin locally, which spreads via blood to distant organs and has a special affinity for the heart muscles, the peripheral nervous system and the adrenal glands.

Exotoxin

- It produces an exotoxin—a protein having two fragments: A and B.
- Enzymatic activity is present in A and B is responsible for binding and transport of a toxin to cells.
- **Mechanism of action** It acts by inhibiting protein synthesis.
- Fragment A inhibits polypeptide chain elongation in presence of nicotinamide adenine dinucleotide (NAD) by inactivating elongation factor 2 and thus protein synthesis is inhibited.

Clinical disease—diphtheria

- Commonly seen in children aged between 2 and 12 years.
- Infection occurs by inhalation.
- The site of infection is the upper respiratory tract—nasopharynx, where it initiates inflammatory exudate and causes necrosis of the cells.
- Pathogenesis is the formation of characteristic pseudomembrane—white to grey in colour.
- Membrane first appears on tonsils and may spread to larynx and trachea.
- Occasionally, the membrane forms on uvula, soft palate, gingiva, buccal mucosa and at the site of tooth eruption.
- Different types of diphtheria depending on sites affected are faucial, laryngeal, nasal, conjunctival, genital, cutaneous and otitic.
- **Faucial diphtheria** is the commonest type.
- Depending on severity, it is of three types:
  - ***Malignant*** This form shows severe toxaemia, marked adenitis, circulatory failure and high incidence of paralytic complications.
  - ***Septic*** It is characterized by ulceration, cellulitis and gangrene around pseudomembrane.
  - ***Haemorrhagic*** It shows bleeding from membrane, epistaxis, conjunctival haemorrhages and purpura.

Clinical manifestation

- High-grade fever
- Malaise
- Pain in throat
- Ulceration of membrane followed by cellulitis or gangrene of surrounding area
- Sometimes, haemorrhages at the edges of membrane
- Cervical adenopathy (bull neck) in severe cases
- Death due to circulatory failure or mechanical asphyxiation

Complications

- Asphyxia due to mechanical obstruction
- Acute circulatory failure
- Post-diphtheritic paralysis
- Septic complications such as pneumonia and otitis media

Laboratory diagnosis

- **Collection of specimen** Swabs are collected from lesions (throat, nose, larynx, ear, etc.). Two swabs are collected—one for smear and one for culture.
- **Direct microscopy** Microscopy is not reliable, as other corynebacteria which are morphologically similar to *C. diphtheriae* are normally present in throat.
  - Gram stain shows Gram-positive bacilli.
  - Albert stain shows beaded green rods with typical Chinese letter arrangement.
- **Culture** On blood agar, Loeffler's serum slope and blood potassium tellurite agar
  - Incubated at 37°C for 48 hours
  - Growth is confirmed by microscopic examination of colony smear stained by Albert's stain (shows beaded green rods with bluish-black metachromatic granules and typical Chinese letter arrangement) and by biochemical reactions
- **Virulence tests**
  - Virulence testing in vivo (subcutaneous test and intracutaneous test in experimental animals—guinea pig and rabbit)
  - Virulence testing in vitro for exotoxin by Elek's gel precipitation test or tissue culture test

Treatment

- In clinically diagnosed cases, treatment should be initiated immediately before the laboratory confirmation.
- Antidiphtheric serum to neutralize the effect of toxin is given as antibiotics have no effect on preformed toxin.
- Antibiotics are given to eradicate the organisms and to terminate toxin production.
  - Penicillin is the drug of choice.
  - Erythromycin is more effective in carriers.

Prophylaxis

- For active immunization, alum precipitated toxoid (APT) or other preparations are used.
- As a routine part of immunization in children, diphtheria toxoid is given in combination with tetanus toxoid and pertussis vaccine as triple vaccine DPT. Three doses are given intramuscularly at an interval of 4–6 weeks, with starting dose at 6 weeks and booster doses (DT) at 18 months and 5 years.
- For passive immunization, subcutaneous administration of 500–1000 units of antitoxin is used. It is an emergency measure used only once when susceptible is exposed to known case of diphtheria.

Self-assessment

Long-answer question

1. Discuss in brief the pathogenicity, laboratory diagnosis and prophylaxis of diphtheria.

Short-answer questions

Write notes on

1. Prophylaxis of diphtheria
2. Laboratory diagnosis of diphtheria
3. Diphtheria

Multiple-choice questions

1. Which of the following types of arrangement is seen in *Corynebacterium diphtheriae?*
   A. Cigar bundle appearance
   B. Thumb print appearance
   C. Chinese letter arrangement
   D. None of the above
2. Which of the following methods is used for staining of *Corynebacterium diphtheriae?*
   A. Albert's stain
   B. Neisser's stain
   C. Ponder's stain
   D. All of the above

3. Which of the following is used as selective medium for *Corynebacterium diphtheriae*?
   A. Chocolate agar
   B. Blood agar
   C. Loeffler's serum slope
   D. Blood potassium tellurite agar
4. Which of the following statements is TRUE regarding the mechanism of action of diphtheria exotoxin?
   A. Acts by inhibiting acetylcholine release
   B. Acts by increasing levels of cAMP
   C. Acts by inhibiting protein synthesis
   D. Acts by activation of cGMP
5. Which of the following statements is FALSE regarding *Corynebacterium diphtheriae?*
   A. It penetrates deeply into the mucosal tissue and produces lesions
   B. Formation of pseudomembrane is the characteristic feature
   C. Its transmission occurs by inhalation
   D. It acts by producing an exotoxin

26 Gram-Positive Bacilli—Clostridia

- Clostridia are Gram-positive, spore-forming anaerobic bacilli.
- Spores are bulging; their position is different in different species and it helps in their identification.
- They grow on media like blood agar under anaerobic conditions.
- Robertson's cooked meat (RCM) broth is commonly used for culture of clostridia.
- Temperature range is 20–50°C, optimum temperature is 45°C.
- pH range is 5.5–8.0, optimum pH is 7.2–7.4.
- Sporulation is favoured in alkaline medium.
- The vegetative cells of clostridia are similar to other bacilli in their resistance to physical and chemical agents.
- Spores are resistant to heat and require 121°C for 20 minutes for killing.
- Spores are also resistant to chemical agents—phenolic disinfectants and others. However, they are sensitive to halogens, glutaraldehyde and iodine.
- *Clostridium welchii, C. tetani* and *C. botulinum* are the important species causing infections in human beings.

Clostridium welchii (Clostridium perfringens)

- Gram-positive bacilli, arranged singly, in chains and bundles
- Size is 4–6 µm by 1 µm with blunt ends
- Spore forming—forms bulging spores, subterminal in position
- Non-motile but capsulated
- Anaerobic but can grow under microaerophilic condition
- Grows on blood agar and in RCM
- On blood agar, it produces a **target haemolysis**—a narrow zone of complete haemolysis due to theta toxin and wider incomplete haemolysis due to alpha toxin
- In RCM it grows rapidly, turning meat particles pink in colour but there is no digestion of meat particles (saccharolytic activity)

Virulence factors

Toxins

- Produces at least 12 different types of toxins in addition to many enzymes and biologically active substances
- Alpha, beta, epsilon and iota are the major lethal toxins
- Some other toxins and soluble substances which are important in pathogenicity include the following:
  - Theta toxin—haemolytic and necrotizing
  - Deoxyribonuclease (nu toxin)
  - Hyaluronidase (mu toxin)
  - Collagenase (kappa toxin)
  - Haemolysin
  - Fibrinolysin

Enterotoxin

- Some strains produce powerful enterotoxin, especially when they grow in meat dishes. It is heat labile protein (molecular weight 36000).
- It causes hypersecretion in the jejunum and ileum leading to loss of fluids and electrolytes. It induces intense diarrhoea in 6–18 hours.

Pathogenicity

C. welchii causes the following infections:

- Gas gangrene
- Food poisoning
- Other infections

Gas gangrene

- **Sources of infection**
  - Important sources are animal and human excreta
  - Spores are also present in soil and dust
  - Organisms may also originate from the skin areas, which are contaminated with organisms from the intestinal tract
- **Modes of infection** Infection occurs by contamination of a wound with faecal matter or soil.
- **Clinical features**
  - Impairment of the normal blood supply due to tissue damage causes reduction in oxygen tension and creates anaerobic condition that favours infection by clostridia.
  - *C. welchii* proliferates and releases necrotizing toxin and hyaluronidase, thus, causing devitalization of the adjacent tissues which leads to tissue necrosis.
  - Gas gangrene is characterized by
    - Rapidly spreading oedema—swelling of infected tissue
    - Crepitation in the subcutaneous tissue and muscle
    - Myositis
    - Necrosis and gangrene of the tissue
    - Gas production
    - Rapidly spreading necrosis leads to generalized symptoms such as fever, toxaemia, shock and death

Food poisoning

- It is caused by strains producing enterotoxin.
- **Sources of infection** is warm meat.
- **Modes of infection** is ingestion.
- Spores resistant to heat survive cooking process, germinate and increase in number in warm meat and when ingested along with food, bacteria grow in intestine, form and release toxin and produce symptoms of food poisoning.
- **Clinical features**
  - Diarrhoea without vomiting
  - Cramps and abdominal pain

Other infections

C. welchii can also cause the following:

- Necrotizing enteritis
- Urogenital infections
- Meningitis
- Gangrenous appendicitis
- Panophthalmitis
- Biliary tract infections
- Septicaemia and endocarditis
- Anaerobic cellulitis

Laboratory diagnosis

Laboratory diagnosis of gas gangrene

- **Specimens** Material from wound, exudates, excised or necrosed tissue. Specimens should be collected from deeper sites.
- **Transport** To avoid the death of anaerobes, they should be collected and transported in RCM medium or thioglycolate broth.
- **Direct microscopy**
  - **Gram stain** shows a large number of Gram-positive bacilli without spores and scanty pus cells, which is a char-

acteristic feature of gas gangrene and helps in presumptive diagnosis.

- **Culture**
  - The specimen is inoculated on fresh blood agars, neomycin blood agar and RCM medium.
  - One blood agar plate and neomycin blood agar are incubated anaerobically at 37°C for 48–72 hours. One blood agar is incubated aerobically.
  - The cultures are observed for typical colonies and subjected for identification using
    - Litmus milk test
    - Nagler reaction

Nagler reaction It is a toxin neutralization test performed on agar medium containing 20% human serum or 5% egg yolk. *C. welchii* produces a zone of opacity surrounding the colonies in media containing serum or egg-yolk due to lecithinase activity of alpha toxin.

- The test bacterium is inoculated on this medium.
- To one-half of the plate, antitoxin is spread on the surface.
- Plate is incubated at 37°C in an anaerobic condition for 24 hours and growth is observed.
- Colonies on the side containing no antitoxin show a zone of opacity while the colonies on the other half with antitoxin show no opacity due to neutralization of alpha toxin by antitoxin (Fig. 26.1).
- **Animal pathogenicity**
  - 0.1 mL of 24 hours growth in RCM is injected intramuscularly on the hind limb of guinea pig.
  - Death occurs within 24 hours.
  - On autopsy, *C. welchii* can be recovered from heart and spleen.

Laboratory diagnosis of food poisoning

- Specimen—faeces and suspected food.
- Specimen is collected in RCM medium and subcultured on selective medium and incubated anaerobically.

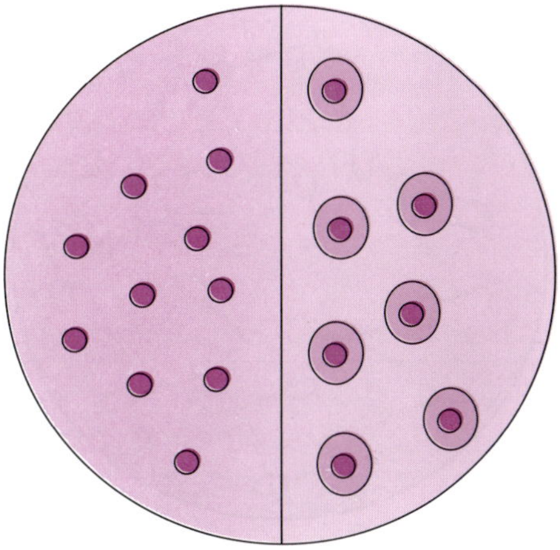

Figure 26.1 Nagler reaction.

- The typical colonies are identified by morphology, cultural characters and Nagler reaction.
- As *C. welchii* may be normally present in the intestine, hence isolation from faeces in a large number is meaningful.

Treatment

- Surgical removal of damaged and dead tissue, foreign body, etc.
- Antibiotics—metronidazole, penicillin, sulphonamides, etc.
- Treatment with hyperbaric oxygen
- Passive immunization with antitoxin containing concentrated immunoglobulins
- Treatment of food poisoning requires only symptomatic care

Clostridium tetani

- Gram-positive, straight, slender rods with bulging spherical spores, terminal in position that gives characteristic drumstick appearance (Fig. 26.2)
- Size is 2–5 μm by 0.4–0.5 μm
- Larger filaments may occur
- Motile but non-capsulated
- They are obligate anaerobes

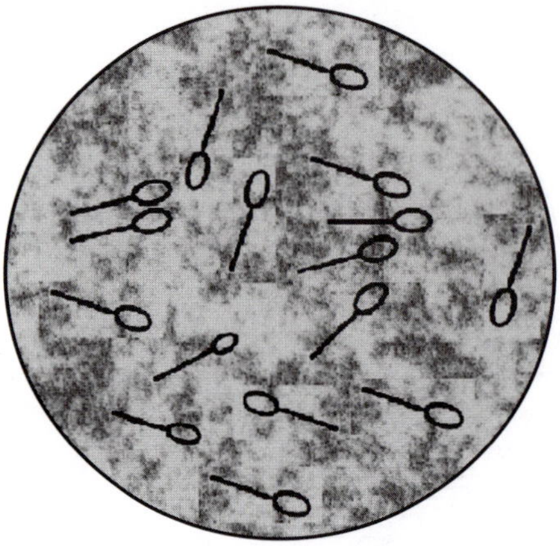

Figure 26.2 *Clostridium tetani.*

- Grow on blood agar; RCM and thioglycolate broth
- On blood agar, swarming—spreading type of growth with alpha haemolysis followed by beta haemolysis. In agar stab culture, fir tree-like appearance
- RCM becomes turbid, meat is not digested but slightly blackened showing a slight proteolytic effect

Virulence factors

Toxins

- **Tetanolysin**—heat labile and oxygen labile haemolysin. Pathogenic role is unknown
- **Tetanospasmin**
  - Heat labile and oxygen stable toxin—a neurotoxin
  - Protein in nature
  - Antigenic
  - Can be toxoided
  - Is specifically neutralized by antitoxin

Pathogenicity

C. tetani is a cause of tetanus.

- **Sources of infection**
  - Important sources are animal faeces, soil, manure and dust
  - Spores are also present in the human intestine, air, plaster, etc.
- **Modes of infection**
  - Infection occurs by wound contamination by spores
  - Tetanus occurs following:
    - Injury
    - Unsterile injections
    - Dirty practices such as application of cow dung on the umbilical stumps
    - Rituals such as circumcision or ear boring
    - Septic abortion

Clinical features

- Incubation period is two to several weeks (commonly 6–12 days).
- It is characterized by muscle stiffness and spasms. Initially, jaw muscles are affected; hence the common name is **lockjaw**. As the disease progresses, spasms develop in other muscles.
- Tonic muscle spasms at the site of infection become generalized involving the whole of somatic muscular system.

Other types

- Tetanus neonatorum
- Uterine tetanus
- Otogenic tetanus

Laboratory diagnosis

- **Specimens** Necrotic tissue from the depth of wound
- **Collection** Necrotic tissue beats excised and collected in anaerobic transport media
- **Microscopy** Demonstration of *C. tetani* is unreliable, as non-pathogenic clostridia such as *C. tetanomorphum* and *C. sphenoides* may be present normally
- **Culture** It is the best and confirmatory method.
  - The specimen is inoculated on blood agar, RCM medium and thioglycollate broth. The typical spreading type of growth with alpha haemolysis followed by beta haemolysis is observed on blood agar and the RCM becomes turbid, meat

is not digested but slightly blackened showing slight proteolytic effect.
  - Three RCM bottles are used. The first bottle is heated at 80°C for 15 minutes, the second is heated at 80°C for 5 minutes to kill vegetative forms and the third bottle is left unheated. All bottles are incubated at 37°C for 24–48 hours, subcultured on blood agar and observed for a typical spreading type of growth.
- **Toxigenicity testing**
  - Two mice are inoculated with 0.2 mL broth suspension into root of tail.
  - One is protected with 1000 U of antitoxin that serves as a control.
  - The test animal develops stiffness of tail and rigidity of leg on inoculated site, followed by opposite side leg, trunk and forelimbs. It dies in 2 days.

Treatment

- Isolation—protection from noise and light
- Human antitetanus immunoglobulin (TIG) followed by a full course of active immunization
- Control of spasms
- To maintain airway and feeding

Prophylaxis

- **Surgical** Removal of foreign body, necrotic tissue and blood clots to prevent development of anaerobic environment
- **Antibiotic prophylaxis**
  - Penicillin and tetracycline administered in 4 hours may destroy or inhibit bacilli and toxin production is prevented
  - Bacitracin or neomycin applied locally
- **Immunization** are of three types: active, passive and combined
  - ***Active immunization***
    - Tetanus toxoid (formal toxoid or toxoid absorbed on aluminium phosphate or hydroxide)—three doses (intramuscularly at an interval of 4–6 weeks, between the first and second doses, and 6 months between the second and third dose) gives immunity for 10 years. It can also be given as triple vaccine (DPT).
    - Booster after 10 years or after 3 years, if wounding occurs.
  - ***Passive immunization***
    - Antitetanus serum (ATS) or human antitetanus immunoglobulin is given as an emergency measure in an individual suffering from tetanus
    - Recommended only in non-immune persons at risk and only once
  - ***Combined immunization*** TIG on one hand and toxoid on another site (hand) followed by second and third dose of toxoid

Clostridium botulinum

- Gram-positive bacilli with bulging spores which are subterminal in position
- Motile but non-capsulated
- Strictly anaerobic
- Found in soil, vegetables, animal manure, etc.
- Produce a potent neurotoxin in food
- Causes botulism—a fatal paralytic illness
- There are three types of botulism:
  - Food-borne botulism (ingestion of food that contains clostridium toxin)
  - Infant botulism (ingestion of spores of *C. botulinum* which grow and release toxin)
  - Wound botulism (wound contaminated with *C. botulinum* which produce toxin)

Lab diagnosis

- Demonstration of Gram-positive, sporing bacilli or toxins in food or patient's faeces

Treatment and prophylaxis

- Antibotulinum serum for treatment as well as prophylaxis in those who consumed contaminated food
- Supportive therapy to maintain respiration

Clostridium difficile

- Isolated in 1935 from the faeces of newborn infants
- Named so because it is difficult to isolate
- Gram-positive bacilli
- Form a large oval and terminal spore
- Non-haemolytic, saccharolytic and weekly proteolytic
- It causes antibiotic-associated pseudomembranous colitis
- Antibiotics such as ampicillin, tetracycline, chloramphenicol, lincomycin, clindamycin suppress the drug-sensitive flora, allowing multiplication of *C. difficile* and production of enterotoxin and cytotoxin
- Demonstration of toxin in faeces by enzyme-linked immunosorbent assay (ELISA)
- *C. difficile* can be isolated from faeces on selective media and tested for toxigenicity
- Current antibiotic therapy should be stopped. Metronidazole is a drug of choice. Vancomycin can also be used

Self-assessment

Long-answer questions

1. Discuss in brief the virulence factors, pathogenicity and laboratory diagnosis of infections caused by *Clostridium welchii.*
2. Discuss in brief the virulence factors, pathogenicity, laboratory diagnosis and prophylaxis of tetanus.

Short-answer questions

Write notes on

1. Virulence factors of *Clostridum welchii*
2. Gas gangrene
3. Food poisoning caused by *C. welchii*
4. Laboratory diagnosis of gas gangrene
5. Nagler reaction
6. *C. botulinum*
7. Laboratory diagnosis of tetanus
8. Prophylaxis of tetanus

Multiple-choice questions

1. Which of the following toxins is responsible for Nagler reaction in *Clostridum welchii?*
   A. Theta toxin
   B. Alpha toxin
   C. Beta toxin
   D. Delta toxin
2. Which of the following species of clostridia is non-motile?
   A. *Clostridum welchii*
   B. *C. tetani*
   C. *C. botulinum*
   D. None of the above
3. Which of the following toxins is responsible for target haemolysis in *Clostridum welchii?*
   A. Beta and iota toxins
   B. Epsilon and alpha toxins
   C. Beta and alpha toxins
   D. Theta and alpha toxins
4. Which of the following species of clostridia is a cause of food poisoning?
   A. *Clostridum welchii*
   B. *C. tetani*
   C. *C. difficile*
   D. None of the above
5. Which of the following statements is FALSE regarding gas gangrene?
   A. Is caused by enterotoxin producing strains of *Clostridum welchii*
   B. Is a rapidly spreading oedema
   C. Is characterized by gas production
   D. Is characterized by necrosis and gangrene of the tissue
6. Which of the following statements is FALSE regarding food poisoning caused by *Clostridum welchii?*
   A. Is caused by enterotoxin producing strains
   B. Warm meat is an important source
   C. Diarrhoea without vomiting is an important symptom
   D. Diarrhoea with vomiting is an important symptom

7. Which of the following toxins is produced by *Clostridum botulinum?*
   A. Enterotoxin
   B. Cytotoxin
   C. Neurotoxin
   D. Verotoxin
8. Tetanospasmin produced by *Clostridum tetani* is
   A. Enterotoxin
   B. Cytotoxin
   C. Neurotoxin
   D. Verotoxin
9. Which of the following is a cause of antibiotic associated pseudomembranous colitis?
   A. *Clostridum botulinum*
   B. *C. welchii*
   C. *C. difficile*
   D. *C. tetani*

27 Gram-Positive Bacilli—*Bacillus* Species

These are aerobic, Gram-positive, spore-bearing bacilli. Important *Bacillus* species include

- *Bacillus anthracis*
- *B. cereus*

Bacillus anthracis

- It is a Gram-positive, spore-forming bacillus.
- Size is large, 3–10 µm by 1–1.6 µm.
- Capsulated but non-motile.
- Spores are non-bulging, oval in shape, central in position. They are formed in soil and in culture and not in animal body (Fig. 27.1).
- It is an aerobe and facultative anaerobe.

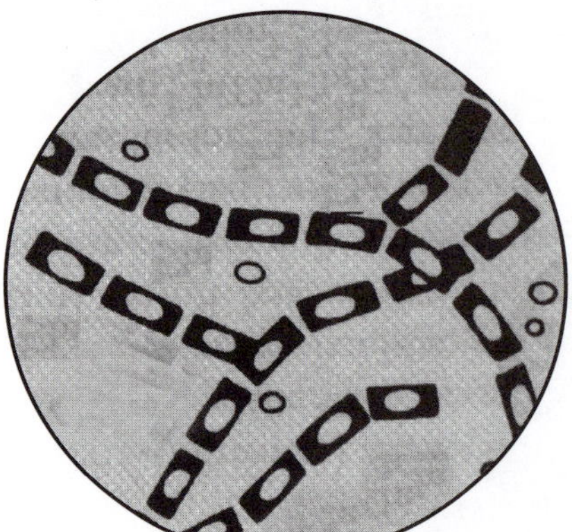

Figure 27.1 *Bacillus anthracis.*

- Optimum temperature is 35°C.
- Grows on ordinary media such as nutrient agar and blood agar.
- Form large, 2–3 mm in diameter, raised, opaque, grey-white colony with irregular edge; edge of the colony shows **'Medusa head appearance'**—wavy margin and small projections.
- Vegetative form is killed at 60°C in 30 minutes but spores are resistant to heat (resist dry heat at 140°C for 1–3 hours and boiling for 10 minutes).
- Spores are resistant to phenol but are destroyed by potassium permanganate solution in 15 minutes.

Virulence factors

- **Capsule**—inhibits opsonization and phagocytosis
- **Exotoxin**—consists of oedema factor, protective antigen factor and lethal factor

Pathogenicity

- *B. anthracis* causes a zoonotic disease—**anthrax** in animals such as sheep and cattle
- Modes of acquiring infection in human beings are
  - Through skin by inoculation
  - Inhalation

- Ingestion
- Anthrax in human beings is of three clinical types:
  - **Cutaneous anthrax**—skin infection
    - Common in dock workers carrying loads of hides on their back, hence called **'Hide porter's disease'**. Also called as **malignant pustule**
    - Lesion starts as papule, become vesicular containing clear or blood-stained fluid
    - Necrosis at the centre of the pustule leads to formation of black eschar
  - **Pulmonary anthrax**—lung infection, also known as **woolsorters's disease**
    - Infection is acquired by inhalation of spores from infected wool
    - Clinically, it manifests as haemorrhagic pneumonia
    - Complication—haemorrhagic meningitis
  - **Intestinal anthrax**—intestinal infection, rarely seen and is characterized by bloody diarrhoea

If the above-mentioned anthrax infections are not treated in time, they lead to fatal septicaemia or meningitis.

Laboratory diagnosis

- **Collection of specimens** Pus, sputum, stool and blood
- **Direct microscopy**
  - Gram staining shows Gram-positive bacilli in chain
  - Demonstration of capsule by negative staining
  - Staining with polychrome methylene blue stain shows capsular material as amorphous purplish material—this is known as M'Fadyean's reaction
  - Demonstration of lipid granules—fat globules by Sudan black B stain
- **Culture** On nutrient and blood agar, growth is confirmed based on colony morphology, Gram stain, etc.
- Ascoli's thermoprecipitation test for antigen detection in tissue

Treatment

- Penicillin is the drug of choice.
- Macrolides, aminoglycosides, tetracycline, chloramphenicol and fluoroquinolones are also effective.

Bacillus cereus

- Is a large, Gram-positive, non-capsulated and motile bacillus which occurs in short chains
- Closely resembles *B. anthracis* in cultural characters
- Is an important agent causing food poisoning
- When food contaminated with *B. cereus* is stored at warm temperature, spores of *B. cereus* germinate into vegetative bacilli, which multiply and elaborate toxin causing food poisoning

Clinical types of food poisoning

It is of two types:

1. **Emetic form**—characterized by acute nausea and vomiting, diarrhoea is not common. Fried rice from Chinese restaurant is the food article responsible
2. **Diarrhoeal form**—characterized by abdominal pain and diarrhoea, vomiting is not common. Cooked meat and vegetables are the food articles responsible

Laboratory diagnosis

- Isolation of bacteria from stool or food by routine methods of culture
- Demonstration of toxin

Treatment

No specific treatment is needed.

Self-assessment

Short-answer questions

Write notes on

1. *Bacillus anthracis*
2. *B. cereus*

Multiple-choice questions

1. Which of the following is a characteristic feature of *Bacillus anthracis*?
   A. Gives positive Nagler's reaction
   B. Colony shows Medusa head appearance
   C. Forms bulging spores
   D. Is non-capsulated but motile
2. Ascoli's thermoprecipitation test for antigen detection in tissue is used for diagnosis of
   A. Tuberculosis
   B. Plague
   C. Anthrax
   D. Tetanus
3. Hide porter's disease caused by *Bacillus anthracis* is an example of
   A. Pulmonary anthrax
   B. Cutaneous anthrax
   C. Septicaemic anthrax
   D. Intestinal anthrax
4. Which of the following types of colony is formed by *Bacillus anthracis*?
   A. Daisy head appearance
   B. Fried egg appearance
   C. Poached egg appearance
   D. Medusa head appearance
5. Which of the following statements is FALSE regarding *Bacillus cereus?*
   A. It causes food poisoning
   B. Fried rice from Chinese restaurant is the food article responsible
   C. Cooked meat and vegetables are the food articles responsible
   D. It is a large Gram-positive, capsulated, non-motile bacillus
6. Woolsorter's disease caused by *Bacillus anthracis* is an example of
   A. Pulmonary anthrax
   B. Cutaneous anthrax
   C. Septicaemic anthrax
   D. Intestinal anthrax

28 Mycobacteria

Mycobacteria of medical and dental importance include

- *Mycobacterium tuberculosis* and *M. bovis*
- Atypical mycobacteria
- *M. leprae*

Mycobacterium tuberculosis and *Mycobacterium bovis*

- These are straight or slightly curved bacilli (Fig. 28.1)
- Size is 2–4 µm by 0.2–0.8 µm
- Non-sporing, non-motile and non-capsulated
- Acid-fast—when stained with Ziehl–Neelsen stain appear bright red in colour

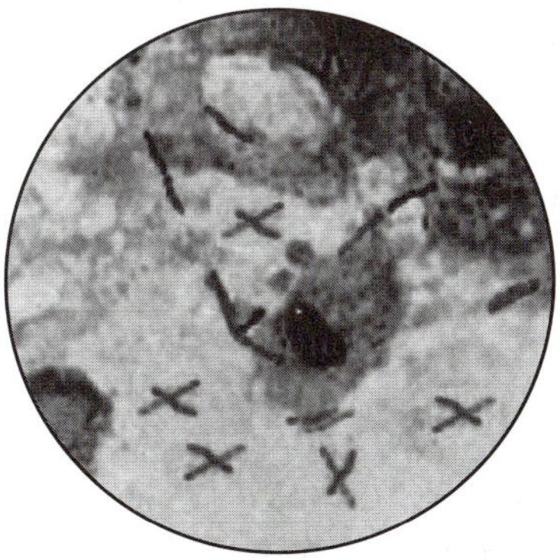

Figure 28.1 *Mycobacterium tuberculosis. See the color image at the end of the book (Color Plates).*

- *M. bovis* is more straight, stout and short as compared to *M. tuberculosis*
- *M. tuberculosis* is an obligate aerobe and *M. bovis* is microaerophilic
- Optimum temperature is 37°C, optimum pH is 7.0
- Grow well on enriched media containing serum, potato, blood and egg
- Grow slowly—growth appears in 2–8 weeks on enriched media such as Lowenstein–Jensen (L–J) medium, Dorset egg medium and Petragnani medium
- *M. tuberculosis* forms dry, rough, raised wrinkled, irregular colonies
- *M. bovis* grows sparsely forming small, smooth, moist colonies, which break up easily
- Sensitive to heat—death occurs at 60°C in 15–20 minutes
- More resistant to chemical disinfectants and destroyed by tincture iodine and 80% ethanol. Ethanol is recommended as disinfectant for skin, rubber gloves, etc.
- They can survive in sputum for 20–30 hours and in droplet nuclei for 8–10 days

Pathogenicity—tuberculosis

- **Sources of infection**
  - ***M. tuberculosis*** originates from infected human cases of tuberculosis.

- *M. bovis* originates from infected animals suffering from bovine tuberculosis—milk being the most common source of infection.
- **Modes of infection** Infection is acquired by inhalation of droplets containing bacilli or by consumption of raw milk in case of *M. bovis* causing bovine tuberculosis.
- **Clinical infections** Tuberculosis occurs in two forms:
  - ***Primary tuberculosis*** It is the most common form and occurs as a pulmonary lesion known as **primary complex** or **Ghon focus** in the lower lobe or lower part of the upper lobe with enlarged hilar lymph nodes. It is often asymptomatic. It may occur as intestinal tuberculosis following consumption of raw milk.
  - ***Secondary tuberculosis*** It occurs because of reactivation of dormant mycobacteria in the primary lesion or exogenous reinfection. Reactivation occurs due to decreased level of immunity. Clinically, one or more lesions commonly in the apex of lungs occur that progress to caseation and cavitation. Cavities may rupture into blood vessels, spreading mycobacteria to various organs and causing generalized infection known as miliary tuberculosis, for example, tuberculosis meningitis, renal, bone and joint tuberculosis.
  - ***Oral lesions*** Tuberculous lesions of the oral cavity may occur rarely. Lesions may occur at any site, but the tongue is the most commonly affected, followed by palate, lips, buccal mucosa, gingiva, etc. Oral lesions occur as
    - A painful and irregular, superficial or deep ulcer which slowly increases in size
    - Tuberculous gingivitis
    - Involvement of bone of the maxilla and mandible may lead to periapical granuloma or tuberculoma and tuberculous osteomyelitis in the later stage of disease

Clinical features

- Fever—evening rise of temperature
- Fatigue
- Headache
- Loss of appetite
- Haemoptysis
- Weight loss
- Weakness
- Cough—sputum coughed out may be bloodstained
- Signs of pleural effusion/consolidation/cavity

Laboratory diagnosis

- **Collection of specimens** Fresh sputum in the morning before meal, gastric washings (in small children who swallow sputum), urine, pleural fluid, peritoneal fluid, cerebrospinal fluid, pus and other infected material.
- **Decontamination and concentration of specimens**
  - Decontamination of sputum is important because it is contaminated with different bacteria and fungi.
  - Concentration of sputum is important because it increases the sensitivity of direct microscopy, which remains the mainstay of diagnosis of TB in the developing countries.
  - The decontaminated specimen is liquefied, neutralized and then centrifuged before using it for microscopy and culture.
- **Direct microscopy**
  - Ziehl–Neelsen staining of specimen shows bright red acid-fast bacilli.
  - Alternatively, fluorescent stain can be used.
- **Concentration of specimens** When acid-fast bacilli (AFB) are not detected by direct microscopy then specimen is concentrated by different techniques. Petroff's method is commonly used. In this method, equal volume of sputum and 4% sodium hydroxide are mixed, incubated at 37°C for 20–30 minutes with intermittent shaking and centrifuged at 3000 rpm for 30 minutes and sediment is used for microscopy and culture.

- **Culture** The concentrated specimen is inoculated into two bottles of L–J media, incubated aerobically at 37°C for 4–8 weeks. Colonies developed on L–J media are studied and identified using Z–N stain and biochemical reactions.
- **Serological tests** are available but nonspecific. They are not helpful in the diagnosis of tuberculosis.
- **Tuberculin test** (Mantoux test) is a delayed hypersensitivity reaction to tuberculoprotein. The test is performed by inoculating purified protein derivative (PPD) intradermally on the forearm and observed after 72 hours for erythema and induration. Erythema and induration about 10 mm indicates positive test. It does not differentiate between clinical disease and subclinical disease; however, a negative test is helpful to exclude the diagnosis of the tuberculosis.

Treatment

• Isoniazid • Rifampicin	Major drugs—first line
• Streptomycin • Ethambutol • Pyrazinamide • Para-aminosalicylic acid	Other first-line drugs
• Kanamycin • Cycloserine • Ofloxacin • Ciprofloxacin • Capreomycin	Second-line drugs

- Currently, short course regimen for 6–7 months is used
- A combination of four drugs (isoniazid, rifampicin, pyrazinamide and ethambutol) three times a week for 2 months followed by isoniazid and rifampicin three times a week for 4–5 months is given in a new smear-positive cases

Prophylaxis

- Prompt and effective treatment of patients and asymptomatic cases
- Adequate nutrition to improve host resistance
- Good housing
- Health education
- Immunization with BCG (Bacillus Calmette–Guerin—a live vaccine) vaccine by intradermal injection soon after the birth offers protection for 10–15 years. A single dose of BCG is sufficient in India.

Atypical mycobacteria

Mycobacteria other than typical mycobacteria causing a disease resembling tuberculosis are called as atypical mycobacteria. They are classified into four groups:

1. **Photochromogens** Produce yellow-orange pigment when culture is exposed to light, for example, *M. kansasii, M. simiae, M. marinum*
2. **Scotochromogens** Produce yellow-orange pigmented colonies even in dark, for example, *M. scrofulaceum, M. szulgai*
3. **Non-photochromogens** These mycobacteria do not produce pigment even on exposure to light, for example, *M. avium, M. intracellulare, M. xenopi, M. ulcerans*
4. **Rapid growers** Capable of growing rapidly, that is, within 7 days of incubation. They include some photochromogens, scotochromogens and non-photochromogens species, for example, *M. fortuitum, M. chelonei*

Pathogenicity

- Pulmonary infection like tuberculosis is caused by *M. kansasii, M avium, M. intracellulare, M. simiae* and rarely by *M. szulgai, M. xenopi* and *M. chelonei.*
- Cervical lymphadenopathy is caused by *M. szulgai, M. avium—intracellulare, M. scrofulaceum* and rarely by *M. kansasii.*
- Cutaneous and subcutaneous lesions such as chronic ulcers, swimming pool granuloma are caused by *M. marinum,* abscesses by *M. fortuitum, M. chelonei*

and Buruli ulcer by *M. ulcerans,* surgical wound infections by *M. chelonei* and *M. fortuitum.*

- Systemic disseminated disease is caused by *M. avium* and *M. intracellulare.*

Laboratory diagnosis

It is same as tuberculosis. Steps in the diagnosis are as follows:

- Collection of specimen
- Microscopy
- Culture on L–J incubated at 25°C, 37°C and 45°C. Slants observed for pigment production
- Identification based on pigment production, rate of growth and based on biochemical reactions

Treatment

- They may respond to prolonged treatment with isoniazid (INH), rifampicin and ethambutol.
- Other drugs used are clofazimine, quinolones and macrolides.

Mycobacterium leprae

- It is a mycobacteria—causing leprosy, which affects skin and peripheral nerves.
- It was first described by Hansen (1873), hence leprosy is also called **Hansen disease**.
- It is a straight or slightly curved, slender, acid-fast bacillus.
- Size is 1–8 × 0.3 µm.
- It is less acid-fast than *M. tuberculosis*; hence, it is decolourized by 5% sulphuric acid.
- Arranged singly or in groups intra- and extracellular.
- Intracellular bacilli usually form parallel bundles called globi, which gives cigar bundle appearance.
- Non-motile, non-sporing and non-capsulated.
- It cannot be cultivated in artificial culture media.
- Animals are used for isolation and culture.
- Animals used are
  - Mice—footpads of mice are used for inoculation
  - Nine-banded armadillo
- Generation time is 13–15 days.
- Can survive in humid climate for 9–15 days.
- Survive exposure of sunlight for 2 hours.

Pathogenicity and clinical features

- It causes leprosy, a disease specially affecting the skin, nerves and nasal mucosa.
- Mode of infection is exactly not known. Organism may infect via respiratory tract and skin-to-skin contact.

Clinical types

According to Ridely and Jopling, there are five clinical types:

1. Tuberculoid (TT)
2. Borderline tuberculoid (BT)
3. Borderline (BB)
4. Borderline lepromatous (BL)
5. Lepromatous (LL)

Two polar forms are tuberculoid and lepromatous leprosy (Table 28.1).

Oral lesions in leprosy

The oral lesions produced in leprosy include the following:

- Small tumour-like masse called lepromas on the tongue, lips or hard palate, which have tendency to breakdown and ulcerate
- Gingival hyperplasia and loosening of the teeth

Lepromin test

- It is a skin test for delayed hypersensitivity and used to study immunity in leprosy patients.
- Antigen used is Mitsuda's antigen or bacillary lepromin.

Table 28.1 Differences between two polar forms of leprosy

	Tuberculoid (TT)	Lepromatous (LL)
CMI	Good	Deficient/absent
Host resistance	Good	Low
Lesions		
• Number	Few	Many
• Appearance	Macular dry, scaly lesions	Nodular, shiny lesions
Infectivity	Usually non-infective form	Highly infective form
Bacteria	Paucibacillary form	Multibacillary form
• Skin smears	Scanty or not seen	Plenty in number
• Nasal smears	Not seen	Plenty in number
Lepromin test	Positive	Negative
Prognosis	Good	Bad

CMI, cell-mediated immunity.

Procedure

- 0.1 mL of antigen is injected intradermally on forearm
- Response shows two types of reactions:
  - ***Early or Fernandez reaction*** It is an acute inflammatory area of more than 10 mm in diameter appearing in 24–48 hours and disappears in 3–4 days.
  - ***Late or Mitsuda's reaction*** It appears 3–4 weeks after injection in the form of a nodule, which may ulcerate or subside in few weeks.
- Mitsuda's reaction is more meaningful as it is a manifestation of cell-mediated immunity, induced by lepromin while Fernandez reaction indicates past reaction.

Uses

- To classify lesions of leprosy—it is positive in tuberculoid and negative in lepromatous
- To assess prognosis and response to treatment—positive reaction indicates good prognosis and negative reaction indicates bad prognosis. Conversion of negative test to positive indicates improvement
- To assess resistance of an individual to leprosy—those showing positive reaction can respond to *M. leprae* infection

Laboratory diagnosis

- **Specimens**
  - **Skin clippings** From peripheral margin of lesions, ear lobules, forehead, cheek or chin
  - **Nasal samples** Nasal scraping, nasal swab, nasal washing and nasal blow
    - Skin nerve biopsy
    - Lymph node puncture
- **Microscopic examination** Smears stained by modified Z–N stain by using 5% sulphuric acid and observed for acid-fast bacilli
- **Culture** is not routinely practicable
- **Serological tests** Antibodies against phenolic glycolipid antigen can be detected by
  - Latex agglutination
  - Enzyme-linked immunosorbent assay (ELISA)
- **Lepromin test** Mitsuda's reaction is not used for diagnosis but to see resistance of patients

Treatment

- **Paucibacillary leprosy** Rifampicin once a month and dapsone daily for 6 months
- **Multibacillary leprosy** Rifampicin once a month, dapsone and clofazimine daily for 2 years

Self-assessment

Long-answer questions

1. Discuss in brief the pathogenicity, clinical features and laboratory diagnosis of tuberculosis.
2. Discuss in brief the pathogenicity, clinical features and laboratory diagnosis of leprosy.

Short-answer questions

Write notes on

1. Lepromin test
2. Atypical mycobacteria
3. Tuberculin test
4. Difference between tuberculoid and lepromatous leprosy
5. Laboratory diagnosis of tuberculosis

Multiple-choice questions

1. Which of the following statements is FALSE regarding tuberculin test?
   A. It is a delayed hypersensitivity reaction
   B. Erythema and induration about 10 mm indicates positive test
   C. It does not differentiate between clinical disease and subclinical disease
   D. Negative test is not helpful in excluding the diagnosis of tuberculosis
2. The following are the atypical mycobacteria, EXCEPT
   A. *Mycobacterium bovis*
   B. *M. avium*
   C. *M. kansasii*
   D. *M. scrofulaceum*
3. Which of the following is highly infective form of leprosy?
   A. Tuberculoid
   B. Borderline tuberculoid
   C. Borderline lepromatous
   D. Lepromatous
4. Which of the following species of mycobacteria is transmitted by consumption of raw milk?
   A. *Mycobacterium tuberculosis*
   B. *M. avium*
   C. *M. bovis*
   D. *M. kansasii*
5. Bacillus Calmette–Guerin vaccine is a
   A. Killed vaccine
   B. Live attenuated vaccine
   C. Subunit vaccine
   D. Recombinant vaccine
6. *Mycobacterium chelonei* belongs to which of the following group of mycobacteria?
   A. Rapid growers
   B. Non-photochromogens
   C. Scotochromogens
   D. Photochromogens
7. Which of the following statements is FALSE regarding *Mycobacterium leprae*?
   A. Is less acid-fast than *M. tuberculosis*
   B. Shows cigar bundle appearance
   C. Is first described by Hansen
   D. Can be cultivated on Lowenstein–Jensen medium
8. Generation time in *Mycobacterium leprae* is
   A. 13–15 minutes
   B. 13–15 hours
   C. 13–15 days
   D. 13–15 months
9. Lepromin test is positive in which of the following clinical types of leprosy?
   A. Tuberculoid
   B. Borderline
   C. Borderline lepromatous
   D. Lepromatous
10. Which of the following reactions is more meaningful in lepromin test?
    A. Fernandez reaction
    B. Mitsuda's reaction
    C. Both of these
    D. None of the above

29 Non-Sporing Anaerobes

Anaerobes are bacteria, which can live in relative or total absence of oxygen. Anaerobes are of two types:

1. Spore forming or clostridial anaerobes—Clostridia species, for example, *Clostridium welchii, C. tetani, C. difficile, C. septicum, C. novyi* and other species
2. Non-sporing or non-clostridial anaerobes

Non-sporing or non-clostridial anaerobes are the most common causes of anaerobic infections. These infections are always endogenous, as the non-clostridial anaerobes are obligate parasites that form the part of the normal bacterial flora of oropharynx, alimentary canal and female genital tract. These organisms from their normal habitat may invade adjacent tissues, which are debilitated or are the seat of some other pathological changes, such as reduction of tissue oxygen because of poor blood supply, tissue necrosis and primary infection with aerobic or facultative anaerobic bacteria.

Non-sporing anaerobes of medical importance

Cocci

- **Gram-positive cocci**
  - *Peptococcus* species—*Pc. niger*
  - *Peptostreptococcus* species—*Ps. anaerobius, Ps. magnus, Ps. prevotii, Ps. asaccharolyticus*
  - *Sarcina* species—*S. ventriculi*
  - **Anaerobic streptococci**—*Streptococcus intermedius, Str. morbillorum*
- **Gram-negative cocci**
  - *Veillonella* species—*V. parvum*
  - *Acidaminococcus* species
  - *Megasphaera* species

Bacilli

- **Gram-positive bacilli**
  - *Actinomyces* species—*A. israelii*
  - *Arachnia* species
  - *Bifidobacterium* species
  - *Eubacterium* species
  - *Lactobacillus* species
  - *Propionibacterium* species—*P. acnes*
- **Gram-negative bacilli**
  - *Bacteroides* species—*B. fragilis, B. vulgatus, B. thetaiotaomicron*
  - *Prevotella* species—*P. melaninogenicus, P. buccalis, P. oralis, P. corporis*
  - *Porphyromonas* species—*P. gingivalis, P. endodontalis, P. asaccharolyticus*
  - *Capnocytophaga* species
  - *Fusobacterium* species—*F. necrophorum, F. nucleatum*
  - *Leptotrichia* species—*L. buccalis*
- **Spirochaetes**
  - *Treponema* species—*Treponema pallidum*
  - *Borrelia* species

Pathogenesis

- The most important factor in developing anaerobic infections is lowering of Eh (oxidation-reduction potential), which favours multiplication of anaerobes.
- Eh is lowered by
  - Poor blood supply
  - Tissue necrosis
  - Growth of facultative anaerobes
  - A concomitant aerobic bacterial infection may at times contribute synergistically in occurrence and progress of anaerobic bacterial infection
- Once the conditions become suitable, the anaerobes invade the surrounding tissue with the help of different virulence factors, for example, toxins, various enzymes such as hyaluronidase, heparinase, proteases, superoxide dismutase, catalase, peroxidase, immunoglobulin proteases, which contribute to the pathogenesis. Anaerobes also produce various extracellular products, while some anaerobes produce capsule, which prevents phagocytosis and help in pathogenesis.

Common infections caused by non-sporing anaerobes

Orodental infections

- Gingivitis
- Dental abscess
- Mandibular space infections
- Periodontal infections
- Stomatitis

Most commonly caused by fusobacteria, spirochaetes, actinomycetes and other anaerobes present in the mouth.

Ear, nose and throat infections

- Otitis media
- Mastoiditis
- Sinusitis
- Peritonsillar infections
- Deep neck space infections

Most commonly involved anaerobes are fusobacteria.

Respiratory infections

- Aspiration pneumonia
- Lung abscess
- Empyema
- Bronchiectasis

Most commonly caused by fusobacteria, *P. melaninogenicus, B. fragilis,* anaerobic cocci and others.

Female genital tract infections

- Vaginitis
- Bartholin's abscess
- Puerperal sepsis
- Post-abortal sepsis
- Pelvic abscess
- Endometritis and pyometritis

Most commonly caused by *P. melaninogenicus, B. fragilis,* peptococci, peptostreptococci, fusobacteria, etc.

Abdominal infections

- Appendicitis
- Diverticulitis
- Peritonitis
- Perirectal abscess
- Biliary tract infections
- Postoperative wound infections
- Wound infections due to abdominal wound contamination after surgery or trauma

Most commonly caused by *Bacteroides* species and anaerobic cocci.

Other anaerobic infections

- Bacteraemia
- Brain abscess
- Bone and joint infections
- Cellulitis
- Necrotizing fasciitis
- Ophthalmic infections
- Skin and soft-tissue infections

Most commonly caused by *Bacteroides* species, *Prevotella* species, anaerobic cocci and others.

Laboratory diagnosis

Specimens

Specimens are collected depending on the site of infection by using appropriate procedures and transported in an anaerobic condition to protect them from lethal effect of oxygen. Specimens are transported in transport media such as Stuart's medium or Robertson's cooked meat medium.

Direct microscopy

Gram-stained smear examination is important because the culture results should be compared with the Gram-stained smear results and every effort should be made to isolate all the cell morphotypes observed in the direct smear of the specimen.

Gram stain usually shows polymicrobial picture, for example, consists of mixture of bacteria.

Culture

Specimen is inoculated on selective and non-selective media, to ensure the culture of all anaerobes present in specimen. The following media are used:

- Plain freshly prepared blood agar—for all anaerobes
- Neomycin blood agar—for all anaerobes
- Neomycin-kanamycin blood agar—for all anaerobes
- Phenylethyl alcohol blood agar—for all anaerobes
- Kanamycin-vancomycin blood agar—for Gram-negative anaerobes

After inoculation, plates are incubated anaerobically in McIntosh-Filde's jar, gas-pak jar or anaerobic glove box. Gas-pak jar is the most reliable and most commonly used now-adays.

Identification scheme

The colonies formed are studied in detail. Each type of colony is Gram-stained and subcultured for oxygen tolerance by inoculating on blood agar and incubating aerobically.

The oxygen-sensitive colony is considered as anaerobe and the identification scheme is continued. The identification of anaerobes can often be made based on colony morphology, pigmentation, haemolysis, pitting of agar, fluorescence under ultraviolet light, motility, catalase test, indole test, sugar fermentation tests, bile resistance and esculin hydrolysis.

Rapid identification methods

Rapid identification with the help of gentamicin and metronidazole discs The rapid presumptive identification of anaerobes can be made using discs of gentamicin (10 μg) and metronidazole (5 μg) applied on heavily inoculated plate at the primary and secondary streaking, respectively. Majority of anaerobes are susceptible to metronidazole and resistant to gentamicin. The culture plates after incubation are observed for zone of inhibition surrounding metronidazole disc and a representative colony at the margin of zone is tested for aerobic growth. A colony failing to grow aerobically from such margin is identified as an obligate anaerobe.

Treatment

Antibiotics commonly used in the treatment are

- Penicillin
- Tetracycline
- Chloramphenicol
- Clindamycin—not in common use
- Metronidazole—drug of choice
- Fucidin
- Trimethoprim
- Some infections require surgical intervention also
- Metronidazole can also be used as a prophylactic agent in large bowl surgery

Self-assessment

Short-answer questions

Write notes on

1. Common infections caused by non-sporing anaerobes
2. Orodental infections caused by non-sporing anaerobes
3. Laboratory diagnosis of non-sporing anaerobic infections

Multiple-choice questions

1. Which of the following species is the most common anaerobe causing orodental infections?
   A. *Bacteroides* spp.
   B. *Fusobacterium* spp.
   C. *Lactobacillus* spp.
   D. *Propionibacterium* spp.
2. *Actinomyces* spp. are most commonly associated with
   A. Ear, nose and throat infections
   B. Respiratory infections
   C. Female genital tract infections
   D. Orodental infections
3. Which of the following statements is FALSE regarding non-spore forming anaerobes?
   A. They are obligate parasites that form the part of the normal bacterial flora
   B. They are non-clostridial anaerobes
   C. Metronidazole is the drug of choice for their treatment
   D. They are associated with female genital tract infections only
4. Which of the following is the drug of choice for treatment of non-spore forming anaerobes?
   A. Clindamycin
   B. Penicillin
   C. Metronidazole
   D. Fucidin
5. Which of the following is the most reliable and most commonly used method for anaerobiosis?
   A. McIntosh-Filde's jar
   B. Gas-pak jar
   C. Anaerobic glove box
   D. Candle jar

30 Spirochaetes

Spirochaetes are slender, unicellular, helical or spiral rods. Important spirochaetal pathogens include the following:

- ***Treponema***
  - *Treponema pallidum*—causing syphilis
  - *T. pertenue*—causing yaws
  - *T. carateum*—causing pinta
  - *T. endemicum*—causing endemic syphilis
- ***Borrelia***
  - *Borrelia recurrentis*—causing relapsing fever
  - *B. burgdorferi*—causing Lyme disease
  - *B. vincentii*—along with Fusobacteria causes Vincent's angina
- ***Leptospira***
  - *Leptospira interrogans*—causing leptospirosis

Treponema pallidum

- Gram-negative, long, slender, helically-coiled, spiral or corkscrew-shaped bacterium with tapering ends (Fig. 30.1)
- Size is about 10 µm long (range 5–15 µm by 0.2 µm)
- It has 10 regular spirals at regular distance of 1 µm
- Actively motile, non-sporing and non-capsulated

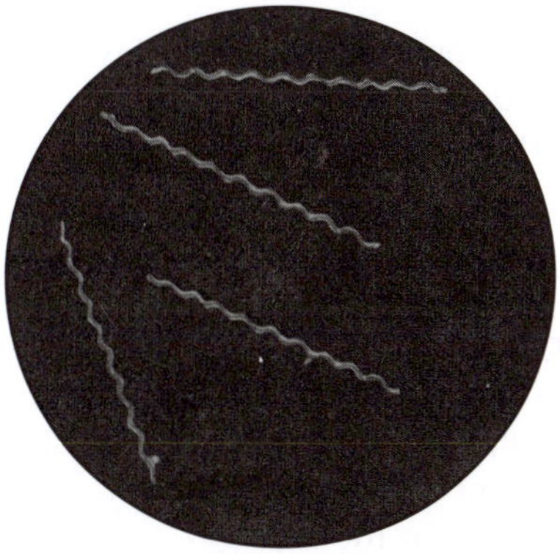

Figure 30.1 *Treponema pallidum.*

- Under dark field microscopy, it exhibits motion around the long axis
- It is a strict anaerobe with forward and backward motion and flexion
- Can be seen with negative staining with India ink
- Difficult to grow, cannot be cultivated on artificial media or in tissue culture
- It can be maintained by subculture in animals—by serial testicular passage in rabbits
- Sensitive to drying, inactivated by heat (41–42°C for 1 hour), also sensitive to low temperature, it is killed at 0–4°C in 1–3 days, hence transfusion syphilis can be prevented by storing blood for 4 days in refrigerator before transfusion

- Inactivated by contact with oxygen, distilled water, soap, arsenicals and common antiseptic agents

Pathogenicity—syphilis

- It is a sexually transmitted disease.
- It occurs as
  - Acquired syphilis
  - Congenital syphilis
  - Non-venereal syphilis

Acquired syphilis

- Infection acquired by sexual contact
- Entry through minute abrasions on mucosa or skin
- Incubation period is 10–90 days
- It occurs in three stages:
  - Primary
  - Secondary
  - Tertiary

Primary lesion It is characterized by a painless ulcer called hard **chancre** on genital organ, mouth, nipple, intrarectal or perianal with the involvement of regional lymph nodes. The chancre heals in 10–14 days.

Oral lesions In the mouth, the chancre occurs as an ulcerated lesion covered by a greyish-white membrane, which may be painful because of secondary infection. The ulcer can occur on the lips, tongue, palate, gingiva and tonsils.

Secondary lesions They occur in 2–6 months after the primary lesion, characterized by eruptions of skin and mucous membranes. On the skin, the lesions occur as macular or papular skin rashes. The lesions on the mucous membrane are known as mucous patches. At mucocutaneous junctions, it manifests as condylomata.

Oral lesions In the **oral cavity,** mucous patches occur as multiple, painless, greyish-white plaques overlying an ulcerated surface and commonly seen on the tongue, gingival and buccal mucosa. The patient is highly infectious during this stage. The lesions subside spontaneously or infection remains in a latent stage.

Tertiary lesions In 50% cases, tertiary lesions develop after several years. These consist of

- Cardiovascular lesions
- Chronic granulomata (gummata)
- Meningovascular manifestations
- The chronic granulomata (gummata) are the main tertiary lesions that occur frequently on the skin and mucous membranes, liver, testes and bone

Oral lesions In the oral cavity, it most commonly occurs on the tongue and palate as a firm nodular mass in the tissue, which may ulcerate and may cause perforation, when it is on the palate. Atrophic or interstitial glossitis is also the characteristic lesion.

Congenital syphilis

- Transmitted from mother to foetus in utero through placenta.
- It may lead to death of the foetus in utero and miscarriage, stillbirth or live birth with symptoms of congenital syphilis.

Non-venereal syphilis

Occupational syphilis may occur in doctors or nurses due to close contact with the patient. The course of disease is same except for the primary chancre is extragenital.

Laboratory diagnosis

Collection of specimens

Specimens include tissue fluid, exudates from the primary lesion, lymph node aspirate and blood for serological tests. For diagnosis of oral chancre, a material from affected regional lymph node is used as the material from oral lesion with saliva is frequently contaminated with *T. microdentium*—a spirochaete normally present in the mouth, which may be confused with *T. pallidum.*

Microscopic examination

Demonstration of spirochaetes by

- **Dark ground microscopy** Specimen of tissue fluid, exudates or lymph node aspirate is placed directly on the slide and observed for motile slender, spirals with pointed ends.
- **Direct immunofluorescence test** Smear is prepared from specimen and stained with fluorescein labelled monoclonal antibody to *T. pallidum*. If *T. pallidum* are present in smear, fluorescence is observed. It is more sensitive than dark ground microscopy.
- **Treponemes in tissue** can be demonstrated by immunofluorescence or silver impregnation technique such as Levaditi stain.

Serological tests

For demonstration of antibodies in the serum of the patient against *T. pallidum*, two types of tests are used. These are as follows:

1. **Standard tests using non-specific antigen (non-specific tests)**
   - Wasserman test
   - Kahn test
   - Venereal disease research laboratory (VDRL) test—most widely used
   - Rapid plasma reagin test—alternative test for VDRL
2. **Treponemal tests using specific antigen (specific tests)**
   - **By using Reiter's strain**—Reiter's protein complement fixation test (RPCFT)
   - **By using Nichol's strain**
     - ***Test using live strain***—*T. pallidum* immobilization (TPI) test
     - ***Test using killed treponemes***
       - Fluorescent treponemal antibody test (FTA)
       - *T. pallidum* agglutination test (TPA)
       - *T. pallidum* immune adherence (TPIA) test
     - ***Test using extract of treponemes***
       - *T. pallidum* haemagglutination (TPHA) test
       - Enzyme immunoassay (EIA) test

VDRL test

- The test was developed in venereal disease research laboratory, New York.
- **Principle** It is a slide flocculation test, a type of precipitation reaction.
- **Procedure**
  - ***Qualitative test***
    - It is carried out on VDRL tile
    - A drop of serum inactivated by heating in water bath at 56°C is added to concavity on the VDRL tile
    - A drop of VDRL antigen is then added
    - Mixed with a stick and the tile is rotated manually or mechanically on VDRL rotator giving 180 oscillations/minute for 4–8 minutes
    - Result read under microscope
  - ***Interpretation***
    - Presence of floccules—reactive
    - Absence of floccules—non-reactive
  - ***Quantitative test*** Serial doubling dilutions of serum are prepared and placed in different concavities and a drop of VDRL antigen is then added in each concavity and the tile is rotated manually or mechanically on VDRL rotator giving 180 oscillations/minute for 4–8 minutes.

Highest dilution giving positive result is taken as titre. A titre of 1:8 or more is considered as significant.

Treatment

- Penicillin—treatment of choice
- Erythromycin
- Tetracycline
- Doxycycline
- Ceftriaxone
- Azithromycin

Prophylaxis

- Avoidance of sexual contact with infected person
- Use of physical barriers (condoms)
- Use of antiseptics (potassium permanganate) or antibiotics

Borrelia

- These are Gram-negative spiral forms
- Size is 8–20 µm long, 0.2–0.5 µm in width
- Actively motile with the help of endoflagella
- They have coarse irregular, uneven, wide, open spirals with pointed ends
- Demonstration can be seen with light microscope by using Giemsa stain (Fig. 30.2)
- They are microaerophilic, optimum temperature for growth is 28–30°C
- Grow in Noguchi's medium, chorioallantoic membrane of chick embryo and peritoneal cavity of rat and mouse

Pathogenicity

- *B. recurrentis, B. duttoni* and few other species cause **relapsing fever** characterized by fever of sudden onset which lasts for 3–5 days followed by afebrile period of 4–10 days. It is followed by another bout of fever in 3–10 days.
- *B. burgdorferi* is a causative agent of **Lyme disease** characterized by localized infection—**erythema chronicum migrans**. It is characterized by a macule at the site of the bite surrounded by redness and induration associated with fever, headache and chills. Infection may become disseminated and spread to variety of organs causing neurological and cardiac symptoms such as meningitis, myopericarditis and heart failure. It may also lead to persistent infection characterized by chronic arthritis and arthralgia.
- *B. vincentii* along with Fusobacteria causes **Vincent's angina**—ulcerative oropharyngitis and gingivostomatitis.

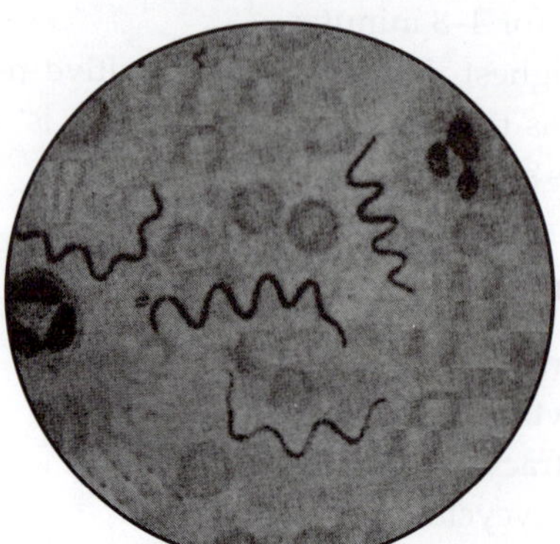

Figure 30.2 *Borrelia.*

Laboratory diagnosis

- **Specimens** Blood, cerebrospinal fluid (CSF), specimen from local lesion
- **Microscopic examination**
  - Demonstration by Giemsa stain or Leishman's stain
  - Dark ground microscopy
  - Phase contrast microscopy
  - Silver impregnation method
  - Immunofluorescence
- **Serology** Antibody detection by immunofluorescence test and ELISA
- **Nuclei acid detection** Polymerase chain reaction (PCR) for detection of nucleic acids in tissue and body fluids
- **Animal inoculation**
  - 1–2 mL blood inoculated intraperitoneally in white mice
  - *Borrelia* multiply and appear in blood within 2 days
  - Smears prepared from blood collected from tail vein examined for *Borrelia*

Treatment

- Doxycycline
- Amoxicillin
- Cefuroxime
- Penicillin
- Metronidazole

Leptospira

- *Leptospira* are Gram-negative, tightly coiled, thin and flexible spirochaetes with characteristics hooked ends (Fig. 30.3)
- Size is 5–15 µm by 0.1–0.2 µm
- Actively motile, non-sporing and non-capsulated
- Aerobic and microaerophilic
- Grow on media enriched with rabbit serum, in chick embryo and in guinea pigs
- Susceptible to heat (50°C in 10 minutes) and acidic pH. Sensitive to salts, chlorine and other antiseptic agents
- Two species—*L. interrogans* and *L. biflexa*

Pathogenicity—leptospirosis

- *Leptospira icterohaemorrhagiae*—belonging to *L. interrogans* is pathogenic
- Causes **Weil disease** characterized by jaundice, haemorrhages and necrosis of tissue, fever, enlargement of spleen and nephritis
- Wild rat is important reservoir
- Human infection results from ingestion of contaminated water or food or through mucous membrane or breaks in the skin

Laboratory diagnosis

- **Collection of specimens** Blood, urine and CSF

Figure 30.3 *Leptospira* species.

- **Direct microscopy** For demonstration of *Leptospira* by
  - Fluorescent antibody technique
  - Silver impregnation technique
  - Phase contrast microscopy
  - Dark ground microscopy for motility
- **Culture** On special media, it takes more time
- **Animal inoculation** It is more sensitive than culture for isolation. Specimen is inoculated intraperitoneally in hamster or guinea pigs and *Leptospira* are demonstrated in peritoneal cavity and many other organs after death (8–15 days)
- **Serological tests** For demonstration of antibodies, following tests are used:
  - Microscopic agglutination test
  - Indirect fluorescent antibody test
  - Complement fixation test

Treatment

- Penicillin
- Tetracycline

Self-assessment

Long-answer question

1. Discuss in brief the pathogenicity and laboratory diagnosis of syphilis.

Short-answer questions

Write notes on

1. Laboratory diagnosis of syphilis
2. VDRL
3. *Borrelia*
4. *Leptospira*

Multiple-choice questions

1. Which of the following tests is a specific test for syphilis?
   A. VDRL test
   B. Kahn test
   C. Wasserman test
   D. *Treponema pallidum* haemagglutination test

2. Which of the following tests is a non-specific test for syphilis?
   A. Rapid plasma reagin test
   B. Fluorescent treponemal antibody test
   C. *Treponema pallidum* immune adherence test
   D. *T. pallidum* haemagglutination test
3. Which of the following titres is considered as significant in VDRL test?
   A. 1:2
   B. 1:4
   C. 1:6
   D. 1:8
4. Which of the following statements is FALSE regarding *Treponema pallidum*?
   A. Is a strict anaerobe
   B. Cannot be cultivated on artificial media
   C. Is non-motile, non-sporing and non-capsulated
   D. Has 10 regular spirals at regular distance of 1 µm
5. Cardiovascular lesions are seen in which of the following stages of syphilis?
   A. Primary
   B. Secondary
   C. Tertiary
   D. None of the above
6. Which of the following specimens is used for diagnosis of oral chancre?
   A. Saliva
   B. Material from affected regional lymph node
   C. Material from chancre itself
   D. None of the above
7. Which of the following species of *Treponema* causes confusion in the diagnosis of oral chancre?
   A. *Treponema pertenue*
   B. *T. carateum*
   C. *T. endemicum*
   D. *T. microdentium*
8. Which of the following techniques is used for demonstration of treponemes in tissue?
   A. Silver impregnation technique
   B. Dark ground microscopy
   C. Negative staining technique
   D. Gram staining method
9. Which of the following spirochetes is a cause of Weil disease?
   A. *Borrelia recurrentis*
   B. *Leptospira icterohaemorrhagiae*
   C. *B. burgdorferi*
   D. *B. duttoni*
10. Which of the following spirochetes is a cause of relapsing fever?
   A. *Borrelia recurrentis*
   B. *B. vincentii*
   C. *B. burgdorferi*
   D. *Leptospira icterohaemorrhagiae*
11. Which of the following spirochetes is a cause of Lyme disease?
   A. *Borrelia recurrentis*
   B. *B. vincentii*
   C. *B. burgdorferi*
   D. *Leptospira icterohaemorrhagiae*

31 Actinomycetes

- Actinomycetes are Gram-positive, non-acid-fast, non-motile, non-sporing and non-capsulated filamentous bacteria that resemble fungi.
- They grow in mycelial forms and break up into coccal and bacillary forms.
- They form sulphur granules—white or yellow in colour and are found in tissues. When these granules are crushed between slides and examined by Gram staining, they show a central filamentous Gram-positive mycelium surrounded by Gram-negative swollen club-shaped structures of host origin. This gives a sunray-like appearance.
- They grow anaerobically or microaerophilically on brain–heart infusion agar and thioglycollate broth.
- The optimum temperature is 37°C.
- On brain–heart infusion agar, small spidery colonies are formed after 48–72 hours that become heaped up, white, irregular and smooth giving molar teeth appearance.
- The important species are *Actinomyces israelii* (most common in humans), *A. naeslundii, A. viscosus, A. odontolyticus* and *A. meyeri.*

Pathogenicity—actinomycosis

- **Source** It is usually an endogenous infection. Bacteria are present as commensals in the mouth, intestine and vagina.
- **Predisposing factors** Trauma, foreign bodies, poor oral hygiene and intrauterine devices.

Actinomycosis

It is a chronic granulomatous disease characterized by indurated swelling of the connective tissue with suppuration and discharge of sulphur granules from multiple sinuses. It occurs in four main clinical forms:

1. **Cervicofacial**—indurated lesions on the cheek and submaxillary region, which may extend to the mandible or the maxilla and may involve maxillary bone causing osteomyelitis. Further invasion may involve the apex of teeth. Dental caries are a predisposing factor. Infection occurs following tooth extraction or other dental procedures
2. **Thoracic**—lesion in the lungs that may involve pleura, pericardium and chest wall. Sinuses often appear on the chest wall. Source of infection is actinomycetes from the oral cavity. Mode of infection is aspiration of actinomycetes from the oral cavity
3. **Abdominal**—lesion around the caecum and abdominal wall
4. **Pelvic**—common in females using intrauterine devices

Oral infections

Actinomycetes are also involved in gingivitis and periodontitis—inflammatory diseases of the gums and root surface caries.

Other infections

They are also the cause of mycetoma.

Laboratory diagnosis

- **Collection of specimens** Pus, sinus discharge, granules, infected tissue and sputum
  - Pus is collected in a test tube containing normal saline, granules sediment at bottom after shaking, which can be used for further examination.
  - Granules can be collected by applying gauge pads to the sinuses.
  - They can also be collected by using probe or loop.
- **Macroscopic (naked eye) examination** For presence of sulphur granules—white or yellow about 5 mm in size
- **Microscopic examination**
  - **Gram stain**—crushed granules are stained with Gram stain observed for Gram-positive filaments showing **sun-ray appearance**
  - **Ziehl–Neelsen stain**—modified Z–N stain using 1% sulphuric acid as decolourizing agent shows the zone of radiating acid-fast clubs
- **Culture** Washed granules are inoculated in thioglycollate broth and brain–heart infusion agar and incubated anaerobically at 37°C for 48 hours and observed for minute colonies identified by microscopy, biochemical reactions and fluorescent antibody method

Treatment

- Surgical removal of affected tissue along with antibiotics
- Penicillin is commonly used
- Ampicillin or co-amoxiclav
- Tetracycline in persons allergic to penicillin
- Aminoglycosides, clindamycin and metronidazole in concomitant infections
- Co-trimoxazole
- Pyrimethamine
- Rifampicin

Self-assessment

Short-answer questions

Write notes on

1. Actinomycosis
2. Cervicofacial actinomycosis
3. Laboratory diagnosis of actinomycosis

Multiple-choice questions

1. Which of the following species of actinomycetes is most common in humans?
   A. *Actinomyces naeslundii*
   B. *A. viscosus*
   C. *A. israelii*
   D. *A. odontolyticus*
2. Which of the following statements is FALSE regarding actinomycetes?
   A. White or yellow sulphur granules in tissues
   B. Sunray-like appearance
   C. Filamentous bacteria resembling fungi
   D. They are Gram-negative bacilli
3. Which of the following is NOT the characteristic feature of actinomycosis?
   A. Sunray-like appearance
   B. Medusa head appearance
   C. White or yellow sulphur granules
   D. Multiple discharging sinuses

32 Gram-Negative Bacilli—Enterobacteriaceae

The members of family Enterobacteriaceae include a large number of closely related bacterial species that inhabit the large intestine of man and animals and are present in soil, water and decaying organic matter.

- Also referred as enteric bacteria.
- The family includes some of the most important intestinal pathogens for humans, for example, *Salmonella* and *Shigella*.
- Many members do not cause disease when they are in the gut but when their habitat is changed they become pathogenic.
- They are Gram-negative bacilli classified based upon lactose fermentation as given in Table 32.1.

Table 32.1 Classification of Enterobacteriaceae based upon lactose fermentation

Lactose fermenters	Non-lactose fermenters	Late lactose fermenters
Ferment lactose, producing pink colonies on MacConkey's agar, e.g., *E. coli*, *Klebsiella*	Do not ferment lactose, producing colourless colonies on MacConkey's agar, e.g., *Salmonella*, *Shigella*, *Proteus*	Ferment lactose late, hence initially colourless colonies, which become pink after prolonged incubation, e.g., *Shigella sonnei*

Escherichia coli

- These are Gram-negative bacilli
- Size is 1–3 µm by 0.4–0.7 µm
- Non-sporing but motile
- Non-capsulated (few strains especially isolated from extraintestinal site are capsulated)
- They are aerobes and facultative anaerobes; grow at wide range of temperature 10–40°C (optimum temperature is 37°C)
- They grow easily on ordinary media such as nutrient agar, blood agar and MacConkey's agar
- On MacConkey's agar, they form pink colonies due to lactose fermentation
- They are comparatively more resistant to physical and chemical agents
- They are found in human and animal intestine
- Outside the body, they remain viable for few days only
- They are killed at 55°C in 1 hour and at 60°C in 15 minutes

Biochemical reactions

G	L	S	M	I	M	Vi	C	Urease	H_2S
+	+	–	+	+	+	–	–	–	–

Virulence factors

It produces

- Enterotoxin
- Haemolysins
- Verotoxin (VT)

Enterotoxin

E. coli produces two different enterotoxins:

1. Heat-labile toxin
2. Heat-stable toxin

Heat-labile toxin (LT) It activates adenylate cyclase in the enterocytes, which converts adenosine triphosphate (ATP) to cyclic adenosine monophosphate (cAMP). The increase in cAMP causes profuse watery diarrhoea.

Heat-stable toxin (ST) It acts by activation of guanylate cyclase leading to formation of cGMP in epithelial cells, which causes inhibition of co-transport of sodium chloride into the wall leading to diarrhoea.

Haemolysins

Some strains, especially those isolated from extraintestinal specimens are haemolytic. They cause lysis of red blood cells.

Verotoxin (VT)

- Is like *Shigella* toxin—two types: VT 1 and VT 2
- Is cytotoxic to both Vero and Hela cells

Pathogenicity

- *E. coli* is commensal in human intestine.
- It is a pathogen associated with two main clinical syndromes:
  - Urinary tract infections (UTIs)
  - Gastroenteritis or diarrhoea
- It also causes
  - Pyogenic infections
  - Septicaemia
  - Meningitis, etc.

Urinary tract infections

- *E. coli* is the predominant agent causing UTI (60–80%).
- It is more common in females than males as the urethra is short and wide. Other factors include infrequent voiding, pregnancy and sexual intercourse.
- Less common in males because of long urethra and bactericidal activity of prostate fluid.
- Other factors that predispose to UTIs are enlarged prostate, urinary calculi, congenital malformation of urinary tract and catheterization.

Gastroenteritis and diarrhoea

- *E. coli* normally present in the intestine is non-pathogenic.
- There are four groups of *E. coli* which can cause gastroenteritis or diarrhoea, particularly in infants and children. These are
  - Enteropathogenic *E. coli* (EPEC)
  - Enterotoxigenic *E. coli* (ETEC)
  - Enteroinvasive *E. coli* (EIEC)
  - Enterohaemorrhagic *E. coli* (EHEC)

Enteropathogenic *E. coli* (EPEC)

- Cause of diarrhoea in infants and children and less often in adults
- **Mechanism of action** They attach to the mucosa of small intestine causing disruption of brush border of microvilli

Enterotoxigenic *E. coli* (ETEC)

- Cause mild diarrhoea or cholera-like disease. Also cause traveller's diarrhoea
- **Mechanism of action** Adhesion of bacteria and production of heat-labile and heat-stable toxins

Enteroinvasive E. coli (EIEC)

- Cause disease like shigellosis
- **Mechanism of action** Cause disease by invading intestinal mucosa—invasiveness

Enterohaemorrhagic E. coli (EHEC)

- Cause mild diarrhoea to fatal haemorrhagic colitis and haemorrhagic uremic syndrome in children and adults
- **Mechanism of action** Action mediated by verotoxin, which acts on vascular endothelial cells

Laboratory diagnosis

- **Collection of specimens** The following specimens are collected:
  - Midstream urine sample in UTI
  - Faeces or rectal swab in diarrhoea
  - Pus from wound infections
  - Cerebrospinal fluid (CSF) in meningitis
  - Blood in septicaemia
- **Microscopy** Gram stain is observed for Gram-negative bacilli—not useful in cases of diarrhoea
- **Culture** On blood agar and MacConkey's agar, pink colonies on MacConkey's agar are subjected to biochemical reactions for identification
- **Confirmation**
  - For EPEC—slide agglutination test using type-specific antisera
  - For ETEC—demonstration of toxin production
  - For EIEC—Sereny test—instillation into guinea pig eyes and observed for conjunctivitis and keratitis
  - For EHIC—demonstration of verocytotoxin directly in faeces or culture
- **In UTI,** detection of significant bacteriuria (i.e., counts more than 100000 organisms/mL [10^5 organisms/mL]) is important by counting the number of bacteria per mL by using quantitative and semi-quantitative methods. The urine sample allows the growth of bacteria; hence, it should be transported immediately for processing to get accurate count.
- **Antibiotic sensitivity testing** is important as *E. coli* shows multiple antibiotic resistance.

Treatment

Treatment should be decided based on sensitivity testing as multiple resistance to antibiotics may occur. Sometimes, a combination of antibiotics is required. The following are the antimicrobial agents used for treatment:

- Ampicillin
- Cephalosporins
- Chloramphenicol
- Tetracycline
- Furadantin
- Nalidixic acid
- Gentamicin
- Norfloxacin

Klebsiella

- Gram-negative, capsulated, non-motile, non-sporing bacilli
- Size is about 1–2 μm by 0.5–0.8 μm
- Aerobe and facultative anaerobe
- Optimum temperature is 37°C, optimum pH is 7.2–7.4
- Can grow on ordinary media such as nutrient agar forming large, mucoid, greyish-white colonies. On MacConkey's agar, it forms lactose-fermenting mucoid colonies

Biochemical reactions

G	L	S	M	I	M	Vi	C	Urease	H_2S
+	+	+	+	–	–	+	+	+	–

Pathogenicity

Two important pathogenic species for humans are

- *K. pneumoniae*
- *K. oxytoca*
  - Klebsiella cause respiratory infections—bronchopneumonia, pleuritis, multiple abscesses in lung
  - Hospital-acquired UTIs
  - Wound and burn infections
  - Bacteraemia

- Nosocomial infections
- Pyogenic infections such as abscesses and meningitis
- Atrophic rhinitis with ozaena is caused by *K. ozaenae*
- Rhinoscleroma—chronic upper respiratory tract disease with lesions in nose, larynx and throat caused by *K. rhinoscleromatis.* **Oral lesions** appearing as proliferative granuloma may also occur

Laboratory diagnosis

- **Specimens** Sputum, urine, wound or burns swab, pus, throat or nasal swab and CSF
- **Microscopic examination** Gram stain shows capsulated, Gram-negative bacilli
- **Culture** Specimen is inoculated on blood agar and MacConkey's agar aerobically. MacConkey's agar showing lactose-fermenting mucoid colonies are further identified by biochemical reactions

Treatment

- Cephalosporins such as cefuroxime and cefotaxime
- Other agents are chloramphenicol, nitrofurantoin, co-amoxiclav and gentamicin

Proteus

Pr. vulgaris and *Pr. mirabilis* are the two important species

- These are Gram-negative coccobacilli
- Pleomorphic (named *Proteus* after the Greek god who could assume any shape)
- Size is 1–3 × 0. 6 µm; long filaments are also seen
- Actively motile by peritrichous flagella
- Non-sporing and non-capsulated
- Aerobe and facultative anaerobe
- Can grow on ordinary media such as nutrient agar
- **On blood agar** Shows **swarming**—a spreading type of growth. This is a characteristic feature of *Proteus*
- **On MacConkey's agar** Colourless colonies because of non-lactose fermentation

Biochemical reactions

G	L	S	M	I	M	Vi	C	Urease	H_2S	PPA
+	–	–	–	V	+	V	V	+	+	–

Pr. mirabilis and *Pr. vulgaris* are common isolates and are differentiated by indole test. *Pr. mirabilis*—indole negative and *Pr. vulgaris*—indole positive

Pathogenicity

Proteus spp. are saprophytic bacteria widely distributed in nature. They are opportunistic pathogens and may cause the following infections:

- UTIs
- Pyogenic infections—wound infections, bedsores, osteomyelitis and infection of umbilical stump leading to meningitis or bacteraemia
- They can cause ear and respiratory tract infections. They are also involved in nosocomial infections

Laboratory diagnosis

- **Specimens** Urine, pus, ear swab, wound swab, CSF and sputum
- **Microscopic examination** Gram stain—Gram-negative pleomorphic rods
- **Culture**
  - Blood agar—swarming
  - MacConkey's agar—non-lactose fermenting colonies
  - Confirmation by using biochemical reactions
- **Antibiotic sensitivity testing** by Kirby–Bauer disc diffusion method to guide the therapy, as resistance to antibiotics is common. Isolate is tested against various antibiotics

- Usually, they are resistant to many common antibiotics
- Sensitive to ampicillin, cefotaxime, cefuroxime and aminoglycosides

Shigella

- The members of genus *Shigella* are the cause of bacillary dysentery
- They are
  - Gram-negative bacilli
  - Size is 2–4 × 0.6 μm
  - Non-motile, non-sporing and non-capsulated
  - Aerobes and facultative anaerobes; optimum pH is 7.4, optimum temperature is 37°C
  - Grow on ordinary media—nutrient agar, blood agar, MacConkey's agar, etc. On MacConkey's agar, it forms non-lactose fermenting (colourless) colonies, except *Sh. sonnei,* which is late lactose fermenter and forms pink colonies after prolonged incubation
  - Deoxycholate citrate agar and *Salmonella–Shigella* agar are used as selective media for *Shigella* species
  - Shigella bacilli are killed at 56°C in 1 hour, by 1% phenol in 30 minutes and by chlorination

Biochemical reactions

Important biochemical reactions are as follows:

- Catalase—positive except *Sh. dysenteriae* Type I

I	MR	VP	C	Urease	H_2S
V	+	–	–	–	–

- Produce acid from glucose
- Mannitol—fermented by all, except *Sh. dysenteriae*
- Lactose—not fermented, except *Sh. sonnei* which ferments lactose late

Based on the antigenic structure, there are four groups:

1. Group A—*Sh. dysenteriae*
2. Group B—*Sh. flexneri*
3. Group C—*Sh. boydii*
4. Group D—*Sh. sonnei*

Virulence factors

Endotoxin

- It is thermostable lipopolysaccharide (LPS) of cell wall
- Acts on the intestinal wall causing diarrhoea and ulcers

Exotoxin

- Produced only by *Sh. dysenteriae* Type I, it acts as enterotoxin and neurotoxin
- Enterotoxin acts on intestinal mucosa causing transudation of fluid in lumen
- Neurotoxin damages endothelial cells of small blood vessels of the central nervous system, which result in neurological complications such as polyneuritis, coma and meningism
- Some strains of *Sh. dysenteriae* also produce cytotoxin, which acts on Vero cells and is known as verocytotoxin

Pathogenicity

Shigellosis

- **Sources** Infected human beings/carriers
- **Modes of transmission**
  - ***Fingers*** Through contaminated fingers
  - ***Fomites*** Through door handles, water taps, lavatory seats
  - ***Flies*** Mechanical vectors—transmit organisms from faeces to food
  - Through contaminated food and water
  - Faeco–oral route
- Pathogenesis is given in Flow chart 32.1.

Clinical features

- Symptoms vary from acute dysentery characterized by passage of blood and mucus in stools to mild diarrhoea with watery stools

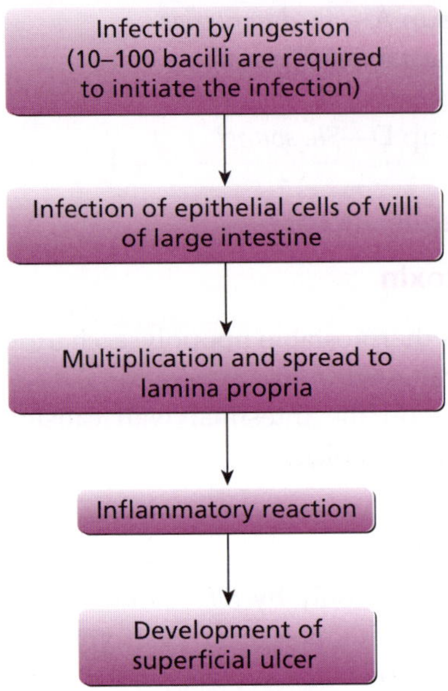

Flow chart 32.1 Pathogenesis of shigellosis.

- The typical presentations are
  - Passage of bloody mucoid stools without faeces
  - Abdominal cramps
  - Tenesmus
  - Fever and vomiting may be present
- Severity of the disease varies with species
  - *Sh. dysenteriae*—most severe
  - *Sh. sonnei*—mild diarrhoea with watery stools

Laboratory diagnosis

- **Collection of specimens**
  - Freshly passed stool or swab from ulcer
  - Stool is collected in a bed pan and portion of it containing mucus flakes is transferred to transport media such as glycerol saline transport medium
- **Microscopy** Wet mount shows plenty of pus cells, RBCs and non-motile bacilli
- **Culture** On blood agar, MacConkey's agar, etc. The colonies grown are confirmed by
  - Biochemical reactions
  - Slide agglutination test
  - Motility
- **Antibiotic sensitivity testing** is done to guide the treatment

Treatment

- Replacement of fluid by oral or intravenous routes as required
- Antibiotics such as ampicillin, tetracycline, nalidixic acid and ciprofloxacin

Prevention and control

- Isolation of patient
- Improvement of environmental sanitation
- Improvement of personal hygiene
- Protection of food from flies

Salmonellae

- The most important member of the genus *Salmonella* is *S. typhi*—the causative agent of typhoid fever
- Other members are *S. paratyphi A*, *S. paratyphi B* and *S. paratyphi C*, *S. typhimurium*, *S. cholerae-suis*, *S. enteritidis*, *S. gallinarum-pullorum* and *S. anatum*
  - Salmonellae are Gram-negative bacilli
  - Size is 1–3 × 0.5 µm
  - Motile, non-sporing and non-capsulated
  - These are aerobes and facultative anaerobes
  - Optimum pH is 7.2–7.4 (pH range 6–8)
  - Optimum temperature is 37°C (range 15–41°C)
  - Grow well on ordinary media such as nutrient agar, blood agar and MacConkey's agar
  - On MacConkey's agar—non-lactose fermenting (colourless) colonies
  - Selective medium—Wilson and Blair medium and *Salmonella–Shigella* agar
  - Killed at 60°C in 15 minutes
  - Survive in water, ice and snow for weeks and months
  - Sensitive to mercuric chloride and phenol

Biochemical reactions

G	L	S	M
+	–	–	+

- All species ferment glucose and mannitol with acid and gas except *S. typhi* (anaerogenic—ferments glucose and mannitol without gas). Lactose and sucrose are not fermented

I	M	Vi	C
–	+	–	+

- *Salmonella* spp. are methyl red positive and all species are citrate positive except *S. typhi* and *S. paratyphi A*, and H_2S positive except *S. paratyphi A* and *S. cholerae-suis*

Pathogenicity

- The disease caused is known as salmonellosis
- Salmonellae cause three types of clinical syndrome:
  - Enteric fever
  - Septicaemia
  - Gastroenteritis

Pathogenesis of enteric fever is given in Flow chart 32.2.

Enteric fever

- It is a septicaemic disease that includes
  - Typhoid fever caused by *S. typhi*
  - Paratyphoid fever caused by *S. paratyphi A, B, C*
- **Sources** Patient or carrier
- **Mode of transmission** Infection occurs by ingestion of contaminated food and water
- The bacilli invade the submucosa of the small intestine, reach the mesenteric lymph nodes, multiply there and enter the bloodstream causing bacteraemia
- The bacilli reach various internal organs such as liver, gallbladder, spleen, lungs, kidneys and bone marrow via blood circulation **(primary bacteraemia)**
- The bacilli multiply in various internal organs and re-enter the bloodstream causing heavy **secondary bacteraemia** and symptoms of enteric fever
- The symptoms are
  - Constant high-grade fever (40°C)
  - Abdominal discomfort with diarrhoea or constipation
  - Hepatosplenomegaly
  - Rose spots on the skin
  - Headache, malaise, anorexia, a coated tongue with bradycardia and leucopenia
- Enteric fever is endemic in India

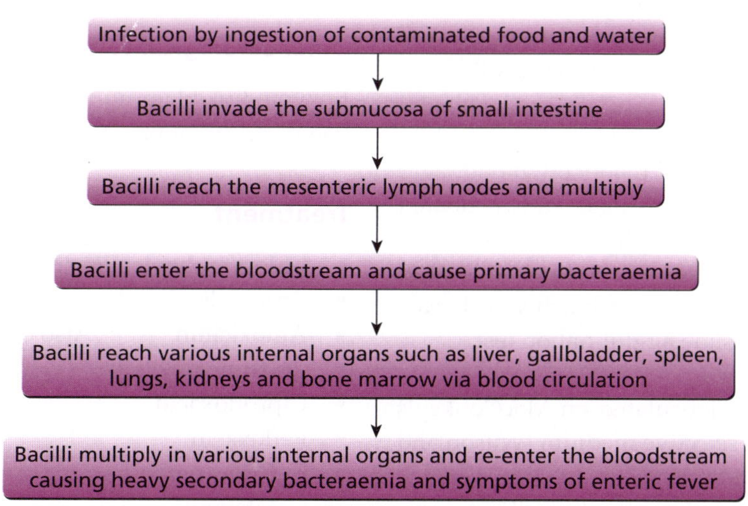

Flow chart 32.2 Pathogenesis of enteric fever.

Septicaemia

- Commonly caused by *S. cholerae-suis* or *S. paratyphi C*
- It occurs with focal suppurative lesions such as osteomyelitis, pneumonia, meningitis and endocarditis

Gastroenteritis (food poisoning)

- Caused by ingestion of food such as meat, milk and egg contaminated with certain *Salmonella* species, which are primarily animal pathogens (*S. enteritidis, S. indiana* and other species)
- Characterized by fever, vomiting, abdominal pain and diarrhoea
- It is infection type of food poisoning

Laboratory diagnosis

Two types of diagnostic methods:

1. Isolation and identification of bacteria
2. Demonstration of antibodies

Isolation and identification of bacteria

- **Collection of specimens** Blood, faeces, urine, bile, bone marrow, etc.
- **Blood culture** 10 mL of blood is collected by taking all sterile precautions into blood culture bottles (5 mL in 50 mL of glucose broth and 5 mL in 50 mL of bile broth).
  - Both blood culture bottles are incubated at 37°C for overnight
  - Subcultures are made on blood agar and MacConkey's agar and incubated at 37°C for overnight
  - After incubation growth is observed and identified using biochemical reactions and slide agglutination test
- **Faeces culture**
  - Faeces are inoculated on MacConkey's agar and selective medium (Wilson and Blair medium)
  - Typical colonies of *Salmonella* are processed further for identification by using biochemical reactions and slide agglutination test
- **Other specimens** Urine, bile and other specimens are processed routinely for isolation and identification

Demonstration of antibodies

Antibodies in patient's sera can be demonstrated by various serological tests.

Widal test

- It is a tube agglutination test used for detection of antibodies (antibody titre is detected).
- The test is positive in the second week of illness.
- In this test O (TO) and H (TH) antigens of *S. typhi* and H antigens of *S. paratyphi* A (AH) and *S. paratyphi* B (BH) are used.
- Four rows of serial dilutions of patient's serum (1:10–1:640) are prepared and to these tubes equal volume of O and H antigens are mixed and incubated at 37°C overnight.
- The tubes are observed for agglutination; the highest dilution of serum showing a positive result is noted.
- The test is considered positive, if antibody titre for O antigen is more than 1:100 and H antigen more than 1:200.

Other serological tests

Enzyme-linked immunosorbent assay (ELISA), haemagglutination, etc., are also used

Treatment

- Chloramphenicol is drug of choice
- Ampicillin, Amoxicillin, Co-trimoxazole } Also effective
- Ciprofloxacin
- Pefloxacin
- Ceftazidime
- Cefotaxime
- Cefoperazone

Prophylaxis

- Typhoid-paratyphoid A and B (TAB) (*S. typhi, S. paratyphi A* and *S. paratyphi B)* vaccine—two doses at an interval of 4–6 weeks give protection for 3 years. Booster dose may be given after 3 years.
- Live oral vaccine is also available and better than TAB. Ty21a is an example of oral vaccine.

Pasteurella pestis (Yersinia pestis)

- It is a Gram-negative, short ovoid bacillus
- Size is 1.5 × 0.7 µm with rounded ends and convex sides
- Non-motile, non-sporing and capsulated
- When stained with methylene blue, it shows **safety pin appearance** with two ends darkly stained and clear central area (Fig. 32.1)
- Grows on ordinary media such as nutrient agar, blood agar and MacConkey's agar
- It is heat labile, destroyed by heat at 55°C in 15 minutes
- Also sensitive to sunlight, drying and chemical disinfectants (0.5% phenol in 15 minutes) but remains viable in cold and moist environment

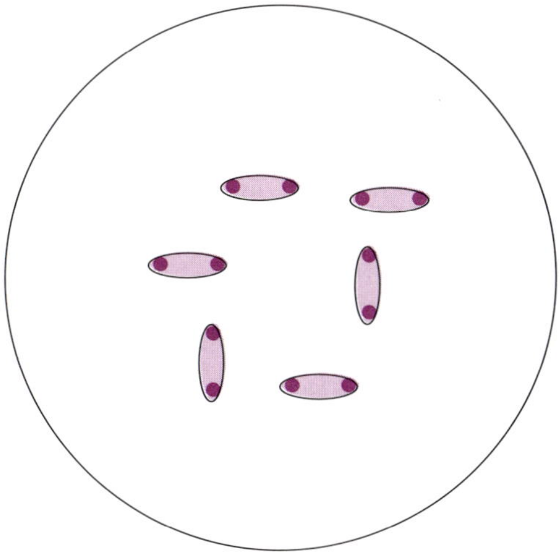

Figure 32.1 *Yersinia pestis*—safety pin appearance.

Pathogenicity

Plague

- Natural disease of rodents (rats)
- Transmitted from animal to animal and animal to man by bite of infected flea—*Xenopsylla cheopis*
- In man, disease occurs as
  - Bubonic plague
  - Pneumonic plague
  - Septicaemic plague
- **Bubonic plague** Characterized by enlargement of inguinal lymph nodes (bubo means groin), fever, chills and malaise following the bite of infected rat flea on the legs.
- **Pneumonic plague** Characterized by haemorrhagic pneumonia—highly infectious, transmitted from man to man by droplet infection (inhalation).
- **Septicaemic plague** Characterized by haemorrhages in the skin and mucosa—named as **Black Death**. It occurs as primary infection or more commonly as a complication of bubonic or pneumonic plague.

Laboratory diagnosis

- **Collection of specimens** Pus or fluid aspirated from bubo, sputum, blood, CSF, etc.
- **Direct microscopy** Observed for characteristic safety pin appearance by methylene blue staining
- **Culture** On blood agar, growth confirmed by biochemical tests
- **Animal inoculation** in guinea pigs or white rats observed for characteristic lesions after death
- **Serological tests** for demonstration of antibodies—passive haemagglutination or complement fixation test

Treatment

Tetracycline is the drug of choice, streptomycin, kanamycin, chloramphenicol, sulphonamides and ciprofloxacin can also be used.

Prophylaxis

- Control of fleas and rodents by spraying insecticides (DDT) and rodenticides
- Vaccination—killed or live attenuated vaccine. It is recommended for those exposed to an occupational risk of infection

Self-assessment

Long-answer questions

1. Discuss in brief the pathogenicity and laboratory diagnosis of enteric fever.
2. Discuss in brief the pathogenicity and laboratory diagnosis of shigellosis.

Short-answer questions

Write notes on

1. Laboratory diagnosis of typhoid fever
2. Laboratory diagnosis of bacillary dysentery
3. Laboratory diagnosis of urinary tract infection
4. Widal test
5. *Yersinia pestis*
6. *Proteus* spp.
7. *Klebsiella*
8. *Escherichia coli*

Multiple-choice questions

1. Which of the following *Escherichia coli* produces verotoxin?
   A. Enteropathogenic *E. coli*
   B. Enterotoxigenic *E. coli*
   C. Enteroinvasive *E. coli*
   D. Enterohaemorrhagic *E. coli*
2. Which of the following group of *Escherichia coli* is responsible for traveller's diarrhoea?
   A. Enteropathogenic *E. coli*
   B. Enterotoxigenic *E. coli*
   C. Enteroinvasive *E. coli*
   D. Enterohaemorrhagic *E. coli*
3. Which of the following bacteria is NOT a lactose fermenter?
   A. *Escherichia coli*
   B. *Klebsiella* spp.
   C. *Salmonella typhi*
   D. *Shigella sonnei*
4. Which of the following bacteria is a lactose fermenter?
   A. *Proteus* spp.
   B. *Klebsiella* spp.
   C. *Salmonella* spp.
   D. *Shigella* spp.
5. Which of the following bacteria is a late lactose fermenter?
   A. *Escherichia coli*
   B. *Klebsiella* spp.
   C. *Salmonella typhi*
   D. *Shigella sonnei*
6. Select the most appropriate count, which detects significant bacteriuria
   A. Counts more than 1000 organisms/mL
   B. Counts more than 10000 organisms/mL
   C. Counts more than 100000 organisms/mL
   D. Counts more than 1000000 organisms/mL
7. Which of the following statements is FALSE regarding *Proteus* spp.?
   A. Named so after the Greek god who could assume any shape
   B. Swarming is a characteristic feature
   C. Form colourless colonies because of non-lactose fermentation
   D. Non-motile but capsulated
8. Swarming is a characteristic feature seen in
   A. *Proteus* spp.
   B. *Klebsiella* spp.
   C. *Salmonella* spp.
   D. *Shigella* spp.
9. Which of the following species of *Shigella* causes most severe disease?
   A. *Shigella sonnei*
   B. *Sh. flexneri*
   C. *Sh. boydii*
   D. *Sh. dysenteriae*
10. Which of the following species of *Salmonella* is anaerogenic?
    A. *Salmonella paratyphi A*
    B. *S. paratyphi B*
    C. *S. typhi*
    D. *S. paratyphi C*

11. Which of the following is a selective medium for typhoid bacilli?
    A. Wilson and Blair medium
    B. Thiosulfate-citrate-bile salts-sucrose agar
    C. Deoxycholate citrate agar
    D. MacConkey's agar
12. The following statements are TRUE regarding *Salmonella* food poisoning, EXCEPT
    A. Caused by ingestion of food such as meat, milk, egg
    B. Caused by *Salmonella* species which are primarily animal pathogens
    C. Is toxin type of food poisoning
    D. Characterized by fever, vomiting, abdominal pain and diarrhoea
13. The following are the antigens used in Widal test, EXCEPT
    A. H antigen of *Salmonella typhi*
    B. H antigen of *S. paratyphi*
    C. O antigen of *S. typhi*
    D. O antigen of *S. paratyphi*
14. Safety pin appearance is the characteristic feature of
    A. *Proteus vulgaris*
    B. *Pr. mirabilis*
    C. *Yersinia pestis*
    D. *Shigella flexneri*
15. Plague is transmitted from animal to animal and animal to man by bite of
    A. Infected flea
    B. Female anopheline mosquito
    C. Sand fly
    D. Infected bed bug

33 Other Gram-Negative Bacilli

Pseudomonas and *Burkholderia*

These are a group of obligatory, aerobic, non-fermentative, oxidase positive, Gram-negative bacilli, which are motile owing to polar flagella.

Pseudomonas aeruginosa

- These are slender Gram-negative bacilli
- Size is 1.5–3 × 0.5 µm
- Actively motile by one or two polar flagella
- Non-sporing and non-capsulated, but many strains have mucoid slime layer
- They are obligate aerobes, require optimum temperature of 37°C and optimum pH of 7.2–7.4
- Can grow on ordinary media
- On nutrient agar, they form large colonies that are 2–3 mm in diameter, irregular, convex, smooth and opaque greenish-blue in colour and emit a characteristic fruity odour or earthy smell
- On blood agar, they form haemolytic colonies
- On MacConkey's agar, they form non-lactose fermenting (NLF) colonies
- Cetrimide agar is used as selective medium
- Survive well in wet environment and susceptible to heat
- Resistant to common disinfectants and antiseptics, and can grow in some disinfectant solutions such as iodine, hexachlorophene, soap solutions and quaternary ammonium compounds
- They have considerable natural resistance to many antibiotics

Pigments

P. aeruginosa produces a number of pigments. These are as folllows:

- **Pyocyanin** It is a bluish-green, diffusible phenazine pigment soluble in water and chloroform. It helps in identification of *P. aeruginosa*.
- **Fluorescein (pyoverdin)** It is a greenish-yellow pigment, soluble in water but not in chloroform. It gives a yellowish tinge to the culture which can be better observed when examined under UV light.
- **Pyorubin** It is a bright red-coloured phenazine pigment soluble in water and insoluble in chloroform.
- **Pyomelanin** It is a brown-black pigment.

Biochemical reactions

- It is a non-fermenter; metabolism is oxidative.
- It oxidatively utilizes glucose only with acid but not gas.

I	M	Vi	C	H_2S	Urease	Oxidase	Catalase
–	–	–	+	–	–	–	+

Virulence factors (toxins and enzymes)

- **Extracellular products** Pyocyanin inhibits mitochondrial enzymes and favours colonization of respiratory mucosa.
- **Extracellular enzymes and haemolysins** It produces proteases, haemolysins and lipases which help in the formation of local lesion.
  - **Elastase** It digests elastin of arterial wall leading to destructive vascular lesions along with haemorrhages. It causes tissue necrosis along with alkaline protease.
- **Exotoxin** It produces the following exotoxins:
  - **Exotoxin A** It is a polypeptide that inhibits protein synthesis.
  - **Exotoxins S and T** These are believed to facilitate the spread of *P. aeruginosa* and tissue invasion by damaging epithelial cells.
- **Endotoxin** It is a cell wall lipopolysaccharide. It exhibits all the properties of enterobacterial lipopolysaccharides (LPS).

Pathogenicity

- It can cause infection in a community; outside the hospitals as well as hospital-acquired infections (HAI).
- Because of its resistance to disinfectants and antibiotics, it is able to persist in moist environments in hospitals and plays an important role in HAI such as
  - Infections of wounds, burns and bed sores
  - Eye infections
  - Urinary tract infections following catheterization
  - Acute purulent meningitis following lumbar puncture or cranial injury
  - Necrotizing pneumonia following colonization of ventilators in debilitated persons
  - Septic arthritis and endocarditis in drug addicts
  - Septicaemia and endocarditis in debilitated persons
  - Infantile diarrhoea and sepsis

Laboratory diagnosis

- **Specimens** Pus, wound swab, urine, sputum, blood, etc., depending on the site involved
- **Transport** Transported immediately to a microbiology laboratory
- **Microscopic examination** Gram stain shows pus cells along with Gram-negative bacilli, non-capsulated and non-sporing, arranged singly or in short chains
- **Culture** Specimen is plated on blood agar and MacConkey's agar
  - Cetrimide agar is the selective medium required especially for isolation of *P. aeruginosa* from stool or wound swab where mixed flora is present
  - The typical growth with bluish-green pigment is identified by using biochemical reactions
- **Antibiotic susceptibility testing** It is obligatory because of multiple antibiotic resistances. It is performed by Kirby–Bauer disc diffusion method using amikacin, carbenicillin, azlocillin, ticarcillin, cefotaxime, ceftazidime, gentamicin, tobramycin, ciprofloxacin and other quinolones, and cephalosporins.

Burkholderia pseudomallei

- Earlier it was known as *P. pseudomallei*
- Small, Gram-negative bacilli, about 2.5 × 0.5 µm and motile
- It is a causative agent of **meliodosis (glanders)**
- In humans, clinical features are
  - Benign pulm onary infection resembling tuberculosis
  - Multiple abscesses in internal organs
  - Fulminating septicaemia

Laboratory diagnosis

- It is done by microscopic demonstration and isolation of bacilli from exudates, urine, pus and blood.
- **Antibody detection** Detection of IgM and IgG by enzyme-linked immunosorbent assay (ELISA) and indirect haemagglutination test

Vibrio cholerae

- Gram-negative, comma-shaped bacilli (Fig. 33.1)
- Size is 1.5 × 0.2 μm
- Non-sporing, non-capsulated but actively motile with the help of a single polar flagellum that shows darting motility
- They are strongly aerobic; require optimum temperature of 37°C and pH is 8.2–8.6
- Grows well on ordinary media such as nutrient agar, blood agar, MacConkey's agar
- On MacConkey's agar, colonies are colourless (NLF) initially; on prolonged incubation they become pink in colour because of late fermentation of lactose (LLF)
- On blood agar, they cause haemodigestion
- TCBS (thiosulfate-citrate-bile salts-sucrose) medium, alkaline bile salt agar, Mansur's gelatin taurocholate trypticase tellurite agar (GTTTA), etc., are selective media. On TCBS, it forms yellow-coloured colonies due to sucrose fermentation
- Susceptible to heat and drying (55°C for 15 minutes to kill), sensitive to common disinfectants and a pH below 5

Biochemical reactions

- Catalase and oxidase positive

G	L	S	M	I	MR	VP	C	Urease	H_2S
+	–	+	+	+	–	V	–	–	–

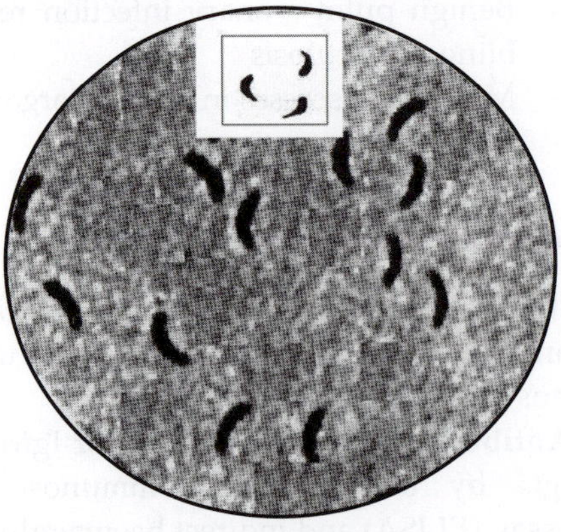

Figure 33.1 *Vibrio cholerae.*

Virulence factors

- Produce two types of toxins:
  - Heat-stable endotoxin like other Gram-negative bacilli
  - **Enterotoxin** known as **cholera** toxin—protein in nature, having two fragments A and B
    - A (active) stimulates adenyl cyclase activity of epithelial cells converting ATP to cAMP and causes dehydration
    - B (binding) binds to ganglioside receptor on the intestinal epithelial cells

Pathogenicity

Cholera

- Cholera is an acute diarrhoeal disease that occurs by ingestion of contaminated foods or drink.
- Cholera bacilli adhere to epithelium of the small intestine and produce enterotoxin which causes secretion of large quantities of water and electrolytes into the intestinal lumen and inhibits intestinal absorption of sodium and chloride. These changes result in
  - Dehydration leading to haemoconcentration
  - Anuria
  - Hypovolemic shock due to massive loss of water and electrolytes
- El Tor vibrio identical to classical *Vibrio* with minor differences cause milder disease than *V. cholerae.*

Laboratory diagnosis

- **Collection of specimen** Rice water stool is collected and transported immediately for processing. If any delay is expected, stool should be collected in a suitable transport media such as Venketraman–Ramkrishnan medium (V–R medium) or Cary–Blair medium.
- **Direct microscopy**
  - Gram stain—observed for comma-shaped bacilli

- Hanging drop preparation—observed for darting type of motility
- **Culture** On selective media, bile salt agar or TCBS medium is used. After overnight incubation, growth is observed and identified by using biochemical reactions and confirmed by slide agglutination tests.

Treatment

- The most important part in the treatment is prompt water and electrolyte replacement to correct dehydration—orally or by giving intravenous fluids or both.
- Antibiotic therapy is recommended for severely ill patients. Though multiple drug-resistant strains have developed, doxycycline in adults and azithromycin in pregnant women and children are effective and recommended as first-line treatment.

Prophylaxis

- Purification of water supplies
- Proper disposal of sewage
- Isolation and treatment of patient
- Vaccination—killed parenteral vaccine, killed oral vaccine and live vaccine can be used

Francisella tularensis

- Was earlier known as *Pasteurella tularensis*
- Is a causative agent of tularaemia—a disease of rabbits (rabbit fever) and other rodents
- Infection is transmitted by ticks and other arthropod vectors
- Is a Gram-negative bacillus about 0.3–0.7 × 0. 2 μm
- Is capsulated, non-motile and non-sporing
- Infection in humans occurs by direct contact with animals, can also occur by ingestion of contaminated meat or water and inhalation
- **In humans, tularaemia may present** as local ulceration with lymphadenitis, typhoid-like fever with glandular enlargement or influenza like respiratory infection. It may also produce **oral lesions** manifested as necrotic ulcers of the oral mucosa or pharynx or it may occur as generalized stomatitis
- **Laboratory diagnosis** May be made by smear examination, culture or by animal inoculation (guinea pigs) of pus, blood, sputum or specimen from the oral lesions. Serological diagnosis may be made by demonstrating antibodies by agglutination test
- **Treatment** Antibiotics—streptomycin is the drug of choice

Bordetella pertussis

- Gram-negative coccobacilli
- Size is 1–1.5 × 0.3 μm
- Non-motile, non-sporing but capsulated
- Is biochemically inactive and does not attack sugars
- Is indole, catalase and oxidase positive
- Three species: *B. pertussis, B. parapertussis* and *B. bronchiseptica*
- Require a complex medium for growth therefore Bordet–Gengou medium is commonly used. After 72 hours of incubation, a small dome-shaped, smooth, opaque, viscid, grey-white, refractile and glistening colony giving the appearance of ***bisected pearls*** or ***mercury drops*** is formed
- Killed by heating at 56°C for 30 minutes. Sensitive to drying and disinfectants but survive in dried droplets for up to 5 hours

Virulence factors

Produces different virulence factors, which include the following:

- Heat-labile toxin
- Lipopolysaccharides—endotoxin
- Tracheal cytotoxin
- Pertussis toxin
- Adenylate cyclase
- Haemolysins
- Filamentous haemagglutinin

Pathogenicity

Whooping cough

- *B. pertussis* causes whooping cough (95% cases).
- *B. parapertussis* (5% cases) and *B. bronchiseptica* (0.1% cases) are responsible for a milder form of whooping cough.
- Whooping cough is a prominent childhood disease.
- Infection is transmitted by droplet inhalation.
- Whooping cough occurs in three stages:
  - ***Catarrhal stage*** Characterized by sneezing, running nose and coughing
  - ***Paroxysmal stage*** Characterized by episodes of uncontrolled cough and a characteristic whooping sound
  - ***Convalescent stage*** During this stage, the frequency and severity of coughing gradually decreases

Laboratory diagnosis

- **Collection of specimens** Prenasal swab, postnasal swab and respiratory secretions
- **Direct microscopy** Gram staining not helpful, hence the fluorescent antibody technique is used
- **Culture** On Bordet–Gengou medium, typical growth of *Bordetella* is confirmed by microscopy and slide agglutination text
- **Serological tests** such as agglutination, complement fixation and indirect immunofluorescence tests are used. ELISA can be used to demonstrate IgA in nasopharyngeal secretions

Treatment

- Erythromycin is the drug of choice
- Tetracycline
- Chloramphenicol
- Ampicillin

Prophylaxis

- Immunization with killed pertussis vaccine is effective. This vaccine is given in combination with tetanus and diphtheria toxoid as triple vaccine—DPT.

Brucella

- These are small, Gram-negative coccobacilli causing a zoonotic disease called brucellosis, which primarily affect goats, sheep, cattle, buffaloes, pigs and other animals
- Medically important species include
  - *B. melitensis*
  - *B. abortus*
  - *B. suis*
- Size is 0.5–0.7 × 0.6–1.5 µm
- Non-motile, non-capsulated and non-sporing
- They are strict aerobes
- Some species are capnophilic requiring 5–10% CO_2
- Optimum temperature is 37°C and optimum pH is 6.6–7.4
- Can grow on ordinary media but growth is slow. Growth is improved by addition of blood and serum
- **Media used**
  - Serum dextrose agar
  - Serum potato infusion agar
  - Trypticase soy agar
  - Tryptose agar
- Addition of bacitracin, polymyxin and cycloheximide makes the medium selective
- On MacConkey's medium, NLF colonies are formed
- They are destroyed by heat at 60°C in 10 minutes
- Also destroyed by pasteurization of milk
- Survive for 6–10 weeks in dust and soil

Biochemical reactions

I	MR	VP	C
–	–	–	–

- They utilize carbohydrates oxidatively
- They are catalase, oxidase and urease positive
- Some species produce H_2S
- Reduce nitrates

Pathogenicity

- They cause **brucellosis,** which is also known as **Mediterranean fever, Malta fever** and **undulant fever.**
- *B. melitensis* is the most pathogenic, *B. abortus* and *B. suis* are of intermediate pathogenicity
- It is a zoonotic disease; infected animals shed bacteria in vaginal secretions, urine and milk
- Infection is transmitted to humans by
  - Direct contact with animal tissue as in dairy workers, farmers and veterinarians
  - Ingestion of contaminated meat, raw vegetables and infected milk
  - Inhalation of aerosolized organisms
  - Accidental injection as in laboratory workers

Clinical features

Brucellosis is of three types:

1. **Latent infection** The patient is serologically positive but clinical features are not seen
2. **Acute infection** Prolonged bacteraemia, irregular fever with chills, malaise, night sweat, myalgia, arthralgia, lymphadenopathy and hepatosplenomegaly
3. **Chronic brucellosis** It is non-bacteraemic, low-grade infection with periodic exacerbation, lasts for years

Laboratory diagnosis

- **Specimens** Blood, bone marrow and lymph nodes and rarely urine, sputum, cerebrospinal fluid (CSF), milk, vaginal discharge and seminal fluid
- **Diagnosis by culture**
  - **Trypticase soy broth** is inoculated with blood. Subcultures are made on serum dextrose agar from blood culture bottle every 3–5 days and growth is studied further for identification.
  - **Castaneda's method** is a biphasic culture medium containing both liquid and solid media in a same bottle.
  - Specimen is inoculated into the broth and the bottle is incubated in upright position. For subculture, bottle is tilted so that the broth runs over the solid slant and then incubated upright again.
  - ***Advantages***
    - It minimizes manipulation of material and reduces the chances of contamination
    - Reduces the risk of infection to laboratory workers
- **Diagnosis by serological methods**
  - **Agglutination test** detects IgM
  - Tube agglutination test—equal volumes of serial dilutions of serum mixed with standard antigen and incubated for 24 hours at 37°C and observed for agglutination
  - Titre of 1:160 or more is considered significant in a single test
  - False negative—sera with blocking antibodies and prozone phenomenon may give negative results
  - False positive—cholera, tularaemia and Yersinia infection may give false-positive results
  - **Complement fixation test (CFT)** detects both IgM and IgG
  - **ELISA** and **radioimmunoassay (RIA)** can detect IgG and IgM, IgA separately

Treatment

Doxycycline and streptomycin

Prophylaxis

- **Vaccine** is available for cattle but not for humans.

Haemophilus influenzae

- Gram-negative, small (1.5 × 0.3 µm) coccobacilli
- Non-motile, non-sporing but capsulated
- It is a strict pathogen; grows on enriched media such as blood agar or chocolate agar
- Growth is better in aerobic condition

- Need 5–10% CO_2 for growth, optimum temperature is 35–37°C
- Growth requirements include factors X (iron porphyrin-haematin) and V (nicotinamide adenine dinucleotide [NAD] or nicotinamide adenine dinucleotide phosphate [NADP])—bacterial vitamins present in blood for growth
- It is a delicate organism, sensitive to heat—moist heat at 55°C kills it within 30 minutes. Sensitive to low temperature also (dies in a few days at 4°C)
- Sensitive to common disinfectants and to drying

Virulence factors

- Capsular polysaccharide—resists phagocytosis
- Pili—help in attachment
- Outer membrane protein—contributes to adhesion and invasion
- IgA protease—cleaves IgA-1

Pathogenicity

- Infection occurs by inhalation—entry by respiratory route
- It spreads either by local invasion along the mucosal surfaces or through bloodstream
- It causes
  - Meningitis
  - Acute epiglottitis
  - Pneumonia
  - Bronchitis
  - Otitis media
  - Cellulitis
  - Pericarditis
  - Endocarditis
  - Conjunctivitis
  - Nasopharyngitis

Laboratory diagnosis

- **Collection of specimens** CSF, sputum, throat swab, pus, blood and other specimens according to the site of infection
- **Direct microscopy**
  - Gram stain shows Gram-negative coccobacilli
  - Direct immunofluorescence test
  - Capsule swelling reaction (Quellung reaction) can be used for direct demonstration
- **Detection of antigen** Latex agglutination and coagglutination tests can be used for demonstration of antigen
- **Culture** On blood agar and chocolate agar—after incubation observed for growth. Growth is confirmed by Gram staining and immunological tests used for direct microscopy

Treatment

- Cefotaxime
- Ceftazidime
- Amoxicillin-clavulanic acid
- Ampicillin
- Co-trimoxazole
- Chloramphenicol
- Sulphonamides
- Tetracycline
- Ciprofloxacin

Prophylaxis

- **Vaccination** Haemophilus b conjugate (Hib) vaccine in children of 18–24 months—two doses at an interval of 2 months

Self-assessment

Long-answer questions

1. Discuss in brief the pathogenicity and laboratory diagnosis of cholera.
2. Discuss in brief the pathogenicity and laboratory diagnosis of brucellosis.

Short-answer questions

Write notes on
1. *Pseudomonas aeruginosa*
2. *Burkholderia pseudomallei*
3. *Francisella tularensis*

4. *Bordetella pertussis*
5. *Haemophilus influenzae*
6. Laboratory diagnosis of cholera
7. Castaneda's method

Multiple-choice questions

1. Which of the following media is used as a selective medium for cultivation of *Pseudomonas aeruginosa?*
   A. Cetrimide agar
   B. Deoxycholate citrate agar
   C. Muller–Hinton agar
   D. Milk salt agar
2. Melioidosis is caused by
   A. *Burkholderia pseudomallei*
   B. *B. cepacia*
   C. *B. maltophilia*
   D. *Pseudomonas aeruginosa*
3. Which of the following statements is TRUE regarding pyocyanin?
   A. Is a greenish-yellow pigment soluble in water but not in chloroform
   B. Is a greenish-yellow pigment soluble in water and chloroform
   C. Is a bluish-green pigment soluble in water and chloroform
   D. Is a bluish-green pigment soluble in water but not in chloroform
4. Which of the following media is NOT selective for cultivation of *Vibrio cholerae?*
   A. Thiosulfate, citrate, bile salt, sucrose medium
   B. Deoxycholate citrate agar
   C. Alkaline bile salt agar
   D. Mansur's gelatin taurocholate trypticase tellurite agar
5. Venketraman–Ramkrishnan medium is a
   A. Selective medium for *Vibrio cholerae*
   B. Enrichment medium for *V. cholerae*
   C. Sugar medium for *V. cholerae*
   D. Transport medium for *V. cholerae*
6. Darting type of motility is the characteristic feature of
   A. *Pseudomonas aeruginosa*
   B. *Vibrio cholerae*
   C. *Escherichia coli*
   D. *Salmonella typhi*
7. Which of the following statements is FALSE regarding tularaemia?
   A. Is a disease of rabbit (rabbit fever) and other rodents
   B. Is transmitted by ticks and other arthropod vectors
   C. May also cause gingivitis
   D. Infection in humans occurs by direct contact with animals, by ingestion of contaminated meat or water and inhalation
8. Majority of the cases (95% cases) of whooping cough are caused by
   A. *Bordetella avium*
   B. *B. parapertussis*
   C. *B. bronchiseptica*
   D. *B. pertussis*
9. Castaneda's method of blood culture is commonly used for diagnosis of
   A. Plague
   B. Brucellosis
   C. Pertussis
   D. Tularaemia
10. Which of the following bacteria is a causative agent of undulant fever?
    A. *Bordetella avium*
    B. *Burkholderia pseudomallei*
    C. *Brucella melitensis*
    D. *Francisella tularensis*
11. Which of the following growth factors is required for growth of *Haemophilus influenzae?*
    A. X factor
    B. V factor
    C. X and V factors
    D. None of the above

34 Other Bacterial Pathogens

Other bacterial pathogens of medical and dental importance include the following:

- *Calymmatobacterium granulomatis*
- Rickettsiae
- *Chlamydia trachomatis*
- *Mycoplasma* and *Ureaplasma*

Calymmatobacterium granulomatis

- Also called as *Donovania granulomatis*
- Gram-negative coccobacillus shows bipolar or safety pin appearance
- Size is 1–2 × 0.5–1.5 µm
- It is capsulated but non-motile and non-sporing
- These microbes are present inside the phagosomes of large macrophages and are known as **Donovan bodies**
- It causes a venereal disease, donovanosis or granuloma inguinale, which starts as a painless papule or nodule on genitalia that ulcerates to form a granular lesion. Inguinal ulceration occurs secondary to genital lesion and is present initially as a fluctuant swelling known as a pseudobubo. The granuloma inguinale may be confused with lymphogranuloma venereum—a venereal disease caused by *Chlamydia trachomatis*
- Extragenital lesions of donovanosis may occur on the oral mucous membranes (usually through autoinfection and not as a primary infection), pharynx, oesophagus and larynx
- In the oral cavity, lesions may occur on the lips, buccal mucosa or palate and they occur as
  - Painful ulcerated lesions
  - Proliferative granular masses
  - Fibrous scar formation
- Disease is diagnosed by demonstration of Donovan bodies in Giemsa stained or Wright's stained smears
- Cultured on egg yolk medium or on modified Levinthal agar. It can also be cultivated in the yolk sac of embryonated hen's eggs

Treatment

- Tetracycline
- Chloramphenicol
- Erythromycin
- Streptomycin
- Co-trimoxazole
- Extensive fibrous scar formation on the cheek or lip needs surgical relief

Rickettsiae

- These are minute organisms having properties in between bacteria and viruses.
- Like viruses, they are obligatory intracellular parasites and unable to grow in cell-free culture.
- Like bacteria, they are Gram-negative pleomorphic rods which divide by binary fission, contain muramic acid in cell wall and possess both DNA and RNA.
- They are Gram-negative coccobacilli.
- Size is 600 × 300 nm.
- Non-motile, non-sporing and non-capsulated.
- Do not grow in cell-free media and are cultivated in embryonated hen's egg, tissue culture or animals.
- Readily inactivated by heat (56°C) and chemical agents.

Pathogenicity

- Transmitted to man by insect vectors, except for Q fever which occurs by ingestion or inhalation.
- They cause
  - Epidemic typhus *(Rickettsia prowazekii)*
  - Endemic typhus (*R. mooseri)*
  - Spotted fever (*R. akari)*
  - Scrub typhus (*R. tsutsugamushi)*
  - Trench fever (*Rochalimaea quintana)*
  - Q fever (*Coxiella burnetii)*

Laboratory diagnosis

- **Specimen** Blood
- **Culture** On chick embryo or tissue culture
- **Animal inoculation** In guinea pigs and mice
- **Serological tests**
  - Weil–Felix test is a tube agglutination test used for detection of antibodies against *Rickettsia* using antigens of *Proteus* strains. The test is positive in endemic typhus, spotted fever, scrub typhus and epidemic typhus
  - Complement fixation test
  - Indirect haemagglutination test
  - Toxin neutralization
  - Microimmunofluorescence test are also used

Treatment

- Tetracycline
- Chloramphenicol

Chlamydia trachomatis

These are Gram-negative, small bacteria which exist in two forms:

1. **Elementary bodies** Spherical, 200–300 nm in diameter, extracellular infectious particles
2. **Initial bodies** Elementary body inside the host cell increases in size from 200 to 1000 nm and becomes initial body. This form reproduces by binary fission to form a large number of elementary bodies

Chlamydiae are heat labile (50°C for few minutes for inactivation), susceptible to ethanol, ether, phenol and formalin.

Pathogenicity

C. trachomatis causes

- **Trachoma** Infection transmitted from eye to eye by finger, fomites (e.g., face towel), flies, dust, etc. It occurs as chronic keratoconjunctivitis
- **Sexually transmitted diseases** such as
  - In male, non-gonococcal urethritis and epididymitis
  - In female, urethritis, cervicitis and pelvic inflammatory diseases
  - In newborn, inclusion conjunctivitis
  - Lymphogranuloma venereum, characterized by suppurative inguinal adenitis
- **Respiratory tract infections** such as
  - Pneumonia in newborn
  - Upper respiratory tract infections in adults with inclusion conjunctivitis

Laboratory diagnosis

- **Specimens**
  - Conjunctival scrapings in trachoma
  - Vaginal or cervical swab in female genital infections
  - Pus or biopsy material in lymphogranuloma venereum
- **Direct microscopy**
  - Giemsa stain shows typical inclusion of epithelial cells
  - Direct fluorescent antibody test for detection of antigens of *C. trachomatis*
  - ELISA can also be used for detection of antigen in specimen
- **Culture** On yolk sac of chick embryo or tissue culture, growth identified by morphology and serologic tests
- **Serologic tests** for demonstration of antibodies
  - Complement fixation test
  - Indirect immunofluorescence test

Treatment

- Sulphonamides
- Erythromycin
- Tetracycline
- Azithromycin

Mycoplasma and *Ureaplasma*

- These are the smallest microorganisms measuring about 0.2–0.3 µm in diameter.
- They are highly pleomorphic because they lack rigid cell wall.
- They are Gram-negative, non-sporing, non-capsulated and non-flagellated but may be motile.
- They are aerobes and facultative anaerobes.
- Optimum temperature for growth is 37°C.
- Require sterol and cholesterol as essential growth factor.
- They can be grown in **mycoplasma** broth, mycoplasma agar and biphasic media.
  - On mycoplasma agar, colonies are very small ranging between 200 and 500 µm in diameter and show 'Fried egg appearance' in transmitted light.

Biochemical reactions

Biochemical reactions of different species of *Mycoplasma* and of *Ureaplasma urealyticum* are given in Table 34.1.

Table 34.1 Biochemical reactions of *Mycoplasma* and *Ureaplasma*

	Utilization of		
	Glucose	**Arginine**	**Urea**
M. pneumoniae	+	–	–
M. hominis	–	+	–
U. urealyticum	–	–	+

- They are susceptible to heat.
- They are susceptible to lysis by surface-active agents and lipolytic agents such as taurocholate.
- They are resistant to penicillin, cephalosporins and lysozyme as these act on the cell wall.

Pathogenicity

Mycoplasma and *Ureaplasma* are responsible for respiratory and urogenital infections.

Respiratory infections

- *M. pneumoniae* is responsible for primary atypical pneumonia
- *M. hominis* is responsible for mild respiratory infections

Urogenital infections

- Caused by *U. urealyticum* and *M. hominis*
- Diseases caused are non-gonococcal urethritis, balanitis, epididymitis and balanoposthitis in males
- In females, it causes acute salpingitis PID (pelvic inflammatory disease), cervicitis and vaginitis

Laboratory diagnosis

- **Specimens** Sputum, throat swab, nasal swab, cervical swab, vaginal swab, semen, prostatic secretion and urine
- **Transport** As mycoplasma is a delicate bacterium, samples should be inoculated immediately. If immediate culture is not possible, then specimen should be held at 4°C
- **Culture** On mycoplasma agar, after 5–7 days of inoculation, *M. pneumoniae* shows characteristic fried egg colonies—200–500 µm with central opaque area
  - Colonies of *Ureaplasma* are tiny about 15–50 µm in diameter
  - Colonies of *M. pneumoniae* are identified by haemadsorption test, tetrazolium reduction test and by serological tests
- **Antigen detection** An antigen can be detected in respiratory specimens by
  - Immunofluorescence test
  - Counterimmunoelectrophoresis
  - Enzyme immunoassay
  - Immunoblotting with monoclonal antibodies
- **Antibody detection**
  - ***Specific tests***
    - Significant titre in recent infection is 1:64
    - Indirect haemagglutination
    - Enzyme immunoassay for detection of IgM, IgG, IgA. The test is more sensitive than complement fixation test (CFT)
  - ***Non-specific tests***
    - Cold agglutination test using 'O' blood group RBCs as antigen
    - Streptococcal MG test using heat killed suspension of Streptococcus MG as antigen

Treatment

- Tetracyclines are effective
- They are resistant to penicillins and cephalosporins

Self–assessment

Short-answer questions

Write notes on

1. *Calymmatobacterium granulomatis*
2. *Rickettsia*
3. *Chlamydia trachomatis*
4. Laboratory diagnosis of chlamydial infections

Multiple-choice questions

1. Which of the following is a causative agent of donovanosis (granuloma inguinale)?
   A. *Chlamydia trachomatis*
   B. *Coxiella burnetii*
   C. *Ureaplasma urealyticum*
   D. *Calymmatobacterium granulomatis*
2. Which of the following rickettsiae is a causative agent of epidemic typhus?
   A. *Rickettsia mooseri*
   B. *R. prowazekii*
   C. *R. akari*
   D. *R. tsutsugamushi*
3. Weil–Felix test is used for diagnosis of all of the following, EXCEPT
   A. Typhus fever
   B. Spotted fever
   C. Scrub typhus
   D. Typhoid fever
4. Which of the following sexually transmitted diseases is caused by *Chlamydia trachomatis?*
   A. Granuloma inguinale
   B. Lymphogranuloma venereum
   C. Balanoposthitis
   D. None of the above
5. Mycoplasma infections are sensitive to which of the following antibiotics?
   A. Penicillin
   B. Tetracycline
   C. Cephalosporins
   D. Ampicillin

6. Which of the following is a characteristic feature of mycoplasma colony?
   A. Fried egg colony
   B. Poached egg colony
   C. Daisy head colony
   D. Medusa head colony

7. Cold agglutination test using 'O' blood group RBCs as antigen is used for diagnosis of infections caused by which of the following microbes?
   A. *Chlamydia*
   B. *Coxiella*
   C. *Rickettsia*
   D. *Mycoplasma*

35 General Properties of Viruses

- Viruses are the smallest (20–300 nm in diameter) obligate intracellular infectious agents without cellular organization, whose genome is an element of nucleic acid, either deoxyribonucleic acid (DNA) or ribonucleic acid (RNA).
- The genome is enclosed in a protein shell known as **capsid**.
- The capsid may be surrounded by a lipid and protein-containing membrane called **envelope**. The entire infectious unit is called '**virion**' which is an extracellular infectious virus particle.
- They differ from bacteria in the following aspects:
  - Are much smaller than bacteria
  - Contain only one type of nucleic acid, either DNA or RNA
  - Do not have cellular organization and ribosomes
  - Are inert in extracellular environment and replicate only inside the living cells
  - Lack the enzymes necessary for synthesis of proteins and nucleic acid
  - Are obligate intracellular parasites not affected by antibiotics
  - Are filterable through bacteriological filters because of their small size

Morphology of viruses

Size

- Viruses are much smaller in size than other microorganisms
- Ultramicroscopic—as they are too small to be seen under the light microscope
- The size ranges from 20 to 300 nm in diameter
  - The largest virus is 300 nm, for example, smallpox virus
  - The smallest virus is 20 nm, for example, parvovirus
- The size of a virus can be measured by
  - Direct observation under the electron microscope
  - Passing them through the filters of different pore size
  - Based on the rate of sedimentation in the ultracentrifuge

Structure and chemical nature

- The two major components are
  - Nucleic acid—core or genome
  - Protein sheath—capsid
- The nucleic acid core is surrounded by a protein coat known as capsid

- The protein nucleic acid complex—the capsid together with the enclosed nucleic acid is known as **nucleocapsid**

Nucleic acid

Viruses contain a single kind of nucleic acid as genome, either DNA or RNA in which genetic information necessary for the replication of virus is present. The nucleic acid may be

- Single-stranded or double-stranded
- Circular or linear
- Segmented or unsegmented

These properties form the basis of classification of viruses into different families.

Capsid

It is a protein shell that encloses nucleic acid (genome). It is composed of polypeptide chains (protomers) that aggregate in groups of 5–6 to form capsomeres and the capsid is formed by a number of capsomeres. Its functions are

- Protection of nucleic acid, that is, genome
- Promotion of attachment of virus to the susceptible host cell

Envelope

Some viruses possess a membrane surrounding the nucleocapsid is known as envelope.

- It is 10–15 nm thick and is acquired from host cell membrane during replication process.
- Chemically, it is a protein covalently attached to carbohydrate (glycoproteins), also contains lipids derived from the host cell.
- In some viruses, for example, myxoviruses, the proteins (glycoproteins) are present as projections called spikes or peplomers about 10 nm long, which function as haemagglutinin or have neuraminidase activity.
- It functions to confer chemical, antigenic and biological properties.
- The peplomers help to attach virus particle to a host cell by interacting with a cellular receptor (Fig. 35.1).

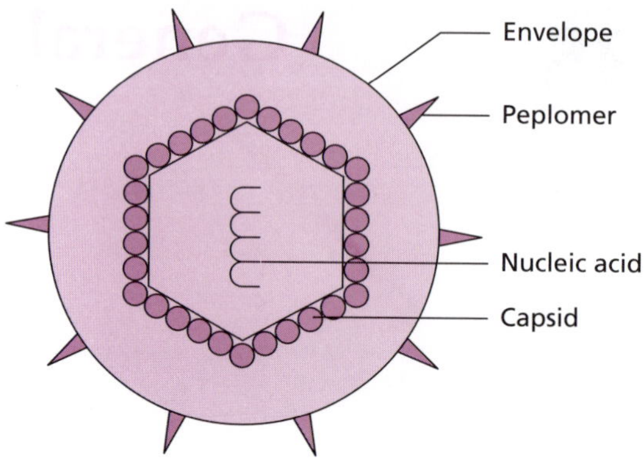

Figure 35.1 Structure of a virus.

Shape and symmetry

- The shape is different in different groups of viruses.
- The shape of virus may be
  - Brick-shaped, for example, poxvirus
  - Bullet-shaped, for example, rabies virus
  - Rod-shaped, for example, tobacco mosaic virus
  - Irregular and pleomorphic in some viruses
- The symmetry varies according to the number of capsomeres and their arrangement.
- Three types of symmetry are determined based on the arrangement of capsid around the nucleic acid core. These are as follows:
  - Icosahedral symmetry
  - Helical symmetry
  - Complex symmetry

Icosahedral symmetry

- An icosahedron is a polygon with 12 corners (vertices) and 20 sides (facets).
- It has a rigid structure.
- Two types of capsomeres, that is, pentons and hexons constitute the icosahedral capsid.
- Pentons are present at the corners and hexons to make up the sides (Fig. 35.2).

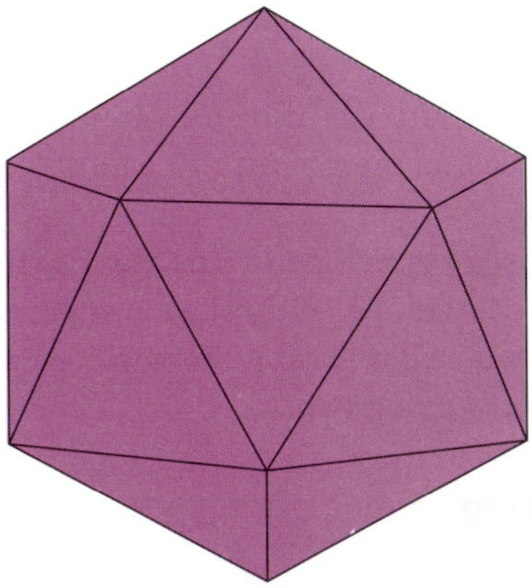

Figure 35.2 An icosahedron symmetry of a virus.

- Icosahedron symmetry is found in
  - DNA viruses such as herpes, parvo, papova and adenoviruses
  - RNA viruses such as picorna and reovirus

Helical symmetry

- In this, the protein subunits (capsomeres) are packed in the helical array around the viral nucleic acid to form a spiral tube or helical (Fig. 35.3).
- Helical symmetry is found in RNA viruses and most of them are enveloped viruses. It is unsuitable for DNA viruses
- Examples—myxo, arbo, tobacco mosaic virus and rhabdoviruses

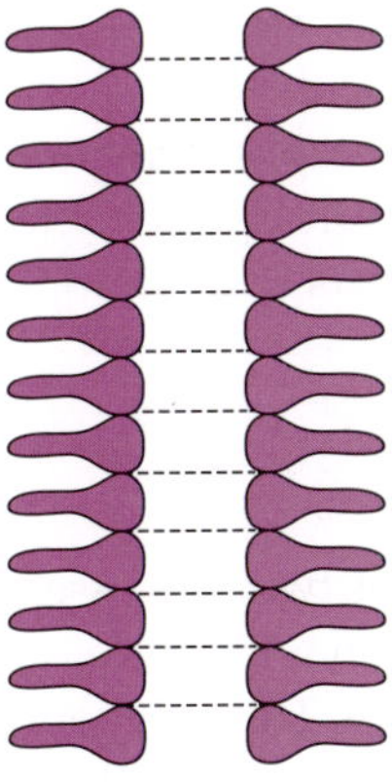

Figure 35.3 Helical symmetry of a virus.

Complex symmetry

Some viruses have a very complicated structure, which is neither icosahedral nor helical, for example, poxviruses (Fig. 35.4).

Susceptibility to physical and chemical agents

- Viruses are sensitive to sunlight, ultraviolet rays and ionizing radiations.
- They are sensitive to heat and are inactivated by heating at 56–60°C in 30 minutes, exceptions are hepatitis B virus and poliovirus.
- Viruses are resistant to cold and can survive up to –70°C.
- pH range is 5–9, but viruses are destroyed by extreme acidity or alkalinity.
- Viruses are sensitive to oxidizing agents such as hydrogen peroxide, potassium permanganate and organic iodophores.
- Enveloped viruses containing lipids are sensitive to ether.
- Some viruses are sensitive to phenols and cresols.
- Glutaraldehyde is effective against viruses and has an important role in the disinfection of apparatus used in renal dialysis units.
- Formaldehyde is active but slow in action.
- Viruses are resistant to antibiotics and chemotherapeutic agents.

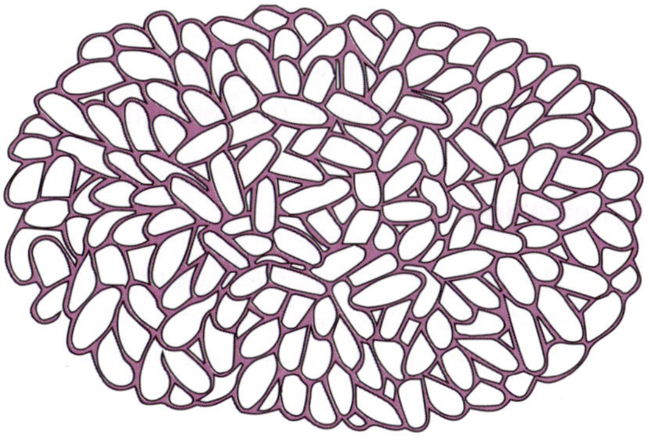

Figure 35.4 Complex symmetry of a virus.

- Chlorination of water kills most viruses but hepatitis A and polioviruses are relatively resistant to chlorination, especially when present with organic or faecal material.

Replication of viruses

As viruses lack enzymes necessary for biosynthesis, they utilize the biochemical machinery of the host cell to synthesize virus-specific macromolecules. The host cell provides the energy, synthetic machinery and the low molecular weight precursors for synthesis of viral proteins and nucleic acids required for the production of the virus progeny.

The viral nucleic acid carries the genetic information necessary for viral replication. As soon as it enters the cell, the cellular metabolism is redirected exclusively towards the synthesis of new viral particles and replication occurs in sequential phases. The different phases in virus replication are

- Adsorption or attachment
- Penetration
- Uncoating
- Biosynthesis
- Maturation
- Release

Adsorption or attachment

The first step in viral replication is attachment to the host cell surface with the help of specific receptors—a highly specific interaction of virus with receptors on the host cell surface results in attachment of the virus to the host cell.

Penetration

It is the taking of virus particle inside the cell. This occurs in the following ways:

- By a process called **viropexis** or **endocytosis** in which the host cell membrane forms a vesicle around the virus particle and detaches from the cell membrane and carries the virus particle deep into the cytoplasm.
- The virus may be directly admitted through the plasma membrane, for example, adenovirus.
- In case of enveloped virus, there is fusion of virus envelope with plasma membrane of the host cell releasing the nucleocapsid into the host cytoplasm.

Uncoating

- It is removal of capsid and release of nucleic acid into the host cell.
- This process of physical separation of the viral nucleic acid is carried out by the action of lysosomal enzymes of the host cell.

Biosynthesis

- This phase includes synthesis of viral nucleic acid, capsid and enzymes necessary in various stages of viral replication.
- In both DNA and RNA viruses, biosynthesis occurs in the following steps:
  - The first step is transcription, that is, formation of messenger RNA (mRNA) from viral nucleic acid. Specific encoded information is transferred to mRNA by viral genome.
  - The second step is translation of the mRNA into early proteins or non-structural proteins (enzymes) necessary for synthesis of viral components.
  - The third step is replication of viral nucleic acid.
  - The last step is formation of late protein or structural proteins (capsid protein). This occurs in the cytoplasm of the host cell.

Maturation

- It consists of two processes: assembly and its association with nucleic acid.
  - ***Assembly*** The polypeptide chains (late proteins) are rapidly assembled into capsomeres to form procapsid.

- *Association with nucleic acid* The procapsid finally incorporates nucleic acid and becomes complete virion—daughter virus.
- The enveloped viruses acquire envelope through the process of budding. The envelope is derived from the nuclear membrane in viruses such as herpes virus, as the maturation occurs in nucleus. However, in other viruses such as orthomyxo and paramyxoviruses, in which maturation occurs in cytoplasm, it is derived from plasma membrane.

Release

It occurs by three different mechanisms:

1. **By cell lysis**—non-enveloped viruses are released by rupturing the host cell and causing its death
2. **By budding**—enveloped viruses are released by a process of budding without rupturing the host cell
3. **By cell degeneration**—viruses such as parvoviruses accumulate in the host nucleus and are released after the cell death, which follows the degeneration of the cell (Fig. 35.5)

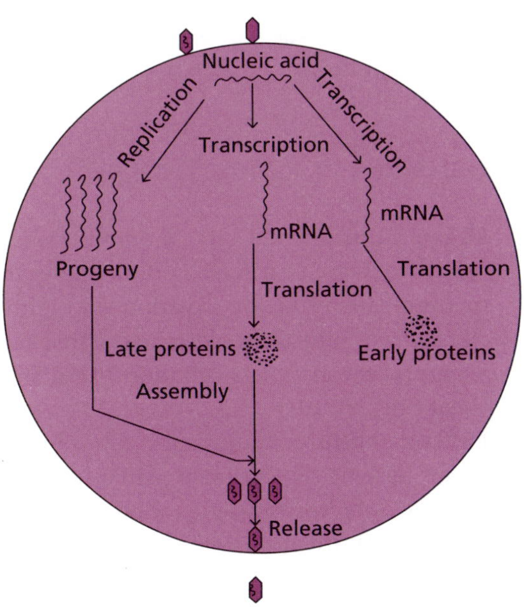

Figure 35.5 Replication of viruses.

Cultivation of viruses

- Viruses are obligate intracellular parasites; hence, they require living cells for their growth.
- Three types of methods have been developed for their cultivation which are as follows:
  - Animal inoculation
  - Embryonated eggs
  - Tissue cultures

Animal inoculation

- Because of the availability of other simple methods, animal inoculations are less in use
- Animals are used for
  - Primary isolation of viruses, which do not grow in eggs and tissue cultures
  - To study pathogenesis of viral diseases
  - To study immune response
  - To study efficacy of vaccines and drugs
  - To study oncogenesis
- **Animals commonly used** include
  - Suckling mice—most commonly used
  - Rabbits
  - Guinea pigs
  - Monkeys
- **Route of inoculation**
  - Intracerebral
  - Intraperitoneal
  - Intranasal
  - Subcutaneous
- **Indicator of growth** Growth of virus in animals may be indicated by
  - Disease or visible lesions
  - Death
  - Demonstrating presence of virus in tissue
  - Demonstration of inclusion bodies

Embryonated eggs

Embryonated hen's eggs, usually 7–12 days old are inoculated by one of the following routes (Fig. 35.6):

- Chorioallantoic membrane (CAM)
- Allantoic cavity
- Amniotic cavity
- Yolk sac

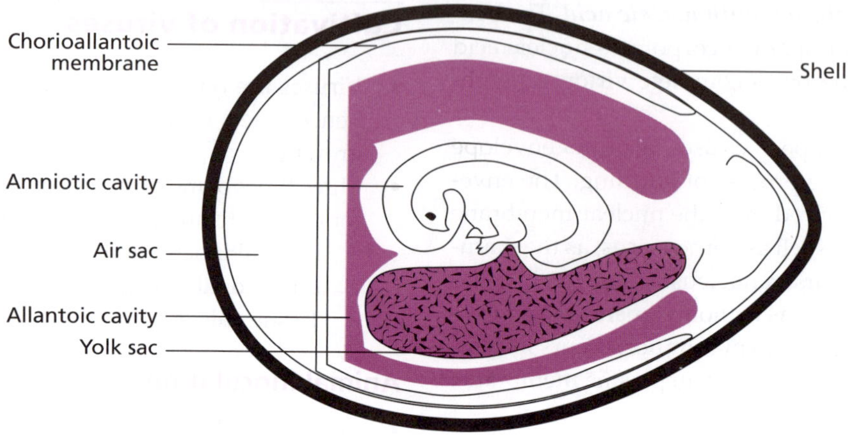

Figure 35.6 Embryonated egg—routes of inoculation.

After inoculation, eggs are incubated for 2–9 days based on the type of virus and route of inoculation.

Chorioallantoic membrane

- Some viruses can grow on CAM producing visible lesions called pocks
- Each virus particle forms one pock; hence, the number of pock indicates the number of virus particles in the inoculum. Thus, it helps in the assay of pock-forming viruses
- **Uses** Used for isolation, diagnosis and assay of pock-forming viruses, for example, poxviruses and herpes simplex virus

Allantoic cavity

- Viruses such as influenza, some paramyxoviruses, yellow fever virus and rabies virus are grown in allantoic cavity
- It is mainly used for growing viruses for vaccine production, because of high yield of virus in this cavity
- The growth of virus is detected by haemagglutination test

Amniotic cavity

- Used for the primary isolation of influenza virus
- Also for obtaining high yield of virus for vaccine production
- The growth of virus is detected by haemagglutination test

Yolk sac

Used for the cultivation of some viruses and bacteria such as chlamydiae and rickettsiae.

Tissue cultures (cell lines)

Three types of tissue cultures are available which are as follows:

1. Organ culture
2. Explant culture
3. Cell culture

- **Organ culture** Small bits of organs maintained in vitro in a tissue culture growth medium are used for isolation of highly specialized viruses of certain organs, for example, corona virus isolation using tracheal ring culture
- **Explant culture** Fragments of minced tissue grown as explants embedded in plasma clots, for example, adenoid tissue explant culture for isolation of adenoviruses
- **Cell culture** Most commonly used, usually in monolayers

Preparation of monolayers

- Desired tissue is cut into small pieces
- By treating with a proteolytic enzyme, for example, trypsin and mechanical shaking, tissues are dissociated into the component cells
- The dissociated cells are suspended in a suitable growth medium containing all the essential nutrients (amino acids, vitamins, salts, glucose, etc.) and supplemented with up to 5% calf or foetal calf serum
- The cell suspension is distributed in a glass or plastic container
- On incubation, the cells adhere to glass or plastic surface and divide to form a confluent monolayer sheet of cells within a period of 1 week

Types of cell cultures

Based on their origin, chromosomal characters and the number of generations through which they can be maintained, cell cultures are classified into three types:

1. Primary cell cultures
2. Diploid cell strains
3. Continuous cell lines

Primary cell cultures

- These are normal cells, freshly taken from the organs of animal or human being and cultured
- These are capable of only 5–10 divisions
- **Examples**
  - Rhesus monkey kidney cell culture
  - Human amnion cell culture
  - Chick embryo fibroblast cell culture
- **Uses** For the primary isolation of viruses and their cultivation for vaccine production

Diploid cell strains

- These are cells of a single type that retain the original diploid chromosome and karyotype during serial subcultivation for a limited number of times based on the lifespan of the species of animal from which it is obtained
- The human diploid cells undergo around 50 divisions, for example
  - WI-38—human embryonic lung cell strain
  - HL-8—rhesus embryo cell strains
- **Uses**
  - Used for isolation of some fastidious pathogens
  - Also used for commercial production of vaccine, for example, WI-38 for rabies vaccine

Continuous cell lines

- These are immortal cell lines capable of indefinite growth in vitro.
- They are usually derived from cancerous tissue or originate by the spontaneous transformation of a diploid cell strain.
- These cells can be maintained indefinitely by serial subcultures at regular intervals or stored at −70°C for use when necessary and when large numbers of cells are required they can be grown in suspension culture.
- These cell lines are derived from monkeys, cattle, mouse, rabbit, human beings, etc.
- **Examples**
  - HeLa—human carcinoma of cervix cell line
  - HEP-2—human epithelioma of larynx cell line
  - KB—human carcinoma of nasopharynx cell line
  - Vero—vervet monkey kidney cell line
- **Uses**
  - Isolation of viruses from clinical specimens
  - For production of antigens
  - Some cell lines are used for vaccine production, for example, vero cell line for rabies vaccine

Detection of virus growth in cell cultures

The growth of a virus can be detected by various techniques.

Cytopathic effects (CPE)

- Many viruses kill the cell in which they grow and many of them cause detectable morphological changes known as CPE. The viruses causing CPE are known as cytopathogenic viruses.
- The CPE are different in different groups and help in the presumptive identification of virus isolates.
- Some viruses produce detectable CPE however others produce CPE which require visualization under the microscope.
- CPE induced by viruses are as follows:
  - Rounding of cells and degeneration in picornavirus group
  - Syncytium formation—fusion of infected cell with adjacent cells to form giant cells containing several nuclei in measles and respiratory syncytial viruses
  - Rounding and aggregation of cells into grape-like clusters in adenoviruses
  - Formation of intracytoplasmic or intranuclear inclusion bodies

Haemadsorption

- The growth of haemagglutinating viruses such as myxoviruses and togaviruses can be detected by adding guinea pig RBCs to the cell cultures.
- The adsorption of RBCs to the surface of cells indicates multiplication of viruses. No adsorption indicates absence of viruses.
- This phenomenon is known as haemadsorption.

Immunofluorescence

- The growth of virus in infected cells can be detected by staining with specific antiviral antibody conjugated with a fluorescent dye.
- This method gives rapid results, earlier than other methods, hence used to identify many viral isolates.

Electron microscopy

Viruses grown in culture can be demonstrated by electron microscope.

Classification of viruses

Viruses are classified into two main classes based on the type of nucleic acid they possess:

1. Riboviruses—viruses containing RNA. These are RNA viruses
2. Deoxyriboviruses—viruses containing DNA. These are DNA viruses

RNA viruses

These include the following:

- Picornaviridae family includes the following viruses:
  - Enteroviruses, for example, poliovirus
  - Rhinoviruses, for example, rhinoviruses
  - Hepatovirus, for example, hepatitis A virus
- Orthomyxoviridae family, for example, influenza virus
- Paramyxoviridae family, for example, mumps virus, parainfluenza virus and respiratory syncytial virus
- Rhabdoviridae family, for example, rabies virus
- Coronaviridae family, for example, corona virus
- Retroviridae family, for example, HIV
- Reoviridae family, for example, rotavirus
- Other families include arboviruses, hantavirus and many other viruses

DNA viruses

These include the following:

- Poxviridae family, for example, poxvirus
- Herpesviridae family, for example, herpes viruses
- Adenoviridae family, for example, adenoviruses

- Hepadnaviridae family, for example, hepatitis B virus
- Papovaviridae family, for example, papilloma virus and polyomavirus
- Parvoviridae family, for example, parvovirus

Self-assessment

Long-answer questions

1. Discuss in detail the morphology of viruses.
2. Discuss in detail the cultivation of viruses.
3. Discuss in detail the replication of viruses.

Short-answer questions

Write notes on
1. Viral capsid
2. Viral envelope
3. Icosahedral symmetry
4. Helical symmetry
5. Tissue cultures
6. Cytopathic effects
7. Classification of viruses

Multiple-choice questions

1. Following are the characteristic features of viruses, EXCEPT
   A. Do not have cellular organization
   B. Lack enzymes necessary for protein synthesis
   C. Contain DNA as well as RNA
   D. Are much smaller than bacteria
2. Which of the following is the largest virus?
   A. Parvovirus
   B. Tobacco mosaic virus
   C. Chickenpox virus
   D. Smallpox virus
3. Icosahedron symmetry is NOT seen in which of the following viruses?
   A. Rabies virus
   B. Adenoviruses
   C. Picorna viruses
   D. Herpes virus
4. Which of the following viruses shows helical symmetry?
   A. Adenoviruses
   B. Rabies virus
   C. Picorna viruses
   D. Herpes virus
5. Which of the following viruses shows complex symmetry?
   A. Adenoviruses
   B. Tobacco mosaic virus
   C. Herpes virus
   D. Poxviruses
6. Viropexis in virus replication is a process of
   A. Adsorption
   B. Uncoating
   C. Penetration
   D. Biosynthesis
7. Transcription in virus replication is a process by which there is a formation of
   A. Progeny virus
   B. Transfer RNA
   C. Ribosomal RNA
   D. Messenger RNA
8. Translation in virus replication is a process by which there is a formation of
   A. Protein synthesis
   B. Transfer RNA
   C. Ribosomal RNA
   D. Messenger RNA
9. Pocks on chorioallantoic membrane (CAM) are produced by
   A. Adenoviruses
   B. Tobacco mosaic virus
   C. Herpes virus
   D. Parvoviruses
10. HeLa—human carcinoma of cervix cell line is an example of
   A. Primary cell culture
   B. Diploid cell strains
   C. Continuous cell lines
   D. Explant culture
11. Which of the following statements is FALSE about primary cell cultures?
   A. These are normal cells—freshly taken from the organs
   B. Used for the primary isolation of viruses
   C. They are usually derived from cancerous tissue
   D. These are capable of only 5–10 divisions

12. Following are the DNA viruses, EXCEPT
    A. Adenoviruses
    B. Poxviruses
    C. Picorna viruses
    D. Herpes viruses
13. Following are the RNA viruses, EXCEPT
    A. Rabies virus
    B. Influenza virus
    C. Rotavirus
    D. Hepatitis B virus
14. Which of the following animals is most commonly used for cultivation of viruses?
    A. Monkeys
    B. Rabbits
    C. Suckling mice
    D. Guinea pigs
15. Monolayers are a type of
    A. Organ culture
    B. Cell culture
    C. Explants culture
    D. None of the above

36 Virus–Host Interaction

- Interaction of a virus with a host may cause various effects, ranging from no apparent cellular damage to rapid cell destruction, for example
  - Cytocidal or cytolysis—poliovirus
  - Malignant transformation—oncogenic viruses
  - Latent infection—herpes simplex virus
  - Steady state infection without any cellular injury—echovirus 6
  - Morphological change in cells to form inclusion bodies—rabies virus
- The mechanism by which cellular injury is produced is different in different viruses
- The mechanisms of cell damage include the following:
  - Shutting down of protein and DNA synthesis of the host cell
  - Accumulation of viral macromolecules causing toxic effects
  - Alteration of permeability of plasma membrane causing the release of lysosomal enzymes and autolysis
  - Alterations in the cytoplasmic membrane of infected cells, for example, fusion of adjacent cell membranes leading to syncytium formation
  - Damage to the host cell chromosome
  - Formation of inclusion bodies

Inclusion bodies

- These are virus-specific intracellular globular masses with distinct size, shape, location and staining properties that are produced during the replication of virus in the host cells.
- These can be demonstrated in virus-infected host cells under the light microscope.
- The inclusions may be
  - Cytoplasmic
  - Intranuclear
  - Both
- Cytoplasmic inclusions are produced by viruses that assemble in the cytoplasm.
  - These are mainly RNA viruses, for example
    - Negri bodies by rabies virus
    - Guarnieri bodies by vaccinia virus
- Intranuclear inclusions are produced by viruses that assemble in the nucleus. These are usually DNA viruses and are of two types:
  - Cowdry type A are of variable size and granular appearance, for example, herpes virus and yellow fever virus
  - Cowdry type B often multiple and more circumscribed, for example, adenovirus and poliovirus
- Both cytoplasmic and intranuclear inclusion bodies are produced by measles (RNA) virus.

- Inclusion bodies may be crystalline aggregates of virions or made up of virus antigens present at the site of virus synthesis.
- They are generally acidophilic (pink) when stained with Giemsa or eosin methylene blue stains. Some are basophilic, for example, adenovirus inclusion bodies stained by haematoxylin.
- Their demonstration helps in the diagnosis of some viral infections, for example, Negri bodies in the cytoplasm of brain cells help in the presumptive diagnosis of rabies.

Pathogenesis of viral infections

Entry of virus into the host

The various routes by which viruses may enter the host are as follows:

- Mucous membranes such as
  - Conjunctival sac—some adeno and enteroviruses
  - Nose and throat—influenza, rhinovirus, mumps, measles, etc.
  - Gastrointestinal—hepatitis A, polio, rotavirus, etc.
  - Genital—HIV, hepatitis B virus, hepatitis C virus, herpes simplex virus, etc.
- Skin—entry of viruses occurs through
  - Abrasions—papilloma
  - Insect bites—arboviruses
  - Animal bites—rabies virus
  - Injections—HIV, hepatitis B virus, etc.
- Subcutaneous and muscular tissue—by insect and animal bite or by injection
- Placenta—congenital transfer of virus from mother to foetus may occur through placenta, for example, rubella and cytomegalovirus

Spread of virus within the host

After entry in the host, spread of virus occurs in the following ways:

Direct cell to cell spread Viruses may spread directly from cell to its neighbouring cells by forming intracellular bridge, for example, common cold virus.

Role of macrophages Viruses resistant to the phagocytic activity of macrophages, if ingested, grow inside the macrophage and spread to various parts along with phagocytic mobility.

Role of lymphatic system After entry through skin, subcutaneous tissue or mucous membrane, viruses may reach the regional lymph nodes and if immune mechanisms fail to overcome the infection in the node, they may be carried in the lymph and to the bloodstream from where they finally reach the target organ.

Role of blood and vascular system

- After local multiplication in lymph nodes, virus may enter the bloodstream causing **viraemia** and it is then transported to the different organs.
- Alternatively, virus may reach the circulating blood with the help of leucocytes in the tissues, which ingest viruses and make their way into the blood through the walls of blood vessels.
- In blood, virus may be associated with granulocytes, monocytes, RBCs or platelets (cell-associated viraemia) or may move freely in plasma.

Spread by nerve fibres Neurotropic viruses such as herpes, rabies and arboviruses can spread along the nerve fibres

Localization of virus in target organs

- Viruses have selective affinity for one or more target organs in the body.
- This property is known as **tropism**.
- The skin and central nervous system are the main target organs. Liver, lungs, muscles, abdominal viscera, mucous membrane and heart may also get infected.
- Based on tropism, viruses may be classified as dermotropic, neurotropic, pneumotropic, enterotropic or hepatotropic.

Incubation period (IP)

- It is the interval between the first entry of infective virus and the first onset of symptoms. It includes the time from entry to spread to the target organs to produce lesions and symptoms. The duration of IP is influenced by the relation between the site of entry, target organ, multiplication rate and lesions.
- IP short—1–3 days when site of entry and site of multiplication are same, for example, respiratory viral infections.
- IP long—10–20 days when site of entry and site of multiplication are different, for example, systemic diseases such as poliomyelitis.
- IP in hepatitis B virus may be 2–6 months and in slow viruses may be many years.

Damage to the host

- Once the defence mechanisms of the host are overcome, the virus can initiate damage to the host tissues producing a mild, sever or fatal illness.
- The damage to the host tissue is produced in the following ways:
  - ***Direct cytotoxicity*** Occurs by viral components and virus-specified products (viral cytotoxins).
  - ***Immunopathological reactions*** Damage to the infected host cell may be produced by Type II (antibody-mediated) or Type IV (cell-mediated) cytotoxic reactions. Uninfected host cells may also be damaged by the immune response evoked by the host to viral antigens or by Type I (anaphylaxis) and Type III (immune complex) reactions.
- This damage may result in
  - Death of the host cell
  - Proliferation of the host cell
  - Formation of multinucleated giant cells by fusion of membranes of adjacent cells
  - Malignant transformation of the host cell

Release of virus from the host

- The final step in pathogenesis is the release of virus.
- Viruses are released from the host in the last few days of IP, during the acute phase of illness and only for a short period thereafter.
- Chronic release as happens in tuberculosis does not occur; however, in some viral diseases, virus may persist in a latent phase after initial or primary infection, which may be stimulated to resume infective condition and cause release of virus, for example, herpes and cytomegalovirus.
- The viruses are released from the site of local multiplication, upper and lower respiratory tract, gastrointestinal tract, genitourinary tract, etc.

Host response to viral infections

The host response to viral infections may be

- Specific immune response
- Non-specific response

Specific immune response

It is of two types:

1. Antibody-mediated immunity or humoral immunity
2. Cell-mediated immunity (CMI)

Antibody-mediated or humoral immunity

- IgG, IgM and IgA antibodies are produced in response to virus infection, which offer protection against viruses.
- IgG and IgM play a major role in blood and tissue spaces and IgA is produced locally and is selectively concentrated in seromucous secretions of respiratory, intestinal and urogenital tracts. It offers major protection at local level and acts as a barrier to prevent

systemic spread of viruses from localized surface areas.

- Specific antibodies formed in response to viral infections may act in the following ways:
  - Neutralize the viruses and prevent their attachment, penetration and uncoating
  - Attach to viral antigens on the surface of the infected cells making these cells prone to lysis by complement or to destruction by phagocytic cells or killer (K) cells
  - Cause immune opsonization of virus and phagocytosis

Cell-mediated immunity

- It is primarily mediated by T lymphocytes, which have virus-specific receptors on their surface with the help of which they respond to the viruses.
- The cells other than T cells such as natural killer (NK) cells, K cells and macrophages directly attack the viruses.
- The different mechanisms of action are as follows:
  - T lymphocytes (cytotoxic T cells) are directly cytotoxic to virally infected host cells.
  - Lymphokines released by sensitized T cells, encourage macrophages to discourage the intracellular bridge formation and limit the intracellular transfer.
  - NK cells attack on virally infected host cells and cause cytolysis.
  - K cells attack on virally infected host cells with the help of antibodies (antibody-dependent cell-mediated cytotoxicity [ADCC]).
  - There may be an antibody and complement-mediated cytotoxicity.
  - T cells produce interferon, which interferes with multiplication of virus and limit the infection.

Non-specific response

Important physiological defences

Phagocytosis Macrophages play an important role in clearing viruses from the bloodstream. Polymorphonuclear leucocytes do not play any significant role.

Body temperature As most viruses are inhibited by temperature above 39°C, fever acts as a natural defence against virus infections.

Interferons (IFNs) They are antiviral substances produced by cells in response to viral infection. They are proteins (glycoproteins) having molecular weight of 20000–40000, susceptible to proteolytic enzymes and resist heating at 56–60°C for 30–60 minutes.

- IFNs have antiviral activity by inhibiting protein synthesis and act by conferring on cell's resistance to the multiplication of number of different viruses.
- They are not virus-specific. Hence, interferon produced in response to one virus can confer protection against infection by same or unrelated viruses.

Types of IFNs

They are of three types:

1. IFN-alpha—produced by leucocytes in response to viral infection. It has antiviral activity
2. IFN-beta—produced by fibroblasts and epithelial cells in response to viral infection and it has antiviral effect
3. IFN-gamma—produced by T lymphocytes and NK cells in response to antigens and mitogens. It is a lymphokine that has modulatory/regulatory effect on immune system. It activates cytotoxic T cells, macrophages and NK cells

Mechanism of action

Flow chart 36.1 shows the mechanism of action of interferon.

Biological effects

- Antiviral activity inhibits the replication of viruses

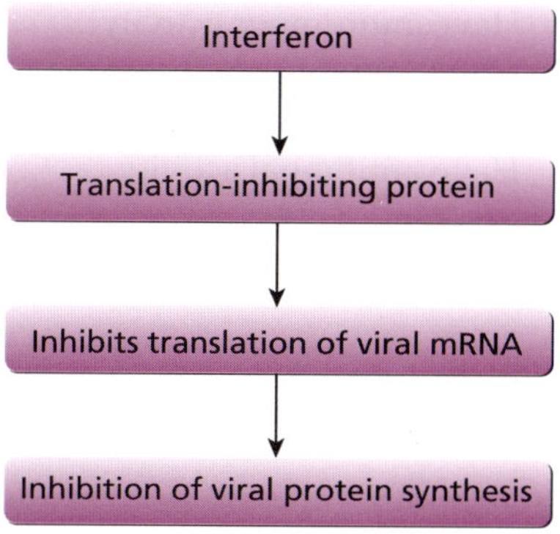

Flow chart 36.1 Mechanism of action of interferons.

- Antimicrobial activity against intracellular pathogens such as toxoplasma, chlamydia and malarial parasites
- Immunoregulatory effects enhance cytotoxic activity of macrophages, NK, K and T cells
- Antitumour activity inhibits the growth of tumour cells by tumour necrosis factor like cytokine

Applications

It can be used in the treatment of viral infections, benign tumours and malignant tumours.

Self-assessment

Long-answer question

1. Discuss in brief the pathogenesis of viral infections.

Short-answer questions

Write notes on

1. Inclusion bodies
2. Interferons

Multiple-choice questions

1. Which of the following viruses produce intranuclear inclusion bodies?
   A. Rabies virus
   B. Vaccinia virus
   C. Poliovirus
   D. Poxvirus
2. Which of the following viruses produce intracytoplasmic inclusion bodies?
   A. Rabies virus
   B. Herpes virus
   C. Poliovirus
   D. Yellow fever virus
3. Following are the examples of viruses that enter through skin, EXCEPT
   A. Rabies virus
   B. Arboviruses
   C. Poliovirus
   D. Hepatitis B virus
4. Which of the following viruses is transferred from mother to foetus through placenta?
   A. Mumps virus
   B. Measles virus
   C. Poliovirus
   D. Rubella virus
5. Which of the following interferons (IFNs) is produced by T lymphocytes?
   A. IFN-alpha
   B. IFN-beta
   C. IFN-gamma
   D. IFN-alpha and IFN-beta
6. Which of the following viral infections is not transmitted sexually?
   A. Hepatitis B virus
   B. Hepatitis A virus
   C. Hepatitis C virus
   D. Herpes simplex virus type 2
7. Following are the neurotropic viruses, EXCEPT
   A. Herpes simplex virus
   B. Rabies virus
   C. Arboviruses
   D. Mumps virus
8. Which of the following statements are TRUE regarding interferons, EXCEPT
   A. Are virus-specific
   B. Are antiviral substances produced by cells in response to viral infection
   C. Are glycoproteins having molecular weight 20000–40000
   D. Inhibit synthesis of viral proteins

9. IFNs act by inhibiting
   A. DNA synthesis
   B. RNA synthesis
   C. Protein synthesis
   D. Both DNA and RNA synthesis
10. Which of the following statements is FALSE regarding IFNs?
   A. Have antiviral activity
   B. Have antitumour activity
   C. Have antimicrobial activity against intracellular pathogens
   D. Have antifungal activity

37 Laboratory Diagnosis, Immunoprophylaxis and Chemotherapy of Viral Diseases

Laboratory diagnosis of viral diseases

Isolation and identification of viruses is routinely impracticable because of technical difficulties and also because of long duration of time required for isolation and identification, and lack of specific therapy for virus infections. Therefore, it is rarely carried out. However, because of simplicity and availability of rapid results serological tests are commonly used.

Laboratory diagnosis of viral infections is given in Flow chart 37.1.

Collection and transport of specimens

- Specimens should be collected during the acute phase of the disease.
- The appropriate specimens should be collected according to the site of infection.
- The specimens collected are as follows:
  - ***Respiratory infections*** Throat swab, nasal swab, nasal washing, nasopharyngeal aspirates, sputum, etc. Stool is also collected
  - ***Gastrointestinal tract infection*** Stool and rectal swab
  - ***Central nervous system infections*** Faeces, blood, cerebrospinal fluid (CSF), brain biopsy, throat swab, rectal swab, saliva, etc.
  - ***Skin infections*** Macular/papular scrapings, vesicular/pustular fluid, ulcer scrapings, crust, faeces, etc.
  - ***Ophthalmic infections*** Conjunctival scrapings or swabs
  - ***Urinary tract infections*** Urine
  - Blood is collected in HIV, hepatitis B, C and D virus infections
- Specimen should be transported immediately to the laboratory to avoid death of delicate viruses (many viruses are labile) and to avoid overgrowth of bacteria and fungi.
- If delay is expected, specimen should be placed in Stuart's viral transport media and transported.

Direct microscopy

The direct microscopic methods are used for

- Demonstration of cytopathic changes in infected cells, for example, Tzanck cells in herpes simplex virus
- Demonstration of virus inclusion bodies in a stained smear under the light microscope (Giemsa or eosin methylene blue stains)
- Demonstration of virus by electron microscope or by immunoelectron microscopy
- Demonstration of virus in lesions by direct immunofluorescence test

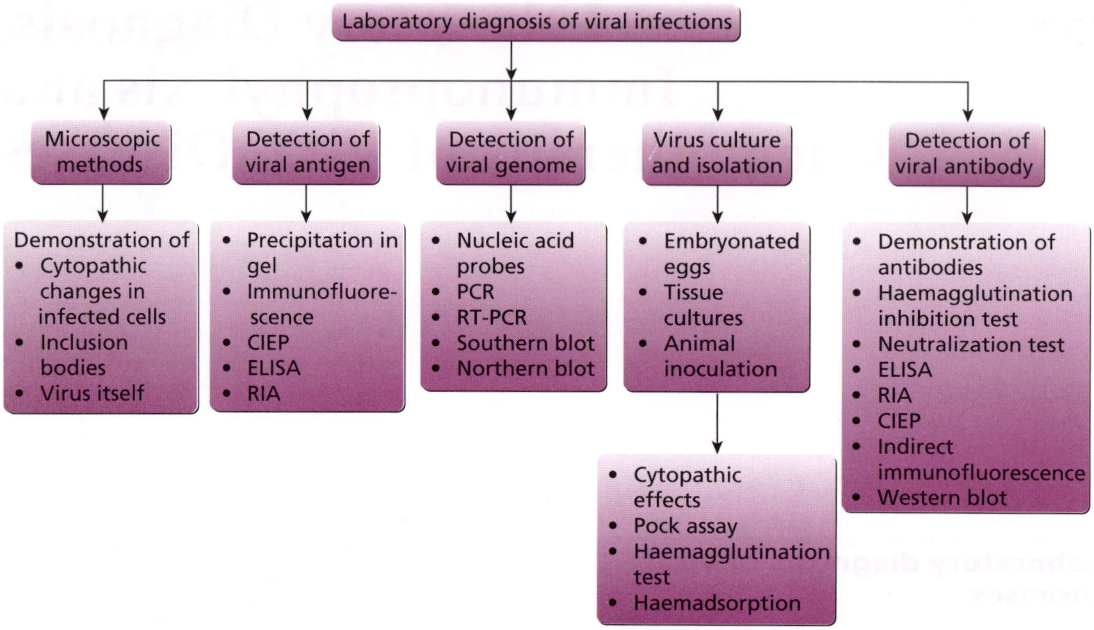

Flow chart 37.1 Summary of laboratory diagnosis of viral infections. *CIEP*, countercurrent immunoelectrophoresis; *ELISA*, enzyme-linked immunosorbent assay; *PCR*, polymerase chain reaction; *RIA*, radioimmunoassay; *RT-PCR*, reverse transcription polymerase chain reaction.

Demonstration of virus antigen

When virus antigen is abundantly present in the lesions, it can be demonstrated/detected by serological methods such as

- Precipitation in gel
- Immunofluorescence test
- Countercurrent immunoelectrophoresis (CIEP)
- Radioimmunoassay (RIA)
- Enzyme-linked immunosorbent assay (ELISA)

Detection of viral genetic material

Detection of viral genetic material can be performed by

- Nucleic acid probes (DNA probe analysis)
- Polymerase chain reaction (PCR)
- Reverse transcriptase PCR

Isolation of virus

Isolation of virus is a gold standard method. It is done in animals, embryonated eggs and tissue cultures. Animals such as

- Suckling mice
- Rats
- Monkeys
- Chimpanzees

Embryonated eggs The various sites are

- Chorioallantoic membrane
- Allantoic cavity
- Amniotic cavity
- Yolk sac

Tissue cultures

- Organ culture
- Explant culture
- Cell culture (primary, diploid, continuous)

Identification

After an appropriate period, the isolates are identified by using appropriate methods according to the culture method used.

Serological methods

Collection of blood specimens

- Blood for serological methods is collected

aseptically in a sterile test tube without anticoagulant.

- The serum is separated as soon as possible and stored at 4°C or −20°C.
- For virus-specific IgM antibodies, the test should be performed before freezing, as IgM may form insoluble aggregates upon thawing.
- Serial samples of blood are collected to demonstrate the rise in titre. In general, first sample should be collected as soon as possible after the onset of the illness and second sample after 2–3 weeks.
- Heating of serum (56°C for 30 minutes) may be necessary to remove non-specific, substances and complement in serum, which may affect the results in complement fixation test and neutralization test in certain viral infections.
- Demonstration of a rise in titre of antibodies to a virus during the course of an illness is considered as strong evidence, hence the examination of paired sera is essential and demonstration of antibodies in a single sample may not be meaningful.
- If paired sera are not available, demonstration of IgM antibodies to the virus can make a presumptive diagnosis.
- The serological tests used would depend on the infecting virus but in general the following tests are used
  - Neutralization test
  - Complement fixation test
  - Haemagglutination inhibition test
  - Passive haemagglutination test
  - Indirect immunofluorescence test
  - Radioimmunoassay
  - Agar gel diffusion test
  - ELISA
  - CIEP test
  - Western blot test

Immunoprophylaxis of viral disease

- Because of obligate intracellular parasitism of viruses, only a few drugs are available, which are useful against viral infections. Hence, prevention of infection by using vaccines is very important
- Two types of vaccines: live and killed vaccines

Live vaccines

- They contain live virus with reduced virulence.
- They initiate infection without causing disease and hence offer greater and longer lasting protection.

Preparation Prepared by using naturally attenuated strain or they are attenuated by cultivating the virus serially into various hosts or cultures. Alternatively, vaccine strains with desired antigens can be developed by DNA recombinant technology.

Advantages

- A single dose is usually sufficient as virus multiplies in the host, providing a prolonged antigenic stimulus.
- They can be administered by the route of natural infection to induce local immunity—both IgA and IgG are produced when the vaccine is administered by natural route of infection.
- Induce a long-lasting immunity hence booster doses are generally not required.

Disadvantages

- Risk of reversion of virulence as it contains a live virus
- Virus may spread from vaccinee to contact. This may be advantageous, if the spread immunizes others and may be dangerous if a virulent revertant of vaccine strain spreads to a susceptible person
- Interference by pre-existing virus, if present, may prevent a good immune response
- **Examples** OPV (oral poliovirus vaccine) for polio, MMR (mumps, measles, rubella vaccine), live attenuated influenza vaccine, varicella vaccine and measles vaccine

Killed vaccines

- They contain killed viruses.
- They do not initiate infection like live vaccines, hence immunity developed is less and the protection lasts for a shorter duration.

Preparation Prepared by inactivation of virus by heat, phenol, formalin or beta-propiolactone

Advantages
- Safe and stable
- No risk of spread of virus from vaccinee to contacts
- Can be given in combination as polyvalent vaccine

Disadvantages
- It offers less protection and also the immunity induced lasts for short duration
- Usually administered by parenteral route (oral route is not suitable); hence do not stimulate IgA response (local immunity), cell-mediated immunity is also not induced
- Multiple injections are needed (booster doses)
- May sometimes cause hypersensitivity reactions
- **Examples** Salk polio vaccine, rabies vaccine and inactivated influenza vaccine

Passive immunization

Passive immunization using human gamma globulin, convalescent serum or specific antiserum provides a temporary protection against many viral diseases, for example, measles, mumps, infectious hepatitis.

Antiviral agents

A large number of antiviral drugs are synthesized continuously but only a few of them are approved for use in human beings. The antiviral agents approved and used for the treatment are given in Table 37.1.

Table 37.1 Antiviral agents approved and used for the treatment

Name	Disease
Idoxuridine	Herpes infection of eye
Amantadine	Influenza virus A
Acyclovir	Herpes virus, varicella zoster virus
Vidarabine	Herpes simplex virus-1 (HSV-1)
Ganciclovir	Cytomegalovirus
Adenine arabinoside	Herpes infection of brain
Trifluorothymidine	HSV-1 (herpetic keratoconjunctivitis)
AZT	HIV
Foscarnet	HIV
Dideoxyinosine (didanosine)	Substitute to AZT in AIDS
Dideoxycytidine (zalcitabine)	Substitute for AZT
Ribavirin	Many DNA and RNA viruses
Methisazone	Poxviruses
Tamiflu (Oseltamivir)	Swine flu virus
Relenza (Zanamivir)	Swine flu virus

AIDS, acquired immunodeficiency syndrome; *AZT*, azidothymidine; *HIV*, human immunodeficiency virus.

Self-assessment

Long-answer question

1. Discuss in detail the laboratory diagnosis of viral infections.

Short-answer questions

Write notes on

1. Live vaccines
2. Killed vaccines
3. Antiviral agents

Multiple-choice questions

1. Which of the following statements is FALSE about live vaccine?
   A. A single dose is usually sufficient and booster doses are generally not required
   B. They can be administered by the route of natural infection
   C. Protection lasts for short duration
   D. Risk of reversion of virulence
2. Which of the following is a live vaccine?
   A. Salk polio vaccine
   B. Mumps, measles, rubella vaccine
   C. Rabies vaccine
   D. All of the above
3. Which of the following statements is FALSE about killed vaccine?
   A. Immunity developed is less
   B. Booster doses are not required
   C. Protection lasts for short duration
   D. No risk of reversion of virulence
4. Which of the following is a killed vaccine?
   A. Sabin polio vaccine
   B. Mumps, measles, rubella vaccine
   C. Rabies vaccine
   D. All of the above
5. Which of the following is an antiviral agent used for the treatment of HIV infection?
   A. Idoxuridine
   B. Azidothymidine
   C. Ganciclovir
   D. All of the above
6. Which of the following is an antiviral agent used for the treatment of swine flu?
   A. Acyclovir
   B. Ribavirin
   C. Ganciclovir
   D. Zanamivir

38 Bacteriophages

- Bacteriophages (phage means to eat, bacteriophage means bacteria-eater) are viruses that infect and parasitize bacteria
- Widely distributed in sewage, faeces, polluted water, soil, etc.
- First described by Twort (1915)
- d' Herelle (1917) coined the term bacteriophage

Morphology

- **Genome** in most phages is a single, linear, double-stranded DNA molecule. However, in some phages, RNA molecule is a genome, for example, phages attacking male strains of *Escherichia coli* contain RNA as genome.
- **Phage capsid** is the protein covering of the genome. The large phages, for example, T-even phages (phages affecting *E. coli*) are tadpole-shaped and possess a head and a tail.
  - **Head**—hexagonal in shape. It encompasses the genome (double-stranded DNA enclosed in a capsid). Size of the head ranges from 28 to 100 nm
  - **Tail**—cylindrical part composed of hollow core surrounded by a contractile sheath and a terminal base plate. Plate has attached pins or tail fibres or both (Fig. 38.1)
- Though most phages have the above-described morphology, they show considerable variations in their morphology—some are spherical or filamentous in shape, some have single-stranded DNA and some have RNA as genome.

Important characteristics of phages

- Host specificity phages have high host specificity
- They are filterable through filters, which hold back the bacteria
- Sensitive to heat—inactivated by boiling

Life cycle

Bacteriophages have two different types of life cycle:

1. **Lytic cycle**—virulent cycle
2. **Lysogenic cycle**—temperate cycle

Lytic cycle

Lytic cycle of phages passes through different phases as follows:

- Adsorption
- Penetration

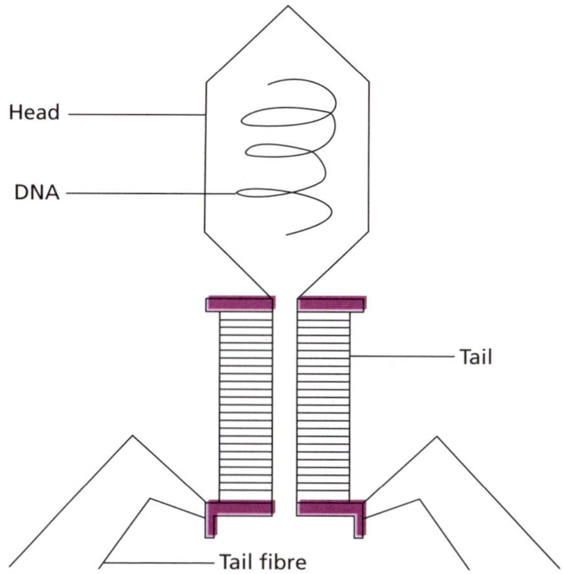

Figure 38.1 Morphology of T-even phage.

- Synthesis of phage components
- Maturation
- Release of progeny phages

Adsorption

During this phase, phages come in contact with the bacterial cells by random collision. They attach to specific receptor sites on bacterial cell surface with the help of complementary chemical groups on the receptor site at the terminal base plate of the phage.

It is a specific process and occurs rapidly (within minutes) under optimal conditions.

Penetration

During this phase, the base plate and tail fibres are held firmly against the bacterial cell causing the hollow core to inject the phage DNA through cell walls. This process resembles injection through a syringe that keeps the empty head (capsid) and tail outside the bacterial cell.

Synthesis of phage components

During this phase, the synthesis of phage components is initiated. Initially early proteins that include specific enzymes, necessary for synthesis of phage components, are synthesized. After that, the synthesis of late proteins, which are protein subunits of phage head and tail, are synthesized.

Maturation

During this process, the protein subunits of phage head and tail and phage DNA assemble to form the mature infective phage particle.

Release of progeny phages

The release of phages occurs by lysis of the bacterial cell. The cell bursts/ruptures because the cell wall is weakened by phage enzymes (lysozyme) and because of osmotic pressure releasing progeny viruses (Fig. 38.2).

Lysogenic cycle

- Infection with phages does not always result in lytic cycle. Some phages after infection, insert their nucleic acid (genome) into bacterial chromosome.

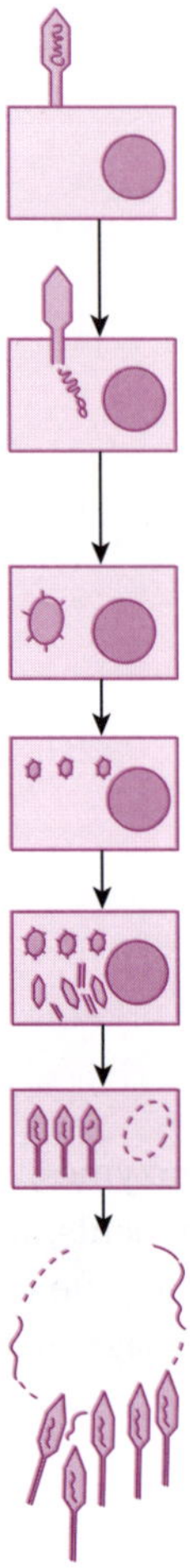

Figure 38.2 Lytic cycle.

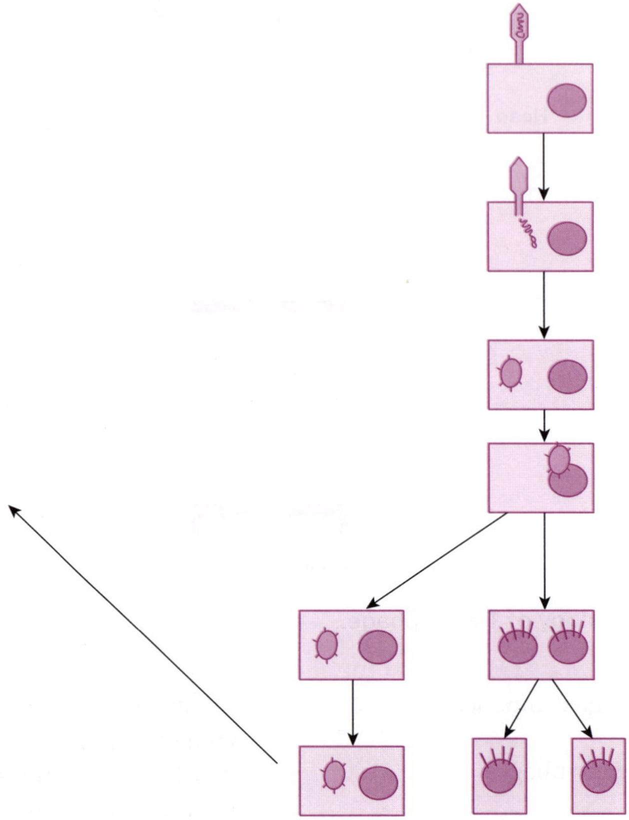

Figure 38.3 Lysogenic cycle.

- The integrated phage genome in bacterial chromosome is known as **prophage**, which behaves like a segment of the host chromosome and replicates synchronously with it. This phenomenon is known as **lysogeny**.
- The bacterium that carries prophage integrated into its chromosome is known as a **lysogen** or **lysogenic bacterium** and the phage that persists in a bacterium without causing lysis of bacterium is known as **lysogenic** or **temperate phage** (Fig. 38.3).
- The prophage confers certain new properties on the lysogenic bacteria. This is known as **lysogenic conversion** or **phage conversion**, for example
  - Phage-mediated toxigenicity of *Corynebacterium diphtheriae*, that is, exotoxin production in this bacterium is mediated by beta phage. Elimination of beta phage makes the bacterium non-toxic.
  - Phage-mediated toxicity in *Clostridium botulinum* produces toxin only when infected by phages.

Bacteriophage typing

- Phage typing is used as epidemiological marker to discriminate different bacterial strains that are biochemically and serologically identical and indistinguishable from each other. Such bacterial strains are differentiated by using strain or type-specific bacteriophages.

- For phage typing, the strain to be typed is inoculated on agar plate to produce lawn culture. The suspension of phages is then applied on a lawn culture and incubated overnight.
- The result is lysis of susceptible bacteria indicated by clear area known as plaques.
- On the basis of formation of plaque, a bacterial species can be divided into various types.
- Phage typing is used in epidemiological tracing of infections or outbreaks caused by *Staphylococcus aureus, Salmonella, Vibrio cholerae* and other bacteria.

Significance of phages

- Phage typing is used as epidemiological marker to establish the path of transmission of infectious agent and to identify the reservoir of infection.
- Differentiation of bacterial species or genus into subtypes by phage typing.
- Bacteriophages may act as carriers of genes from one bacterium to another—a process known as transduction, for example, plasmid-mediated drug resistance in *Staph. aureus*.
- Bacteriophages confer the property of toxin production in some bacteria.
- Bacteriophages have been extensively used in studying host-parasite relationships.

Self-assessment

Long-answer question

1. Discuss in detail the life cycle of bacteriophages.

Short-answer questions

Write notes on

1. Bacteriophages
2. Lytic cycle
3. Lysogenic cycle
4. Bacteriophage typing

Multiple-choice questions

1. Which of the following statements is FALSE regarding bacteriophages?
   A. Are widely distributed in sewage, faeces, polluted water, soil, etc.
   B. Have high host specificity
   C. Are filterable through filters, which hold back the bacteria
   D. Show considerable resistance to heat and are not inactivated by boiling
2. Which of the following statements is TRUE regarding lytic cycle?
   A. It is a virulent cycle
   B. It is a temperate cycle
   C. There is insertion of phage nucleic acid into bacterial chromosome
   D. The phage nucleic acid confers certain new properties on the lysogenic bacteria
3. Which of the following statements is FALSE regarding lysogenic cycle?
   A. It is a virulent cycle
   B. There is insertion of phage nucleic acid into bacterial chromosome
   C. Phage that persists in bacterium without causing lysis is known as temperate phage
   D. Phage nucleic acid confers certain new properties on the lysogenic bacteria
4. Bacteriophage typing is used as
   A. A diagnostic marker
   B. An epidemiological marker
   C. A serological marker
   D. A virological marker

39 Herpes Viruses

- The family Herpesviridae consists of enveloped DNA viruses affecting man and animals.
- It includes four important human pathogens:
  - Herpes simplex virus (HSV) t ype 1 and 2
  - Varicella zoster virus (VZV)
  - Cytomegalovirus (CMV)
  - Epstein–Barr virus (EBV)

Herpes simplex virus

- **Size** One of the largest viruses measuring 150–200 nm in diameter
- **Capsid** Icosahedral capsid
- **Envelope** Loose, amorphous envelope derived from the nuclear membrane of the host cell
- **Genome** Double-stranded DNA
- Envelope contains lipid, carbohydrate and protein and shows glycoprotein projections in the form of spikes from its surface (Fig. 39.1)
- Grows in eggs and in a variety of primary and continuous cell cultures such as
  - Monkey or rabbit kidney
  - Human amnion
  - HeLa, human epithelial type 2 (HEp-2) cell line and Vero cell lines

Figure 39.1 Herpes simplex virus.

- Produces characteristic cytopathogenic effects (CPE) in cell cultures, that is, formation of syncytium or giant cell formation
- On chorioallantoic membrane (CAM) of chick embryo, HSV produces small (less than 0.5 mm), white, shiny and non-necrotic pocks

Types of herpes simplex virus

HSV is of two types: type 1 and 2.

- Type 1 (HSV-1)—usually affecting the face, lips, oral cavity and skin above the waist

- Type 2 (HSV-2)—usually affecting the genitals and skin below the waist

Pathogenicity

- Saliva, skin lesions or respiratory secretions from infected cases or asymptomatic carriers (especially in genital infection) are the important sources.
- HSV-1 is transmitted primarily in saliva—infections occur mainly on the face.
- HSV-2 is transmitted by sexual contact causing lesions in the genital area.
- In persons indulging in abnormal sexual practices (oral–genital sex), HSV-1 can cause infections of the genitals and HSV-2 can cause lesions in the oral cavity.
- The virus primarily infects and replicates in the epithelial cells in the skin or the mucous membrane. After local multiplication, cell-to-cell spread occurs and involves local lymph nodes.
- The virus secondarily infects the nervous tissue and becomes latent in the sensory ganglion cells.
- Periodic reactivation of the virus from the latent state can occur during which the virus migrates down the neuron and replicates in the skin and mucous membrane causing lesions.
- The reactivation is associated with certain non-specific stimuli such as exposure to sunlight or ultraviolet lamps, hormonal changes, trauma, fatigue, emotional stresses, fever, allergy and upper respiratory tract infections.

Pathogenesis of herpes simplex virus is given in Flow chart 39.1.

Clinical findings

Both HSV-1 and HSV-2 cause primary and recurrent diseases.

Lesions by HSV-1

- **Herpetic stomatitis** Acute gingivostomatitis in children and young adults characterized by fever, irritability and vesicular lesions in the mouth, which ulcerate and become secondarily infected. Lesions heal spontaneously in 7–14 days. Pharyngitis may also occur. Recurrent herpetic stomatitis is usually seen in adults, which is milder than the primary disease.
- **Herpetic labialis (fever blisters or cold sores)** It is characterized by crops of vesicles, usually at the mucocutaneous junction of the lips or nose. Recurrent herpetic labialis is usually seen in adults, which is milder than the primary disease and may occur at varying intervals.

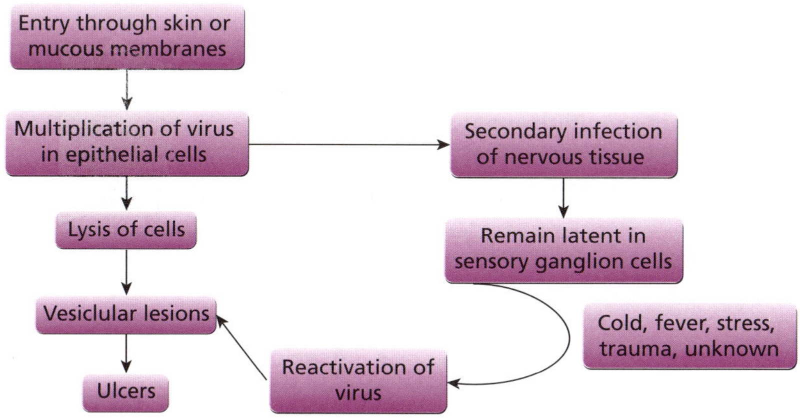

Flow chart 39.1 Pathogenesis of herpes simplex virus.

- **Cutaneous lesions** These are characterized by vesicular lesions that contain serous fluid filled with virus particles and cell debris. It is commonly seen on the face, cheeks, chin, around the mouth, forehead and also on the buttocks as napkin rash.
  - ***Herpetic whitlow*** Occupational disease in **dentists**, doctors and nurses—occurs as a pustular lesion of the finger or hand
  - ***Eczema herpeticum*** Generalized eruption in children suffering from eczema
- **Herpetic conjunctivitis or acute keratoconjunctivitis** It is characterized by corneal ulcers and lesions of conjunctival epithelium.
- **Lesions of central nervous system**
  - Aseptic meningitis
  - Encephalitis in premature babies
  - Acute necrotizing encephalomyelitis in older children and adults associated with high mortality rate

Lesions by HSV-2

- **Genital herpes** It is characterized by vesiculoulcerative lesions on the penis and urethra in male and the cervix, vulva, vagina and perineum in female. The lesions may be associated with fever, malaise and inguinal lymphadenopathy. Infection may be asymptomatic in female.
- **Neonatal herpes** Infection may be acquired in utero, during birth or after birth. The infection may be
  - Localized to the skin, mouth or eyes
  - Generalized involving multiple organs, including central nervous system and is associated with high mortality

Laboratory diagnosis

Specimens

- Vesicle fluid
- Skin swab
- Corneal scrapings
- Throat swab
- Saliva
- Cerebrospinal fluid
- Brain biopsy

Microscopic examination

- Demonstration of Tzanck cells—multinucleated giant cells in the scrapings obtained from the base of vesicles and stained with toluidine blue (1%)
- Giemsa stain—for demonstration of Cowdry type A intranuclear inclusion bodies in the smear
- Electron microscopy—for demonstration of virus particles in smear
- Direct immunofluorescence test for demonstration of virus antigen in the smears or sections from lesions
- Isolation of virus—the specimen is inoculated in tissue culture and observed for typical CPE in 2–3 days. The identification of HSV is confirmed by using neutralization test or immunofluorescence test with specific antisera

Serological tests

- Useful in the diagnosis of primary the infections only
- Antibodies develop in 4–7 days after the infection and reach the peak in 2–4 weeks
- Antibodies can be measured by
  - Neutralization (quantitative) test
  - Complement fixation test (CFT)
  - Enzyme-linked immunosorbent assay (ELISA)
  - Radioimmunoassay (RIA)
  - Immunofluorescence test
  - Passive haemagglutination test for rapid diagnosis of encephalitis

Treatment

- Acyclovir
- Iododeoxyuridine
- Trifluorothymidine
- Vidarabine

Varicella zoster virus

- Morphologically, similar to HSV
- Is a DNA virus, 100–150 nm in size and is lipid-enveloped virus
- Does not grow in experimental animals and chick embryos
- Can be grown in human fibroblasts, human amnion or HeLa cells with typical intranuclear inclusion bodies
- By using highly specific antisera, it can be distinguished from HSV-1 and HSV-2
- Sensitive to ether and chloroform

Pathogenicity

- Infection occurs through the mucosa of the respiratory tract or conjunctiva.
- The virus circulates in blood, multiplies and finally localizes in the skin and causes chickenpox.

Pathogenesis of varicella zoster virus is given in Flow chart 39.2.

Clinical infections

Varicella (chickenpox)

It is a mild and highly contagious disease of children characterized by generalized vesicular eruption of the skin and mucous membranes. In the initial stage, fever and malaise is followed by successive crops of eruptions—first on the trunk and then on the face, limbs and oral mucosa.

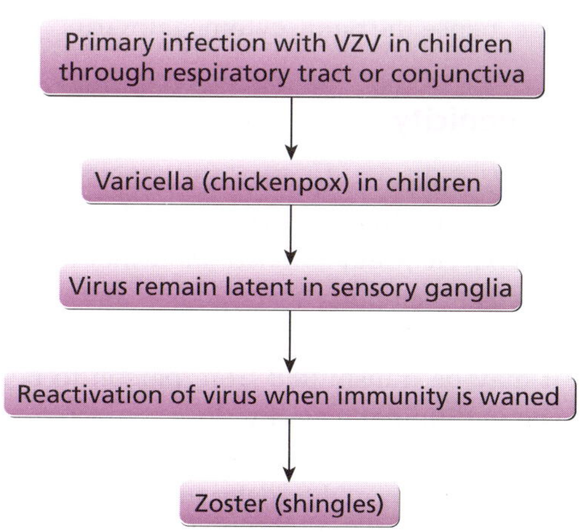

Flow chart 39.2 Pathogenesis of varicella zoster virus (VZV).

Oral manifestations Small blister-like lesions on the buccal mucosa, tongue, gingiva, palate and pharynx are seen occasionally. These lesions initially appear as slightly raised vesicles, which rupture and form small eroded ulcers with a red margin

Complications

- Secondary bacterial infections
- Reye syndrome—acute hepatic failure, encephalopathy and hypoglycaemia
- Varicella encephalitis—may be fatal or lead to brain damage
- Varicella pneumonia in children
- The virus may cross placenta and infect the foetus during pregnancy—causing congenital malformations

Zoster (shingles)

It is a sporadic disease of the adults that occurs due to the reactivation of the latent virus present in the sensory ganglia when immunity drops to an ineffective level. It is characterized by

- Localized vesicular eruption of skin limited to the skin supplied by the affected nerves
- Fever and malaise
- Severe neurotic pain

Ophthalmic zoster Occasionally

Oral manifestations

Painful vesicles which rupture to leave areas of erosion on the buccal mucosa, tongue, uvula, pharynx and larynx. Hunt syndrome involving external ear and oral mucosa with facial paralysis, pain of the external auditory meatus and pinna of the ear, vesicular eruption of oral cavity, hoarseness, tinnitus, vertigo, etc. It occurs owing to the infection of the geniculate ganglion

Complications

- Lower motor neuron paralysis
- Generalized zoster in immunocompromised individuals with vesicles scattered throughout the skin

Laboratory diagnosis

Specimens

Scrapping or swabs from the base of vesicular lesions

Microscopic examination

- Demonstration of multinucleated giant cells by H&E staining
- Demonstration of intranuclear inclusion bodies by Giemsa or Papanicolaou's stain
- Demonstration of intranuclear virus antigen by fluorescent antibody technique using monoclonal antibodies
- Electron microscopy to differentiate VZV from poxviruses
- Isolation of virus using human tissue cultures such as human fibroblast, human amnion or Vero cells. CPE may take more time to develop hence for early confirmation of isolates of VZV, immunofluorescence or other immunologic tests using specific antisera are used

Serological tests

- Demonstration of antibodies against virus in the patient serum by complement fixation, neutralization, indirect immunofluorescence test or gel precipitation test
- VZV-specific IgM antibody detection by ELISA
- Countercurrent immunoelectrophoresis—rapid and simple test for detection of virus antigen

Treatment

Acyclovir and vidarabine are effective. VZV immunoglobulin of high-specific antibody titre prepared from pooled plasma of patients can be used to prevent the development of illness in immunocompromised children

Prophylaxis

- One attack of chickenpox gives lifelong immunity
- Vaccination—live attenuated vaccine (Oka strain) induces good antibody response and provides protection for several years, but it is very labile. A modified lyophilized form of the vaccine is now available, which is safe and effective

Cytomegalovirus

- Is morphologically similar to HSV and VZV
- Is the largest virus in the herpes virus family—150–200 nm
- DNA content is more than HSV
- Exhibits strict host specificity. Human CMV replicates in humans only and is unable to grow/replicate in animals
- Human CMV can be grown in human fibroblast cultures. It grows slowly, requires longer period of incubation to produce CPE—perinuclear cytoplasmic inclusions in addition to the intranuclear inclusions and multinucleated cells
- Many affected cells are greatly enlarged in size, hence the name cytomegalovirus

Pathogenicity

- CMV replicates in the epithelial cells of respiratory tract, salivary glands, kidney, cervix, etc., and is shed in urine, saliva, cervical secretions, tears, semen and breast milk.
- It may be transmitted from person to person in different ways by close contact.
- Transmission may occur by
  - Transplacental transfer in foetus
  - Exposure to maternal body fluids during delivery and maternal breastfeeding in infants

- Contact with saliva or urine of infected individuals in younger children
- Sexual intercourse, kissing, blood transfusion in adults

- The virus after gaining entry into the body remains associated with lymphocytes and polymorphonuclear cells and may cause cell-associated viraemia.

Clinical features

Most of the infections are asymptomatic—lead to prolonged latency with occasional reactivation

Congenital infections

- May remain asymptomatic at birth or may lead to cytomegalic inclusion disease, which often proves to be fatal
- It is characterized by hepatosplenomegaly, jaundice, thrombocytopenic purpura, haemolytic anaemia, microcephaly, permanent mental abnormalities and chorioretinitis

Postnatal infections

- These are usually unapparent but may sometimes lead to insidious hepatitis or pneumonitis
- Primary infection in older children and adults is usually unapparent but may lead to infectious mononucleosis-like syndrome characterized by malaise, myalgia, protracted fever, liver function abnormalities and lymphocytosis without heterophile antibodies (cytomegalovirus mononucleosis). The patient shows cytomegalouria, rise of CMV antibodies and presence of virus in the peripheral blood leucocytes
- In immunocompromised hosts—in patients with malignancy, immunodeficiency, AIDS and transplant recipients, CMV causes more severe infections. Pneumonia, hepatitis or generalized disease are caused by reactivation of latent infection or by exogenous infection. It often causes disseminated disease in AIDS patients

Laboratory diagnosis

- **Specimens** Urine, saliva, breast milk, cervical secretions, semen and blood leucocytes
- **Microscopic examination**
  - Demonstration of cytomegalic cells—enlarged cells with large intranuclear inclusions (Owl's eye) in centrifuged deposits of urine or saliva
  - Demonstration of virus by electron microscopy
- **Molecular technique** DNA hybridization
- **Isolation of virus** In human fibroblast culture—most reliable
  - CPE becomes visible after 1–2 weeks
  - Identification can be confirmed by staining culture cells by immunofluorescence or immunoperoxidase technique using monoclonal antibodies
- **Serological tests** Antibodies may be detected by
  - Neutralization test
  - CFT
  - RIA
  - Immunofluorescence test
  - ELISA to detect specific IgM antibody

Treatment

- Ganciclovir is the drug of choice
- Acyclovir is also beneficial

Epstein–Barr virus

- It is structurally and morphologically similar to other herpes viruses but is antigenically different.
- Grows well in human blood lymphocytes—human B lymphocytes.
- It causes transformation of B lymphocytes, which undergo continuous multiplication. The transformed cells contain many EBV genomes.

Pathogenicity

- EBV is transmitted by infected saliva.

- It initially replicates in the epithelial cells of the oropharynx and parotid glands. Subsequently, B lymphocytes are infected, where it persists in latent state.

Pathogenesis of Epstein–Barr virus is given in Flow chart 39.3.

Clinical features

- EBV is ubiquitous in all human populations.
- By the age of 3 years, about 80% children in developed countries and 99% children in developing countries acquire infection.
- Once infected, the virus remains in an individual for life.
- In most cases, it remains silent.
- The following clinical manifestations may result
  - Infectious mononucleosis (glandular fever)
  - Burkitt's lymphoma
  - Nasopharyngeal carcinoma
  - Lymphomas in immunodeficient hosts and transplants recipients
  - Oral hairy leucoplakia—wart-like growth on the tongue, seen in HIV infected patients and transplant recipients

Laboratory diagnosis

- **Specimens** Saliva, peripheral blood or lymphoid tissue
- Isolation of virus is extremely difficult, time consuming (6–8 weeks); hence most EBV infections are diagnosed serologically
- **Serology** Two types of tests:
  - Tests for detection of EBV-specific antibodies
  - Tests for detection of heterophile antibodies
- **Test for detection of EBV-specific antibodies** Commonly used serological tests are
  - Indirect immunofluorescence test
  - ELISA
  - CFT
  - Gel diffusion
- **Test for detection of heterophile antibodies** During the acute phase of infectious

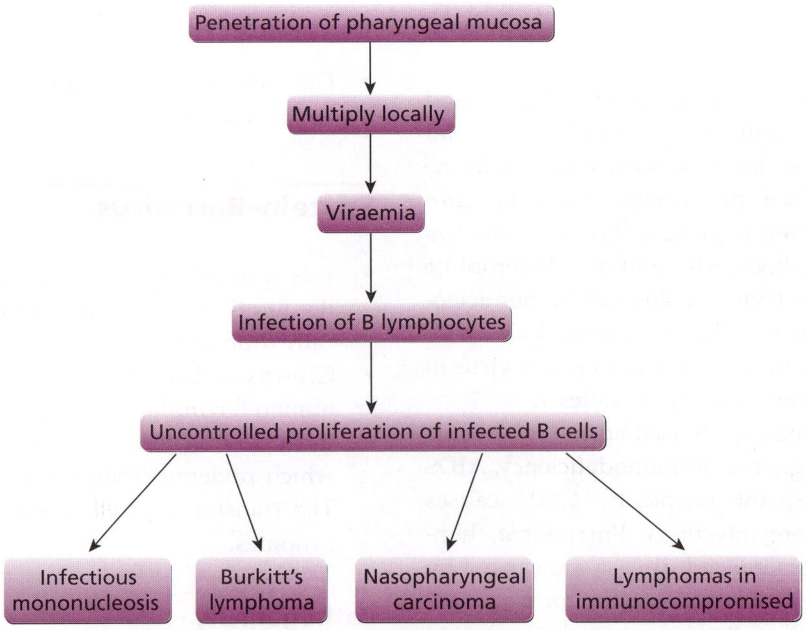

Flow chart 39.3 Pathogenesis of Epstein–Barr virus.

mononucleosis, most patients (85–90%) develop IgM antibodies, which are the heterophile antibodies. These antibodies agglutinate sheep erythrocytes. The heterophile antibodies are detected by **Paul–Bunnel test**.

Treatment

- Antiviral therapy is not necessary in uncomplicated cases of infectious mononucleosis
- Acyclovir has little activity
- **Prevention**—no EBV vaccine is available

Self-assessment

Long-answer questions

1. Discuss in brief the pathogenicity and laboratory diagnosis of herpes simplex virus.
2. Discuss in brief the pathogenicity and laboratory diagnosis of cytomegalovirus.

Short-answer questions

Write notes on
1. Herpes simplex virus
2. Chickenpox
3. Herpes zoster
4. Cytomegalovirus
5. Epstein–Barr virus

Multiple-choice questions

1. Which of the following lesions is NOT caused by herpes simplex virus type 1?
   A. Herpetic stomatitis
   B. Acute keratoconjunctivitis
   C. Eczema herpeticum
   D. Neonatal herpes
2. Which of the following lesions is produced by herpes simplex virus type 2?
   A. Herpetic stomatitis
   B. Acute keratoconjunctivitis
   C. Eczema herpeticum
   D. Genital herpes
3. Which of the following statements is FALSE regarding herpes simplex virus type 2?
   A. Produces lesions of central nervous system
   B. Affects the genitals and skin below the waist
   C. Also causes neonatal herpes
   D. Is transmitted by sexual contact
4. Which of the following statements is TRUE regarding herpes simplex virus type 1?
   A. Is transmitted by sexual contact
   B. Causes acute keratoconjunctivitis
   C. Affects the genitals and skin below the waist
   D. Also causes neonatal herpes
5. Which of the following herpes virus infections occurs as an occupational disease in dentists?
   A. Herpetic stomatitis
   B. Herpetic conjunctivitis
   C. Herpetic labialis
   D. Herpetic whitlow
6. Small blister-like lesions on the buccal mucosa, tongue, gingiva, palate and pharynx are seen occasionally in which of the following infection?
   A. Varicella zoster virus infection
   B. Herpes simplex virus infection
   C. Epstein–Barr virus infection
   D. Cytomegalovirus infection
7. Which of the following statements is FALSE about zoster (shingles)?
   A. Is a sporadic disease of adult
   B. Occurs as a result of reactivation of the latent virus present in the sensory ganglia
   C. Is caused by varicella zoster virus
   D. Is characterized by generalized vesicular eruption of the skin and mucous membranes
8. Which of the following statements is TRUE regarding varicella (chickenpox)?
   A. Is a mild and highly contagious disease of children
   B. Is a sporadic disease of adult

C. Occurs as a result of reactivation of the latent virus present in the sensory ganglia
D. Is characterized by localized vesicular eruption of skin limited to the skin supplied by the affected nerves

9. Infectious mononucleosis-like syndrome is caused by
   A. Varicella-zoster virus
   B. Herpes simplex virus
   C. Epstein–Barr virus
   D. Cytomegalovirus
10. Infectious mononucleosis is caused by
   A. Varicella zoster virus
   B. Herpes simplex virus
   C. Epstein–Barr virus
   D. Cytomegalovirus
11. Oral hairy leucoplakia in HIV infected patients and transplant recipients is caused by
   A. Varicella zoster virus
   B. Epstein–Barr virus
   C. Herpes simplex virus
   D. Cytomegalovirus
12. Which of the following tests is used for detection of heterophile antibodies in Epstein–Barr virus infection?
   A. Paul–Bunnel test
   B. Weil–Felix test
   C. Ascoli's thermoprecipitation test
   D. Cold agglutination test

40 Hepatitis Viruses

Viral hepatitis

- Viral hepatitis is caused mainly by hepatitis viruses. Six hepatitis viruses—A, B, C, D, E and G—have been identified so far.
- Hepatitis A, C, D, E and G are RNA viruses.
- Hepatitis B is a DNA virus and causes more severe kind of hepatitis than other hepatitis viruses.

Hepatitis A virus (HAV)

- Is a typical enterovirus classified in Picornaviridae family
- Size is 27 nm
- Single-stranded RNA genome surrounded by non-enveloped icosahedral capsid
- It is resistant to inactivation by heat (60°C for 1 hour), ether and to pH 3. However, it is inactivated by ultraviolet rays, autoclaving, boiling for 5 minutes, formaldehyde (1:4000) and chlorine at 10–15 parts per million for 30 minutes
- Grows in human and simian cell cultures–no cytopathogenic effects

Pathogenicity

Infectious hepatitis

- HAV is transmitted by faeco–oral route.
- Infection occurs by ingestion (oral route) of contaminated water or food grown in polluted water and eaten raw.
- The virus multiplies in the intestinal epithelium and reaches the liver by haematogenous spread—infects hepatocytes.
- Common in children and young adults.

Clinical features

- Incubation period is 2–6 weeks
- Majority of infections are asymptomatic
- The clinical disease occurs in two stages:
  - **The prodromal stage or preicteric stage** It is characterized by fever, anorexia, nausea, vomiting and liver tenderness. The symptoms usually subside with the onset of icteric stage.
  - **The icteric stage** It is characterized by jaundice. Most cases resolve spontaneously in 4–6 weeks.
- Rarely, a rapidly fatal fulminant hepatitis may occur
- The disease is milder in children, in whom many infections may be anicteric
- Mortality is very low with most of the deaths occurring in adults
- Occurs sporadically or as an outbreak
- Overcrowding and poor sanitation favour its spread

Laboratory diagnosis

- Demonstration of the virus in faeces by immune electron microscopy
- Detection of HAV in faeces by enzyme-linked immunosorbent assay (ELISA)
- Isolation is difficult but possible
- Detection of IgM antibody to HAV in the blood by ELISA

Treatment and prophylaxis

- No antiviral therapy is available
- Prevention of contamination of food and water with faeces of patient (improved sanitation)
- Vaccination—HAV vaccine available which is safe and effective; two injections intramuscularly offer protection for 10–20 years

Hepatitis B virus (HBV)

- Is a complex double-layered sphere
- Size is 42 nm in diameter
- Shape is spherical
- The outer surface or envelope contains hepatitis B surface antigen (HBsAg) and surrounds a 27 nm inner dense core that contains hepatitis B core antigen (HBcAg). It also possesses HBeAg, which is a hidden antigenic component of core
- The core (nucleocapsid) possesses icosahedral symmetry
- Inside the core is a genome—a single circular double-stranded DNA with DNA-dependent DNA polymerase
- This particle is also known as **Dane particle** (Dane, 1970) and is a complete HBV (Fig. 40.1)
- Under electron microscope, sera from HBV hepatitis patients show three types of particles (Fig. 40.2):
  - Spherical particle approximately 22 nm in diameter—most abundant
  - Tubular or filamentous from 22 nm in diameter and of varying length
  - Dane particle—a complete HBV

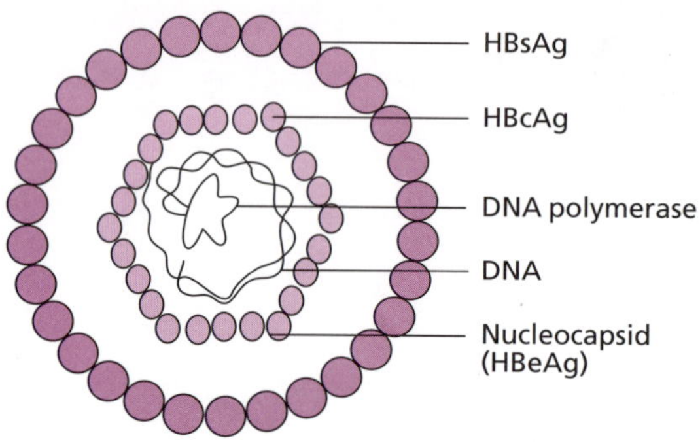

Figure 40.1 Hepatitis B virus.

The spherical and tubular particles are antigenically identical and are the surface subunits of HBV

- It cannot be cultivated in the laboratory
- It is relatively more resistant to heat and survives at 60°C for 60 minutes but is inactivated at 100°C when exposed for 5 minutes. It is inactivated by formaldehyde (1:4000) and 2% glutearaldehyde

Antigenic structure

Two major antigens are as follows:

- The surface antigen—HBsAg—also known as Australia antigen (Blumberg, 1965)
- The core antigen—HBcAg
- Also contains nucleocapsid antigen—HBeAg

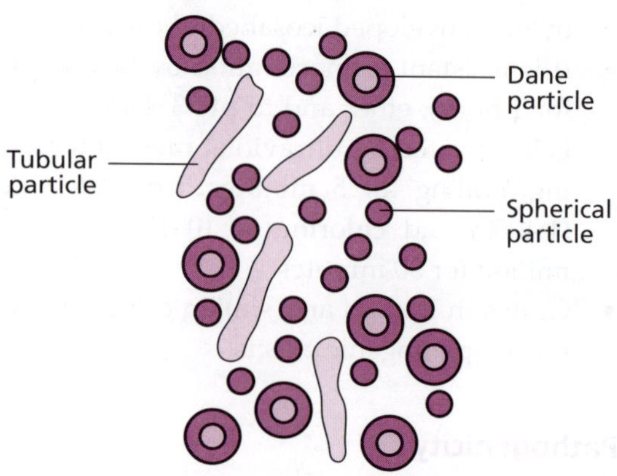

Figure 40.2 Different types of particles of hepatitis B virus.

Pathogenicity

Serum hepatitis

Infection occurs in the following ways:

- Parenteral transmission by accidental inoculation of infected blood, blood products or fluids (such as saliva, tears, urine, faeces) during medical, surgical or dental procedures
- Blood transfusion, intravenous drug abuse, tattooing, ear piercing may also transmit infection
- Perinatal infection from the infected mother to newborn during birth
- By sexual intercourse with infected individuals

Clinical picture

- Incubation period is 6 weeks to 6 months.
- The clinical disease occurs in three phases:
  - **Preicteric phase** It is characterized by malaise, anorexia, weakness, myalgia, nausea and vomiting.
  - **Icteric phase** It is characterized by jaundice, pale stools and dark urine.
  - **Convalescent phase** It is characterized by mild symptoms of hepatitis—may persist for 1 year. Majority of the patients recover completely. About 5–10% cases do not clear the virus completely—may become asymptomatic carriers or develop chronic hepatitis that may advance to cirrhosis and/or hepatocellular cancer.
  - Extrahepatic manifestations are common and include
    - Rash
    - Arthralgia
    - Polyarteritis nodosa
    - Glomerulonephritis
    - Serum sickness
- These complications are believed to result from antigen–antibody combination in vivo.
- Carrier state with minimal or no liver damage may occur. In 10–20% of adults and 35% children, HBsAg persists in blood for extended period, but few of them become chronic carriers. Carrier state is commonly seen in medical and paramedical workers such as doctors, dentists, nurses and professional blood donors.
- Two types of carriers
  - **Super carriers** Highly infectious, show presence of HBeAg and high titre of HBsAg and DNA polymerase in blood. HBV may also be demonstrated in blood. Very minute amount of blood can transmit infection
  - **Simple carriers** More common, show no HBeAg and low level of HBsAg in blood. HBV and DNA polymerase in blood are absent. Transmission is possible only when the large volumes of blood or serum are transferred

Laboratory diagnosis

- Diagnosis by detection of hepatitis B antigens and antibodies by using serological techniques
- A variety of serological tests are available, these include the following:
  - Agar gel diffusion
  - Countercurrent immunoelectrophoresis
  - Haemagglutination test
  - Complement fixation test
  - Reverse passive latex agglutination test
  - Radioimmunoassay (RIA)
  - ELISA
- Demonstration of virus under the electron microscope
- Nucleic acid detection by polymerase chain reaction (PCR) is a highly sensitive test for detection of HBV DNA in serum

Treatment

- No specific antiviral therapy is available for HBV infection
- Interferon-alpha and antiviral drug such as lamivudine, adefovir and telbivudine are generally used for treatment purpose

Prophylaxis

- Health education
- Improvement of personal hygiene and strict attention to sterility
- Vaccination—plasma-derived vaccine is available, but very costly
  - Recombinant yeast hepatitis B vaccine is currently used. It is safe and effective
  - Given in three doses at 0, 1 and 6 months intramuscularly

Hepatitis C virus (HCV)

- Is a small, 50–60 nm RNA virus with a single-stranded RNA as a genome belonging to the family Flaviviridae
- Is an enveloped virus carrying glycoprotein spikes
- Cannot be grown in culture

Pathogenicity

- Infection occurs by percutaneous exposure to blood and plasma derivatives.
- Needlestick injuries, use of contaminated needles and syringes, sharing of needles by intravenous drug users, transfusion of blood and blood products, tattooing and skin piercing are the common modes of transmission.
- Sexual transmission and mother to neonatal transmission are also possible.

Clinical features

- Incubation period is 5–12 weeks
- Majority of cases are asymptomatic/subclinical
- It causes a less severe disease with milder symptoms
- Jaundice is absent or less marked
- About 50–80% patients develop chronic hepatitis and slowly progressive liver damage

Laboratory diagnosis

- Detection of viral antigen in blood or biopsy specimens by immunofluorescence
- Detection of nucleic acid (HCV RNA) by reverse transcription polymerase chain reaction (RT-PCR)
- Detection of specific antibodies by ELISA and confirmation by recombinant immunoblot assay

Treatment and prophylaxis

- Interferon-alpha alone or in combination with ribavirin may be useful
- No vaccine is available
- General control measures against HBV are applicable to HCV, which include safe blood and safe injection

Hepatitis D virus (HDV)

- HDV was considered a defective virus that needs HBV as a helper for replication and expression.
- First detected in Italy (1977) and named as delta agent.

Properties of virus

- Is spherical, 35–38 nm in diameter
- It consists of a single-stranded small circular molecule of RNA; delta antigen or HDAg, a nucleoprotein encoded by RNA; and an outer envelope of HBsAg encoded by HBV genome indicating that HBV is necessary for the production of HDV virions

Pathogenicity

- HDV enters by parenteral route.
- As presence of HBV is essential for the replication of HDV, HDV infection occurs only in the HBV-infected persons.

Clinical features

- Incubation period is 2–12 weeks.

- HDV infection results in hepatitis of increased severity than the HBV infection and may progress to fulminant hepatitis.

Laboratory diagnosis

- Detection of delta antigen in the nuclei of hepatocytes by direct immunofluorescence test
- Delta antigen can also be visualized in the liver biopsy specimens by indirect immunoperoxidase staining
- Detection of HDV RNA by hybridization using a radiolabelled probe
- Antibody detection by ELISA and RIA

Prevention and treatment

- No specific therapy
- No specific immunoprophylaxis
- Immunization with HBV vaccine is effective as HDV is unable to infect a person's immune to HBV

Hepatitis E virus (HEV)

- Belongs to the family Calciviridae and genus *Calcivirus*
- **Size** Small; 27–38 nm in diameter
- **Shape** Round
- **Genome** Single-stranded RNA
- **Capsid** Icosahedral capsid without an envelope

Pathogenicity

Infection occurs by ingestion of contaminated drinking water.

Clinical features

- Incubation period is 2–8 weeks.
- Clinically, the disease resembles hepatitis A.
- Generally, mild and self-limited and does not lead to chronic hepatitis, cirrhosis, cancer or carrier state.

Laboratory diagnosis

Diagnosis can be achieved by

- Demonstration of virus particles in faeces using monoclonal antibodies under the electron microscope
- Detection of antibodies—IgM or IgG antibodies to HEV by ELISA or Western blot test
- Detection of HEV RNA in faeces or acute phase sera of the patients

Treatment and prophylaxis

- No specific therapy
- No vaccine is available
- The disease can be prevented by
  - Provision of safe drinking water
  - Improving standards of sanitation

Hepatitis G virus (HGV)

- A new flavivirus-like agent, isolated from a patient with chronic hepatitis in 1994.
- This agent is different from HCV and named as HGV.
- It is an RNA virus.

Pathogenicity

- Entry of the virus occurs through blood transfusion and by other parenteral routes.
- HGV RNA has been found in patients with acute, chronic and fulminant hepatitis, but its role in hepatitis is not clear.

Self-assessment

Long-answer question

1. Enumerate the viruses causing hepatitis. Discuss in brief the pathogenicity and laboratory diagnosis of serum hepatitis.

Short-answer questions

Write notes on

1. Hepatitis A virus
2. Dane particle
3. Hepatitis C virus
4. Hepatitis D virus
5. Hepatitis E virus

Multiple-choice questions

1. Hepatitis A virus belongs to which of the following families?
   A. Picornaviridae
   B. Papovaviridae
   C. Parvoviridae
   D. Hepadnaviridae
2. Which of the following statements is FALSE regarding hepatitis A virus?
   A. Belongs to Picornaviridae family
   B. Has a single-stranded DNA genome
   C. Has an icosahedral nucleocapsid not surrounded by an envelope
   D. Causes infectious hepatitis
3. Which of the following statements is FALSE regarding hepatitis B virus?
   A. Has a single circular double-stranded DNA genome
   B. Cannot be cultivated in the laboratory
   C. Is transmitted by faeco–oral route by ingestion of contaminated water or food
   D. Causes serum hepatitis
4. Which of the following statements is TRUE about Dane particle?
   A. Is a spherical particle approximately 22 nm in diameter
   B. Is a filamentous structure, 22 nm in diameter and of varying length
   C. Is a tubular structure, 22 nm in diameter and of varying length
   D. Is a complex double-layered sphere, 42 nm in diameter
5. Serum hepatitis is caused by
   A. Hepatitis A virus
   B. Hepatitis B virus
   C. Hepatitis C virus
   D. Hepatitis E virus
6. Which of the following viruses is needed as a helper virus by hepatitis D virus?
   A. Hepatitis A virus
   B. Hepatitis B virus
   C. Hepatitis C virus
   D. Hepatitis E virus
7. Which of the following statements is FALSE regarding hepatitis C virus?
   A. Is a small, 50–60 nm virus with a single-stranded RNA
   B. Is an enveloped virus carrying glycoprotein spikes
   C Infection occurs by percutaneous exposure to blood and plasma derivatives
   D. Causes a severe disease with severe symptoms
8. Extrahepatic manifestations are common in which of the following hepatitis viruses?
   A. Hepatitis A virus
   B. Hepatitis B virus
   C. Hepatitis C virus
   D. Hepatitis E virus
9. Delta agent is associated with
   A. Hepatitis G virus
   B. Hepatitis E virus
   C. Hepatitis C virus
   D. Hepatitis B virus

41 Human Immunodeficiency Virus

Morphology of HIV

- Human immunodeficiency virus (HIV) belonging to retrovirus group is the causative agent of AIDS.
- It belongs to a subgroup of retrovirus known as lentivirus (slow virus with a long incubation period).
- Retroviruses are RNA viruses, which generate DNA copy from their RNA templates with the help of reverse transcriptase enzyme.
- HIV is a spherical, enveloped RNA virus.
- Size is 90–120 nm in diameter.
- Nucleocapsid has an outer icosahedral shell and an inner core.
- Genome consists of two identical single-stranded RNA and reverse transcriptase enzyme.
- HIV is surrounded by a lipoprotein envelope with projecting spikes of glycoproteins on the surface.
- Envelope antigens
  - **Spike antigen** gp120
  - **Transmembrane pedicle antigen** gp41
- Core and shell antigens
  - **Shell** Nucleocapsid antigen—p18
  - **Core** Major antigen—p24; other core antigens—p55, p15
- Reverse transcriptase antigens are p31, p51 and p65 (Fig. 41.1).

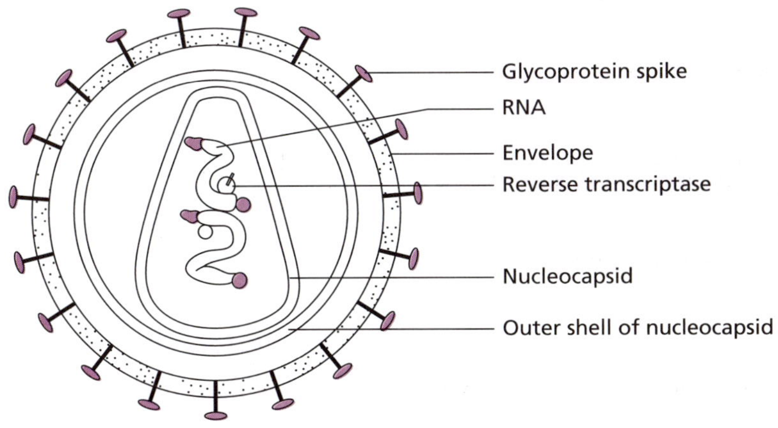

Figure 41.1 Human immunodeficiency virus.

- It is heat labile, inactivated in 30 minutes at 56°C and in seconds at 100°C.
- It is susceptible to alcohol, lysol, glutaraldehyde, sodium hypochlorite, hydrogen peroxide and detergents.

Pathogenicity

- The virus is present in lymphoid cells, semen, blood, vaginal secretions, saliva, breast milk, tears, urine, serum, cerebrospinal fluid, etc., of the patient.
- Infection occurs by
  - Sexual contact with an infected person
  - Transfusion of blood and blood products
  - Transmission from mother to child before birth via placenta after birth through breast milk
  - Needlestick injuries and blood splash on open wound
  - Sharing of needles in drug addicts

Pathogenesis

Flow chart 41.1 depicts pathogenesis of HIV.

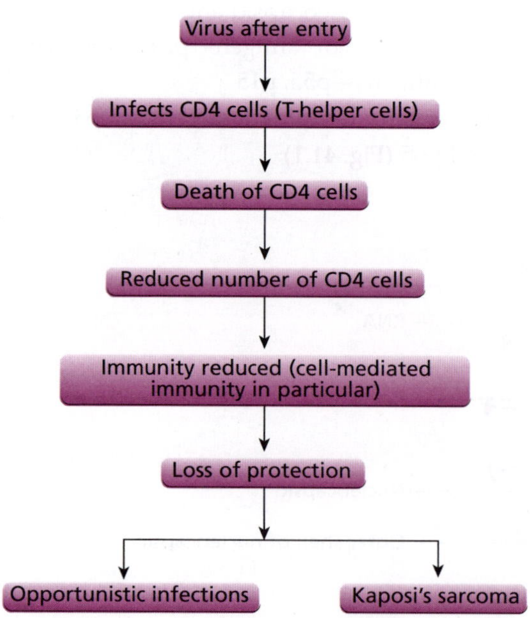

Flow chart 41.1 Pathogenesis—HIV.

Clinical picture

AIDS is characterized by

- Fever
- Malaise
- Weight loss
- Chronic diarrhoea
- Night sweats
- Cervical lymphadenopathy
- White patches on tongue
- Shortness of breath
- Kaposi's sarcoma—a dermal malignancy
- Opportunistic infections caused by
  - **Parasites** such as *Pneumocystis carinii, Cryptosporidium, Toxoplasma gondii* and *Isospora*
  - **Bacteria** such as *Mycobacterium tuberculosis,* atypical mycobacteria and *Salmonella* species
  - **Fungi** such as *Candida albicans, Cryptococcus, Histoplasma* and *Aspergillus*
  - **Viruses** such as herpes virus, cytomegalovirus, adenovirus and varicella-zoster virus

Oral manifestations

A variety of oral lesions are produced by opportunistic pathogens. These include

- Gingivitis, periodontitis and submandibular cellulitis caused by opportunistic bacterial pathogens
- Herpetic stomatitis, oral zoster, hairy leucoplakia, etc., caused by viruses
- Oral candidiasis (most commonly seen) and histoplasmosis—opportunistic fungal infections
- Recurrent aphthous ulceration, salivary gland enlargement, oral ecchymoses
- Oral cancers, for example, Kaposi's sarcoma of oral cavity

Laboratory diagnosis

Direct methods

- Detection of virus antigen by ELISA test

- Detection of reverse transcriptase enzyme by radiolabelling
- Demonstration of virus by electron microscopy
- Isolation of virus possible but very difficult
- Detection of virus RNA by polymerase chain reaction

Indirect methods

- Demonstration of antibody in the patient serum is the simplest and most commonly used method for diagnosis.
- Antibodies appear in serum after several weeks or months. This period till which antibodies are not detectable in serum is known as **window period**; serological tests are negative during this period in spite of infection with HIV.
- The different serological tests used are
  - **Screening tests**
    - ELISA
    - Rapid tests
      - *Dot blot assay* It is a technique used for detection and identification of proteins (antigens).
      - Latex agglutination
      - *HIV spot and comb tests* These are immunodot assays in which the antigen–antibody reaction is visualized as a chromogenic reaction (nine colour–producing reaction). These tests use recombinant or synthetic peptide antigens separately that allow differentiation of HIV-1 and HIV-2 infections.
    - Simple tests
      - Particle agglutination test
  - **Supplemental tests**
    - Western blot test—most confirmatory
    - Indirect immunofluorescence test
    - Radioimmunoprecipitation test

A positive result by a single screening test is not accepted without confirmation; it should be confirmed by either another screening test or Western blot test.

Prevention and control

- Health education through television, radio, newspapers, etc., regarding the basic concepts of HIV transmission
- Avoidance of sexual contact with unknown person/multiple sex partners
- Use of physical barriers such as condoms
- Avoiding use of same needle and syringe
- Screening of blood and blood products
- Change of lifestyle
- Isolation and treatment of AIDS patient
- Vaccine (no effective vaccine is available; many vaccine preparations are under trial)

Treatment

- Various drugs are available to treat HIV infection. These include azidothymidine, didanosine, zalcitabine, stavudine, lamivudine, nevirapine and many others.
- These drugs can be used as monotherapy or in various combinations.
- Because of severe adverse reactions and high cost, their use is restricted.

Self-assessment

Long-answer question

1. Discuss in brief the pathogenicity and laboratory diagnosis of AIDS.

Short-answer questions

Write notes on

1. Laboratory diagnosis of AIDS
2. Opportunistic infections in AIDS

Multiple-choice questions

1. Which of the following is a transmembrane pedicle antigen in human immunodeficiency virus?
   A. gp120
   B. gp41
   C. p24
   D. p55
2. Which of the following cells is commonly attacked by HIV?
   A. T-suppressor cells
   B. T-regulator cells
   C. T-helper cells
   D. Cytotoxic T cells
3. Which of the following parasites is the commonest opportunistic pathogen in AIDS?
   A. *Cryptosporidium parvum*
   B. *Toxoplasma gondii*
   C. *Isospora belli*
   D. *Pneumocystis carinii*
4. Which of the following is the commonest oral lesion produced by opportunistic pathogens in AIDS?
   A. Herpetic stomatitis
   B. Oral candidiasis
   C. Oral zoster
   D. Oral histoplasmosis
5. Which of the following tests is NOT used as a direct method for diagnosis of HIV infection?
   A. Polymerase chain reaction
   B. Electron microscopy
   C. Latex agglutination
   D. Radiolabelling
6. Which of the following is used as the most confirmatory test for the diagnosis of HIV infection?
   A. ELISA test
   B. Radioimmunoprecipitation test
   C. Indirect immunofluorescence test
   D. Western blot test
7. Which of the following tests is NOT used as a screening test for diagnosis of HIV infection?
   A. ELISA test
   B. Particle agglutination test
   C. Indirect immunofluorescence test
   D. Latex agglutination test
8. Which of the following is the commonest bacterial infection in AIDS?
   A. Pneumocytosis
   B. Salmonellosis
   C. Tuberculosis
   D. Shigellosis
9. Which of the following statements is TRUE about window period?
   A. Period after antibodies appears
   B. Period before antibodies disappears
   C. Period after antibodies disappears
   D. Period before antibodies appears

42 Myxoviruses

- Myxoviruses are spherical or filamentous RNA viruses.
- They have the characteristic ability to adsorb mucoprotein receptors of erythrocytes that lead to haemagglutination.
- They are divided into two families:
  - Orthomyxoviridae
  - Paramyxoviridae

Orthomyxoviridae—influenza virus

- Influenza virus is a RNA virus, 80–120 nm in size, spherical in shape.
- Nucleocapsid has a helical symmetry and consists of eight sRNA segments and RNA-dependent RNA polymerase.
- Nucleocapsid is surrounded by an envelope, which is lipoprotein in nature and possesses two types of spikes: the haemagglutinin and the neuraminidase (Fig. 42.1).
- It is susceptible to heat (56°C for 30 minutes), ether, phenol, formaldehyde, salts of heavy metals and iodine.
- It grows in chick embryo and in human and monkey kidney tissue cultures.
- It is of three types: A, B and C.

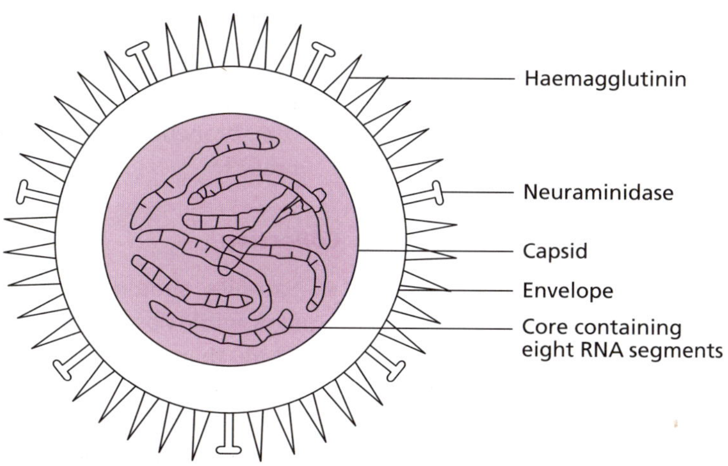

Figure 42.1 Influenza virus.

Pathogenicity—influenza or flu

- Infection occurs by inhalation. The virus multiplies in the ciliated epithelial cells of the respiratory tract and destroys them leaving the underlying basal cells exposed to secondary infection by bacterial pathogens.
- Influenza is an acute respiratory disease characterized by an abrupt onset of fever, chills, sore throat, non-productive cough, headache, generalized myalgia and malaise.
- **Complications** These include pneumonia due to secondary bacterial infections, congestive heart failure and encephalitis. Occasionally, Reye syndrome, Guillain–Barré syndrome and fatty liver may develop.

Laboratory diagnosis

- Demonstration of virus antigen in nasopharyngeal secretions or throat swab by direct immunofluorescence test
- Detection of viral RNA by polymerase chain reaction
- Isolation of virus in chick embryo or tissue culture
- Serological tests such as complement fixation, haemagglutination inhibition test and radial immunodiffusion test in agarose gel used for demonstration of antibodies in patient serum

Prophylaxis

Two types of vaccines are available:

1. Inactivated vaccine—subunit vaccine
2. Live attenuated vaccine

The major difficulty in prophylaxis is the frequent change in the antigenicity of influenza virus. Hence, a vaccine containing a mixture of all important antigens may be useful.

Swine flu

- Swine influenza or swine flu or 'H1N1 influenza' is a highly contagious acute respiratory disease caused by the influenza virus endemic in pigs (swine) that regularly causes outbreaks of influenza among pigs.
- Strains endemic in swine are called swine influenza virus.
- The virus is morphologically identical to influenza virus but antigenically different.
- Pigs play an important role in swine flu; their cells possess receptors that can bind to swine, human and avian influenza viruses; therefore, two or more types of viruses may coinfect swine cells and combine to produce a novel virus by reassortment and new viruses that are a mix of swine, human and/or avian influenza viruses can emerge.

Transmission of swine flu

- Swine flu is transmitted like seasonal flu.
- It spreads from person to person.
- It is passed to other people by exposure to infected droplets through inhalation of infected droplets expelled by coughing or sneezing.
- Infected droplets can also contaminate hands or surfaces, such as door handles, computer keyboards, mobiles, ordinary phones and TV remote controls.

Laboratory diagnosis of swine flu

Specimens

- Nasal swab, nasal washing, nasopharyngeal aspirate, oropharyngeal swab, sputum, bronchoalveolar lavage, tracheal aspirate, etc.

Collection

- Samples should be collected by hospital staff while observing safety measures.
- More than one specimen should be collected before antiviral treatment.
- Swab with a synthetic tip polyester or Dacron with aluminium or plastic shaft should be used. Dry swab should be inserted

in nostrils back to nasopharynx and left in place for 10 seconds and slowly removed while rotating it slightly and placed in viral transport medium and labelled.

Transport

- Store specimen at 4°C before and during transportation.
- It should be transported within 48 hours of collection to the laboratory.
- Process specimen immediately; if it is not possible to process within 48 hours, store the specimen at –70°C.
- Do not store in freezer and avoid freeze–thaw cycles.
- Transport in a viral transport medium in appropriate packing.

Processing of specimen

- Specimens should be processed with all safety measures in a class 3 safety cabinet.

Confirmatory test

- **Real-time RT-PCR** It is a quantitative PCR which detects viral RNA in less than 1 hour.
- It is diagnostic; however, it does not indicate stage of disease.

Viral culture

- Cell cultures are used for cultivation.
- They detect viral growth in 2–10 days.

Neutralization test

- A fourfold rise in virus-specific antibodies in paired sera is diagnostic.
- **Immunofluorescence** can be used for rapid diagnosis.
- Genomic sequencing is performed by using RT-PCR.

Treatment and prevention of swine flu

Prevention

- Social distancing
- Respiratory etiquettes
- Hand hygiene
- Personal protective equipment—use of apron, mask, eye glasses, gloves, etc.
- Avoiding spitting
- Avoiding direct contact with hands
- Vaccine
- Chemoprophylaxis

Treatment

- Tamiflu (oseltamivir)
- Relenza (zanamivir)

Paramyxoviridae

- **Family** Paramyxoviridae includes three genera and four important pathogens. The three genera are the following:
  - Genus *Paramyxovirus*
  - Genus *Morbillivirus*
  - Genus *Pneumovirus*
- Four important pathogens are the following:
  - Mumps virus
  - Parainfluenza virus
  - Measles virus
  - Respiratory syncytial virus

Mumps virus

- Mumps is caused by mumps virus belonging to Paramyxoviridae family.
- It is a spherical virus with a diameter of 100–250 nm.
- Genome contains single-stranded RNA.
- It is surrounded by an envelope containing lipoprotein membrane and covered by projections of haemagglutinin; it may also have neuraminidase activity and fusion protein.
- It grows in chick embryo and human or monkey kidney cell culture. It produces characteristic cytopathic effects—syncytium formation and acidophilic cytoplasmic inclusions.
- It is inactivated at room temperature, by ultraviolet rays and by disinfectants such as formaldehyde and ether.

Pathogenicity

Mumps or epidemic parotitis

- Incubation period is 12–15 days.
- Infection occurs through the respiratory tract (inhalation) and through conjunctiva.
- After multiplication in the respiratory tract and cervical lymph nodes, the virus spreads via blood to the salivary glands, testes, ovaries, pancreas, kidneys and brain.
- It is a disease of childhood characterized by a prodromal stage of fever, malaise and anorexia followed by tender swelling of the parotid glands—either unilateral or bilateral.
- **Complications** These include meningitis, meningoencephalitis, **orchitis,** pancreatitis, oop- horitis and nephritis.

Laboratory diagnosis

- Most cases are diagnosed clinically and laboratory support is not required generally.
- Demonstration of the virus in saliva or throat secretions is done by immunofluorescence test.
- Isolation of virus is done in chick embryo or cell culture.
- For rapid diagnosis, ELISA for detection of mumps-specific IgM antibodies is undertaken.

Prophylaxis

- Mumps infection gives a lifelong immunity.
- A live attenuated vaccine can be administered subcutaneously in combination with attenuated measles and rubella vaccine as MMR vaccine.

Parainfluenza virus

Morphologically, it is identical to other paramyxoviruses.

Pathogenicity

- Infection via respiratory route—by inhalation
- Causes upper and lower respiratory tract disease without viraemia
- **Clinical features** Main cause of
  - **Croup**—acute laryngotracheobronchitis in children under 5 years, characterized by harsh cough and hoarseness
  - Other respiratory diseases such as
    - Common cold
    - Pharyngitis
    - Bronchitis
    - Pneumonia

Laboratory diagnosis

- **Isolation of virus** Best method
- **Specimens** Throat swab, nasal swab
- Primary monkey kidney cell cultures or continuous monkey kidney cell lines
- Growth confirmation by haemadsorption test as cytopathogenic effect not easily apparent
- **Serological tests** ELISA, neutralization and CFT are helpful in diagnosis

Measles

- Measles is caused by measles virus belonging to Paramyxoviridae family.
- Like other paramyxoviruses, it is spherical in shape with a diameter of 120–250 nm and is surrounded by a lipoprotein envelope having haemagglutinin spikes only.
- Other properties are similar to those of mumps virus.
- This virus does not grow in chick embryo. Human or kidney cell culture is used for growing.
- It is a labile virus—readily inactivated by heat, ultraviolet light, ether and formaldehyde.

Pathogenicity

- Measles is a highly infectious childhood disease transmitted by inhalation of virus present in respiratory secretions of the patient.
- Incubation period is 9–11 days.
- After multiplication in the respiratory tract and regional lymph nodes, the virus invades the bloodstream and spreads to the

reticuloendothelial system where it multiplies further and is transported via the blood to skin, mouth, respiratory tract and conjunctiva.

Clinical features

- Measles is characterized by a prodromal phase (3–5 days) of high fever, cough and conjunctivitis, followed by a generalized maculopapular rash which appears first on the face and then spreads downwards.
- **Koplik's spots** appear on the buccal mucosa 1–2 days before the appearance of rash.
- **Oral manifestations**
  - Small, irregular, bluish white specks surrounded by a bright red margin called Koplik's spots on buccal mucosa
  - Palatal and pharyngeal petechiae
  - Generalized inflammation, congestion, swelling and focal ulceration of the gingiva, palate and throat
- **Complications** Rarely secondary bacterial infections, bronchitis, pneumonia and meningoencephalitis may occur.
- **Subacute sclerosing panencephalitis (SSPE)** A rare and late complication. It is a fatal disease of the central nervous system.

Laboratory diagnosis

- Most cases are clinically diagnosed.
- In atypical cases
  - Demonstration of multinucleated giant cells in Giemsa-stained smears of nasal secretions
  - Demonstration of the virus in nasal secretions by direct immunofluorescence test
  - Isolation of the virus from nose, throat, conjunctiva and blood, and from urine using primary human or monkey kidney cell culture or human amnion (as CPE takes a longer time, early detection of growth is done by immunofluorescence test)
- **Serological tests**—such as ELISA for detection of IgM. Haemagglutination inhibition, complement fixation and neutralization tests can also be used for detection of antibodies.

Prophylaxis

- Live attenuated vaccine is given to children at the age of 9 months.
- This vaccine can be given in combination with mumps and rubella as MMR.

Respiratory syncytial virus

- Morphologically, it is identical to other paramyxoviruses.
- It is pleomorphic, 150–300 nm.
- The envelope has two surface spikes—glycoproteins.
- The G protein by which it attaches to cell surfaces and the fusion protein cause cell to fuse, forming syncytium, which gives rise to the name of the virus.
- The virus does not grow in eggs.
- Cultivation is done in heteroploid human cell cultures such as HeLa and HEP-2.
- It is highly labile, inactivated rapidly at room temperature.
- It is preserved by lyophilization.

Pathogenicity

- Infection occurs by inhalation or direct contact of contaminated hands with nose or mouth. Infection is localized to respiratory tract and no viraemia occurs.
- RSV causes outbreaks of respiratory infections every winter.
- Infection is more severe in infants and often involves lower respiratory tract in comparison to that in older children and adults, in whom it causes mild upper respiratory tract infections.

Clinical picture

- In infants, it manifests as lower respiratory tract diseases such as

- Tracheobronchitis
- Bronchiolitis
- Pneumonia
- Secondary bacterial pneumonia—rare
- In older children and adults
  - Upper respiratory tract infections resemble the common cold
  - Otitis media in young children
  - Pneumonia may occur

Laboratory diagnosis

- **Specimens** Nasopharyngeal swab or nasal washings
- **Microscopy** Rapid detection of virus by immunofluorescence on smears of respiratory epithelium
- **Culture** In HeLa or HEP-2 cell cultures observed for CPE—characteristic giant cell and syncytium formation takes a longer time, 10 days
- Early detection of growth by immunofluorescence test
- **Serological diagnosis** By demonstration of rising antibody titre of at least fourfold by ELISA, CFT, neutralization or indirect immunofluorescence test

Treatment Ribavirin administration by continuous aerosol in severely ill hospitalized infants

Prevention No effective vaccine available

Self-assessment

Long-answer question

1. Discuss in brief the pathogenicity and laboratory diagnosis of influenza virus. Add a note on swine flu.

Short-answer questions

Write notes on

1. Influenza virus
2. Mumps virus
3. Measles

Multiple-choice questions

1. Koplik's spots on buccal mucosa are seen in which of the following infections?
   A. Mumps virus
   B. Measles virus
   C. Parainfluenza virus
   D. Influenza virus
2. Segmented RNA and RNA-dependent RNA polymerase is the characteristic feature of?
   A. Mumps virus
   B. Measles virus
   C. Parainfluenza virus
   D. Influenza virus
3. Which of the following viruses is a cause of croup—an acute laryngotracheobronchitis in children under 5 years?
   A. Mumps virus
   B. Measles virus
   C. Parainfluenza virus
   D. Influenza virus
4. Which of the following viruses is the cause of orchitis?
   A. Mumps virus
   B. Poliovirus
   C. Parainfluenza virus
   D. Respiratory syncytial virus
5. Which of the following animals play a key role in H1N1 infection?
   A. Dogs
   B. Horses
   C. Guinea pigs
   D. Pigs
6. Reye syndrome is a complication of which of the following viral infections?
   A. Parainfluenza virus
   B. Influenza virus
   C. Measles virus
   D. Mumps virus

43 Rubella Virus

- Rubella virus is the cause of **German measles**.
- Rubella virus is an RNA virus belonging to Togaviridae family.
- It is pleomorphic.
- Shape is spherical.
- Size is 50–70 nm in diameter.
- It is an enveloped virus.
- Genome: It is a single-stranded RNA.
- Envelope carries haemagglutinin spikes.
- Cultivation: It grows in tissue culture—primary and continuous cell lines such as rabbit kidney-13 and BHK-21.
- Resistance: It is susceptible to heat, ether and chloroform.

Pathogenicity

German measles or rubella

- It is a virus causing mild fever with macular rash and lymphadenopathy.
- Disease in pregnant women causes **congenital rubella syndrome** leading to congenital malformation and mental retardation.
- **Mode of infection** Infection occurs by inhalation. After multiplication in the cervical lymph node via blood, it is disseminated throughout the body.
- Incubation period is 2–3 weeks.
- **Clinical features** It is characterized by prodromal phase (1–5 days) of fever, malaise, lymphadenopathy and upper respiratory tract infections followed by maculopapular, pruritic rash which appears first on the face and then spreads to neck, trunk and extremities (spare palm and sole).
- **Congenital rubella** The virus can cross the placenta and infect foetus in utero causing congenital abnormalities such as cataract, deafness and cardiac defects (classical congenital rubella syndrome) or death of foetus.
- Foetal damage is related to the stage of pregnancy in which exposure to infection occurs; earlier infection in pregnancy causes more damage to the foetus.
- It may cause abortions, foetal death or congenital malformations.
- Other symptoms are
  - Hepatosplenomegaly
  - Thrombocytopenic purpura
  - Myocarditis
  - Bone lesions
  - Developmental retardation of foetus

Laboratory diagnosis

- Rubella in pregnancy needs confirmation. It is done by virus isolation and serology.

- **Specimens** These include blood, throat swab and nasopharyngeal swab.
- **Isolation** Virus can be cultivated in primary and continuous cell lines and the growth of virus is detected by detection of virus antigen by immunofluorescence.
- **Serology** It involves haemagglutination inhibition test and ELISA for IgM and IgG detection.
- Presence of IgG denotes immunity.
- To confirm recent rubella infection, rise in titres of either IgG in two samples collected 10 days apart or IgM must be demonstrated in a single sample.

Prophylaxis

- Rubella infection provides lifelong immunity.
- Live attenuated vaccine is given to young girls (11–13 years) and women immediately after delivery.
- A combined measles–mumps–rubella (MMR) vaccine is recommended at the age of 15 months followed by a booster dose at the age of 4–6 years.

Self-assessment

Short-answer questions

Write notes on

1. Rubella virus
2. Congenital rubella

Multiple-choice questions

1. Which of the following viruses is the cause of German measles?
   A. Mumps virus
   B. Measles virus
   C. Parainfluenza virus
   D. Rubella virus
2. Which of the following statements is FALSE about congenital rubella?
   A. The virus can cross the placenta and infect foetus in utero
   B. The virus causes congenital abnormalities such as cataract, deafness and cardiac defects or death of foetus
   C. Foetal damage is not related to the stage of pregnancy
   D. It may cause abortions

44 Other Viral Pathogens in General and Dental Infections

This chapter discusses the viral pathogens which are occasionally associated with oral and dental infections and not included in earlier chapters.

DNA viruses

Poxviruses

- Poxviruses are the largest and most complex viruses. They can be seen under a light microscope.
- Poxviruses causing human infections are summarized in Table 44.1.

Table 44.1 Poxviruses causing human infections

Virus	Disease
Variola	Smallpox
Vaccinia	Vaccine virus
Monkeypox	Smallpox-like disease
Cowpox	Localized primary vaccinia-like lesion
Orf	Contagious pustular dermatitis
Milker's node	Small ulcerating node
Molluscum contagiosum	Benign skin lesion
Tanapox	Pox-like lesion

Smallpox virus (variola virus)

- **Size** 230 × 300 nm (largest virus)
- **Shape** Brick-shaped
- **Genome** Double-stranded DNA
- **Capsid** Double-layered
- **Envelope** Lipoprotein envelope
- Contains DNA-dependent RNA polymerase (Fig. 44.1)
- Grows on chorioallantoic membrane of 11–13-day-old chick embryos producing small, shiny, white, convex, non-necrotic and non-haemorrhagic pocks in 48–72 hours
- Produces eosinophilic inclusion bodies—**Guarnieri bodies**—in tissue cultures such as monkey kidney and HeLa
- Also grown in monkeys

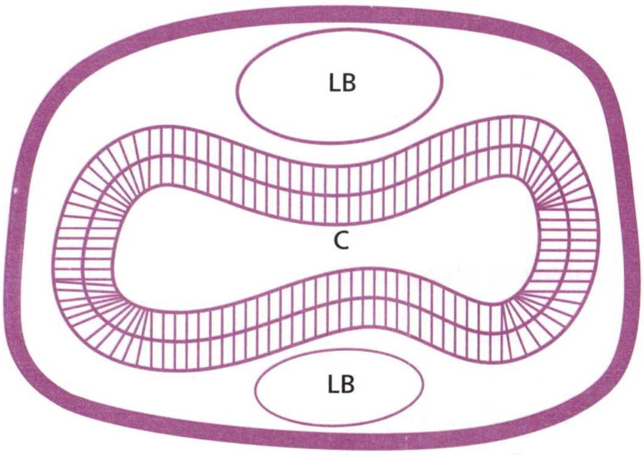

Figure 44.1 Poxvirus.

- Resistant to 50% glycerol and phenol; is susceptible to ultraviolet rays, formalin, oxidizing agents and acids
- Destroyed at 60°C in 10 minutes in moist state; is resistant to drying, can withstand drying for months and in dry state can resist a temperature of 100°C for 5–10 minutes

Pathogenicity

Smallpox

- Infection occurs through the mucosa of upper respiratory tract.
- After multiplication in the lymphoid tissue, it enters the blood causing primary viraemia and reaches the reticuloendothelial cells throughout the body where they multiply in large numbers and are finally transported to the skin and mucosa to produce clinical disease via blood (secondary viraemia).

Clinical features

- Incubation period is 7–14 days.
- It is characterized by prodromal symptoms such as fever, malaise, vomiting and headache, followed by the rash. The rash first appears on the buccal mucosa (exanthem) and then spreads over the body. The rash evolves through stages from macules, papules, vesicles and pustules. Pustules develop into scabs and finally form crusts that leave deep, pitted scars behind, some of which may be permanent. This course takes about 2 weeks.
- Rash occurs most abundantly on the face and involvement of the eyes may result in conjunctivitis or blindness.
- **Oral manifestations** These include ulceration of the oral mucosa, pharynx and oesophagus.

Laboratory diagnosis

- **Specimens** Scrapings from lesions, vesicle fluid, contents of pustule, scabs and blood
- **Methods of diagnosis**
  - Demonstration of the virus in skin lesions by electron microscope
  - Demonstration of the virus by silver impregnation method under a light microscope
  - Demonstration of virus antigen by immunofluorescence
  - Demonstration of viral antigen by complement fixation, haemagglutination or precipitation in gel
  - Isolation of virus by inoculation of vesicular fluid in chorioallantoic membrane of chick embryo or cell culture
  - Demonstration of antibodies after the first week of illness by ELISA, neutralization, RIA, indirect immunofluorescence test and agar gel diffusion test

Prophylaxis

- Smallpox has been eradicated by global use of live attenuated vaccinia virus vaccine.
- Routine vaccination is now stopped.

Molluscum contagiosum

- It is a disease caused by a virus belonging to poxvirus group.
- The disease is more common in children and young adults.
- It is a benign epidermal tumour-like lesion. There are pink or pearly white, wart-like nodules on the skin of the arms, legs, buttocks and genitals.
- **Oral manifestations** Lesions similar to those on the skin may occur on the lips, tongue and buccal mucosa.
- Sections of the nodules show eosinophilic hyaline inclusion bodies called molluscum bodies composed of a large number of virus particles, embedded in a protein matrix.
- Virus cannot be grown in tissue culture, egg or animals.

Adenoviruses

- **Size** 70–90 nm in diameter
- **Shape** Like a space vehicle (Fig. 44.2)
- **Capsid** Icosahedral capsid
- **Genome** Double-stranded DNA

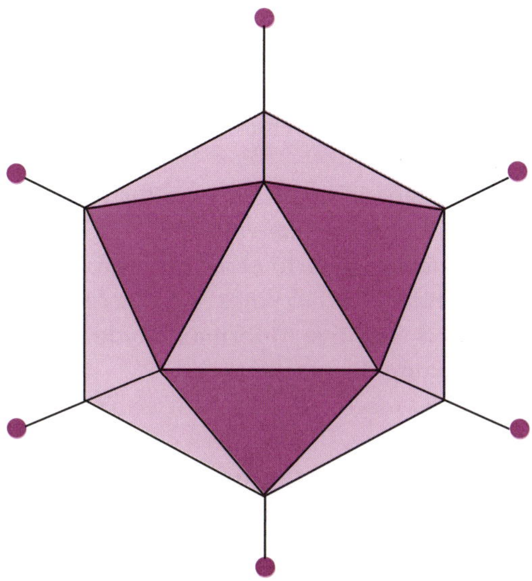

Figure 44.2 Adenovirus.

- **Envelope** No envelope is present
- Human adenoviruses can be cultured in tissue cultures of human origin, for example, human amnion, HeLa or HEP-2
- CPE includes cell rounding and aggregation into grape-like clusters—take several days
- Intranuclear inclusion bodies may be seen in stained preparations
- They remain viable for a week at 37°C but are readily inactivated at 50°C
- They resist ether and bile salts

Pathogenicity

- Entry of adenovirus occurs by
  - Droplet (aerosol) inhalation
  - Faecal–oral route
  - Direct inoculation of conjunctiva
- After entry in the host, the virus attaches to mucosal epithelial cells of the respiratory tract (both upper and lower), the gastrointestinal tract or conjunctiva and enters the cell.
- It causes death of the cell in acute infection or it may cause a latent infection, particularly in the adenoid and tonsillar tissue of the throat.

Clinical features

In the upper respiratory tract, it causes

- Acute febrile pharyngitis in infants and children
- Pharyngoconjunctival fever in children
- Acute respiratory disease in young adults
- Epidemic keratoconjunctivitis
- Acute follicular conjunctivitis
- Acute haemorrhagic cystitis in children
- Meningoencephalitis
- Gastroenteritis with non-bloody diarrhoea in children
- Generalized exanthem

Laboratory diagnosis

The commonly used methods are as follows:

- Demonstration of virus in cells aspirated from the nasopharynx by direct immunofluorescence stain using group-specific antibodies
- Isolation of virus from the throat, conjunctiva, urine or stool by using cell cultures (HeLa, HEP-2 or KB); growth identified by characteristic CPE—enlarged rounded cells in grape-like clusters or by CFT using adenovirus antiserum
- **Serological tests**
  - Demonstration of a fourfold or greater rise in antibody titre is diagnostic.
  - CFT, haemagglutination inhibition neutralization and RIA can be used.

Treatment No antiviral therapy

Prevention A live non-attenuated vaccine is used in the form of enteric-coated capsule in military recruits; it produces subclinical infection and confers protection against respiratory disease.

Human papillomaviruses (HPVs)

- These are DNA viruses with double-stranded, circular DNA molecule.
- Size is 55 nm in diameter.
- Symmetry is icosahedral symmetry.
- These viruses cannot be grown in culture.

Pathogenicity

- Warts on hand and feet—HPV types 1, 2, 3 and 4
- Genital warts (condylomata acuminatum)—HPV types 6 and 1
- May be transmitted venereally
- May become malignant
- **Oral lesions** of condylomata acuminatum may occur as small, multiple, white or pink nodules on the tongue, buccal mucosa, palate, gingiva or alveolar ridge, which enlarge, proliferate and coalesce
- Uterine cervical cancer—HPV types 16 and 18

Diagnosis

- Diagnosis is clinical. History can confirm the diagnosis.
- There are no culture and serological methods for diagnosis.
- Identification of viral genotype is done by DNA hybridization method.

RNA viruses

Picornaviruses

Picornaviruses are small, 27–30 nm in size, non-enveloped, RNA viruses belonging to the family Picornaviridae. This family includes two genera:

1. Enteroviruses—affecting enteric tract
2. Rhinoviruses—affecting nasal mucosa

Enteroviruses

Enteroviruses of medical importance are

- Polioviruses—1–3
- Coxsackie viruses
  - A—1–24 except 23
  - B—1–6
- Enteric cytopathic human orphan (ECHO) viruses—1–34 except 10 and 28
- Enteroviruses—68–71

Polioviruses

- **Size** Very small; 27 nm in diameter
- **Shape** Spherical
- **Capsid** Icosahedron
- **Genome** Single-stranded RNA
- **Envelope** No envelope
- Resistance
  - In faeces, it can survive for months at 4°C and for years at –20°C
  - It is resistant to ether, chloroform, bile, proteolytic enzymes and detergents
  - It is sensitive to formaldehyde and oxidizing disinfectants
  - It is inactivated by heat at 55°C for 30 minutes
  - Chlorination destroys virus
- **Cultivation** Virus grows in tissue cultures of simian and human origin, for example, primary monkey kidney culture
- In culture, it produces cytopathic effects in 2–3 days; infected cells round up and become refractile and pyknotic, and show eosinophilic intranuclear inclusion bodies

Pathogenicity—poliomyelitis

Infection occurs by ingestion; virus multiplies in epithelial and lymphoid cells of GIT and reaches the regional lymph nodes, from where it enters the bloodstream to cause primary viraemia and then reaches reticuloendothelial tissue and multiplies. It again enters the bloodstream to cause major or secondary viraemia. It reaches the brain and spinal cord, multiplies in neurons and destroys them.

Clinical features

Infection with poliovirus may result in

- **Inapparent infection** During this, the patient is asymptomatic but virus can be isolated from samples of stool or throat swab.
- **Minor illness** Characterized by fever, sore throat, headache and malaise associated with primary viraemia, it may progress to paralytic form.
- **Major illness** Characterized by headache, neck stiffness, back pain and other features of aseptic meningitis and it marks the stage of viral invasion of CNS.

- **Paralytic poliomyelitis** Characterized by flaccid paralysis, it occurs after a stage of meningitis.

Laboratory diagnosis

- **Specimens** Blood, cerebrospinal fluid (CSF), throat swab and faeces
- **Direct demonstration** By electron microscope and immune electron microscopy
- **Isolation** Grows in tissue cultures of human or simian origin such as primary monkey kidney and HEP-2; growth indicated by characteristic cytopathic effect in 2–3 days or identified by neutralization test
- **Serological tests** Are not much useful in the diagnosis; can use complement fixation and neutralization tests for demonstration of antibodies

Prophylaxis

Vaccination—two types of vaccines are available:

1. **Oral** or **Sabin vaccine** is a live attenuated vaccine. It is given orally. It is more effective, economical, safe and easy to administer. Theoretically, single dose gives lifelong immunity, but in practice five doses are given. It produces both systemic immunity and local immunity in the intestinal epithelium—the primary site of multiplication for poliovirus.
2. **Injectable** or **Salk vaccine** is a killed vaccine. It is given by parenteral route. It is also effective and safe and produces systemic immunity only but fails to produce optimal level of local immunity in the intestinal epithelium. Hence, it is less protective than oral vaccine.

Coxsackieviruses

- The virus was first isolated from the village of Coxsackie in New York, so labelled as coxsackievirus.
- Coxsackieviruses are members of the family Picornaviridae.
- They are morphologically similar to other picornaviruses.
- They grow well in suckling mice following intracerebral and intraperitoneal inoculation and produce the following changes in suckling mice:
  - **Group A** produce generalized myositis and flaccid paralysis leading to death in a week.
  - **Group B** produce patchy focal myositis, spastic paralysis, necrosis of brown fat and pancreatitis, hepatitis, myocarditis and encephalitis.
- They also grow in monkey kidney tissue culture.
- Based on the pathological changes produced in suckling mice, viruses have been classified into two groups:
  - Coxsackie A virus
  - Coxsackie B virus
- By neutralization test group A is classified into 24 types and group B into 6 types.

Clinical features

- **Herpangina** It is a vesicular pharyngitis caused by coxsackie A viruses and characterized by sore throat, fever, headache and formation of small ulcers on the anterior faucial pillars and sometimes also on the hard and soft palates, posterior pharyngeal wall, buccal mucosa and tongue.
- **Acute lymphonodular pharyngitis** It is caused by coxsackievirus A10 and characterized by sore throat, fever, headache, anorexia and formation of raised, discrete, white to yellow papules surrounded by a narrow zone of erythema on the uvula, soft palate, anterior pillars and posterior oropharynx.
- **Hand, foot and mouth disease** It is caused by coxsackievirus A16 and characterized by maculopapular, exanthematous and vesicular lesions of the skin of the hands, feet, legs, arms, etc., fever, coryza, anorexia and lymphadenopathy.
- **Oral manifestations** They include formation of small, multiple, vesicular and ulcerative lesions.

- Coxsackieviruses also cause the following:
  - Aseptic meningitis and encephalitis
  - Minor respiratory tract infections such as common cold
  - Epidemic pleurodynia
  - Myocarditis and pericarditis in the newborn
  - Juvenile diabetes
  - Orchitis
  - Transplacental and neonatal transmission resulting in disease in the newborn
  - Postviral fatigue syndrome

Laboratory diagnosis

It involves isolation by using suckling mice inoculation and identification by studying histopathological findings.

ECHO viruses

- They resemble other picornaviruses in morphology.
- They infect enteric canal of humans.
- They are called ECHO viruses because they are unrelated to any disease in particular.
- They are cultivated in monkey kidney tissue culture and growth is detected by cytopathic effect.

Clinical features

- Most of the ECHO viruses cause asymptomatic infection.
- They can cause
  - Common cold
  - Aseptic meningitis
  - Rash with fever
  - Gastroenteritis

Laboratory diagnosis

Faeces, throat swab and CSF are inoculated in monkey kidney tissue culture. Growth is confirmed by studying cytopathic effects and neutralization test.

Enteroviruses 68–72

Enterovirus 68–72 are associated with human diseases.

- Enterovirus 68 causes pneumonia and bronchitis.
- Enterovirus 70 causes acute haemorrhagic conjunctivitis.
- Enterovirus 71 causes meningitis.
- Enterovirus 72 is hepatitis A virus and causes hepatitis.

Rhinovirus

- Virus belongs to the family Picornaviridae and causes common cold.
- Rhinoviruses are small RNA viruses, 30 nm in diameter, non-enveloped viruses.
- They resemble other picornaviruses except for
  - More resistance to heat
  - Growth being best at 33°C
  - More acid labile—destroyed at pH 3–5
- Grow on human or monkey cell cultures (humans are the only natural hosts)

Pathogenicity

- Infection is transmitted by inhalation.
- It grows in nasal mucosa and causes upper respiratory tract infections.
- It causes common cold characterized by coryza (watery discharge with nasal obstruction), sneezing, cough, headache, sore throat and malaise. Fever may be present. Other viruses such as coronaviruses, respiratory syncytial viruses, parainfluenza viruses and adenoviruses can also cause common cold.
- Complications—these include sinusitis, bronchitis and otitis media.

Laboratory diagnosis

- Demonstration of virus antigen by ELISA
- Demonstration of virus by polymerase chain reaction
- Isolation of virus from nose and throat swabs or nasopharyngeal washings in human tissue cultures; growth identified by study of cytopathic effects and confirmed by neutralization test

Prophylaxis

No ideal vaccine is available due to more than 100 types of rhinoviruses—difficult to prepare.

Arboviruses

- Arboviruses are arthropod-borne viruses that are transmitted by blood-sucking arthropods.
- Arboviruses are RNA viruses measuring 40–100 nm in size and are spherical in shape.
- They can be grown in tissue culture and suckling mice.
- They are susceptible to heat, bile salts, ether and other lipid solvents.
- Arboviruses belong to the five taxonomic families as follows:
  - Togaviridae
  - Flaviviridae
  - Bunyaviridae
  - Reoviridae
  - Rhabdoviridae

Togaviridae Important members of this family are

- Chikungunya virus
- Eastern equine encephalitis virus
- Western equine encephalitis virus
- Venezuelan equine encephalitis virus and many other

Flaviviridae Important members of this family are

- Japanese encephalitis virus
- Yellow fever virus
- Dengue fever virus
- Kyasanur Forest disease virus and so on

Bunyaviridae Important members of this family are

- California encephalitis virus
- Sandfly fever viruses
- Ganjam virus
- Hantan virus and so on

Reoviridae Colorado tick-borne virus

Rhabdoviridae Important members of this family are

- Vesicular stomatitis virus
- Chandipura virus

Pathogenesis

Arbovirus infections are transmitted from animals to humans (zoonoses); arthropods get infected by biting viraemic vertebrates and after extrinsic incubation period they become infective.

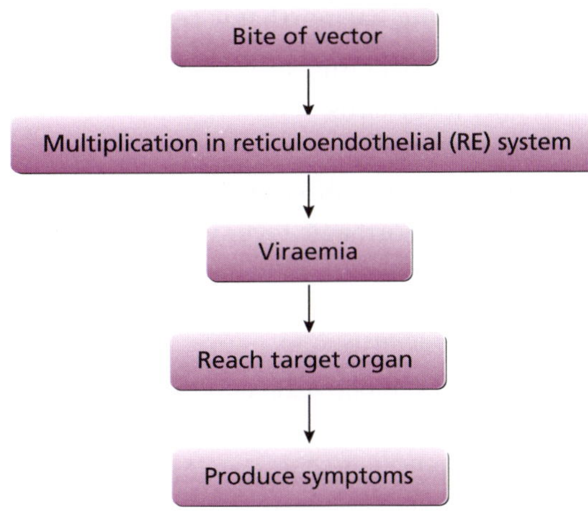

Clinical features

- Fever with or without rash and arthralgia
- Encephalitis
- Haemorrhagic fever
- Characteristic systemic disease of target organ

Viruses causing fever with or without rash and arthralgia

- Chikungunya virus
- O'nyong-nyong virus
- West Nile virus
- Ross River virus
- Dengue fever virus
- Sandfly fever viruses

These viruses are transmitted by mosquitoes or by ticks.

Viruses causing encephalitis

- Eastern equine encephalitis virus
- Western equine encephalitis virus

- Venezuelan equine encephalitis virus
- Japanese encephalitis virus
- West Nile virus
- St. Louis encephalitis virus
- Murray Valley encephalitis virus
- California encephalitis virus

These viruses are transmitted by mosquitoes.

Viruses causing haemorrhagic fever

- Chikungunya virus
- Yellow fever virus
- Dengue fever virus
- Kyasanur Forest disease virus
- Omsk haemorrhagic fever virus
- Crimean-Congo haemorrhagic fever viruses

Laboratory diagnosis

- **Specimens** Blood, CSF and brain tissue
- **Culture**
  - Animal inoculation—suckling mice inoculated by intracerebral route
  - Tissue cultures
    - Chick embryo fibroblast—Vero and HeLa
    - Embryonated hen's eggs—yolk sac
- Isolate is identified by
  - Haemagglutination test
  - CFT
  - Gel precipitation test
  - Immunofluorescence test
  - ELISA
  - Neutralization test

Important arboviruses

Chikungunya virus

- It is a virus causing febrile illness with arthralgia.
- Vector is transmitted by *Aedes aegypti.*
- Clinical features—severe joint pain is a characteristic feature.
- Fever, lymphadenopathy, conjunctivitis and maculopapular rash are other symptoms.

Japanese B encephalitis virus

It is the most common agent causing encephalitis.

Pathogenicity

- Human infection occurs by bite of mosquitoes.
- Virus after multiplication in reticuloendothelial system is transmitted via blood to the central nervous system and causes encephalitis characterized by fever, headache, vomiting, neck rigidity, convulsions and coma that may lead to death.

Laboratory diagnosis

- Isolation of virus in suckling mice or tissue culture from CSF or blood
- Can use serological tests such as ELISA, complement fixation test, haemagglutination test or neutralization test for demonstration of antibodies can be used

Prophylaxis

- Control of mosquitoes
- Keeping pigs away from residential areas
- Vaccination—using formalin-inactivated vaccine or live attenuated vaccine

Kyasanur Forest disease virus

- Geographical distribution—Karnataka
- Transmission—by bites from ticks
- Clinical features—acute-onset fever, headache, myalgia, vomiting and haemorrhages in skin, mucosa and viscera
- Prevention—control of ticks and vaccination with killed KFD vaccine

Dengue fever

- Dengue fever is caused by arbovirus belonging to the family Flaviviridae—dengue virus.
- It is an RNA virus, 40–50 nm in size.
- Other properties are similar to those of arboviruses causing encephalitis and yellow fever virus.

Pathogenicity

- Dengue fever is a mosquito-borne disease characterized by fever of sudden onset, headache, conjunctival infection, pain in the back and limbs, lymphadenopathy and maculopapular rash.
- In more serious forms, haemorrhagic manifestations—dengue haemorrhagic fever or shock (dengue shock syndrome)—are seen.

Laboratory diagnosis

- Detection of dengue NS1 antigen by ELISA and immunochromatography
- Demonstration of virus by immunofluorescence techniques or by using radiolabelled RNA probes
- Virus isolation difficult
- Detection of antibodies by haemagglutination test, dot ELISA IgM capture test and fluorogenic ELISA for rapid diagnosis
- Polymerase chain reaction

Prophylaxis

- Elimination of mosquitoes
- No effective vaccine available (a live attenuated vaccine is under trial)

Yellow fever virus

- Yellow fever is caused by arbovirus belonging to the family Flaviviridae—yellow fever virus.
- It is an RNA virus, 40–50 nm in size.
- Other properties are similar to those of arboviruses causing encephalitis.

Pathogenicity

- Yellow fever is a mosquito-borne acute febrile illness—transmitted by mosquitoes.
- It is characterized by
  - Fever with chills
  - Headache, myalgia and vomiting
  - Severe jaundice due to liver destruction
  - Haemorrhagic manifestations
  - Death, which may occur due to hepatic or renal failure

Laboratory diagnosis

- Histopathological examination of liver tissue
- Virus isolation from liver tissue and blood
- Serological tests for demonstration of antibodies

Prophylaxis

- Control of mosquitoes
- Vaccination—two vaccines available (the 17 D vaccine is safe and effective)

Rabies virus

- Rabies virus (rhabdovirus) causes rabies—hydrophobia.
- It is a bullet-shaped RNA virus measuring 75–180 nm, surrounded by a membranous envelope with spikes (Fig. 44.3).
- Core of virion consists of helically arranged ribonucleoprotein, which is unsegmented, linear, single-stranded RNA.
- Nucleocapsid also contains RNA-dependent RNA polymerase.
- The virus is susceptible to ultraviolet rays, heat (heating at 56°C for 1 hour and at 60°C

Figure 44.3 Rabies virus.

for 5 minutes), ether, strong acids and alkalis, trypsin, detergents, etc.
- The virus grows in all warm-blooded animals. It also grows on chick embryo and duck embryo, and in tissue cultures.

Pathogenicity

- Rabies is primarily a disease of animals and is transmitted to humans by bites of rabid animals or by contact with saliva of the infected animals (dogs).
- It is acute, fulminant and fatal encephalitis.
- Incubation period is generally 1–3 months, but may be as long as 3 years.
- Clinically, it occurs in three phases:
  - ***Prodromal phase*** It lasts for 2–10 days, and is characterized by fever, malaise, nausea, vomiting, anorexia, headache, photophobia, etc.
  - ***Acute neurological phase*** It is characterized by nervousness, apprehension, hallucinations and **hydrophobia** (fear of water), that is, difficulty in drinking together with intense thirst, which is an important feature. The patient can swallow dry solids but not liquid. Attempt to drink brings painful spasms of pharynx and larynx producing choking.
  - ***Coma*** The neurological phase is followed by convulsions or coma and death. The major cause of death is respiratory paralysis.

Laboratory diagnosis

- Demonstration of viral antigen in facial skin biopsy and in corneal smear by immunofluorescence or immunoperoxidase staining
- Demonstration of inclusion bodies (Negri bodies) in the brain or the spinal cord after death—definitive diagnosis
- Demonstration of virus antigen in the brain
- Isolation of virus by mouse inoculation or tissue cultures or eggs
- Serological tests—complement fixation, neutralization, ELISA or indirect immunofluorescence test for detection of antibodies
- **Detection of nucleic acid**
  - RT-PCR
  - Dot blot hybridization
  - Probes

Prophylaxis

Prophylaxis includes
- The wound is washed with soap and water.
- Prompt cauterization of wound with carbolic acid, quaternary ammonium compounds (such as citavlon), tincture or aqueous iodine or alcohol is done.
- In a severe wound, antirabies serum may be applied topically.
- Vaccination—suitable antirabic vaccine is given. Two types of vaccines are available:
  - Neural vaccines are cheap but less antigenic and encephalitogenic.
  - Non-neural vaccines are highly antigenic, safe and effective but costly.

Neural	Non-neural
Fermi vaccine—not used	Duck egg vaccine
Semple vaccine—widely used	Tissue culture vaccine—safe
Beta-propiolactone vaccine	Live attenuated chick embryo vaccine
Infant brain vaccine	Subunit vaccine

Viruses causing diarrhoea

Viruses causing diarrhoea are as follows:
- Rotavirus
- Norwalk virus
- Corona viruses
- Astroviruses

Rotavirus

- It is a major cause of diarrhoea in infants.
- It is an RNA virus with double-stranded RNA.
- Size is about 65 nm in diameter.
- Shape is spherical.
- Symmetry is icosahedral symmetry.

- It has a characteristic wheel-like appearance.

Pathogenicity

- Infection is acquired by ingestion of contaminated food and water or directly from contaminated fingers.
- Rotavirus gastroenteritis is observed in children aged 6–24 months. Stool is green-yellow without blood and mucus.
- Diarrhoea and vomiting can lead to severe dehydration.
- It is usually associated with fever.

Laboratory diagnosis

- **Specimen** Stool sample or rectal swab
- Demonstration of virus under electron microscope or by immune electron microscope
- Virus antigen detection in stool by complement fixation test, countercurrent immunoelectrophoresis, ELISA or passive agglutination test
- Antibody detection in serum—IgM and IgG detection by ELISA

Norwalk virus

- It is a 27-nm, small, round, RNA virus.
- It cannot be cultured.

Pathogenicity

- It is transmitted by faeco–oral route.
- Incubation period is 24–48 hours.
- It is a cause of epidemic viral gastroenteritis in adults characterized by rapid-onset diarrhoea, vomiting, nausea, fever, abdominal cramps, headache and malaise.

Laboratory diagnosis

- Virus or antigen detection by RT-PCR
- Virus demonstration in stool by electron microscope
- Antibody detection by ELISA

Coronaviruses

- Spherical, 120–160 nm in diameter with helical nucleocapsid
- RNA virus with non-segmented single-stranded RNA
- Enveloped virus with petal-shaped spikes
- Difficult to grow in cell cultures; can use Vero cell lines

Pathogenicity

These are viruses causing common cold, severe acute respiratory syndrome (SARS) in adults and gastroenteritis in infants.

Laboratory diagnosis

- Antigen detection by ELISA
- Virus demonstration by electron microscopy in stool
- Nucleic acid detection by PCR
- Isolation of virus from respiratory secretions and stool in Vero cell lines
- Antibody detection by passive haemagglutination and ELISA

Astro viruses

They are 28–30-nm, star-shaped, single-stranded RNA viruses causing diarrhoeal disease in children and immunocompromised hosts.

Self-assessment

Long-answer questions

1. Enumerate the arboviruses prevalent in India. Discuss in detail one of them.
2. Enumerate the picornaviruses. Discuss the pathogenicity and laboratory diagnosis of polio.

Short-answer questions

Write notes on

1. Poxvirus
2. Molluscum contagiosum
3. Adenoviruses
4. Human papillomaviruses
5. Polioviruses
6. Coxsackieviruses
7. Rhinovirus
8. Yellow fever virus

9. Dengue fever virus
10. Japanese encephalitis virus
11. Rabies virus
12. Rotavirus

Multiple-choice questions

1. Condylomata acuminatum as small, multiple, white or pink nodules on the tongue, buccal mucosa, palate, gingiva or alveolar ridge are caused by
   A. Papillomaviruses
   B. Adenoviruses
   C. Smallpox virus
   D. Molluscum contagiosum
2. Which of the following is a brick-shaped virus?
   A. Papillomaviruses
   B. Adenoviruses
   C. Smallpox virus
   D. Molluscum contagiosum
3. Guarnieri bodies are the inclusion bodies produced by which of the following viruses?
   A. Papillomaviruses
   B. Adenoviruses
   C. Smallpox virus
   D. Molluscum contagiosum
4. A benign epidermal tumour-like lesion, pink or pearly white, wart-like nodule on the skin is produced by which of the following viruses?
   A. Papillomaviruses
   B. Adenoviruses
   C. Smallpox virus
   D. Molluscum contagiosum
5. Which of the following is a route of entry of poliovirus in human body?
   A. Inhalation
   B. Insect bite
   C. Ingestion
   D. Skin cuts
6. Which of the following is a hepatitis A virus?
   A. Enterovirus 68
   B. Enterovirus 70
   C. Enterovirus 71
   D. Enterovirus 72
7. Which of the following is a tick-borne disease?
   A. Kyasanur Forest disease
   B. Yellow fever
   C. Dengue fever
   D. Japanese encephalitis
8. Which of the following arboviruses does not cause haemorrhagic fever?
   A. Chikungunya virus
   B. Yellow fever virus
   C. Japanese encephalitis virus
   D. Kyasanur Forest disease virus
9. Negri bodies are the inclusion bodies produced by which of the following viruses?
   A. Poliovirus
   B. Adenovirus
   C. Smallpox virus
   D. Rabies virus
10. Which of the following vaccines is NOT a neural vaccine?
    A. Semple vaccine
    B. Beta-propiolactone vaccine
    C. Tissue culture vaccine
    D. Infant brain vaccine
11. The following are the viruses causing diarrhoea, EXCEPT
    A. Coxsackie A virus
    B. Rotavirus
    C. Norwalk virus
    D. Astrovirus
12. Which of the following viruses has space vehicle–like shape?
    A. Smallpox virus
    B. Adenovirus
    C. Coxasackievirus
    D. Poliovirus

45 Introduction to Mycology

- **Medical mycology** is the branch of mycology that deals with the study of human diseases caused by fungi.

Morphology of fungi

- Fungi are eukaryotic microbes devoid of chlorophyll.
- They are broadly divided into two groups as yeast and mould.
- The simplest type of fungus is the unicellular budding **yeast.**
- Elongation of yeast cell produces a tubular thread-like branching filament called **hypha** (plural: hyphae).
- An aggregate of hyphae is called **mycelium** (plural: mycelia).
- Fungi which form mycelia are called moulds or filamentous fungi.
- Fungi form both sexual and asexual spores.

Differences between fungi and bacteria

Fungi are differentiated from bacteria in the ways given in Table 45.1.

Important terms

- **Budding** It is an asexual method of reproduction in yeast. Daughter bud arises from

Table 45.1 Differences between fungi and bacteria

Fungi	Bacteria
Eukaryotes	Prokaryotes
Larger in size	Smaller in size
Possess rigid cell wall containing chitin, mannan and polysaccharides	Cell wall consists of peptidoglycan, teichoic acid and lipopolysaccharides
Cytoplasmic membranes contain sterols	Lack sterol
Cytoplasm consists of organelles such as mitochondria and endoplasmic reticulum	Mitochondria and endoplasmic reticulum absent
True nucleus with nuclear membrane and paired chromosomes is present	Primitive nucleus—single chromosome without nuclear membrane is present
Most of them divide by sexual or asexual method	Divide by binary fission
Resistant to antibiotics	Sensitive to antibiotics

parent bud, enlarges and separates from the parent cell.

- **Pseudohyphae** Yeast produces a chain of elongated cells known as pseudohyphae.
- **Spores** These are structures produced as a result of asexual or sexual reproduction of fungi.
  - ***Asexual spores*** They are produced because of budding, fission and mitosis. Asexual spores include the following:
    - *Chlamydospores* These are large with thick double refractile wall produced from hyphal cell.
    - *Arthrospores* These are produced as a result of fragmentation of hyphae. They are cuboidal, rectangular spores formed in chains, with a slightly thick wall, and are released at maturity.
    - *Blastospores* These are asexual spores produced as a result of budding.
    - *Sporangiospores* These are asexual spores present inside the sporangium.
    - *Conidia* These are asexual reproductive structures borne exogenously on specialized hyphae called conidiophore. They are of two types: macroconidia (large) and microconidia (small).
  - ***Sexual spores*** They are produced as a result of meiosis.
    - *Ascospores* Sexual spores inside a sac-like structure called ascus are ascospores and are seen in ascomycetes.
    - *Zygospores* These are sexual spores in zygomycetes.
    - *Basidiospores* These are sexual spores formed on basidium.

Classification

Morphological

Based on morphology, fungi are classified into four groups:

1. **Yeasts** These are unicellular fungi occurring as spherical or ellipsoidal cells, which reproduce by simple budding, for example, *Cryptococcus neoformans* (Fig. 45.1).
2. **Yeast-like fungi** Fungi which grow partly as yeast and partly as elongated cells resembling hyphae called pseudohyphae are yeast-like fungi, for example, *Candida albicans* (Fig. 45.2).
3. **Moulds or filamentous fungi** Fungi which form true hyphae and mycelia and reproduce by forming different types of asexual spores are called moulds or filamentous fungi, for example, dermatophytes (Fig. 45.3).
4. **Dimorphic fungi** Fungi which occur in two forms as yeast as well as moulds based on growth conditions are called dimorphic fungi. These fungi grow as yeast in host tissue and in cultures at 37°C while they occur as moulds in soil and in cultures at

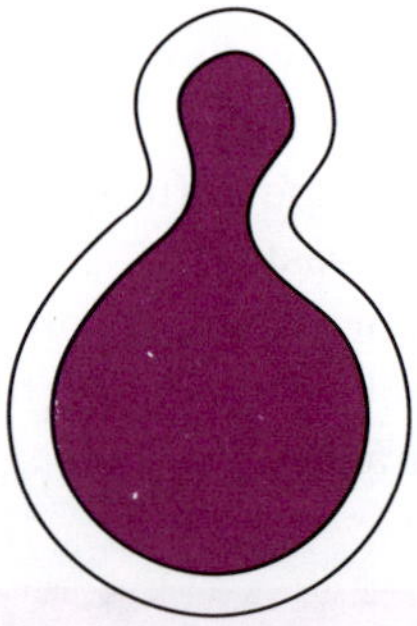

Figure 45.1 Budding yeast.

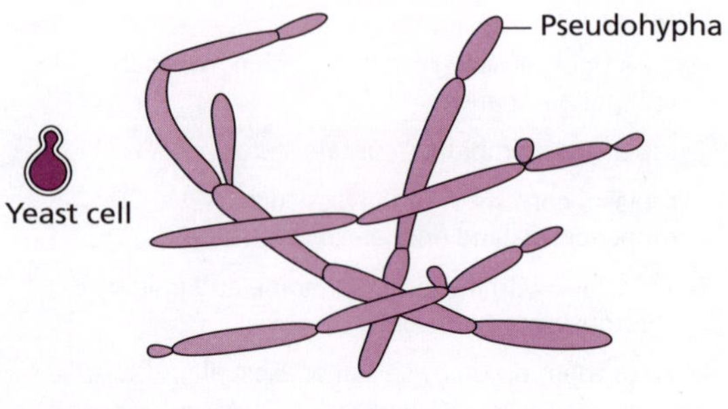

Figure 45.2 Yeast-like fungi.

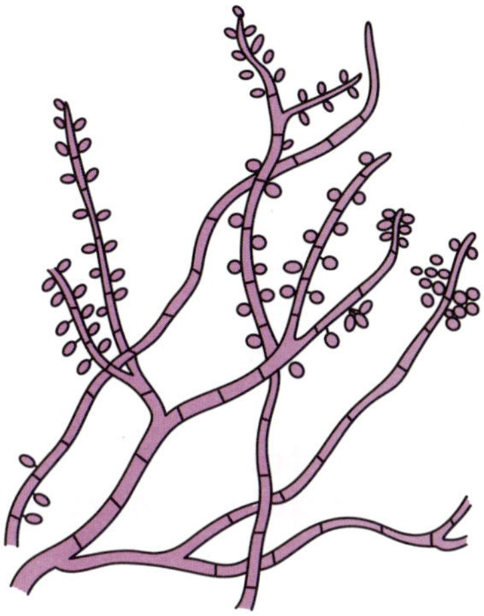

Figure 45.3 Moulds.

room temperature, for example, *Histoplasma capsulatum* (Fig. 45.4).

Classification based on sexual reproduction

Based on the sexual method of reproduction, fungi are classified into four groups as follows:

1. **Zygomycetes** form zygospores.
2. **Ascomycetes** form ascus and ascospores.
3. **Basidiomycetes** form basidium and basidiospores.
4. **Fungi imperfecti** refer to the fungi in which sexual process is not observed.

Laboratory diagnosis of fungal diseases

Collection and transport of specimens

Proper collection and transport of specimen is an important step in the isolation and identification of medically important fungi.

Collection of skin and nail scrapings

- The affected area is sponged with 70% alcohol or sterile water (if the lesion is tender and painful) to remove surface contamination and topical medication.
- Scrapings from the active edge of the lesion preferably from the deeper epithelium of the skin and from friable or discoloured areas or from under the thick hyperkeratotic nails are collected with the help of a flame-sterilized scalpel.
- They are transported in an envelope, Petri dish or an other convenient container.

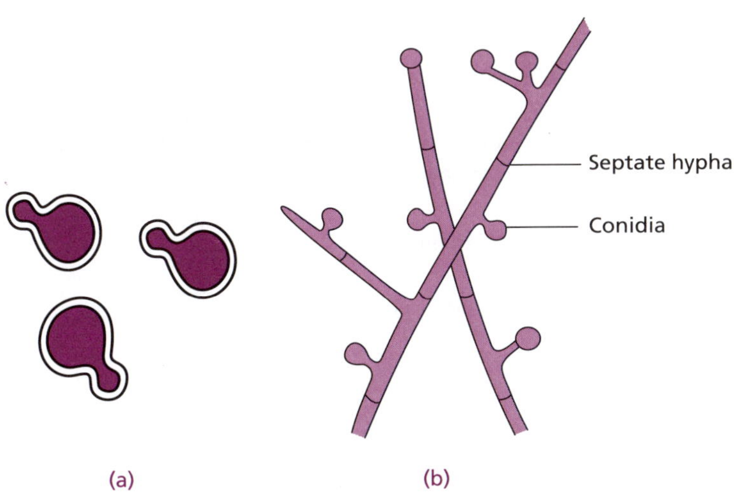

Figure 45.4 Dimorphic fungi. (a) Yeast form. (b) Mycelial form.

Collection of infected hairs

- Infected hairs are plucked with forceps.
- They are transported as mentioned in the preceding text.

Corneal scrapings

These are collected from the margin of corneal ulcer with the help of a needle under local anaesthesia, for example, xylocaine.

Sputum

- Early morning sputum sample is preferred.
- It is collected in a sterile, clean, wide-mouthed, screw-capped container.
- It is transported and processed immediately to avoid growth of commensals and to increase chances of isolation of the causative agent.

Pus/discharge/crusts

- They are aspirated with the help of a syringe and needle or collected with the help of swab.
- Crusts removed from the surface of lesion are collected in a sterile container.
- They are transported immediately for further processing.

Urine

- Midstream urine sample is collected by a **clean-catch method**.
- It is collected in a sterile container and transported immediately to avoid delay in processing.
- If delay is unavoidable, it can be refrigerated at 4°C up to 12 hours.
- Urine is centrifuged and the sediment is used for further processing.

Cerebrospinal fluid (CSF)

- It is collected in a sterile container by **lumbar puncture**.
- It is transported and processed immediately.
- If delay is expected, CSF should be kept at room temperature or in an incubator.

Blood

- Approximately 8 mL of blood is collected aseptically by venipuncture in a brain–heart infusion broth.

Procedures used for diagnosis of fungal diseases

Direct microscopy

- The purpose of microscopy is to detect spores, mycelial elements, yeast cells, spherules or granules.
- The different procedures used include the following:
  - Direct wet mount
  - Potassium hydroxide (KOH) mount
  - Mounting and staining methods

Direct wet mount

- Specimens such as sputum, bronchoscopic secretions, pus, exudates, CSF and urine which are not too thick are observed by direct wet mount.
- The specimen is placed on a clean glass slide and coverslip is applied.
- It is observed under low-power and high-power objectives.

Potassium hydroxide (KOH) mount

- Specimens such as skin, hairs, nail and sputum which are too thick to observe are to be cleared with sodium or potassium hydroxide.
- It is used most commonly.
- KOH or NaOH dissolves keratin and cellular material and makes the fungal elements clearer.

Method

- The specimen is placed on a slide.

- One or two drops of 10–20% KOH or NaOH is added.
- A thin coverslip is placed.
- The slide is heated gently over the flame (should not be boiled) or kept in an incubator for 20 minutes at 37°C to digest keratin.
- It is observed under low- and high-power objectives.

Mounting and staining methods

These include the following:

- **India Ink wet mount** For demonstration of capsule of *C. neoformans*
- **Lactophenol cotton blue stain**
- **Calcofluor white stain**
- **Gram stain** For demonstration of mycelium and budding yeasts in sputum, urine, vaginal secretions and other specimens (all fungi are Gram-positive)
- **Wright's stain** For demonstration of intracellular fungal parasites
- **Direct immunofluorescence stain** For demonstration of fungi in tissues and smears
- **Special stains**
  - For demonstration of fungi in tissues (biopsy specimens)
  - Following staining methods are used:
    - Periodic acid–Schiff (PAS) stain
    - Gomori's methenamine silver nitrate stain
    - Haematoxylin and eosin stain

Culture methods

- For isolation of fungi, specimens are inoculated on Sabouraud's dextrose agar (SDA) and other media (pH 5.4–5.6). SDA with chloramphenicol (50 mg/L) and that with cyclohexamide (500 mg/L) help to prevent growth of bacteria and saprobic fungi, respectively. Brain–heart infusion agar and brain–heart infusion agar with chloramphenicol and cyclohexamide can also be used as alternative.
- Slants of media are used commonly as slants in tubes are resistant to drying.
- Two slants of SDA are inoculated routinely. One of them is incubated at room temperature (25°C) and another at body temperature (37°C) for 2–3 weeks (up to 6 weeks). Most of the cultures become positive in 10 days.

Identification

The culture media are observed for growth and identification of fungi is done based on the following:

- Macroscopic appearance
- Microscopic morphology—wet mount or tease mount in lactophenol cotton blue
- Physiological and nutritional tests
- Nucleic acid probes

Antifungal susceptibility testing

Antifungal susceptibility testing can be performed by

- Disc diffusion method
- Broth dilution method

Indirect methods

Serological tests

Many serological tests can be used for diagnosis of various fungal infections. These include the following:

- Complement fixation test for blastomycosis, coccidioidomycosis, histoplamosis, paracoccidioidomycosis, etc.
- Agar gel diffusion for aspergillosis, blastomycosis, candidiasis, coccidioidomycosis, paracoccidioidomycosis, histoplasmosis, etc.
- Indirect immunofluorescence test for cryptococcosis
- Latex agglutination test for candidiasis, cryptococcosis, sporotrichosis, etc.

Animal inoculation

- Animal inoculation test is used
  - To determine pathogenicity
  - To demonstrate the yeast form of fungus causing systemic infections
- Animals used are mice, rats, guinea pigs, rabbits, hamsters, etc.

- Route of inoculation are percutaneous, subcutaneous, intravenous, intraperitoneal or intratesticular.
- Results are obtained after 2–3 weeks—lesions are studied and fungi are demonstrated microscopically or isolated from the lesions.

Antifungal agents

- Amphotericin B
- Nystatin
- Griseofulvin
- Miconazole
- Tolnaftate
- Clotrimazole
- Ketoconazole
- Fluconazole
- Itraconazole
- Flucytosine
- Potassium iodide
- Selenium sulphide
- Gentian violet
- Sodium hyposulphate
- Salicylic acid

Self-assessment

Long-answer question

1. Discuss in detail the laboratory diagnosis of fungal infections.

Short-answer questions

Write notes on

1. Difference between fungi and bacteria
2. Classification of fungi

Multiple-choice questions

1. Which of the following is true yeast?
   A. *Candida albicans*
   B. *Histoplasma capsulatum*
   C. *Cryptococcus neoformans*
   D. *Blastomyces dermatitidis*
2. Fungi with true mycelium are called
   A. Moulds
   B. Yeast
   C. Yeast-like fungi
   D. Dimorphic fungi
3. Fungi in which sexual process is not observed are placed in a group known as
   A. Dimorphic fungi
   B. Yeast
   C. Yeast-like fungi
   D. Fungi imperfecti
4. Asexual reproductive structures borne exogenously on specialized hyphae are called
   A. Arthrospores
   B. Blastospores
   C. Chlamydospores
   D. Conidia
5. Fungal spores formed by fragmentation of hyphae are called
   A. Arthrospores
   B. Blastospores
   C. Chlamydospores
   D. Basidiospores
6. Which of the following is a component of fungal cell wall?
   A. Teichoic acid
   B. Lipopolysaccharides
   C. Chitin
   D. Peptidoglycan
7. Which of the following is a dimorphic fungus?
   A. *Candida albicans*
   B. *Histoplasma capsulatum*
   C. *Cryptococcus neoformans*
   D. *Aspergillus niger*
8. Which of the following is the most commonly used technique for direct demonstration of fungi in clinical specimens?
   A. India Ink wet mount
   B. Lactophenol cotton blue mount
   C. KOH mount
   D. Gram stain
9. Which of the following statements is TRUE about chlamydospores?
   A. Are sexual spores
   B. Are asexual spores
   C. Are formed by fragmentation of hyphae
   D. Are formed by budding

46 Common Fungal Pathogens in General and Dental Infections

Fungal infections are called mycoses. Mycoses can be divided into two types:

1. Superficial mycoses
2. Deep mycoses

Superficial mycoses

Superficial mycoses are of two types:

1. Surface infections
2. Cutaneous infections

Surface infections

Infections of the outermost epithelial tissue produce cosmetic effects only. These fungi do not elicit allergic response because they are not in contact with living tissue. These include

- Tinea versicolor (pityriasis versicolor)
- Tinea nigra
- Piedra

Tinea versicolor (pityriasis versicolor)

Causative agent

Tinea versicolor is caused due to *Pityrosporum orbiculare,* also known as *Malassezia furfar*—a lipophilic yeast-like fungus that requires oil or fat for its growth.

Clinical features

Infection of the horny layer of the epidermis characterized by

- White-, brown- or fawn-coloured superficial macular areas on the chest, abdomen, back and upper limbs
- Non-inflammatory
- Occasional redness of skin and pruritus

Laboratory diagnosis

KOH mount of skin scrapings is observed for the presence of short, curved, non-branched, mycelial filaments (2.5–4 μm in size) and clusters of spherical yeast cells.

Treatment

Application of

- Mild sulphur ointments—sodium thiosulphate (20%)
- Mild fungicidal and keratolytic ointment, Whitfield ointment
- Imidazole cream

Tinea nigra

Causative agent

Tinea nigra is caused due to *Cladosporium mansoni* in Asia and Africa, and *Cladosporium werneckii* in America.

Clinical features

It is characterized by brown to black macular areas on thick epidermis (stratum corneum) of palms and soles.

Laboratory diagnosis

- KOH mount of skin scrapings shows brown, branched, septate hyphae (1–5 μm) and budding yeast cells (1–3 μm).
- Culture on SDA shows a greenish black colony.

Treatment

- Fungicides and keratolytic ointments such as Whitfield ointment
- Topical miconazole

Piedra

It is of two types: black piedra and white piedra (Table 46.1).

Laboratory diagnosis

- KOH mount of infected hair shows nodules containing asci having ascospores in black piedra.
- Arthrospores are seen in white piedra.

Treatment

- Removal of hair by shaving
- 5% salicylic acid
- 1% iodine
- Imidazole derivatives

Table 46.1 Differences between black and white piedra

Black piedra	White piedra
• **Causative agent** *Piedraia hortae*	*Trichosporon beigelii*
• **Clinical features** Black, hard nodules along the hair shaft	Soft, mucilaginous, white to light brown nodules on or within hairs
• Firmly adherent	Loosely adherent

Cutaneous infections

Cutaneous infections include the infections of the cornified layer of the skin and its appendages. These infections are caused by dermatophytes, which elicit allergic and inflammatory response.

- These are infections of superficial keratinized tissues—the skin, hair and nails.
- These infections are caused by dermatophytes and are called dermatophytosis, also known as 'ringworm' or tinea.
- Dermatophytes break down and utilize keratin and are unable to penetrate the subcutaneous tissue.

Classification of dermatophytes

Dermatophytes are moulds or filamentous fungi with true mycelia and are classified into three genera based on asexual spores known as macroconidia (Fig. 46.1).

Trichophyton Microscopic examination shows abundant club- or pear-shaped microconidia arranged in clusters and a few pencil-shaped macroconidia. They infect skin, nails and hair.

- **Important species** are *T. rubrum, T. mentagrophytes, T. violaceum, T. tonsurans* and others.

Microsporum It shows few microconidia which are not distinctive, and many large fusiform to spindle-shaped, 5–150 μm in size, rough-walled macroconidia. They infect hair and skin.

- **Important species** are *M. gypseum, M. canis* and *M. audouinii.*

Epidermophyton Microconidia are absent, and macroconidia are multicellular, club- or pear-shaped, one to five celled, 8–30 μm in size,

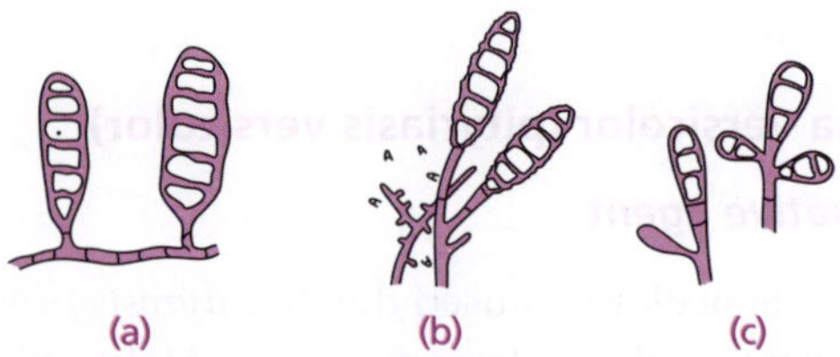

Figure 46.1 Macroconidia of dermatophytes. (a) Trichophyton. (b) Microsporum. (c) Epidermophyton.

thin walled and typically arranged in clusters. They infect skin and nails.

- **Important species** is *E. floccosum.*

Clinical features

They cause dermatophytoses (ringworm or tinea).

Transmission

- It occurs by
  - Direct contact with an infected human or animal
  - Agency of an object on which dermatophytes may survive for months
  - Infected hair of animal
- A single species of dermatophyte may be involved in several types of diseases and the same clinical entity may be caused by different species.
- Clinically, ringworm can be classified based on the site of involvement as follows:
  - Tinea capitis—ringworm of scalp
  - Tinea corporis—ringworm of non-hairy skin
  - Tinea cruris—ringworm of groin
  - Tinea pedis—ringworm of foot (athlete's foot)
  - Tinea barbae—ringworm of beard (barber's itch)
  - Tinea unguium—ringworm of nails
  - Tinea manuum—ringworm of hand

Laboratory diagnosis

- **Collection of specimens** Infected hair, nails or skin scrapings are collected for direct microscopy and culture
- Specimens must be processed immediately
- **Microscopy** KOH mount of specimen is observed for fungal elements
- **Culture** On SDA—incubated at 25–30°C for 3 weeks; any growth on SDA is identified based on
  - Colony morphology
  - Pigment production
  - Microscopic morphology of hyphae, microconidia, macroconidia, etc., by lactophenol cotton blue preparation
- **Serological tests** These are generally not useful in the diagnosis

Treatment

- Oral griseofulvin, ketoconazole and itraconazole
- Topical antifungal agents
  - Clotrimazole
  - Tolnaftate

Deep mycoses

Deep mycoses may be classified as follows:

- Subcutaneous mycoses—mycoses of subcutaneous tissues
- Systemic mycoses—mycoses of internal organs (deep-seated mycoses)

Subcutaneous mycoses They include

- Mycotic mycetoma
- Chromomycosis
- Sporotrichosis
- Rhinosporidiosis
- Subcutaneous phycomycosis

Systemic mycoses They include

- Cryptococcosis
- Blastomycosis
- Paracoccidioidomycosis
- Coccidioidomycosis
- Histoplasmosis

Subcutaneous mycoses

Mycetoma

- Mycetoma is a chronic granulomatous infection of the subcutaneous tissue, usually of the foot and rarely of other parts of the body.
- It was first observed in Madura region of India and hence known as Madura foot or Madura mycosis.

Aetiology (causative agents)

Soil fungi, Actinomycetes and bacteria are the causes of mycetoma.

- **Fungi** Mycetoma caused by fungi is known as **eumycetoma**. The fungi causing mycetoma are
  - *Acremonium* species
  - *Madurella mycetomi*
  - *Madurella grisea*
  - *Pseudallescheria boydii*
- **Actinomycetes** Mycetoma caused by Actinomycetes is known as **actinomycetoma**. The Actinomycetes causing mycetoma are
  - *Actinomyces israelii* and other species
  - *Nocardia brasiliensis* and other species
  - *Actinomadura madurae*
  - *Streptomyces somaliensis*
- **Bacteria** Mycetoma caused by bacteria is known as bacterial mycetoma or **botryomycosis**. The bacteria causing mycetoma are
  - *Staphylococcus aureus*
  - Streptococci
  - *Pseudomonas*
  - *Proteus*

Pathogenesis

- The causative agents enter through minor trauma into the subcutaneous tissue (usually foot, hand or back) and may extend through muscle up to bone.
- The disease begins as a small subcutaneous swelling of the foot, which enlarges burrowing into the deeper tissues—produces abscess.
- The abscess bursts with the formation of chronic multiple sinuses discharging viscid, seropurulent fluid containing granules.

Laboratory diagnosis

- Aetiological diagnosis—it is important in choosing proper treatment.
- Demonstration of granules—it is of diagnostic value.
- Colour of granules—they are white in actinomycetoma and usually black in mycotic mycetoma.
- Examination of crushed smear of granules helps in differentiation of actinomycetoma from eumycetoma.
- Culture helps in definitive diagnosis.

Treatment

- Actinomycetoma—tetracycline, streptomycin, amikacin, sulphonamides and sulphones
- Eumycetoma—oral ketoconazole or itraconazole and radical surgery

Chromomycosis

It is a slowly progressive granulomatous infection of the skin and subcutaneous tissue.

Aetiological agents

It is caused by several species of darkly pigmented fungi. These include

- *Fonsecaea* species
- *Cladosporium* species
- *Phialophora* species

Pathogenesis

- The fungi enter through skin or subcutaneous tissue of legs or feet by traumatic implantation.
- Lesions are developed slowly around implantation.
- The most common form of chromomycosis is known as **chromoblastomycosis** or **verrucous dermatitis.**
- The lesions are wart-like nodules, which resemble the flower of cauliflower.
- They also cause phaeohyphomycosis.
- Phaeohyphomycosis includes localized or systemic infections—cutaneous, subcutaneous, deeper tissues or organs such as brain or lung.

Laboratory diagnosis

- KOH mount for demonstration of fungi
- Culture on SDA—black colonies and characteristic conidiophore
- Histopathological demonstration of sclerotic bodies in KOH mounts and H&E staining

Treatment

- Amphotericin B, 5-fluorocytosine and thiabendazole
- May require surgical removal and skin grafting
- Cryotherapy, laser therapy, surgery and thermotherapy

Sporotrichosis

It is a chronic granulomatous disease of the skin and subcutaneous tissue.

The aetiological agent is *Sporothrix schenckii.* It is a dimorphic fungus which occurs as yeast (3–5 μm in diameter), as well as in filamentous form—small, ovoid branching with septate hyphae.

Pathogenicity

- Fungus is introduced through thorn pricks or other minor injuries.
- It usually affects hand or forearm.
- It is characterized by
  - Pustule, abscess or ulcer
  - Multiple subcutaneous nodules, which break down to form indolent ulcers—sluggish, painless, slow to heal
- The fungus spreads through lymphatics up to regional lymph nodes.
- Sometimes disseminated lesions are present, especially in debilitated patients.
- **Oral manifestations** It causes non-specific ulceration of the oral, nasal and pharyngeal mucosa, usually associated with regional lymphadenopathy.

Laboratory diagnosis

- **Direct microscopy** Demonstration of fungus in pus or tissue by Gram stain or Giemsa stain
- **Culture** On SDA—as fungus may not be demonstrable by direct microscopy
- **Animal inoculation** In mice or rat. It produces characteristic disease in 2–3 weeks
- **Serology text** Latex agglutination test

Treatment

- Generally, self-limited
- Saturated solution of potassium iodide for cutaneous and lymphatic form
- In systemic disease—amphotericin B, itraconazole and ketoconazole

Rhinosporidiosis

- It is a chronic granulomatous disease caused by *Rhinosporidium seeberi*—an endosporulating fungus seen in the tissues.
- The fungus forms a characteristic thick-walled sporangium filled with endospores (Fig. 46.2).

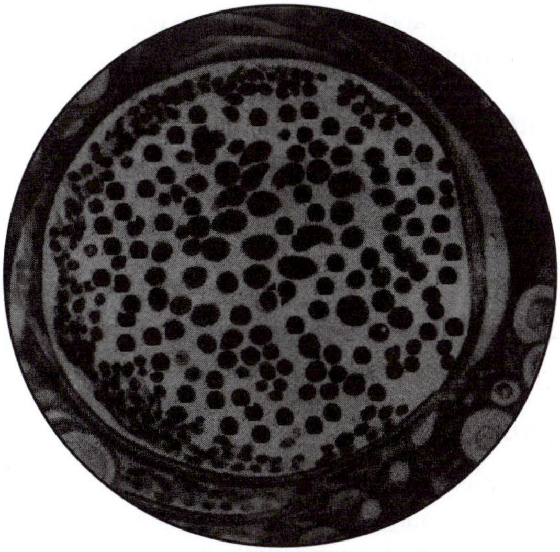

Figure 46.2 *Rhinosporidium seeberi*—sporangium filled with endospores.

Pathogenicity

- The fungus produces small tumour-like masses (friable polyps) usually in the nose, mouth or eyes and rarely affects the vagina, rectum, male urethra and bronchi.
- The oropharyngeal lesions appear as friable, red-coloured, highly vascular, polypoid mass, which spreads to pharynx and larynx. It bleeds easily on touching.
- The infection is probably acquired by bathing or diving in infected water.

Laboratory diagnosis

- Demonstration of sporangia in connective tissue by H&E stain. The sporangium is 10–200 µm in diameter and contains thousands of endospores.
- Fungus cannot be cultivated on laboratory media.

Treatment

- Radical surgery is the first choice.
- Dapsone is used for treating recurrences.

Subcutaneous phycomycosis

It is caused by *Basidiobolus haptosporus*—it is a saprophytic phycomycete found in decaying vegetation and in the intestine of many reptiles and amphibians.

Pathogenesis

It produces a painless subcutaneous nodule, which enlarges to involve a whole limb or a large area of the body.

Systemic mycoses

Cryptococcosis

Causative agent

It is caused by *Cryptococcus neoformans*—Gram-positive, round or oval budding yeast cells, 4–20 µm in diameter with a polysaccharide capsule (Fig. 46.3). It is a true yeast that grows on SDA.

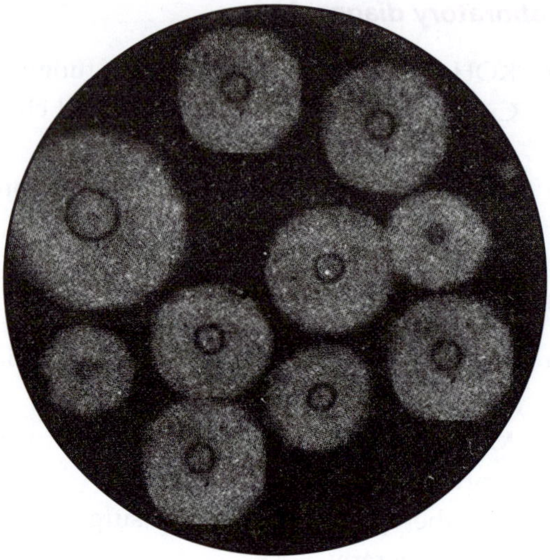

Figure 46.3 *Cryptococcus neoformans.*

Pathogenicity

- Infection occurs by inhalation, sometimes through skin or mucus.
- **Clinical features** It causes opportunistic infections.
- Pulmonary cryptococcosis may lead to mild pneumonia.
- Dissemination of infection leads to visceral, cutaneous and meningeal diseases.
- Cryptococcal meningitis—serious disease occurs in patients with AIDS and other immunocompromised individuals.
- Visceral cryptococcosis resembles tuberculosis or cancer clinically.
- **Oral cryptococcosis** rarely occurs in patients with cutaneous or visceral cryptococcosis. It occurs as non-specific single or multiple ulcers.

Laboratory diagnosis

- **Specimens** Sputum, cerebrospinal fluid, pus, etc.
- Demonstration of fungus by
  - Simple wet mount
  - Negative stain (India ink)
  - Gram stain
  - Immunofluorescence stain

- Histopathological stains
- **Culture** On SDA
- **Animal inoculation** For pathogenicity testing in mice
- **Serological tests**
  - For antigen detection—latex agglutination and countercurrent immunoelectrophoresis (CIEP)
  - For antibodies detection—indirect immunofluorescence test

Treatment

- 5-Fluorocytosine
- Amphotericin B
- Miconazole

Blastomycosis

Causative agent

- ***Blastomyces dermatitidis*** It is a dimorphic fungus, which grows as a round, 8–15 µm, multinucleated budding yeast in the tissue and as a mould in a culture at room temperature.
- Mycelia show septate hyphae—form blastospores.

Pathogenicity—North American blastomycosis

- It is present in soil—infection occurs by inhalation.
- Primary infection of lung may resemble tuberculosis or histoplasmosis.
- Infection from lung may spread to other parts of the body such as skin, bone and urogenital tract, and form multiple abscesses in various parts of the body.
- Cutaneous lesions on the skin of face or other exposed parts of the body. The initial lesion is a papule around which secondary nodules develop and coalesce to form large elevated ulcerative lesions.
- **Oral manifestations** May occur as primary lesion or secondary to lesions elsewhere in the body. Clinically, it may resemble actinomycosis. Tiny ulcer formation may be the main feature and abscess formation is not as prominent as seen in actinomycosis.

Laboratory diagnosis

- **Specimens** Sputum, pus and skin scrapings
- **Direct microscopy** For demonstration of fungus by
  - KOH mount
  - Direct immunofluorescence test
  - Histopathological staining techniques
- **Culture** On SDA
- **Animal inoculation** Done in mice or guinea pigs or rabbit; blastospores are injected intravenously or intraperitoneally and observed for death of animal in 6–20 days. The fungi are demonstrated in lesions
- **Serological tests** Include complement fixation test and immunodiffusion test

Treatment

- Amphotericin B
- Ketoconazole

Paracoccidioidomycosis

Causative agent

- *Paracoccidioides brasiliensis* is a dimorphic fungus. In tissues it forms thick-walled, 10–60 yeast cells that have more than one bud. At room temperature (25°C) in culture, it grows as mycelial phase.

Pathogenicity—paracoccidioidomycosis (South American blastomycosis)

- Infection occurs by inhalation.
- Primary lesions in lung—spread to spleen, liver, skin and mucous membrane may occur by haematogenous route producing chronic granulomatous reaction.
- Lymph node enlargement and gastrointestinal disturbances are also seen.
- **Oral manifestations** Ulcerative granulomas of the buccal and nasal mucosa are prominent features. Papillary lesions of the oral mucosa

occur following teeth extraction. Widespread oral ulceration is also commonly seen.

Laboratory diagnosis

It is the same as for blastomycosis.

- **Specimens** Sputum, pus, biopsies from granulomatous lesions
- **Direct microscopy** For demonstration of characteristics yeast cells by
  - KOH mount of specimen
  - Histopathological techniques
- **Culture** On SDA
- **Animal inoculation** By intratesticular route
- **Serological tests** CFT and immunodiffusion

Treatment

- Itraconazole
- Fluconazole with amphotericin B
- Ketoconazole

Coccidioidomycosis

Causative agent

- *Coccidioides immitis* is a dimorphic fungus. In the body it occurs as a spherule, 20–100 µm in size, with double wall and contains a large number of endospores. At room temperature (25°C), it grows as a mould—forms arthrospores.

Pathogenicity

- Infection occurs by inhalation of arthrospores, which develop into spherules in the body.
- Generally, infection is asymptomatic.
- Many persons develop a self-limited influenza-like fever to severe pneumonia.
- In less than 1% of persons, disseminated disease (coccidioidal granuloma) occurs, which is highly fatal and resembles disseminated tuberculosis.
- Meningitis, skin and mucosal lesions, and bone lesions may also occur.
- **Oral manifestations** Proliferative granulomatous and ulcerated lesions on oral mucosa—non-specific in clinical appearance. Lytic lesions of the jaws may also occur.

Laboratory diagnosis

- **Specimens** Sputum, pus, CSF and biopsy specimens
- **Direct microscopy** For demonstration of spherules in specimens
- **Culture** On SDA
- **Animal inoculation** In mice—intraperitoneally
- **Serological tests** Latex agglutination test, CFT, etc.

Treatment

- Amphotericin B
- Ketoconazole

Histoplasmosis (Darling disease)

Causative agent

- *Histoplasma capsulatum* is a dimorphic fungus. At room temperature (25°C), it grows as mould and in tissues and at 37°C it forms oval uninucleate cells, 2–4 µm in size (Fig. 46.4). The mould form shows two types of conidia:
  - Macroconidia—large (8–14 µm)
  - Microconidia—small (2–4 µm)

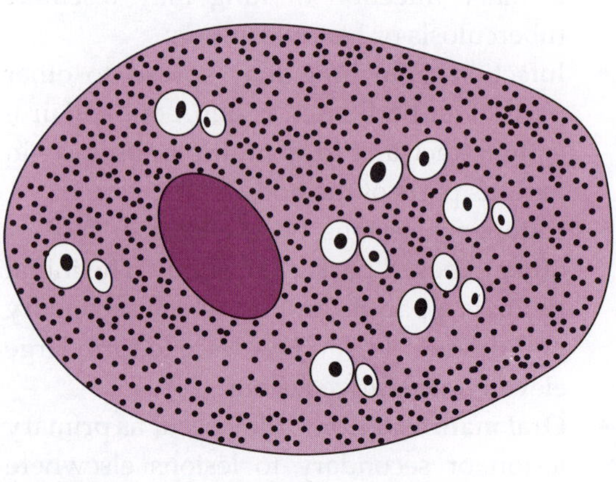

Figure 46.4 *Histoplasma capsulatum.*

Pathogenicity

- Infection occurs by inhalation of conidia, which are engulfed by alveolar macrophages and converted into yeast cells.
- Generally, infection is asymptomatic.
- Some individuals develop pulmonary disease, which resembles tuberculosis.
- Severe disseminated histoplasmosis develops in infants, aged or immunocompromised individuals.
- The reticuloendothelial system may be invaded with resultant lymphadenopathy, hepatosplenomegaly, anaemia and high-grade fever, and it could be the cause of a high rate of fatality.
- Granulomatous and ulcerative lesions may develop on skin and mucosa.
- **Oral manifestations** It manifests as nodular, ulcerative or vegetative lesions on the buccal mucosa, gingiva, tongue, palate or lips.

Laboratory diagnosis

- **Specimens** Sputum, urine, blood, scrapings from lesions, biopsies from lymph node and other lesions
- **Direct microscopy** For demonstration of intracellular yeast cells in specimens by
  - Direct immunofluorescence test
  - Giemsa or Wright stain
  - Histopathological techniques
- **Culture** Grows on SDA
- **Serological tests** Latex agglutination, precipitation, CFT and immunodiffusion test

Treatment

- Amphotericin B
- Ketoconazole

Opportunistic mycoses

Candidiasis

Causative agents

- *Candida albicans* and other species of *Candida* are the causative agents.
- *C. albicans* is a yeast-like fungus that produces both yeast-like cells and pseudohyphae.
- Yeast-like cells are oval, budding cells, 2–3 µm by 4–6 µm in size and Gram-positive.
- Pseudohyphae are Gram-positive, elongated budding cells resembling hyphae.
- It forms blastospores and chlamydospores (Fig. 46.5).

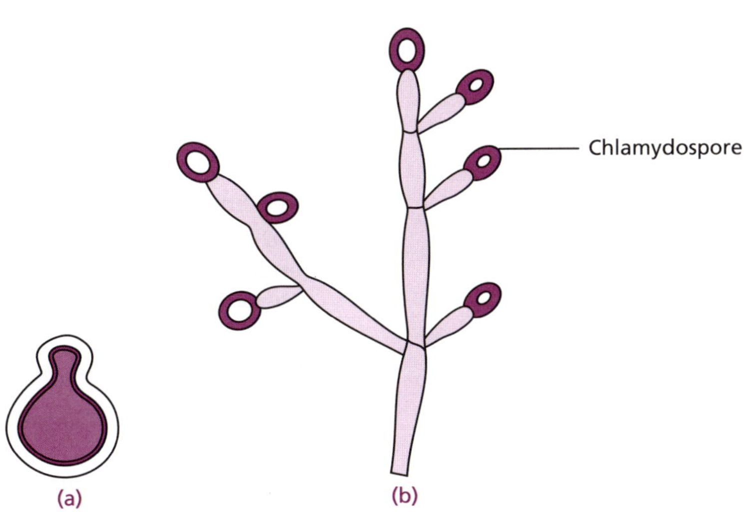

Figure 46.5 *Candida albicans.* (a) Budding yeast. (b) Pseudohyphae with chlamydospores.

- Culture grows on SDA. It also grows on blood agar and nutrient agar.

Pathogenicity

- It is normally present on skin, in mouth, in the intestine and in vagina, and produces infection when natural resistance is compromised; therefore, it is known as an opportunistic pathogen.
- The important predisposing factors are
  - Diabetes
  - Immunodeficiency
  - Malignancy
  - Prolonged administration of antibiotics
  - Immunosuppressive therapy
  - IV drug abuse

Clinical picture

- **Mucosal lesions**
  - Oral thrush
  - Vulvovaginitis
  - Balanitis
  - Conjunctivitis
  - Keratitis
- **Skin infections**
  - Infections of moist and warm parts of the body such as the maxilla, intergluteal fold, groin and submammary folds
  - Infections of interdigital webs of the hands in a person immersing hands in water repeatedly
- **Nail infections**
  - Paronychia
  - Onychia
- **Systemic candidiasis**
  - Urinary tract infections
  - Pulmonary candidiasis
  - Candida endocarditis
  - Intestinal candidiasis—following prolonged oral antibiotic therapy
  - Meningitis
  - Septicaemia
- Candida granuloma and chronic mucocutaneous candidiasis in immunodeficiencies
- **Oral manifestations** The oral lesions in candidiasis include
  - Acute pseudomembranous candidiasis (oral thrush)—characterized by soft, milky white and slightly elevated plaques commonly seen on the buccal mucosa and tongue, also seen on the palate, gingiva and floor of the mouth
  - Acute atrophic candidiasis—characterized by red or erythematosus lesions, which may occur at any site in the oral cavity
  - Chronic hyperplastic candidiasis—characterized by formation of firm, white, persistent leucoplakia type of plaques on the lips, tongue and cheeks (these lesions may persist for years together)
  - Chronic atrophic candidiasis—characterized by a diffuse inflammation of the denture bearing area often with angular cheilitis (more common in females)

Laboratory diagnosis

- **Specimens** Skin scrapings, material from nail, mouth, vagina, urine, sputum, blood, CSF, etc.
- **Direct microscopy** *C. albicans* normally present in most specimens, hence only abundant presence significant
- Material is observed for pseudohyphae and budding yeast cells by
  - Gram staining
  - Wet mount
  - KOH mount
- **Culture** On SDA—growth identified by biochemical reactions, germ tube formation, chlamydospores formation, etc.
- **Serological tests** As positive in normal individuals also not much important in diagnosis

Treatment

- Nystatin, miconazole, clotrimazole and ketoconazole for topical application
- Amphotericin B, ketoconazole, itraconazole, fluconazole and 5-fluorocytosine for systemic infection

- Gentian violet for oral thrush

Aspergillosis

Causative agent

- *Aspergillus fumigatus, A. flavus, A. niger* and other species (Fig. 46.6)

Clinical picture

Three clinical forms:

1. Respiratory disease such as
   - Allergic pulmonary aspergillosis—aspergillus asthma
   - Bronchopulmonary aspergillosis
   - Colonizing aspergillosis—aspergilloma
2. Invasive aspergillosis—fungus invades lung tissue causing necrotizing pneumonia or haemoptysis and secondarily disseminates to organs such as kidney, brain and heart
3. Superficial infections—sinusitis, mycotic keratitis, otomycosis, etc.

Laboratory diagnosis

- **Specimens** Sputum, bronchoalveolar lavage, tissue biopsies, etc.
- **Direct microscopy** For demonstration of fungus by KOH mount and by histopathological staining techniques
- **Culture** On SDA—colonies appear within 1–4 days
  - *A. fumigatus*—green colonies
  - *A. niger*—black colonies
- **Serological tests** For antibody detection include immunodiffusion, CFT, immunoelectrophoresis and indirect immunofluorescence test

Treatment

- Amphotericin B
- Itraconazole

Zygomycosis

It includes mucormycosis and entomophthoromycosis.

Causative agents

Three genera of class Zygomycetes (Fig. 46.7):

1. *Mucor* species
2. *Rhizopus* species
3. *Absidia* species

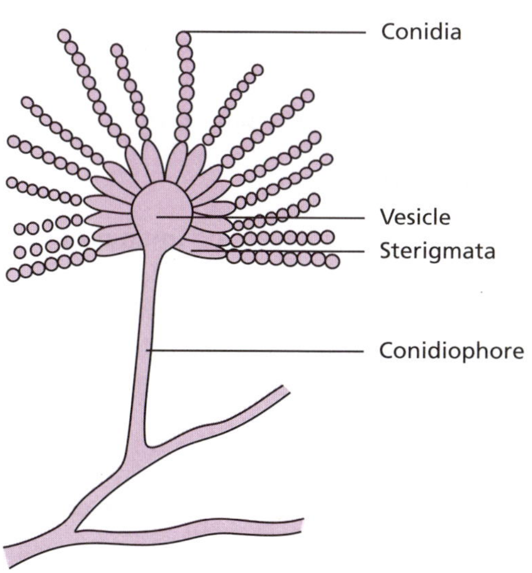

Figure 46.6 *Aspergillus* species.

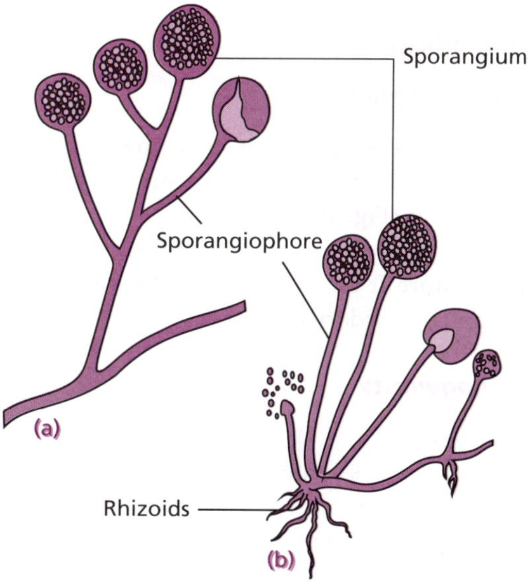

Figure 46.7 Zygomycetes. (a) *Mucor* species. (b) *Rhizopus* species.

Pathogenicity

- Cause disease in immunocompromized persons
- Primary infection—in upper respiratory tract or nose
- Rhinocerebral infection may occur because of spreading of fungus from nasal mucosa to turbinate bone, paranasal sinuses, orbit and brain
- Other infections include
  - Pulmonary mucormycosis—pneumonia
  - Gastrointestinal mucormycosis
  - Invasion of artery leading to thrombosis and infarction
- Entomophthoromycosis is infection of the subcutaneous tissue or paranasal sinuses

Laboratory diagnosis

- **Specimens** Nasal discharge, sputum, pus and scrapings from the lesions
- **Direct microscopy** Demonstration of non-septate hyphae by
  - KOH mount
  - Histopathological staining technique
- **Culture** On SDA
- **Treatment** Amphotericin B

Penicilliosis

Causative agent

- *Penicillium* species is a saprophytic fungus and has a brush-like arrangement of conidia (Fig. 46.8).
- Very rarely, it causes opportunistic infections.
- **Culture** It grows on SDA and forms blue-green powdery colony.

Pathogenicity

It causes
- Otomycosis—infection of external ear
- Keratitis
- Deep infections—rarely

Laboratory diagnosis

- **Specimens** Scrapings from ear and eyes

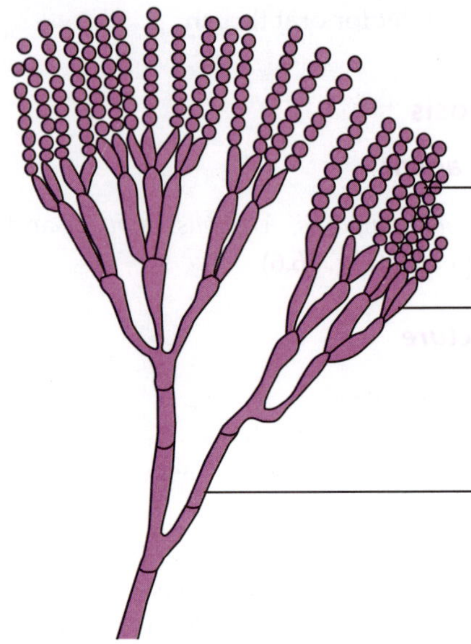

Figure 46.8 *Penicillium* species.

- **Microscopy** KOH mount
- **Culture** On SDA

Other types of opportunistic mycoses

Pneumocystis pneumonia

Causative agent

- *Pneumocystis carinii* is divided into two stages:
  - Trophozoite—1–4 μm in size
  - Cysts—four to eight nucleated, spherical in shape, 4–6 μm in size

Pathogenicity

- Causes pneumonia in immunocompromised patients
- Most common opportunistic pathogen in AIDS and major cause of death among patients with AIDS

Laboratory diagnosis

- **Specimens** Bronchoalveolar lavage, lung biopsy and sputum
- **Direct microscopy** For demonstration of fungus by

- Giemsa stain
- Silver methenamine stain
- Direct fluorescent antibody staining
- Calcofluor white stain

Treatment

- Trimethoprim–sulphamethoxazole
- Pentamidine

Otomycosis

- Fungal infection of the external auditory canal—very common
- Caused by *Aspergillus, Penicillium, Candida* species, etc.
- Symptoms—itching pain and deafness
- Secondary bacterial infections by *Pseudomonas* and *Proteus* species may occur
- **Laboratory diagnosis** Demonstration of fungus in scrapings and culture on SDA

Oculomycosis

- A fungal infection of the cornea—keratomycosis (mycotic keratitis or fungal keratitis) usually occurs following the corneal trauma
- Fungal spores—colonize the injured tissue and initiate the inflammatory reaction leading to hypopyon ulcer and endophthalmitis
- Use of corticosteroids—increase the risk of keratomycosis
- Causative agents—*Aspergillus, Fusarium* and *Candida* species
- **Laboratory diagnosis** Examination of deep scrapings for fungus
- **Treatment** Local application of amphotericin B, nystatin and pimaricin

Self-assessment

Long-answer questions

1. Discuss in brief the deep mycotic infections.
2. Enumerate opportunistic fungi. Discuss in brief the pathogenicity and laboratory diagnosis of candidiasis.

Short-answer questions

Write notes on

1. Surface infections
2. Tinea versicolor
3. Piedra
4. Tinea nigra
5. Dermatophytes
6. Mycetoma
7. Rhinosporidiosis
8. Cryptococcosis
9. Histoplasmosis
10. Candidiasis
11. Oral manifestations in candidiasis
12. Blastomycosis
13. Aspergillosis
14. Opportunistic fungi
15. Otomycosis and oculomycosis
16. *Pneumocystis carinii*

Multiple-choice questions

1. Which of the following fungi is a cause of pityriasis versicolor?
   A. *Malassezia furfar*
   B. *Cladosporium mansoni*
   C. *Trichosporon beigelii*
   D. *Piedra hortae*
2. All of the following are the surface fungal infections, EXCEPT
   A. Tinea versicolor
   B. Tinea nigra
   C. Dermatophytosis
   D. Piedra
3. Which of the following fungi is the cause of cutaneous infections?
   A. *Malassezia furfar*
   B. *Cladosporium mansoni*
   C. *Trichophyton rubrum*
   D. *Piedra hortae*
4. Which of the following statements is FALSE about ringworm?
   A. Is caused by dermatophytes
   B. Is subcutaneous mycosis
   C. Is also known as tinea or dermatophytoses

D. Is transmitted by direct contact with infected human or animal

5. Which of the following genera is NOT included in the dermatophytes?
   A. *Epidermophyton* spp.
   B. *Microsporum* spp.
   C. *Trichophyton* spp.
   D. *Trichosporon* spp.

6. All of the following are the fungi causing mycetoma, EXCEPT
   A. *Actinomadura madurae*
   B. *Acremonium* species
   C. *Madurella mycetomi*
   D. *Pseudallescheria boydii*

7. Which of the following is a subcutaneous fungal infection?
   A. Dermatophytoses
   B. Mucormycosis
   C. Sporotrichosis
   D. Coccidioidomycosis

8. Which of the following is the commonest site for rhinosporidiosis?
   A. Nose
   B. Mouth
   C. Eyes
   D. Vagina

9. Which of the following is capsulated fungus?
   A. *Candida albicans*
   B. *Histoplasma capsulatum*
   C. *Cryptococcus neoformans*
   D. *Blastomyces dermatitidis*

10. Which of the following fungi is responsible for oral thrush?
    A. *Candida albicans*
    B. *Histoplasma capsulatum*
    C. *Cryptococcus neoformans*
    D. *Blastomyces dermatitidis*

11. All of the following are the opportunistic fungal infections, EXCEPT
    A. Rhinosporidiosis
    B. Mucormycosis
    C. Candidiasis
    D. Aspergillosis

12. Which of the following is a causative agent of South American blastomycosis?
    A. *Coccidioides immitis*
    B. *Histoplasma capsulatum*
    C. *Paracoccidioides brasiliensis*
    D. *Blastomyces dermatitidis*

13. Which of the following fungi occurs as a spherule in the body?
    A. *Histoplasma capsulatum*
    B. *Coccidioides immitis*
    C. *Paracoccidioides brasiliensis*
    D. *Blastomyces dermatitidis*

14. Which of the following fungi is a cause of Darling disease?
    A. *Coccidioides immitis*
    B. *Histoplasma capsulatum*
    C. *Paracoccidioides brasiliensis*
    D. *Blastomyces dermatitidis*

15. Which of the following fungi is the most common opportunistic pathogen in HIV/AIDS disease?
    A. *Coccidioides immitis*
    B. *Histoplasma capsulatum*
    C. *Paracoccidioides brasiliensis*
    D. *Pneumocystis carinii*

16. Which of the following fungi is a cause of otomycosis?
    A. *Penicillium* spp.
    B. *Histoplasma* spp.
    C. *Paracoccidioides* spp.
    D. *Blastomyces* spp.

17. Which of the following fungi is commonly associated with oculomycosis?
    A. *Coccidioides* spp.
    B. *Aspergillus* spp.
    C. *Paracoccidioides* spp.
    D. *Blastomyces* spp.

18. Which of the following refers to infection of hairs?
    A. Tinea versicolor
    B. Tinea nigra
    C. Piedra
    D. None of the above

47 Introduction to Parasitology

- Parasitology is the branch of microbiology that deals with the study of parasites.
- Medical parasitology is the study of medically important parasites—parasites causing diseases in humans.

Important terms used in the study of parasites

- **Parasite** An organism that is dependent on another living organism for its survival. It infects other living beings, lives in or on the body of another living being and obtains shelter and nourishment from it.
- **Host** An organism which harbours the parasite is known as host.
- **Ectoparasite** It is a parasite that lives outside on the surface of the body without penetrating the tissues, for example, lice, ticks and mites.
- **Endoparasite** It is a parasite that lives within the body of the host: in blood, tissues, body cavities and other organs, for example, all protozoan and helminthic parasites of humans.
- **Facultative parasite** It is a parasite which leads a parasitic life when it gets opportunity.
- **Obligatory parasite** It is a parasite which is completely dependent on the host and cannot exist without a parasitic life.
- **Definitive host** The host in which the adult stage of parasite lives or the sexual mode of reproduction takes place is called the definitive host.
- **Intermediate host** The host in which the larval stage of parasite lives or the asexual mode of reproduction takes place is called the intermediate host.
- **Reservoir host** The invertebrate species in which the parasite passes its life cycle and the host may act as the source of infection for humans is called reservoir host.
- **Paratenic host** It is a carrier or transport host (a vertebrate host) in which the parasite remains viable without further development or multiplication.
- Medical parasitology includes
  - Protozoology—study of protozoa
  - Helminthology—study of helminthes

Protozoology

- Protozoa are single-celled eukaryotic organisms possessing animal-like characteristics.
- They are the lowest form of animal life (*proto* means primitive, *zoo* means animal).
- They vary in size, shape, structure and physiological characteristics.
- They are microscopic in size but much larger than bacteria (1–70 μm).

- They are unicellular organisms with one or more nuclei. A single cell contains all structures required to perform various functions.
- The nucleus of cell controls various activities of the cell and regulates the process of reproduction.
- The multiplication occurs by binary fission or multiple fission or by sexual means.

Classification

Based on the organ of locomotion (motility), pathogenic protozoa are classified into four types:

1. **Rhizopoda** Protozoa which are motile with the help of pseudopodia. An example is, *Entamoeba histolytica,* causative agent of amoebiasis, amoebic dysentery, liver abscess and abscess in other organs
2. **Mastigophora** Protozoa which are motile with the help of flagella are of two types:
   - **Intestinal flagellates** Flagellates infecting intestine and vagina, for example, *Giardia lamblia* causing giardiasis and *Trichomonas vaginalis* causing trichomoniasis (vaginitis)
   - **Haemoflagellates** Flagellates infecting blood and tissues, for example, *Leishmania* species causing leishmaniasis and *Trypanosoma* species causing trypanosomiasis
3. **Sporozoa** Protozoa which are non-motile, for example, malarial parasites (*Plasmodium* species) causing malaria and *Toxoplasma* species causing toxoplasmosis
4. **Ciliata** Protozoa which are motile with the help of cilia, for example, *Balantidium coli* causing balantidiasis (dysentery)

Helminthology

- Helminthes are worms—metazoan parasites—multicellular, bilaterally symmetrical animals having three germ layers.
- Two main groups of importance:
  - **Platyhelminthes**—include cestodes and trematodes
  - **Nemathelminthes**—include nematodes
- The important differentiating features are summarized in Table 47.1.

Cestodes

- Cestodes are tape-like segmented worms with no separate sexes.
- Their size ranges from few millimetres to several metres.
- They occur in three different morphological forms:
  - **Adult worm**—found in the intestine of the definitive host, human and animal (definitive host, host in which the adult worm lives)

Table 47.1 Important differences between cestodes, trematodes and nematodes

Feature	Cestodes	Trematodes	Nematodes
Shape	Tape-like	Leaf-like	Elongated, cylindrical
Segmentation of body	Segmented	Unsegmented	Unsegmented
Sexes	• Not separate • Hermaphrodite (monoecious)	• Not separate • Hermaphrodite (monoecious), except schistosomes	Separate (diecious)
Head end	Suckers present, with hooks in some species	Suckers present, no hooks	• No suckers, no hooks • Some species have well-developed buccal capsule
Alimentary canal	Absent	Incomplete, no anus	Complete, anus present
Body cavity	Absent	Absent	Present

- **Eggs**—laid by adult worms passed in faeces
- **Larval stage**—seen in intermediate host (intermediate host— host in which larval stage of parasite lives)

- Adult worms have three parts as follows:
  - **Head (scolex)** is provided with slit-like or cup-like suckers and in some species hooks are present on scolex, which serve as organs of attachment.
  - **Neck** is the region behind the scolex.
  - **Strobilla (body or trunk)** consists of a series of segments called **proglottides**.
- Proglottides are formed continuously during the entire course of life of the adult worm. The newly formed proglottides are small and immature. The process of maturation progresses as the immature segments are pushed away from the neck due to formation of new proglottides. Mature proglottides contain fully developed reproductive organs. Each mature segment contains ovaries and testes (monoecious).
- Eggs are produced by self-fertilization or cross-fertilization. Eggs containing proglottides are the **gravid segments**.
- No body cavity and no mouth or digestive system is present. Food is absorbed through its body surface.
- They have a simple excretory system.

Classification of cestodes

Cestodes infecting humans are classified into two types:

1. **Pseudophyllidean cestodes** are cestodes possessing false or slit-like grooves, for example, *Diphyllobothrium latum* (fish tapeworm) causing diphyllobothriasis.
2. **Cyclophyllidean cestodes** are cestodes possessing cup-like round suckers, for example
   - *Taenia solium* (pork tapeworm) causing taeniasis or cysticercosis
   - *Taenia saginata* (beef tapeworm) causing taeniasis
   - *Echinococcus granulosus* (dog tapeworm) causing hydatid disease
   - *Hymenolepis nana* (dwarf tapeworm) causing hymenolepiasis

Trematodes

- Trematodes are leaf-like, unsegmented, flat worms with no separate sexes called flukes.
- Size varies from 1 mm to several centimetres in length.
- Sexes are not separate (monoecious) except the schistosomes, which are diecious.
- Head is with cup-shaped suckers but no hooks are present. Suckers serve as organs of attachment.
- Body cavity is absent.
- The alimentary canal is present but incomplete; the anus is absent.
- Excretory and nervous systems are present. Well-developed and complete reproductive system is present.
- Trematodes occur in three different morphological forms:
  - **Adult worm**—in definitive host, generally humans
  - **Eggs**—laid by adult worms gain access to the water
  - **Larval stage**—develops in water and enters a proper intermediate host (snail or crabs) for further development
- The worm is oviparous—liberates eggs. Eggs are operculated (except in schistosomes) and develop only in water.
- **Examples of important trematodes**
  - *Schistosoma* species causing schistosomiasis
  - *Fasciola hepatica* causing fascioliasis
  - *Fasciolopsis buski* causing fasciolopsiasis

Classification of trematodes

Trematodes infecting humans are classified as follows:

- **Intestinal trematodes (intestinal flukes)**
  - *F. buski*

  - *Gastrodiscoides hominis*
- **Hepatic trematodes (liver flukes)**
  - *F. hepatica*
  - *Clonorchis sinensis*
- **Lung trematodes (lung flukes)**
  - *Paragonimus westermani*
- **Blood trematodes (blood flukes)**
  - *Schistosoma haematobium*
  - *Schistosoma mansoni*
  - *Schistosoma japonicum*

Nematodes

- Nematodes are elongated, cylindrical, unsegmented worms with separate sexes (diecious). Male is smaller than female and its posterior end is curved ventrally.
- Size varies from 5 mm to 1 m.
- Nematodes possess a tough, acellular, hyaline cuticle.
- They possess a body cavity in which the various organs float.
- Digestive system is complete and consists of mouth, oesophagus, intestine and anus.
- Nematodes are diecious, that is, sexes are separate.
- Females are viviparous (produce larvae), oviparous (lay eggs) or ovoviviparous (lay eggs, which hatch immediately producing larvae).
- Moulting is a feature in development of nematode larvae. Moulting involves shedding of the old cuticle.

Classification of nematodes

Nematodes are classified into two types based on the habitat of the adult worms:

1. Intestinal nematodes
2. Tissue nematodes

Intestinal nematodes

- These are the nematodes inhabiting the intestine of a definitive host.
- Humans are the optimum host for all the nematodes.
- Only one host is required for intestinal nematodes.
- They occur in three different morphological forms:
  - **Adult worm**—found in the intestine of humans
  - **Eggs**—passed in stool
  - **Larvae**—develop from egg
- **Examples of the intestinal nematodes**
  - *Ascaris lumbricoides*—causing ascariasis
  - *Enterobius vermicularis*—causing enterobiasis
  - *Strongyloides stercoralis*—causing strongyloidiasis
  - *Ancylostoma duodenale* and *Necator americanus*—causing hookworm disease
  - *Trichinella spiralis* (eggs are not formed)—causing trichinellosis
  - *Trichuris trichiura*—causing trichuriasis

Tissue nematodes

- Nematodes invading tissues and organs
- Require two hosts to complete their life cycle
- Second host required for larval development
- Occur in two different morphological forms:
  - **Adult worm**—in a definitive host
  - **Larval stage**—in an insect vector or Cyclops
- **Examples of tissue nematodes**
  - *Wuchereria bancrofti*—causing lymphatic filariasis
  - *Brugia malayi*—causing lymphatic filariasis
  - *Loa loa*—causing loiasis
  - *Onchocerca volvulus*—causing onchocerciasis
  - *Dracunculus medinensis*—causing dracunculosis

Procedure used in the diagnosis of parasitic diseases

Laboratory diagnosis is an important part in the diagnosis of parasitic diseases. Each parasite possesses distinctive morphological feature; hence, study of morphology is helpful in the identification of parasitic organisms. As culture methods are routinely impracticable and serological methods are relatively less important in diagnosis, morphological criteria for the identification of parasites form the major part in the diagnosis of parasitic infections and majority of the parasites are identified based on the morphological features.

Faecal specimens

Examination of faeces is an important part in the diagnosis of intestinal parasitic infections and also for those helminthes which localize in the biliary tract and discharge their eggs into the intestine.

General guidelines for collection of faecal specimens

- Fresh specimen before radiological examination of barium sulphate and before giving medications should be collected.
- Contamination of faeces with water (which may contain free-living organisms) and urine (which may cause destruction of motile organisms) should be avoided during collection.
- Specimen should be collected in clean, wide-mouthed containers.
- Specimen should be identified with all necessary information including time and date of collection.
- It should be transported immediately within 30 minutes to laboratory for examination.
- If delay is expected, approximately one-half teaspoon of sample is collected into a bottle of 7–9 mL of polyvinyl alcohol (PVA).

Macroscopic examination

Important points to be noted are as follows:

- Colour
- Consistency—whether it is formed, semi-formed, soft or liquid because trophozoites are usually found in soft or liquid specimen and rarely in a formed or semiformed specimen. However, cystic forms are normally found in formed specimen. Helminthes eggs or larvae may be found in any type of specimen
- Blood, mucus and/or pus may be present in certain parasitic infections, hence should be noted
- Adult worms or segments of adult worms may be seen in or on the surface of stool or at the bottom of container

Methods used for stool examination

Saline preparation

- **Procedure**
  - Mix a small amount of faecal matter (approximately 2 mg) in a drop of saline on a clean glass slide to make a smooth suspension
  - Apply coverslip (22 × 22 mm)
  - Observe under low power with low intensity of light , and then under high power
- **Uses** The saline preparation is used to demonstrate
  - Motile trophozoite stage
  - Helminthic eggs
  - Helminthic larvae
  - RBCs
  - WBCs
  - Cysts of protozoa may also be seen

Iodine preparation

- **Procedure** It is the same as saline preparation. Instead of saline, iodine is used. A weak iodine solution, such as Lugol's iodine, is used.
- **Uses** This preparation is used mainly for demonstration of cystic stage.
  - Trophozoite stage can also be demonstrated
  - Eggs and larvae can also be demonstrated

Blood specimen

Examination of blood is an important part in the diagnosis of those parasitic infections in which the parasite itself or in any stage of its development circulates in the bloodstream. The examples are

- Malarial parasites—inside the red blood cells
- *Trypanosoma* species—in the blood plasma
- Filarial parasite (microfilaria of *W. bancrofti, B. malayi, L. loa, Mansonella* species are found in the blood plasma)

Collection of blood

- Blood sample is collected by pricking the pulp of any finger or lobe of the ear with a surgical cutting needle taking all sterile precautions.
- Blood can also be collected with the help of a sterile syringe and needle when a large quantity (5–10 mL) is required (for concentration).

Methods used for examination of blood

- **Wet mount** Direct wet mount of blood is used for detection of microfilaria and trypanosoma for their characteristic shape and motility.
- **Permanent stained smears**
  - Permanent stained smears are necessary for the specific identification of the causative agent.
  - There are two types of blood smears: thick and thin smear.
    - *Thick smear* It allows examination of a larger amount of blood, which increases the possibility of detecting light infections. The procedure for thick smears is as follows:
      - Take a big drop of blood on a slide and spread it with a needle or with the corner of another slide to form an area of a 0.5 inch square.
      - Alternatively, take three to four small drops of blood on a slide and with the corner of another slide mix the drops and spread over an area of 2 cm in diameter.
      - Allow to air dry or keep the slide in an incubator to accelerate drying (air drying may take a longer time).
      - After drying, place the slide in buffer to remove haemoglobin.
      - Stain it by an appropriate staining method.
    - ***Thin smears*** It allows species identification. The procedure for preparation of thin smear is as follows:
      - Take a drop of blood (not larger than a pin's head) on a glass slide.
      - Hold spreader at an angle of 45° in contact with the drop of blood.
      - Lower it to an angle of 30° and push gently to the left, till the blood is exhausted.
      - Allow it to dry.
      - Stain.

Alternatively, thin smear can be prepared on the same slide on which thick smear is prepared. For this, after thick film (2 cm) is prepared, if the same slide is spread further 2 cm long, it gives thin film.

Staining of blood smears

The blood smear can be stained by

- Leishman's stain—commonly used
- Giemsa stain
- Wright's stain
- Field's stain
- JSB stain (Singh and Bhattacharji)

Stained smears are observed under high power and oil immersion objectives for parasites and findings are noted and reported.

Sputum

Examination of sputum is performed in respiratory tract infections caused by parasites. These include

- *E. histolytica*—trophozoites found in sputum
- *E. granulosus*—solices and hooklets in hydatid cyst disease of respiratory tract
- *A. lumbricoides*—rhabditiform larvae
- *S. stercoralis*—filariform larvae

Methods used for examination of sputum Sputum is usually examined as a saline or iodine mount under low- and high-power objectives.

Urine

Examination of urine is performed in urinary tract infections caused by parasites. These include

- *S. haematobium*—eggs
- *W. bancrofti*—microfilaria
- *T. vaginalis*—trophozoites

The urine is collected in a sterile container and observed as a wet mount.

Genital specimens

Specimens such as vaginal swab, urethral discharge and parasitic secretions are observed for *T. vaginalis.*

Aspirates

The diagnosis of certain parasitic infections requires examination of aspirated material. These include

- Lung aspirate—*Pneumocystis carinii*
- Lung and liver aspirates—*E. histolytica*
- Hydatid aspirates—hydatid disease
- Lymph nodes, spleen, bone marrow, etc., in trypanosomiasis, leishmaniasis or amoebiasis

Methods for examination

The specimen is processed as

- Wet mount
- Impression smears stained with Giemsa stain
- Culture
- Animal inoculation

Cerebrospinal fluid (CSF)

- Examination of CSF is performed in primary amoebic meningoencephalitis caused by free-living amoebae—*Naegleria* and *Acanthamoeba* species and also in *E. histolytica* causing meningoencephalitis secondarily.
- CSF is collected by lumbar puncture in a sterile container by taking all aseptic precautions.
- The CSF is processed as
  - Wet mount—for motile organisms
  - Fixed preparations stained with iron haematoxylin stain
  - Culture

Culture methods

- The culture methods are routinely impracticable and facilities for culture are not available in a routine clinical laboratory.
- Few parasites can be cultivated successfully for research purpose.
- Culture methods are mainly employed for
  - Research purpose
  - Identification of species
  - To obtain antigen
  - For sensitivity testing
  - For teaching purpose

Animal inoculation

Animal inoculation is not a routine diagnostic method employed in parasitic infections. Occasionally, it may be required in some parasitic infections such as toxoplasmosis, leishmaniasis and trypanosomiasis.

Xenodiagnosis

In this method, the causative organism is demonstrated in the animal host or arthropod host (vectors), for example

- The bugs are allowed to feed on the patient's blood in Chagas disease and after 30–60 days, faeces of bugs are examined for *Trypanosoma cruzi.*
- In trichinosis, the rat is fed on muscle biopsies of the suspected patient and rats are then checked for the presence of encysted larvae of *T. spiralis.*
- In *W. bancrofti,* mosquitoes are allowed to feed on the suspected patient and microfilaria are demonstrated microscopically in the sucked blood obtained from the stomach of these mosquitoes.

Immunodiagnostic methods

- A number of immunodiagnostic methods based on the detection of specific antibodies or antigens are available.

- Detection of antigen is difficult but helps in definitive diagnosis and indicates present infection.
- Detection of antibody—detection of IgM indicates recent infection; it is more meaningful than IgG detection, as it persists for a long time in the serum even after infection has been cured. Cross-reaction due to complex antigen structure is another problem in antibody detection.
- Tests used for detection of antibodies in various parasitic infections include
  - Precipitation test
  - Agglutination test
  - Indirect haemagglutination test
  - Latex agglutination test
  - Immunodiffusion
  - Immunoelectrophoresis
  - Indirect immunofluorescence test
  - Enzyme-linked immunosorbent assay (ELISA) test
  - Radioimmunoassay (RIA)
  - Complement fixation test (CFT)
- Tests used for detection of antigens in parasitic infections include
  - Direct immunofluorescence test
  - Countercurrent immunoelectrophoresis
  - ELISA
  - RIA
  - Direct agglutination test
  - Circumoval precipitin test
  - Automated fluoroimmunoassay

Newer diagnostic methods

The following are some examples of newer techniques:

- Polymerase chain reaction (PCR)
- DNA probes
- Restriction fragment length polymorphism (RFLP)
- Flow cytometry which is useful for diagnosis of various parasitic diseases

Self-assessment

Long-answer question

1. Discuss in brief the laboratory diagnosis of parasitic infections.

Short-answer questions

Write notes on

1. Cestodes
2. Trematodes
3. Intestinal nematodes
4. Tissue nematodes
5. Examination of stool
6. Examination of blood
7. Thick and thin smears

Multiple-choice questions

1. Protozoa which are motile with the help of pseudopodia are known as
   A. Rhizopoda
   B. Mastigophora
   C. Sporozoa
   D. Ciliate
2. Tape-like segmented worms with no separate sexes are known as
   A. Trematodes
   B. Nematodes
   C. Cestodes
   D. None of the above
3. Leaf-like unsegmented, flat worms with no separate sexes are called
   A. Trematodes
   B. Nematodes
   C. Cestodes
   D. None of the above
4. Elongated, cylindrical, unsegmented worms with separate sexes are called
   A. Trematodes
   B. Nematodes
   C. Cestodes
   D. None of the above
5. Which of the following is a tissue nematode?
   A. *Ascaris lumbricoides*
   B. *Enterobius vermicularis*

C. *Ancylostoma duodenale*
D. *Wuchereria bancrofti*

6. Which of the following is an intestinal nematode?
   A. *Wuchereria bancrofti*
   B. *Ancylostoma duodenale*
   C. *Onchocerca volvulus*
   D. *Brugia malayi*
7. Which of the following iodine preparations is used for examination of stool sample?
   A. Gram's iodine
   B. Tincture iodine
   C. Lugol's iodine
   D. All of the above
8. Which of the following statements is TRUE regarding thick blood smear?
   A. Allows examination of a small amount of blood
   B. Increases the possibility of detecting light infections
   C. Helps in detailed study of parasite
   D. All of the above
9. Which of the following stains is most commonly used for examination of blood smear?
   A. Giemsa stain
   B. Wright's stain
   C. Field's stain
   D. Leishman's stain
10. Xenodiagnosis is a method of diagnosis used in which of the following parasitic infections?
   A. *Wuchereria bancrofti*
   B. *Plasmodium falciparum*
   C. *Leishmania donovani*
   D. *Brugia malayi*

48 Common Parasitic Diseases—Protozoal

Entamoeba histolytica

Entamoeba histolytica causes amoebiasis. It is worldwide in distribution and more common in tropics and subtropics. Its habitat is the large intestine of humans.

Morphology of *Entamoeba histolytica*

It occurs in three stages:

1. **Trophozoite or vegetative form (feeding stage of parasite)**
   - **Shape** Irregular
   - **Size** 10–40 μm (average—20–30 μm)
   - **Motility** Actively motile with the help of pseudopodium
   - **Cytoplasm** Differentiated into **ectoplasm** (thin, clear, translucent outer layer) and **endoplasm** (granular inner layer containing nucleus, food vacuoles, red blood cells [RBCs], occasionally white blood cells and tissue debris)
   - **Nucleus** Spherical, 4–6 μm in size, contains small dot-like structure, central in position called karyosome (Fig. 48.1a)
2. **Precystic stage** It is the transitory stage formed during the conversion of trophozoite to cyst.
   - **Shape** Round or oval with blunt pseudopodium

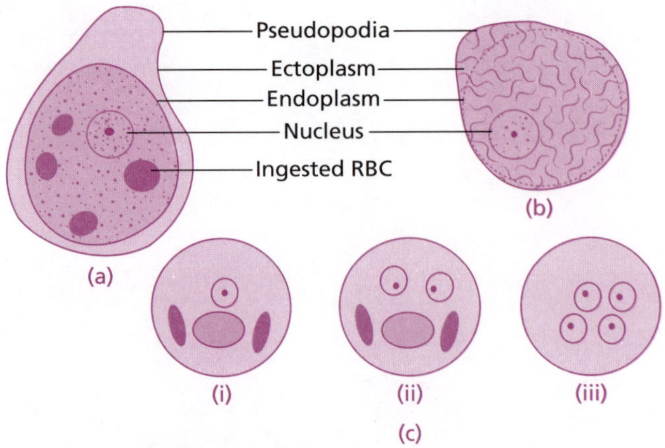

Figure 48.1 *Entamoeba histolytica*. (a) Trophozoite. (b) Precystic stage. (c) Cyst stage: (i) uninucleated (ii) binucleated (iii) quadrinucleate. *RBC*, red blood cell.

- **Size** 10–20 µm
- **Endoplasm** Free of RBCs and other ingested particles
- **Nucleus** retains the features of trophozoite stage (Fig. 48.1b)

3. **Cyst stage**
   - **Shape** Spherical
   - **Size** 10–15 µm
   - **Nucleus** Early cyst contains single nucleus and a mass of glycogen and one to four cigar-shaped chromatoid bodies. As it matures, the glycogen mass and chromatoid bodies disappear. The nucleus undergoes two successive mitotic divisions to form two and finally four nuclei (mature cyst—quadrinucleate) (Fig. 48.1c)

Life cycle of *Entamoeba histolytica* (Flow chart 48.1)

- **Definitive host** Humans
- **Intermediate host** Not required, passes life cycle in one host

Pathogenicity (Flow chart 48.2)

- Trophozoites in lumen do not cause any illness when they invade the intestinal tissue—cause disease.
- **Ulcers**—multiple and confined to the colon
  - ***Size*** Pinhead to 1 inch or more
  - ***Shape*** Round or oval, flask shaped in cross-section
  - ***Margin*** Ragged or undermined
  - ***Base*** Generally formed by the muscular coat and filled up by the necrotic material, yellowish or blackish slough

Spread to other organs

During the invasion of intestinal wall, amoebae penetrate the radicals of portal vein and are transported to the liver where they initiate lytic necrosis with an inflammatory reaction leading to formation of an abscess (few millimetres to few centimetres) containing thick, chocolate brown pus

Mature cyst—passed in faeces of convalescents and carriers; contaminates food and drinks. Infection occurs by ingestion of contaminated food or drink

↓

Cysts enter the small intestine. Excystation occurs in the caecum or lower part of the ileum and a tetranucleate amoeba (metacyst) comes out

↓

Nuclei and cytoplasm of metacyst divide to form eight amoebulae, which lodge in the submucous tissue of the large intestine where they grow and multiply by binary fission

↓

Produce characteristic lesions of amoebiasis

↓

When conditions become unsuitable for survival of trophozoite form, some of them get converted into precystic stage and finally into cystic stage

↓

Cysts are passed in faeces to repeat the cycle

Flow chart 48.1 Life cycle of *Entamoeba histolytica*.

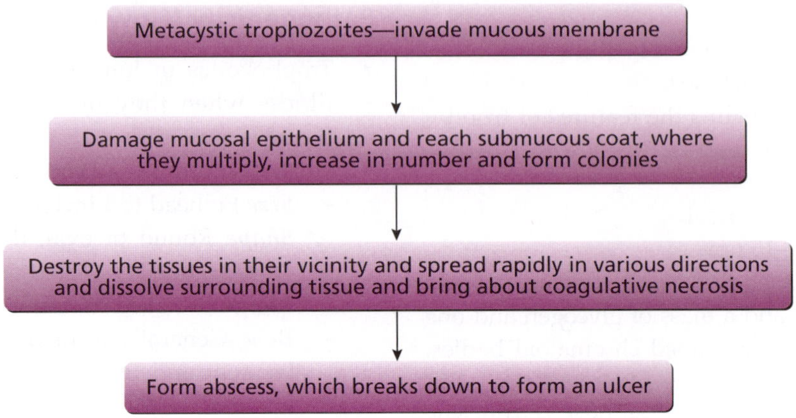

Flow chart 48.2 Pathogenicity of *Entamoeba histolytica*.

(anchovy sauce pus--containing liquefied necrotic liver tissue and blood). Untreated abscess may rupture into the surrounding organs and tissues such as lung, pleural cavity, pericardium, peritoneal cavity, stomach, intestine, inferior vena cava, abdominal wall and skin. Spread to lung and skin may also occur by haematogenous route (via blood) and amoebae may also spread to organs such as brain, kidneys, spleen and adrenals by haematogenous route.

Clinical features

The disease caused is known as **amoebiasis,** which is of two types:

1. Intestinal amoebiasis also known as **primary amoebiasis**
2. Extraintestinal amoebiasis also known as **secondary** or **metastatic amoebiasis**
   - **Intestinal amoebiasis** is characterized by
     - The passage of blood and mucus in stool
     - The stool is foul smelling and brownish black in colour
     - The patient is usually afebrile and non-toxic
     - Sometimes only diarrhoea and vague abdominal symptoms are present
   - **Extraintestinal amoebiasis—hepatic amoebiasis** is characterized by
     - Pain and tenderness in the right hypochondrium
     - Shoulder pain due to irritation of phrenic nerve
     - Fever with chills
     - Weight loss
     - Jaundice is infrequent

It also causes pulmonary amoebiasis, cutaneous amoebiasis, cerebral amoebiasis, splenic abscess, etc.

Laboratory diagnosis

Diagnosis of intestinal amoebiasis

- **Specimen** Faeces are collected and transported immediately.
- **Microscopy**
  - *Saline preparation* To demonstrate motile trophozoite
  - *Iodine preparation* To demonstrate trophozoite in killed state and cysts in stained state
- **Serological tests** They are negative in early cases and in the absence of deep invasion.

Diagnosis in hepatic amoebiasis

- **Specimens** Pus is aspirated from liver or liver biopsy for trophozoites.

- Stool sample may show cysts in about 15% of cases.
- **Serological tests** Positive test indicates the presence of specific antibodies in the blood.

  The antibodies can be detected by complement fixation test, agar gel diffusion, latex agglutination, indirect haemagglutination test, countercurrent immunoelectrophoresis, ELISA, immobilization test and immunofluorescence test. The antigen can be detected by radioimmunoassay.

Diagnosis in pulmonary amoebiasis

- Demonstration of trophozoites in anchovy sauce sputum (the *Entamoeba gingivalis* normally present in mouth may cause confusion in diagnosis)
- By serological tests

Prophylactic measures

For personal prophylaxis

- Use of boiled drinking water
- Protection of food and drink from contamination by flies, cockroaches and rats
- Avoiding use of raw vegetables and fruits
- Personal cleanliness and elementary hygienic conditions during meals

For community prophylaxis

- Effective sanitary disposal of faeces
- Protection of public water supplies from faecal pollution

Treatment

- Metronidazole and tinidazole are the drugs of choice.
- Chloroquine is effective in hepatic and pulmonary amoebiasis.
- Emetine and dehydroemetine are the other drugs.

Other amoebae

- ***E. gingivalis*** It is a harmless commensal normally present in gingival pockets and tonsillar crypts. It has no cystic stage.
  - The trophozoite stage is 5–15 μm in diameter and is actively motile with the help of multiple pseudopodia. Cytoplasm is differentiated into clear ectoplasm and granular endoplasm. Nucleus is round and 2–4 μm in diameter. The endoplasm shows presence of food vacuoles, digested leucocytes and epithelial cells. There are usually no RBCs.
  - *E. gingivalis* spreads from one person to another by kissing and other methods that are able to transfer oral secretions.
  - Its medical significance is as follows:
    - It causes confusion in the diagnosis of pulmonary amoebiasis.
    - It is commonly associated with lesions of periodontal diseases, but its role in causation of periodontal diseases is not exactly known and most probably it may act as bacterial vector in these lesions.
- ***E. coli*** It is a harmless commensal normally present in the intestine. It causes confusion in the diagnosis of intestinal amoebiasis. Its medical significance is that it needs to be differentiated from *E. histolytica* causing intestinal amoebiasis.
- ***Naegleria* spp.** These are pathogenic free-living amoebae causing primary amoebic meningoencephalitis.
- ***Acanthamoeba* spp.** These are pathogenic free-living amoebae causing primary amoebic meningoencephalitis.

Giardia lamblia

Giardia lamblia is a parasite causing giardiasis. It is worldwide in distribution and its habitat is **duodenum** and **jejunum**.

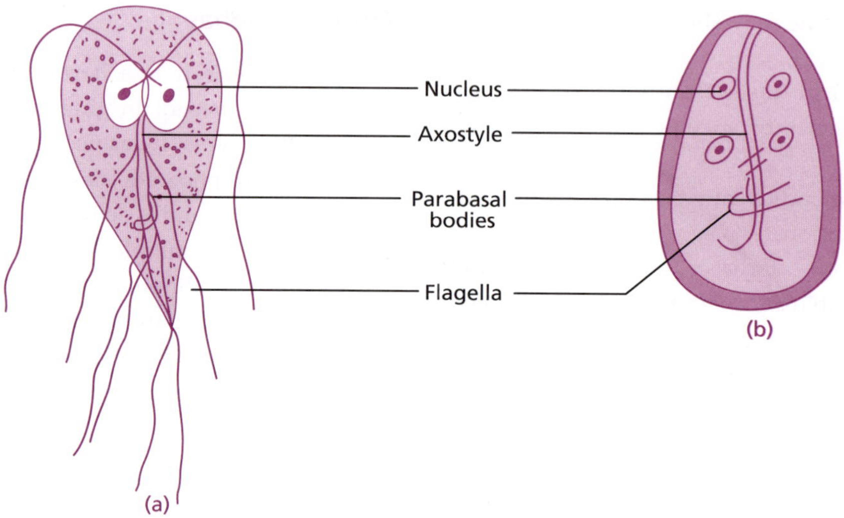

Figure 48.2 *Giardia lamblia*. (a) Trophozoite. (b) Cyst.

Morphology of *Giardia lamblia*

It occurs in two forms:

- **Trophozoite or vegetative form**
  - **Shape** Tennis or badminton racket, or heart shaped
  - **Size** 14 × 7 µm
  - **Motility** Actively motile with the help of four pairs of flagella
  - **Nucleus** Two nuclei, one on each side
  - **Axostyles** Slender rod-like structure, two in number, formed by the fusion of axonemes of flagella and associated groups of microtubules
  - **Symmetry** Bilaterally symmetrical
  - **Parabasal bodies** Two curved median bodies posterior to sucking disc
  - **Division** Longitudinally following duplication of all organelles (Fig. 48.2a)
- **Cyst stage**
  - **Shape** Oval, football shaped
  - **Size** 12 × 7 µm
  - **Nucleus** Four nuclei in a cluster or in pairs at opposite pole
  - **Cyst wall** Tough hyaline (Fig. 48.2b)

Life cycle of *Giardia lamblia*

- **Definitive host** Humans
- **Intermediate host** Not required, passes life cycle in one host (Flow chart 48.3)

Pathogenicity

The disease caused is known as **giardiasis** and is characterized by

- Diarrhoea—five to six stools a day; explosive watery stools
- Indefinite abdominal pain, nausea and vomiting
- Steatorrhoea—passage of yellowish and greasy stool with excess fat
- Malabsorption
- Severe flatulence
- Children may develop chronic diarrhoea, malabsorption, weight loss, anaemia, impairment of growth and chronic indigestion
- Occasionally, cholecystitis and jaundice

Laboratory diagnosis

- **Specimen** Faeces should be collected in a clean, wide-mouthed container and transported immediately within 30 minutes to the laboratory for examination.
- **Microscopy**
  - ***Saline preparation*** To demonstrate motile trophozoite

Mature cyst—passed in faeces; contaminates food and drinks

↓

Infection occurs by ingestion of contaminated food or drink

↓

Cyst hatches out in two trophozoites within 30 minutes

↓

Multiply in intestine by binary fission

↓

When conditions in duodenum are unfavourable for survival of trophozoite form

↓

Encystment occurs in large intestine

↓

Mature cysts are passed in faeces and cycle is repeated

Flow chart 48.3 Life cycle of *Giardia lamblia*.

 - ***Iodine preparation*** To demonstrate trophozoite in killed state and cysts in stained state; only cysts seen in asymptomatic carriers
- **Demonstration of cysts** Cysts are demonstrated in a concentrated stool sample, when they are less in number.

Prophylactic measures

- Protection of food and drink from contamination
- Personal hygiene
- Protection of public water supplies from faecal pollution
- Water disinfection by iodine

Treatment

- Metronidazole and tinidazole are drugs of choice.
- Atabrine (quanacrine) and furazolidone are also effective.

The other protozoa causing intestinal infections are as follows:

- *Balantidium coli*—balantidiasis (dysentery)
- *Isospora belli*—self-limited diarrhoea in healthy persons, severe disease in patients with AIDS
- *Cryptosporidium parvum*—cryptosporidiosis (self-limited diarrhoea in healthy persons, severe diarrhoea in patients with AIDS).

Haemoflagellates—*Leishmania donovani*

Leishmania donovani is a haemoflagellate causing kala-azar. It is endemic in many places in India, China, Bangladesh, Middle East, around Mediterranean region, Africa, South and Central America, and Russia. It is a parasite of the reticuloendothelial system.

Morphology of *Leishmania donovani*

It occurs in two stages:

1. **Amastigote form (LD body, leishmanial form or aflagellar stage)** This stage occurs in

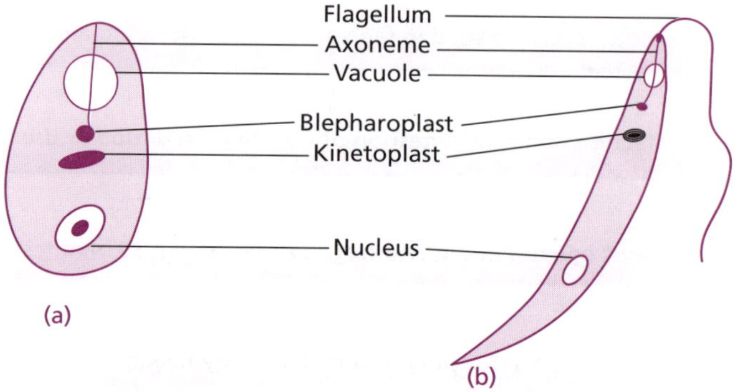

Figure 48.3 *Leishmania donovani*. (a) Amastigote form. (b) Promastigote form.

vertebrate host (human, dog, hamster). It is intracellular, and resides in the macrophages, monocytes, neutrophils or endothelial cells.

- **Shape** Round or oval
- **Size** 2–4 µm along the longitudinal axis
- **Cytoplasm** Pale blue when stained by Romanowsky stain
- **Nucleus** Small, red in colour
- **Kinetoplast** Rod-like or tiny dot–like body at right angle to the nucleus, red in colour
- **Axoneme** A root of flagellum arising from blepharoplast to the margins of the body
- **Vacuole** Clear, unstained space lying alongside the axoneme (Fig. 48.3a)

2. **Leptomonad form (promastigote or flagellar stage)**
   - **Shape** Long, slender, spindle-shaped
   - **Size** 15–20 µm long and 1–2 µm broad
   - **Nucleus** Red, central in position
   - **Kinetoplast** Lies transversely near the anterior end
   - **Vacuole** Present near the root of flagellum
   - **Flagellum** Single flagellum, 15–30 µm in length (Fig. 48.3b)

Life cycle of *Leishmania donovani* (Flow chart 48.4)

- **Definitive host** Humans, also dog in some areas
- **Intermediate host** Sand fly—*Phlebotomus* spp. (*Phlebotomus argentipes* in India and Pakistan)

Pathogenicity

The disease caused is known as **kala-azar** or **visceral leishmaniasis**. It is characterized by

- Fever—continuous, remittent or irregular type
- Splenomegaly
- Skin becomes dry, rough and darkly pigmented, hence the name kala-azar
- Jaundice because of liver damage
- Epistaxis and bleeding gums common
- In 75–95% of untreated cases, death occurs in about 2 years. Death occurs due to complications such as amoebic or bacillary dysentery, pneumonia, pulmonary tuberculosis, cancrum oris and other septic infections

Post–kala-azar dermal leishmaniasis About 10–20% of cases recovered from kala-azar develop non-ulcerative cutaneous lesions, which develop after the completion of treatment. These lesions are of three types:

1. Depigmented macules appear commonly on the trunk and extremities.
2. Erythematous patches on the nose, cheeks and chin having butterfly distribution and being photosensitive; they become prominent during the middle of the day.
3. Granulomatous nodules—painless, yellowish pink nodules on skin and mucous membrane of tongue **(lesions in the oral cavity)**

Human infection occurs by bite of sand fly—releases promastigote forms, which are engulfed by macrophages

↓

Promastigote forms—change to amastigote forms and multiply, forming a large number of daughter cells

↓

This results in enlargement and rupture of infected host cell releasing daughter cells in circulation, which are again engulfed by macrophages and histiocytes

↓

Cycle is repeated and the entire reticuloendothelial system becomes infected

↓

Some of the LD bodies are found in peripheral blood inside the neutrophils and monocytes

↓

A sand fly, when feeds on infected persons, takes the amastigote forms, which develop into promastigote forms

↓

Promastigote forms divide by binary fission and form a large number of daughter cells, which are transported from the midgut to the pharynx and buccal cavity

↓

When infected sand fly bites, parasites are released in puncture wound and cycle is repeated

Flow chart 48.4 Life cycle of *Leishmania donovani.*

and eyes. Nodules mostly appear on face but may appear on other parts also.

Laboratory diagnosis

- **Specimens** Blood, spleen aspirate, bone marrow or biopsy from splenic pulp tissue
- **Direct methods**
  - ***Microscopy*** Amastigote forms are demonstrated by Romanowsky stain.
  - ***Culture*** In Novy–MacNeal–Nicolle (NNN) medium. Specimen is inoculated into water of condensation and incubated at 22°C for 1–4 weeks. At the end of every week, a drop of condensation fluid is examined for promastigote forms.
  - ***Animal inoculation*** The specimen is inoculated intraperitoneally or intradermally into hamster and spleen impression smears are observed for the presence of parasites as death of animal takes several months.
- **Indirect methods**
  - ***Serological tests*** Different serological tests are used to demonstrate specific antibodies using leishmanial antigens prepared from cultures. These tests include the following:
    - Complement fixation test
    - Countercurrent immunoelectrophoresis
    - Indirect haemagglutination test
    - Indirect immunofluorescence test
    - ELISA
  - ***Complement fixation test with WKK antigen*** (antigen prepared by Witebsky, Klingenstein and Kuhn)
  - ***Other tests*** Infection with *L. donovani* results in hypergammaglobulinaemia—increase in the level of IgG. These antibodies are detected by

- Napier's aldehyde (formol gel) test
- Chopra's antimony test

Prophylactic measures

- Attack on parasite—treatment of all cases
- Attack on vector—eradication of sand fly
- Personal prophylaxis by using anti-sand fly measures such as
  - Use of mosquito net or screen
  - Avoiding ground floor for sleeping
  - Periodic fumigation of sleeping quarters

Treatment

- Pentavalent antimony compounds such as sodium antimony gluconate and urea stibamine
- Pentamidine, which is an alternative
- Amphotericin B for drug-resistant organisms

Other haemoflagellates

Other flagellates found in blood and tissues of human beings are as follows:

- *L. tropica* causing oriental sore
- *L. braziliensis* and *L. mexicana* causing espundia
- *Trypanosoma brucei* causing African trypanosomiasis (sleeping sickness)
- *T. cruzi* causing South American trypanosomiasis (Chagas disease)

Trichomonas vaginalis

Trichomonas vaginalis causing trichomoniasis is worldwide in distribution. Its main habitat is the vagina. It is also found in urinary tract of both males and females.

Morphology

It occurs as a trophozoite only and there is no cystic stage.

Trophozoite or vegetative form

- **Shape** Pear-shaped or ovoid
- **Size** 10–30 μm long and 5–10 μm
- **Motility** Motile, shows characteristic wobbling or rotatory movement
- Flagella are five in number, four directed anteriorly, one directed posteriorly forming the margin of an undulating membrane, which is supported at its base by a flexible rod—the costa
- **Nucleus** Single nucleus
- **Axostyle** Originates anteriorly and terminates posteriorly as a tail-like appendage
- Cytoplasm shows granules, which are most numerous alongside the axostyle and costa (Fig. 48.4)
- **Division** By binary fission

Life cycle of *Trichomonas vaginalis*

- **Definitive host** Human. It inhabits vagina and cervix in females, and urethra, seminal vesicles, epididymis and prostate in males.
- **Intermediate host** No intermediate host is required.
- The trophozoite passes from person to person by sexual contact. Transmission in females also occurs by the exchange of contaminated towels, underclothing or other toilet articles.

Pathogenicity

- The disease caused is known as **trichomoniasis.** In females, it causes **vaginitis** characterized by vaginal inflammation, burning

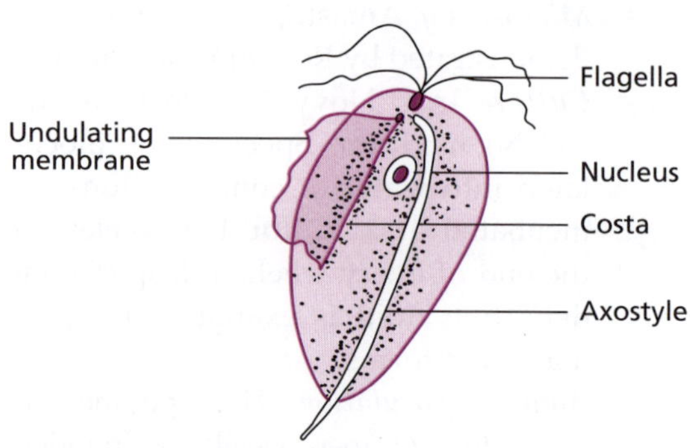

Figure 48.4 *Trichomonas vaginalis*—trophozoite.

and itching sensation and frothy, offensive, yellow vaginal discharge.
- In males, the infection is usually asymptomatic. Some patients may develop urethritis or prostatitis.

Laboratory diagnosis

- **Specimens** Vaginal discharge, urethral discharge and prostatic fluid in males
- **Microscopy** Examination of specimen in a drop of saline to demonstrate motile trophozoites

Prophylactic measures

- Avoidance of unprotected sexual intercourse
- Avoidance of exchange of towels and undergarments

Treatment

- Metronidazole is the drug of choice.
- The simultaneous treatment of sexual partner

Other *Trichomonas*

- ***T. tenax*** It is a parasite smaller than *T. vaginalis* (8–10 µm). It is normally present in the mouth as a harmless commensal.
- ***T. hominis*** It is a parasite smaller than *T. vaginalis* (8–12 µm). It is normally present in the caecum as a harmless commensal.

Malarial parasites

Malarial parasites are found in all countries extending from 40°S to 60°N. *Plasmodium vivax* and *P. falciparum* are common in tropical countries, *Plasmodium malariae* in subtropical zone and *P. ovale* has been reported from Africa. Their habitat is liver cells and RBCs—via blood they are carried to all the organs in the body.

The species of Plasmodia causing malaria are as follows:
- *P. vivax*
- *P. falciparum*
- *P. malariae*
- *P. ovale*

Morphology of malarial parasites

The morphological features of four different species of *Plasmodium* are summarized in Table 48.1.

Life cycle of malarial parasites

- **Definitive host** Female anopheline mosquito—sexual phase
- **Intermediate host** Human—asexual phase

Human cycle

Human infection occurs by bite of an infected mosquito—releases **sporozoites**. The human cycle shows the following stages:

Pre-erythrocytic schizogony Sporozoites released in blood capillaries reach the liver and enter the parenchymal cells (hepatocytes) to initiate pre-erythrocytic schizogony. Sporozoites in liver cells change to form pre-erythrocytic schizont, which matures and bursts releasing thousands of pear-shaped merozoites—two types:
1. Micromerozoites—enter the circulation
2. Macromerozoites—re-enter the liver cells

Erythrocytic schizogony Micromerozoites invade the RBCs. Inside the RBC, the merozoite becomes a rounded body with a vacuole in the centre, peripheral cytoplasm and nucleus at one pole. When stained with Romanowsky stain, the cytoplasm stains blue, nucleus red and central vacuole remains unstained. It appears like an annular or ring; hence, it is called **ring stage—early trophozoite stage**.

The ring stage develops into amoeboid stage—increases in size, becomes irregular in shape and shows amoeboid motility; it is the **late trophozoite stage**. When amoeboid

Table 48.1 Morphology of malarial parasites

Morphological form	*Plasmodium vivax* (Fig. 48.5)	*Plasmodium falciparum* (Fig. 48.5)	*Plasmodium malariae*	*Plasmodium ovale*
Trophozoite				
• **Ring stage**	Size (μm)—2.5–3 Cytoplasm—blue	1.25–1.5 Ring attached to margin of RBC—form appliqué or accole form	2.5 Resembles *P. vivax*	2–2.5 Resembles *P. vivax*
	Nucleus—red; vacuole—unstained	Binucleate rings—common	Thicker and more intensely stained	–
• **Amoeboid form**	Large, irregular Accumulates pigment	Large, irregular 6–12 brick red Maurer's dots	Band-like Dark brown or black pigment	Bilobed –
	Infected RBC becomes irregular	No increase in size	No increase in size	Oval in shape
	Loses red colour—colourless	RBC—reddish violet	Not decolourized	–
Schizont				
• **Early schizont**	Size (μm)—9–10 Round, vacuole disappears, large nucleus lies at the periphery	4.5–5 Not seen in peripheral blood, develop in capillaries of internal organs	6.5–7	6.2
• **Late and mature schizonts**	Nucleus divides to form daughter nuclei and develops into merozoites with central nucleus and surrounding cytoplasm	Same as in *P. vivax*	Same as in *P. vivax*	Same as in *P. vivax*
	Size—1.5–1.75 × 0.75 μm Number—12–24 Arrangement—rosette form	0.5–0.7 μm in diameter 8–32 Grape-like cluster	2–2.5 μm in diameter 6–12 Daisy head	2–2.5 μm in diameter 6–12 Irregular

Gametocyte	*P. vivax* Male	*P. vivax* Female	*P. falciparum* Male	*P. falciparum* Female	*P. malariae* Male	*P. malariae* Female	*P. ovale* Male	*P. ovale* Female
Size (μm)	9–10	10–12	8–10 × 2	10–12 × 2–3	7–7.5	7–7.5	9	9
Shape	Spherical	Spherical	Kidney-shaped	Crescent-shaped	Round	Round	Oval	Oval
Cytoplasm	Light blue	Deep blue	Light blue	Deep blue	Pale blue	Deep blue	Pale blue	Deep blue
Nucleus	Large, diffuse	Small, compact	Scattered, fine granules	Small, compact	Same as *P. vivax*	Same as *P. vivax*	Same as *P. vivax*	Same as *P. vivax*

RBC, red blood cell.

stage reaches a certain stage of development and when its nucleus starts division, the stage is called **schizont**. Initially the nucleus divides to form small nuclei without the division of cytoplasm known as **early schizont**. Then each daughter nucleus is surrounded by cytoplasm. This stage is known as **late schizont**. The late schizont develops into **mature schizont** in which small merozoites are seen, each having a nucleus with

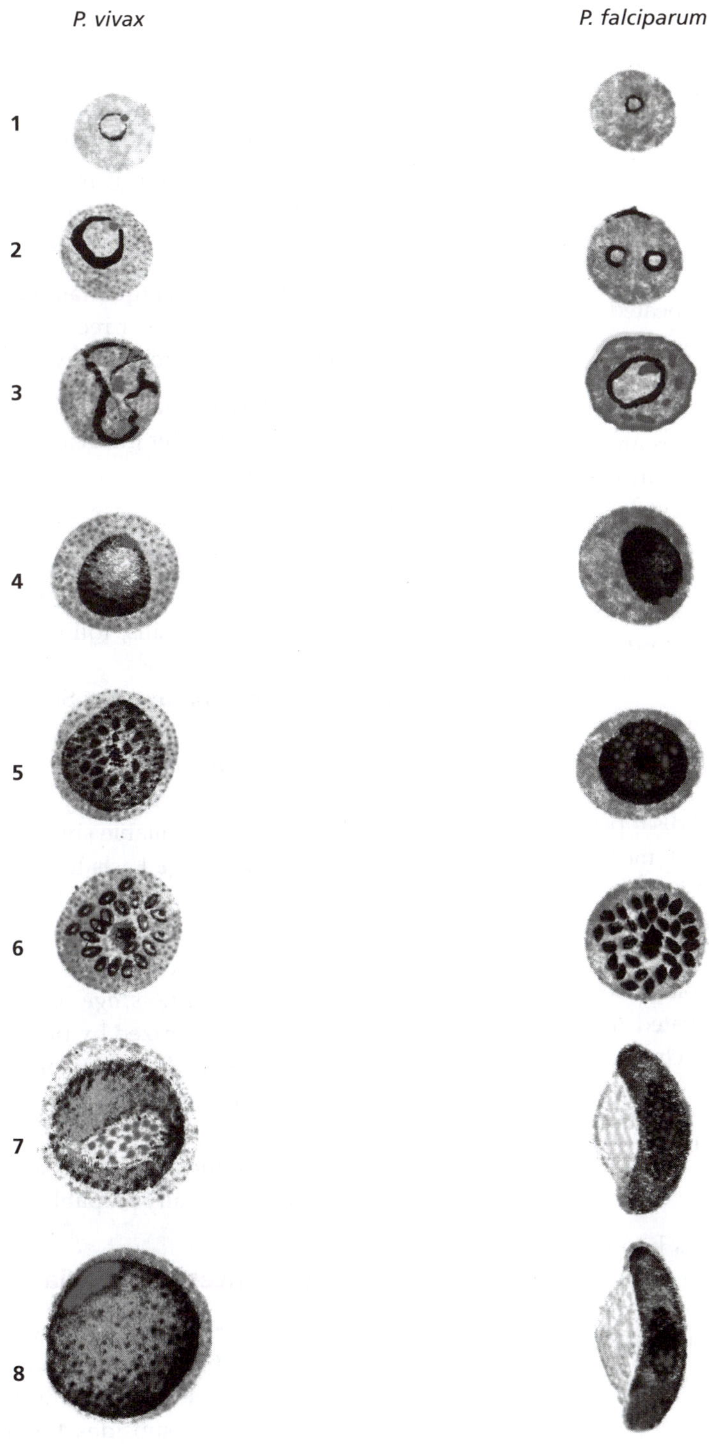

Figure 48.5 Morphology of *Plasmodium vivax* and *P. falciparum*. (1–3) Trophozoites. (4–6) Schizonts. (7–8) Male and female gametocytes. *See the color image at the end of the book (Color Plates).*

surrounding cytoplasm. The mature schizont bursts releasing the merozoites into circulation, which again invade the fresh RBCs and the cycle is repeated.

The rupture of the mature schizont releases large quantities of pyrogens responsible for clinical attack of malaria.

This cycle lasts for 48 hours in *P. vivax, P. falciparum* and *P. ovale,* and 72 hours in *P. malariae.*

Gametogony After repeated cycles of erythrocytic schizogony, some merozoites develop into sexually differentiated forms called **gametocytes**. This process is known as **gametogony**. The mature gametocytes are round, except in *P. falciparum* in which they are crescent-shaped. The female (macrogametocyte) is larger than male (microgametocyte) and females are more in number. They do not produce any febrile reaction. They are produced for continuation of species and are taken up by mosquito. The individuals who harbour gametocytes are known as **carriers**.

Exoerythrocytic schizogony It is a local liver cycle that persists even after the establishment of blood infection. It is seen in *P. vivax, P. ovale* and probably in *P. malariae* but disappears in *P. falciparum.* It acts as a source of merozoites and causes relapses. Recently, it has been found that in *P. vivax* and *P. ovale,* some sporozoites on entering the hepatocytes remain dormant in a cryptobiotic phase called hypnozoites (sleeping sporozoites). These forms are activated from time to time to form merozoites, which infect RBCs and cause recurrence of malaria. It is known as relapse.

Mosquito cycle (Flow chart 48.5)

Pathogenicity

The disease caused is known as **malaria.** The incubation period is generally 9–30 days, shortest in *P. falciparum* (12 days) and longest in *P. malariae* (28–30 days). In *P. vivax* and *P. ovale,* the incubation period is 13–17 days. Each species causes a characteristic fever, designated as follows:

Vivax malaria (benign tertian malaria) It is caused by *P. vivax.* Fever recurs after intervals of 48 hours or every third day, hence tertian. It is less dangerous, hence benign.

Falciparum malaria (malignant tertian malaria) It is caused by *P. falciparum.* Fever recurs after intervals of 48 hours or every third day, hence tertian. It is dangerous and malignant. It is also called subtertian because fever may recur before 48 hours.

Malariae malaria (quartan malaria) It is caused by *P. malariae.* Fever recurs after intervals of 72 hours or every fourth day.

Ovale tertian malaria It is caused by *P. ovale.* Fever recurs after intervals of 48 hours or every third day.

Clinical Features

The typical picture consists of periodic bouts of fever with chills, followed by anaemia and splenomegaly.

- **Febrile paroxysms** Show three successive stages:
  - ***Cold stage*** Lasts for 15–60 minutes, characterized by intense cold and uncontrollable shivering
  - ***Hot stage*** Lasts for 2–6 hours, characterized by high-grade fever, severe headache, nausea, vomiting and abdominal discomfort
  - ***Sweating stage*** Lasts for 2–3 hours, characterized by profuse sweating
- **Anaemia** Microcytic or normocytic, hypochromic type, more pronounced in *P. falciparum*
- **Splenomegaly** Important physical sign, spleen usually palpable by the second week

Recurrences in malaria

Recurrences in malaria are of two types:

1. **Recrudescence** In *P. falciparum,* following the development of immunity, the clinical attack subsides but the parasites are not entirely eliminated and they persist in some RBCs. The number of these forms may increase in number and cause fresh

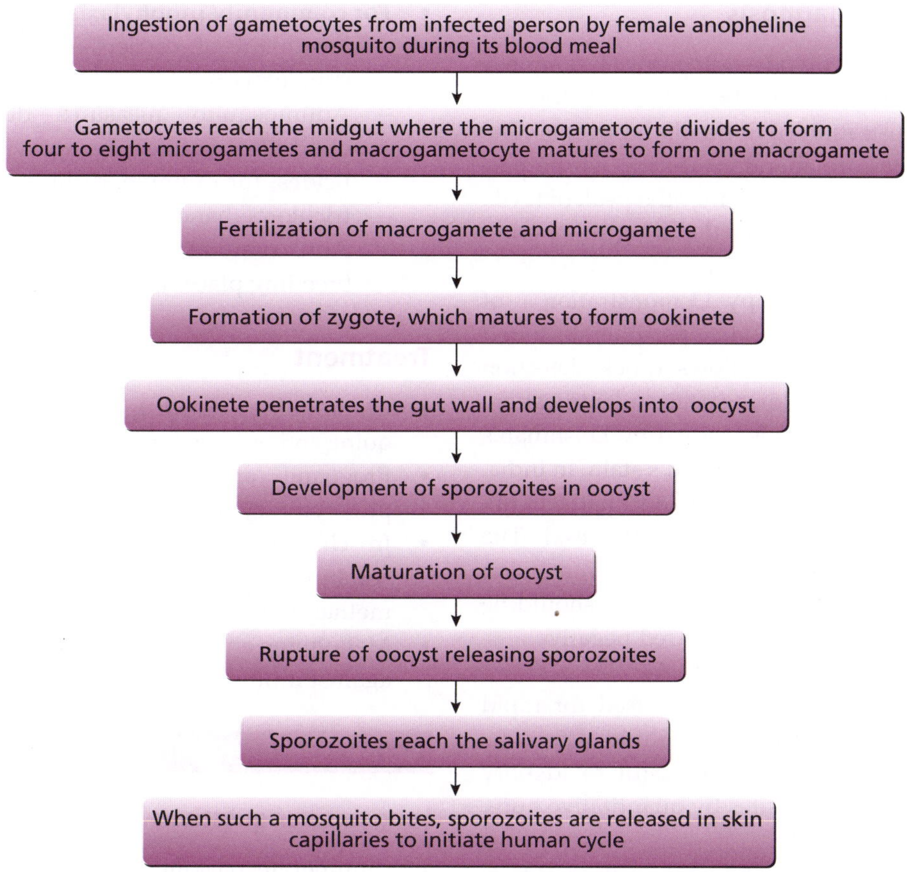

Flow chart 48.5 Mosquito cycle.

attack of malaria within 1 or 2 years. This is known as **recrudescence.**

2. **Relapse** In *P. vivax* and *P. ovale,* some sporozoites on entering the hepatocytes remain dormant as hypnozoites (sleeping sporozoites), which are activated from time to time to form merozoites, which infect RBCs and cause recurrence of malaria. It is known as **relapse.**

Complications of *Pseudomonas falciparum* infection

Pernicious malaria (malignant malaria) It is a life-threatening complication of *P. falciparum* infection, and occurs if infection is not effectively treated. Clinically, it may present as

- **Cerebral malaria** Characterized by hyperpyrexia, convulsions, coma and paralysis
- **Algid malaria** Characterized by cold and clammy skin, peripheral circulatory failure, hypotension and gastrointestinal symptoms
- **Septicaemic malaria** Characterized by high-grade fever, bilious remittent fever, pneumonia and cardiac syncope

Black water fever It is also a complication of *P. falciparum* infection and it occurs due to massive intravascular haemolysis caused by antierythrocyte antibodies. It is characterized by haemoglobinuria—passage of dark red or blackish urine, hence the name black water, circulatory collapse and acute renal failure. Chloroquine is the drug of choice for treatment.

Laboratory diagnosis

- **Specimens** Blood—a fingerprick sample is sufficient. It should be collected before the administration of antimalarial agents. The parasites are abundant during febrile paroxysm—a few hours after the peak of fever. Blood sample collected during this period gives positive results.
- **Direct microscopy** Demonstration of malarial parasite in peripheral blood smear; thick film allows quick detection and thin film allows species identification. The blood smear is stained by Leishman's stain, Giemsa stain or Field's stain. In India, JSB stain (Jaswant Singh and Bhattacharji), a rapid method, is commonly used. The smear is observed under oil immersion objective and at least 200 fields should be observed before it is declared negative.
- **Other stains**
  - **Fluorochromes** can be used for rapid staining and rapid screening of smears.
  - **Acridine orange** is useful to identify malarial parasites by quantitative buffy coat method.
- **Serological tests** Different serological tests are used to demonstrate specific antibodies. These tests include the following:
  - Immunoprecipitation test
  - Flocculation test
  - Complement fixation test
  - Countercurrent immunoelectrophoresis
  - Indirect haemagglutination test
  - Indirect immunofluorescence test
  - ELISA
  - RIA

Prophylactic measures

- **For personal prophylaxis**
  - Protection against mosquito bite
  - Chemoprophylaxis—the drugs recommended are chloroquine, amodiaquine and pyrimethamine. It gives effective protection to travellers visiting endemic areas
- **For community prophylaxis**
  - Treatment of carriers—destruction of gametocytes
  - Antimosquito measures—destruction of adult mosquitoes by spraying insecticides, for example, dichlorodiphenyltrichloroethane (DDT)
  - Antilarval measures—elimination of breeding places and use of larvicides

Treatment

- Chloroquine is the drug of choice—amodiaquine and quinine for resistant *P. falciparum.*
- Proguanil and pyrimethamine act on pre-erythrocytic schizont and on sporozoites.
- In chloroquine-resistant *P. falciparum,* a combination of sulphadoxine and pyrimethamine is effective.
- Mefloquine and halophantrine are effective against multidrug-resistant *P. falciparum.*

Self-assessment

Long-answer questions

1. Enumerate parasites causing gastrointestinal infections. Discuss in brief the morphology, life cycle, pathogenicity and laboratory diagnosis of *Entamoeba histolytica.*
2. Enumerate haemoparasites. Discuss in brief the morphology, life cycle, pathogenicity and laboratory diagnosis of *Leishmania donovani.*
3. Enumerate haemoparasites. Discuss in brief the morphology, life cycle, pathogenicity and laboratory diagnosis of *Plasmodium falciparum.*

Short-answer questions

Write notes on

1. Laboratory diagnosis of amoebiasis
2. *Giardia lamblia*
3. Haemoflagellates
4. LD body
5. Kala-azar
6. Laboratory diagnosis of kala-azar
7. *Trichomonas vaginalis*

8. Laboratory diagnosis of malaria
9. *Plasmodium ovale*
10. Gametogony
11. Pernicious malaria

Multiple-choice questions

1. Which of the following parasites does not have cystic stage?
   A. *Entamoeba histolytica*
   B. *Giardia lamblia*
   C. *Trichomonas vaginalis*
   D. None of the above
2. Which of the following parasites is the cause of kala-azar?
   A. *Leishmania donovani*
   B. *Trypanosoma cruzi*
   C. *Trypanosoma brucei*
   D. *Leishmania tropica*
3. Which of the following is an infective form of malarial parasite to humans?
   A. Trophozoite
   B. Sporozoite
   C. Merozoite
   D. Schizont
4. Black water fever is a complication of which of the following species of *Plasmodium?*
   A. *Plasmodium vivax*
   B. *Plasmodium malariae*
   C. *Plasmodium ovale*
   D. *Plasmodium falciparum*
5. Select the most appropriate statement regarding definitive host.
   A. Is a carrier or transport host
   B. The host in which the sexual mode of reproduction takes place
   C. The host in which the asexual mode of reproduction takes place
   D. The invertebrate species in which the parasite passes its life cycle
6. Select the most appropriate statement regarding intermediate host.
   A. Is a carrier or transport host
   B. The host in which the sexual mode of reproduction takes place
   C. The host in which the larval stage of parasite lives
   D. The invertebrate species in which the parasite passes its life cycle
7. Which of the following is an intermediate host for *Leishmania donovani?*
   A. Female anopheline mosquito
   B. Body louse
   C. Rat flea
   D. Sand fly
8. Which of the following is a definitive host for *Plasmodium falciparum?*
   A. Female anopheline mosquito
   B. Human being
   C. Rat flea
   D. Sand fly
9. Which of the following species of *Plasmodium* causes most serious illness?
   A. *Plasmodium vivax*
   B. *Plasmodium malariae*
   C. *Plasmodium ovale*
   D. *Plasmodium falciparum*
10. Which of the following is a drug of choice for the treatment of malaria?
    A. Primaquine
    B. Chloroquine
    C. Quinine
    D. Amodiaquine
11. Which of the following amoebae does not have cystic stage?
    A. *Entamoeba histolytica*
    B. *Entamoeba gingivalis*
    C. *Entamoeba coli*
    D. None of the above
12. Which of the following is an intermediate host for *Trichomonas vaginalis?*
    A. Female anopheline mosquito
    B. Body louse
    C. Rat flea
    D. None of the above
13. Which of the following statements is FALSE about *Giardia lamblia?*
    A. Its trophozoite is racket shaped
    B. Its cyst is football shaped
    C. It passes its life cycle in one host only

D. It is the cause of dysentery

14. Which of the following amoebae causes confusion in the diagnosis of pulmonary amoebiasis?
    A. *Entamoeba histolytica*
    B. *Entamoeba gingivalis*
    C. *Entamoeba coli*
    D. *Acanthamoeba* spp.

15. Which of the following statements is FALSE about giardiasis?
    A. Diarrhoea
    B. Dysentery
    C. Steatorrhoea
    D. Malabsorption

49 Common Parasitic Diseases—Helminthic

Ascaris lumbricoides (roundworm)

It is the intestinal nematode, worldwide in distribution. It is more prevalent in China, India and South East Asia. Its habitat is the lumen of the small intestine (jejunum) in the humans.

Morphology of *Ascaris lumbricoides*

It occurs as

- **Adult worm** (Fig. 49.1a)
  - ***Shape*** Cylindrical with tapering ends
  - ***Freshly passed worm*** Light brown or pink in colour that changes gradually to white
  - ***Male worm*** 15–25 cm in length and 2–4 mm in diameter with a curved posterior (tail) end
  - ***Female worm*** 25–40 cm in length and 5 mm in diameter, stouter than male with straight and conical posterior end. The vulva is situated at the junction of anterior and middle thirds of the body. This part is narrow and is called vulvar waist. It is **oviparous—mature female** can liberate about 200,000 eggs daily
- **Eggs** Two types of eggs:
  - ***Fertilized egg*** *(Fig. 49.1b)*
    - *Shape* Round or oval
    - *Size* 60–70 × 40–50 μm
    - *Colour* Yellow-brown—bile stained
    - *Eggshell* Thick and an uneven outer albuminous coat
    - *Ovum* Large, unsegmented ovum
    - Floats in saturated solution of common salt
  - ***Unfertilized egg*** *(Fig. 49.1c)*
    - *Shape* Narrower, longer and more elliptical than fertilized egg
    - *Size* 80–90 × 45–55 μm
    - *Colour* Brownish—bile stained
    - *Eggshell* Thinner, with irregular outer albuminous coat

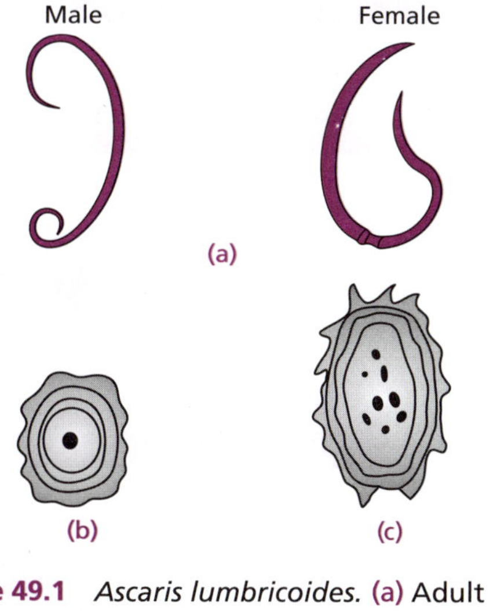

Figure 49.1 *Ascaris lumbricoides.* (a) Adult worm. (b) Fertilized egg. (c) Unfertilized egg.

- *Ovum* Small, atrophied ovum
- Does not float in saturated solution of common salt

Life cycle of *Ascaris lumbricoides* (Flow chart 49.1)

- **Definitive host** Humans
- **Intermediate host** Not required, passes life cycle in one host—the humans

Pathogenicity and clinical features

The disease caused is known as **ascariasis**. The symptoms are produced by both larvae and adult worms.

Symptoms due to larvae

***Ascaris* pneumonia (Loeffler syndrome)** is characterized by fever, non-productive cough and dyspnoea. Occasionally, blood-tinged sputum containing *Ascaris* larvae may be expectorated. Urticaria and eosinophilia may also be seen in 20% of cases.

Symptoms due to adult worms

The adult worms produce pathogenic effects in the following ways:

- **Spoliative action** They interfere with digestion and absorption of food and cause protein–energy malnutrition and vitamin A deficiency (night blindness).

Fertilized eggs with unsegmented ovum passed in faeces develop in soil to form rhabditiform larva

↓

Infection occurs by ingestion of food, drink or raw vegetables contaminated with eggs containing rhabditiform larva

↓

Eggs release motile rhabditiform larvae in the upper part of small intestine

↓

Rhabditiform larvae penetrate the intestinal mucosa, enter the portal circulation and reach the liver and then enter the systemic circulation and reach the lungs via right heart

↓

From lungs, larvae penetrate through the capillaries and reach the lung alveoli

↓

From alveoli, larvae ascend the bronchi and trachea, larynx and pharynx and are swallowed with saliva

↓

Finally, larvae reach the upper part of small intestine where they grow into adult worms and after mating, the females lay fertilized eggs

↓

The cycle is repeated

Flow chart 49.1 Life cycle of *Ascaris lumbricoides.*

- **Toxic action** The body fluid (*ascaron* or *ascarase*) of an adult worm produces toxic effects such as typhoid-like fever and hypersensitivity reactions such as fever, urticaria, oedema of face, conjunctivitis and irritation of the upper respiratory tract.
- **Mechanical effects** Presence of large numbers of entangled worms may cause intestinal obstruction and occurrence of intussusceptions.

The adult worm may enter appendix causing **appendicitis**. It may enter the biliary passage causing **obstructive jaundice** and **acute haemorrhagic pancreatitis**. It may enter the stomach and pass through the oesophagus and may reach the larynx causing **asphyxia** or may come out through the mouth or nose.

Laboratory diagnosis

Diagnosis of intestinal ascariasis includes the following:

- Demonstration of the characteristic eggs in faeces by saline and iodine preparation
- Demonstration of eggs in concentrated faeces if routine examination is negative
- Demonstration of adult worms passed in faeces, in vomit or through nose
- Demonstration of larvae in sputum or gastric aspirate in *Ascaris* pneumonia

Treatment

- Piperazine salts (citrate, hydrate, phosphate, adipate)—drug of choice
- Mebendazole and albendazole
- Pyrantel pamoate, hetrazan and thiabendazole can also be used

Prophylactic measures

- Proper sanitation—effective sanitary disposal of faeces
- Avoiding consumption of raw vegetables and fruits grown in soils contaminated with human faeces
- Personal cleanliness and elementary hygienic conditions during meals

Hookworms

Two species of hookworms are infectious to humans—*Ancylostoma duodenale* and *Necator americanus. A. duodenale* is prevalent in southern Europe, Northern Africa and Northern Asia (known as Old World hookworm). *N. americanus* is prevalent in Central and South America, Central and Southern Africa, far East Asia and Australia (known as New World hookworm). Both the species are common in India. *A. duodenale* is prevalent in Northern India and *N. americanus* is prevalent Southern India. Their habitat is the small intestine of humans.

Ancylostoma duodenale

Morphology

It occurs as

- **Adult worm**
  - *Shape* Small, greyish white and cylindrical
  - *Anterior end* Is bent dorsally, hence the name hookworm
  - *Freshly passed worm* Reddish brown in colour because of ingested blood in its intestine
  - *Mouth* Has six teeth, four hook-like on the ventral surface and two knob-like on the dorsal surface
  - *Male worm* Smaller, 8–11 × 0.4 mm. Its posterior end has umbrella-like copulatory bursa with two copulatory spicules
  - *Female worm* 10–13 × 0.6 mm. Its posterior end is tapering and no expanded bursa is present like in male worm. The vulva opens ventrally at the junction of posterior and middle thirds of the body. It is **oviparous—mature female** can lay 10,000–25,000 eggs
- **Eggs** (Fig. 49.2)
  - *Shape* Oval or elliptical
  - *Size* 60 × 40 μm
  - *Colour* Colourless—non-bile stained
  - *Eggshell* Transparent hyaline
  - *Ovum* Segmented ovum generally with four blastomeres

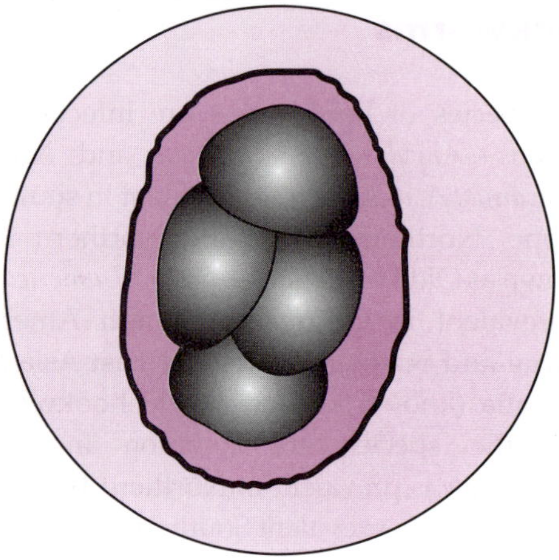

Figure 49.2 Egg of *Ancylostoma duodenale*.

– Floats in saturated solution of common salt

Life cycle of *Ancylostoma duodenale* (Flow chart 49.2)

- **Definitive host** Human
- **Intermediate host** Not required, passes life cycle in one host—the humans

Pathogenicity and clinical features

The disease caused is known as **ancylostomiasis (hookworm disease)**. The symptoms are produced by both larvae and adult worms.

Symptoms due to larvae

- **Ground itch or dermatitis** is characterized by pruritic maculopapular dermatitis. It is more common with *N. americanus.*
- **Creeping eruption** is characterized by a reddish itchy papule along the path traversed by the larval stage of *N. americanus,* which wander aimlessly through the skin layers producing symptoms—termed **larva migrans**.
- **Bronchitis or bronchopneumonia** may also occur.

Symptoms due to adult worms

Adult worms produce epigastric pain, vomiting and diarrhoea.

Anaemia Microcytic hypochromic anaemia. The causes of anaemia are

Eggs passed in faeces, develop in soil to form rhabditiform larva, which develops further into filariform larva

↓

Infection occurs by penetration of filariform larva through the skin. Filariform larva, on reaching the subcutaneous tissue, enter the lymphatics or small venules

↓

Larvae pass through the lymphatic vascular system into venous circulation and via right heart reach the pulmonary capillaries and enter the alveolar spaces

↓

From alveolar spaces, larvae migrate to the bronchi, trachea, larynx and pharynx, and are swallowed

↓

Finally, larvae reach the small intestine where they grow into adult worms. In 3–4 weeks, they sexually mature and after mating, the females lay eggs

↓

The cycle is repeated

Flow chart 49.2 Life cycle of *Ancylostoma duodenale*.

- Sucking of blood by adult worm through the wound produced in intestinal mucosa during its attachment (a single adult worm of *A. duodenale* sucks 0.2 mL of blood a day and *N. americanus* sucks 0.03 mL blood a day)
- Continuous bleeding from the punctured sites

Hypoproteinaemia Malnourished individuals may have hypoproteinaemia.

Laboratory diagnosis

Diagnosis includes the following:

- Demonstration of the characteristic eggs in faeces by saline and iodine preparation
- Demonstration of eggs in concentrated faeces if routine examination is negative
- Demonstration of adult worms passed in faeces spontaneously or after a vermifuge
- Demonstration of worms or eggs in duodenal contents obtained by duodenal intubation may also be possible sometimes

Treatment

- Mebendazole, albendazole or pyrantel pamoate
- Oral iron and appropriate nutritional support for correction of hypoproteinaemia and anaemia

Prophylactic measures

- Treatment of infected persons—carriers and diseased persons
- Effective disposal of sewage to prevent soil pollution
- Disinfection of faeces or soil
- Personal protection by wearing of boots and gloves

Necator americanus

N. americanus is similar to *A. duodenale* in many aspects with slight differences in morphological features. These are as follows:

- **Shape** Smaller and more slender than *A. duodenale*
- **Anterior end** Bends in opposite direction
- Buccal capsule has four chitinous plates, two on ventral surface and two on dorsal surface
- **Male worm** 7–9 × 0.3 mm. Copulatory bursa is long and wide
- **Female worm** 9–11 × 0.4 mm. The vulva is placed in the middle of the body. Its life cycle, morphology, pathogenicity, diagnosis, treatment and prophylactic measures are similar to those of *A. duodenale* but *N. americanus* is comparatively less pathogenic than *A. duodenale*

Enterobius vermicularis (pinworm, threadworm, seat worm)

It is worldwide in distribution, more common in temperate than in tropical regions and more common in children. Its habitats are the caecum, vermiform appendix and adjacent parts of ascending colon.

Morphology

It occurs as

- **Adult worm** (Fig. 49.3a)
  - *Shape* Small, white, spindle-shaped—resembles a piece of white thread
- A double bulb oesophagus is the characteristic feature
  - No buccal cavity is present
  - **Male worm** 2–4 × 0.1–0.2 mm. The posterior end is curved and has a coiled tail with a single spicule. It dies after fertilization of female.
  - **Female worm** 8–13 × 0.3–05 mm. The posterior third of the body is pointed like a pin, hence the name pinworm. It is **oviparous**—mature female lays eggs and after oviposition dies in 2–3 weeks.
- **Eggs** (Fig. 49.3b)
  - *Shape* Planoconvex—flattened on ventral side and convex on dorsal side
  - *Size* 50–60 × 30 μm

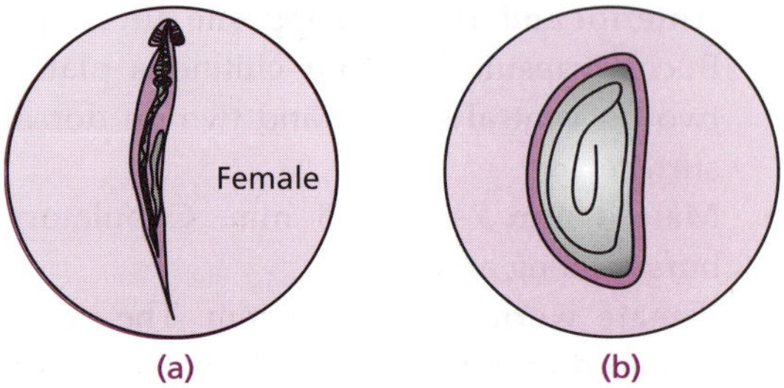

Figure 49.3 *Enterobius vermicularis.* **(a)** Adult worm. **(b)** Egg.

- *Colour* Colourless—non-bile stained
- *Eggshell* Transparent shell
- *Ovum* Fully developed—a coiled tadpole-like larva
- Floats in saturated solution of common salt

Life cycle (Flow chart 49.3)

- **Definitive host** Human
- **Intermediate host** Not required, passes life cycle in one host—the humans

Pathogenicity

The disease caused is known as **enterobiasis,** common in children. The eggs deposited on perianal skin contaminate night clothes and bed linens of infected persons—handling of night clothes and bed linens can transmit infection due to contamination of hands. Infection by inhalation of eggs that become airborne during bed making can also occur. Reinfection of same host (autoinfection) is also possible; it occurs in two ways:

1. **By hand-to-mouth** In this, fingers contaminated with eggs because of scratching of the affected itching part around the anus are transferred to food articles and swallowed or transferred directly from anus to mouth.
2. **Retrograde infection** In this, the eggs laid on perianal skin hatch out into larvae, which migrate back through the anus up to caecum and develop into adult worms.

Clinical features

- Perianal pruritus
- An eczematous condition around the anus and perineum
- Nocturnal enuresis
- Inflammation of the vermiform appendix may also occur
- Vulvovaginitis
- Cystitis in young girls

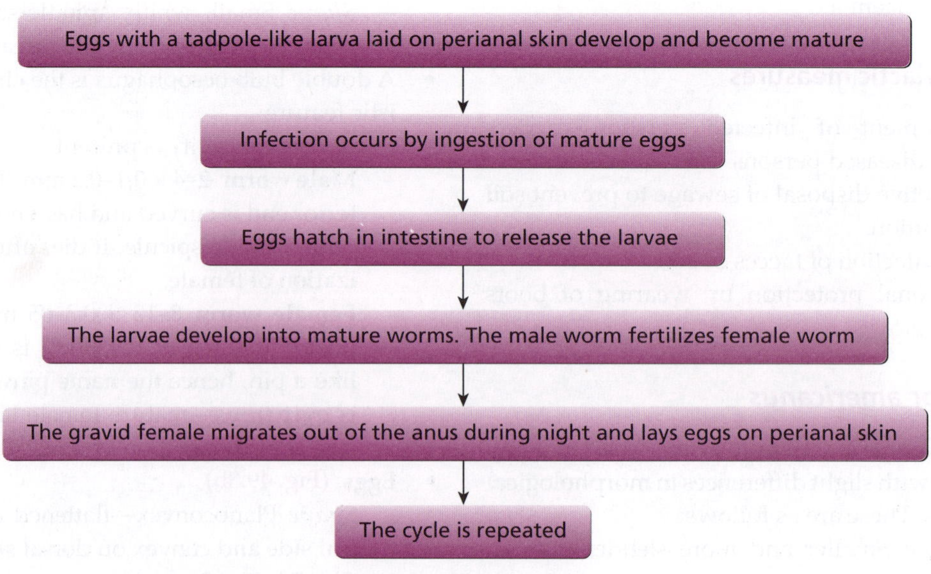

Flow chart 49.3 Life cycle of *Enterobius vermicularis.*

- Salpingitis
- Pelvic or peritoneal granulomas

Laboratory diagnosis

Diagnosis includes the following:

- Demonstration of adult worms in faeces after a purge or an enema
- Demonstration of the characteristic eggs in faeces by direct smear examination or in concentrated faeces may be negative as eggs are deposited on perianal skin; hence, demonstration of eggs in the scrapings from the perianal skin by NIH swab is a better method

Treatment

Mebendazole or pyrantel pamoate

Prophylactic measures

- Health education on personal and community hygiene
- Mass treatment of infected persons to prevent infection by contact

Other intestinal nematodes

- *Strongyloides stercoralis* causing **strongyloidiasis**
- *Trichinella spiralis* causing **trichinelliasis (trichinosis)**
- *Trichuris trichiura* causing **trichuriasis**

Wuchereria bancrofti (Bancroft's filaria)

It is a tissue nematode, cosmopolitan in distribution, common in tropics and subtropics. It is found in India, China, Japan, West Indies, West and Central Africa, and South America. The adult worm is found in the lymphatic vessels and lymph nodes of human beings only.

Morphology

It occurs as

- **Adult worm**
  - Long, hair-like, transparent, and creamy white in colour; ends are tapering and rounded (Fig. 49.4a)
  - ***Male worm*** 2.5–4 cm in length and 0.01 mm in thickness
  - ***Female worm*** 8–10 cm long and 0.2–0.3 mm in thickness; is **ovoviviparous** and liberates eggs with well-developed sheathed embryos (microfilaria)
- **Embryo (microfilaria)**
  - It is the first-stage larva, found in peripheral blood, hydrocele fluid and chylous urine.
  - ***Size*** It is 275–300 μm long and 8–10 μm in breadth.

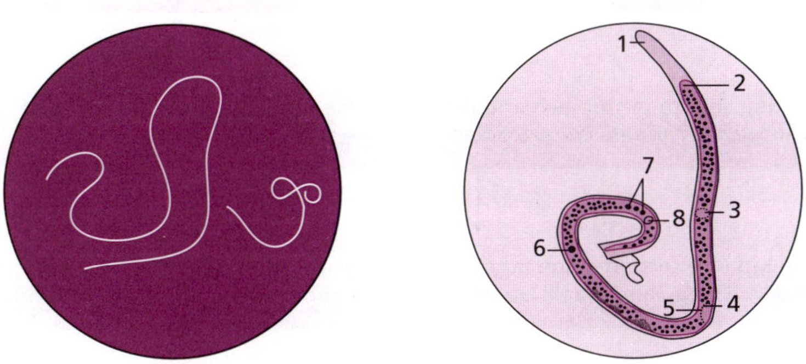

(a) (b)

1. Sheath 2. Cephalic space
3. Nerve ring 4. Excretory pore 5. Excretory cell
6. G cell-1 7. G cells-2–4 8. Anal pore

Figure 49.4 *Wuchereria bancrofti*. (a) Adult worm. (b) Microfilaria.

- *Motility* It is actively motile with the help of coiling and uncoiling of its tail.
- *Hyaline sheath* It is a structureless sac covering the embryo; it is longer than the larval body and measures 350 µm. The larva moves forward and backward in sheath.
- In a stained smear (Romanowsky stain), it is stained pink with a column of violet nuclei (somatic cells) extending from head to tail end but absent at the tip of the head and tail (Fig. 49.4b).

Life cycle (Flow chart 49.4)

- **Definitive host** Human beings
- **Intermediate host** Mosquitoes of genus *Culex*, *Aedes* and *Anopheles*

Pathogenicity and clinical features

The disease caused is known as **wuchereriasis (bancroftian** or **lymphatic filariasis)**.

The pathogenic and clinical effects are due to inflammatory damage to the lymphatics by adult worms. Clinically it occurs as

Human infection occurs by bite of infected mosquito, which deposits **third-stage larvae** on the skin near the site of the mosquito bite

↓

The larvae reach the subcutaneous tissue and subsequently reach the lymphatic channels

↓

The larvae the draining lymph nodes to develop into adult worms and mature sexually

↓

The male fertilizes the female and the gravid female then gives birth to microfilaria

↓

Microfilariae enter the blood circulation through thoracic duct or the right lymphatic duct

↓

Mosquito ingests microfilaria in peripheral circulation during its blood meal

↓

Microfilariae lose their sheath in stomach and penetrate the gut wall to reach thorax of the mosquitoes, where they grow to form the first-stage larvae

↓

First-stage larvae develop into second-stage larvae and finally into the third-stage larvae, which is infective to humans. These third-stage larvae enter the proboscis sheath of the mosquito

↓

When this mosquito bites, it releases the third-stage larvae and the cycle is repeated

Flow chart 49.4 Life cycle of *Wuchereria bancrofti*.

- **Lymphatic filariasis** It is characterized by
  - Lymphangitis
  - Lymphoedema
  - Lymphadenitis
  - Lymphangiovarix
  - Elephantiasis
  - Chyluria, chylothorax, chylous ascitis and chylous diarrhoea
  - Hydrocele
- **Occult filariasis** It is characterized by tropical pulmonary eosinophilia.

Laboratory diagnosis

Diagnosis includes the following:

- Demonstration of the microfilariae in peripheral blood
  - ***Time of blood collection*** Between 10 pm and 4 am, as *W. bancrofti* has nocturnal periodicity; alternatively, blood can be collected during daytime by giving diethylcarbamazine (100 mg) orally and collecting and examining blood for microfilariae in 30–45 minutes.
  - ***Methods for demonstration*** Microfilariae in blood can be demonstrated in
    - A wet mount (unstained preparation)—motile microfilaria can be seen under low power
    - Stained preparation—in a thin or thick blood film stained with Romanowsky stain
    - Demonstration of microfilariae in the chylous urine, exudates of lymph varix and hydrocele fluid
    - Demonstration of the adult worm in lymph node biopsy
    - Demonstration of antibodies using passive haemagglutination test, fluorescent antibody test, complement fixation test, ELISA and radioimmunoassay test
    - Demonstration of circulating antigen in serum using ELISA

Treatment

Diethylcarbamazine is the drug of choice.

Prophylactic measures

- Vector control—destruction of mosquitoes
- Protection against mosquito bite
- Treatment of patients and carriers with diethylcarbamazine

Other tissue nematodes

- *Brugia malayi* causing **lymphatic filariasis**
- *Loa loa* causing **loiasis**
- *Onchocerca volvulus* causing **onchocerciasis**
- *Dracunculus medinensis* causing **dracunculosis**

Echinococcus granulosus/Taenia echinococcus (dog tapeworm/ hydatid worm)

It is a cestode causing hydatid disease and is worldwide in distribution; it is also reported from many states of India. This parasite lives in adult tapeworms found attached to intestinal mucosa of dogs and the larval stage lives in humans and other herbivorous animals.

Morphology

- **Adult worm** (Fig. 49.5a)
  - It is a small cestode.
  - Size is 3–6 mm in length; it has head, neck and body.
  - Scolex has four suckers with two rows of hooks.
  - Neck is short and thick.
  - Strobilla or body consists of three segments: first, immature; second, mature; and third, gravid.
- **Egg**
  - ***Shape*** Ovoid
  - ***Size*** 32–36 × 25–32 μm

- *Colour* Brown (bile stained)
- *Embryo* Contains six hooklets (hexacanth embryo)
- *Eggs* Infective to humans, cattle and sheep

- **Larval form**
  - It is a hydatid cyst, which develops in tissues of the intermediate host.
  - Hydatid cyst in humans is
    - Typically, it is unilocular, subspherical in shape and is filled with fluid.
    - The cyst wall secreted by embryo has two layers:
      - *Ectocyst (outer—cuticular layer)* Laminated hyaline membrane, appears as white of hard-boiled egg, 1 mm thick and elastic
      - *Endocyst (inner—germinal layer)* It is cellular, nucleate and thin, 22–25 µm. This is the vital layer and gives rise to
        - Brood capsules with scolices
        - Specific hydatid fluid highly toxic—when absorbed, causes anaphylactic shock
        - Ectocyst—outer layer (Fig. 49.5b)

Life cycle (Flow chart 49.5)

- **Definitive host** Dog (also fox, wolf, jackals)
- **Intermediate host** Sheep, cattle, pigs, goat, and horse, and human beings are the accidental hosts

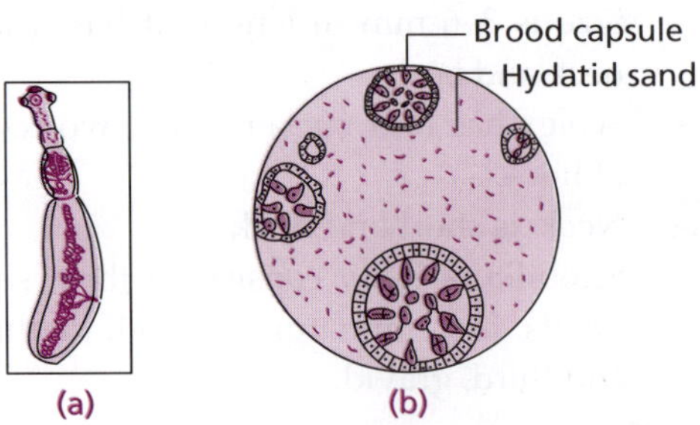

Figure 49.5 *Echinococcus granulosus.* (a) Adult worm. (b) Hydatid cyst.

Pathogenicity

The disease caused is known as **hydatid disease**. It is characterized by the following features:

- Hydatid cyst in subcutaneous tissue may be visible and can be palpable.
- Its presence can be detected at autopsy or by its pressure effects on the surrounding tissue or suppuration of cyst or rupture of cyst producing anaphylactic symptoms along with secondary echinococcosis.
- Liver is the commonest site followed by lungs and other organs.
- Liver hydatid cyst may manifest with pain and swelling, nausea and vomiting.
- Lung hydatid cyst presents with cough and chest pain.

Laboratory diagnosis

Diagnostic aspiration is not recommended due to danger of anaphylaxis and secondary echinococcosis. Diagnosis includes the following:

- **Casoni test (skin test)** Intradermal injection of 0.2 mL of sterile hydatid fluid in one arm—development of large wheel, 5 cm in diameter, with multiple pseudopodia in 30 minutes indicates a positive reaction.
- **Antigen detection test**
  - Antigen in serum can be detected by ELISA, countercurrent immunoelectrophoresis, coagglutination test and latex agglutination test.
  - Antigen in urine can be detected by countercurrent immunoelectrophoresis.
- **Detection of antibodies**
  - Antibodies can be detected by indirect haemagglutination test, fluorescent antibody test, countercurrent immunoelectrophoresis, latex agglutination test, ELISA and Western blot test.
  - The tests are of low sensitivity and low specificity and cannot differentiate old and new infection.
- **Radiological diagnosis** Plain X-ray, ultrasonography, CT scan and magnetic resonance imaging (MRI) can be used for diagnosis.

Eggs in faeces of definitive host

↓

Ingestion of eggs by intermediate hosts; in humans it occurs by
- Handling and fondling infected dogs
- Allowing infected dog to eat from same dish
- Eating of raw vegetables infected with canine faeces

↓

Ingestion of eggs in sheep and other domestic animals (intermediate hosts) occurs while grazing in the field

↓

Eggs reach small intestine—hexacanth embryos penetrate intestinal mucosa and reach portal circulation

↓

Eggs reach liver, lungs and other organs and are filtered out from the systemic circulation to the various organs and tissues. Finally develop into hydatid cyst (in humans, it is a dead end)

↓

Infection of definitive host–dog, occurs due to consumption of infected tissues of sheep, cattle, etc.

↓

Attachment of scolices to intestinal mucosa

↓

Development of adult worm in dogs

↓

Release of eggs from gravid segment, which pass out in faeces

↓

Cycle is repeated

Flow chart 49.5 Life cycle of *Echinococcus granulosus*.

Treatment

- Surgical removal of cyst is the treatment of choice.
- Albendazole, mebendazole and praziquaentel may be used.

Prophylactic measures

- Deworming of infected dogs
- Elimination of street dogs
- Personal hygiene such as washing of hands and utensils used by dogs

- Maintenance of slaughterhouse, that is, prevention of dogs from eating tissues of animals

Taenia saginata (beef tapeworm) and *Taenia solium* (pork tapeworm)

T. saginata and *T. solium* are cestodes causing taeniasis, worldwide in distribution. Their habitat is small intestine—jejunum.

Morphology

They occur in three different morphological forms—as adult worm, larva and egg. Morphological features of *T. saginata* and *T. solium* are summarized in Table 49.1.

Life cycle (Flow chart 49.6)

- **Definitive host** Human beings
- **Intermediate host** Cow, buffalo in *T. saginata*, pig or rarely humans in *T. solium*

  Infection occurs by eating inadequately cooked pork (*T. solium*) or beef (*T. saginata*) containing cysticerci (larval stage).

Pathogenicity—intestinal taeniasis (tapeworm infection)

It is characterized by abdominal discomfort, diarrhoea, vomiting, chronic indigestion and anaemia.

Table 49.1 Morphological features of *Taenia saginata* and *Taenia solium*

	T. saginata	*T. solium*
Adult worm	• Tape-like, 5–10 m in length • White, semitransparent	• Tape-like, 2–3 m in length • White, semitransparent
Number of proglottides	1000–2000	800–900
Scolex	• Quadrate with four suckers • Pigmented	• Globular with four suckers • Non-pigmented
Head	Head without rostellum and hooklets	Head with rostellum and pigmented hooklets
Neck	Long, thin and fragile	Short and thick, 5–6 mm long
Proglottides	• Size—20 × 5 mm (Fig. 49.6a) • Expelled—singly • Uterus—with 15–30 lateral branches on each side • Testicular follicles—300–400 • Vaginal sphincter—present	• Size—12 × 6 mm (Fig. 49.6a) • Expelled—in chains of five or six • Uterus—with 5–10 compound lateral branches on each side • Testicular follicles—150–200 • Vaginal sphincter—absent
Larvae	• Ovary—two without accessory lobes • *Cysticercus bovis* • Found in muscles of cow, buffalo • Not found in human beings	• Two with accessory lobes • *Cysticercus cellulosae* • Muscles of pig • Also found in human beings
Eggs	• Shape is spherical (Fig. 49.6b) • Size—33–43 µm in diameter • Colour—brown (bile-stained) • Embryo contains six hooklets (hexacanth embryo) • Does not float in saturated salt solution	• Same as *T. saginata*

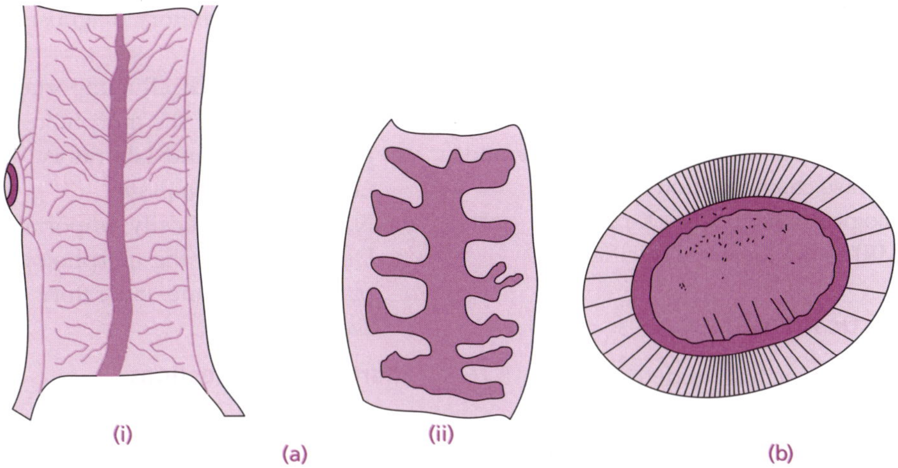

Figure 49.6 *Taenia saginata* and *T. solium*. (a) Proglottides: (i) *T. saginata* (ii) *T. solium*. (b) Egg.

Larval stage develops into adult worm in small intestine and attains sexual maturity and fertilization occurs in the segment and eggs develop

↓

Eggs are passed in faeces after rupture of gravid segments

↓

Animals ingest egg while grazing (human beings also may get infection by ingestion of water vegetables contaminated with eggs; this happens in *T. solium* only and not in *T. saginata*)

↓

Eggs reach systemic circulation by penetrating the gut wall and filtered in muscle tissues, where the embryos develop into infective cystic larvae called cysticerci

↓

The cycle is repeated when improperly cooked pork (*T. solium*) or beef (*T. saginata*) containing cysticerci (larval stage) is consumed

Flow chart 49.6 Life cycle of *Taenia saginata* and *T. solium*.

T. solium also causes diseases that are similar to those caused by *T. saginata* but it is less conspicuous. In addition, it causes **cysticercosis**—a fatal systemic condition clinically manifested as epileptic fits, headache, blurred vision, etc. Cysticerci are found in muscle and subcutaneous tissue, eyes and brain.

Laboratory diagnosis

This includes the following:

- Demonstration of eggs
- Demonstration of segments of worms in faeces
- Demonstration of *Taenia* antigen in faeces and CSF by ELISA

- Demonstration of antibodies by indirect haemagglutination test, complement fixation test, indirect immunofluorescence test and ELISA
- Molecular diagnosis by DNA probes and polymerase chain reaction (PCR)
- Radiological diagnosis—X-ray, CT scan and MRI to demonstrate calcified cyst

Prophylactic measures

- Avoidance of eating undercooked pork or beef
- Inspection of beef/pork for cysticerci
- Treatment of infected persons

Treatment

- Praziquantel is the drug of choice.
- Niclosamide is also effective.

Other cestodes infecting human beings

- *Diphyllobothrium latum* (fish tapeworm) causing diphyllobothriasis
- *Hymenolepis nana* (dwarf tapeworm) causing hymenolepiasis or hymenolipidosis

Self-assessment

Long-answer questions

1. Enumerate helminthic parasites found in gastrointestinal tract. Discuss in brief the morphology, life cycle, pathogenicity and laboratory diagnosis of *Ascaris lumbricoides.*
2. Enumerate helminthic parasites found in gastrointestinal tract. Discuss in brief the morphology, life cycle, pathogenicity and laboratory diagnosis of *Ancylostoma duodenale.*
3. Enumerate helminthic parasites found in gastrointestinal tract. Discuss in brief the morphology, life cycle, pathogenicity and laboratory diagnosis of *Enterobius vermicularis.*
4. Enumerate haemoparasites. Discuss in brief the morphology, life cycle, pathogenicity and laboratory diagnosis of *Wuchereria bancrofti.*
5. Name the medically important cestodes. Discuss in brief the morphology, life cycle, pathogenicity and laboratory diagnosis of *Echinococcus granulosus.*
6. Name the medically important cestodes. Discuss in brief the morphology, life cycle, pathogenicity and laboratory diagnosis of *Taenia solium.*

Short-answer questions

Write notes on

1. *Necator americanus*
2. Laboratory diagnosis of filariasis
3. Lymphatic filariasis
4. Enterobiasis
5. Hydatid cyst
6. Laboratory diagnosis of hydatid disease
7. *Taenia saginata*

Multiple-choice questions

1. Which of the following is a bloodsucking parasite?
   A. Roundworm
   B. Hookworm
   C. Pinworm
   D. Seat worm
2. Which of the following is a cause of vitamin A deficiency?
   A. *Ancylostoma duodenale*
   B. *Enterobius vermicularis*
   C. *Ascaris lumbricoides*
   D. *Echinococcus granulosus*
3. Vitamin A deficiency in *Ascaris lumbricoides* infection occurs as a result of
   A. Toxic action of adult worm
   B. Spoliative action of adult worm
   C. Mechanical effects of adult worm
   D. None of the above
4. The scrapings from the perianal skin by NIH swab are to be collected in which of the following infections?
   A. *Ancylostoma duodenale*
   B. *Necator americanus*

C. *Ascaris lumbricoides*
D. *Enterobius vermicularis*

5. Which of the following is an intermediate host in *Wuchereria bancrofti?*
   A. *Anopheles* mosquito
   B. *Culex* mosquito
   C. *Aedes* mosquito
   D. All of the above
6. The best time for collection of blood to demonstrate microfilariae in peripheral blood is
   A. Between 10 pm and 4 am
   B. Between 10 am and 4 pm
   C. Between 5 pm and 10 pm
   D. Any time during night
7. Which of the following is a definitive host in *Echinococcus granulosus?*
   A. Dog
   B. Sheep
   C. Human
   D. Cattle
8. Which of the following adult worms is not found in the intestine of a human?
   A. *Taenia saginata*
   B. *T. solium*
   C. *Echinococcus granulosus*
   D. None of the above
9. Which of the following is an intermediate host in *Taenia solium?*
   A. Pig
   B. Cow
   C. Buffalo
   D. Sheep
10. *Cysticercus cellulosae* is a larval stage of which of the following parasites?
   A. *Taenia saginata*
   B. *T. solium*
   C. *Echinococcus granulosus*
   D. None of the above
11. Casoni test is a skin test used in the diagnosis of
   A. *Taenia saginata*
   B. *T. solium*
   C. *Echinococcus granulosus*
   D. None of the above
12. Which of the following parasites is the most common cause of anaemia?
   A. *Echinococcus granulosus*
   B. *Ancylostoma duodenale*
   C. *Ascaris lumbricoides*
   D. *Enterobius vermicularis*
13. Eggs showing four blastomers is the characteristic feature of which of the following parasites?
   A. *Echinococcus granulosus*
   B. *Ascaris lumbricoides*
   C. *Ancylostoma duodenale*
   D. *Enterobius vermicularis*
14. Which of the following is a non-bile stained egg?
   A. *Echinococcus granulosus*
   B. *Taenia saginata*
   C. *Ascaris lumbricoides*
   D. *Enterobius vermicularis*
15. Which of the following is an intermediate host in *Taenia saginata?*
   A. Pig
   B. Cattle
   C. Dog
   D. Sheep

50 Oral and Dental Infections

The organisms normally present in the oral cavity are responsible for a large proportion of oral and dental infections. Organisms other than normal flora are also involved in these infections.

Predisposing factors

Predisposing factors for oral and dental infections are depicted in Flow chart 50.1.

Aetiology

Bacterial causes

- *Streptococcus mutans*
- *Str. sanguis*
- *Str. sobrinus*
- *Str. salivarius*
- *Str. milleri*
- *Str. oralis*
- *Str. faecalis*
- *Str. pyogenes*
- *Corynebacterium diphtheriae*
- *Mycobacterium tuberculosis* and *Mycobacterium leprae*
- Lactobacilli
- *Actinomyces israelii* and other species
- *Staphylococcus aureus*
- *Prevotella melaninogenica*
- *Fusobacterium* species
- *Borrelia vincentii* and *Treponema pallidum*
- *Neisseria gonorrhoeae*
- *Calymmatobacterium granulomatis*
- *Klebsiella rhinoscleromatis*
- *Bacteroides* species
- Anaerobic Gram-positive cocci

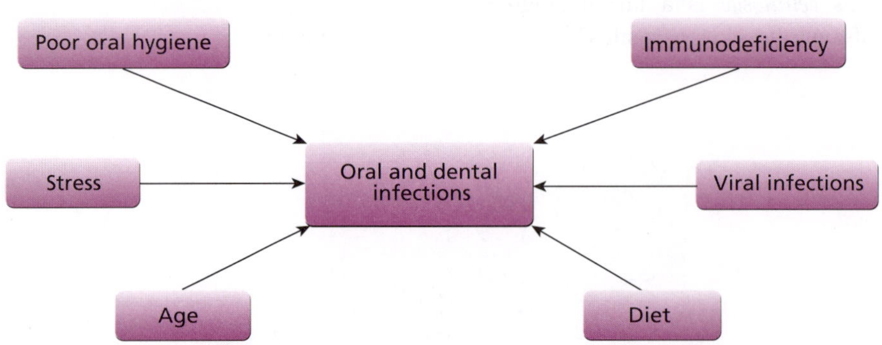

Flow chart 50.1 Predisposing factors for oral and dental infections.

- *Francisella tularemia*
- *Pseudomonas pseudomallei*
- *Rothia* spp.
- *Veillonella* spp.
- *Actinobacillus* spp.
- *Campylobacter* spp.
- *Bifidobacterium* spp.
- *Leptotrichia* spp.
- *Mycoplasma* spp.

Viral causes

- Herpes simplex viruses
- Varicella-zoster virus
- Cytomegalovirus
- Coxsackie A and B viruses
- Measles virus
- Mumps virus
- Rubella virus
- Smallpox virus
- Molluscum contagiosum
- Human papillomaviruses

Fungal causes

- *Candida albicans*
- *Fonsecaea* species
- *Cladosporium* species
- *Phialophora* species
- *Sporothrix schenckii*
- *Rhinosporidium seeberi*
- *Cryptococcus neoformans*
- *Blastomyces dermatitidis*
- *Paracoccidioides brasiliensis*
- *Coccidioides immitis*
- *Histoplasma capsulatum*
- *Geotrichum* species
- *Mucor* species
- *Rhizopus* species
- *Absidia* species

Parasitic causes

- *Leishmania donovani*
- *Trypanosoma cruzi*
- *Toxoplasma gondii*
- *Taenia* species
- *Echinococcus granulosus*
- *Trichinella spiralis*
- *Ascaris lumbricoides*
- *Strongyloides stercoralis*

Pathogenicity

The important oral and dental infections include the following:

- Dental caries
- Periodontal diseases
  - Acute gingivitis
  - Chronic gingivitis
  - Periodontitis
  - Juvenile periodontitis
- Endodontic infections
  - Pulpitis
  - Periapical abscess
- Cellulitis
- Acute sialadenitis
- Oral candidiasis
- Dental abscess
- Stomatitis (herpetic)
- Vincent's angina
- Herpangina
- Periapical abscess
- Osteomyelitis of the jaw, etc.

The knowledge regarding the structure of tooth helps in better understanding of pathogenicity (Fig. 50.1).

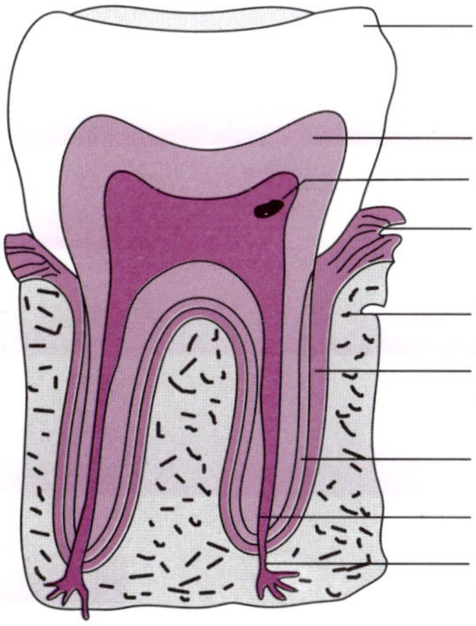

Figure 50.1 Structure of tooth.

Dental caries

Dental caries is a microbial disease of the calcified tissues of the teeth, characterized by demineralization of the inorganic portion and destruction of the organic substances of the tooth. It is the most prevalent chronic disease affecting both sexes, all age groups and all socioeconomic strata.

Contributing factors

Following are the contributing factors in dental caries:

- The tooth factors such as composition of tooth—the structure of enamel, morphological characteristics of the tooth, position of tooth, etc.
- Salivary factors such as composition of saliva, pH, quantity, viscosity and antibacterial factors in saliva
- Diet factors such as the physical nature, carbohydrate content, vitamin content of the diet and fluoride content (the calcium and phosphorus intake in diet also contribute to the occurrence of caries)
- Dental plaque
- Heredity

Microbes associated with caries

Str. mutans is considered as the most important agent causing dental caries as it is almost invariably isolated from carious lesions. The following are the bacterial agents capable of causing dental caries:

- *Lactobacillus* species—*L. acidophilus* and *L. casei*
- *Streptococcus* species—*Str. mutans, Str. sobrinus, Str. sanguis, Str. salivarius, Str. mitior, Str. milleri, Str. oralis* and *Str. faecalis*
- *Actinomyces—A. viscosus, A. naeslundii, A. israelii*
- *Rothia* species

Other organisms Following organisms have been isolated from dental caries but their role in causing dental caries is not clear, although protective role of *Veillonella* species has been observed in germ-free animals. *Veillonella* spp. reduces the incidence of caries.

- Staphylococci
- *Arachnia* species
- *Bacillus* species
- *Bifidobacterium* species
- *Eubacterium* species
- *Propionibacterium* species
- *Veillonella* species

Mechanism of caries development

The development of caries occurs as depicted in Flow chart 50.2.

Some bacteria degrade the proteins present in the enamel or the protein phase is also destroyed by acidic demineralization. The enamel protein goes into the solution along with

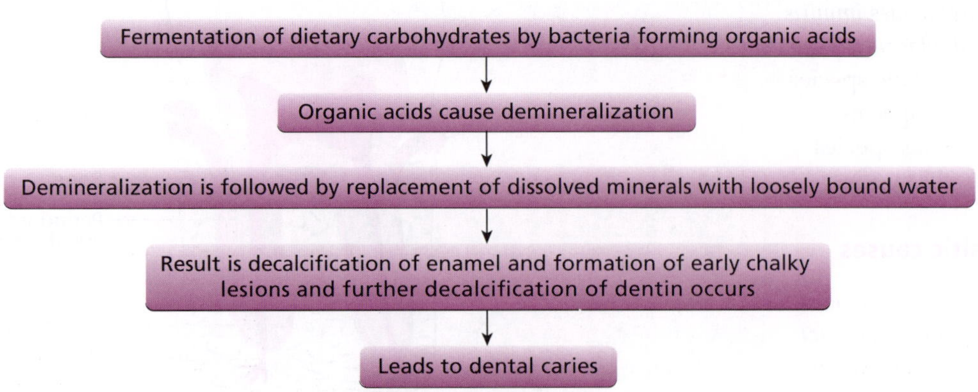

Flow chart 50.2 Mechanism of development of caries.

loss of minerals. In dentin, demineralization leaves the collagenous matrix intact. The residue is either digested by proteases produced by bacteria or converted into leather-like material.

Role of *Streptococcus mutans*

Str. mutans has a unique feature of utilizing dietary sucrose and convert it into glucan and dextran. Glucan acts as a carrier for other bacteria and helps bacteria to attach to solid surface forming matrix. Dextran causes clumping of these bacteria. Once this process of attachment occurs with the help of glucan and dextran, continuous acid production occurs leading to initiation of destruction of enamel. Once the process of caries is initiated by *Str. mutans,* the process of progression is taken up by other bacteria associated with dental caries, in which lactobacilli takes the major lead in the further process.

Clinical aspects of dental caries

Clinical classification

According to location on the individual tooth

- **Pit or fissure caries** Develop in the occlusal surface of molars and premolars, in the buccal and lingual surface of the molars and in the lingual surface of the maxillary incisors
- **Smooth surface caries** Develop on the proximal surfaces of the teeth or on the gingival third of the buccal and lingual surfaces (proximal caries usually begins just below the contact point)
- **Root surface caries** Develop on the cementum and/or dentine when the root is exposed to oral environment

According to the rapidity of process

- **Acute dental caries** Caries that run a rapid clinical course and lead to early pulp involvement by the carious process. Commonly occurs in children and young adults. It may occur as a rampant form of caries in infants because of prolonged use of a nursing bottle, breastfeeding or sugar or honey-sweetened pacifiers and is called nursing bottle caries or nursing caries.
- **Chronic caries** Caries that progress slowly and pulp involvement occurs much later as compared to that in acute caries. It is more common in adults.

According to whether the lesion is a new or whether it is associated with existing restoration

- **Primary or virgin caries** Caries that attack a previously intact surface
- **Secondary or recurrent caries** Caries that occur in the immediate vicinity of existing restoration

Arrested caries Caries that become static or stationary and do not progress further

Clinical appearance of caries

Initial lesion seen in caries is a chalky white spot, which can heal or remineralize. Up to this stage, the disease is reversible. This lesion is undermined because of the lateral spreading. This causes continuous destruction that progresses to cavitation. Further lateral spread of caries leads to penetration into the dentin, which undermines the enamel. Further spread of microorganisms along the tubules leads to penetration into the pulp, which becomes infected, inflamed and necrosed. Subsequently, the invasion of periapical tissue by microbes leads to the formation of a periapical abscess, which may expand into cancellous bone and establish a fistula—a tiny point of opening with a large carious lesion.

Microbiological tests for assessment of caries

No microbiological diagnostic tests are available for diagnosis; however, the following microbiological tests are available:

- To highlight the patients with a higher number of potentially pathogenic microorganisms in their oral cavity
- To assess the efficacy of preventive measures, for example, efficacy of antimicro-

bial agents, diet and oral hygiene measures taken by the patient

For this, a sample of saliva is collected and appropriate dilution of it is cultured on mitis-salivarius-bacitracin agar for *Str. mutans* and Rogosa SL agar for lactobacilli. Alternatively, a commercially available dip-slide kit is used, which gives equally comparable results with culture technique.

The tests are used to find out the high and low counts of *Str. mutans* and lactobacilli per millilitre of saliva. Counts more than 1 million/mL are considered as high count and counts lower than 100,000/mL are considered as low count for *Str. mutans* and counts more than 100,000/mL are considered as high count and counts lower than 1000/mL are considered as low count for lactobacilli. The presence of these bacteria in high count is considered as one of the indicators of increased risk of developing dental caries, but the presence of high count alone does not mean that the patient has an increased risk of developing dental caries.

Methods of caries control

These include the following:

- Using chemical substances, which alter the tooth surfaces or tooth structures and make them less soluble to acid attack. These include:
  - ***Fluorides*** They can be administered through the communal supply in a concentration of 1 ppm, by topical application in the form of gel and solution, or through the medium of a dentifrice.
    - *Mechanism of action of fluorides* They can exert their effects in different ways:
      - Prevent degradation of carbohydrates by bacteria in the oral cavity and decrease the acid production and thereby offer protection against cariogenic process
      - Alter the structure of the developing tooth—through incorporation of fluoride in the enamel with the formation of a fluoroapatite producing less acid-soluble enamel and thus making it more resistant to attack by acid decalcification
      - Promote the remineralization of early enamel and dentine caries
  - Other chemical substances such as chlorhexidine and alexidine, silver nitrate, zinc chloride and potassium ferrocyanide can also be used.
- By using substances, which interfere with bacterial growth and metabolism, and thereby reducing the bacterial flora in the oral cavity. These substances include antibiotics such as penicillins, erythromycin, kanamycin, tetracycline and vancomycin and agents such as nitrofurans, urea and ammonium compounds, and chlorophyll.
- By changing dietary habits, that is, by restricting the refined carbohydrate intake, especially avoidance of sucrose-rich diet, caries can be controlled.
- By sealing anatomical sites, which are prone to develop caries and sites where stagnation of food occurs. Sealing can be achieved by fissure sealants.
- By mechanical measures, that is, by removing plaque from tooth surface. This can be achieved by routine periodic scaling and polishing of rough tooth surfaces, toothbrushing, mouth rinsing, using dental floss or tooth picks and incorporating detergent foods in the diet.

Periodontal diseases

Periodontal diseases are the diseases of the periodontium. The periodontium includes the following structures:

- Alveolar bone
- Cementum
- Periodontal ligament
- Gingiva

The periodontal diseases with a microbial aetiology are grouped into two categories:

1. Gingivitis—inflammation of the gingival tissue
2. Periodontitis—inflammation of the deeper tissue of the periodontium

Gingivitis

It is the inflammation of the gingival tissue. It may occur in acute or chronic form.

Acute ulcerative gingivitis (AUG)

AUG is an acute inflammation of the gingival tissue with irregularly shaped ulcers. The inflammation involves primarily the free gingival margin, the crest of the gingiva and the internal papillae; however, the ulcers first appear on tips of interdental papillae and if untreated may spread to marginal and finally to attached gingiva.

Aetiology Many microbes have been found to be associated with AUG, but whether they are really the causative agents or not is not conclusively known. The microbes isolated from the cases of AUG include the following:

- *Fusobacterium* species
- *B. vincentii*

These two are almost invariably present. In addition, other organisms are also isolated. These include

- *Treponema* species
- Streptococci
- *Veillonella* species
- *Actinomyces* species
- *Selemonas* species
- *Vibrio* species

Clinical features AUG is characterized by the development of painful, hyperaemic gingiva and sharply punched out erosions of the interdental papillae. The ulcers are covered by a grey, necrotic pseudomembrane or slough. The ulcer has a tendency to spread and may involve all gingival margins. The tendency for gingival bleeding, severe gingival pain or tenderness makes eating difficult. A typical unpleasant breath (odour) and bad taste are common. Fever, headache and malaise are the other symptoms.

In serious cases, generalized or systemic manifestations such as leucocytosis, gastrointestinal disturbances and tachycardia are seen.

Sequelae Occasionally, gangrenous stomatitis or noma, septicaemia, toxaemia and death may occur following AUG.

Laboratory diagnosis The cases are diagnosed clinically—clinical diagnosis is final. Laboratory findings are non-specific, hence are not much helpful; however, they may be of value in the diagnosis of atypical cases.

- **Specimen**—material from gingiva
- **Gram staining**—shows fusobacteria, an oral spirochete (medium sized), other spirochetes, filamentous bacteria, *Vibrios*, cocci and polymorphonuclear leucocytes. The diagnosis is strongly suspected only when the leucocytes, spirochetes and fusobacteria are seen in smear

Treatment Treatment modalities include

- Superficial cleansing of the oral cavity followed by thorough scaling and polishing
- Use of oxygenating agents or antibiotics with local treatment

Chronic gingivitis

This is a chronic inflammation of the gingival tissue. The inflammation is limited to the gingiva. It occurs in both sexes at any age, but is more common in women in the age group of 40–55 years.

Aetiology Microbes associated with chronic gingivitis include the following:

- *Str. sanguis*
- *Str. milleri*
- *Fusobacterium nucleatum*
- *Veillonella* species
- *A. israelii*
- *A. naeslundii*

- *Bacteroides intermedius*
- *Capnocytophaga* species

Clinical features It is characterized by the red and swollen gingiva with rounded ends, and the tendency for gingival bleeding even with mild irritation, such as toothbrushing. Severe gingival pain, discomfort and unpleasant bad taste are not seen.

Periodontitis (pyorrhoea)

It is the involvement of periodontal ligament, cementum and alveolar bone following untreated or improperly treated gingivitis. It is most common in adults and occasionally found in children.

Aetiology Microbes commonly isolated from the lesions include the following:

- *F. nucleatum*
- *P. melaninogenica*
- *Bacteroides gingivalis*
- *B. intermedius*
- *Bacteroides corrodens*
- *Bacteroides capillosus*
- *Eikenella corrodens*
- *Str. milleri*
- *Treponema* species
- *Eubacterium* species
- *Wolinella recta*
- *Actinomyces actinomycetemcomitans*

Pathogenicity Gingivitis of chronic persistence progresses to destructive chronic periodontitis causing destruction of the connective tissue attached to the teeth.

It begins as a simple marginal gingivitis. Further progress of disease leads to ulceration of crevicular epithelium. It proliferates further and gradually involves deeper portions of the periodontium leading to the advanced lesion of the periodontitis (severe periodontitis).

Clinical features

- Gingival inflammation and hyperaemia of the gingiva
- Presence of periodontal pocket
- Bleeding gums
- Bad taste
- Foul type of halitosis
- Tooth mobility and migration
- Gingival recession preceded by alveolar bone loss

Juvenile periodontitis (periodontosis)

It is the disease of periodontium, which is commonly seen in healthy adolescents 12–20 years old, especially in females from Africa and Asia, and is characterized by rapid destruction of periodontal tissue and a rapid loss of alveolar bone about more than one tooth of the permanent dentition.

Aetiology Microbes commonly isolated from the lesions include the following:

- *A. actinomycetemcomitans*
- *Capnocytophaga* species
- *E. corrodens*
- *B. gingivalis*

Pathogenicity It begins with the destruction of periodontal tissue that commences usually from the first permanent molars and then the anterior teeth. Gradually, it spreads to other teeth. There is generalized alveolar bone loss and loss of teeth may also occur in many cases.

Clinical features

- Deep pocket formation, often on only one tooth, which is the first clinical evidence
- Alveolar bone loss
- Inflammatory symptoms
- Rapid bone resorption
- Tooth mobility and migration
- Degenerative changes in the periodontal tissue
- Lateral abscesses in the periodontal tissue

Rapidly progressive periodontitis

It may be the late stage of juvenile periodontitis. It frequently occurs in young adults.

Aetiology Microbes commonly isolated from the lesions include the following:

- *A. actinomycetemcomitans*
- *B. gingivalis*
- *B. intermedius*
- *Treponema* species

Pathogenicity It occurs as acute exacerbations and remissions and is characterized by marked gingival inflammation and active destruction of periodontal tissue and rapid alveolar bone loss.

Endodontic infections

Endodontic infections are the infections of the dental pulp (pulpitis) and periapical tissues—periapical infections (apical periodontitis).

Aetiology

These infections are caused by bacteria and fungi. The exact cause is not yet known.

The following agents are frequently isolated from the lesions of endodontic infections.

Bacterial isolates

- *Str. milleri*
- *Bacteroides endodontalis*
- *B. gingivalis*
- *Fusobacterium* species
- *Str. salivarius*
- *Str. mutans*
- Enterococci
- *Actinomyces* species
- Anaerobic cocci
- *Lactobacillus* species

Rare isolates

- *Treponema* species
- *Veillonella* species
- *Campylobacter* species
- *Staphylococcus* species
- *Bifidobacterium* species
- *Leptotrichia* species
- *Mycoplasma* species
- *Actinobacillus* species
- Members of Enterobacteriaceae family

Fungal isolates

- *Candida* species
- *Cryptococcus* species
- *Saccharomyces* species

Pathogenicity

Pulpitis

The dental pulp is a delicate connective tissue with limited capacity to withstand microbial infections. Like other connective tissues in the body, it reacts to microbial infection by an inflammatory response, but the overall immune response is inadequate to defend the challenge. Hence, once the microbes gain access to the pulp and produce infection, it becomes difficult for the host to eliminate the infection completely. It occurs most commonly from dental caries in which invasion of the dentin and pulp tissue by microbes occurs.

Types Pulpitis is classified into different types which are as follows:

- **Focal reversible pulpitis** It is an early mild transient form of pulpitis in which inflammatory process is confined to a portion of the pulp, usually to the pulpal ends of irritated dentinal tubules. Clinically, a tooth with focal pulpitis is sensitive to cold. The application of ice or cold fluids to tooth results in pain. The pain disappears after the removal of irritant or restoration of the normal temperature.
- **Acute pulpitis** It is an acute inflammation of the dental pulp that occurs immediately after focal reversible pulpitis or occurs as an acute exacerbation of a chronic inflammatory process. Clinically, a tooth with acute pulpitis is sensitive to thermal changes, particularly to cold. The application of ice or cold fluids to tooth results in severe pain. The pain persists even after the removal of irritant or restoration of the normal temperature.

- **Chronic pulpitis** It is a chronic inflammation of the dental pulp. It occurs as a chronic type of disease from the onset or may arise from acute pulpitis. Clinically, the signs and symptoms are considerably milder than those of acute pulpitis. The pain is not a prominent feature; it is mild, dull and of intermittent type.
- **Irreversible pulpitis** Untreated acute or chronic pulpitis leads to irreversible pulpitis characterized by complete necrosis of the pulp tissue. This necrosis is caused by any microbe (any microbe that invades the tissue) present in the oral cavity, nasopharynx or gastrointestinal tract or its toxic products.

Periapical infections

Periapical infections occur due to spreading microbes or their toxic products from dental pulp (from acute or chronic pulpitis) through root canals into the periapical tissue. This spreading results in activation of non-specific inflammatory reaction as well as specific immunological responses. The failure of the defence mechanisms leads to acute inflammation, which further progresses and leads to the following:

- Periapical granuloma (apical periodontitis—acute or chronic)
- Periodontal cyst
- Periapical abscess

These periapical lesions may lead to

- Cellulitis of the face and neck
- Ludwig's angina—a severe form of cellulitis that begins in the submandibullar space and then spreads to other tissue spaces bilaterally
- Osteomyelitis of the jaw

Laboratory diagnosis

- **Collection of specimen** Specimen from root canal is collected aseptically by using sterile paper points.
- **Transport of specimen** The specimen collected with the help of paper points is placed in suitable anaerobic transport media, for example, Robertson's cooked meat medium or thioglycollate broth, and transported to microbiology laboratory.
- **Processing of specimen** Specimen can be processed for qualitative as well as quantitative analysis. It is processed aerobically and anaerobically and the organisms grown are identified using standard aerobic and anaerobic techniques. Antibiotic susceptibility is performed by disc diffusion method or broth dilution method.

Treatment

- **Treatment of acute pulpitis** There is no successful treatment available. However, in early cases, pulpotomy and placing of material such as calcium hydroxide that favours calcification may be helpful in survival of tooth.
- Teeth involved with acute pulpitis may be treated by filling of root canals with an inert material.
- Treatment of chronic pulpitis may be treated by extraction of the tooth or by pulp extirpation.
- Treatment of periapical abscess includes:
  - Removal of infected and non-vital tissue
  - Establishment of drainage
  - Root canal therapy
  - Antimicrobial agents in the form of
    - Irrigants, for example, sodium hypochlorite, hydrogen peroxide and iodine
    - Topical agents, for example, formocresol and paraformaldehyde
    - Systemic agents, for example, penicillin, amoxicillin, metronidazole and erythromycin

Self-assessment

Long-answer questions

1. Enumerate the microbes causing orodental infections. Discuss in detail the periodontal diseases.

2. Enumerate the microbes causing orodental infections. Discuss in detail the dental caries.

Short-answer questions

Write notes on

1. Dental caries
2. *Streptococcus mutans*
3. Classification of dental caries
4. Methods of caries control
5. Periodontal diseases
6. Acute ulcerative gingivitis
7. Chronic gingivitis
8. Juvenile periodontitis
9. Periodontitis
10. Endodontic infections
11. Pulpitis
12. Periapical infections

Multiple-choice questions

1. Which of the following is an endodontic infection?
   A. Acute gingivitis
   B. Periodontitis
   C. Pulpitis
   D. None of the above
2. Which of the following is a periodontal disease?
   A. Periapical abscess
   B. Periodontitis
   C. Pulpitis
   D. None of the above
3. Which of the following streptococci is the most important agent causing dental caries?
   A. *Streptococcus sobrinus*
   B. *Str. sanguis*
   C. *Str. mutans*
   D. *Str. milleri*
4. The following statements are TRUE regarding dental caries, EXCEPT
   A. It is a microbial disease of the calcified tissues of the teeth
   B. *Streptococcus mutans* is considered as the most important agent
   C. There is demineralization of the inorganic portion and destruction of the organic substances of the tooth
   D. Chlorhexidine and alexidine are most commonly used agents for their control
5. Following are the chemical agents used for the control of dental caries, EXCEPT
   A. Potassium permanganate
   B. Fluorides
   C. Silver nitrate
   D. Chlorhexidine
6. Which of the following statements is FALSE regarding acute ulcerative gingivitis?
   A. It is an acute inflammation of the gingival tissue with irregularly shaped ulcers
   B. The ulcers are covered by a grey, necrotic pseudomembrane or slough.
   C. It is characterized by the development of painful, hyperaemic gingiva and sharply punched-out erosions of the interdental papillae
   D. It is characterized by the red and swollen gingiva with rounded ends
7. Ludwig's angina—a severe form of cellulitis of the submandibullar space occurs in which of the following?
   A. Periapical infections
   B. Chronic pulpitis
   C. Juvenile periodontitis
   D. Chronic gingivitis
8. Which of the following microbes is commonly isolated from the lesions of juvenile periodontitis?
   A. *Streptococcus mutans*
   B. *Bacteroides fragilis*
   C. *Actinomyces actinomycetemcomitans*
   D. *Prevotella melaninogenica*
9. Which of the following microbes is commonly isolated from the lesions of rapidly progressive periodontitis?
   A. *Streptococcus mutans*
   B. *Bacteroides fragilis*
   C. *Actinomyces actinomycetemcomitans*
   D. *Prevotella melaninogenica*

51 Septicaemia, Pyaemia and Toxaemia

- **Septicaemia** (means **sepsis of blood**) is a condition in which there is presence of actively multiplying bacteria in the bloodstream and formation of toxic products in the blood.
- **Pyaemia** is the septicaemia caused by pyogenic bacteria with multiple abscesses in internal organs such as spleen, lungs, liver, kidneys, brain and heart.
- **Toxaemia** is formation of toxic products in the blood. When the bacterial endotoxin circulates in the blood, the condition is called endotoxaemia. Endotoxaemia can occur in the absence of bacteria in the bloodstream, for example, endotoxins produced by Gram-negative bacteria present in the gut can enter the bloodstream by passing across the gut wall.
- **Bacteraemia** is a condition in which there is transient presence of bacteria in the bloodstream without multiplication. Clinical signs of septicaemia are absent.

Predisposing factors

Impaired host defences

- Deficiency of cell-mediated immunity, humoral immunity or both
- Decreased complement level
- Diminished phagocytic activity and poor natural killer cell activity
- Diminished inflammatory response
- Diabetes mellitus
- Malignancy
- Severe neutropenia
- Prematurity and low birth weight
- Intravenous drug abuse
- Old age
- Immunosuppressive therapy
- Splenectomized patients
- Uraemia, nephrotic syndrome
- Myeloma

Pre-existing infections

- Abdominal sepsis—peritonitis, liver abscess, retroperitoneal abscess
- Pneumonia caused by Gram-negative bacteria
- Gram-negative infections of burns, wounds, abscesses, etc.
- Gynaecological sepsis—puerperal sepsis, pelvic abscesses, salpingitis
- Meningitis
- Food poisoning
- Urinary tract infections (UTIs)
- Osteomyelitis, septic arthritis, etc.

Instrumentation and surgery

- Surgery on urinary tract
- Surgery on gastrointestinal tract
- Radiological invasive techniques

- Catheterization, cystoscopy
- Prosthetic devices
- Tooth extraction in immunocompromised individuals
- Endotracheal tubes, etc.

Other factors

- Difficult delivery
- Exposure to infected incubators
- Exposure to infected ventilators, etc.

Microorganisms encountered in blood

Bacteria

Common pathogens

- *Escherichia coli*
- *Streptococcus pneumoniae*
- *Staphylococcus aureus*
- *Klebsiella* species
- *Proteus* species
- *Haemophilus influenzae*
- *Salmonella* species
- *Streptococcus pyogenes*
- *Pseudomonas aeruginosa*
- Group B streptococci
- *Str. viridans*

Rare pathogens

- *Staph. epidermidis*
- Enterococci
- *Serratia marcescens*
- *Citrobacter* species
- *Bacteroides* species
- *Fusobacterium* species
- Anaerobic cocci—peptococci and peptostreptococci
- *Neisseria meningitidis*
- *Brucella* species
- *Bacillus* species
- *Clostridium welchii*
- *Rickettsia* species
- *Coxiella* species
- *Leptospira* species
- *Borrelia* species

Fungi

- *Candida albicans* and other species
- *Cryptococcus neoformans*
- *Mucor* species
- *Aspergillus* species
- *Histoplasma capsulatum*
- *Coccidioides immitis*
- *Blastomyces dermatitidis*

Pathogenesis

The vascular compartment is sterile. Bacteria may enter the bloodstream from

- An infective focus with the help of phagocytic cell or from a surface with normal flora causing breakages of blood vessels
- By introduction of contaminated material directly into the vascular system

Organisms that enter the bloodstream are quickly eliminated by various immune mechanisms. But when the immune system is overwhelmed or evaded, the microorganisms persist in the blood and multiply producing signs and symptoms of septicaemia.

Clinical features

Septicaemia is characterized by

- Fever or hypothermia
- Rigors
- Tachycardia
- Tachypnoea
- Hypoxia
- Dyspnoea
- Cyanosis
- Hypotension
- Mental confusion, Agitation, Behavioural changes } in elderly patients
- **Complications**
  - Septic, endotoxic or bacteraemic shock
  - Disseminated intravascular coagulation

- Acute renal failure
- Shock may lead to multiple organ failure (e.g., heart, lungs, liver, kidneys)

Laboratory diagnosis

Blood culture

- **Collection of blood for culture**
  - Apply 2% tincture iodine to the skin over the area of the vein
  - Allow it to dry
  - Remove the iodine with the help of sponges saturated with 80% isopropyl alcohol
  - The entire procedure is repeated
  - Apply tourniquet
  - Collect 10 mL of blood with the help of sterile syringe and needle
  - The blood is diluted to inactivate antimicrobial component present in the blood. Minimum dilution of blood required is 1:10. Hence, 5 mL of blood is collected in 50 mL of glucose broth and 5 mL of blood is collected in 50 mL of bile broth (total 10 mL of blood is collected as the number of organisms in the blood may be very less, may be 1/mL)
  - Other broth media which can be used for collection of blood are brain–heart infusion broth, trypticase soya broth and even nutrient broth can be used
  - For anaerobes, thioglycollate broth or Robertson's cooked meat medium can be used
  - Sodium polyanethol sulphonate (SPS) is added to broth media, which acts as an anticoagulant, antiphagocytic and anticomplementary, and interferes with the activity of certain antimicrobial agents such as aminoglycosides, enhances growth rate and increases rate of isolation

Processing of blood culture

After collection of blood, blood culture bottles are incubated aerobically and blind subcultures are made after 24 hours, 48 hours, 72 hours, on 6th and 10th day.

The subcultures are made on

- Blood agar
- MacConkey's agar
- Chocolate agar
- Anaerobic supplemented blood agar—for anaerobes
- Sabouraud's dextrose agar for fungi
- Other selective media as indicated

One blood agar is incubated anaerobically, chocolate agar under 5–10% CO_2 and other media under ordinary conditions. After incubation, colonies obtained on solid media are studied further for identification and antibiotic susceptibility by conventional methods.

Castaneda's method

This method is used for

- Rapid detection of causative agents
- To minimize the materials and manipulations
- To reduce the problem of contamination
- To reduce the risk of infection in laboratory workers

Castaneda's medium is a diphasic medium containing both liquid and solid media in the same bottle. It contains brain–heart infusion broth and agar in the same bottle. The blood specimen is collected into liquid medium and the bottle is incubated in an upright position. For inoculation of agar, the bottle is tilted at intervals so that the broth flows over the agar slant. Again, it is incubated in an upright position. The colonies formed on agar slant are studied and identified (Fig. 51.1).

Automated blood culture system

Various newer non-conventional methods for detecting bacteria in blood are now available which detect bacterial growth by various techniques such as the detection of carbon dioxide by radiometric or optical methods. One such instrument commonly used is Bactec system.

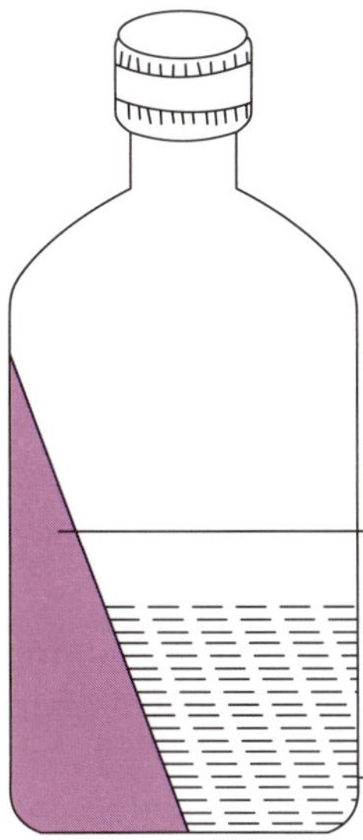

Figure 51.1 Castaneda's medium.

Cultures of other specimens

Cultures of the following specimens may be useful in the diagnosis of septicaemia:

- Culture of intravenous catheter tips
- Swab from infected burns
- Swab from wounds or abscesses
- Urine in UTI
- Sputum in respiratory tract infections
- Stool in intestinal infections

Non-culture methods

Various non-culture methods are used to detect the circulating antigens and other microbial products. These are

- Latex agglutination test—used for detection of antigen of Group B streptococci, *H. influenzae* type B, *Str. pneumoniae, N. meningitidis*, staphylococci and some yeasts
- Counter immunoelectrophoresis (CIEP)—used for detection of pneumococci, *Klebsiella, H. influenzae* and other microbial agents
- Limulus amoebocyte lysate assay test—used for detection of circulating lipopolysaccharide (endotoxin) of Gram-negative bacteria in blood. The test is specific and extremely sensitive for detection of endotoxin and detects as little as 0.1 ng of endotoxin
- Gas liquid chromatography—used for detection of metabolic end products of microbial activity in serum

Treatment

- Immediate parenteral antibiotic therapy (IV route is the best) in adequate dosage is necessary as soon as the specimen for culture is collected
- Surgical intervention—urgent surgical drainage of abscesses, wounds, etc.
- Intravenous fluids to prevent shock
- Blind drug therapy is given before the availability of antibiotic susceptibility testing report, based on the
  - Clinical symptoms and signs
  - Likely focus and cause of infection
  - Knowledge of the underlying conditions
- The correct antibiotic therapy is started after the availability of antibiotic susceptibility testing report
- The antibacterial agents used for blind drug therapy include
  - Penicillin, Cloxacillin, Fusidic acid, Vancomycin, Ampicillin } for Gram-positive bacteria
  - Gentamicin, Carbenicillin, Tobramycin, Azlocillin, Cefotaxime } for Gram-negative bacteria
  - Metronidazole } for anaerobes
- Combination of drugs can be given in combined infections

Prevention

- By minimizing cross-infection and self-infection in hospital. This is possible by

maintaining standard labour room and nursery and also by maintaining proper aseptic conditions in the theatres, wards during surgical procedures
- By preventing localized sepsis
- Prophylactic antibiotic administration before surgery, tooth extraction or instrumentation
- By taking due care of localized infection—the likely focus
- By avoiding indiscriminate use of antibiotics

Self-assessment

Long-answer question

1. Enumerate the organisms causing septicaemia and discuss in brief the pathogenesis and laboratory diagnosis.

Short-answer questions

Write notes on
1. Blood culture
2. Castaneda's method of blood culture
3. Septicaemia

Multiple-choice questions

1. Which of the following bacteria is most commonly encountered in blood?
   A. *Staphylococcus aureus*
   B. *Streptococcus pneumoniae*
   C. *Escherichia coli*
   D. *Pseudomonas aeruginosa*
2. Which of the following fungi is most commonly encountered in blood?
   A. *Aspergillus* species
   B. *Histoplasma capsulatum*
   C. *Cryptococcus neoformans*
   D. *Candida albicans*
3. Which of the following media are most commonly used for collection of blood for culture?
   A. Glucose broth and bile broth
   B. Brain–heart infusion broth and trypticase soya broth
   C. Peptone water and nutrient broth
   D. Robertson's cooked meat medium and thioglycollate broth
4. Which of the following statements are TRUE regarding Castaneda's method, EXCEPT
   A. Is a diphasic medium containing both liquid and solid media
   B. Contains nutrient broth and nutrient agar
   C. Is used for rapid detection of causative agents
   D. Reduces the risk of infection in laboratory workers
5. Presence of actively multiplying bacteria in bloodstream with the formation of toxic products in the blood is known as
   A. Toxaemia
   B. Pyaemia
   C. Septicaemia
   D. Bacteraemia

52 Hospital Waste Management

Hospital waste refers to all waste, biological or non-biological material, that is discarded and is not intended for further use in the hospital. It is the waste generated in the hospital during the clinical management of patients (diagnosis or treatment), immunization, human or animal research and waste generated in hospital kitchens, offices, etc. Two classes of hospital waste are recognized: infectious waste and non-infectious waste.

Infectious waste

A waste that can cause infectious disease or disability. It includes

- Microbiological waste
- Blood and body fluids
- Contaminated laboratory wastes
- Sharps
- Pathological waste
- Soiled dressing and cotton plaster
- Other materials contaminated with blood and body fluids
- Cotton swabs
- Animal wastes generated by animal experiments, etc.

Non-infectious waste

A waste that is not infectious and does not cause any hazard is known as non-infectious waste.

The amount of waste generated per bed per day varies with the type of hospital. However, on an average, 1–5 kg of waste per bed per day is generated. The type of waste generated is 80–85% non-infectious, 10–15% infectious and 5% chemical waste, which is non-infectious but hazardous.

The main aim of hospital waste management is to prevent injury and accidental transmission of microbial infections to

- Hospital staff
- Patients
- Attendants of patients
- Visitors
- General public who are at a potential risk of getting infected

Hence, a proper hospital waste management programme for disposal of waste is of utmost importance for the safety of health care personnel as well as for the community. Now, it is mandatory for every hospital to have proper waste management programme for waste disposal.

Segregation and waste treatment

Generation of waste is a continuous process. Hence, proper collection and segregation is essential. As 80–85% of waste generated in a hospital is non-infectious, hence it is important to segregate (separate) the non-infectious waste from infectious waste. If the effective separation is done at the source, that is, at the point of generation, it prevents the mixing of infectious and non-infectious wastes. This is the most important step to safeguard the occupational health of healthcare personnel and it also avoids any significant health hazard to the general public. Thus, an effective segregation is the golden key to a good management plan. Segregation of waste is done in different colour-coded plastic (polythene) bags and containers (biomedical waste [BMW] rules 1998, which are further modified in the year 2016) as different types of wastes need different type of treatment for their disposal. The recommended segregation, colour coding, waste treatment and disposal as per the BMW rules 2016 is given in Table 52.1. All of the containers should have the biohazard symbol (Fig. 52.1).

Figure 52.1 Biohazard symbol.

Table 52.1 Colour coding, type of containers, type of waste and waste treatment

Colour coding	Type of containers	Type of waste	Waste treatment
Yellow	Plastic bag	Infectious nonsharp waste such as • **Human/animal anatomical waste** • **Soiled waste** Items contaminated with blood and body fluids (cotton, gauze, bandages and plasters soaked/in contact with blood, urine, pus or other body fluids, soiled mattresses, beddings, etc.) • **Microbiological and biotechnological wastes**	• Incineration or deep burial • Incineration or deep burial • Chemical disinfection followed by incineration
Red	Disinfected container/plastic bag	**Contaminated recyclable waste** Plastic bags, bottles, tubing, etc.	Autoclaving or microwaving/hydroclaving followed by shredding or mutilation. After treatment may be recycled
White translucent	Plastic bag and puncture-proof container	**Waste sharps** Needles, syringes, scalpels, blades, lancets, butterfly needles, suturing needles, etc.	Autoclaving or dry heat sterilization followed by shredding or mutilation or encapsulation in metal container or cement concrete. Final disposal in sharp pit or sent to authorized iron foundries
Blue	Blue cardboard box with blue labell	**Glassware** Broken or discarded and contaminated glass items such as cut ampoules, glass vials other than those contaminated with cytotoxic wastes, metallic body implants	Chemical disinfection with detergent and sodium hypochlorite or autoclaving or microwaving or hydroclaving. Final disposal sent for recycling

Treatment technologies for infectious waste

The following techniques are available for treatment of infectious material:

Double-chambered incineration

- An incinerator burns waste at high temperature and reduces waste volume. The double-chambered incinerator contains two chambers:
  - Primary chamber—in which the waste is burnt at 800°C
  - Secondary chamber—combustion of volatiles and gases emitted from the primary chamber occurs in this chamber where the gases are subjected to conditions of high temperature (1000°C) and excess air. The negative pressure maintained inside the incinerator forces the end gases out of the chimney
- **Uses** Used for treatment of
  - Microbiological and pathological waste
  - Soiled dressings
  - Anatomical waste
  - Cytotoxic waste
- **Disadvantages**
  - Generates highly toxic gases, if polyvinyl chloride plastic material is present
  - Not recommended for sharps and plastic wastes

Autoclaving/steam sterilization

- Two kinds of autoclave:
  - The gravity displacement type
  - The prevacuum type
- In the prevacuum type, steam is created outside the chamber loaded with waste.
- Air in the chamber is then gradually removed as steam is injected in.
- A temperature of 134°C is achieved for 30 minutes and the waste in the bags is sterilized.
- The prevacuum type tries to eliminate 'cold spots' and 'air pockets' (region where the steam is unable to penetrate) by creating vacuum and ensures complete elimination of air (only 5% air remains in the main chamber). Because of this, there is quicker heating of the chamber and greater sterilization.
- In the gravity displacement type, about 25% of air remains in the main chamber because of which heating is not quick—requires longer duration and the sterilization is less efficient as compared to prevacuum type.
- **Uses** Autoclaving is used for the treatment of:
  - Microbiological and pathological waste
  - Blood and blood products
  - Body fluids
  - Sharps and plastic wastes

Chemical disinfection

- Chemicals such as formaldehyde (6–8%), glutaraldehyde, hydrogen peroxide (6–30%) and chlorine in various forms (most commonly as hypochlorite solution—1%) are commonly used for the treatment of waste.
- Several factors influence the effectiveness of chemical treatment such as
  - Type of disinfectant
  - Quantity and concentration of disinfectant
  - Contact time and temperature

Microwaving

- This technology involves the use of radiation produced by the microwave to break apart molecular chemical bonds and thus disinfect infectious waste.
- This process involves pre-shredding of the waste, injecting it with steam in a special treatment chamber and evenly heating it for 25 minutes at 97°C–100°C under a series of microwave units (radiation spectrum between the frequencies of 300 and 300,000 MHz).
- Cannot be used for cytotoxic, hazardous and radioactive waste.

Hydroclaving

- Hydroclave is an expansion of the autoclave technology.
- There is indirect heating without direct contact with the waste by introducing steam into the outer jacket while the waste is kept inside the other chamber and turned mechanically with the help of a series of large rotating rods, which spin continuously, rupturing the waste bags and ensuring complete exposure to the heat.
- The moisture content in the waste turns into steam and builds pressure inside the vessel.
- The sterilization is carried out at 132°C for 15 minutes or at 121°C for 30 minutes.
- This treatment results in fragmentation and dehydration with 80–85% reduction in volume and 65–70% reduction in weight.
- After sterilization is completed, the waste is passed into the shredder, which renders the waste unrecognizable.
- The waste after shredding can be recycled or land filled.
- **Advantages**
  - No pretreatment of waste is required
  - Complete fragmentation and dehydration is achieved
  - Reliable for the treatment of pathological and highly infectious waste
  - Reduction in volume and weight reduces the transportation and land filling costs
  - Environment friendly with no harmful emissions or discharges

Plasma technology

It is a technology (plasma torch) used to burn materials at a very high temperature, that is, 2000–3000°C sometimes up to 10,000°C that allows complete destruction of the waste.

Waste management programme

All healthcare establishments including dental OPD/IPD and minor operation theatres attached to dental set-up should have waste management programme according to the specific needs. The policies and procedures should be incorporated in the operating manuals. Special emphasis should be given to

- Minimization of waste by reducing, reusing and recycling the waste
- Proper segregation
- Health and safety of workers

All workers concerned with the healthcare waste management programme must be trained in

- Principles of medical waste management
- Responsibilities of employees (job description)
- Roles of employees and employers in biosafety management

Self-assessment

Short-answer questions

Write notes on

1. Infectious waste
2. Segregation of waste
3. Waste treatment and disposal in hospital
4. Incineration
5. Hydroclaving

Multiple-choice questions

1. The chemical waste generated in hospital accounts for
   A. 10%
   B. 5%
   C. 20%
   D. 2%
2. The quantity of non-infectious waste generated in hospital accounts for
   A. 10–15% B. 5–10%
   C. 60–80%
   D. 80–85%

3. Which of the following bags is used for collection of the human anatomical waste?
   A. Red bag
   B. Blue bag
   C. Yellow bag
   D. White bag
4. Rubber gloves are collected in
   A. Blue bag
   B. Yellow bag
   C. Red bag
   D. White bag
5. Which of the following wastes needs special treatment?
   A. Anatomical waste
   B. Sharps
   C. Bandages
   D. Plasters
6. Which of the following categories of waste can be sent for recycling?
   A. Sharps
   B. Radioactive waste
   C. Heavy metals
   D. Rubber disposables
7. The sharps should be collected in which of the following containers?
   A. Red container
   B. Yellow container
   C. White translucent puncture-proof container
   D. Blue container
8. Following categories of the waste are treated by incineration, EXCEPT
   A. Sharps
   B. Soiled dressing
   C. Microbial waste
   D. Anatomical waste
9. Autoclaving is used for treatment of
   A. Microbiological and pathological waste
   B. Body fluids
   C. Sharps and plastic wastes
   D. All of the above
10. The following are the chemical agents used for treatment of waste, EXCEPT
    A. Iodine
    B. Formaldehyde
    C. Glutaraldehyde
    D. Hypochlorite solution
11. The temperature range used in plasma technology is
    A. 900–1200°C
    B. 2000–3000°C
    C. 121°C
    D. 160°C
12. Microwaving involves
    A. Direct heating
    B. Indirect heating
    C. Radiation
    D. None of the above
13. No pretreatment of waste is required in
    A. Hydroclaving
    B. Incineration
    C. Microwaving
    D. None of the above

53 Hospital-Acquired Infections

The terms 'hospital infections' or 'hospital-acquired infections' are applied to infections developing in hospitalized patients, which were not present or were not in incubation at the time of their admission. The term 'nosocomial infections' is used synonymously for hospital-acquired infections.

Predisposing factors (Flow chart 53.1)

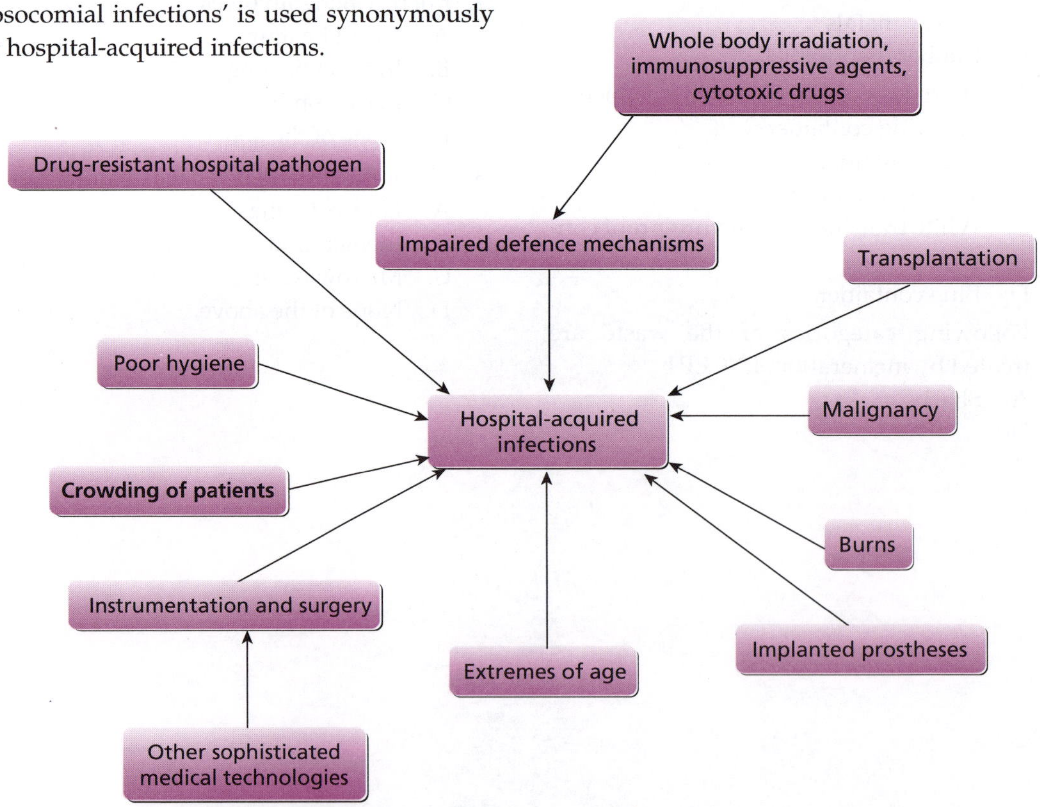

Flow chart 53.1 Predisposing factors of hospital-acquired infections.

Microbiology of hospital infections

Almost any pathogen can cause hospital infections, but those that are able to survive in a hospital environment for longer periods and develop resistance to antibiotics and disinfectants are particularly important.

Gram-negative bacilli are the major causes, constituting about 60% infections, Gram-positive cocci constitute about 30% infections and 10% infections are caused by fungi, viruses and parasites.

Bacteria

Both aerobes and anaerobes are involved. Common bacterial agents are as follows:

Aerobic Bacteria

- *Staphylococcus aureus*
- *Pseudomonas aeruginosa*
- *Escherichia coli*
- *Klebsiella* species
- *Proteus* species
- *Staph. epidermidis*
- *Streptococcus pyogenes*
- *Str. pneumoniae*
- *Haemophilus* species
- *Salmonella* species
- *Shigella* species
- *Mycobacterium* species

Anaerobic Bacteria

- *Bacteroides fragilis*
- *Clostridium* species
- Anaerobic cocci
- *Campylobacter* species

Viruses

The commonly involved viruses are as follows:

- Hepatitis B virus
- Hepatitis C virus
- Hepatitis D virus
- Herpes simplex virus
- Cytomegalovirus
- Influenza virus
- Enteroviruses
- Rhinovirus
- Rotavirus

Fungi

The commonly involved fungi are as follows:

- *Candida* species particularly *C. albicans*
- *Aspergillus* species
- *Mucor* species
- *Cryptococcus* species
- *Histoplasma* species

Parasites

The commonly involved parasites are as follows:

- *Entamoeba histolytica*
- *Toxoplasma gondii*
- *Pneumocystis carinii*

Sources

Endogenous

Many microorganisms normally present in and on the body of a patient (patient's own flora) may act as opportunistic pathogens and may invade the patient's tissues. These infections are known as endogenous infections, auto infections or self- infections (Fig. 53.1).

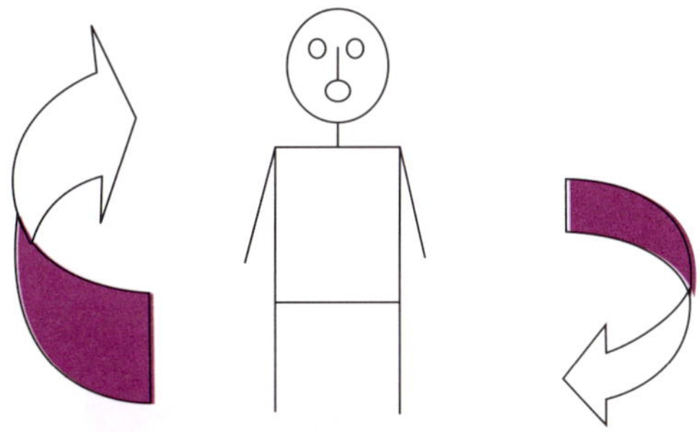

Figure 53.1 Endogenous infections.

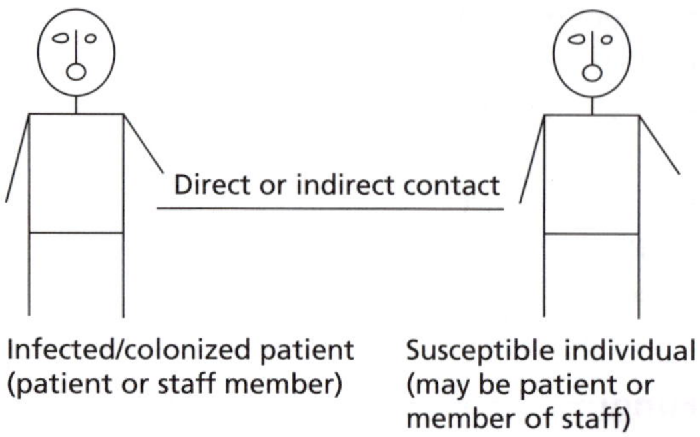

Figure 53.2 Exogenous infections.

Exogenous

Infection from other people or from inanimate objects in the environment is known as exogenous. Hospital infection is mostly exogenous.

- **Cross infection** Infection from another patient or a member of hospital staff (Fig. 53.2)
- **Environmental infection** Infection from environmental sources such as inanimate objects, air, water and food (Fig. 53.3)

Modes of transmission

Infection spreads by various routes, which are as follows:

- **Contact** Transmission by hands or clothing of hospital personnel and even by the patient himself. Transmission may happen by contact with inanimate objects.
- **Air-borne route** Transmitted by inhalation of droplets, dust from bedding, floors, exudates dispersed from wound, skin, etc., and aerosols produced by nebulizers, humidifiers and air conditioning apparatus.
- **Oral route** Transmitted by ingestion of contaminated food or water.
- **Parenteral route** Transmitted by use of contaminated syringes, needles and other instruments, by administration of contaminated blood, blood products, infusion fluids or tissue.
- **Inoculation route** Infection by inoculation occurs when the infected material is inoculated directly into tissue. For example, in hepatitis B virus infection, virus is inoc-

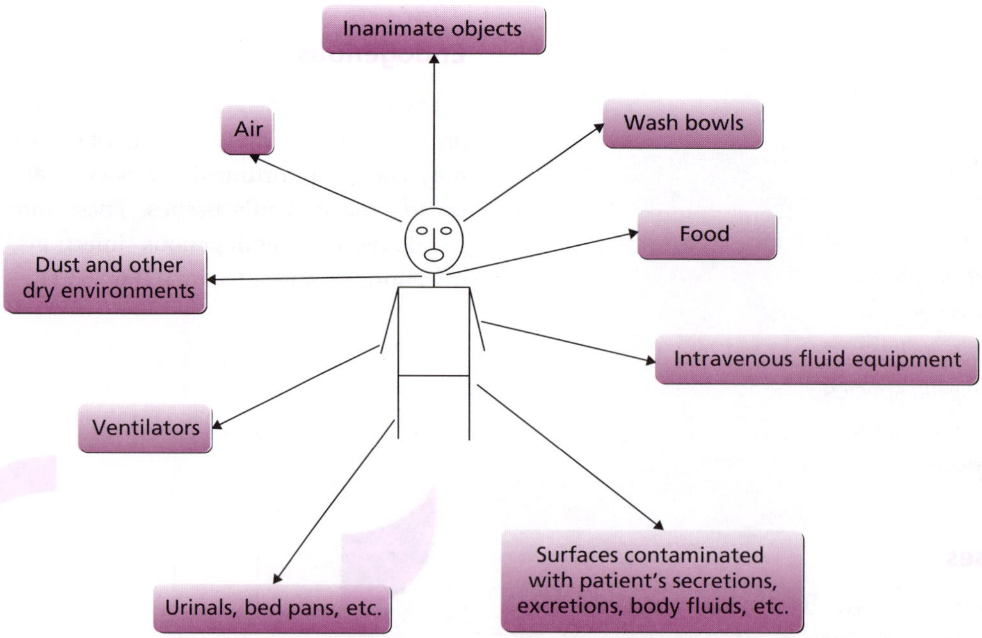

Figure 53.3 Sources of environmental infection.

ulated by transfusion of contaminated blood or by inoculation of material containing the virus.

- **Iatrogenic transfer** Infections may also occur during diagnostic or therapeutic procedures, if proper care is not taken.

Common types of hospital infections

Urinary tract infections

- Associated with catheterization or instrumentation of urinary tract
- Manifested as pyelonephritis, cystitis, pyelitis or urethritis
- *E. coli*, *Proteus* species, *P. aeruginosa*, *Klebsiella* species are common organisms

Respiratory tract infections

- Nosocomial bronchopneumonia
- *Staph. aureus, H. influenzae, Str. pneumoniae,* Enterobacteriaceae and respiratory viruses are common organisms

Wound and soft tissue infections

- Post-operative wound infections—incidence is high, particularly in elderly patients (above 60 years)
- *Staph. aureus, P. aeruginosa*, Enterobacteria and other Gram-negative bacteria are commonly involved
- Are of two types: surgical and non-surgical
  - ***Surgical***
    - Post-operative wound infections such as intra-abdominal and pelvic abscesses, infections after orthopaedic surgery and gynaecological surgery
  - ***Non-surgical***
    - Stitch abscesses
    - Umbilical stumps
    - Ulcers
    - Burns
    - Injection abscess, etc.

Gastrointestinal (GIT) infections

- Diarrhoea
- Dysentery
- Enteric fever
- Food poisoning
- GIT infections are most commonly caused by *Salmonella* species, *Shigella sonnei*, viruses, etc.

Genital infections

- Puerperal sepsis
- Septic abortion
- Intrauterine sepsis
- Pelvic inflammatory diseases, etc.

Neonatal infections

- Neonatal sepsis
- Infection of eye, skin and umbilical cord, etc.

Other infections

- Bacteraemia and septicaemia
- Hepatitis
- Tuberculosis
- Influenza, etc.

Laboratory diagnosis

- Hospital infection may occur sporadically or as outbreaks.
- Aetiological diagnosis is made by routine diagnostic methods of smear, culture and identification.
- Susceptibility testing is very important because of multiple drug (antibiotic) resistance in nosocomial pathogens.
- When it occurs as outbreak, identification and elimination of source is an important part to control the infection.
- In case of an outbreak, the source needs to be identified. It requires sampling of possible sources—various inanimate objects and hospital personnel including patients who are suspected to be colonized—and also the sampling of water, food, air, blood products, transfusion fluids, disinfectants, antiseptics, etc.
- Detection of carriers among the staff and patients.

- Typing of isolates from patients and hospital environment to find out the source of infection.

Prevention of hospital infections

- Education of medical and nursing staff regarding the basic concepts of infection control.
- Universal safety precaution procedures to control transmission route.
- Proper sterilization and disinfection of the inanimate objects and use of disinfectants in the hospital environment to control the source or reservoir of infection.
- Asepsis in operation theatre, hygiene in wards and kitchens and special attention to the disposal of excreta, soiled dressings, etc.
- Provision of sterile instruments, dressings, surgical drapes, etc., and use of disposable items such as syringes, catheters and tubing.
- Aseptic and antiseptic procedures during and after surgery (post-operative care)—good surgical techniques.
- Early recognition and isolation of infected cases.
- Overcrowding of patients or mingling of susceptible patients in a ward should be avoided.
- Carriers among patients and staff should be detected and treated accordingly.
- Protection of highly susceptible patients, for example, premature babies and immunocompromised individuals.
- Bacterial interference—is colonization of a newborn with commensal microorganisms to prevent the colonization of carriage sites by more virulent or antibiotic-resistant strains.
- Prophylactic antibiotic therapy in specific situations for a short period, for example, before surgical technique.
- Limitation of use of antibiotics and a rational use of antibiotics as per antibiotic policy.
- Vaccination—to protect the susceptible host.
- Other important precautions are as follows:
  - Frequent hand washing
  - Limitations of transfusion
  - Frequent change of intravenous lines
  - Frequent change of working clothes
  - Staff suffering from infection, for example, infected lesions and respiratory infections, should not be allowed to attend the patients

Control of hospital infections

Each hospital should have an effective hospital infection control team (HICT) consisting of a microbiologist, medical and nursing staff, hospital administrator and clinician.

Functions of HICT

- Surveillance programme to assess various aspects of infections such as
  - Investigation of infection
  - Extent of infection
  - Site of occurrence
  - Investigation of possible source
  - Microbial cause
  - Control of outbreak
- Conduct training courses for staff to educate them in the basic concept of infection control
- Prepare training manuals for different categories
- Prepare and execute guidelines for admission, nursing and treatment
- Surveillance on sterilization and disinfection practices
- Monitoring of hygiene practices
- Conduct audits for evaluation of effectiveness of various programmes under taken by HICT committee

Self-assessment

Long-answer question

1. Enumerate the microbes causing hospital-acquired infections. Describe briefly the

different sources and modes of transmission. Add a note of prevention and treatment.

Short-answer questions

Write short notes on

1. Hospital infection control team
2. Factors predisposing to hospital-acquired infections

Multiple-choice questions

1. Which of the following is the most common microbe causing hospital-acquired infections?
   A. *Escherichia coli*
   B. *Proteus* spp.
   C. *Klebsiella* spp.
   D. *Pseudomonas aeruginosa*
2. Infections transferred in hospitalized patients during diagnostic or therapeutic procedures is known as
   A. Transfer by contact
   B. Parenteral transfer
   C. Iatrogenic transfer
   D. Transfer by inoculation
3. Transfer of infection from another patient or a member of hospital staff is
   A. Environmental infection
   B. Parenteral infection
   C. Iatrogenic infection
   D. Cross infection

54 Biosafety Measures

Infections of special concern

Following are the infections of special concern to those who are working in a healthcare set-up and especially in a microbiology laboratory:

- Tuberculosis
- Hepatitis B virus
- Hepatitis C virus
- AIDS virus/HIV
- Enteric infections such as enteric fever, dysentery
- Other infections include the ones caused by
  - Staphylococci
  - Streptococci
  - *Brucella* species
  - *Neisseria* species
  - *Coxiella*
  - *Rickettsia*
  - *Chlamydia*
  - *Francisella*

Routes of transmission in healthcare set-up

In a healthcare set-up and especially in a microbiology laboratory, the different routes of infection are as follows:

Inoculation Accidental introduction of infection into the body, particularly by a breach of an epithelial surface, for example

- Introduction of microbe into the human eye by splashing or by rubbing with contaminated fingers
- Injection through skin by needlestick injury or by bite of an ectoparasite
- Incision with a sharp or broken glass
- Rubbing of infectious material onto the skin or mucous membrane

Ingestion Infection by ingestion may occur because of licking, sucking or accidental swallowing of infectious material. This may occur in the following ways:

- Splashing of infectious material on lips
- Touching the mouth with contaminated fingers
- Licking of labells contaminated by fingers
- Mouth pipetting

Inhalation Infection is transmitted by inhalation of infected aerosols, droplet nuclei or dust into the upper or lower respiratory tract.

Contact Contact with patient's contaminated specimen containers, contaminated equipment and instruments, linen soiled with blood or body fluids, and other inanimate objects soiled with infectious material can also transmit the infection to healthcare workers.

Biosafety measures to be adopted

General safety measures

General safety measures include the following:

Protective clothing Protective clothing, such as aprons, masks and gloves, are designed as a barrier to reduce the likelihood of injury and infection. Most healthcare personnel do not wear aprons and work in ordinary clothes, thereby spreading infection to others and themselves.

- **Gloves**
  - Health care personnel should wear
    - Disposable vinyl gloves in all patient care areas
    - Latex surgical gloves for operative procedures
    - Heavy duty thick rubber gloves for waste handlers
  - Routinely single gloves are sufficient but in high-risk patients, double gloves must be used and disposed suitably after use. It is most ideal to use disposable gloves. Gloves should be checked for gross defects every time
- **Masks**
  - Use of mask is obligatory as the patient's breath may contain infected aerosols
  - Well fitting, simple, reusable plastic masks or disposable masks should be used to protect healthcare workers from aerosols and splashes
  - Masks should be disinfected with liquid bleach before washing
  - Mask should be changed for any surgical procedure lasting more than 20 minutes or any procedure where an aerosol spray is expected or in a high-risk patient (e.g., known HIV/tuberculosis patient)
- **Aprons**
  - Full sleeved, knee length cotton apron must be worn at all time
- **Protective eyewear**
  - Protective glasses or eye shield of transparent material to protect eyes should be used, especially for procedures where aerosol is produced
- **Dressing**
  - Dressings of break in skin (cuts or wounds) and areas that are oozing blood should be covered with waterproof strong adhesive plastic dressings

Hands washing Hand washing before and after coming in contact with a patient or specimen is the most effective method for preventing the transfer of any infectious microbe. Hand washing with soap and water or with an appropriate disinfectant solution is advised in the following situations:

- Before handling food and eating
- After visiting the toilet
- Before and after handling the patient for various reasons such as specimen collection, special procedures, bathing of patient and bed making
- Whenever hands are soiled
- After collection of specimens and after handling the infectious materials such as specimens and culture of infectious microbes

Safe disposal Safe disposal of specimens, infectious material, contaminated waste, etc.

Proper handling and sterilization Proper handling of sharps (such as needle, syringes and lancets, which are used during therapeutic and diagnostic procedures to puncture the skin), specimen containers and other infectious material, and proper sterilization and disinfection practices of these materials in the healthcare set-up must be followed. All specimens should be considered potentially infectious, and handling and processing should be performed accordingly.

Safety measures in dentistry

Dentists are exposed to various microorganisms transmitted by inoculation and inhalation. Control of cross-infection is the basic requirement for the ethical and professional practice of medicine. It encompasses measures not only against HIV but also against other infectious diseases such as tuberculosis and hepatitis B. Uniform high standards of disinfection control measures must be practised for all patients. However, additional precautions may be practised while treating patients in the high-risk group for any infectious disease and not only HIV seropositive patients. Wherever possible, disposable items should be used, particularly the so called critical instruments, for example, blades and injection needles.

The following safety measures must be practised in addition to the general safety measures mentioned above:

- Routinely, single gloves are sufficient but in high-risk patients, double gloves must be used and disposed suitably after use. It is most ideal to use disposable gloves.
- Change gloves after 1 hour preferably, continuous wear may be detrimental. In no case, it should never be used for more than 3 hours.
- While treating multiple patients, the gloved hands should be disinfected with a suitable disinfectant, for example, 1% sodium hypochlorite solution, Betadine, 1% available iodine or at least soap for minimum 30 seconds.
- After starting the dental procedure, do not touch areas which are not directly involved in the diagnostic or treatment procedure.
- Wash hands thoroughly with a soap before wearing gloves and after degloving.
- Check gloves for gross defects every time you wear them. Cover cuts or wounds in the hand with waterproof band aid before gloving.
- Use of masks
  – Masks are mandatory as patient's breathes may contain infected aerosols.
  – Mask should of good fitting and preferably disposable.
  – Masks should be changed after any surgical procedure lasting more than 20 minutes or any procedure where an aerosol sprays is expected (e.g., use of hand piece) or in a high-risk patients (e.g., known HIV/Koch's patients).
  – The mask should be disinfected with liquid beach before washing.
- Protective eyewear is recommended for all dental procedures, especially for procedures where aerosols are produced.

Self-assessment

Short-answer questions

Write notes on

1. Biosafety measures
2. Safety measures in dentistry

Multiple-choice questions

1. Which of the following is NOT the infection of special concern to those who are working in healthcare set-up?
   A. Hepatitis B virus
   B. AIDS virus
   C. Hepatitis C virus
   D. Hepatitis A virus
2. In dental procedures, the gloves should never be used for more than
   A. 1 hour
   B. 2 hours
   C. 3 hours
   D. 4 hours

55 Animal Experiments

Use of animals

- Laboratory animals are used in microbiology laboratories for various purposes such as
  - For virulence and pathogenicity testing
  - For cultivation of some pathogens, which are not cultivable using artificial media
  - For preparation of antisera
  - For obtaining blood or serum for preparation of media and as a source of complement
  - For raising desired antibody (monoclonal and polyclonal)
  - For the study of in vivo interactions of antigens–antibodies
  - For testing and production of vaccines
  - For testing the in vivo effect of antimicrobial agents
- The animals commonly used for experiments include the following:
  - Mice
  - Guinea pigs
  - Chickens
  - Hamsters
  - Sheep
  - Horses
  - Rabbits
  - Rats
  - Cats
  - Monkeys
  - Dogs
  - Frogs, etc.
- These animals are commonly used for diagnosis or research purpose
- Nowadays, the use of animals for experiment purpose has been restricted because of strict rules/laws governing the usage of animals in a laboratory

Animal experiments

Materials to be inoculated

The following materials/specimens can be used for inoculation by injection:

- Body fluids such as urine, cerebrospinal fluid and blood
- Cultures—fluid cultures are to be used. Growth on solid medium is to be suspended in broth or saline and then used for injection
- Tissues—small fragments of tissue are to be homogenized with a diluent and used for injection

Selection of experimental animals

Important considerations

For selection of suitable animals for an experiment, specific anatomical, physiological and pathological characteristics need to be taken into consideration. The choice of animals is also influenced by the type of study/experiment. The following points are to be taken into consideration for the selection of an appropriate animal for experiment:

- Availability of animals
- Size and anatomic characteristics
- Age and life expectancy
- Feeding habits
- Genetic characteristics
- Reproduction
- Health status
- Indigenous factors
- Nutritional, environmental, space and caging requirements
- Type of agent being investigated
- Dosage of the drug and route of administration

Routes of inoculation

The different routes of inoculation in various laboratory animals include the following:

- Intradermal
- Subcutaneous
- Intravenous
- Intramuscular
- Infracerebral
- Intranasal
- Intracranial
- Intra-abdominal
- Intraperitoneal
- Intraspinal, etc.

The route of inoculation is selected based on the nature of the inoculation and tissue tropism.

Information to be recorded

- Information is to be recorded before and after inoculation of animal
- The important information to be recorded include the following:
  - Number of animals
  - Age of animals
  - Physiological condition
  - Nature of the specimen
  - Date of inoculation
  - Route of inoculation
  - Changes observed on a daily basis
  - Test results on a regular basis
  - If death occurs, the date of death is to be recorded—the animal is to be disinfected and incinerated

Procedure

Steps in animal experiments include the following:

- Preparation of specimen for inoculation
- The experimental animal is to be labelled properly
- The syringe loaded with the appropriate specimen is introduced by using appropriate route to inoculate the specimen
- After inoculation, it is to be kept in its cage and to be kept away from other animals
- The animals under experiments are to be observed and monitored for
  - Physical properties
  - Health and other activities of the animals
- The test results are to be monitored and recorded regularly

Animals commonly used in microbiology laboratory

Rabbit

- It is one of the most commonly used animals for various experiments.
- Different routes of inoculation are used for different purposes.
- These routes include the following:
  - Scarification
  - Subcutaneous injection
  - Intravenous injection
  - Intraperitoneal injection
  - Intramuscular injection
  - Installation into eyes
- The appropriate route is selected based on the experiment to be performed.

Uses of rabbit

Some of the most important uses of a rabbit in microbiology are as follows:

- For testing virulence and pathogenicity of

- *Streptococcus pneumoniae*
- *Mycobacterium tuberculosis*
- Herpes simplex viruses
- *Candida albicans*

- To differentiate *M. tuberculosis* and *M. bovis*
- For maintenance of *Treponema pallidum*
- Sereny's test for demonstration of Enteroinvasive *Escherichia coli*
- Toxigenicity testing of enteropathogenic organisms
- To increase the virulence of rabies virus and vaccinia virus
- To raise antibodies (antisera) to antigen

Raising of antisera

- Apart from other uses, rabbit is the most commonly used for raising of antisera, that is, raising of antibodies against specific antigen.
- For this purpose, rabbit is immunized with desired antigen. After the desired level of antibodies are produced, the same can be obtained from the marginal vein of the ear.
- Alternatively, antibodies can be obtained by collecting blood from the central artery of the ear or directly from the heart by cardiac puncture.

Guinea pig

- Guinea pigs are most easy to handle
- Different routes of inoculation are as follows:
  - Subcutaneous injection
  - Intradermal injection
  - Intraperitoneal injection
  - Intramuscular injection
  - Installation into eyes

Uses of guinea pigs in microbiology

- Guinea pigs are used for isolation of
  - *M. tuberculosis*
  - *M. bovis*
  - *Yersinia pestis*
  - *Brucella abortus*
  - *Toxoplasma gondii*, etc.
- Guinea pigs are used for toxigenicity testing of
  - *Corynebacterium diphtheriae*
  - *Clostridium welchii*
  - *C. tetani*
  - *C. botulinum*
- They are also used for pathogenicity testing of
  - *Bacillus anthracis*
  - *C. welchii*
  - *Cryptococcus neoformans*
  - *M. tuberculosis*
- Guinea pig is the richest source of complement; hence, its serum is used as a source of complement in the complement fixation test
- Used for pyrogen testing
- Used in Sereny's test

Collection of blood To obtain complement and antibodies raised in Guinea pigs, blood is collected from marginal ear vein (around 0.5 mL can be collected) or alternatively directly from the heart (up to 5 mL can be collected).

Mouse

- Mouse is the most commonly used lab animal for different animal experiments.
- It is a very suitable animal for different types of pathogens.
- It is very easy to handle with little practice.

Different routes of inoculation

- The common routes used for inoculation of different specimens include the following:
  - Subcutaneous injection
  - Intravenous injection
  - Intraperitoneal injection
  - Intracerebral injection
  - Intranasal instillation, etc.
- Intravenous inoculation into the tail vein is the most commonly used route in addition to intraperitoneal injection.

Uses of mouse

- Suckling mouse less than 48 hours old is used for isolation and cultivation of viruses, for example, arboviruses.

- The suckling mouse is also used for testing of enterotoxins of enteropathogenic bacteria.
- An adult mouse is used for isolation and cultivation of organisms such as
  - *M. leprae*—foot pad
  - *Toxoplasma gondii*—intraperitoneal
  - *Cryptosporidium* species—intestinal
- Mouse is used for isolation of pathogens such as
  - *Borrelia recurrentis*
  - *Rickettsia* species
  - *Trypanosoma brucei*
  - Rabies virus
  - *Histoplasma capsulatum*
- Mouse is also used for pathogenicity and virulence testing of
  - Pneumococci
  - Anthrax bacilli
  - *Leishmania* species
  - Herpes simplex virus
  - *C. neoformans*

Collection of blood from mouse Blood from mouse can be collected from the tail (about 0.3 mL), from the retro-orbital plexus (up to 0.7 mL) and from the heart (up to 1.5 mL)

Monkey

- Monkeys are considered very suitable for lab testing, as they are genetically evolved animals.
- They are extensively used in laboratories.

Different routes of inoculation

The most common routes of inoculation are intracerebral and intraspinal.

Uses of monkey

- Monkeys are used for raising of antisera.
- For testing pathogenicity of poliovirus.
- For cultivation of hepatitis A virus and *Plasmodium falciparum.*
- The red blood cells of monkeys are used in serological tests.
- They are also used for testing of virulence of *Entamoeba histolytica.*

Self-assessment

Short-answer questions

Write notes on

1. Raising of antisera
2. Uses of rabbits
3. Uses of guinea pigs
4. Uses of mice
5. Monkeys

Multiple-choice questions

1. Rabbit is most commonly used for
   A. Virulence testing
   B. Maintenance of bacteria
   C. Raising of antisera
   D. Sereny's test
2. Which of the following animals is used as the richest source of complement?
   A. Rabbit
   B. Guinea pig
   C. Mice
   D. Monkey
3. Suckling mouse of less than 48 hours old is commonly used for
   A. Raising of antisera
   B. Isolation and cultivation of arboviruses
   C. Sereny's test
   D. Maintenance of bacteria

56 Microbiology—Practicals

Stained preparations

Gram stain

- It is the most commonly used staining method devised by the histologist Christian Gram (1884) to stain bacteria in tissue.
- It is a differential staining method, which differentiates organisms into Gram-positive and Gram-negative according to their Gram reaction.

Preparation of smear

- In case of liquid material, for example, urine, sputum, pus, cerebrospinal fluid and broth culture, a loopful of material is taken with the help of inoculating loop and spread thinly on the slide.
- In case of solid material, for example, colonies on culture plates, a minute quantity of material is obtained by just touching the growth on culture plate and emulsified in a drop of sterile water or saline on a glass slide and spread evenly on the slide.
- The smear prepared as above is dried in the air and fixed by passing the dried slide three times slowly through the flame.
- The fixed smear is used for staining.
- Prepare smear on a clean glass slide, allow it to air dry and fix it by flaming.

Staining procedure

- **Primary staining** Apply crystal violet, methyl violet or gentian violet to smear and allow it to act for 1/2–1 minute
- **Application of mordant** Apply Gram's iodine for 1–2 minutes and wash with water
- **Decolourization** Decolourize the smear with an organic solvent such as absolute alcohol, acetone, acetone-ether mixture or aniline for 10–30 seconds or until the colour oozes from the slide. Wash with water
- **Counter staining** Counter stain with a safranine, carbol fuchsin or neutral red for 15–30 seconds
- Wash with water and blot dry
- Observe the slide under 100X after putting a drop of cedar wood oil

Role of staining reagents

- **Primary stain** It is the first staining reagent, which gives violet colour to the smear.
- **Mordant** It is the agent that enhances the attraction between primary stain and cell cytoplasm. Mordant helps to fix the primary stain in bacterial cytoplasm.
- **Decolourizer** It is the agent that removes the primary stain from cytoplasm of the Gram-negative bacteria and other Gram-negative structures in the smear, for example, pus cells.

- **Counter stain** It is the staining reagent used in the last step to stain the bacteria and structures that are decolourized by decolourizer.

Observations (Fig. 56.1)

Gram stain divides bacteria in two broad groups:

1. **Gram-positive bacteria** They resist decolourization and retain the colour of primary stain and appear violet in colour, for example
   - Pneumococci, streptococci, staphylococci are Gram-positive cocci
   - Clostridia, corynebacteria and *Bacillus* species are Gram-positive bacilli
2. **Gram-negative bacteria** They are decolourized by alcohol and therefore take counter stain and appear red in colour, for example
   - Gonococci, meningococci and *Veillonella* species are Gram-negative cocci
   - *Escherichia coli, Salmonella, Shigella, Vibrio cholerae, Pseudomonas aeruginosa, Klebsiella* species, etc., are Gram-negative bacilli
   - Background/pus cells and their nuclei appear red in colour

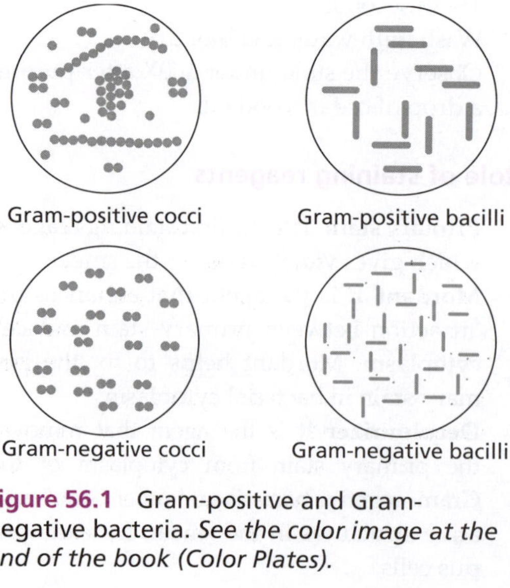

Figure 56.1 Gram-positive and Gram-negative bacteria. *See the color image at the end of the book (Color Plates).*

Mechanism of Gram reaction

Different theories have been proposed to explain the mechanism. These are

- Acidic protoplasm theory
- Lipid content theory
- Cell wall permeability
- Magnesium ribonucleate theory

Acidic protoplasm theory According to this theory, the cytoplasm is acidic in Gram-positive bacteria and the primary stain used is basic in nature. Hence, they retain the primary stain more strongly than Gram-negative bacteria. Also, the iodine makes the cytoplasm more acidic and acts as mordant increasing the attraction of primary stain and cell cytoplasm and thus helps to fix the stain in the bacterial cell.

Lipid content theory According to this theory, the lipid content of cell wall is more in Gram-negative bacteria and less in Gram-positive bacteria. There is formation of a complex containing primary stain and iodine in both Gram-positive and Gram-negative bacteria which gives violet colour. But, on the application of alcohol, the lipid in the cell wall of Gram-negative bacteria gets dissolved in the alcohol. This causes an increase in the pore size through which a dye-iodine complex diffuses out during the process of decolourization and subsequently the bacteria are stained by counter stain and appear red in colour.

Cell wall permeability The cell wall of Gram-positive bacteria contain more mucopeptide because of which it is thicker and stronger, hence dye-iodine complex does not come out of the Gram-positive cell. However, in Gram-negative bacteria because of less content of mucopeptide, the cell wall is not strong and thick, hence dye-iodine complex diffuses freely out of the cell and they take up the colour of counter stain.

Magnesium ribonucleate theory According to this theory, magnesium ribonucleate is present in Gram-positive bacteria and there is formation of magnesium ribonucleate–dye-iodine complex, which is insoluble in alcohol, but magnesium ribonucleate is absent in Gram-negative bacteria; hence, there is formation of dye-iodine complex only, which is soluble in alcohol.

Acid-fast stain (Ziehl–Neelsen stain)

- The organisms which are not easily stained by ordinary staining method, but once stained resist decolourization by acids, are known as acid-fast organisms and the method used for staining these organisms is known as acid-fast stain.
- The method was devised by Ehrlich (1883) and modified by Ziehl and Neelsen (1885), hence known as Ziehl–Neelsen staining (Z–N staining) method.
- It is a differential staining method, which differentiates acid-fast organisms (mycobacteria) from other organisms (non-acid-fast).

Procedure

- Prepare smear on a clean glass slide, allow it to air dry and fix it by flaming
- **Primary stain** Apply filtered carbol fuchsin and heat it until steam rises. Carbol fuchsin is not allowed to boil. It is applied for 5–10 minutes with intermittent heating
- The stain must not be allowed to evaporate and dry on the slide, if needed more stain is added to the slide and reheated. Heating is necessary for penetration of stain into the cell wall
- Wash with water
- **Decolourization** Slide is covered with 20% sulphuric acid (H_2SO_4). The red colour of smear changes to yellowish brown
- Wash with water and observe the colour of smear, if it is red, repeat decolourization till it becomes yellowish brown
- Wash with water
- Apply 90% alcohol for 2 minutes for decolourization. (This step is optional and may be omitted, if the specimen is not urine)
- Wash with water
- **Counter staining** Counter stain with methylene blue or malachite green for 1–2 minutes. Picric acid can also be used as a counter stain
- Wash, blot dry and observe under 100X after putting a drop of cedar wood oil

Role of staining reagents

- **Primary stain** It is the first staining reagent, which gives pink colour to the smear.
- **Mordant** It is the agent that enhances the attraction between primary stain and cell cytoplasm. It helps to fix the primary stain in bacterial cytoplasm. The mordant used is phenol, which is incorporated with primary stain (basic fuchsin + phenol = carbol fuchsin).
- **Decolourizer** It is the agent that removes the primary stain from cytoplasm of the non-acid-fast bacteria and other non-acid-fast structures in the smear, for example, pus cells.
- **Counter stain** It is the staining reagent used in the last step to stain the non-acid-fast bacteria and structures that are decolourized by decolourizer.

Observations (*see* Fig. 28.1)

- Acid-fast bacilli appear bright red in colour
- Pus cells, epithelial cells and other organisms blue or green in colour

Mechanism of acid-fast stain

- Acid-fast organisms are not easily stained because they are coated with lipids, fatty acids and higher alcohols in their cell wall.
- Mycolic acid (waxy substance) present in the cell wall does not allow the stain to penetrate easily inside these organisms.
- In Z–N staining, carbol fuchsin (a phenolic solution of basic fuchsin) is applied with heat. Heat and phenol facilitate the penetration of dye.
- Subsequently, when acid-fast organisms are decolourized by acid, the dye does

not come out because the dye is soluble in phenol and phenol is more soluble in lipid substances, hence there is no decolourization and they retain the colour of the basic fuchsin (primary stain).

Unstained preparations

Wet mount

- It is an unstained preparation in which specimens can be observed directly, for example, urine or in an emulsified suspension, for example, stools.
- A drop of urine or other specimen, which does not require emulsification, is taken on a glass slide.
- Cover slip is placed and observed under low power and high power or a drop of saline is placed on a glass slide and specimens such as stool, which require emulsification, are emulsified in saline.
- Cover slip is placed and observed under low power and high power.

Uses

- To assess and enumerate inflammatory cells
- For examination of urine deposits
- For examination of parasites such as *Trichomonas*, amoeba and *Giardia*

Hanging drop preparation

Procedure

- A ring of petroleum jelly is applied around the concavity of the depression of the cavity slide
- A drop of liquid culture or specimen such as stool is placed on the cover slip by taking all sterile precautions and the cover slip is inverted over a cavity slide so that drop remains hanging
- This preparation is then observed under low power to adjust edge of the drop and under high power to study the motility of organisms

Uses

- To study the motility of *Vibrio cholerae* in stool sample
- To study the motility of organisms in fluid culture

Self-assessment

Short-answer questions

Write notes on
1. Gram stain
2. Acid-fast stain

Multiple-choice questions

1. The following are the counter stains used in Gram staining, EXCEPT
   A. Safranine
   B. Carbol fuchsin
   C. Picric acid
   D. Neutral red
2. Which of the following is used a decolourizer in Gram stain?
   A. Alcohol
   B. Acetone
   C. Acetone-ether mixture
   D. All of the above
3. The following reagents can be used as primary stain in Gram stain, EXCEPT
   A. Methyl violet
   B. Methylene blue
   C. Gentian violet
   D. Crystal violet
4. Which of the following can be used as decolourizer in acid-fast staining?
   A. 20% sulphuric acid
   B. Absolute alcohol
   C. Acetone
   D. All of the above
5. Which of the following is the mordant used in Ziehl–Neelsen stain?
   A. Iodine
   B. Phenol
   C. Alcohol
   D. None of the above

6. Which of the following is the mordant used in Gram stain?
   A. Iodine
   B. Phenol
   C. Alcohol
   D. None of the above
7. Acid fastness is due to
   A. Butyric acid
   B. Lipid A
   C. Mycolic acid
   D. None of the above
8. The following are used as counter stains in Ziehl–Neelsen stain, EXCEPT
   A. Methylene blue
   B. Methyl violet
   C. Malachite green
   D. Picric acid
9. The acid-fast staining is devised by
   A. Ehrlich
   B. Ziehl–Neelsen
   C. Robert Koch
   D. Hansen
10. Which of the following components of bacterial cell wall is responsible for Gram positiveness?
   A. Acidic cytoplasm
   B. Basic cytoplasm
   C. Neutral cytoplasm
   D. All of the above
11. Which of the following components of bacterial cell wall is considered to be responsible for Gram negativeness?
   A. Magnesium ribonucleate
   B. Peptidoglycan
   C. Lipid
   D. All of the above

Answers to MCQs

Chapter 1

1. B	2. D	3. C	4. D	5. C	6. D	7. C	8. B	9. D	10. A
11. B	12. D	13. B	14. B	15. A	16. D	17. A	18. D	19. B	

Chapter 2

1. C	2. D	3. D	4. C	5. B	6. A

Chapter 3

1. C	2. D	3. B	4. A	5. C	6. D	7. D	8. B	9. B
10. C	11. A	12. D	13. B	14. B	15. B	16. D	17. A	18. A

Chapter 4

1. B	2. D	3. A	4. B	5. C	6. D	7. B	8. C	9. A	10. B
11. D	12. A	13. D	14. C	15. B	16. D	17. C	18. A	19. D	20. B
21. C	22. A								

Chapter 5

1. D	2. C	3. C	4. C	5. C	6. D	7. B
8. D	9. C	10. B	11. A	12. B	13. C	

Chapter 6

1. D	2. C	3. C	4. B	5. C	6. D
7. C	8. B	9. C	10. D	11. C	

Chapter 7

1. A	2. D	3. A	4. C	5. D	6. D
7. B	8. C	9. C	10. B	11. D	

Chapter 8

1. B	2. D	3. C	4. B	5. A	6. D	7. D	8. B
9. B	10. D	11. B	12. A	13. C	14. B	15. C	

Chapter 9

1. A	2. D	3. C	4. B	5. A

Chapter 10

1. D	2. D	3. C	4. C	5. D	6. A	7. D	8. A
9. D	10. D	11. A	12. C	13. B	14. D	15. B	

Chapter 11

1. C	2. B	3. A	4. B	5. D	6. D	7. A	8. D	9. A
10. A	11. C	12. C	13. A	14. B	15. D	16. C	17. B	18. D

Chapter 12

1. D	2. B	3. A	4. D	5. B	6. C	7. D
8. C	9. D	10. A	11. A	12. D	13. B	14. A

Chapter 13

1. C	2. A	3. B	4. D	5. C	6. C
7. C	8. B	9. D	10. D	11. D	

Chapter 14

1. C	2. A	3. B	4. D	5. C	6. B
7. A	8. B	9. D	10. D	11. C	12. C

Chapter 15

1. A	2. C	3. D	4. A	5. D	6. C
7. B	8. B	9. C	10. A	11.D	

Chapter 16

1. C	2. B	3. D	4. A	5. C	6. A	7. C	8. B	9. C

Chapter 17

1. B	2. C	3. D	4. B	5. A	6. D	7. C	8. B	9. A	10. B

Chapter 18

1. A	2. C	3. B	4. A	5. D	6. A
7. C	8. C	9. A	10. C	11. C	

Chapter 19

1. B	2. B	3. D	4. A	5. D	6. D	7. A	8. D

Chapter 20

1. B	2. A	3. C	4. D	5. D	6. C	7. D	8. A

Chapter 21

1. D	2. A	3. C	4. B	5. C

Chapter 22

1. C	2. B	3. D	4. B	5. A

Chapter 23

1. D	2. D	3. A	4. B	5. A	6. B
7. B	8. C	9. D	10. C	11. D	

Chapter 24

1. B	2. D	3. C	4. D	5. A

Chapter 25

1. C	2. D	3. D	4. C	5. A

Chapter 26

1. B	2. A	3. D	4. A	5. A	6. D	7. C	8. C	9. C

Chapter 27

1. B	2. C	3. B	4. D	5. D	6. A

Chapter 28

1. D	2. A	3. D	4. C	5. B	6. A	7. D	8. C	9. A	10. B

Chapter 29

1. B	2. D	3. D	4. C	5. B

Chapter 30

1. D	2. A	3. D	4. C	5. C	6. B
7. D	8. A	9. B	10. A	11. C	

Chapter 31

1. C	2. D	3. B

Chapter 32

1. D	2. B	3. C	4. B	5. D	6. C	7. D	8. A
9. D	10. C	11. A	12. C	13. D	14. C	15. A	

Chapter 33

1. A	2. A	3. C	4. B	5. D	6. B
7. C	8. D	9. B	10. C	11. C	

Chapter 34

1. D	2. B	3. D	4. B	5. B	6. A	7. D

Chapter 35

1. C	2. D	3. A	4. B	5. D	6. C	7. D	8. A
9. C	10. C	11. C	12. C	13. D	14. C	15. B	

Chapter 36

1. C	2. A	3. C	4. D	5. C	6. B	7. D	8. A	9. C	10. D

Chapter 37

1. C	2. B	3. B	4. C	5. B	6. D

Chapter 38

1. D	2. A	3. A	4. B

Chapter 39

1. D	2. D	3. A	4. B	5. D	6. A
7. D	8. A	9. D	10. C	11. B	12. A

Chapter 40

1. A	2. B	3. C	4. D	5. B	6. B	7. D	8. B	9. D

Chapter 41

1. B	2. C	3. D	4. B	5. C	6. D	7. C	8. C	9. D

Chapter 42

1. B	2. D	3. C	4. A	5. D	6. B

Chapter 43

1. D	2. C

Chapter 44

1. A	2. C	3. C	4. D	5. C	6. D
7. A	8. C	9. D	10. C	11. A	12. B

Chapter 45

1. C	2. A	3. D	4. D	5. B	6. C	7. B	8. C	9. B

Chapter 46

1. A	2. C	3. C	4. B	5. D	6. A	7. C	8. A	9. C
10. A	11. A	12. C	13. B	14. B	15. D	16. A	17. B	18. C

Chapter 47

1. A	2. C	3. A	4. B	5. D	6. B	7. C	8. B	9. D	10. A

Chapter 48

1. C	2. A	3. B	4. D	5. B	6. C	7. D	8. A
9. D	10. B	11. B	12. D	13. D	14. B	15. B	

Chapter 49

1. B	2. C	3. B	4. D	5. D	6. A	7. A	8. C
9. A	10. B	11. C	12. B	13. C	14. D	15. B	

Chapter 50

1. C	2. B	3. C	4. D	5. A	6. D	7. A	8. C	9. C

Chapter 51

1. C	2. D	3. A	4. B	5. C

Chapter 52

1. B	2. D	3. C	4.C	5. B	6. D	7. C
8. A	9. D	10. A	11. B	12. C	13. A	

Chapter 53

1. D	2. C	3. D

Chapter 54

1. D	2. C

Chapter 55

1. C	2. B	3. B

Chapter 56

1. C	2. D	3. B	4. A	5. B	6. A
7. C	8. B	9. A	10. A	11. C	

Index

D

E

Color Plates

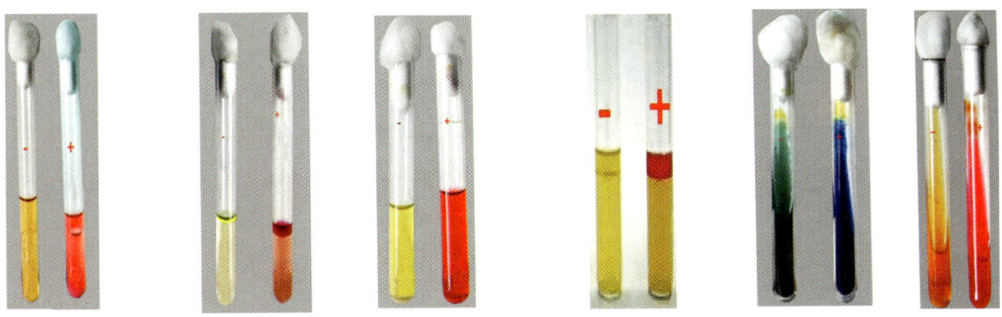

Sugar fermentation test | Indole test | Methyl red test | Voges-Proskauer test | Citrate test | Urease test

Figure 6.2 Biochemical reactions.

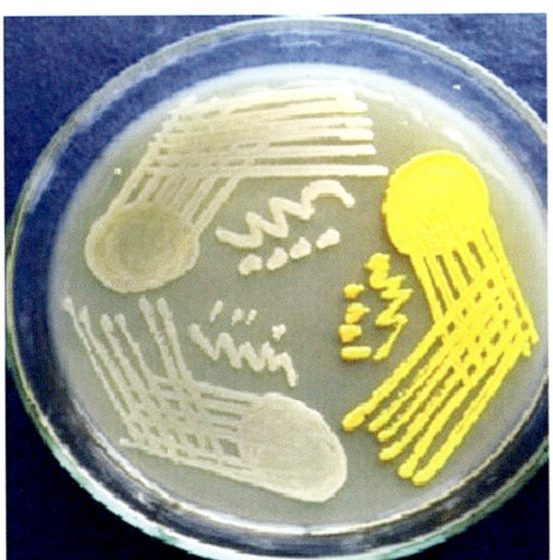

Figure 23.2 Types of pigments produced by staphylococci.

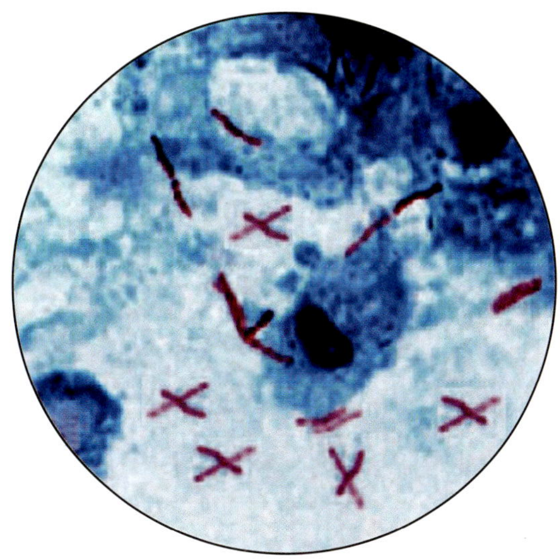

Figure 28.1 *Mycobacterium tuberculosis.*

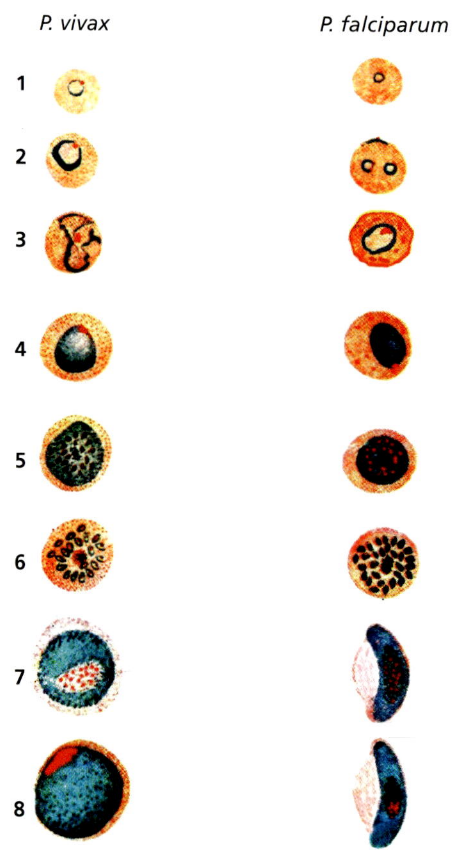

Figure 48.5 Morphology of *Plasmodium vivax* and *P. falciparum*. (1–3) Trophozoites. (4–6) Schizonts. (7–8) Male and female gametocytes.

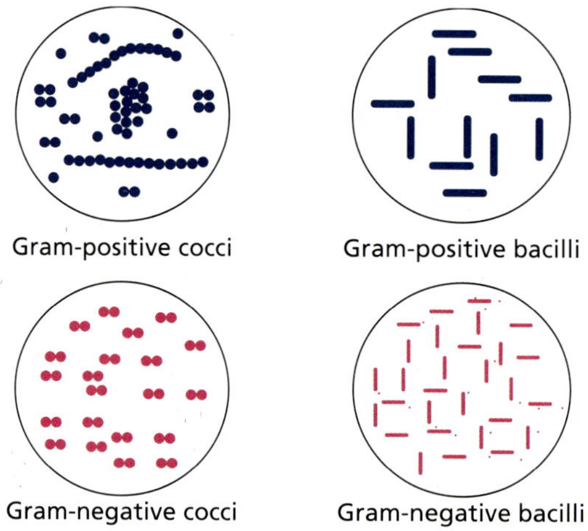

Figure 56.1 Gram-positive and Gram-negative bacteria.